SARA DOUGLASS

Enchanter

Book Two of
The Axis Trilogy

HarperCollins*Publishers*

Voyager
An Imprint of HarperCollins*Publishers*
77–85 Fulham Palace Road,
Hammersmith, London W6 8JB

www.voyager-books.com

Published by *Voyager* 1999
5 7 9 8 6

A catalogue record for this book
is available from the British Library

ISBN 0 00 651107 4

Set in Bembo

Printed and bound in Great Britain by
Omnia Books Ltd, Glasgow

The Axis Trilogy continues for Lynn, Tim and Frances, with a nod and a smile for Pachelbel, whose haunting Canon in D provided the background for the writing of *Enchanter*.

Enchanter is the axis, and it remembers Elinor, who died when she and I were far too young.

Contents

Courage my Soul, now learn to wield
The weight of thine immortal Shield.
Close on thy Head thy Helmet bright.
Ballance thy Sword against the Fight.
See where an Army, strong as fair,
With silken Banners spreads the air.
Now, if thou bee'st that thing Divine,
In this day's Combat let it shine:
And shew that Nature wants an Art
To conquer one resolved Heart.

ANDREW MARVELL,
"A Dialogue Between The Resolved Soul,
and Created Pleasure"

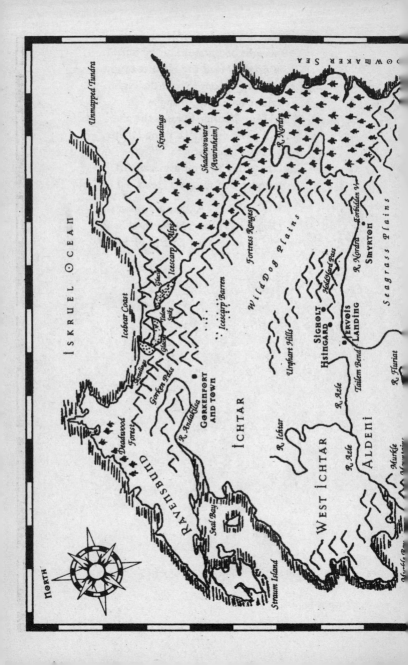

The Prophecy of the Destroyer

A day will come when born will be
Two babes whose blood will tie them.
That born to Wing and Horn will hate
The one they call the StarMan.
Destroyer! rises in the north
And drives his Ghostmen south;
Defenceless lie both flesh and field
Before Gorgrael's ice.
To meet this threat you must release
The StarMan from his lies,
Revive Tencendor, fast and sure
Forget the ancient war,
For if Plough, Wing and Horn can't find
The bridge to understanding,
Then will Gorgrael earn his name
And bring Destruction hither.

StarMan, listen, heed me well,
Your power will destroy you
If you should wield it in the fray
'Ere these prophecies are met:
The Sentinels will walk abroad
'Til power corrupt their hearts;
A child will turn her head and cry
Revealing ancient arts;
A wife will hold in joy at night
The slayer of her husband;
Age-old souls, long in cribs,
Will sing o'er mortal land;
The remade dead, fat with child
Will birth abomination;
A darker power will prove to be
The father of salvation.

Then waters will release bright eyes
To form the Rainbow Sceptre.

StarMan, listen, for I know
That you can wield the sceptre
To bring Gorgrael to his knees
And break the ice asunder.
But even with the power in hand
Your pathway is not sure:
A Traitor from within your camp
Will seek and plot to harm you;
Let not your Lover's pain distract
For this will mean your death;
Destroyer's might lies in his hate
Yet you must never follow;
Forgiveness is the thing assured
To save Tencendor's soul.

Prologue: The Ruins of Gorkenfort

Gorgrael stood in the deserted bedchamber of Gorkenfort Keep, his breath frosting about his tusks in the frigid atmosphere. His bright silver eyes narrowed as he absorbed the lingering memories and emotions of the room. Bending, he scraped a hand across the bed, catching and tearing the bed linen with his hooked claws. Hate and desire, pain and satisfaction lingered here. He snatched a handful of the material to his nostrils, crushing it between his powerful claws. *She* had been here, had slept here, had laughed and cried here. Gorgrael abruptly arched his body back, his muscles rigid, and shrieked his anger, frustration and desire. He hated and wanted this woman almost as much as he hated and wanted Axis.

Outside the Keep's walls the Skraelings stilled and fell silent as they heard their master's voice echo about the frozen wastes. As suddenly as he had given vent to his anger and desire Gorgrael stopped, straightening and relaxing his body. He dropped the fragment of sheet to the floor, and glanced around the ruined chamber. This had been *her* chamber, hers and that pitiful fool's, Borneheld. He was of no account; Gorgrael would brush him aside at the first possible opportunity. But the woman . . . she was the key.

Gorgrael knew the Prophecy almost as well as its maker. He knew that now Axis had escaped to his – *their* – father he would prove a far more formidable opponent. Enough to counter Gorgrael's command of the Dark Music? Gorgrael was not sure. Axis was certainly now too strong to be vulnerable to his SkraeBolds. But as the third verse of the Prophecy gave Axis the key to destroy Gorgrael, so it gave Gorgrael the key to destroy Axis. The Prophet had been kind.

The key was the Lover mentioned in the Prophecy. If Gorgrael could destroy her, he would destroy Axis. Axis was vulnerable to nothing but love, and eventually love could prove his destruction.

Gorgrael shrieked again, but this time in glee. It would take time, but eventually he would have her. The traitor was in place. All he needed was the opportunity.

Faraday. Gorgrael had gleaned much from this room. *She* was the one to whom Timozel had bound himself, *she* had given Axis the power of the emerald fire that had decimated Gorgrael's Skraeling force. For that alone she deserved to die. For the fact that Axis loved her Faraday would die slowly. For her alliance with the Mother and with the Trees she would die alone and friendless. Gorgrael dug his claws deep into the mattress and shredded it with a single twist of his powerful arm. This is what he would do to Faraday's body. After she had begged for her life, pleaded for mercy, screamed as she submitted herself to his will. He would *shred* her!

Gorgrael's eyes drifted towards the shattered window. Most of the hamlets and towns of Ichtar lay in ruins. Hsingard, the one-time seat of the Duke of Ichtar, was useless rubble. Tens of thousands of Ichtar's inhabitants had died. The Skraelings had fed well. But not all had gone according to plan, and satisfaction was still a way off. Axis had escaped, and in doing so had badly damaged Gorgrael's force.

If Gorgrael had enough Skraelings to occupy Ichtar then he did not have a strong enough force left to harry either

Axis or Borneheld. The Duke of Ichtar had managed to flee south with almost five thousand men (and *her*) and even now approached Jervois Landing. There he would no doubt make his stand by the running waters.

Neither Gorgrael nor his creatures liked running water. It made music from beauty and peace, not darkness. It *tinkled*. Gorgrael screamed in frustration and completed his destruction of the bed. He was severely disappointed in his SkraeBolds. Borneheld's escape had been assisted by their inability to focus the Skraelings' attention on attacking the Duke's column as it fled south. While it was true that many Skraelings trembled at the SkraeBolds' screams and threats of retribution, many others did not. Long had the Skraelings hungered to drive into the pleasant southern lands, long had they resented their icy northern wastes. Now, as the defeat of Gorkenfort opened Ichtar to them, they spread across the province in largely unrestrained and undisciplined glee, a misty, whispery mob that destroyed without thought. The SkraeBolds had found it impossible to rally enough Skraelings to make any serious attempt on Borneheld's fleeing force, and had to confine themselves to harrying the flanks and rearguard of his column.

Not only were the Skraelings proving harder to control and the SkraeBolds less effectual than he had hoped, Gorgrael also had to admit that his forces had been so weakened by the fury Axis had unleashed on them above Gorkenfort that it would take him months to rebuild an army strong enough and disciplined enough to push further south than Hsingard.

And as the SkraeBolds trembled and wept at the thought of reporting their failures to Gorgrael, so Gorgrael himself began to construct the arguments he would need to convince his mentor that it *had* been the right time to strike Gorkenfort, it *had* been the right time to begin his drive into Achar. The Dark Man had cautioned him to wait a year or two more, to wait until his army had been built into a more formidable force and his magic was deeper and darker. But Gorgrael had been tired of waiting. While the Dark Man had taught him all he knew, had taught him the use of the Dark Music and crafted him into the power he was today, Gorgrael feared him as much as he loved him.

His claws twitching nervously, Gorgrael began rehearsing his explanations.

I

Jervois Landing — Arrivals

Ho'Demi sat his shaggy horse and contemplated the impenetrable fog before him. His scouts had reported that the Duke of Ichtar and what remained of his command from Gorkenfort drew close. For all Ho'Demi knew they were but ten paces away.

Ho'Demi shivered. He did not like these southern lands with their damp mists. He yearned for the northern wastes of the Ravensbund with its endless leagues of grinding ice. He yearned to be once more hunting the great icebears with the men and women of his tribe – not these Ghostmen whose very whispers defiled the wind.

However, the northern wastes were denied Ho'Demi and his people. For as far back as tribal memory stretched the Skraeling wraiths had existed. Until the past year they had been neither numerous nor brave, and as long as his people hunted in packs, the Skraelings had not attacked. But now, massed by the unseen yet powerful hand of Gorgrael the Destroyer, the Skraelings had driven them from the Ravensbund, down through Gorken Pass, past Gorkenfort and town – where the Duke of Ichtar had stopped the invasion of Gorgrael's Ghostmen – and into these southern lands. Ho'Demi had finally stopped his people's flight here at Jervois Landing. It was here that Borneheld, having somehow escaped the Skraelings, intended to make his stand.

Ho'Demi and his people had always intended to help the Southerners against Gorgrael and his Skraelings; it was part of their heritage. But when he had offered his warriors at Gorkenfort, Borneheld had laughed and said he had no need for Ravensbund assistance. He, Duke of Ichtar, commanded a *real* army. Well, now the Duke and his *real* army might not be so slow to accept the help of the Ravensbund warriors.

Ho'Demi had led as many of his people out of the Ravensbund as he could. But the Ravensbund tribes lay scattered across the vast territory of the northern wastes and Ho'Demi had not been able to get word to the majority of the tribes to flee into the southern lands. Only twenty thousand had pitched their sealskin tents about Jervois Landing, a mere twentieth of the Ravensbund population. Ho'Demi shuddered to think of what had happened to those left behind. He hoped they had found a place to hide among the crevices of the ice packs, there to await the day when Gorgrael was defeated by the StarMan. He hoped they had the courage for a long wait.

The Ravensbundmen were a proud and ancient people who had adapted their culture and society to a life spent almost entirely within the ice-bound regions of northern Achar. Few had any contact with the world beyond the River Andakilsa. The King of Achar (whosoever he currently was) might fondly believe that he ruled Ravensbund as he ruled the rest of Achar, but as far as the Ravensbundmen knew or cared, the Achar King had as much control over them as he did over the Forbidden. Ho'Demi was their Chief, and his was the law they obeyed.

But now, for the sake of the Prophecy and because it was the only thing left for him to do, Ho'Demi would put himself under the command of Borneheld. Ravensbundmen had been aware of the Prophecy of the Destroyer for thousands of years, and Ho'Demi knew that, divided, no-one could defeat Gorgrael. Someone had to begin the alliance that would create Tencendor and crush the Destroyer. As the Skraeling threat grew infinitely worse, he had quickly realised this was a sign that the Prophecy had awoken and now walked. Of all the peoples of this land, perhaps the Ravensbundmen were more loyal to the name of the StarMan than most. When he called, then they would rally.

In groups of never less than a thousand, the Ravensbund people had passed by Gorkenfort, many weeks before Axis had arrived. As yet they did not know where the StarMan was; they did not know who he was. Until they found him, until they could declare their loyalty and their spears for him, Ho'Demi had decided they would fight with Borneheld. *If* he would have them.

Borneheld knew what the bells were the instant their gentle sound reached him through the fog, and he hunched even further beneath his voluminous cloak.

It had been two weeks since they had fled Gorkenfort. As soon as Axis had drawn the Skraelings northwards away from the fort, Borneheld had ordered the gates opened and led his column out through the ruins of Gorkentown. The march south towards Jervois Landing was a desperate trek through icy conditions which hourly weakened his men's resistance to death. Many had died from the freezing cold or from the physical effort of the march. In the past week even more had died as the Skraelings made nibbling attacks on the rear and flanks of Borneheld's retreating column. Others deserted. Even those two old brothers who Axis had dragged north with him from the Silent Woman Keep and who had babbled incessantly about musty prophecies had disappeared one night. As far as Borneheld was concerned, the Skraelings could feed all they wanted on those two as on any others not prepared to stay with him.

Unaccountably, the Skraelings had left them alone for a critical five days after their escape from Gorkenfort. They had ridden as hard and as fast as they could – until the horses started to die beneath them – expecting an attack from Gorgrael's army at any moment. No-one in Borneheld's company knew that it was because Axis and his command had hurt the Skraelings so grievously in the icy wastes above Gorkenfort that the SkraeBolds had needed to regroup the decimated Skraeling forces.

All Borneheld and his company knew was that they'd had five days' start on the Skraelings, and that five days was the difference between life and death. When the Skraelings did finally reappear, they did not do so in force, and Borneheld's column had managed to keep moving further south towards the comparative safety of Jervois Landing. The Skraelings would not push so far south. Surely.

Yet every step they took southwards towards safety increased Borneheld's bitterness. It hadn't been his fault that Gorkenfort had fallen. Traitors had undermined his command and betrayed both Ichtar and Achar. Magariz's actions had confirmed that. His most senior, most trusted commander had chosen to ride with his bastard half-brother rather than fight for Borneheld and the cause of Achar. For thirty years Borneheld's jealousy of Axis had dominated his life; now bitter resentment twisted his gut. Artor curse him, he thought, I hope he died out there in the frozen wastes. Screaming for me to ride to his rescue, screaming my name as the wraiths chewed the flesh from his bones.

But even that thought could not bring a smile to Borneheld's cold-chapped face. Now, after the treachery of Gorkenfort, Borneheld trusted few. If Magariz could turn against him, then who else might prove treacherous? Even Jorge and Roland, riding silent and introspective further back in the column, did not enjoy the same depth of trust as they once had. No, Borneheld truly trusted only Gautier and Timozel. Who would have thought that such a young whelp – and an Axe-Wielder to boot – could grow into such a loyal and devoted servant to the Duke of Ichtar? Timozel had clearly demonstrated his worth on this march south, proving that he could harry men into obedience as well as Gautier, and fight with as much courage as Borneheld himself. Now he rode his horse slightly to the left and behind Borneheld, sitting tall and proud in the saddle, the occasional flare of his visionary eyes keeping Borneheld's own hopes alive.

Artor had graced Timozel with visions, and that meant Artor would eventually grace Borneheld's cause with victory as well.

Borneheld's eyes slipped to the horse that followed a few paces behind Timozel's. His wife, Faraday, clung to the saddle and to Yr, as she had since her horse succumbed to the cold three days ago. Could he trust Faraday? Borneheld frowned under the hood of his cloak. He had thought that she loved him, for had she not whispered words of love and devotion to him night after night, and fled to his arms when Axis had proved incapable of protecting her? But what was it she had murmured to Axis as they said goodbye in the courtyard of Gorkenfort?

Curse her, he swore silently. Her future would be with *him*, not with Axis. She would provide *Ichtar* with an heir, not whatever shadowland Axis currently ruled. He would rather see her dead than betray him as Magariz had.

The loss of Gorkenfort and, subsequently, Ichtar had hurt Borneheld to the core of his soul. As a young boy growing up in a loveless household, deserted by his mother, ignored by his father, Borneheld had always had Ichtar. And when his father died and Borneheld became Duke of Ichtar at only fourteen, he finally felt that his life had meaning. Ignored by so many when he was simply the son of Searlas, Borneheld revelled in the power he wielded as the new Duke. Power brought him the attention he craved, the respect he demanded, the command that was his due, and, eventually, the woman that he desired above all others.

Now most of Ichtar was lost to him, and Borneheld felt the loss as keenly as a physical wound. What power would he command as the man who had lost Ichtar? What respect? Even if he could win back Ichtar – and he *would* – he would still feel vulnerable. He would only feel safe if he commanded ultimate power over all of Achar, if he sat the throne itself. As King, Borneheld would have all the power, the respect and the love he craved. As King, he would surely be able to flush out the traitors about him once and for all. Desperate as he was to get it back, Ichtar was no longer enough for Borneheld.

And didn't Timozel's visions indicate that Borneheld *would* become King? Yes, it was Artor's wish that he take the throne.

Now, as he approached Jervois Landing, Borneheld reviewed the forces he still commanded. Despite the losses at Gorkentown – all of which had been the fault of either the demon-spawned Axis or that traitor Magariz – he still controlled a powerful force. The original column of five thousand he had led from Gorkenfort had been swelled by the refugees from Ichtar. As sorry as these refugees were now, they could work and some could be trained to fight. There were also troops still stationed in Achar that Borneheld could command. There was still a cohort of five hundred Axe-Wielders guarding the Brother-Leader at the Tower of the Seneschal. All these could be his. And, if those soft chimes meant what he hoped they did, he would also have the Ravensbundmen. Uncouth savages to be sure, but they had both spears and horses. If they could stick an enemy in the gut then they would be useful. Finally, there were the resources of the Corolean Empire to the south of Achar. If that simpering fool of a King, Priam, hadn't yet thought about arranging a military alliance with the Coroleans then Borneheld would make sure that he soon would.

Suddenly a stationary horseman loomed out of the mist and Borneheld barked an order to halt. He sat for a moment and looked at the inscrutable Ravensbundman's face. It was even more intricately tattooed in blue and black than most of his race. Dizzying whorls and spirals covered not only his cheeks, but his forehead and chin as well – although, strangely, there was a circular area right in the centre of his forehead that remained naked and untattooed. As with all his race, the savage had tiny chips of blue glass and miniature bells threaded through his myriad greasy black braids. Even his mount – ugly, stunted, yellow-furred nag that it was – had glass and bells woven into its mane and tail. Uncivilised savages. Still, if they could kill they might yet serve a purpose.

Ho'Demi let the Duke stare at him a moment, then spoke, demonstrating a fluent command of the Acharite language. "Duke Borneheld. Gorgrael has taken my land and murdered my people. He drives his Ghostmen south. The Ravensbundmen live only to defeat Gorgrael. If you fight against Gorgrael then we will stand by your side."

Borneheld narrowed his eyes at the barbarian. "I *do* fight Gorgrael. But if you want to fight with me then you will place yourself and your people under *my* command."

Ho'Demi wondered at the implicit threat in Borneheld's tone, but it did not perturb him. He nodded. "Agreed."

"Good." Borneheld peered into the mists behind the Ravensbundman, trying to see how many men he had with him. "How many will you bring to my command?"

"Of the twenty thousand in my camp, eleven thousand can fight."

"You have done well to choose my cause," Borneheld said quietly. "Together we will make our stand here at Jervois Landing against whichever of our enemies attack first. This time, *I* will prevail."

2

Talon Spike

Four weeks after StarDrifter tore the crossed axes from his breast, Axis – BattleAxe no longer – sat in his favourite spot on Talon Spike letting the wind ruffle through his blond hair and beard. Every few days Axis found he had to spend time alone, to lose himself in contemplation of these beautiful northern alps rather than in the intricacies of the magical Star Dance, Icarii society and his new life.

From his eyrie perch on the rock ledge Axis gazed at the blue-white glacier a thousand paces below, crashing a path through the lesser Icescarp Alps beyond Talon Spike to calve its massive icebergs into the Iskruel Ocean. One month ago the bergs in the Iskruel Ocean would simply have been flecks at the edge of his vision. Now he could see that the huge icebear on the smallest of the bergs had lost an ear in some past ursine dispute.

He sighed. Even the wonders of his new-found powers could not make him forget that Faraday was still trapped with one half-brother while the other, Gorgrael, was undoubtedly remarshalling his forces to invade Achar. And if Faraday or either one of his despised half-brothers did not occupy his thoughts, then Axis found himself worrying over the problems of his new life.

Father, mother, sister, uncle, grandmother. All exciting, all troubling in their own right. But it was StarDrifter who dominated Axis' days. His father, the man who had only existed in court gossip and innuendo for almost thirty years and whose conspicuous absence had given Gorgrael the grist to torment Axis in his nightmares for so long, was as compulsively drawn to Axis as Axis was to him.

Their relationship was not easy. StarDrifter was a forceful man with powerful expectations. He drove his son from first waking until Axis, exhausted, lay down his head late at night. And Axis, having been alone for so long, having been his own man for so long, both resented his father's intrusions and yearned for his father's attention. It was not easy reconciling resentment and need every minute of the day.

Axis' mouth twisted as he thought of their morning's training session. After hours confined in the one chamber, they had fought, bitterly, savagely. MorningStar, StarDrifter's mother and Axis' grandmother, who was often present, had finally dismissed Axis as she tried to reason with her son. Yet all Axis wanted to do was stay in that chamber and ask StarDrifter another question about his heritage and powers.

"You fought again."

Startled, Axis turned his head towards the voice. It was Azhure, dressed in a pale-grey woollen tunic and leggings, walking confidently along the narrow rock ledge. She halted a few paces away. "May I join you? Am I intruding?"

Axis smiled. "No, you're not intruding. Please, join me."

She sat down gracefully, curling her legs underneath her. "It is a superb view."

"Can you see the icebear?" He pointed to the distant iceberg.

Azhure laughed. "I have not your Enchanter's vision, Axis SunSoar."

Axis relaxed. Since he had come to Talon Spike, Azhure had become a good friend. She was the one person he felt he could talk to, who understood the problems he encountered as he embraced his heritage.

"You have developed a good head for heights since living among the Icarii, Azhure. Few Groundwalkers could even stand on this ledge, let alone wander along it as if strolling the flat plains of Skarabost."

"Why fear when I have an Enchanter to hand to save me should I tumble?"

Axis laughed and changed the subject. "How did you know StarDrifter and I had fought?"

"He came back to the apartments and snapped at Rivkah. She snapped back. I left them bickering and thought to find the source of such marital disharmony so that he could explain himself."

"Do you think I should have re-entered their lives, Azhure?" Axis asked.

"If there are problems between them, you are not the cause, Axis," Azhure replied. "I am sorry if I implied, even laughingly, that you were."

Axis leaned his arms on his raised knees and considered his parents. Tension marked the relationship between himself and his father, while with his mother there was nothing but warmth. When the five Icarii had escorted him into Talon Spike she had been the first to step forward. She had said nothing, just folded him in her strong arms. For long minutes they had stood, each weeping silently, holding each other as close as they could. Axis recalled how he had summoned the memory of her struggle to give him birth and fight for his life. For so long he'd believed that she had cursed him as she died in his birth. Those long minutes holding each other had been a time of healing for them both.

But things between Rivkah and StarDrifter were not idyllic. That they loved each other, Axis had no doubt. But their passionate affair atop Sigholt had not transferred easily to Talon Spike. Perhaps Axis had arrived in their lives only in time to watch the sad disintegration of their marriage.

"It must be hard to look into the face of your husband and see a man who looks no older than your son."

Axis' expression hardened a little. His Icarii blood ran much stronger than his human and, like his sister, he would live the full span of an Icarii lifetime – perhaps some five hundred years, should he be left in peace to do so. What would it be like to watch his friends age and die while he still enjoyed youthful vitality? What would it be like to see the sods thrown on their grandchildren's coffins before he had reached his middle years?

"Do I like it that in four hundred years I might still be sitting here watching the icebears hunt seals on the icebergs, trying desperately to recall the name and face of a lovely woman who had once sat here with me? Whose bones have turned to dust in some forgotten tomb? No, Azhure. I do not like it. I find it . . . hard."

Azhure reached out and took his hand. Axis stiffened briefly, then he forced a smile. "But these powers I daily learn as an Icarii Enchanter give me a few compensations. Such as making the woman who sits here with me a small gift for the friendship she offers me."

For an instant Azhure thought she caught the hint of a faraway melody in the wind. Then she was laughing in delight as the soft, velvety blooms of the violet Moonwild-flower rained down about her. She let Axis' hand go and tried to catch as many as she could.

"How did you know?" she gasped. She had not seen a Moonwildflower for over twenty years – when she was a tiny girl her mother had occasionally taken her on walks during full moon to find the flower.

Axis plucked a flower out of the air and threaded it into her wavy black hair. He was mildly disturbed, for he had meant to shower her with soft spring roses. "A lucky guess, Azhure. You sometimes remind me of the Moonwildflower. Hidden in darkness, desperate not to be found or touched."

Suddenly awkward, Azhure gently cradled a flower in her hands. The cascade drifted to a halt and she spoke, changing the subject. "EvenSong wants me to join her at training this afternoon. She says I show aptitude."

EvenSong had been impressed by Azhure's extraordinary fighting ability so clearly demonstrated during the battle in the Earth Tree Grove at Yuletide. While the Icarii Strike Force had faltered helplessly, unsure of how to combat the Skraeling wraiths, Azhure had discovered the Skraelings' vulnerability – their eyes – and almost single-handedly rallied the Icarii and Avar to fight back. During the battle she had also saved StarDrifter from certain death.

EvenSong admired Azhure for her cool head and bravery, and for some weeks she and her Wing-Leader, SpikeFeather TrueSong, had been pressing Azhure to join weapons training with the Strike Force.

Axis could see Azhure's doubts and knew the reasons for them. Had he not reviled her for the death of her father and the assault on Belial as she escaped into the Avarinheim with Raum and Shra? Had not the Avar rejected her, suspicious of her violence, even though she had saved so many of their lives?

"Azhure," he said gently. "You did what you had to. Now do what you want with your life. *Would* you like to go with EvenSong this afternoon?"

Azhure hesitated, then nodded. "I have seen the Strike Force practise at archery. They look so smooth, so graceful. I would like to try that. SpikeFeather has offered to demonstrate for me and," her mouth quirked, "teach me the proper use of the arrow." Again she hesitated, then forged on. "I am sick of feeling helpless, directionless. I feel as though I have spent my life in a deep, dark well. Now, after so long buried in Smyrton, I am starting to make my way towards the surface – but the surface is still so very far away. Each day away from Smyrton, each new experience, brings me a little closer, wakes me up a little more from the torpor of my previous life. You are right. I must seek my own path."

She laughed now, her good humour returning. "I am glad I'm not an Icarii Enchanter like you, destined for heroic deeds. That would be a heavy burden."

Axis turned away, his face expressionless. "I am no hero."

Azhure lowered her eyes to the flower she still held. If Axis had his moments of denial, then she did not blame him. Not a day passed that Axis did not grieve for those who had already died for him. He despised the thought that yet more would die. And it haunted him that his sister blamed him for FreeFall's death.

"You must bear with EvenSong. She has not yet reconciled herself to FreeFall's death. Her grief needs an outlet."

Axis knew his sister resented him for many other reasons besides his inability to prevent FreeFall's death. She had not begun to come to terms with having an older brother, and one who had inherited their father's powers in full. Where once StarDrifter had lavished attention on EvenSong, now she found herself virtually ignored by her father as he spent almost every waking moment with his son. EvenSong found her father's obsession with Axis difficult to accept.

It was fortunate, Axis mused, that Azhure was here to offer EvenSong companionship. He too appreciated the friendship and understanding she gave him as he fought to adjust to his new life and his new powers. Rivkah spent a good deal of time talking to her as well. If not for Azhure, StarDrifter's entire household might well have self-destructed by now.

"The SunSoars are difficult people to live with," he said, resting his chin in his hand.

"The Icarii people as a whole are," replied Azhure, her eyes distant. "They are very good at passions and very bad at friendships."

Axis studied her closely. This woman from Smyrton displayed more insight than many who had spent years in scholarly or diplomatic training. Where had she got it from? Not from her father, surely; Hagen had demonstrated as much insight as a sack of barley. Her mother? From what Axis knew of Nors women, they thought mainly of the pleasures of the flesh and very little else. And surely the woeful society of her village had contributed little to the inner depths she increasingly revealed.

Azhure shifted under his gaze – those pale-blue eyes seemed to reach to the core of her soul. Unthinking, she said the first thing that sprang to mind.

"Do you worry about her, Axis? Do you wonder if she is all right?" she asked, and then wished desperately she could snatch her words back.

Axis tensed at her side and Azhure could sense his withdrawal. He rarely spoke of Faraday and yet Azhure knew she was always in his thoughts.

Azhure stumbled on, trying to relieve the sudden tension. "I saw her, you know, at Yuletide. She is a woman who combines great beauty with great compassion and selflessness. It is no wonder you love her as you do."

"You saw her?" Axis frowned. "How?"

"Did StarDrifter not tell you how he and Faraday woke the Earth Tree at Yuletide as the Skraelings attacked the Earth Tree Grove?"

Axis nodded, still frowning, and Azhure hurried on. "I don't know what enchantment StarDrifter used, but Faraday appeared as if in a vision above the Earth Tree. No-one else saw her. StarDrifter and Raum were concentrating so hard on the Tree that they did not look up. I don't know if she saw me, but she looked down and smiled." Azhure gave a little shrug. "At least, I like to think she smiled at me."

Axis relaxed a little. "She would like you, and you her. It is a pity you are both caught in the web of this Prophecy."

"If *I* were married to Borneheld he would not have survived his wedding night," Azhure said tightly. Over the past few weeks she had learned much of Faraday's circumstances. "Why did she not escape with you to Talon Spike?"

"Because she honours the vows that she took when she became Borneheld's wife, Azhure. Even her love for me will not make her desert her honour." He sounded bitter. "Do I wonder about her? Do I worry if she is all right? With every breath that I draw, Azhure. I live for her."

"Axis."

They both swivelled towards the voice. StarDrifter stood on the ledge by the archway that led back into the mountain, his white wings a little outstretched to aid his balance.

Axis stood in one fluid motion, feeling his father's intrusion keenly.

StarDrifter held his gaze briefly, then dropped his eyes to Azhure and smiled warmly at her, his face breathtaking in its beauty. "You should not bring Azhure out here, Axis. She does not have our balance." He stepped forward and helped Azhure to her feet, clasping her hand as he led her back into the safety of the mountain.

As they stepped through the archway and down into the wide corridor, Azhure pulled her hand awkwardly from StarDrifter's grasp. "I followed Axis out there, StarDrifter. It was not his fault. And neither the height of the cliff nor the narrowness of the ledge bother me. Truly."

StarDrifter looked back at her. He wished she would abandon the Avar tunic and leggings and wear the loose flowing robes favoured by the Icarii women; she would look superb in their jewelled colours and she had the grace to do their elegance justice.

Axis stepped down into the corridor behind them and StarDrifter glanced at his son. The tensions of their morning argument remained, and this afternoon's training session would not be easy. No doubt they would end this afternoon with angry words as well. Axis was so desperate to learn, but hated being the student.

Yet he learned so well, and so quickly. That was part of the problem, for Axis wanted to learn faster than StarDrifter was willing to teach. While StarDrifter took pride in the knowledge that the Prophecy had chosen him among all Icarii to breed this son, he also found it hard not to resent Axis' power. As EvenSong resented losing her only and most favoured child status, so StarDrifter was battling to come to terms with the fact that very soon Axis' power would surpass his own — and StarDrifter had long revelled in being the most powerful Icarii Enchanter alive.

StarDrifter looked back to Azhure with studied casualness. "Will you join us this afternoon, Azhure?" he asked. With her present, both Enchanters kept a tighter rein on their tempers. Neither MorningStar — who often helped with Axis' training — nor Axis had so far raised any objections to Azhure's occasional presence in the training chamber.

"I thank you for the invitation, StarDrifter, but I will refuse. I promised EvenSong I would spend the afternoon with her. If you will excuse me."

She nodded at both men, then walked down the corridor, disappearing around the first corner.

"Imagine the Enchanters she would bear," StarDrifter said, so quietly that Axis could not believe he was hearing correctly. "I am nothing if not a good judge of blood."

Then he turned his powerful gaze on his son. "Over the past thousand years the Icarii blood has thinned. Before the Wars of the Axe that severed our races many Icarii birdmen chose to get their sons on human women. It was said that human blood added vitality to the Icarii. You are proof enough of that."

Axis felt his anger simmering. Was StarDrifter planning another seduction?

"I love Rivkah," StarDrifter said slowly. "I demonstrated my love through marriage — even though I believed she had lost our son. In ages past Icarii birdmen simply took the babies of human–Icarii unions and never spared a thought for the women they had bedded who had struggled to birth their children."

Appalled at such evidence of Icarii insensitivity, Axis suddenly understood the depth of hate and loathing that had led the Acharites to finally drive the Icarii from Tencendor.

The Icarii had a lot to learn about compassion.

3

The Wolven

Azhure walked through the confusing maze of corridors in the Talon Spike complex, hoping she had remembered EvenSong's instructions correctly. Over at least a thousand years the Icarii had tunnelled and excavated the mountain into myriad chambers, connecting corridors and shafts. The Icarii not only used horizontal corridors, but also vertical shafts – foot travellers needed to be wary of wells opening abruptly at their feet.

Azhure paused at one of the main connecting shafts of Talon Spike, which not only extended up to the very peak of the mountain, but also fell into its dizzying depths. She grasped the waist-high guard rail and peered down. Two Icarii, already several levels below her, slowly spiralled down through the shaft side by side. Both had gorgeously dyed emerald and blue wings, and the soft enchanted light of the shaft shimmered across their jewel-bright feathers. Azhure had to blink back tears at their loveliness. Nothing in her previous life in Smyrton had prepared her for the beauty and passion of life among the Icarii of Talon Spike.

On her arrival six weeks ago Azhure had wondered at the height and width of the corridors – but their spaciousness was explained the moment she saw several Icarii wing their graceful way along the corridor, several paces above her head. Fortunately for her, the complex also had stairs that wound about the walls of the vertical shafts. Icarii children did not develop wings until they were four or five years of age, and did not learn to fly well until they were eight or nine. And occasionally an Icarii who injured a wing might have to walk the corridors or climb the stairs. MorningStar, StarDrifter's mother, was such a one. She had been unable to attend the Yuletide rites in the Earth Tree Grove after snapping a tendon in her left wing, and was still grumbling about the indignity of having to use the stairs.

Leaving the shaft, Azhure passed the doors to the massive Talon Spike Library. The Avar Bane Raum spent most of his days here, teaching the wingless youngsters about the Avar and their forest home. Azhure's thoughts drifted to Rivkah as she walked. Over the many years that Azhure had known Rivkah — or GoldFeather as she had been called until recently — she had never known her so at peace with herself as she had been since Axis' arrival. Rivkah might yet have her unhappinesses with StarDrifter, but the reunion with the son she had long thought dead had healed a festering wound in Rivkah's heart. She spent many hours each day guiding Azhure through the intricacies of Icarii society, teasing the young woman mercilessly when she gaped open-mouthed at some of the more permissive practices of the Icarii.

"You are already a much sought-after prize, Azhure Groundwalker, with your raven-black hair and mysterious smoke-filled eyes," Rivkah had said only this morning. "Will you survive the Beltide festivities without being cradled within some lover's wings?"

Azhure had blushed and turned away, thinking uncomfortably of the way StarDrifter had begun to watch her recently. The last thing she wanted to do was come between StarDrifter and Rivkah, who was rapidly filling the void caused by the loss of Azhure's mother so early in life. Azhure couldn't remember a time when she hadn't woken several nights a week, her cheeks wet with tears of loss; but now she slept soundly, and the unsettling dreams that had troubled her for more than twenty years had vanished entirely.

Azhure abruptly realised that for the past five or six weeks she had been constantly happy. Never had she been accepted before, and the Icarii not only seemed to accept her for who she was, but they actually *liked* her.

She nodded to an Icarii passing overhead, her thoughts returning to EvenSong. Azhure had so far resisted the urge to join the Strike Force in weapons training for fear of giving in to the violent streak the Avar claimed she possessed. She shuddered, remembering how after she had seized the arrow and killed her first Skraeling, she had been consumed with the desire to kill. Perhaps the Avar *were* right to regard her with some degree of apprehension.

But Azhure had made up her mind. Axis was right; she should seek her own path. If her path lay in violence, then perhaps she should simply accept that. Accept the blood and turn it into a mark of respect, not of reproach.

She turned down a corridor to her left, then ran lightly down several levels of stairs, her grace causing the Icarii birdman who soared past her to turn his head and watch for long moments until the Groundwalker woman disappeared into a corridor far below.

EvenSong had a leather thong tied about her pale-skinned forehead to keep the sweat out of her eyes. She had turned twenty-five on the day after Yuletide, and had immediately joined the Strike Force for her five years of compulsory military service.

She grunted as she parried a blow from her sparring partner. She did not like to sweat and thought longingly of the relaxing hot waters of the Chamber of Steaming Water. Once she had looked forward to her years in the Strike Force, but that was only because she had believed she would spend those years with her cousin FreeFall. Born only two months apart, she and FreeFall had grown up together, planned their lives together, and mused over what it would be like when he became Talon. It was not unusual for Icarii to marry or form sexual relationships with close relatives, and FreeFall and EvenSong had become lovers at thirteen.

Of course, neither EvenSong nor FreeFall had considered the possibility that he would be so cruelly murdered at such a young age. EvenSong daily bewailed not only the loss of her friend and lover, but also the prospect of spending the rest of her long life alone.

Her sparring partner and Wing-Leader, SpikeFeather TrueSong, slipped his stave under EvenSong's guard and dealt her a heavy blow to the ribs. She dropped her staff and fell to her knees, badly winded.

"Pay attention," SpikeFeather hissed viciously. "In battle – even in a tavern brawl – you would be dead now! We cannot afford to lose any more SunSoars."

EvenSong glared at him, her hand clutched to her ribs. "Like you lost FreeFall?" SpikeFeather had flown with Free-Fall and HoverEye BlackWing to meet Axis atop Gorkenfort's roof. But their mission had ended in tragedy when Borneheld murdered FreeFall.

SpikeFeather swore and seized EvenSong by her short curls, hauling her to her feet. She winced and tried to twist free, but SpikeFeather's grip was too strong.

"FreeFall had the courage to face life, EvenSong, even when it led him to death. Think how he would frown to see you use his death to give up on life itself!"

The ten other members of the Wing had stopped sparring and watched SpikeFeather and EvenSong soberly. Ever since the disaster of Yuletide, training had taken on a much more serious aspect. Where once good humour and enjoyment had pervaded weapons practice, now the expectation of an eventual conflict with Gorgrael's forces dominated everyone's thoughts.

SpikeFeather let EvenSong's hair go, then stepped back and glared at the rest of his command. He was an experienced Wing-Leader, but in these difficult times his responsibilities weighed heavily on him. And despite what EvenSong apparently thought, SpikeFeather agonised daily over his inability to act quickly enough to save FreeFall. EvenSong seemed to have no heart since FreeFall's murder, and SpikeFeather knew that the inattention of a single member could bring ruin to his entire Wing in battle.

To add to SpikeFeather's woes, all of the Strike Force were on edge, and not simply because of the battle at Earth Tree Grove or the inevitable battle to come with Gorgrael's forces. From the most senior Crest-Leader, FarSight CutSpur, to the lowliest recruit, the Strike Force was keenly aware of the presence of Axis SunSoar in Talon Spike. The Icarii Assembly had agreed to StarDrifter's request to help his son in Gorkenfort partly because after a thousand years of relative peace they needed a true war leader. Someone who actually *had* experience of battle.

Yet Axis SunSoar, one-time BattleAxe of the Axe-Wielders, the force that had been largely responsible for the thousand-year exile of the Icarii in Talon Spike, had shown not an iota of interest in the Strike Force in the month since he'd been in Talon Spike. As much as SpikeFeather, or any other member of the Strike Force, might tell himself that Axis was preoccupied with learning the skills of Enchanter from his father, his lack of interest had stung. When would Axis visit the training chambers? When would he deign to visit the Strike Force? And what would he say when he saw them train? What would he think? Would he praise, or deride?

SpikeFeather was about to call a halt to their afternoon training when a movement at the edge of his vision stopped him. Azhure stood leaning over the balcony rail of the observation gallery, watching them gravely.

"Azhure!" EvenSong exclaimed, and SpikeFeather hoped she felt just a little ashamed that her friend might have witnessed her poor behaviour.

"I do not want to interrupt, SpikeFeather TrueSong," Azhure said courteously, "and if I have broken your concentration then I apologise to you and to your command." One of the first things Azhure had learned in Talon Spike was that the Icarii valued politeness and correct etiquette extremely highly. Two Icarii could get themselves into a murderous argument and never raise their voices or transgress the bounds of civilised language. The scene she had just witnessed between SpikeFeather and EvenSong was extraordinary, and bespoke the tension within the Strike Force.

"I have decided to accept your offer to teach me the use of the bow and arrow, SpikeFeather."

SpikeFeather swept his wings behind him in the traditional Icarii gesture of welcome and goodwill. "You are welcomed, Azhure. And I regret that my command is not at its *best* this afternoon."

EvenSong reddened.

SpikeFeather ignored her. "Both myself and my Wing would be pleased if you joined us, Azhure. We are all beholden to you for your bravery at Yuletide, the SunSoar family perhaps more than most." Another barb for EvenSong. SpikeFeather was truly exasperated with her.

Azhure stepped down from the ladder, took off her boots, and walked across the floor of the spacious training chamber towards the Wing. Soft mats covered every part of the floor, while from the high roof hung several brightly coloured orbs that served as archery targets. Weapon racks and cupboards lined the lower walls.

"I am not dressed for combat, SpikeFeather. Please do not aim any arrows my way." She grinned at the Wing commander, her hand indicating her Avar clothing and bare feet. All the Icarii present, both female and male, wore light leather training armour over brief loin cloths – although the armour did not protect against serious blows. They were sweating after their exertions, and Azhure noticed that several had abrasions and dark bruises on their unprotected arms and legs. Feathers lay scattered across the floor mats.

"I would be hounded from Talon Spike should I land an arrow in a guest, and such an admired guest at that," SpikeFeather said gravely, then turned to one of the members of his Wing. "TrueFlight, would you lift the Wolven from the rack and select a quiver of arrows?" He paused dramatically, ignoring the collective gasp of the Wing.

Azhure watched curiously as TrueFlight retrieved a beautiful bow and a quiver of arrows and handed them to SpikeFeather, who slung the quiver over his shoulder.

"As creatures of the air ourselves we have a special affinity with weapons of flight," SpikeFeather explained as he notched an arrow into the bow. "See."

In one liquid movement, so fast Azhure found it difficult to follow, SpikeFeather lifted the bow, aimed, and loosed the arrow. It soared towards the ceiling and lodged in a small scarlet target ball suspended sixty paces above their heads.

"The stories of your ability don't do you justice, Spike-Feather," Azhure said. "Can I try that bow?" The bow SpikeFeather held was a weapon of elegance as well as of skill, and Azhure found its lure almost irresistible.

SpikeFeather studied her. Since the Wolven's creator had died four thousand years ago, only he had been able to master it. The Icarii had extraordinarily powerful flight muscles in their chests and backs, and SpikeFeather doubted whether Azhure, despite her height and obvious fitness, would even have the strength to draw a notched arrow back in a normal Icarii bow, let alone the Wolven.

He finally shrugged. What would it hurt? He picked another arrow from his quiver and handed the bow to Azhure. Tall, but made of surprisingly light ivory wood, it was patterned with golden tracery and strung and tasselled in vivid blues and scarlets. It was as beautiful as it was deadly.

"Here," SpikeFeather said, showing Azhure how to place her hands, then notching the arrow. Standing behind her, he curled her fingers around the arrow. "Let me help you to . . ."

"No," Azhure said, stepping away from him slightly. "Let me try first, SpikeFeather. What should I aim for?"

SpikeFeather smiled indulgently. "Aim high, Azhure, at any of the targets suspended from the ceiling. If you hit one I will make you a gift of the Wolven itself as a mark of Icarii admiration and fashion you a quiver with my own hands."

Azhure looked at the targets hanging from the ceiling. Then, without lowering her eyes, she raised the bow and started to draw the arrow back.

SpikeFeather saw the exact moment when Azhure found that the Wolven required extraordinary strength. Her shoulders, back, and arms suddenly tensed, and her hands quavered so badly that SpikeFeather was sure she would drop the bow or let the arrow tumble to the floor. He started as if to step forward and help her, but EvenSong caught his elbow. "Let her try for herself," she whispered, and SpikeFeather subsided, although a frown of worry creased his face. What if she couldn't control the flight of the arrow, and skewered one of his command? None of them wore armour that could withstand a loose Icarii arrow.

But Azhure managed to retain control, although Spike-Feather could see what a supreme effort it cost her. Gradually her hands steadied and her back straightened. Then she took a deep breath and pulled the arrow all the way back, raising the bow to her face and sighting along the shaft of the arrow.

SpikeFeather's eyes widened in amazement. Where did she find the strength to control the bow? A *human* woman?

Azhure, as taut and tense as the Wolven itself, finally let fly the arrow in as good an imitation of SpikeFeather's action as she could manage.

As one the Icarii watched the flight of the arrow.

It flew straight and true, striking a golden target the size of a man's head. But Azhure, for all her effort in drawing, aiming and releasing the arrow, could not give the arrow the same power as SpikeFeather had, and the arrow head only penetrated the target superficially. It hung there for a long moment, then slowly slipped from the target and tumbled to the floor.

"I hit it!" Azhure cried triumphantly, lowering the bow and turning to SpikeFeather, who stood with an expression of absolute amazement on his face. "It stuck for a moment. It *did*!" She laughed with joy. "Is the bow mine, SpikeFeather?"

She spun around in an excited circle until she faced SpikeFeather again. "Well?"

SpikeFeather lowered his eyes to the woman before him. If he hadn't witnessed it himself he would never have believed it. It wasn't simply Azhure's strength in drawing the bow and loosing the arrow, it was also the fact that she had actually hit the target she'd aimed at. It usually took a novice Icarii archer several weeks of practice before they even got an arrow within spitting distance of a ceiling target – and the Icarii were flight intuitive. Was it simply luck?

SpikeFeather looked at the magnificent bow that Azhure clutched possessively to her side. It was one of the most valuable and treasured items in the Strike Force's arsenal. What had he *done*?

Azhure's smile died and her eyes narrowed as she watched the welter of emotions play across SpikeFeather's face; emotions mirrored on the faces of the eleven Icarii who stood at his back. EvenSong looked as though she had swallowed the arrow instead of simply watching it hit the target.

Azhure stepped over and lifted another arrow from the quiver on SpikeFeather's back. He flinched a little as her hand brushed the downy red feathers on the back of his neck.

"No fluke," she said, her eyes unexpectedly dark as she stared into SpikeFeather's face. "If I miss this time then I will return the bow. But if I hit the target, then you will not only fashion me the quiver to sling across my back, but fletch the arrows to go in it with your own flight feathers, SpikeFeather TrueSong. Dyed the same blue as my eyes, I think."

Then, in a movement almost as elegant as SpikeFeather's, Azhure notched the arrow, raised the bow, sighted, and loosed the arrow. This time it struck the target true, the solid thunk as it penetrated deep into the golden orb audible around the chamber.

"The Wolven is mine," Azhure said into the utter silence. "I think it likes me. It felt easier the second time."

SpikeFeather dropped his eyes to Azhure, then bowed deep before her, his wings sweeping a wide arc on the floor behind him. When he straightened, his eyes were solemn. "The Wolven is yours, Azhure. I will fashion you a quiver to hold arrows fletched with feathers from my own wings. You are an archer-born, Azhure, and I will welcome you whenever you wish to train with my Wing."

"Yes," Azhure said to the handsome birdman. "I would like to return and train with your command, SpikeFeather TrueSong."

"Then make sure that when the time arrives, you deal death with the Wolven, Azhure. That is why it was crafted."

Later, the muscles in her back, arms and chest burning with the effort required to use the bow, Azhure mounted the ladder, the bow slung across her back. SpikeFeather caught her arm. "Azhure, you speak to Axis SunSoar more than most. When will he visit the Strike Force? When?"

Azhure stepped down from the ladder and turned to face him. "I do not know, SpikeFeather. He is consumed by his need for his father now, and by his need to discover what lies beneath his surface. Wait. He will come."

4

Learning the Star Dance

MorningStar took a deep breath to calm herself and turned back to StarDrifter. He had been a late child, born when MorningStar was already close to four hundred years old. Because he was so unexpected – and had inherited his mother's Enchanter powers at that – both MorningStar and her husband, RushCloud, had spoiled him abominably. And whereas her eldest son, RavenCrest, had been groomed from birth to inherit the mantle of Talon, leader of all the Icarii, the much younger StarDrifter had been indulged. At least, MorningStar sighed, StarDrifter's lack of discipline had got him a son who might well prove the last hope of the SunSoars, if not the Icarii race as a whole.

She glanced over at Axis, sitting calmly on a stool in the small, unadorned chamber, StarDrifter pacing irritably about him. He had learned well since arriving in Talon Spike – far better than either MorningStar or StarDrifter had thought possible. Who could have imagined that an Enchanter, left without training for thirty years, could grasp the intricacies of the Star Dance so quickly and easily?

As Axis' father, StarDrifter had borne the major burden of his son's training, but MorningStar helped, and that was at the heart of their current troubles. Although an Enchanter was usually trained by his or her parent – the one who had bequeathed the Enchanter blood – another Enchanter of the same House, or family, could also act as an instructor. The closer the blood link, the easier the teaching. MorningStar was only one generation removed from Axis, so the blood link was strong, and she wanted to help.

But StarDrifter, having been separated from his son for so long, found it hard to share him with anyone, even his mother. MorningStar could understand that, but there were some things that MorningStar knew she could teach Axis better than StarDrifter.

And that is what they were fighting about now.

"StarDrifter," MorningStar said reasonably, "you are so good using the power of the Star Dance in conjunction with the elements of fire, earth and air. In those areas you are by far the most powerful we have seen in generations, and you pass your skills to your son well. But if you have a weakness, it is with the element of water. Since I have skill in that area, it only makes sense that I take charge of Axis' training when it comes to the water music."

StarDrifter stopped his pacing. "I have more power," he snapped.

"Yes, you have more power," she agreed. "But the element of water does not need power so much as subtlety, and you are often too impatient for such subtlety."

StarDrifter glared at her, then suddenly backed down. "Then teach!" he snarled.

Axis felt MorningStar's hand rest lightly on his shoulder. "Good," she said quietly and moved around to face him. Their relationship was still awkward, and neither knew quite what to think of the other. Axis was aware that his grand-mother vaguely disapproved of him. He knew she'd have preferred the StarMan to be of full Icarii blood, and he suspected that she, like StarDrifter, was just a little resentful of the extent of his power.

MorningStar was a determined and forceful woman who wielded enormous power within Talon Spike – not only as a senior Enchanter, but also as the widow of the previous Talon. Axis still found it difficult to come to terms with MorningStar's age. She approached the limit of her life, five hundred years, but she looked no older than himself. She had the same colouring as StarDrifter, short curly golden hair, pale blue eyes, and luminous white feathered wings. Only the vast experience evident in her eyes and the assurance of her manner gave some indication of her age.

MorningStar closed her eyes as she ran a prayer to Flulia, the Goddess of Water, through her mind. Then she took Axis' head between her hands and closed his eyes with her thumbs. "Hear the Star Dance," she said softly.

The first thing StarDrifter had taught Axis was to hear the Star Dance – the music that the Stars made as they whirled through the universe, and the source of power for all Icarii Enchanters. The music of the Star Dance was of astounding beauty, and when Axis first heard it, he had burst into tears at its unexpected splendour. Although the music was not particularly loud it pervaded every aspect of life. Now its faint melodies surrounded Axis through every moment, in the beat of his heart, in the conversations about him, in the sound of feathers rustling in the wind, in the shadows of his dreams.

Icarii Enchanters harnessed the power of the Stars by manipulating the music of the Star Dance. From the Dance they wove a melody that served as a conduit for the power of the Stars. For each purpose, a melody. Enchanters spent their developing years learning all the different melodies, or Songs, and the purpose of each. Once they had learned a Song – no mean feat – to use it they ran its melody through their minds, sometimes physically giving voice to the music they manipulated. The more powerful the Enchanter, the more complex the Song they could manipulate. For thousands of years Icarii Enchanters had debated the possibility that one day an Enchanter might learn to use the entire Star Dance, rather than lifting more manageable fragments of melody. The debate had finally been solved seventeen hundred years previously when one Enchanter had tried to grapple with the power of the entire Star Dance – he had died so horribly, warped out of existence, that no-one had been tempted to try it again.

Axis had learned so quickly because he had the remarkable gift of remembering a melody after only one hearing. Usually Icarii Enchanters had to have a Song repeated to them scores of times before they could use it effectively. It was one of the many ways in which the depth and extent of Axis' ability constantly astounded MorningStar and Star-Drifter.

"Listen," MorningStar said, and began to sing for her grandson the Songs which were particularly effective for manipulating the element of water and of all matter associated with water. Before she sang each Song, MorningStar whispered its purpose.

StarDrifter watched Axis carefully. Axis had already learned virtually all there was to know about the other groups of Songs and had displayed equal (and remarkable) talent in each. Would he now display a similar talent for water music?

Within an hour StarDrifter had his answer. There was not one Song MorningStar sang for him that Axis could not instantly repeat, even strengthen. He must be beloved of all the Star Gods, StarDrifter mused, to be so favoured.

In training, Enchanters usually only learned the melodics of the Songs, they did not yet attempt to manipulate the power of the Stars. It would be disastrous for an Enchanter only beginning to develop his skills to manipulate power at the same time as he sang a Song for the first time. Yet Axis never made a mistake, and on those rare occasions when StarDrifter and MorningStar had let him actually reach for the power of the Stars, Axis had demonstrated his ability to control the power that flowed through the melody.

Finally MorningStar stepped back, exhausted.

"Enough," she said, letting Axis' head go. "You have learned enough for today. We will resume tomorrow."

"How many more?" Axis asked, opening his eyes.

"Thirty-eight Songs."

"And you have shown me fourteen this afternoon." Axis stood up and stretched. "Fifty-two. It is not many."

For each Song there was only one purpose, and there were only a finite number of Songs that the Icarii Enchanters had discovered in ten thousand years of searching. The restrictions of his powers frustrated Axis as much as they excited him. What was the use of such ability if there was no Song for the purpose you had in mind? And as yet nothing that StarDrifter or MorningStar had taught him seemed powerful enough to combat Gorgrael or his mass of Skraelings.

He turned to his father in frustration. "Do the Icarii Enchanters have no Songs that will aid in war, StarDrifter?"

"Perhaps once the Icarii had Songs of War, Axis." StarDrifter's earlier ire had faded and now he clasped his son's shoulder affectionately. "But if they ever existed they have been lost for thousands of years. Perhaps they were too dangerous. Too potent. Once the Icarii were more warlike, and could fashion weapons that themselves wielded Star Power."

"Such a weapon is the Wolven," RavenCrest said from the doorway. Anger laced his words. He was furious with SpikeFeather for promising the bow to Azhure if she could hit a target with it. *Stupid*! No matter that he, too, would have thought Azhure could not possibly loose an arrow from it, let alone hit a ceiling target. In the week since Azhure had gained possession of the Wolven, it had not once left her side, and she had practised with it every day, spending long hours afterwards in the Chamber of Steaming Water, easing her aching chest and back muscles.

"The Wolven is an enchanted weapon?" Axis frowned at his uncle, although he smiled inwardly at RavenCrest's anger.

Azhure had won her gift fairly, displaying remarkable skill in doing so.

"Yes, enchanted," StarDrifter cut in, "but we have lost the key to use it. Whatever Song it requires has been lost. It died with," he hesitated, "WolfStar SunSoar, the Enchanter-Talon who originally crafted the weapon."

MorningStar's mouth thinned at the mention of WolfStar, but Axis did not notice. "Is there is no way of remembering the Song of the Wolven?" he asked. "Or of any other of the Songs of War?"

"We rely on *you* to save us!" RavenCrest hissed, his anger fully apparent as he strode across the room. He was vividly coloured, far more so than his mother or brother, with violet eyes, raven-black hair and wingbacks, and gorgeous speckled blue underwings. Yet his vivid anger made him menacing, and Axis had to fight from taking a pace back as RavenCrest stepped up to him. "Seek not legends from our past to lead us to victory, Axis! Rely on what skills you have inside you!" He paused, then dropped his voice to a harsh whisper. "And remember, Axis SunSoar, that you will have to win the loyalty and trust of the Icarii nation if you are to succeed against Gorgrael, and enchanted weapons will not win for you our trust."

Axis fully understood RavenCrest's anger. With the death of FreeFall SunSoar, RavenCrest had lost his only son and heir. Not only did RavenCrest daily have to live with the grief of losing his beloved son, he also had to battle with the fact that the heir to the Talon throne would be Axis – StarDrifter might be a powerful Enchanter, but he would be a hopeless leader of the Icarii nation. Axis knew that RavenCrest was also deeply resentful that his heir was not only of Icarii–human parentage, but also a former BattleAxe of the loathed Seneschal.

Nothing had been said, but everyone knew the situation – and Axis intended to fight for his right to be named

RavenCrest's heir. He knew he had to weld the Icarii, Acharite and Avar races together in order to fight Gorgrael, and if he could control the thrones of both Icarii and Acharite nations then he'd have a much better chance of success. Through his mother, Rivkah, once Princess of Achar, Axis was second in line to the Acharite throne behind Borneheld. And Axis did not intend to let Borneheld live.

He turned his mind away from his half-brother and considered the implications of what RavenCrest had said. Axis would have to win the trust of the Icarii nation if he wanted to not only be accepted as heir, but also use the Icarii Strike Force in his battle against Gorgrael. Axis knew the Icarii trust would be hard to win, and as yet he had not even made a start. In the five weeks he'd been in Talon Spike he hadn't met any Icarii beyond his immediate family.

"RavenCrest," he said. "It is time I met with your Crest-Leaders. It is time I took control of the Strike Force." Axis assumed a great deal with that statement. As the Icarii Talon, RavenCrest was in overall command of the Strike Force. Now Axis demanded that *he* assume overall control.

RavenCrest may have been angry, and resentful of this man who stood so calmly before him asking for control of the Strike Force, but he was no fool. He knew that Axis alone had the skills and the experience to transform the Strike Force into an effective command – and he would need total leadership to do so.

He nodded. "I'll arrange a meeting for three days' time," he said, then turned on his heel and walked out of the room.

StarDrifter and Axis made their excuses and left MorningStar alone in the small training chamber. She waited until the door closed behind them, then sat down heavily and rested her head in her hands.

Training Axis was physically demanding work and MorningStar was tired. But she was also sorely troubled. Axis learned well. Too well. That point had been driven home forcibly this afternoon. Many of his other skills could be waved off with the explanation that he had absorbed them from StarDrifter when he had sung to his son in Rivkah's womb as they sat on the sunny rooftop of Sigholt.

But StarDrifter just could not have taught Axis the skills associated with the water music – his own abilities in that area were too poor.

Natural ability, then, on Axis' part? Perhaps. But MorningStar did not think that natural ability explained everything. She shook herself and stood up. She did not want to think just yet about *why* Axis was so good at learning the Songs when other Icarii Enchanters had so much difficulty.

Perhaps he was not learning them for the first time.

"Stars, woman!" MorningStar muttered to herself. "Don't even *think* it!"

5

The Rebel Army

Belial's hazel eyes restlessly scanned the leaden-grey sky.
Either side of him reared the barren walls of Hold-
Hard Pass, their starkness relieved only by the
occasional stunted bush or tree. It was eleven days since they
had entered the eastern end of the Pass, and five since Belial
had ordered they set up camp and sent Arne, the most
experienced unit commander Belial still had with him, and a
small number of men to scout Sigholt and its environs.

Belial hardly dared hope Sigholt would provide them with
a base. He desperately wished that he'd some of those Icarii
farflight scouts with him. Instead he had been forced to send
men on what might well be a dangerous and fruitless mission.

That any of them were alive at all was due principally to
Magariz — and the foresight of Borneheld, of all people.
Beside him Lord Magariz sat a fidgeting Belaguez. The two
men took turns to exercise Axis' war horse. Belaguez had
already thrown Magariz twice today, and Belial had his own
fair share of bruises from the cursed grey stallion. We should
just let the horse run wild, Belial thought, before he kills one
of us. I can ill afford to lose Magariz.

Lord Magariz had been Duke Borneheld's most senior and
trusted commander, responsible during the past twelve years
for commanding the garrison at Gorkenfort. Yet Magariz had
deserted Borneheld to follow Axis, even though his disloyalty

would almost certainly result in his death should the Duke ever catch him. Magariz's choice had undoubtedly saved the lives of Belial and those of the three thousand men he led. After they'd watched the Icarii claim Axis at the foot of the Icescarp Alps, they had ridden into the dreadful territories of the Icescarp Barren and the northern WildDog Plains. Only Magariz's familiarity with the area, and his knowledge of the reserves of food, fuel and hay that lay secreted across northern Ichtar, had saved them from starvation during the five weeks it took them to reach the southern Plains.

In the months leading up to the siege of Gorkenfort, Borneheld and Magariz had planned for every eventuality. Among the less palatable had been a retreat from Gorkenfort. But neither had been sure of which direction they'd be able to retreat in — south through central Ichtar to Jervois Landing or east across the Icescarp Barren and through the WildDog Plains to Skarabost? In the end, Borneheld had ordered that supplies be secreted across both lines of retreat. And while Borneheld and his command had undoubtedly made effective use of the reserves in central Ichtar, so Belial and his command had benefited from the supply route across the Icescarp Barren and the WildDog Plains.

Borneheld would be horrified to realise that his planning had saved the lives of men openly allied with the Forbidden.

Surprisingly, the Skraelings had hardly bothered Belial's force as they moved east and then south. Belial wished he knew what the Skraelings were up to. Had they hurt them so badly in the ice fields above Gorkenfort they'd gone to ground to lick their wounds? Or were they even now massing for a devastating assault on Achar through Ichtar? Belial irritably brushed his sandy hair off his forehead, the green thread Faraday had given him to tie about his biceps catching his eye. Perhaps the Mother's magic still protects us, he thought. Whatever the reason, there had been a few half-hearted attacks on stragglers and nothing else.

While they were still close to the Icescarp Alps the Icarii farflight scouts had kept in contact, occasionally sweeping down to share a meal in the evenings. Only Belial and Magariz had ever seen the Icarii at close range previously – during the tragic meeting atop Gorkenfort's Keep – and the first evening two of the farflight scouts had alighted in the camp had caused a sensation. Scores of men suddenly found pressing need to consult with either Belial or Magariz.

The Icarii had taken the curiosity of the men in good humour – indeed, they had been almost as curious themselves. They were fascinated with the type and composition of the armour the Acharite soldiers wore, and Belial had to restrain them from stroking the soldiers in much the same fashion as they had the strange and wondrous horses.

Whenever they'd visited, the Icarii gave Belial what news of Axis they had, although he spent so much time with his father that few of the Icarii had yet seen him. They did have news of Azhure, however, and Belial fully intended to wring an apology from her for clubbing him unconscious in her bid to free an Avar man and child from their cell in Smyrton.

The Icarii had disappeared as Belial led his force into the central WildDog Plains some two and a half weeks ago. They were as yet reluctant to fly too far from the relative safety of the Alps, and Belial missed their company as much as he missed their mobility.

Belial was looking for a suitable site to base Axis' rebel army. On farewelling Axis at the Icescarp Alps he had thought to move down to Smyrton with its extensive grain fields. But Sigholt was far more defensible and had better facilities for training and barracking troops. And the daily company of the stolid villagers of Smyrton held little appeal for Belial – not to mention that his army now supported a cause which their beloved Seneschal found heretical.

Had Sigholt been destroyed by the advancing Skraelings who even now lurked in its cellars? Was there a contingent of

Borneheld's command there who would resist their arrival? Too many unknowns – and Belial did not like unknowns. He chewed his cold-chapped lip and cursed when it cracked and split in the bitter wind.

So now here he sat, anxiously awaiting the return of Arne and his men, the bulk of his army lying half a league behind, as anxious as Belial was. All wanted to find somewhere to dig in for the inevitable attack from the Skraelings and to shelter from this cursed weather that roiled down from the north. If nothing else, the worsening weather conditions – not as bad as they had endured in Gorkenfort, but still abnormal for this part of Ichtar – told Belial that Gorgrael's influence was finally spreading south after the fall of Gorkenfort.

And with the wind and ice would come the Skraelings.

Belial shifted in his saddle. Five days was plenty of time for Arne to ride to Sigholt, scout the garrison from a safe distance, and return. If they weren't back by this evening then Belial would be forced to admit that something was wrong. He hunkered down a little further in his saddle, pulling the hood of his cloak far over his face in an effort to keep the freezing wind out.

They waited.

At dusk Belial finally stirred and turned to Magariz, the man only a dark shape in the deepening twilight.

"My friend," he croaked, his voice hoarse from the cold. "We have waited long enough. Tomorrow we will break camp, turn for Smyrton, and take our chances with home-spun village life."

Magariz kneed Belaguez closer. "Yes. Only adversity could have kept Arne from returning by now."

"Only adversity or a good meal," a dour voice interrupted from behind them. Belial and Magariz both swore in surprise and swung their horses about. Only a few paces behind them stood Arne, his face no more cheerful or less austere than it normally was. He was alone, but looked fit and uninjured.

"Arne, how did you –" Belial began.

"Your men?" Magariz barked. "Where are they?"

Arne chewed on a piece of dry grass, then abruptly spat it out. "At Sigholt, my Lord."

"Prisoners?"

Arne actually laughed. "In a manner of speaking. They are trapped before a roaring fire, hearing tales of adventure from an arthritic old cook and a genial pig-herder as they sip good dark ale. They were too comfortable to move, so I returned on my own."

As Magariz took a deep breath and fought to keep from swearing at the man's misplaced sense of humour, Belial slid from his horse and stepped closer to Arne. "What did you find, Arne? *What*?"

"Sigholt is ours once we overcome the resident force," Arne said. "An old retired cook and a pig-herder. There is no-one else. None of Borneheld's men. Not even a Skraeling. They reached Hsingard and destroyed it, but according to the pig-herder, they have not approached Sigholt."

"Why?" Belial asked Arne. "*Why* has Sigholt been left untouched? Surely it is too important for Gorgrael to leave it alone?" After the events of the past few months, Belial no longer believed much in good news or good luck.

"The pig-herder said the Skraelings did not like Sigholt." Arne paused, debating whether to continue.

"Speak up, man!" Belial snapped.

"I have seen this pig-herder before," Arne said finally. "Outside the Silent Woman Woods. He had his pigs there."

Belial frowned. This pig-herder had been outside the Silent Woman Woods – two hundred leagues to the south? It seemed a lifetime ago since they'd camped at the Silent Woman Woods. Then Axis had simply been the BattleAxe of the Seneschal and Belial his second-in-command. No-one knew then what they were riding into. "What is his involvement in this, Arne? Do you know?"

"He is involved, Commander. I know not how." Again Arne paused. "But I trust him. And he seems eager that you move this rag-tag army to Sigholt. He says he has a job for some strong backs."

Belial frowned. These were strange words for a pig-herder. He looked at Magariz. "My friend. What do you think?"

"I am surprised," said Magariz, "that Sigholt should be sitting there waiting for us as eager and as open as an Ysbadd whore – and I wonder if it has as many traps. I say we should approach . . . carefully. Why has Gorgrael not attacked?"

"Jack said he could answer that when you arrived," Arne replied, giving Belial and Magariz the pig-herder's name. "He said to remind you that Sigholt was where Axis was conceived, and," Arne hesitated, "that Sigholt was an Icarii stronghold long before the Acharites and the pox-cursed Dukes of Ichtar made it their home. He said Sigholt has some secrets that you could make good use of."

"A most unusual pig-herder, Belial," Magariz murmured. "Either a friend or a cunningly laid trap for us."

Belial considered a moment. "Then we will break camp in the morning and ride west to Sigholt. But we ride carefully."

Arne spat on the ground. "If you had been an enemy, the first you would have known of my approach was the feel of my blade in your neck. Perhaps it is as well you only have a cook and a pig-herder to battle with at Sigholt."

Belial grimaced and swung onto his horse. Arne was right. He should have been more careful.

Three days later Belial sat Belaguez a half-league from Sigholt. Approaching him was an open- and genial-faced middle-aged man in peasant garb. Dark blond hair flopped untidily over his forehead and he carried a heavy staff with a curiously worked metal head. At his heels trotted a number of well-fed pigs, grunting and rolling cheerfully as they picked their way across the stony ground.

Belial had ridden out alone, leaving Magariz and the three thousand some one hundred paces behind him.

He risked taking his eyes off the approach of the pig-herder to glance at Sigholt itself, standing stark but peaceful in the cold morning air. If there were troops waiting to surprise him, then they were hidden well.

"Peace, Belial," said the pig-herder and stopped a few paces from him. "Sigholt is yours. Use it."

"Jack," Belial said by way of brief greeting. "I hope you mean that. Why should I trust you?"

Jack smiled. "You have known my friends well, Belial. Through them, I know you."

"Your friends?"

"Ogden and Veremund. My friends and my companions."

Belial's mouth dropped open. "You're one of the . . . ?"

"My task is to serve the Prophecy, Belial TrueHeart, as yours is to serve Axis." His eyes suddenly glowed a vivid emerald.

"You're a Sentinel!" Belial gasped, his shock making Belaguez sidestep nervously.

"Then trust me," Jack said, as the light died in his eyes.

Belial still hesitated. "Jack. I come from Gorkenfort. I have had enough of sieges at the mercy of the Skraelings. What chance is there that once I have this army settled into Sigholt the Skraelings will lay siege to us? I have no wish to endure another Gorkenfort."

"I understand your concern," Jack replied. "But there are good reasons why the Skraelings would hesitate to come within leagues of Sigholt. They have destroyed Hsingard, which is not a great distance from here. Do you not think that if they destroyed Hsingard they would have destroyed Sigholt if not for very good reasons?"

"Such as?"

"Come inside, Belial, and bring your army. It is a long story."

6

New Responsibilities,
Old Friends

Axis stood at the open window and watched two Wings of the Strike Force wheel and somersault through the sky in a dazzling but utterly useless display of grace and fluidity.

He sighed and turned into the spacious meeting chamber. Soft light shone from concealed ceiling lamps on a massive round table of highly polished dark-green stone that dominated the room. The mottoes of the various Crests were carved in elegant gilded Icarii script into the walls above pennants and standards.

Around the stone table sat the twelve Crest-Leaders of the Icarii Strike Force, their wings draped across the gleaming floor behind their stools. Each Crest-Leader commanded twelve Wings of twelve members; the total Strike Force composed over seventeen hundred Icarii. Not overly large, Axis mused, but their flight abilities *should* give them the advantage over any ground force. But Axis had severe doubts about the capabilities of the Strike Force. Currently they were more gorgeously decorative than practically potent.

Axis gazed at the Crest-Leaders, all with their wings dyed in the black of war, all staring back at him flintily. He, too, had dressed entirely in black; it was the colour he'd worn as BattleAxe. Except now the twin crossed axes were gone from his chest. He felt naked without a badge of office.

RavenCrest SunSoar, sitting with the jewelled torc of his office glowing about his neck and his black brows meeting at an acute angle above sharp eyes, had called the Crest-Leaders together to meet Axis. FarSight CutSpur, the senior among the Crest-Leaders, had made a gracious speech of welcome. Axis had made, he hoped, an equally gracious reply. And now no-one quite knew what to say next.

Finally Axis broke the uncomfortable silence. "You have the makings of a good Strike Force. But I need to take command and shape it to make it more effective."

Backs stiffened noticeably about the table and wings rustled in agitation. Looking each Crest-Leader in the eye as he slowly circled the table Axis continued, his voice low but intense. "Do you really think the Strike Force can harm Gorgrael in its current state?"

There were low murmurs of protest, but Axis ignored them. "You have a Strike Force, but what are its accomplishments? What its experience? Where its battle honours?" he asked. "Where its successes?"

Crest-Leader SharpEye BlueFeather suddenly pushed his stool back and stood. "Do you accuse us of failure, BattleAxe?" he hissed, his neck feathers rising aggressively.

SharpEye's use of this title was an indication of the depth of ill will that some in the room bore him. For a thousand years the person and the office of BattleAxe had been reviled and loathed among both Icarii and Avar.

Axis held the birdman's eyes in a fierce stare. "I am Axis SunSoar," he retorted. "And, yes, it is true, I have the experience of a *successful* BattleAxe behind me. But I am BattleAxe no longer, SharpEye. I am SunSoar born and it is with that right and heritage that I stand here today." SharpEye dropped his eyes a fraction, and Axis shifted his gaze about the table. "*Should* I accuse you of failure? If not, then inform me of your successes."

There was a telling silence about the table.

"Was Yuletide a success?" Axis asked, anger creeping into his voice. "How many died, FarSight?"

"We lost several hundred, the Avar lost more." FarSight looked steadily at Axis. "I am not proud of that, Axis Sun-Soar. But we rallied after the surprise of the initial attack."

"You rallied after *Azhure* showed you how to kill!" Axis snapped. "Did not Azhure kill most of the wraiths until the Earth Tree struck? And would you have triumphed over the Skraelings if StarDrifter had not roused the Earth Tree?"

"What would you have done differently, Axis?" FarSight challenged, his fists clenching.

"You gave them a feast, Crest-Leader, with the Icarii and Avar herded tight into that grove," Axis said. "The Strike Force should have remained in the air, FarSight, where the Skraelings could not have reached them – *and* where they might have actually seen the wraiths approach. What would I have done differently? I would have had the Strike Force ready to *strike*, FarSight, and I would not have allowed the Yuletide rites to go ahead with so many people packed into one place waiting to be killed!"

"We could not have known the Skraelings were going to attack!" RavenCrest shouted, self-reproach raising his voice.

"What?" Axis said, turning to his uncle, who subsided back onto his stool at the expression on his nephew's face. "*What*? You *knew* they were massing to the north of the Avarinheim. You *knew* that the Prophecy walked, that Gorgrael was ready to drive his Ghostmen south. What do you mean *you did not know they were going to attack*?"

Again there was silence for a full minute. Axis slowly shifted his gaze from face to face, knowing he had struck home. He walked back to the window and watched the Icarii manoeuvre in the sky.

"How did you lose the Wars of the Axe?" he asked finally. "How did you let yourself be driven from the southern lands? How could you let Tencendor be destroyed?"

"The Acharites – the Axe-Wielders – were too fierce," FarSight replied grudgingly. "They hated too much. We could not withstand them."

"I have spent years with the Axe-Wielders," Axis said. "I was their leader for five of them. I know what they are capable of. And I know that no ground force, no matter how motivated by hatred, could do so well against an airborne force unless that force was pitifully weak to start with. You should have won the Wars of the Axe." He paused, then repeated his words to drive his message home. "You should have won. Why didn't you? Why?"

"We lacked the determination," said FarSight CutSpur, almost whispering. "We were so horrified that the Acharites had actually attacked that we fled instead of fighting. We lacked the resolve. We lacked – lack – the instinct to attack and defend the instant it is needed."

Axis nodded. "Good. Shall I tell you your other major flaw?"

FarSight, as the others in the room, stared at him levelly.

"Your Icarii pride constantly leads you to underestimate your opponents. You underestimated the ill will the Acharites bore you, which fed their desire to drive you from Tencendor. You underestimated their fierceness and *their* determination in doing just that. You underestimated Gorgrael's ability to drive his Skraelings through the Avarinheim to attack the Earth Tree Grove. And most recently SpikeFeather underestimated Azhure's ability to use the Wolven, leading to the loss of one of your most prized weapons. Have I made my point?"

FarSight CutSpur nodded once, jerkily.

"What do you use the Strike Force for, FarSight?" Just one more humiliation, Axis thought, then he would begin to rebuild their hopes.

"To scout, to observe and to defend."

"Then why call it a *Strike* Force?" Axis commented dryly. "At the moment you have a force that is incapable of defence, let alone a strike." He paused to let it sink in, then his face and voice softened. "My friends, you have the makings of an elite force, one that could defeat any other in these lands. But at the moment you have neither the means nor the knowledge to create that elite force from the ineffective one you now have."

Axis pulled out the spare stool and sat down among the Crest-Leaders. "You need a war leader," he said finally. "You need *me*. You know that. It is why you are all here. Give me the Strike Force. Let me realise its fabulous potential. Let me turn you from birds of paradise into hawks. Killers. Don't you want to regain your pride? To avenge Yuletide?"

FarSight glanced at RavenCrest. The Talon looked furious, but he jerked his head in assent. FarSight looked about the table at the other Crest-Leaders, seeking their decision. Slowly, one by one, they inclined their heads.

FarSight finally turned back to Axis. "You have command, Axis SunSoar." Stars, he thought, what would my ancestors think now that I hand over command of the Icarii Strike Force to a former BattleAxe?

Axis nodded. "Thank you. You honour me with your trust and with the command of the Strike Force. I will not fail you, nor will I betray you or your traditions."

Gradually the other faces about the table relaxed. "What are your plans?" one of the younger Crest-Leaders asked.

"I need to watch the Strike Force train," Axis replied, a small knot of excitement in his belly at the title. "I need you to tell me what you are capable of, and we all need to talk about what it is we face. Then we can decide what to do."

"How will we fight Gorgrael?" Another of the Crest-Leaders leaned forward. "How?" The mood among the Crest-Leaders was quickly turning from shame to eagerness.

Axis looked about the room. "Eventually we must unite with the Avar and the Acharites. That is the only way we can defeat Gorgrael." That last they did not particularly like but they realised the need for it. "I have a force of some three thousand men in eastern Achar. Eventually I want the Strike Force to join them. A combined air and ground force will give us our best chance to drive Gorgrael back."

FarSight leaned forward. "Yes. Our farflight scouts kept in contact with Belial. The last they saw of him he was leading your three thousand into the southern WildDog Plains."

"Why is this the first I have heard of it?" Axis snapped.

"You have hardly been accessible," FarSight bit back, then subsided and went on more mildly. "Our Strike Force *does* have its uses, Axis SunSoar."

Axis smiled a little guiltily at the birdman. "I think we both have a good deal to learn about each other, FarSight."

FarSight inclined his head. "Then let us tell you about your Strike Force."

Azhure hurried along the corridor clutching the Wolven. She was late for archery practice with SpikeFeather's Wing, delayed by an errand Rivkah had sent her on, and was anxious to get there. Her skill had improved to the extent that she could now match SpikeFeather arrow for arrow, surprising even herself with her aptitude. And next week SpikeFeather had promised to show her some of the skills required to hit a target while both she and it were moving. Azhure could not wait for the new challenge.

"My dear girl," a cheerful voice said behind her. "Do you by chance know your way about this rabbit warren?"

Azhure whirled around, almost dropping the Wolven in shock. Two Brothers of the Seneschal advanced up the corridor towards her, one tall and skinny, the other short and fat. Both had kindly creased faces and haloes of untidy white hair above tattered and stained habits.

Azhure took a cautious step back and one hand tightened about the Wolven. Her other hand crept towards the quiver of arrows slung about her back.

"Don't you recognise us?" the tall Brother asked. "Don't you remember who we are?"

Azhure stared at them, then finally relaxed a little. "You're the two Brothers who were with Axis in Smyrton. Sentinels." Axis had told her that these Brothers were two of the Sentinels mentioned in the Prophecy.

"Yes. My name is Veremund," the tall one said, then turned to indicate his corpulent companion. "And this is Ogden." Both made courtly bows.

Azhure shook their hands. "My name is Azhure. I'm sure Axis will be delighted to find you here in Talon Spike. Do you want to see him? He is usually with StarDrifter and MorningStar during the afternoons." Her archery practice would have to wait for today.

"My dear, we would be very grateful if you could direct us to him," Veremund said, and Azhure turned and led them up one of the shafts.

Axis had spent all morning and the early part of the afternoon with the Crest-Leaders, and he was now feeling exhausted, both physically and emotionally. But he knew he would be so busy with the Strike Force over the coming weeks that he should take this chance to learn the remaining Songs MorningStar had to teach him.

StarDrifter was once again relegated to a stool in a corner of the training chamber as MorningStar stood before a seated Axis. This afternoon she and StarDrifter would have taught Axis all they could – then it would be up to him to develop his own powers on the foundation they had given him.

Axis relaxed. The music came to him easily this afternoon and he felt as if he might drift off to sleep as MorningStar cradled his head between her hands. Her voice was very soothing, her fingers so sure that Axis let the entire weight of his head sink into their hold. His mind started to wander.

"And this one," MorningStar said, "is the Song of Harmony. It will soothe emotions, calm tempers, turn thoughts to peace rather than violence." She smiled a little. "It is as useful to a military commander as weapons of war, Axis. Listen well and learn."

She opened her mouth to sing, but halted in amazement as her grandson began to hum it himself. She looked wide-eyed over Axis' head towards StarDrifter.

Axis now began to sing rather than hum. It was the Song of Harmony.

MorningStar gently let his head go and took a step backwards, her heart beating wildly. He should not be able to do this.

"When have you sung this for him before, mother?" StarDrifter whispered hoarsely, walking slowly over.

MorningStar shook her head from side to side. "Never. I left it until last. You have not . . . ?"

"You know I have little proficiency with this Song, mother. I have not taught him."

MorningStar's face hardened. So. It was what she had feared. "Wait until he has finished his Song," she whispered. "Then we will have some questions for him."

Oblivious to their reaction, Axis sang the Song to a close. For a moment silence hung in the air, then he opened his eyes. "That was a beautiful Song, MorningStar. Thank you."

Before MorningStar could say anything there was a gentle knock at the door and Azhure and – by the Stars! – two Brothers of the Seneschal walked in.

Azhure saw MorningStar's shocked face and smiled reassuringly. "They are the Sentinels Axis has told us about, MorningStar. Ogden and Veremund."

"Ogden! Veremund!" Axis leapt to his feet and clasped each Sentinel by the hand warmly. "It is good to see you! But what are you doing here? Faraday? Was she well when you left her?"

Ogden laughed. "Axis, m'boy, so many questions! Please, will you introduce us to these two delightful people?"

Axis introduced Ogden and Veremund to his father and grandmother and the two Sentinels fussed over them.

Azhure smiled at Axis' obvious pleasure at seeing the two old men again. "I found them in the corridors of Talon Spike, Axis. I do not know from where they came or how they entered the complex."

Axis gave her a quick kiss on the cheek. "Thank you, Azhure. You have brought me a gift to lighten my day." He stood back and looked fondly at the two old men. "Though there was a time when I found them so irritating that I would have cheerfully pushed them from the peak of Talon Spike itself. You were lucky to survive my temper, gentlemen!"

Ogden and Veremund both beamed. "We are so glad you have found your father, Axis," Veremund said, "and embraced your heritage so completely."

"We did not stay with Borneheld for long, Axis," Ogden broke in. "But they made good their escape from Gorkenfort and, the last we saw them, were riding hard for Jervois Landing. Faraday was as well as could be expected under the circumstances. Yr stays with her."

Axis' eyes shadowed a little. "Thank you, my friend. I was not sure if they'd taken their chance when we drew the Skraelings away from Gorkenfort. To know that Faraday managed to escape eases my heart."

Ogden nodded, then noticed the strained expression on MorningStar's and StarDrifter's faces. "Ah, forgive us, but we have interrupted your training,"

"Such as it is," MorningStar muttered.

"We should excuse ourselves and retire," Ogden continued. "Axis, perhaps we can meet soon to talk. I'm sure there's a lot we must —"

MorningStar broke in. "There's a great deal that must be said, and most of it needs to be said now. No." She held up her hand as Ogden and Veremund bowed and turned for the door. "I think it would be good to have the advice of the Sentinels. Please, stay. Axis, would you sit, please?"

Axis frowned, perplexed, but he took his stool in the centre of the room. Unnoticed, Azhure sat down on the floor by the door.

MorningStar paused and collected her thoughts.

"Axis," she said finally. "Your training has gone so well. You display an extraordinary ability to master a Song the moment you hear it and to control the power that flows through the melody. You hear the Star Dance more clearly, it seems, than anyone else. You are a remarkable Enchanter."

Axis' eyes narrowed at MorningStar's rare praise.

"He *is* the StarMan," Veremund murmured to one side. "One would expect that –"

"I am not a fool!" MorningStar snarled abruptly. "I *understand* that Axis wields remarkable powers. I *understand* that because of who he is it's no wonder he's had little difficulty with a training that normally taxes the most gifted Enchanter for years. I *understand* that!"

She took a deep breath, fighting to keep her temper under control and to keep her face from showing the sheer dread that fed her anger.

"Axis." Her face was now a mask of serenity, its bland lines hiding her fears. "How did you know the Song of Harmony?"

Axis frowned, even more perplexed. "You sang it for me, MorningStar."

"No!" she whispered, her fingers twisting among the golden beads at her throat. "I told you its name, and what it could be used for, but as I took the breath to sing it, you started to sing it yourself. You already knew it."

"I . . ." Axis' voice drifted off as he tried to remember.

"It was not a Song that StarDrifter would have sung for you while you lay cradled in Rivkah's womb. He could not have done it. *I* have not sung it for you before. Yet you already knew it. How, when it takes a SunSoar to instruct a SunSoar, do you know this Song when neither of the two living SunSoar Enchanters has taught it to you?" She glanced briefly at the two Sentinels. "No Enchanter, no matter how powerful, instinctively knows the Songs. He or she *must* be taught them, and by a member of their own blood.

"StarDrifter. When Axis was growing in Rivkah's womb, did you *ever* sing for him the Song of Recreation?"

"No." StarDrifter smiled a little at the memory. "I sang for him many things, but not that. It is no thing to sing to a developing baby."

MorningStar nodded. "And yet, Axis knew what to sing for the Avar girl. Raum has told me of this."

"Yes," Ogden nodded slowly. "Veremund and I heard it too. He sang beautifully."

"Yes," MorningStar repeated woodenly, her face set into hard lines. "Axis. You have learned well since your arrival in Talon Spike. Too well. Far too well. I have wondered why many times. When you sang the Song of Harmony it confirmed my worst fears. Axis, StarDrifter and I have not been training you at all. We have simply been *reminding* you. You have already been trained, probably as a very small child."

She paused, and when she resumed her words were chill stones in the absolute silence of the chamber. "Who trained you as a child, Axis? *Who?*"

Axis gaped at her. She looked fierce, almost ready to attack, and he stood slowly. "MorningStar, what do you mean? Trained? How? Who by? If I have been already trained then why haven't I been able to use my powers all my life? No. No, you must be wrong."

MorningStar held his eyes steadily. If he was only pretending confusion, then he was doing a good job. "You must have been trained at a very young age and undoubtedly you do not remember it. Because you never used your powers they fell into disuse as you grew older. But over the past year, as the Prophecy and its Sentinels unlocked your past, as you discovered your true identity, the Songs have drifted back."

"But, MorningStar," Veremund began, "I thought that only another Enchanter of the same family could teach an Enchanter."

MorningStar gave a curt nod. "You are right."

"Then who else is there in your family who could have had access to Axis? What other Enchanters?"

MorningStar lifted her chin. "StarDrifter and I are the only two SunSoar Enchanters – apart, of course, from Axis himself. I received my powers from my mother, DriftStar, also a SunSoar, but she died some three hundred years ago."

"Are you saying that there is *another* SunSoar Enchanter running about?" Azhure asked. Everyone in the room jumped slightly; they had forgotten her presence. "Someone you aren't aware of? Someone who taught Axis as a baby?"

MorningStar stared at Azhure, who had risen slowly to her feet. She nodded. "Yes. I was afraid to say the words, but yes. That is what I think."

"But *who*?" Axis said. "Why hide from me? And how did an Icarii Enchanter have access to me in the Seneschal? *How*? I don't understand."

"My son," StarDrifter stepped up to Axis and placed a comforting hand on his shoulder. "I fear there might be worse. If there is another SunSoar Enchanter about then . . . then . . ." he hesitated, "then it might explain who taught Gorgrael as well."

MorningStar visibly rocked on her feet, and her hand drifted to her throat in horror. "Gorgrael?"

"After Yuletide FreeFall asked me how Gorgrael had learned his powers," StarDrifter said, dropping his hand from

Axis' shoulder and moving to his mother's side. "I said then that he'd obtained his powers from the music of discord, the Dance of Death, rather than the Star Dance. But I evaded the real issue. Gorgrael had to be taught how to use that music as well, and he had to be taught by someone of the same blood. A family member. A SunSoar Enchanter."

"But *who*? And who would teach *both*? And teach them each such *different* music?" MorningStar turned to the Sentinels. "Ogden, Veremund, can you help us? Please?"

They shook their heads and Veremund spread his hands helplessly. "There are many riddles within the Prophecy we do not understand, but I do not think the Prophecy even alludes to this problem, MorningStar. All the Prophecy tells us is that the same man fathered both the Destroyer and the StarMan – StarDrifter, as we now know. It says nothing about who trained them. But a SunSoar presumably, as they are both of SunSoar blood."

"Axis." Now MorningStar addressed her grandson. "Do you know? Is there anything you should be telling us?"

Axis' temper boiled over. "I do not lie to you, Morning-Star, and I do not dissemble! If I knew anything I would tell you!"

Azhure moved to his side and rested a soothing hand against his back. "Axis, shush. Is there nothing you remember?"

Axis' eyes snapped at her but he did not attempt to pull away from the comforting touch of her hand. "No," he said finally. "All I know is that over the past few months, ever since Ogden and Veremund gave me the Prophecy written in Icarii script to read, memories and melodies have been bubbling to the surface. I did not think to ask myself who put them there in the first place."

"Veremund and I should have noticed," Ogden said. "We should have asked ourselves how Axis knew the Song of Recreation. Why he seemed to know so many melodies.

But," he shrugged his shoulders, "we were so thrilled to have finally found the StarMan after so many thousands of years, so thrilled that finally the Prophecy walked after such a long wait, that we did not think to ask ourselves these questions."

MorningStar let her eyes drift over the people before her, finally bringing them to rest on Axis. "So. You have been taught, as Gorgrael has been taught, by an unknown SunSoar Enchanter. Unknown, because where could he or she have come from? Only from the loins of myself or my mother, and I can assure you that is not the case. I have only borne two children, and I was my mother's only child – through complications sustained in birthing me she was never able to have another infant." She paused, and when she resumed her voice was so soft that the others could hardly hear it. "And this SunSoar Enchanter is not only unknown, but incredibly powerful. No-one has been able to use the Dark Music previously – its use has been only theorised until now – yet this SunSoar Enchanter was able to teach it to Gorgrael. I think we have a right to be afraid of him."

For a long time there was silence as everyone stood wrapped in their own thoughts. Ogden and Veremund took each other's hands. StarDrifter turned away to hide his face as he thought. Azhure leaned a little closer to Axis, slipping her arm about his waist and giving him a quick hug; Axis smiled at her gratefully. She was a good friend.

"Again I think we might be evading the real questions here," StarDrifter finally said into the silence, turning back to the others. "And they are: Where is this SunSoar Enchanter now? What does he plan? What does he plot? Is he for Axis? Or is he for Gorgrael?"

7

Dark Man, Dear Man

The four SkraeBolds grovelled at Gorgrael's feet. Even SkraeFear, senior and bravest of them, thrust himself against the stone flagging as a man might against the body of his lover. His clawed hands clutched at Gorgrael's toes, and he begged for forgiveness, begged Gorgrael to love him again.

Gorgrael wallowed in their misery. The Yuletide attack on the Earth Tree Grove had been a miserable failure. Not only had the SkraeBolds failed to kill the Earth Tree – and she now sang so loud that the northern Avarinheim was denied to him – but SkraeFear had almost killed StarDrifter, and Gorgrael had expressly ordered that he be brought to him alive and in good working order. They deserved to be punished *horribly* for their failure.

"Get up!" he snarled. "But only as far as your knees. You are not yet fit to stand in my presence!"

He swaggered away from the SkraeBolds as they inched to their knees. This was the first time he'd managed to have them all in the same room since the fall of Gorkenfort, and he intended to drag out their fear as long as he could.

"Sssss!" he hissed in frustration, swinging his head from side to side, and the four SkraeBolds behind him whimpered as his tusks glinted in the dim light. They knew they had a right to fear the fury of his tusks.

Gorkenfort had started so well. The town had fallen quickly and thousands had died. Gorgrael, watching his forces from the safety of his ice fortress far to the north of the Avarinheim, had shrieked in delight as each man died.

But Axis had escaped. Escaped with a significant force of men. Escaped to the arms of his father whom Gorgrael had so desperately desired to have here with him. Escaped, and in escaping, had destroyed so many Skraelings.

Now Gorgrael would be forced to curtail his drive south, for it was all he could do to keep a tight grip on those territories in Ichtar that he held – from the Andeis Sea to the Urqhart Hills. It was now a dead land, peopled only by frozen corpses and the Skraelings who fed on them. He could take pleasure in that, at least.

But if Gorgrael was pushed into simply consolidating rather than pushing further south, then now was the time to instil some order among the Skraelings. Bring them back under his control. Breed some more IceWorms. Fashion some new creations from the raw material surrounding him to breach the Acharite lines and break the force that Axis would inevitably throw at him. As Axis needed time to build his numbers, so Gorgrael needed time to rebuild his.

"You are failures!" he rasped venomously. The flickering light twisted his part-man, part-bird, part-beast form into an even more hideous shape.

"We tried our best!" "But so hard to remember orders amid such excitement!" "And those Skraelings, so un- reliable!" "Nasty, nasty brights!" Their excuses littered the air.

"Your failure tells me that you do not love me!" Gorgrael screeched. The SkraeBolds cried out in denial. They loved Gorgrael, lived for him!

Gorgrael's face twisted in derision. "Let me show you the price of your failure."

He reached for SkraeFear, who had failed him the most. SkraeFear still had the arrow Azhure had plunged into his neck embedded in his flesh, the wound festering and black, oozing pus down his chest. Gorgrael grasped the arrow and twisted it viciously, and SkraeFear screamed in agony. Gorgrael waited until SkraeFear's screams had bubbled away into low sobs, then he twisted the arrow again, twice as hard, the arrow head tearing through SkraeFear's flesh with a sound like wet cloth ripping.

"Will you fail me again?" Gorgrael hissed in SkraeFear's ear. "Will you?"

"No, no, no," SkraeFear moaned. "Never again, never again!"

Suddenly Gorgrael let the arrow go and SkraeFear sagged to the floor. Gorgrael grimaced in disgust. He needed a more intelligent and reliable lieutenant.

Timozel. Gorgrael's lip curled. But Timozel was bound to Faraday, and until those bonds were broken Timozel could continue to escape Gorgrael's need for him.

Well, for the moment the SkraeBolds would have to do. He patted SkraeFear on the head comfortingly.

"I still love you, SkraeFear, you and your brothers here."

SkraeFear whined in adoration and clung to one of Gorgrael's legs. "I will be good," he whispered. "Good, good, good!"

"Yes, yes," Gorgrael said absently, gently prising SkraeFear loose. "Be gone for the moment. I will speak to you soon. Give new orders. Impart a new mission. But for now, be gone."

SkraeFear gave one last grateful whimper, then scurried out of the room on his hands and knees, his brothers hurrying after him, gladdened beyond measure that their beloved master had not seen fit to chastise them as well.

Gorgrael prowled among the massive pieces of dark wooden furniture of his chamber; twisted and ensorcelled into strange and tormented shapes, they flung shadows into every corner.

He loved the room's gloom and clutter, its darkness and malformed purpose. It was where he did his best work.

One corner of the chamber was dominated by a massive plate-iron fireplace. Though Gorgrael constructed many of his creatures from mist and ice, he was warm-blooded himself and needed the heat and comfort of fire from time to time. He wandered over to the cold grate and snapped his fingers. Flames licked their way about the misshapen pieces of wood piled at the back of the grate, and Gorgrael murmured to himself. Sometimes he saw strange shapes in the flames, and it bothered him.

He turned to a sideboard, its undulating planes and angles polished smooth so that the wood shone, and lifted a crystal decanter from its depths. Gorgrael smiled. This decanter and its delicate matching glasses he had brought home from Gorkenfort, and the fact that Borneheld and Faraday had been forced to leave them behind when they fled pleased Gorgrael. He hummed a broken and grating tune as he lifted a glass with one scaled, clawed hand and filled it with good wine from the decanter.

He was civilised. He was as good as anyone else. Certainly as good as Axis. Perhaps Faraday would enjoy the time she spent with him. Perhaps she would think him polite company. Perhaps he might not kill her after all.

Gorgrael sipped the wine, clinking the crystal against a tusk and dribbling a little of the wine down his chin as his cumbersome mouth and tongue tried to cope with the delicacy of the glass. He reached into the depths of the sideboard again and lifted out a large parcel. Crystal was not the only item Gorgrael had brought home from Gorkenfort.

He grunted in satisfaction and wandered over to his favourite chair, scraping it towards the fire. It was a good chair, throne-like, with a high carved back and wings that reached even higher towards the ceiling. He sat down and ripped open the parcel with his free hand. For a long time he sat there, looking at the parcel's contents, stroking it gently, careful to keep his claws retracted. Then he drained his wine in a gulp and irritably threw the crystal into the fire where it shattered among the flames.

In his lap, tumbled and crushed, lay the emerald and ivory silk of Faraday's wedding gown. Looking at it, absorbing the smell and the feel of the woman who had worn it, Gorgrael felt strange, painful emotions well up inside him. They made him feel merciful – and Gorgrael did not want to feel merciful. Worse, they made him feel lost – and that feeling Gorgrael did not like very much at all.

There was a movement in the air, swirling about the room, and the flames leapt and spat in the turbulence.

"She is a very beautiful woman, Gorgrael," the loved voice said gently behind him, "and it is no wonder you sit there with her silks to comfort you."

"Dear Man," Gorgrael breathed. It had been months since the Dark Man had visited him.

A heavily shrouded figure brushed past his chair and stood for a moment in front of the fire, his back to Gorgrael. The hood of his black cloak was pulled close about his face.

"Have you met her?" Gorgrael asked, desperate for closer knowledge of Faraday. "Have you spoken with her?"

The shrouded figure turned and sat down on the hearth. "I know Faraday, yes. And we have passed the occasional word."

Gorgrael gripped the silk in his hands. "Have you desired her?"

The Dark Man laughed, genuinely amused. "Many desire her, Gorgrael, and perhaps I am one of them. It is of no account. If you want her then I will not stand in your way. You may enjoy her as you wish."

For a while they sat there in silence, Gorgrael fingering the silken dress, the Dark Man contemplating the flames.

Gorgrael had long given up trying to see the face of the Dear Man. No matter how hard and how craftily he'd peered, always the Dark Man, the Dear Man, appeared as he was now, shrouded so heavily that no-one, not even Gorgrael with his dark talent, could understand or know what lay beneath the folds.

The Dark Man had been a part of Gorgrael's life since he was small. The five Skraelings who had midwifed Gorgrael's terrible delivery had brought him back to their burrow in the northern tundra, had somehow managed to feed him until he was able to crawl out of the burrow and forage in the snow, catching first small insects, then the white mice of the northern wastes, then finally the small mammals, hot and juicy, that fed his growing flesh and provided the stiff furs that kept him warm at night. The Skraelings had sheltered him and loved him, but Gorgrael had led a miserable life among the silly wraiths until the day that, scampering across a small ice field, he had seen the cloaked figure striding towards him. At first the tiny Gorgrael had been afraid of this tall and mysterious man, but the Dark Man had picked him up and whispered to him of things which soon had him cooing in delight and squirming in the stranger's arms. The Dark Man had sung dreams to the child, had offered him hope.

No-one but Gorgrael knew about the Dark Man – the five Skraelings, later transformed by Gorgrael into Skrae-Bolds, had never known he existed. The Dark Man, the Dear Man, had come to Gorgrael almost every day when he was little. Singing strange songs of power and enchantment, teaching him about his heritage, teaching him about his path for the future. Gorgrael had learned well from the Dark Man, and had come to love and respect as well as fear this stranger who taught him. He had learned very early that it was not a good thing to cross the Dark Man.

But through all these years he had never found out who the Dark Man was. Whenever he asked, whenever he tried to pry, the Dark Man would laugh and evade his questions and inquisitive eyes. There were some things he knew about him. The Dark Man knew Axis, for he had told Gorgrael about his hated half-brother very early in life and had taught Gorgrael the Prophecy of the Destroyer. Gorgrael knew also that the Dark Man lived a dark and crafty life, using his disguises to fool many who loved him. He knew that the Dark Man was a manipulator of considerable skill, and some-times Gorgrael wondered just how much he had been manipulated as well.

Gorgrael knew that the Dark Man had a purpose, but he did not know exactly what that purpose was.

"It was her wedding gown," Gorgrael mumbled. "Timozel's sleeping mind told me that. Dear Man," he lifted his gaze to the still figure before him. "I need a trustier lieutenant than these SkraeBolds. I want Timozel, but he is tied to Faraday. What can you tell me?"

"You will have him eventually," the Dark Man assured him. "Many bonds that have been forged will tear apart. Many vows that have been spoken will become meaningless."

"Will I have Faraday?"

"You have read the Prophecy. You know it as well as any." The Dark Man's voice was a little harder now.

"Axis' Lover. The only one whose pain can break his concentration enough for me to kill him. Faraday."

"Axis' Lover. Yes," the Dark Man agreed. "Only love can provide the means to destroy him. You know the Prophecy well."

Faraday, Gorgrael thought, I *must* have her!

The Dark Man sat and watched Gorgrael's thoughts play across his face. Gorgrael would do well – he had proved his worth already – but he would have to learn to curb his impatience.

"You moved too fast," the Dark Man said abruptly, his voice harsh.

"How much longer was I supposed to wait? My forces were massed, my magic was strong, and Axis knew little about his true identity, his true ability. It was a good time to move."

"You should have waited another year. Waited until you had more Skraelings, more ice creatures who could work your will for you. Waited until you had more *control* over your creatures!" The Dark Man's voice was scathing now, and he leaned forward from the hearth, stabbing his finger at Gorgrael. "Now you have gained Ichtar, true, but you can go no further until next winter. And meantime the forces of opposition are forming against you. Six months ago Axis had no idea of his true nature. But your precipitate action has flushed out all the major actors in this little drama. Now Axis has cast aside the lies of the Seneschal and absorbs his lessons from StarDrifter as a sponge absorbs water. You have woken the StarMan, Gorgrael, but you have weakened yourself so seriously in the process that you cannot yet move against him!"

Gorgrael twisted his head away from the Dear Man, sulking. "I *will* win." Did the Dark Man not believe in him?

"Oh, yes," the Dark Man said. "Undoubtedly. Trust me."

8

The Brother-Leader Plans

The silvery, secretive waters of Grail Lake lapped against the foundations of the white-walled, seven-sided Tower of the Seneschal. Deep within, Jayme, Brother-Leader of the Seneschal and most senior mediator between the one god Artor the Ploughman and the hearts and souls of the Acharites, paced across his chamber.

"Is there no news?" he asked Gilbert for the fourth time that afternoon.

The fire blazing in the mottled-green marble fireplace behind the Brother-Leader's desk was stacked high and the light it threw off shimmered along the edge of the fine crystal and gold that stood atop the mantel. Before the fire lay an exquisite rug of hand-woven emerald and ivory silk from the strange hot lands to the south of Coroleas. The Brother-Leader's private chambers lacked no comforts.

"Brother-Leader." Gilbert, his junior adviser, bowed respectfully, his hands tucked away in the voluminous sleeves of his habit. "The only word from the north comes from Duke Borneheld's camp at Jervois Landing. And the last Borneheld saw of your BattleAxe, he was whooping and screaming as he led his depleted Axe-Wielders to the north in an attempt to draw the Skraelings away from Gorkenfort."

Jayme frowned at the referral to Axis as "your BattleAxe". Gilbert had never liked Axis, and felt justified in his dislike when news of Axis' appalling betrayal of the Seneschal's cause reached the Brotherhood. Yet Jayme was so sick at heart he said nothing to reprove Gilbert.

"An attempt that nevertheless succeeded, Brother Gilbert," murmured Moryson, Jayme's senior adviser and closest friend for over forty-five years. He sat close by the fire to warm his creaking joints. "Axis' self-sacrifice saved many lives, Borneheld's the most important."

Gilbert continued. "Since the forces of this Gorgrael have moved through Ichtar I have received no word from north of Jervois Landing. Who knows if Axis lives or moulders?" As Borneheld had, so too had Jayme and his advisers reluctantly accepted that the foe they faced, Gorgrael, was something even more terrible than the Forbidden.

Jayme paced about the centre of the chamber. "Artor curse it, I did not love Axis and raise him from a baby to lose him like this! How many hours did I nurse that parentless child, sing him cradle-songs to comfort him to sleep?"

"Better to have lost him in the service of Artor than to lose him to the service of the Forbidden," Gilbert intoned.

"How *could* Axis betray the Seneschal – and *me* – like this!" shouted Jayme.

"Blame it on Rivkah for bedding with one of those damn lizards!" spat Gilbert. Borneheld's report had been very detailed. "Women ever were the weaker vessel!"

"Gilbert! Enough!" Moryson stood up from his chair, wavered for a moment, then walked over to put a comforting arm about Jayme. "Recriminations will not help us at this point, Brother Gilbert. We need to plan for the future."

Gilbert's lip curled at the two old men. What the Seneschal needed was an infusion of blood strong enough to save the Brotherhood from the possibility that the Forbidden would one day re-enter Achar. Artor needs young men to save the Seneschal, Gilbert thought, his eyes expressionless, not old men afraid of fighting words and deeds.

"Thank you, my friend," Jayme muttered, patting Moryson's arm. "I am all right now. Just for a moment . . ."

Moryson nodded in understanding and let Jayme go. When word of Axis' defection to the Forbidden had reached the Tower of the Seneschal it had almost caused Jayme a fatal apoplexy. That a man entrusted with such a position of responsibility within the Seneschal could defect to the *Forbidden* of all things – the races he was committed to destroy – was almost beyond belief. But what cut even deeper was that Jayme had raised Axis from a new-born infant. Cared for him, loved him, taught him, indulged him. And for that care and love Axis had not only led the military wing of the Seneschal, the Axe-Wielders, to the service of the Forbidden, but he had betrayed both his god and everything Jayme believed in. Jayme's hurt was the pain of a father betrayed as much as that of a Brother-Leader deceived.

"I must assume he is still alive," Jayme said. "I must prepare for the worst scenario – that Axis survived, the command he led survived, and all are now in the employ of those," he paused, "flying lizards." His voice strengthened as he spoke, and by the time he was finished Jayme's back was straight and his eyes gleamed with renewed strength. The Seneschal needed him and he would serve. If Axis had abandoned Jayme and the Seneschal, then Jayme and the Seneschal would abandon Axis.

"I am told that news of this cursed Prophecy spreads within Achar," he said with new resolve.

Gilbert nodded. "Yes. Those of Borneheld's soldiers who brought his report from the north, also – Artor damn them – brought this evil Prophecy. Once they had delivered Borneheld's report to King Priam they took their worthless and pox-infected bodies off to a tavern where they recited the Prophecy for the edification of the tavern patrons."

"Is it too late to stop word of the Prophecy spreading?" asked Jayme.

"Unfortunately so, Brother-Leader. Gossip will spread – and the Prophecy is so damnably ensorcelled that all who hear it remember it instantly."

"And curse those two Brothers Ogden and Veremund for finding and showing the Prophecy to Axis!" Jayme rasped. He still found it hard to believe that the Brotherhood's small outpost in the Silent Woman Keep had been so corrupted by the isolation and the records of the Forbidden they had found there.

Of course, none of the three in the room had yet heard news of the true identity of the two beings who wore the shapes of the long-dead Ogden and Veremund.

"Axis hardly needed those two fools to read him the Prophecy," Gilbert said. "He could read the depraved script in the Forbidden's books as easily as you would read the word of Artor himself. I, for one, do not find it hard to believe that Axis is of such tainted and ungodly breeding. None else could have read those ghastly lines. He was betrayer-bred, Brother-Leader, and his blood would always lead him to forsake you and the one true god Artor."

Gilbert paused, watching the older men carefully. "Axis' capitulation to the forces of evil may not be our worst threat. There may be traitors closer to home."

Jayme narrowed his eyes. What did Gilbert know now? Over the past months Jayme had learned to respect Gilbert's sources of information. "Well?" he barked finally, his entire frame tense and wary.

"I have heard word of Priam's private deliberations," Gilbert said casually.

Artor, but the little turd-faced bastard must have spies at the keyhole to Priam's privy chamber, thought Jayme. No doubt he has word on how many times Priam mounts his wife at night. Jayme rarely let the language and imagery of his peasant youth intrude into his conscious mind. It was a measure of his unease that he did so now.

"Priam has become obsessed with the Prophecy," Gilbert observed. "He believes its advice more than he believes the advice of the Brother-Leader. It is rumoured that Priam wavers towards supporting Axis and his cause. That he begins to think that alliance with the Forbidden might be a way to defeat Gorgrael."

Jayme cursed under his breath, staring into the fire in order to hide the expression on his face. Even Moryson looked mildly surprised at Gilbert's news.

"It is rumoured," Gilbert continued, staring at Jayme's back, "that Priam is . . . disappointed . . . with Borneheld. That he now wonders if Borneheld was such a good choice for WarLord. Priam believes Ichtar's loss underscores the need to pay close attention to the advice of the Prophecy."

The Brother-Leader's clenched fist slammed into the mantel above the fire, sending chills of music rattling around the room.

"I would rather see Priam *dead*!" Jayme seethed, staring first at Gilbert and then at Moryson. "*Has he lost his mind to consider an alliance with the Forbidden?*"

Moryson and Gilbert were stunned by Jayme's violent outburst. Moryson's eyes flickered to Gilbert then back to Jayme. He laid a soothing hand on Jayme's shoulder.

"Priam ever was a waverer," he said gently. "'Tis perhaps not unexpected that he should vacillate in this present crisis."

Jayme shook Moryson's hand off his shoulder and stalked into the centre of the chamber. "Priam leads the nation!" he snapped. "Should we let him lead it back into subjection under the yoke of the Forbidden?"

Gilbert's bright eyes narrowed. "What do you mean, Brother-Leader?"

"I mean that perhaps we – Achar – would be better off if we had a King whose loyalties were uncompromised."

There was utter silence for several heartbeats; even Jayme was a little surprised by what he had just said.

"Brother-Leader," Moryson said calmly. "It may be best if Borneheld knows of the situation. It might be best if Borneheld himself were here. To stop Priam from wavering, of course."

"Borneheld is an experienced leader and battle commander," Jayme said thoughtfully. "His hatred of the Forbidden and devotion to Artor is well known. He is also heir to the throne. I'm sure that he, too, would be appalled to learn of Priam's treasonous thoughts."

"Treasonous to Achar," Moryson said.

Jayme gave him a hard look. "Treasonous to everything the Seneschal stands for. We *cannot* let the Forbidden back into Achar. *Gilbert!*"

Gilbert jumped to his feet.

"I think it were best that you left for the north on the next river transport."

Gilbert smiled and bowed. He could see nothing but advantages for himself in these developments.

"Borneheld needs to be advised of where Priam's mind is turning," Jayme continued. "We are vulnerable now that the majority of the Axe-Wielders either lie dead or run with the traitor Axis. Only one cohort of Axe-Wielders remain to guard the interests and the persons of the Seneschal."

Not in a thousand years had the Seneschal been as vulnerable as it was now. That thought was uppermost in Jayme's mind. He would do whatever he had to do to ensure the Seneschal's survival. "What we do we must do for the good of the Seneschal."

"For the good of Artor and for the good of Achar," Moryson added mildly.

"Of course," Jayme said blandly, "that's what I meant. Furrow wide, Moryson, furrow deep."

9

The Blood-Red Sun

"Don't try to overpower me through such direct means. You leave yourself open. I grab your wrist and elbow, twist, and you're crippled."

SpikeFeather gave a gasp of pain and dropped the iron-tipped stave he was carrying, his free hand flying to the arm that Axis held in a vice-like grip. Axis casually kicked one leg out from under the Wing-Leader and SpikeFeather collapsed to the ground in an undignified heap.

Each day for over two weeks Axis had worked with individual Wings of the Strike Force, getting to know the Wing commanders and the individual members of the Force. They were obstinate and thin-skinned, Axis had decided, but they had the makings of a fine force, despite having degenerated over the past thousand or more years into little more than a decorative appendage to Icarii society. Axis had transformed the Strike Force's exercises and training from displays of graceful acrobatics in the sky and on ground to difficult manoeuvres that would win them battles rather than parades, lives rather than hearts and cheers.

Axis leaned down and offered SpikeFeather his hand. SpikeFeather was one of the more skilful fighters among the Icarii and he had caused Axis a moment's worry during their demonstration. SpikeFeather hesitated an instant, then took Axis' hand, standing up in a flowing movement.

"You could have killed me, SpikeFeather," said Axis, making sure he spoke loudly enough for the other Icarii standing about to hear, "if you had used your most potent weapon."

"What do you mean, Strike-Leader?" SpikeFeather frowned. "I could not hold the stave while you twisted my arm so."

"Your wings," Axis said, exasperated. "You could have knocked me with one or both of your wings, or so distracted me that I would have let you go. Don't forget your wings. They may save your life one day."

Axis was intent on making the Icarii realise that even defensive fighting should be aggressive, and that surprise and skill would always win over brawn and superior weaponry. But the Icarii needed experienced practice partners before they could develop the instinct necessary to survive the inevitable battles with Gorgrael's forces.

"All right, SpikeFeather, that's enough for today." Axis looked up to the gallery of the main training chamber where FarSight CutSpur and several of the other Crest-Leaders stood watching. Behind them were ranged some thirty or forty Icarii from other Wings who had asked if they could observe the training session. "Eventually when you join up with Belial's command you can train one-on-one with his soldiers. *That* will sharpen your combat skills."

"I don't see why you push us so, Axis," EvenSong remarked a little resentfully. "We are an archer force. What can possibly attack us in the air?" EvenSong made a point of not calling her brother Strike-Leader. Axis suspected she wanted to provoke him into disciplining her in front of the other members of her Wing, but he ignored her jibes.

FarSight CutSpur leaned over the railing of the observation gallery. "She may be right, Strike-Leader. We are vulnerable only to arrows, yet with the tactics we have been working out over the past two weeks soon arrows from below will become only a minor consideration. What will grappling with Belial's Groundwalkers teach us?"

Axis smiled, but his eyes were cold. "Already Gorgrael's SkraeBolds can fly. Once he knows I command your Strike Force he will plan counter-measures. FarSight CutSpur, fellow Strike Force members, you will almost certainly have to fight for your lives at some point with creatures that will attack you in the air. The battle for Tencendor will be a bloody affair on land and in the air. It will not always be fought at the safe distance of an arrow flight but hand to hand, wing to wing. Training with Belial's *battle-hardened* men will teach you instinctive aggression. Learn it . . . or die."

A number of the Icarii looked visibly shocked. Although their training under Axis had been hard, they had comforted themselves with the thought that they were almost impossible to attack while in the air. Now they had to think again.

Axis' eyes circled the assembled Icarii. "Each of you should arm yourself with a good blade. Knives can be carried easily, concealed even more easily, and will save you when another grapples you and restricts your movement, whether in the air or on the ground. Learn how to kill at close quarters. Azhure."

Azhure, who had been standing unobtrusively against the side wall of the chamber, narrowed her eyes in suspicion.

"Come." Axis beckoned impatiently, his eyes on the Icarii fighters.

Azhure walked over to Axis, doubt about his motives making her hesitant.

"Pick up that stave on the floor," he said as she stopped before him, "and see if you can find a way to knock me off my feet."

Her every movement wary, Azhure leaned down to the stave.

At precisely the moment her eyes left him Axis moved as swiftly as a striking cat, his booted foot catching Azhure squarely in the small of her back. She grunted as she fell on top of the stave. Axis leaned down, wound his fingers into the thick twist of hair at the crown of Azhure's head, hauled her to her feet, and manoeuvred her head into the classic handhold needed to twist an enemy's head until the spine snapped.

But in the instant before his hands could fatally tighten on her head and jaw, Axis felt the blade of a knife lightly pierce the skin of his belly.

Azhure's eyes were furious as they stared into his.

Axis laughed softly. Azhure had reacted as quickly and as decisively as he'd hoped. He let her head go and stepped back, dropping one hand to gently clasp her wrist and pull the knife away from his belly.

"Azhure came closer to killing me with that knife than any member of the Strike Force has come to bruising me with a stave," he said finally, his eyes not leaving Azhure's face. "I hesitated with the kill and now *I* should be dead instead. Azhure, I am grateful you stayed that knife." He looked around at the Icarii. "Azhure has shown you two lessons. The deadliness of even a small knife in close combat, and the need to develop that instinct to attack without the slightest hesitation – even if your enemy has got a death grip on you."

Axis let Azhure's wrist go and then turned to face the Icarii. After a moment Axis heard a faint movement behind him as Azhure sheathed the knife.

"Enough for today," he said mildly. "But remember the lessons. Once you begin to train with Belial's men you will develop the killer instinct quickly or risk losing more than a few of your proud feathers. SpikeFeather, you may dismiss your command."

As the Icarii filed from the chamber, Axis climbed the ladder into the gallery and stood talking quietly with FarSight, organising a meeting of all the Strike Force commanders so he could discuss future training plans. Although he hadn't yet discussed it with FarSight or RavenCrest, Axis planned on leaving Talon Spike for some weeks after Beltide in early Flower-month. Axis needed to complete his training else-where — as well as fulfil a vow — and he wanted the Strike Force to continue training in his absence.

When he turned back into the chamber, Axis saw that only Azhure was left. She stood in a far corner, lifting the Wolven from a hook on the wall and slinging its accom-panying quiver over her shoulder.

Axis stood a moment, a soft smile playing about his mouth, then he leapt down to the floor of the chamber and silently walked towards her. Azhure gave a small jump of surprise when she saw him standing only a few paces away.

"I am sorry," he said, "that I used you so poorly. But if I had warned you, you would not have reacted so swiftly or so reflexively. Not only were you the only one I trusted to react so instinctively, you were the only one present I could trust to stay the knife. Even so," he fingered his belly gingerly, "you have added one more scar to my growing collection."

Azhure relaxed a little. "I had to stay the impulse to slide that knife all the way in, Axis, but I thought you should suffer a little for the ache you caused my scalp."

"Are you going to practise with the bow?"

"Yes." Azhure fingered the bow, and Axis wondered at her smile as she touched the weapon.

"I see you have a quiver full of new arrows. Should I blame SpikeFeather's tattered appearance on those blue-feathered arrows?"

Azhure laughed. "He did not think I could use the Wolven. He was willing to bet his own pride and feathers on it."

"It was a lesson not only SpikeFeather, but most of the Icarii, will not readily forget. The Wolven is one of their greatest treasures."

Azhure's smile faded. "Should I give it back?"

"No. I think the Wolven chose you. It is an enchanted thing."

Azhure looked down at the beautiful bow she held in her hands. "But the Wolven let SpikeFeather use it."

Axis remembered a conversation he had overheard between SpikeFeather and EvenSong several days ago. "It took SpikeFeather nine years before he fully mastered the Wolven – and he is the only one who has been able to use it in some four thousand years. It was only late last year that he managed it." Axis paused. "It is as if the Wolven knew you were coming and finally let SpikeFeather use it so he would pick that bow to demonstrate for you. The Wolven tells you it wants you, Azhure. It is yours."

She ran her fingers gently through its blue and scarlet silken tassels. "Then it honours me, though I know not why." She raised her smoky eyes. "Enchanted, you say?"

Axis reached out and ran his fingers along the string of the bow. "WolfStar SunSoar made it, many thousands of years ago. WolfStar was the most powerful of the Enchanter-Talons – there has never been another like him." He stopped, considering. Due to his extraordinary power, WolfStar's name had cropped up many times during Axis' training, but curiously StarDrifter and MorningStar had evaded his occasional questions about the mysterious ninth Enchanter-Talon. After a moment Axis continued. "He wove enchantments into the bow's making. No-one really knew what. No-one has been able to see." He dropped his hand. "*I* cannot see. It is as though a film of ice covers the bow's soul. I can see the shape of the enchantments, but they are hazy, out of focus. I can hear them, especially when you use the bow. But the music lingers at the extreme edge of my hearing, and I cannot quite catch the tune. WolfStar took his enchantments and the key to the Wolven to the grave with him."

"You will prevail even without the knowledge of the ancient Icarii Enchanter-Talons, Axis."

Axis' mouth quirked at the absolute certainty in her voice. "With the faith of such as you by my side then I am bound to," he said softly. Their eyes caught, then Axis turned away slightly. "I am thinking of using you in the Strike Force's aerial training, Azhure, if you would consent."

She laughed, incredulous. "Will you build me wings, then, like StarDrifter offered to do for you?" Axis had vehemently refused StarDrifter's offers to coax his dormant wing buds into flowering. He had lived his life thus far without wings, and he would live the rest of his life without them.

Axis smiled. "No. With FarSight I have been putting the Strike Force through various evasive manoeuvres designed to lessen the risk of arrow strike. But now I want them to have some real arrows to out-manoeuvre. Will you shoot at them?"

Azhure's mouth dropped open. "You can't mean that!"

Axis' eyes twinkled. "Perhaps I still have a trace of Battle-Axe in me, Azhure."

"But I do not know *how* to fire an arrow to miss, Axis! It would be a betrayal to the Wolven to aim to miss."

"Then wrap the arrow heads in cloth or dip them in wax to blunt them. That way you will give them bruises, but not heart-piercing wounds."

Azhure did not want to risk the Icarii's acceptance now that she had finally won it. "They will not resent me?" she asked doubtfully.

"They will resent *me*. It will be my suggestion. My order," said Axis. "Will you do it? You could stand on that ledge that overlooks the Iskruel Ocean. The extent of the air field on the northern face of Talon Spike will give the Strike Force their maximum manoeuvring field."

Azhure thought for a moment. "They'll need it. Yes. I'll do it, so long as we can blunt the arrows sufficiently. And I will have to use less exotic arrows than these. SpikeFeather won't be pleased to see his feather-fledged arrows tumbling down the chasm at Talon Spike's feet."

Axis nodded. "Good. I'll discuss the plan with FarSight and the other Crest-Leaders tomorrow. I will go ahead with it only if they think there is little danger to the Strike Force. Well, I'll leave you to your target practice. Perhaps you will soon have something larger and more difficult to aim for."

Azhure's face darkened. "The sooner I have a Skraeling eye to aim for, the better." She ached to appease the agony she still felt at her friend Pease's terrible death in the Earth Tree Grove, chewed into bloody fragments by the Skraeling wraiths as Azhure stood by, horrified, unable to act through her own terror.

Axis' mood shifted abruptly. "Your first target in war may not be Skraelings, Azhure," he said a little sadly.

She frowned. "What do you mean?"

"I'll discuss it when the time comes. Azhure, I must go. I thank you again for your assistance here this afternoon, and again I apologise for my rude treatment of you. I am glad our friendship has survived this afternoon."

Axis turned to go.

"Wait!" Azhure cried, rummaging in the shoulder sack she carried about with her and withdrawing a bundle of dark golden silk.

She stood, gently fingering the material, her eyes downcast, then she looked up, and Axis felt his heart clench a little at the expression in her beautiful eyes.

"I've noticed you touching the tunic over your left breast, where once the twin crossed axes of your station rested. Now you are no longer BattleAxe, but rather Axis SunSoar, son of Princess Rivkah and StarDrifter, heir to the powers and gifts of the SunSoar Enchanters and to the Prophecy of the Destroyer. You need a new emblem, Axis, a new standard, a sign to mark you the StarMan."

She shook the material out. "Rivkah found the fabric for me, and over the past few weeks I have spent the occasional hour sewing this for you."

Axis took a sharp breath of amazement as the material unfolded in Azhure's hands. It was a finely crafted tunic of deep golden silk, its texture slightly roughened so that it caught the light. Around the bottom of the sleeves and the high neck Azhure had embroidered designs recalling the exotic writing of the ancient Icarii language. The design embroidered in silk on the centre of the golden tunic made him catch his breath anew. It was the SunSoar blazing sun, but in blood-red rather than its usual insipid pale gold.

Azhure relaxed at the expression on Axis' face. She hadn't known whether or not he would accept it. "I have almost finished a battle standard for you in the same design, Axis SunSoar."

"I will be proud to accept tunic and standard and to embrace this emblem as my own, Azhure," Axis whispered, cradling the silken tunic in his hand. It was light, so light. "You have done me honour."

10

Propositions and Endings

Azhure shot off yet another arrow, hitting the scarlet target globe which already bristled with her previous shots. She gazed at the beautiful bow. No-one knew what wood it had been made of. Perhaps WolfStar had altered it with his enchantments, she thought vaguely, running her fingers over its smooth ivory surface. Strange patterns in gold tracery spiralled about the length of the bow, like nothing else she had seen decorating Icarii walls or art works. She wondered what WolfStar had been like. No-one among the Icarii liked talking about him much. Would he have minded that his bow had been lost into the possession of an Acharite woman?

She reached for an arrow and finding her quiver empty, abruptly realised she had a problem. Always there had been an Icarii present to retrieve her arrows for her. But now the target ball swung sixty paces above her head. She could hardly leave the ball bristling with arrows – the next Icarii to use the chamber would be furious at her carelessness. She sighed and hung the Wolven on a wall hook. Either she'd have to climb up herself, a choice she quickly discarded as she glanced about the smooth walls, or she would have to find an Icarii willing to retrieve the arrows for her.

"I should be pleased to retrieve them for you, Azhure," a voice said from behind her, and Azhure whipped about.

StarDrifter stood at the rail of the observation gallery, smiling down at her, then launched himself into the air with his powerful wings. Watching him, Azhure envied the Icarii ability to fly. What would it be like, she thought, to be able to escape into the limitless freedom of the skies?

StarDrifter alighted before her, passing over her arrows.

"Thank you," Azhure said, dropping the arrows into the quiver across her back. "Next time I will make sure someone else is using the chamber whenever I practise."

StarDrifter smiled. She had such a lovely face. For weeks now his desire for her had been growing. Yet she tried to keep herself so distant, avoiding the times he used the Chamber of Steaming Water.

He gazed longingly at her hair. No Icarii woman had long hair, it stopped growing once it reached the level of their neck feathers, and StarDrifter loved the feel of long hair – it was one of the attractions human women had for him. Unable to stop himself, he reached over and cradled the back of her head, feeling the weight of the coiled braid.

Azhure started in alarm. "StarDrifter!" she began, then StarDrifter's other arm was about her and he pressed her against his body, stopping her objections with a deep kiss.

For long minutes Azhure did not resist. She had never been kissed like this before. The few experiences she'd endured from the awkward boys of Smyrton had not pleased her, and their groping fumblings had repulsed her.

This was different. The feel of his chest under her hands, the warmth and taste of his mouth, curiosity at new sensations, the subtle but unmistakable touch of his Enchanter's power, all made her hesitate to break the embrace.

Encouraged by Azhure's initial reaction, StarDrifter's mouth left hers to caress her jaw and throat, gently biting, nibbling. He wrapped his wings about her, cradling her within them so his hands were free. He started to unfasten the buttons of her tunic.

Azhure finally found the resolve to push her hands more firmly against his chest. It was difficult, for part of her mind screamed at her to stay and let him do what he wanted, but another part recalled Rivkah's words about being cradled in a lover's wings during Beltide, and the thought of Rivkah gave Azhure the courage to speak.

"No," she mumbled. "No, StarDrifter. Stop."

He smiled and slipped his hand inside her tunic, cupping a breast. "You do not want me to stop, Azhure."

"If you do not stop then it will be rape, StarDrifter," Azhure insisted, her voice now firm. "I love and respect Rivkah too much to betray her like this. Let me go."

"Rape? But do you not enjoy this, my beautiful woman?" StarDrifter asked, his fingertips drifting over a nipple. "I can feel you tremble. You do *not want* me to stop."

Azhure freed an arm and struck him across the face. The effect was electric. StarDrifter stumbled backwards, a hand clasped to his shocked face.

Azhure jerked her tunic closed, fumbling with the fastenings. "I do not welcome your advances, StarDrifter. Please do not lessen my respect for you by pursuing me like this," she said emphatically, then, picking up the Wolven, she turned and climbed the ladder into the observation gallery with as much dignity as she could muster.

Azhure was as furious with herself as she was with him. She had almost managed to put her scruples aside in order to indulge her curiosity and enjoy what StarDrifter was offering. She crossed the observation gallery, her steps quickening as she got closer to the door and escape. In her haste she did not notice the figure who had sought refuge in a shadowed corner just minutes before.

StarDrifter watched her go, only slowly dropping his hand from his cheek. He was appalled, not that Azhure had hit him, but that she been *forced* to hit him. Rape – sexual force of any kind – was a concept almost totally alien to the Icarii people. All of them loved the chase and the seduction, but no Icarii ever pursued one who was unsure or unwilling.

StarDrifter took a deep breath. He would apologise. But his desire for Azhure was driving him crazy. He had never felt like this about anyone, not even Rivkah during the height of their passion. Why? StarDrifter asked himself. There were more beautiful women than her about, and surely more willing than her. But he felt driven to possess her by a force so deep within him that he did not, could not, understand it.

He looked up to the gallery, hoping Azhure had not left. But the woman standing there was not Azhure.

Rivkah stood with her hands resting lightly on the gallery rail. She looked calm and cool, elegant in a sky-blue gown, her silver and golden-streaked hair left free to trail down her back. "We need to talk, StarDrifter," she said quietly. "And I would appreciate it if you could join me up here."

Oh Stars! StarDrifter thought helplessly, his face, every entire muscle of his body, showing his tenseness.

Rivkah waited until he joined her, then touched his face. "This must end," she said, her eyes inexpressibly sad.

"I do not know what came over me, I will not do it again," StarDrifter began, but Rivkah cut him off.

"No. Our marriage must end while we still respect each other. StarDrifter, it is time we talked plainly."

StarDrifter's face stilled, his pale-blue eyes narrowing. "Very well. Let us talk."

A slight tremor belied Rivkah's calm exterior.

"StarDrifter. We both know that in past years we have been slowly but inexorably drifting apart. We had a grand passion, we loved each other dearly, we both sacrificed dearly for that love and passion. But we must now face the reality that our marriage is no longer viable."

"Rivkah –" He reached out, but Rivkah stepped back.

"No. Let me finish. You are Icarii and I am human. You have, potentially, another four hundred years of life, Star-

Drifter. Already I grow old. I will *not* become an object of pity in your eyes. I must end this marriage while there is still respect – perhaps even a little love – left between us." She paused. "Now I know why the Ferryman thought that resuming the name Rivkah would be a high price for me to pay. GoldFeather may have belonged here, StarDrifter, but Rivkah does not. After Beltide I will return to Achar."

"Rivkah!" StarDrifter reached for her again, and this time she did not attempt to resist. For a long time they stood, holding each other, StarDrifter gently stroking the golden streak through her hair. Despite what she had implied, Rivkah still loved him deeply, but she wanted to walk away from their marriage while she knew that StarDrifter still enjoyed their intimate relationship.

Eventually she pulled back. "StarDrifter," she whispered, grateful for the unforced tears of regret in his eyes, "don't let your consuming need for Azhure destroy her life. Don't make her go through what I am now going through. She is human too, and in another twenty or thirty years I don't want her to be standing here ending her marriage to you because your eye has been caught by a woman younger and more vital than her. Let her go. Respect her enough for that. Find an Icarii woman who will be with you for the rest of your life."

"Azhure was not at fault for what just happened." StarDrifter knew how deep the friendship was between the two women.

"I know." Rivkah forced a smile. "I admire her resistance. If I remember correctly I conceded at a single smile from you. I do not blame her . . . nor you, really. I want us to go to RavenCrest and formally break the marriage." Soon, she thought bleakly, while I still have the strength for this.

"What will you do?" StarDrifter asked. "Where will you go?"

"I will return to my people, StarDrifter. I will find myself a home among them."

II

"Are You True?" Asketh the Bridge

"See?" Jack said, pointing his hand. "Do you see?" Belial, Magariz and Arne stood at his shoulder at the western window of Sigholt's spacious map-room. Behind them Reinald sat comfortably by the fire, sipping some spiced wine.

"There was a lake there, once," Jack said, a little impatient with the three men. "A beautiful lake. Do you not see?"

"Yes, Jack," Belial finally responded, wondering what all this had to do with why the Skraelings seemed to be keeping their distance from Sigholt. "But why is it important?"

"If Jack's going to give us lessons in geological curiosities," Magariz grumbled, "then let us at least fortify ourselves with some of that wine before Reinald drinks it all."

Belial had led his command into Sigholt almost four weeks ago. He, like Magariz, had been stunned to find the garrison both undamaged and deserted, except for Jack and the retired cook. Reinald had grinned toothlessly at his amazement and explained that once word reached Sigholt that Gorkenfort had fallen, the majority of Borneheld's men stationed there had retreated south. Once Hsingard fell, and it seemed that the Skraelings were only a day or two away from Sigholt, the rest had fled in the middle of the night in a mad and cowardly dash that had left three men trampled to death in the gateway of the garrison.

But the Skraelings had never attacked. The day after the last of the garrison fled, leaving only Jack and Reinald to inhabit the huge Keep ("And I would have fled too," Reinald confessed, "save that my arthritis was so bad that week I was bed-bound"), a band of hungry Skraelings had appeared at some distance from Sigholt, sniffing around the perimeters of the old lake bed. But they'd approached no closer, and Jack and Reinald had been bothered no more by the wraiths.

Jack had apparently never been concerned that the Skraelings would attack, and to Reinald's dismay he'd even refused to lock the garrison's gates at night. After two or three weeks of peace, Reinald had relaxed as well, enjoying the company of this strange man who'd sought refuge at the gates of Sigholt during the first week of the new year.

So it was that Sigholt lay waiting for Belial and his three thousand men. They had settled in quickly. The garrison complex – the ancient Keep, its kitchens, orchards, barracks, stables, courtyards, cellars and sundry storage and out-buildings – held easily all the men and their horses. The garrison Borneheld had maintained here had been almost as large, and when his men fled they'd taken their horses but not much else, leaving enough supplies to keep Belial's men fed for some months.

As yet no-one had received an adequate explanation from Jack about why the Skraelings had left Sigholt alone after destroying Hsingard, which was a hundred times the size of Sigholt. In fact, two days after their arrival Jack had disa-ppeared for over three weeks, returning only some four or five days ago. Despite Sigholt's apparent safety, Belial had spent some sleepless nights, wondering if the Skraelings had left the garrison alone only to mass for a surprise attack. But Belial had gradually relaxed, supervising the daily training routines of his men while making sure they spent an equal amount of time in leisure. The horrors of Gorkenfort and the rigours of the march through eastern Ichtar to Sigholt were still evident in some haggard and prematurely lined faces, but generally the men were recovering well from the trials of the previous months.

A week ago Belial had sent a small detachment of men to make contact with the Axe-Wielders left in Smyrton, inquire further south about supply routes, garner what information they could about Priam and Borneheld's plans and, most importantly, to see if news of the Prophecy had spread any further south than the Nordra. "If no-one knows the Prophecy, then repeat it," Belial had instructed. "It will only serve Axis that the Prophecy, and thus the news of his coming, precedes him."

A couple of days after their departure Jack had reappeared as suddenly as he'd disappeared and refused to answer Belial's questions. His stubborn silence sent Belial stamping from the room, but this morning Jack had appeared at the daily command conference in the map-room and announced he was prepared to answer all of Belial's questions as best he could.

"So," Belial said as he accepted a glass of wine from Magariz. "An ancient lake bed. How does that explain why the Skraelings haven't attacked?"

"The ancient lake bed explains both why I am here and why the Skraelings have not attacked – and probably won't attack unless Gorgrael pushes them very hard," Jack replied. "Please, Belial, may I have some of that spiced wine before we continue? Sigholt may be protected from the worst of Gorgrael's cold, but it is still chill enough."

Belial started to move towards the table, but Arne indicated he would fetch Jack a goblet. Since their arrival at Sigholt Arne had made himself Belial's general personal assistant, although Belial was sure that when Axis reappeared Arne would resume service with him.

Jack sipped the wine Arne handed him with pleasure. He had spent the past three weeks exploring the surrounding hills and cliff faces in detail, searching for what he knew must be there. Finally he put his wine down.

"Each of the Sentinels are associated with one of what were known as the sacred Lakes of Tencendor, Belial. There were four, now there remain only three. You have seen one of them, Grail Lake – although Arne has seen two. The remaining two sacred Lakes are Cauldron Lake in the heart of the Silent Woman Woods, and Fernbrake Lake in the highest valley of the Bracken Ranges. All are magical, and the Skraelings – who hate water of any sort – will stay far away from them. The Keep of Sigholt sat on the very edge of the most powerful of the four Lakes – the Lake of Life."

Jack chewed his lip, debating whether to tell them the rest, then made up his mind. The Lake's secrets would be revealed soon enough anyway.

"But the Lake of Life has been drained," he continued. "It has disappeared. And with it has gone its Sentinel, Zeherah."

Belial shifted impatiently. "Yes, I can understand the Sentinels' alliance with the Lakes. I'm aware that the Skraelings dislike water, and I suppose that they would dislike magical Lakes more than ordinary water. But since the water has now disappeared, why don't they attack?"

Jack shrugged. He had discarded his peasant garb and now stood clothed in a fine green woollen tunic and trousers edged with scarlet that would have done a minor noble proud. "Some of the magic lingers, Belial. Enough to discourage them from an attempt on the Keep itself." That the Keep was also magical Jack did not tell Belial and Magariz.

"But they might one day surmount their dislike enough to attack?" asked Magariz, limping over to the window again.

"Perhaps." Jack sighed, worry straining his face. "Especially if Gorgrael decides the garrison might be a worthwhile enough target."

"Gorgrael has spread himself thin," Belial said slowly. "We were hardly bothered in the journey south to Sigholt. My guess is that we damaged him so badly above Gorkenfort that he's concentrating on maintaining his hold, rather than extending it."

"I agree. We're probably safe for the moment, perhaps for the entire summer coming while Gorgrael reinvigorates his Ghostmen. But . . ." Jack paused.

"But?" Magariz prompted, one heavy eyebrow raised.

"But I need your help. I want to make Sigholt secure against the Skraelings, a strong base for Axis as he builds the forces necessary to beat the Destroyer back. And . . ." he hesitated. "And I want to see if I can find Zeherah. Belial, Magariz, if I cannot find her then we may as well turn our backs and let Gorgrael occupy the whole of Tencendor – or Achar, as you still call it. We need the five – *Axis* needs the five – to defeat Gorgrael."

"So," said Reinald wearily from his comfortable chair by the fire. "I suppose you want to reflood the Lake."

Belial and Magariz looked at him in surprise, then turned back to Jack.

Jack nodded. "Yes. If the Lake is reflooded, then Sigholt will be all but impregnable except to Gorgrael himself – and even he would hesitate to ask for entry at the Keep's gates." If Gorgrael got as far as the gates. "And reflooding the Lake may bring Zeherah back."

"You're not sure," Magariz said.

Jack suddenly looked ashen and worn out. "No. I am not sure. She was tied to the Lake, but not completely. She could have left it, as all the other Sentinels have currently left their Lakes. If it was drained – by one of the criminal Dukes of Ichtar, I suspect – that would not of itself automatically have killed her. She could have continued to haunt the Lake site, grieving, but not mortally wounded. But there is no sign of her at all."

For long moments there was silence, then Arne broke in with his customary bluntness. "How do you intend to reflood the Lake?"

Belial smiled. Trust Arne to ask the practical question.

"I have spent the past three weeks making sure that it *can* be done, Arne," Jack replied. "There's a narrow gully behind Sigholt that runs back into the Urqhart Hills about half a league. It is overgrown with shrubs and weeds now, but I think that once it was a waterway.

"The gully leads into a small cavern. Inside the cavern there is a blockage of rocks. It is too neat, too regular to be natural. I think it is a plug placed over the spring that fed the Lake. If we can remove it then the water will once more flow down to the Lake."

"Can we?" Belial asked. "Do you think we can unblock it?"

"You have three thousand men, Belial. If we can't do it with three thousand, then no-one will ever do it." Jack paused. "But it is not simply the blockage in the cavern itself. We will have to clear the gully of some of the obstructions that have fallen from the rocky walls since the water stopped flowing, and we will have to clear a path about Sigholt itself."

Belial frowned. "What do you mean?"

Jack came and stood before the fire. "There is a deep depression about Sigholt that has been filled with rubble and boulders. I think the water flowed down through the gully until it reached Sigholt, then divided in two to flow completely about the garrison, forming a natural moat before it flowed into the Lake. With the water surrounding Sigholt on all sides, this garrison will be virtually impregnable." And will be reinfused with the source of its magical power, Jack thought. Sigholt will live again.

"Well, tomorrow we'll take several of the engineers we have with us and go inspect this gully and cavern, Jack. Magariz, you can organise a detail to inspect this rubble-filled moat that surrounds the walls of the garrison. We will know by tomorrow eve if this feat is possible."

And whether or not we manage to unblock this spring, reflood the Lake and find this missing Zeherah, thought Belial, at least the attempt will keep the men fit and busy.

That it did. With only five hundred men left on garrison duty – not that, according to Jack, Belial even needed to keep five hundred assigned to that task – two and a half thousand set to the unblockage of spring, gully and moat. For twelve days they laboured, fifteen hundred on the moat, and a thousand on the gully and inside the cavern where Jack claimed the spring was.

Eight days after they had started Belial and Magariz stood at the outer edge of the moat and peered inside. A deep, wide watercourse had been uncovered, its sides and floor paved with great slabs of greyish-green rock, fitted together in a patchwork of incredible subtlety and beauty. Even though the builders had not used any mortar, the joints between slabs were so tight that Belial could not even get the blade of his knife between them.

"No stone mason today could create such fine joinery and not use a single handful of mortar," Magariz said quietly.

"I wonder how much Jack knows about this Keep that he does not yet tell us, my friend," Belial said.

Magariz looked up. Today the wind was a little lighter, and he had discarded his heavy black cloak. "Belial, I worry less about what mysteries the Keep might hold than how we're going to get into it should the men currently working in the cavern unblock the spring and allow the water to flow. At the moment we have no bridge worthy of the name."

As the moat had been uncovered, Belial had ordered that a rudimentary bridge be erected across the divide. But it was flimsy and only carried men on foot. The moment a surge of water rushed through it would be destroyed.

"I'd better start the men on building a more permanent replacement," Belial said wearily. "Although where we will find the timber needed for such a structure I do not know." The fifteen hundred working on the moat were close to exhaustion, and Belial had wanted to give them a few days' rest before he sent them to relieve those still labouring in the gully and cavern. But a bridge was vital.

"No need," said Jack behind them. Covered in grey rock dust, Jack looked as tired as Belial's men. His chest heaved as if he had been hurrying. "When the water flows, Sigholt will create her own bridge."

"*What*?" Magariz and Belial said together.

Jack smiled. "Sigholt is a cunning lady. She was created by ancient Icarii Enchanters. Trust her."

"And when will the water flow, Jack? How is the work going in the cavern?" Belial asked.

Jack wiped his forehead, smearing rock dust into the furrows as he did so. "Your three engineers tell me that whoever filled in the spring simply tipped cartload after cartload of rocks into the fissure where the water bubbled out. Although they finished off the outer layers with mortared masonry, once we cleared those layers all we found was rubble such as filled this moat. If they had taken the time to construct tightly mortared layers from the very base of the spring our task would be so much more difficult. But now we reach the lower layers of the rubble," he smiled, "and find that the rubble is wet. Over hundreds of years the force of the spring beneath the rubble has been slowly eroding the base of the fill. What we have started at the top, the spring itself is doing from the bottom. Perhaps, eventually, the spring would have broken free anyway."

"So how close are you to clearing the spring?" Magariz's excitement was clear in his voice. For some reason he could not wait to see the water surround this gracious garrison and fill the Lake again.

"Three days, Magariz. The men in the cavern work slowly now – they have to be careful. The engineers are planning their route through the rubble cautiously. If they have calculated correctly, then they only need remove about four paces more of rubble before the force of the underground spring will blast the rest free."

"And the gully?"

"Will be clear tomorrow morning." Jack's eyes glistened. "In four days at the most the Lake of Life will begin to refill and . . . and perhaps Zeherah will be freed."

Magariz laid a hand on the Sentinel's shoulder. "How long is it since you have seen her?"

A tear escaped and trailed slowly through the rock dust covering Jack's cheek. "Over two thousand years, Magariz. It is a hard thing to be separated from a loved one so long."

"I too have loved and lost and now wait," Magariz said quietly, "although I have not had to wait two thousand years. I hope in a few days' time your waiting, at least, will be over."

Belial regarded Magariz curiously. What did he mean? Belial had always supposed that, like himself, Magariz had been too wedded to his profession to think of a wife as well. But now it appeared Magariz had other, sadder, reasons for remaining unmarried. Yet Magariz was a man of honour and worth, as well as being as handsome a devil as any woman could hope to have warm her bed.

"Stand clear!" shouted Fulbright, the senior of Belial's engineers. "The rocks shift. Stand clear!"

Five men deep within the fissure scrambled to the ropes awaiting them, and teams of men hauled them to the surface as quickly as they could. A rumble deep within the earth confirmed Fulbright's worst fears.

"Haul, damn you!" he screamed at the men pulling the ropes in, and ran to the nearest team, adding his weight and power to theirs. "*Haul!*"

The gods were benign this day, for the water burst forth the instant after all five had been pulled over the edge of the fissure. "Back!" Fulbright screamed again, but the men needed no encouragement. They scrambled to safety as the water shrieked and wailed its way to freedom, carrying with it the final remnants of rubble.

Fulbright's eyes widened as steaming water rushed towards the roof of the cavern in a great spout, then cascaded over the lip of the fissure and down the waterway towards the gully. It was a hot spring.

"Axis save us," he muttered to himself. "We'll all have a hot bath tonight."

Belial and Magariz stood anxiously by the moat as the steaming water surged forwards, destroying the flimsy bridge.

Jack stood unperturbed as the broken pieces of the bridge sailed past them. "Peace, gentlemen, and wait."

"Wait for what?" Magariz muttered. "Someone to hand me a piece of soap? This moat will be good for nothing but bathing if we cannot get into Sigholt."

Jack smiled. These Acharites were so impatient. "Wait for the warmth to penetrate Sigholt's walls, Magariz. Then watch."

For another half an hour they all stood there, Belial and Magariz growing increasingly agitated. There were deep ruby tints in the stream, Belial thought, probably the minerals carried to the surface by the water. Dammit! His temper abruptly broke. *What* were they waiting for?

"Jack," he began, but stopped as the Sentinel turned to him, his emerald eyes agleam.

"Don't you feel it?" Jack asked, excited. "Sigholt awakes. Watch the water as it flows by the gate."

Belial peered, then he realised there was a . . . film . . . between his eyes and the surface of the water. As he watched, it solidified until what appeared to be a solid bridge of grey stone curiously marbled with deep ruby-red veins stood before him spanning the moat.

His eyes bulged. "What? How?" He could not get any other words out. At his side Magariz stood similarly astonished. The bridge *looked* solid and wide enough to support not only mounted men, but heavily laden carts as well.

Jack waved at the bridge. "Cross, Magariz, and see what happens."

Magariz glanced at Belial. Cross? This magical bridge? It might vaporise underneath his feet! He took a deep breath to steady himself then stepped forth to the edge of the bridge. But, just as he prepared to step onto the structure itself, the bridge spoke.

"Are you true?" it asked in a woman's deep melodic voice.

Magariz leapt back a full pace, his eyes wide. "What?"

"Are you true?" the bridge asked again, patiently.

"Answer her, Magariz," Jack said. "She will only ask three times, and after that you may never cross."

"Answer her?" Magariz repeated, dragging his eyes away from the bridge and turning to stare at Jack. "Answer *what*?"

"Answer with whatever is in your heart, Magariz," Jack snapped, "but answer! *Now!*"

Magariz stepped up to the bridge again.

"Are you true?" the bridge asked for the third time.

Magariz hesitated, then answered. "Yes, I am true."

"Then cross, my Lord Magariz, and I will see if you speak the truth."

Magariz stepped onto the bridge and paused, obviously expecting to fall straight through. Then he took another step, then another.

"You speak the truth, Magariz," the bridge suddenly said. "Welcome to my heart." And with that he was across.

Magariz noticed all the men watching him, and walked back across, his gait now confident. "The bridge let me cross back unchallenged?" he asked.

"Yes," Jack said. "It is only the first time that the bridge will ask the question. She knows you now. She will greet you, but she will not challenge you again — unless she feels your heart has been corrupted since last you trod her back. Watch."

Jack stepped up to the bridge and placed a foot upon its surface unchallenged. As his weight bore down on the stone the bridge spoke.

"Welcome, Jack," the voice said warmly. "It has been many years since you have trod my back."

"I greet you well, dear heart," Jack replied softly, "and it gladdens my heart to see that once more the waters flow."

"I have been sad," the bridge said, "but now I am happy."

Later, after the bridge had questioned each member of Belial's force, Belial stood with Jack in the courtyard of Sigholt.

"Well? What of Zeherah?"

Jack shook his head sadly. "Perhaps she needs the Lake to refill before she can return."

But as the Lake gradually filled over the next few days, there was no sign of the fifth Sentinel. After six days of watching from the rooftop Jack retired to his private chamber and did not emerge for many days. When he did, his face was creased and haggard with grief. There was nothing else he could do. Zeherah was lost unless he could discover the enchantments that bound her.

12

"I Will Lead You Back into Tencendor!"

The Assembly Chamber of Talon Spike was vast, tiered with dozens of rows of golden-veined white marble about a circular floor of translucent and very beautiful golden marble veined with violet. Pale gold and blue cushions lay scattered about the benches. The lower circles of benches were reserved for the Elders, the Enchanters and the family of the Talon. These benches were completely lined with crimson cushions for the Elders, turquoise ones for the Enchanters, and royal violet for those of the House of SunSoar. The very top seventeen rows of benches reserved for the Strike Force were uncushioned, as befitted the hard muscles of warriors.

A spectacular circle of gigantic pillars soared above the tiers and supported the domed roof of the Chamber. Five times life height, the pillars were carved into alternating male and female figures, their arms and wings extended joyously, their eyes open in wonder and mouths open in silent song. They were gilded and enamelled, with real gems in their eyes and in the golden torcs about their necks. Each individual hair on their heads and feathers in their wings had been picked out in gold and silver and the muscles in their pale naked bodies were carefully defined in the ivory tones of flesh. They supported a domed roof completely plated in highly burnished bronze mirrors which, due to the enchantments bonded into their making, gave off a gentle golden light that illuminated the entire Chamber.

The Chamber lay empty, awaiting the Icarii and the man of the Prophecy who would lead them back into Tencendor and back into the lands of myth and legend.

In the circular robing room RavenCrest SunSoar faced the man who demanded to be named his heir.

The Icarii Talon, his violet eyes furious, paced to and fro, his black and speckled-blue wings rustling angrily behind.

"I reserve the right not to name an heir!" he shouted.

Axis understood RavenCrest's reluctance to act. The Talon had not yet accepted FreeFall's death, but Axis had to make him realise that an heir needed to be named while Raven-Crest still lived. These were bad and dangerous times, and if an heir could die so precipitously, then so too could a Talon – and nothing was so threatening to the stability of any realm than uncertainty over the succession.

Tonight Axis would address the full Assembly of the Icarii, and he needed to do that with the authority of an heir. He had to unite the three races – Icarii, Acharite and Avar – in order to weld them into a force that could defeat Gorgrael's Ghostmen. He knew tonight could be his only opportunity to pull the Icarii behind him.

He walked deliberately towards his uncle, wearing the golden tunic Azhure had made for him, the blood-red sun blazing triumphantly across his breast. I bless her for this gift of the blood-red sun, he thought as he held RavenCrest's eyes, for it will be the emblem of what I will become.

StarDrifter and MorningStar glanced at each other.

Axis stopped not a pace from RavenCrest, his eyes calm before the Talon's temper.

"Your son is dead. Gone. You have no other children. RavenCrest, you have a duty to your people," Axis paused, "and to your blood. You have no choice but to name me your heir. I demand it as my right. You have no choice."

RavenCrest gestured towards StarDrifter. "My brother stands in direct line to the throne."

Axis' mouth curled ironically. "Uncle, if you follow that line of reasoning, then StarDrifter would be followed by his eldest son." He paused, letting the full implications of his statement sink in. "Would you have Gorgrael knock on Talon Spike's door to claim his heritage, RavenCrest? Gorgrael as Talon? If nothing else, I am the lesser of two evils."

RavenCrest said nothing, the muscles in his jaw flickering.

"The whole mountain seethes with uncertainty over this issue," Axis snapped. "Name me as your heir, or let your beloved people tear themselves to pieces once you have gone. You have no son or full-blood nephew to follow you, Raven-Crest, and I *am* your only choice! You must decide and you must decide *now*! Why did you give me control of the Strike Force if you did not intend to give me the throne as well?"

RavenCrest tore his eyes away from his nephew's and looked at his mother.

MorningStar inclined her head. "He is right, RavenCrest. You have no choice. You must name Axis your heir."

Her eldest son did not like what she said.

"This has *never* happened before!" RavenCrest shouted, wheeling away and resuming his agitated pacing. "The Icarii have *always* had a full-blood Icarii SunSoar as Talon!"

"The whole world is changing and being refashioned beneath our feet, RavenCrest. Nothing will ever be the same again." Not only his voice, but Axis' entire body stance exuded power and confidence.

RavenCrest looked at his nephew. His whole being yearned for his son, but FreeFall was dead. Despite his grief and his resistance to naming Axis his heir, RavenCrest indeed knew that he would have to do it. StarDrifter would be a hopeless Talon, and, even though Axis was not full-blood Icarii – not even winged – he knew how to lead.

The anger on RavenCrest's face faded, and he gestured to his brother. "StarDrifter, call our wives and EvenSong. They must be here so that the entire living House of SunSoar will bear witness to this."

At StarDrifter's summons, BrightFeather, RavenCrest's wife, then Rivkah and EvenSong entered the room.

As soon as the door was closed behind them RavenCrest stepped forward and took Axis' face between his hands, then kissed him softly on the mouth.

"As the head of the House of SunSoar and as Icarii Talon, I not only welcome you who was lost into the House of SunSoar, nephew, but also name you in front of these witnesses as my heir and successor to the titles, ranks, privileges and powers of the hereditary office of Talon."

EvenSong's eyes widened in surprise. Rivkah smiled at StarDrifter; their eyes burned with pride.

RavenCrest's eyes were still locked with Axis' and his hands still gripped his nephew's head; he took no notice of the reactions about the room. "Axis. For the past six thousand years the House of SunSoar has been the guardian of the office and person of the Talon. We have been privileged, and have enjoyed the trust and loyalty of the Icarii people."

If not the trust and loyalty of the Acharite people over whom you once ruled, Axis thought a little sourly.

"Respect that tradition of trust and loyalty." RavenCrest paused. "Axis. You will be the twenty-seventh Enchanter-Talon, the first for over fifteen hundred years. You will wield much power, both in your own right and in your position as StarMan. Do you promise to respect your people?"

"Always," Axis responded softly, his sourness fading.

"Do you promise now, before me and your family, that you will not abuse your power?"

"I will never do so."

"Will you guide your Icarii people through the Prophecy so that they will drift only into sun-bright clear air and not shadowed turbulence?"

"I do so promise."

RavenCrest gently let Axis' head go and kissed each of his nephew's palms before folding them gently over Axis' heart.

"Then accept my blessing and my goodwill, Axis SunSoar. Before the House of SunSoar here gathered I formally name you heir to the Talon throne as I will name you to the Icarii nation in Assembly. Shoulder your responsibilities and fly with them into the future."

"I shall endeavour not to falter, RavenCrest, and I will do my best for our people. I am grateful for your trust and for your belief in me. I will do well." In truth, Axis did not know if he'd ever take the throne of Talon, but this was not the time or place to tell RavenCrest how he intended to structure the new Tencendor. But if he did not become Talon, he would pass it to another of the same blood. The office of Talon would not leave the House of SunSoar.

StarDrifter embraced his son. "Welcome to the House of SunSoar, Axis. Welcome home to your heritage."

He was followed by MorningStar. "Welcome to the House of SunSoar. You are a powerful Enchanter, Axis, heir to the Throne. I am proud of you. Fly high and soar well."

BrightFeather whispered some cordial words of welcome, then Axis was enveloped into a bear hug by his mother. He could feel her cheeks were wet with tears as they brushed his.

"I weep with happiness, my sweet son," she said, "and because at least I have witnessed you seize your heritage in both your hands before I die. Welcome among the SunSoars."

Axis hugged her tightly, tears springing into his own eyes. He wished he had enjoyed her love and support all his life instead of only the past few months.

Rivkah let him go and stepped back for EvenSong.

EvenSong placed her hands on Axis' shoulders and kissed him gently. "I have not been very welcoming, Axis," she said softly. "Please accept my sorrow that I did not more fully embrace your return into our family earlier. I have acted badly, and for that I beg your forgiveness. Welcome into the House of SunSoar, brother."

Axis touched her cheek. "There is no need. I know of your grief. EvenSong," he hesitated, "FreeFall's last words and thoughts were of you. Have faith in his love for you."

EvenSong leaned back, her face expressionless as she fought back tears. Even now, after so many months, words of FreeFall were painful.

"There is one more task that must be done before we enter the Assembly," said RavenCrest, "and it breaks my heart to do this." He held out his hands. "Rivkah. StarDrifter."

When they joined him he took each by the hand. "Are you sure you want to do this?"

Rivkah nodded. Her mind was made up. "Yes, Raven-Crest. This is what we must do."

StarDrifter was silent.

"Many years ago," RavenCrest began, "it was my privilege to announce and witness the marriage vows and bonds between you. Now, by mutual decision, you have decided to break those vows." He dropped each of their hands, the gesture deliberate and grave. "Your marriage has come to an end, StarDrifter and Rivkah. Use your freedom wisely."

Rivkah and StarDrifter had warned their children and family earlier of their decision; none were truly surprised. The true tragedy, Axis thought, was that this passion, this love that had altered lives and would alter nations, could be ended so simply.

"I loved you, Rivkah," StarDrifter said gently. "Know that."

"And I loved you, StarDrifter, with heart and soul. Know that."

"Rivkah," RavenCrest laid a hand on her shoulder. "You are and will always be SunSoar. Talon Spike is still your home if you wish to call it that. You are not cast out of this family because you have ended your marriage to StarDrifter."

Rivkah nodded. "Thank you, RavenCrest. Those are kind – and welcome – words." She hesitated. "I will stay until Beltide, celebrate that with you, and then return to Achar for a time. I do not know how long I will stay, or if I will find a home there."

"Come," RavenCrest said to his family. "I can hear the Assembly Chamber filling. It is time for us to robe. Axis must meet his people."

Axis had lived among the Icarii for some three months now and had yet to meet the Icarii people as an assembly. For the first two months he had been so closeted with MorningStar and StarDrifter that he'd hardly seen anyone else, and for the past month his efforts with the Strike Force had kept him relatively isolated.

However, even though the greater proportion of the Icarii had yet to have the chance to make up their minds about Axis SunSoar, rumour and hearsay had spread like wildfire through the Talon Spike complex. If Axis spent two months closeted with MorningStar and StarDrifter it was because he was teaching them, not they teaching him. He was planning to throw the Strike Force at Gorgrael immediately after Beltide in revenge for the Yuletide attack, while a contrary rumour had Axis planning to drive south and capture Achar for the Icarii first. Five Icarii solemnly swore they'd personally seen the letter of surrender that Gorgrael had sent to Axis, addressed to Talon Spike, while another seven claimed to have seen a similar letter announcing that Gorgrael had been assassinated by a band of Ravensbundmen. Several Icarii women claimed that Axis had proposed marriage to them. One woman claimed to be bearing his child. Others still tried to determine which of the conditions of the Prophecy had been fulfilled and which still waited. Many wondered if RavenCrest had finally made up his mind regarding the succession. If not Axis, then who? A few talked of Azhure and her mastery of the Wolven, and one or two privately wondered if she were one of the Star Gods wearing mortal disguise, returned to play among the Icarii.

Raum sat with Azhure, talking quietly on a tier several rows below those the Strike Force would take. Azhure had hardly seen the Avar Bane in recent months; he had been so busy with his study in the Icarii library and his teaching of the Icarii children.

"What do you think will happen tonight?" Azhure whispered, her eyes on the fidgeting Icarii population squeezed into the benches of the Chamber. She wore a vivid crimson gown, draped low over her shoulders and sashed with deep emerald, her hair loose down her back, making her normally exotic appearance even more striking than usual. Many Icarii eyes had followed her entrance into the Chamber.

Raum smiled at her, his liquid brown eyes gentle. "Who knows, Azhure. Tonight Axis must either win the Icarii or lose them. He will have no other chance."

"Raum!" Azhure exclaimed. "They cannot refuse him! Can they?"

Raum squeezed her hand reassuringly. "No-one can ever tell what the Icarii will do in Assembly, Azhure. They are a flighty lot and can stampede in entirely the wrong direction."

"But Raum, in the Assembly after Yuletide, didn't the Icarii vote to accept Axis as the one to lead them through the battles ahead?"

Raum smiled wryly. "That's not the exact thing they voted on, Azhure. That was discussed, yes, and many agreed to it, but the actual vote was taken on whether or not to open negotiations with Axis in Gorkenfort. The Icarii love to meet and argue, but they are very bad at actually making decisions."

Azhure muttered something about the Icarii under her breath as Raum continued. "But it helps that Axis has already gained control of the Strike Force, Azhure. The Icarii will respect that. At the least he will address them as Strike-Leader." Raum's eyes flickered up to the empty benches of the Strike Force. He smoothed down his dark-green robe. Where were they? Were they not going to support Axis?

As if in answer to his thought there was a rustle of movement, and the various Wings of the Strike Force began to emerge from each of the archways, filing their way silently into their places.

Their appearance stunned the Icarii who crammed the benches below. As necks craned, mouths dropped open.

"What?" Raum gasped. "What is that they wear?"

Azhure's eyes gleamed in satisfaction.

Not only had the entire Strike Force dyed their wings in the ebony of war, but now all wore ebony uniforms of slim-fitting wool as well.

"Axis said he wanted to turn the Strike Force from birds of paradise into hawks," Azhure said, her eyes fixed on the Strike Force. "At least now they look the part."

But it was not their dark and imposing presence, stunning as it was, that made the real impact. Every member of the Strike Force wore a blazing blood-red sun embroidered into the chest of his or her uniform. Wing-Leaders were distinguished by a tracery of gold outlining the blazing sun, Crest-Leaders by a smaller circle of golden stars.

"The blazing sun is the symbol of the House of SunSoar," Azhure explained, "and the blood-red sun is Axis' own."

"You devised it for him?"

Azhure nodded. "And he accepted it, although he does not yet know that the Strike Force now wear it. I approached FarSight with the idea."

And he obviously agreed, thought Raum. If nothing else this will indicate to the Icarii population that the Strike Force stands totally united behind Axis. Again he looked at the woman beside him, her face serene as she gazed at the Strike Force. Did the Prophecy place her in Smyrton for a purpose? Raum wondered. Was it simple coincidence that in Smyrton I should find a woman who would save myself and Shra from death, a woman who would later show the way to save many of the Icarii and Avar from slaughter at Yuletide, a woman who could master the Wolven when in four thousand years only one of the Icarii could, a woman who could plan this stunning show of support for Axis? Coincidence? Hardly. There were so many small things about Azhure that didn't add up. He remembered how, during the last Assembly, Azhure had understood the ancient Icarii tongue that StarDrifter had sung in, a language that Raum had mastered only after many years of hard study.

Who are you, Azhure? Raum wondered. *What* are you?

Five rows below him sat the two Sentinels, Ogden and Veremund. Both had discarded their dirty habits and were dressed in slightly more becoming robes, and both were looking at Azhure with exactly the same amount of speculation as Raum. The sense of deep familiarity they experienced whenever they met the woman puzzled them. It was as if they had known her most of their lives. And the Sentinels had lived very, very long lives. This was no simple peasant girl from Smyrton, caught up in events that were spinning her out of control. No, they thought not. Who *was* this woman who walked so effortlessly through prophecy?

Contemplations were cut short by the entrance of the Elders and Enchanters who took their seats on the lower tiers.

The Assembly held its collective breath, all eyes on the small door that led to the robing room. No-one spoke, not a feather was ruffled to destroy the silence.

The SunSoar women came out finally and took their seats; BrightFeather first, as befitted the wife of the Talon, then MorningStar, Rivkah and EvenSong who, through virtue of her connection with the royal House of SunSoar, sat with them tonight rather than the Strike Force. All the women wore various combinations of the royal violet, intertwined with gold and ivory. The colour combination looked particularly striking on EvenSong with her violet eyes and golden underwings.

There was a movement in the doorway and seventy thousand eyes shifted as one towards the figure who now entered.

It was StarDrifter, looking his magnificent and powerful best in a crimson toga with a pale gold sun across his chest. He did not sit on the benches but moved to stand in the centre of the golden floor that was the heart of the Chamber. There he dropped his eyes and watched the door.

RavenCrest entered – slowly, proudly, his violet toga edged with gold, the jewelled golden torc about his neck proclaiming his position as Talon, leader of all Icarii. He walked to stand with StarDrifter, pausing as he joined him. Then, as one, they saluted the Assembly, bowing low in the traditional Icarii greeting, their arms and wings swept low in a gesture both of respect and of abasement, both swinging in a slow full circle so that all were included in their greeting.

Azhure remembered how incredibly beautiful and graceful she had thought StarDrifter when he had bowed in greeting to the Assembly the last time it met, but the effect of both brothers saluting the Assembly in this manner was staggering in its exquisite beauty and simplicity.

It was very unusual for both to open the Assembly as equals. Normally, either one or the other did it – StarDrifter, in his capacity as the most powerful Enchanter, or Raven-Crest in his capacity as Talon.

Azhure turned to Raum with the question in her eyes.

"It indicates, I think, that who is to follow is even more powerful than either of them," he whispered in Azhure's ear. "This entrance and gesture by RavenCrest and StarDrifter is also intended to show the Icarii that they stand together in their support of who is to follow. It will make opposition to Axis very hard. Especially as the Strike Force so obviously stand united behind Axis."

RavenCrest stepped forward to speak, his eyes widening slightly at the sight of the Strike Force. "There is one more to enter the Chamber, my people. I need not tell you who he is. He is the StarMan. Axis SunSoar, son of the Princess Rivkah of Achar and of my brother, StarDrifter SunSoar, Enchanter. And he is the one whom I name heir to the Talon throne," he said into the utter silence of the Chamber.

"A very formal introduction," Raum explained, "and one that clearly tells the Icarii that this man demands respect, not only through his identity as StarMan, and not only through his breeding and relationship to two royal families, but also as the one named heir to the Talon throne."

"He is my son," said StarDrifter directly, "and he is our saviour." Both he and RavenCrest now turned to the doorway.

Axis walked out from the dark of the hallway into the golden light of the Assembly Chamber, feeling the immense solemnity and magnitude of the moment.

As one, the Strike Force stood and saluted their Strike-Leader with fists clenched over their hearts.

Their movement and the rustling of their wings as they stood far above him caught Axis' attention. For a heartbeat he hesitated as his eyes drank in their ebony uniforms with the blood-red blazing suns and their gesture of support and respect. In that instant Axis realised the full power of his destiny. Confidence and pride surged through him.

He walked into the centre of the golden floor, his uncle and father stepping back to make way for him.

As RavenCrest and StarDrifter had saluted the Assembly, so too did Axis, bowing with his hand clenched over the blazing sun, circling the Chamber to include all in his salute. As he rose from his bow his eyes caught Azhure's, and she felt a strong sense of the emotion that Axis was experiencing at this moment. *You do me honour again, Azhure, and I slip yet further into your debt,* his voice whispered in her head. Her hand clenched the material of her gown as she felt his Enchanter powers wrap around her. For an instant they lingered, caressing, then Axis withdrew them and stood straight and proud to address the Assembly.

Unlike his father and uncle, who wore the togas that Icarii wore on all formal occasions, Axis was dressed as a man of war in the tunic Azhure had made for him over fawn breeches and leather riding boots.

"You are my people," he said, his eyes shining, "and I have escaped the lies that bound me to lead you back into Tencendor."

The Chamber erupted. Many thousands of Icarii leapt to their feet. Some shouted, others shrilled warcries, others yet burst into spontaneous song. Feathers flew, fists punched the air, and cushions were ripped apart in excitement. If any of the Elders still harboured doubts that the younger generation would leave the comforts of Talon Spike for the rigours of reclaiming Tencendor, then those doubts were now lost.

Axis simply stood and watched the ruckus. Again his eyes met Azhure's, and again she felt the soft touch of his power as he shared with her the emotions surging through him. It was at that moment Azhure admitted to herself that she loved him. All her life she had dreamed of a hero. Was there any greater than this man who now stood before this Assembly? She smiled dreamily, a crimson island of stillness in the excitement about her.

As Axis withdrew his power from Azhure he turned his eyes to survey the emotion which swept the Assembly. He had thought long and hard about what to say to them and had finally fallen back on a maxim that Jayme, Brother-Leader of the Seneschal, of all people, had once taught him. "Learn to seize the hearts of your audience with your first words, for those hearts will always remain the most loyal. If someone needs to be persuaded with hours of arguments, then he will forever remain a potential traitor in your camp."

Finally Axis held up a hand for quiet. The Icarii only very gradually subsided into their seats and into silence. When he had the complete attention of the Assembly Axis spoke again.

"I will lead you back into Tencendor, but it will not be easy, nor will it be all that you expect. It may be years before you can reclaim what you lost." This was the dangerous moment, Axis knew – when the Icarii would have to realise that their dreams would not be accomplished overnight. "You know that the Prophecy walks and that I am the StarMan. Even as I speak two of the Sentinels sit among you."

Heads craned and Ogden and Veremund gave small embarrassed waves.

"Whatever I do, wherever I lead you, it must be as the Prophecy dictates, my people. If Tencendor will rise again to defeat Gorgrael, then we must all heal the rift within. Icarii, Avar and Acharite must reunite into one nation. If we cannot find the bridge to understanding, then will Gorgrael earn his name and bring destruction hither," Axis said, quoting the Prophecy to them. "My first task and, I think, my hardest, will be to unite the three races and recreate Tencendor. I face deadly opposition in doing this."

"The Acharites," a voice hissed.

"No, not the people of Achar." Axis paused and stared at the Icarii for a moment. "Not the *people* of Achar, whom I think will accept both you and the concept of Tencendor again, but it will be the Brotherhood of the Seneschal and the Duke of Ichtar who will oppose me . . . us. Was it not the Seneschal who persuaded the Acharites to drive you from

Tencendor during the Wars of the Axe? The Seneschal will oppose us and they will use Borneheld and his army to do it."

"And Priam?" someone asked.

"Priam cannot oppose both the Seneschal and Borneheld. No, my friends, there are two battles ahead of us. One to reunite the three races against the opposition of the Seneschal and Duke Borneheld. The second to throw the combined weight of the united races against Gorgrael."

Again Axis paused and gave the Icarii the chance for speech, but they all sat silent, absorbing his words.

"If you want Tencendor," he continued, "then you will have to fight for it. This summer the Icarii can start to move south again. I already have waiting for us an army of Acharites who are committed to me as StarMan. FarSight CutSpur?" Axis turned and addressed the Crest-Leader where he sat high above the rest of the Icarii. "Have your farflight scouts brought word of Belial's force?"

FarSight stood, the combination of his ebony wings and uniform with his black hair and eyes and swarthy complexion giving him the appearance of a bird of prey. He saluted Axis crisply, then spoke.

"My fellow Icarii. This morning five of our farflight scouts, who have been on a long and dangerous mission to the Urqhart Hills, brought astounding news. Axis' army, commanded at the moment by his loyal lieutenants Belial and Magariz . . ."

Far below, Rivkah's face went ashen with shock.

" . . . has taken possession of the ancient Keep of Sigholt. Sigholt lives, and it waits for us. Our first step back into Tencendor has been taken."

Again cheering broke out, but Axis did not let it go on so long this time.

"My people," he shouted, "listen to me! It is from Sigholt that we will reunite Tencendor, from Sigholt that we will bring the Seneschal and Borneheld to their knees."

Ah, Azhure thought to herself. So that is what he meant when he said my first target in war may not be Skraelings. Well, it will hardly grieve me to take part in the destruction of the Seneschal.

"It is from Sigholt that we will create the momentum which will win us Tencendor and drive Gorgrael from this land!"

Axis stood proud and tall in the centre of the golden floor, his tunic glowing, the blood-red sun blazing on his chest. He raised his hands in appeal to the assembled Icarii.

"I am the StarMan and I will lead you back into Tencendor. I promise you this. Icarii, will you come home with me?"

There was no doubt about the response. Every Icarii in the Chamber surged to his or her feet, screaming Axis' name.

His family, sitting to one side, regarded Axis with mixed emotions. Rivkah and StarDrifter watched with soaring pride that they had created this man. MorningStar watched him and felt regret at the passing of an era. Life for the Icarii would never be the same again. EvenSong watched him and thought of FreeFall. Axis had, to all intents and purposes, usurped FreeFall's position, but could FreeFall ever have united the notoriously divisive Icarii like this?

RavenCrest, like his mother, sat and watched the passing of an age. Tonight he had witnessed the eclipse of his own power. Talon he still might be, but Axis now wielded true authority in the Icarii nation. Already he had grasped power. RavenCrest's shoulders and wings slumped a little. Like EvenSong, he too thought of FreeFall.

Again Axis held his hands up for silence. "Peace, my people. I thank you for your support."

"When will we return to Tencendor?" a voice called from high up in the Chamber.

"When will we mass to fight the Seneschal and Borne-held?" cried a member of the Strike Force.

"We will return and we will fight," Axis said. "But we will do neither tomorrow. The Strike Force still needs training, and especially training with those who await them in Sigholt. In two weeks we go to Beltide celebrations with the Avar, and following Beltide and over the next few months the Strike Force will begin to move down to Sigholt. And I, too, need more training."

"No!" cried one overly excited Icarii. "You are already the most powerful Enchanter we have seen in generations. More training? I think not!" He was supported by a surge of cheers.

Axis grinned. "I will be more powerful with the training I have in mind. Rivkah, my mother," he turned and gave her a small bow and she smiled and inclined her head, "has won for me the right to ask the Charonites for assistance. The assistance I shall ask for will be their secrets."

His words surprised the majority of the Icarii, for not many knew the Charonites still existed. StarDrifter allowed a small flicker of pride to show. *His* son would learn the secrets that the Charonites had guarded for so many thousands of years.

"I shall be gone from you for some time following Beltide," Axis continued, "but I will return. And when I return, then will I lead you out into Tencendor. I will take you home."

The cheering broke out anew. The Icarii had waited a long time for this and they were not going to quibble about a small delay now.

13

Dinner at the Tired Seagull

Timozel sat wrapped in his own peculiar stillness, as if the others seated at the dining table did not exist. The visions came more often now, and far, far more vividly.

He rode a great beast – not a horse, something different – that dipped and soared. He fought for a great Lord, and in the name of that Lord he commanded a mighty army which undulated for leagues in every direction. Hundreds of thousands screamed his name and hurried to fulfil his every wish.

Before him another army, his pitiful enemy, lay quavering in terror. They could not counter his brilliance. Their commander lay abed, unable to summon the courage to meet Timozel in just combat.

In the name of his Lord he would clear Achar of the invading filth.

"Yes," he mumbled, and Borneheld shot him an irritated glance.

A great and glorious battle and the enemy's positions were overrun – to the man (and others stranger that fought shoulder to shoulder with them) the enemy died. Timozel lost not one soldier.

Another day, another battle. The enemy used foul magic, and Timozel's forces were grievously hurt . . . but Timozel still won the field, and the enemy and their commander retreated before him.

Another day. Timozel sat before the leaping fire with his Lord, Faraday at their side. All was well. Timozel had found the light and his destiny.

His name would live in legend forever.

All was well.

The vision dimmed and Timozel heard Borneheld chastise Faraday yet again.

"You are worthless to me!" Borneheld hissed. Faraday stiffened. Her husband's words were clearly audible to all those seated at the table.

"Worthless!" Borneheld said. "How many months have we been married? Four? Five? Your belly should be swollen with my son by now."

Faraday focused on a distant point of the room, refusing to let her cheeks stain red. The Mother had answered her prayers and continued to bless her with barrenness, and she was not going to force false promises past her lips. The line of Dukes of Ichtar would end in her empty womb.

Her calm expression intensified Borneheld's fury. "Your barrenness is not for want of trying on *my* part, Faraday," he said, louder now. "Perhaps I should summon a physician to mix you a herbal."

To his left Gautier grinned, but Duke Roland, sitting on Faraday's other side, looked extremely embarrassed.

Faraday lowered her eyes to her plate of food, hoping her lack of responsiveness would lead to Borneheld tiring of the topic. Yr sat silently in a shadowy corner of the room and Faraday could feel her silent sympathy and support.

If Faraday had managed previously to tolerate her marriage to Borneheld in Gorkenfort, now she could barely keep her distaste for the man safely hidden. She no longer sought to please or humour him in their bed, nor pretended to love him or desire his company.

Borneheld now realised her feelings for Axis and suspected she had lied to him in Gorkenfort. Yet he could tolerate all of this – if only she provided him with an heir.

And yet Faraday remained barren despite his most strenuous exertions. Borneheld had never been charming or courtly, but in Gorkenfort he'd made an effort to treat Faraday with respect. Now that he had been forced to abandon Gorkenfort and Ichtar, Borneheld slipped into almost perpetual surliness, not hesitating to humiliate Faraday in public. Something dark and sinister had taken root in his mind since the fall of Gorkenfort, and daily Faraday watched it grow.

Borneheld abruptly turned aside and began to discuss with Gautier and Timozel the continuing efforts to construct a viable defence system around Jervois Landing.

Faraday let her breath out in relief and looked about the room. Borneheld and the immediate members of his command had taken over the Tired Seagull, the very same inn that she, Yr and Timozel had stayed at on their way to Gorkenfort. The men who had escaped Gorkenfort with them were either quartered about the town, or camped in the massive tent city that had sprung up about Jervois Landing.

Faraday caught the eye of the Ravensbund chief, Ho'Demi. She almost looked away, sure the man would be as embarrassed and uncomfortable as most others in the room, but Ho'Demi smiled at her warmly. There was nothing but sympathy and respect in his dark eyes. Faraday straightened her back a little, and Ho'Demi inclined his head in approval.

Faraday had never had a chance to speak to the man, as Borneheld did his best to keep her sequestered from anyone save Yr and Timozel. But Ho'Demi had such a natural aristocratic bearing for one whose appearance was so savage and frightening that Faraday found him fascinating. Indeed, she was intrigued by the entire Ravensbund population camped about Jervois Landing. On the few occasions Borneheld had allowed her out of their quarters (with a suitable guard), Faraday had seen their multicoloured tents spreading for what seemed like leagues about the town, the air around them filled with the sound of the soft chimes which they threaded through their hair and the manes of their horses, and which hung from every available space in their tents. All of them were tattooed to some degree, the different designs denoting different tribal groups, but all of them, no matter their tribe, had that peculiarly naked circle in the centre of their foreheads where no line crossed.

Little did Faraday know that Ho'Demi was equally interested in her. All Ravensbund people knew the Prophecy. They lived to serve both it and the StarMan, and Ho'Demi instinctively knew that this woman was one of those named in the Prophecy. But he could get near neither she nor her Sentinel maid, so closely watched were they by Borneheld's men. One day. One day. Meantime, why did Borneheld humiliate one so obviously Prophecy-born? He did not understand it.

Faraday turned her eyes away from Ho'Demi, lest her attention draw Borneheld's suspicion on the man's head, and saw Timozel watching her.

There was no sympathy or support in his eyes at all. Over the past months Timozel had, tragically, become Borneheld's man. Timozel was still her Champion, supposedly devoted to her welfare and interests, but he seemed to have decided that the best way he could serve Faraday's interests was by serving her husband. Timozel admired and respected Borneheld, and Faraday found that very hard to understand.

Timozel had not thought to share his visions with her as he had with her husband.

Faraday averted her eyes. If she had known Timozel would turn into this dark, brooding, frightening man, she would have refused his request to be her Champion. Now Timozel stared at her, having sided with Borneheld on the issue of the child.

In her shadowy corner Yr watched Faraday's shoulders straighten as she recognised the sympathy and support in Ho'Demi's eyes, watched them slump again as she saw the accusation in Timozel's. Yr seriously wondered whether she and the other three Sentinels had done the right thing in so forcibly persuading Faraday to deny her love for Axis and marry Borneheld. We thought it might help to keep Axis alive, Yr thought bitterly. So we persuaded the darling girl, so full of sweetness and love, to give herself to Borneheld. *Why* did we find it so necessary for the Prophecy that we force her into this boorish man's bed?

I hope she will eventually find love and peace with Axis, Yr prayed. That Axis loved Faraday Yr had no doubt – everyone had seen that at Gorkenfort. And that Axis would fight through Achar to rescue Faraday from Borneheld's side, Yr also did not doubt. She *could* not doubt it. She didn't want to think that Faraday's heartache would be for nothing.

And, as Faraday had done, Yr also glanced at Timozel. She and he had once been lovers, but Timozel's tastes had become too dark for Yr's liking and she'd ended the affair. As far as Yr was concerned, she and Faraday would have to stand together to survive this dreadful situation.

Pray Axis come quickly, she thought, pray that he come and rescue us both from this.

"My man," Brother Gilbert said, "I represent the Brother-Leader of the Seneschal himself. I *demand* entrance to Duke Borneheld's quarters *immediately!*"

The guard sniffed and looked this pimply, skinny Brother up and down. If *I* were the Brother-Leader, thought the guard, I would find myself a more imposing representative.

"I have papers! Proof of my identity," Gilbert shouted, losing patience. *Both* this dullard's parents must have been riddled with the pox to have birthed a child so grossly under-witted! It had been a hard, fast and dreadfully cold journey up the Nordra from Carlon to reach Jervois Landing, and the sooner Gilbert saw a fire – preferably with Duke Borneheld standing in front of it – the better. Gilbert was just about to shout at him again when a figure loomed in the darkened corridor behind the guard.

The guard snapped to attention, which puzzled Gilbert when he saw who the newcomer was — one of those savages from the northern wastes, a Ravensbundman, with even more lines scribbled across his face than normal.

"Chief Ho'Demi," the guard saluted. "This underfed scrawling claims to be on a mission from the Brother-Leader."

"I have papers," Gilbert said, indignant. Him? An underfed scrawling? He had always thought himself a rather attractive man.

The savage snapped his fingers at Gilbert. "Well? Show them to me!"

Gilbert pulled a sheaf of papers out of the lining of his cloak and handed them to the savage. So, he was going to pretend he could read, was he?

"You have news for Borneheld regarding Priam, Brother Gilbert?" the savage finally asked, looking up from the papers.

Gilbert stopped himself from gawping only through a supreme effort. So the savage had managed to read Priam's name. He would have guessed the rest. "Yes," he finally got out. "Important news regarding Priam and the situation in Carlon. *Important* news," Gilbert repeated slowly in case the savage had not understood him the first time.

Ho'Demi folded the papers and slipped them inside his furred waistcoat, ignoring Gilbert's yelp of disapproval. "I will take him through, Eavan. You have done well."

Gilbert sneered as he pushed past the guard. Done well, indeed. He hurried after Ho'Demi, almost tripping over a broom that some careless slut had left by a door, then stumbled up a similarly darkened stairwell.

"Little fuel about for lamps," Ho'Demi explained as he heard Gilbert trip over the hem of his robe.

At the head of the stairs there was a large door, securely closed, with another two guards before it. Both snapped to attention as Ho'Demi brushed past them into the room, beckoning Gilbert after him.

Gilbert blinked as he accustomed himself to the light in the bright room, then stepped out of the way as two women hurried towards the door.

"Wait up, Faraday," he heard Borneheld call. "Perhaps I will get my son on you tonight."

Harsh laughter followed as Faraday slipped by Gilbert and out the door. It had been some six months since he had seen Faraday. Then she had been a vibrant girl, now the person who brushed past him looked wearied by the sadnesses of the world.

"Well?" Borneheld's voice snapped. "Who's this?"

Ho'Demi turned over the papers he had taken from Gilbert. Borneheld skimmed through them quickly. "Ah," he said. "It seems Brother Gilbert might have some interesting news indeed. Gilbert?"

Well, thought Gilbert, here at least is a man worthy of my regard. Borneheld stood before the fire, a little scruffier than when Gilbert had last seen him, with his auburn hair shaved so short it appeared he had a badly bruised but utterly bald scalp, yet Gilbert still thought he looked the noblest man in the room. He deserves our protection and support, he thought as he stepped up to Borneheld and bowed.

"My Lord Duke," he said respectfully. He did not add "of Ichtar", because that would be insulting in the present circumstances, and Gilbert had strict instructions from Jayme not to offend Borneheld in any way.

"What news?" Borneheld asked, "that the Brother-Leader should send one of his advisers to speak to me personally?"

"My Lord," Gilbert said ingratiatingly. "Brother-Leader Jayme instructed me that my news should be for your ears only."

Borneheld's eyes narrowed. Either the man carried important news or he was an assassin, and these days Borneheld trusted few people. But eventually he turned from Gilbert. "Roland, Ho'Demi, you may leave. Report to me with Jorge at dawn tomorrow. We need to go over the plans for the final flooding of the canals."

Both men bowed and left silently, Gilbert noticing that Roland had lost much weight recently.

"My Lord?" Gilbert whispered, gesturing towards Gautier and Timozel.

"They stay with me," Borneheld said sharply. "I trust them with my life, and they will not hesitate to take yours should you threaten mine."

"I am your servant, Lord," Gilbert grovelled, "not your murderer."

"Well, then, sit down at the table and help yourself to some wine. You look as if you need some refreshment."

Borneheld sat down opposite Gilbert, but Gautier and Timozel remained standing, ready to leap to Borneheld's defence should he require it. Both men looked equally dangerous, and Gilbert wondered what had turned the boyish Timozel into this frightening man who had, quite obviously, transferred his loyalties from Axis to Borneheld.

"My Lord Duke," Gilbert began, "Brother-Leader Jayme has read your reports and listened to the news from the north of Achar with growing alarm."

"I have done my best," Borneheld said, "but . . ."

"But you were betrayed, my Lord, we understand that. Axis and Magariz betrayed you, and they have betrayed the Seneschal as well with their damned pact with the Forbidden."

"*Yes!*" Borneheld said. "I was betrayed from within! There is no-one I can trust! No-one! Except," he hastened, "Gautier and Timozel. No-one else."

To one side both Gautier and Timozel bowed slightly.

"And you are right to fear treachery, my Lord," Gilbert continued smoothly. This was going far better than he had anticipated. "For I bring grievous news."

"By the Blessed Artor!" Borneheld said, rising so quickly that the chair he'd been sitting on fell to the floor with a crash. "Who now?"

Gilbert assumed an expression of deep sorrow. "It grieves me to say this, my Lord —"

"Then bloody say it!" Borneheld shouted, and leaned across the table to seize Gilbert by his habit.

"Priam," Gilbert stammered, frightened by the madness in Borneheld's eyes. "Priam."

Borneheld let Gilbert go. "Priam? Priam betrays me? How?"

"Priam is frightened and alone," Gilbert whispered. "He does not have your resolve or your courage. He listens to the Prophecy of the Destroyer."

Borneheld swore, and Gilbert hurried on. "He wonders if Axis is still alive and, if so, whether he should consider an alliance with the Forbidden."

"He *what*?" Borneheld said. "How can he consider such a thing? Artor himself must be screaming at the thought."

"Yes," Gilbert said. "Your reaction mirrors Jayme's."

"How many know that Priam thinks this way?" Borneheld asked.

"Jayme, Moryson, the four of us in this room, and one or two others, my informants in the palace at Carlon."

"This is something that should not be bruted about," Borneheld said.

"Jayme would entirely agree with that. My Lord, I cannot stress how anxious Jayme is about this development. If Priam were to ally himself with Axis and his ungodly hordes, then the Forbidden could invade Achar and all would be lost."

He took a careful pause. "My Lord. Jayme has instructed me to tell you that you have his, nay, the Seneschal's, entire support in whatever course of action you choose to take in this matter."

Borneheld turned towards the fire so that none could see his face. "And what does 'Jayme's entire support' mean, Gilbert? Has not Axis efficiently destroyed your military power base? Where are your vaunted Axe-Wielders now?"

"We control the hearts and souls of the Acharites, my Lord Duke. We are the mediators between their souls and the rewards of the AfterLife in the care of Artor, or, should they refuse to listen to our message, in the pits of fire where worms will gnaw at their entrails for eternity. My Lord Duke, they listen to us. Should we say, 'Borneheld is your man', then they will listen."

Gilbert took a deep breath, and when he spoke again his voice was heavy with meaning. "If you fight against Axis and the Forbidden, Borneheld, then Jayme and the Seneschal will support you in *whatever* course of action you decide to take."

Borneheld's eyes glinted strangely. "And what does the Brother-Leader advise me to do, Brother Gilbert?"

"Brother-Leader Jayme advises that you return to Carlon, my Lord, should the situation here in Jervois Landing be stable enough. Once back in Carlon you can shore up Priam's resolve, or —"

"Or?"

"Or perhaps you can decide to take some other course of action."

"And what 'course of action' do you advise me to take, Brother Gilbert?"

"I would advise that you are only one step away from the throne, my Lord Duke Borneheld. Priam is childless, and you are the heir," Gilbert said very softly, his eyes steady on Borneheld's. "I would advise that you take that one step closer. We need, *Achar* needs, a King whose loyalties and resolve are uncompromised, who can lead us to victory against the Forbidden."

There was complete and utter silence in the room as Borneheld stared at Gilbert.

At dawn Borneheld met with his senior commanders; Duke Roland of Aldeni, Earl Jorge of Avonsdale, and the savage Ho'Demi who, by virtue of commanding eleven thousand men, sat at Borneheld's table with Gautier and Timozel.

They reviewed the system of canals which the majority of Borneheld's men were digging. Borneheld knew that a battle fought against the Skraelings on their terms was virtually unwinnable. Now he would fight the Skraelings on *his* terms.

He and his commanders had planned a massive series of deep canals between the rivers Azle and Nordra that they would flood when finished. The Skraelings hated water and avoided it whenever possible. If they attacked in force Borneheld hoped they would be driven by the twisting system of canals into small pockets and envelopes where Borneheld's men could pick them off relatively safely.

It was a bold move, but one that all agreed might just work. Especially since the Skraelings had spread themselves so thinly over Ichtar that it would take Gorgrael months to build up a force strong enough to try to push further south. For ten weeks every soldier, plus thousands of ordinary Acharites who were within reasonable distance, had been out digging the canals. Each would be twenty paces wide and more than ten deep, and the entire system of canals would provide a watery barrier almost fifteen leagues wide.

"It is looking good, gentlemen," Borneheld said cheerfully. "Jorge, you have been in charge of the western series of canals. When will they be ready to flood?"

"In two days, WarLord."

"Good!" Borneheld slapped Jorge on the back. "And Roland, your canals are already flooded?"

Roland nodded. What could have happened to put Borneheld in such a good mood?

"Ho'Demi." Borneheld turned to the Ravensbundman. "What do your scouts report?"

Ho'Demi shrugged a little and his hair gently chimed with the slight movement. "Very little activity within two leagues north of here, Lord Duke, though above that distance Skraelings scurry about in small bands. But they seem disorganised. I doubt they will have the strength to attack for some time yet."

"And they will certainly not attack through the warmer months," Borneheld said. "In a week spring will be upon us. Gentlemen! I feel more positive than I have for months! I think we will not only be able to hold the Skraelings with this watery line of defences, but start our reconquest of Ichtar within only a few months."

He beamed at the surrounding men, ignoring the bemused expressions on Roland's, Jorge's and Ho'Demi's faces.

"So!" Borneheld rubbed his hands together. "This is the perfect time for me to make a quick journey down the Nordra to confer with Priam. Besides, Faraday seems . . . ill . . . not herself. Perhaps it would be best if she could see the physicians at the court of Carlon. We will be leaving this afternoon."

"Borneheld!" Roland said. "You can't just leave Jervois Landing like this!"

Jorge concurred. "You are needed more here than in Carlon, WarLord!"

"My dear comrades," Borneheld replied, "with such competent men already in Jervois Landing you can well afford to lose me for a few weeks. Timozel, you will travel with Faraday and myself. Pick a small contingent of men to travel with us and organise some river transport. I want to leave by dusk. Gautier, my good friend, I leave you in charge of Jervois Landing. Roland, Jorge and Ho'Demi will give you their full support as they would give it to me."

He looked carefully at the three men, each of whom fought to restrain their shock. *Gautier?*

Finally all three inclined their heads. "As you wish, WarLord," Jorge said quietly.

"As I wish," Borneheld said menacingly. "Always as I wish. I will not countenance treachery. Timozel? You have much work to do before we can leave this evening. Get to it."

Timozel's face was pale, and uncharacteristically he stood his ground, ignoring Borneheld's orders. "Great Lord," he began. "Surely *I* would be better left to command the troops here in Jervois Landing?"

"*What?*" Borneheld glared at him. "Do you think to contradict me, stripling?"

Timozel swallowed, but his eyes were bright, fanatical. "Lord, you know what I have seen —"

"I know what now *I* see!" Borneheld shouted. "I need you in Carlon, Timozel! Your place is at my side . . . and Faraday's, of course," he added, as an afterthought. His voice regained its strength. "And if you demonstrate that you are incapable of following orders then the only command you will receive is of a blanket in a cell. Do you understand me?"

"Yes, Lord," Timozel mumbled. *When* would Borneheld pass command over to him? He suppressed a niggling doubt. All would be well. It *would*.

14

Through the Mountain Passes

"It is a sadness to see your parents go their separate ways after so many years." MorningStar sighed. "But historically it was *entirely* expected."

Axis looked at his grandmother, puzzled. "What do you mean?"

"Axis. We SunSoars are a peculiar family. Our blood calls to each other so strongly that if we marry out of the family then we generally marry badly."

Axis frowned. Today he, Rivkah, Azhure, Raum and the two Sentinels were starting their trek down through the mountain passes to the Avar groves to celebrate Beltide. "You marry each other, MorningStar? How can that be?"

MorningStar shrugged. "SunSoars are only happy when they marry each other, Axis. No, don't look so horrified. None of us has gone mad yet. Well, not very many of us," she muttered, half to herself. "Generally every second generation SunSoar cousins will marry each other. RushCloud, my husband, was also my first cousin. FreeFall and EvenSong, both first cousins, would have married. This pattern of marriages has kept our blood strong over the years."

"And the generation that marries outside the family – their marriages . . . ?"

"Are generally passable at best, but often miserably unhappy. RavenCrest is SunSoar, but BrightFeather is not.

They respect each other, but they share no passion. While RushCloud and I," MorningStar smiled slowly, "lived our lives among the stars. Like FreeFall and EvenSong, we became lovers at thirteen."

"Lovers at thirteen?" Axis was appalled. His sister? And FreeFall?

MorningStar raised a well-groomed eyebrow. "Well, why not? Thirteen is not young. Whether Icarii, Avar or human, at thirteen one begins to put away childish things and consider more mature pastimes. At what age did you first take a woman to bed?"

Axis reddened, and MorningStar laughed with delight before tipping her lovely silvery head on one side and regarding Axis thoughtfully. "We are both SunSoar and our blood sings strongly, Axis. Do not pretend you cannot hear it. Have you chosen your Beltide companion yet? Shall we let our blood sing together that night?"

Axis took a defensive step backwards, shocked.

"Ah," she said seductively. "I am your grandmother, you say. Well, Axis, it has been done before, and I have no doubt it will be done again." She smiled. "But not this Beltide, I think. Your Acharite reservation holds you back. A pity."

She sat on a stool behind her. "I started to tell you why StarDrifter and Rivkah's marriage ended in unhappiness. She is not SunSoar. They had a passion and a love, but StarDrifter's blood constantly sings, looking for another whose blood sings back to him with the same Song. But," MorningStar sighed, "there are no other SunSoar women for either him or you to marry. No," she said tartly, watching Axis' face, "SunSoars never marry or couple with first blood. It is Unclean. EvenSong is out of bounds to her brother and her father. Father and daughter, mother and son, brother and sister – there we draw the line, but *only* there. All else is freedom."

"I will marry Faraday," Axis said firmly, "when she is free."

"And is she SunSoar?" MorningStar inquired archly.

"You know she is not."

"Then you will have an unhappy marriage. Your blood, like StarDrifter's, like EvenSong's, will constantly crave another SunSoar. Perhaps your children will marry Even-Song's. I hope that will be the case. They, at least, will know happiness."

Angry, Axis turned away.

The journey through the alps was exhilarating. Rivkah had only come down these mountain passes on her own previously, had never shared the grandeur of the Icescarp Alps with anyone else. Now that she had such good companionship, she found herself enjoying the journey as never before. Since the night of the Assembly Rivkah's manner had become more and more light-hearted, and Axis supposed that being freed from the strain of her increasingly unhappy marriage had cast her into a happier frame of mind.

The trails down the Icescarp Alps wound slowly through narrow ravines and valleys, past icefalls and, occasionally, behind them. Sometimes the gradient was steep, sometimes mild, but the view was *always* breathtaking. On either side of the trails great cliff faces of glassy black rock plunged into fern-bracketed glacier-fed rivers thousands of paces below them. In the afternoons, as the light began to fail and the mists thicken, Rivkah would lead them to small caves she'd discovered in her years of travelling up and down these trails. Here they would slip their cumbersome backpacks from their shoulders, laughing and complaining in the same breath, and set up camp for the night.

Before, Rivkah had always had to carry enough fuel, food, and blankets to keep her alive over the week or more it took her to traverse the trails. There was no vegetation this high in the alps to provide firewood, and no game to trap or kill.

Then the journey had been risky, but she had never travelled the mountain passes with an Enchanter before – and such an Enchanter! Axis' powers kept the paths dry where before Rivkah had slipped and skidded dangerously, swept the shifting winds to one side where before they had often threatened to blow Rivkah from the narrow paths, and kept the cold at bay, surrounding the small party with balmy air. In the evenings he conjured up fires of green and red and purple, and provided them all with feather-soft mattresses of warm air.

Apart from the considerable difference Axis' powers made, Rivkah enjoyed having her son virtually to herself. Previously StarDrifter had commanded so much of his attention Rivkah had found little time to talk with Axis. Now they chatted about his likes and dislikes, his life with the Seneschal, his life as BattleAxe, the good times and the bad times, as they walked side by side.

The evenings, when Rivkah shared Axis with their companions, were just as wonderful.

After they'd chosen a cave for the night, eased packs from aching shoulders and cleared the cave floor of debris, Axis would provide a roaring fire that warmed the entire party. Then he would sing to the cave walls, caressing them with his hands, and, as fast-gathering gloom descended outside, the rock gave off a gentle glow that intensified with the night.

Even their food was magical, but Axis had nothing to do with that. As he conjured fire and light each evening, Ogden and Veremund would slip off the light packs they carried, open the top flaps, rustle around mumbling and complaining for a few moments, and then draw out parcel after parcel of beautifully wrapped and packaged food. Honeyed hams, crisp-roasted poultry, peppered joints of beef and sundry other marinated delicacies ready to be warmed at the fire, fresh and dried fruits, a variety of breads and pastries, platters of vegetables, exotic cheeses, bowls of almonds and raisins and gourds of spiced wines – every evening the Sentinels unpacked a veritable feast.

"Ogden always sees to the packing," Veremund said the first evening. "I have no idea how he does it."

Ogden gaped at Veremund. "What? I packed not a crumb of this! I thought you did!" Then he frowned into his pack. "Where did you put the napkins?"

Axis, rising from the fire laughing, had told them to stop arguing and advised the others to simply enjoy the food and not push the Sentinels on where it came from. "They will just argue with each other," he said to Azhure and Raum, "to keep from answering you."

Each evening after they had eaten, Axis entertained with his wonderful voice and his skill on the harp. He sang Icarii melodies for the first part of the evening, but as the night deepened Axis' mood changed and he sang ballads and songs of Acharite extraction, making Rivkah and Azhure smile and tap their fingers in pleasure. He far surpassed any court bard Rivkah had ever heard.

Axis often asked the others to sing with him, or to sing their own songs. Rivkah and Raum both sang well, Ogden and Veremund enthusiastically, but Azhure had one of the most dreadful voices anyone had ever heard, and after one attempt at joining them in song, she had laughed and promised not to sing again.

But they did not simply sing the evenings away. For long hours into each night they talked, Axis walking soft melodies up and down the strings of his harp as he listened. Sometimes they talked of the Icarii or Avar myths and legends, sometimes of the Star Gods. Occasionally Rivkah recalled her early life amid the intrigue of the Carlon court. Ogden and Veremund, rascals that they were, told tales of the exploits of some of the early Icarii, tales of when the Icarii had first learned to fly and had sometimes fallen from the sky in tangled and embarrassing wreckages.

Late one night, early in their trek, Axis stretched out comfortably, his legs extended towards the fire, hands behind his head, his eyes on Azhure as she finished plaiting her raven hair for the night.

Azhure smiled a little uncertainly at him, then spoke to Raum. "Raum, may I ask about the Horned Ones? Are they Avar?"

Raum seemed not to mind answering Azhure's question. "Yes. The Horned Ones were once Avar Banes. But only the strongest of the male Banes are allowed to complete the transformation to Horned Ones. It is the responsibility of the Horned Ones to act as the guardians of the Sacred Grove."

"How do you change?" Axis asked, remembering the frightening beast of his nightmare outside the Silent Woman Woods. How could someone so apparently gentle as Raum metamorphose into such a frightening, angry creature?

Raum's dark face was now unreadable. "There are some mysteries that I will not even tell you, Axis SunSoar. We simply . . . change. The change picks us, we do not pick it. When we feel the change begin, we wander the ways of the Avarinheim alone, for we no longer desire the companionship of our friends and family."

"And no female Banes ever become Horned Ones?" Azhure asked, her thick plait hanging over her shoulder.

"No, Azhure. We do not know why. But no females walk the Sacred Groves as Horned Ones." Raum frowned. "I think female Banes transform, but they guard their mysteries closely, and I do not know into what they transform, or where they go when they do. We each have our mysteries, Azhure, and we do not pry too deeply into them."

As Raum spoke, Axis had sunk deeper into the memory of his dream of the Sacred Groves. "The Horned Ones haunt the trees that line the Sacred Grove, watching," he whispered. "They drift with the power that lives among the trees."

"How do you know that, Axis?" Raum asked.

"I travelled to the Sacred Grove once, Bane Raum, in a dream."

To one side Ogden and Veremund nodded. They had felt this when they tested Axis in the Silent Woman Keep. The Horned Ones would not welcome the intrusion of a hated BattleAxe into their mysterious realms.

"You have?" Raum said. "How?"

"It started with a nightmare," Axis began, sitting up again, and he told them of the night outside the Silent Woman Woods when his old nightmare had claimed him, but had turned instead into a dream of the Grove. He had stood on the cool grass, feeling the power and the eyes that moved among the encircling trees, watching with horror as the man with the magnificent, but terrifying, head of a horned stag approached. When challenged for his identity Axis had said that he was Axis Rivkahson, BattleAxe of the Seneschal, and the puzzlement that he had originally felt from the eyes in the trees turned to rage. As the Horned One neared, swinging his head from side to side with hate, Axis had screamed and woken from the dream.

"Your old nightmare?" Rivkah said after Raum had finished questioning Axis about his dream. "What do you mean?" she asked, thinking of her son, lost and alone without either of his parents and in the grip of nightmare.

Axis had never spoken of the nightmare that had haunted so much of his life to anyone, not even when his long-time lover, Embeth, Lady of Tare, had pressed him about it. Yet now he was telling this group without hesitation about the nightmare entity that had come to him throughout most of his life, the entity that claimed to be his unknown father. The dreams had stopped only after Axis escaped the fury of the head in the clouds outside the Ancient Barrows – when he'd realised that, whoever he might be, his father had loved him and could not have been the hateful voice of his nightmare.

"It was Gorgrael who came to you," Veremund said. "Trying to break your heart and your spirit with lies about your father."

Axis' face flinched with the memory. "He said that my mother died giving birth to me, died cursing me for taking her life. I believed him. I had no choice, none to tell me differently."

Appalled, Rivkah reached out and seized Axis' hand. She finally understood what a lonely childhood he had led, thinking his mother had died hating him, not knowing who his father was. For a time both mother and son sat, holding hands, lending each other comfort.

Then Axis sighed and turned to Azhure, letting his mother's hand go. "Azhure," he said gently, "it is good to let go of old nightmares. Will you tell us how your back came to be so horribly scarred?"

Azhure's reaction caused the only dark moment of the trip. Her whole body went rigid and she stared at Axis, her eyes dark and frightened. For a moment she said nothing, her mouth trembling, then she whimpered.

"No." It was the whimper of a terrified little girl.

"*No!*" she shouted, her voice edging towards hysteria. "No! Stay away!"

Rivkah quickly shifted over to her, wrapping her arms about the terrified woman.

"No!" Azhure shouted again, louder, twisting against Rivkah's hands. "Stay away! Please! *Please!* I will *not* do it again!" She took a deep, shuddering breath. "I *promise!*" she screamed.

Axis leant forward, thinking to add support to that of his mother's, but Azhure almost wrenched herself out of Rivkah's arms in the effort to twist away from him. "No!" she screamed, patently terrified by Axis' approach. "*Forgive me!*"

Veremund hastily placed his hand on Azhure's shoulder. She stopped twisting immediately, but only very slowly did she relax. Veremund exchanged a worried glance with Ogden before looking at Axis.

"Withdraw the question," said Veremund. "She doesn't want to talk about it. The memory is too much for her."

"I am sorry I have caused you pain with my question, Azhure," Axis said, touching her cheek gently with his fingertips. "Please forgive my intrusion. I retrieve my words."

A gentle melody spun through the air and Axis sat back as Rivkah let Azhure go.

"What is it?" Azhure asked, puzzled as she looked about to see everyone in the cave staring at her. "What did I say?"

Veremund caught Axis' eye and nodded, pleased. Axis had learnt well from StarDrifter and MorningStar. Still, more lessons had been learned. One — never ask Azhure about her back. Two — find out what *did* happen, because that knowledge could well unlock some of Azhure's secrets. But Veremund had the dreadful intuition that to unlock that particular secret without proper precautions could well cost either Azhure her life, or that of the person who tried too insistently to make her answer.

Azhure had been the only one to sleep well that night, and Axis had lain awake for many hours, watching her gently breathing. Wondering.

Four days out from Talon Spike Axis abruptly stopped on the path, his face tight with concentration. Then he smiled, laughed, and called ahead to Raum.

"Raum! I hear her! I hear her! She sings beautifully!"

Raum turned back to Axis and smiled. Although he could not hear what Axis did, he knew what it must be. Earth Tree. Earth Tree singing her Song, the Song that had destroyed the Skraeling attack on the Earth Tree Grove at Yuletide, the Song that now protected the entire northern Avarinheim against Gorgrael. If it had not been for StarDrifter and Faraday, Earth Tree might still be asleep and the Skraelings might well have eaten their way through the Avarinheim by now.

Two days later Raum began to catch the first faint strains of Earth Tree's Song himself, and two days later yet, Rivkah and Azhure started to pick it up.

Ogden and Veremund had begun to hear it about the same time as Axis.

The night before they reached the foot of the Icescarp Alps, the group ate a splendid meal of roast partridge stuffed with breadcrumbs, cheese, raisins and almonds, and relaxed about the magical fire.

"Tell me of how you bonded Faraday to the Mother," Axis asked Raum, reluctantly lifting his eyes from the firelight glinting through Azhure's hair. "There is so little I know about her. So much I want to comprehend."

Faraday's connection with the Mother, with the power of the earth and of nature, was one of the deeper mysteries that Axis did not yet understand. There had been so little time or opportunity at Gorkenfort for Faraday and Axis to talk.

And Axis needed someone to speak of her, to remind him how much he loved her. Once her image had been so vivid in his mind, now he had to struggle to recall the exact shade of her hair and the timbre of her laughter.

Raum hesitated a little, then began by explaining the significance of the groves to the Avar people and how those Avar children who had the potential to become Banes had to be presented and bonded to the Mother. Fernbrake Lake, one of the four magical lakes in Achar, lay deep in the Bracken Ranges far to the south of the Avarinheim, and the Avar people had to travel secretly through the hostile Skarabost Plains to reach the lake they called the Mother.

"And Rivkah helped you in this?" Axis asked, smiling at his mother.

"Yes," Raum said. "For many years now she has spent the summer months with us, often helping to take a child or two through to the Bracken Ranges."

"And yet none in Achar knew that the Princess Rivkah walked among them," Axis said, his eyes on the flames. "Did you never want to return to your home, Rivkah?"

"I thought my life dead, Axis. I thought you dead. Had I known you lived I would have kept walking until I reached the Tower of the Seneschal and its BattleAxe."

For a while there was silence, then Azhure prompted Raum to return to the story of the night he had bonded Faraday to the Mother. Ever since Azhure had seen the vision of Faraday awakening the Earth Tree on the night of the Yuletide attack, she had been fascinated by Faraday.

Raum told the story as if every moment of that night was seared into his memory. How he had tested Faraday at Jack and Yr's insistence and, to his shock, had found she talked to the trees as easily as if she had been Avar-born. He told them how Faraday had bonded instantly to the Mother, how the Mother herself had wakened the lake and how he, Faraday and the child Shra had walked into and through the lake, to the Sacred Grove.

All listened intently, astounded by Raum's tale.

"You walked through emerald light into the grove?" Azhure asked, her blue eyes wide. This was magic beyond anything she had yet seen.

Raum told them of how the Horned Ones had greeted Faraday, and how the most ancient and sacred of them all, the silver pelt, had given Faraday the bowl of enchanted wood.

"The bowl is a way for her not only to reach out and touch the Mother," Raum explained, "but also to reach the Sacred Grove whenever she feels the need."

"She has been blessed," Azhure said, admiration and wonder evident in her voice.

Raum let his hand rest on Azhure's shoulder. He had become very attached to this lonely woman and wished that the Avar had accepted her. She had saved his life, but Raum's regard for Azhure went much deeper than gratefulness. "Yes, Azhure, she has truly been blessed."

Axis' eyes lingered on Raum's hand. He raised his gaze to the Bane's face slowly. "Is Faraday's only role in Prophecy that of Tree Friend, Bane?"

"She has many things to do, Axis," Veremund answered for Raum. "As do you. Concentrate on your own path, and let others find theirs as the Prophecy guides them."

Axis nodded. "Has Faraday used the enchanted bowl, Raum? Has she stepped back into the Groves?"

"Yes," Raum answered. "Yes, she has. Several times. Each time Faraday uses the bowl I can . . . feel it."

Ogden and Veremund both studied the Bane closely. You can *feel* it? wondered Ogden. And I would wager that you can feel it changing you, can't you, Bane Raum? How long before you, too, feel the urge to wander the paths of the Avarinheim all by yourself, wander until the pain in your body and your skull drives you mad? Until you are transformed? Do you feel it yet, Bane? Do you *know*?

Azhure sighed and sat back. She envied Faraday greatly. Not only did she have Axis' love, but she had a major role to play in the Prophecy, a role that would one day see her walk at Axis' side. Azhure might love Axis herself, but she knew her love would not be returned. Axis would never be her lover. Faraday and Axis were both heroes, and they would walk together into legend and immortality. She was only a human woman, scarred in mind and body, doomed to drift without a true home or a lifetime lover.

The next day the party walked down from the mountains and into Beltide.

The pigs abandoned Sigholt five days before Beltide.

Saddened, Jack stood and watched as the fifteen who had kept him company for the last three thousand years rolled and grunted their way across the bridge. He had always known they would go one day, always known they would pick the day. What better time to choose than these days when the Prophecy walked?

But Jack was excited as well as saddened. The pigs would only leave him to seek the Blood.

For three days the pigs trotted resolutely along the HoldHard Pass, stopping only to rest or nose around the rocks for whatever they could find to eat. But they did not waste much time foraging for food. Soon there would be better eating than stiff weather-worn grass, so aged and wizened it took true hunger to make it palatable.

On the fourth day the pigs emerged from the HoldHard Pass and turned north-east. For another day and night they trotted.

On Beltide, as the day darkened towards dusk, the pigs began to change. Their limbs lengthened, their bodies became sleeker, their coats lighter. Their teeth began to glint and their mouths began to grin.

As the moon emerged they began to lope, but they made no sound. They would not begin to bay until they had caught the scent they had waited so long for.

Above, the moon gleamed and lit their way before them.

15

Beltide

As they closed the distance between the last of the alps and the Avar groves, Axis drew closer to Azhure. "Azhure, what do you think of the Avar?" he asked.

Azhure thought for a moment. "They are a reserved people, Axis, and they do not accept strangers easily. They are very peaceable and reject those who embrace violence."

Axis nodded. If the Avar had rejected Azhure because of her involvement in her violent father's death, then how would they feel about a former BattleAxe of the Axe-Wielders?

"They are reserved," Azhure repeated. "Shy. They have learned over centuries of persecution to fear the Plains Dwellers, as they call . . ." She almost said "us", "the Acharites. They protest to loathe violence, but . . ." Her voice trailed off.

"But they have an aura of violence about them?"

Azhure glanced at Axis, startled. "Yes. I had not thought of it that way before. But . . . yes. They put their children through a frightening test to see if they have the ability to become Banes — a test that kills many of them. And sometimes the Banes themselves can threaten violence. When I was a girl in Smyrton and stumbled upon Rivkah and a Bane taking two children past the village, the Bane was so angry that I think Rivkah only just managed to prevent him from killing me. Yes," she paused, "they protest violence, but they exude it."

"When I walked into the Sacred Grove in my dream," Axis said, "the feeling of hatred and inherent violence was overwhelming – of course," he laughed humourlessly, "I was BattleAxe, then."

"Do you still fear the reaction of the Avar, Axis? You do not walk into their groves as BattleAxe but as the StarMan."

"Perhaps, but they still have reason enough to distrust me. They will not be easy to win over."

"They are ashamed that it was their blood which birthed Gorgrael but not you," Azhure said softly so Raum, walking just ahead, would not hear. "The Icarii and the Acharites have accepted and will accept you because you have been born of their blood. But to the Avar you will not only be foreign, but also frightening." She paused. "Axis, don't be too confident. The Avar will not be as ready to follow you as the Icarii were."

Axis was taken aback once again by her perceptivity, but did not say anything. Like Ogden and Veremund, more and more he found himself wondering if Azhure was the peasant woman she first appeared to be. An odd memory resurfaced. Strangely, the few times Azhure had discussed Hagen, she had never referred to him as her father.

"Azhure," he said, hesitant.

"Yes?" Azhure replied, her face open and uncomplicated.

"Was Hagen your father? Your real father?"

"What a thing to ask! Of course," she said, but her voice sounded forced. "Who else?"

Axis began to say something, but Azhure broke in. "Look, Axis! We're almost there. How I'm looking forward to seeing Fleat and Shra again!"

The sacred groves and surrounding forest were a confusion of Icarii and Avar as the small party finally arrived in the early afternoon of Beltide. The bulk of the Icarii had arrived an hour earlier and were now laughing and exchanging greetings with the Avar. As they pushed through the crowds, StarDrifter hailed them. "Axis! Rivkah! Azhure!"

Smiling hugely, StarDrifter embraced Axis and then gave Rivkah a warm kiss on the cheek. "I am glad to see that you arrived well and in time for Beltide," he said, giving Azhure a light and blameless kiss on the cheek as well. "Did you travel without incident?"

Raum nodded and grasped StarDrifter's arm. "You look cheerful, StarDrifter. Should I assume that . . . ?" He let the question hang in the air between them.

Both Icarii Enchanters and Avar Banes had been worried about the arrival of spring. The SkraeBold attack on Yuletide had disrupted the rites before they were completed and many feared the sun would not regain the strength it needed to break through the grip of Gorgrael's unnatural winter. What if spring did not arrive? Was there any point in holding Beltide if there was no spring to celebrate?

"Raum," StarDrifter said, stepping closer to the Bane so he could be heard above the din. "Gorgrael's power is strong and winter has a grasp on the northern regions, but Earth Tree sings, and even though we could not finish the Yuletide rites, the sun has strengthened enough to allow the earth to reawaken. Spring has begun. It will be weak and many areas will experience a cold summer, especially Ichtar, but the Banes tell me that the sun will shine strongly over the Avarinheim. Your people will be well."

"And Achar?" Axis broke in. His plans would have to be drastically altered if Achar remained in the grip of ice. "Will winter break in Achar?"

"Yes, Axis," StarDrifter replied. "It will be a cool summer and the crops may not flourish as well as hoped, but it will be a summer. Gorgrael's power has not spread as far south as we had feared."

Axis relaxed visibly. "Good."

StarDrifter looked at his son carefully. Apart from informing the Assembly of his intention to seek further training with the Charonites, Axis had not talked to anyone about his plans after Beltide. All knew that he meant to unite the Icarii and Acharite nations, but to do that he would have to face Borneheld. When? How?

"Strike-Leader!" FarSight CutSpur's voice cut across Star-Drifter's thoughts. "You have arrived. Good."

Axis turned and conferred with the Crest-Leader. He did not want the Strike Force to leave the Beltide rites as exposed as they had at Yuletide, and he confirmed with FarSight the plans they had made in Talon Spike for both air and ground patrols of the northern Avarinheim.

As Axis and FarSight talked, Azhure frowned and peered through the throngs of Avar and Icarii.

"There," Raum pointed. "The GhostTree Clan usually pitches its tents under that stand of trees. Remember?"

"Do you think I should . . . ?" she started, nervous.

Raum smiled reassuringly. "They will be pleased to see you, Azhure. Especially Fleat and Shra. Go on, now."

Azhure took a deep breath and headed in the direction Raum had pointed. Fleat and Shra might welcome her, but what about Grindle? And Barsarbe, if she was with them?

Rivkah hurried after her. The GhostTree Clan had been Rivkah's surrogate family for years now, and she always looked forward to seeing them. Besides, Azhure looked as though she might need some support.

As Azhure and Rivkah disappeared into the crowd, Raum touched Axis' arm. "Axis."

Axis glanced at Raum and brought his conversation with FarSight to a close. "You have done well, Crest-Leader. Speak with me in the hour before dusk, well before the Beltide rites begin."

FarSight nodded, saluted, then left.

Axis turned. "Bane Raum?"

"Axis, it is time that I introduced you to the Avar Banes, the Clan Leaders, and the Earth Tree. Are you ready?"

Axis nodded, briefly touching the blood-red sun on his fawn tunic for reassurance.

As Axis approached the great circle of stone that surrounded and protected the Earth Tree with his father and Raum, he grew more and more tense. Of all the races, Axis knew the Avar would be the most difficult to win to his cause. A thousand years previously the Axe-Wielders, under the direction of their BattleAxe and the Seneschal, had slaughtered hundreds of thousands of trees, decimating the great forests of Tencendor.

And Azhure was probably right in surmising that the Avar would deeply resent the fact that the StarMan had been born of the Icarii and the Acharite races, not of the Avar. Their blood ran in Gorgrael, the Destroyer, but not in Axis, their saviour.

Axis dearly needed Faraday to help win the Avar to his cause. He would not be able to do it on his own.

The Avar Banes and Clan Leaders waited for Axis inside the stone circle. Axis felt their eyes on him as he walked towards the centre of the Earth Tree Grove. His eyes drifted in awe towards the Earth Tree as she soared above the encircling protective stone. Her Song hung in the air, not loud enough to stifle or inhibit conversation, but sufficiently to drift through the thoughts of everyone within the northern Avarinheim, and to keep back Gorgrael and his Skraelings.

While the Earth Tree was far more sacred to the Avar than to the Icarii, both races revered it deeply. It was the living symbol of the harmony that existed between the earth and nature; if that harmony was disrupted, the Earth Tree sickened. But the Earth Tree could also act. On the night of

Yuletide, StarDrifter and Faraday, Tree Friend, had woken the Earth Tree from the slumber in which she had spent several millennia. Earth Tree had immediately realised that her grove was under attack from the creatures of Gorgrael and had responded with her Song. The Skraelings had died as one mass, breaking apart under the force of her anger. Now, awake and aware, Earth Tree continued to sing, protecting the entire northern Avarinheim from the incursions of Gorgrael and his creatures.

Now she waited for the StarMan, as did the Banes and the Clan Leaders of her people.

Each branch of the Earth Tree was covered with densely packed waxy olive-green leaves, and the ends of her branches drooped with fat trumpet-shaped flowers, some gold, some emerald, some sapphire and some ruby in hue. The Earth Tree, thought Axis, is as colourful as a rainbow. And as mysterious. StarDrifter had told Axis that not even the Avar knew the full extent of the Earth Tree's power or of her purpose. They simply revered her and protected her. All the most sacred rites of both Icarii and Avar were conducted under her spreading branches.

"Who built the circle of stone?" Axis whispered to his father as they drew closer. It was massive, each stone ten paces in height and three in width, with similar sized stones laid across their tops to form a series of archways.

"No-one knows," said StarDrifter. "Some say the Star Gods built the circle during a night ringed with fire, some say that the circle was constructed by a long-forgotten race of giants. Now, go ahead with Raum. I will wait for you here."

As they stepped through an archway Axis was struck by the feeling of sanctity within the circle – that this was a holy place no-one could doubt. A group of Banes waited by the Tree, and Axis felt both their nervousness and hostility.

The Sentinels, Ogden and Veremund, waited to one side of the Avar. Somehow, no-one ever rejected the Sentinels.

Raum motioned Axis to a halt and stepped forward to greet the gathered Avar.

A small woman, of dark and delicate form with a garland of flowers and leaves about her forehead and wearing a long loose robe of light rose wool, stepped forward and kissed Raum on both cheeks.

"Bane Raum," she said. "It has been so long. We have missed you greatly. Be well and welcomed back among us. And do not leave us again so quickly."

"Bane Barsarbe," Raum replied, "I am well and am heartened to find you well yourself." He smiled, stepped back and gestured to Axis.

"You know whom I bring," he said clearly. "Axis SunSoar. StarMan and son of StarDrifter SunSoar and Princess Rivkah of Achar. Welcome him."

Barsarbe hesitated, then stepped forward and kissed Axis on both cheeks. "Be well and welcomed among us, Axis SunSoar, StarMan," she said. "We are pleased that you have torn yourself from the lies that bound you and have found both your parents and your heritage."

"Thank you, Bane Barsarbe," Axis replied. "I hope that I will be able to fulfil both your people's and the Prophecy's expectations of me."

There was an awkward silence until one of the Clan Leaders stepped forward. He was a tall man, as dark and swarthy as Raum, but much more heavily muscled. "Brode, of the SilentWalk Clan," he said, his stare hostile. "We understand your wish is that the people of the Horn, Wing and Plough unite to drive Gorgrael from these lands?"

"It is the only way," Axis said. "It is the way the Prophecy describes. It is my task to build the bridge of understanding that will bind the three races as one."

Again, silence from the Avar. Above them the Earth Tree sang her Song, strong and joyous, unperturbed by the tense meeting underneath her branches.

"It is strange," another Avar finally said, a Bane by the look of her, "that the Prophecy should ask us to follow one who once wielded the axe."

Axis kept his voice even. "But I stand before you now as the StarMan, not as the BattleAxe."

"A warrior." This from a Bane almost as forbidding as Brode.

"Yes," Axis said. "Can you think of one better trained to face Gorgrael? The StarMan *needs* to be a warrior."

"Violence," said Barsarbe. "All warriors breed violence."

Axis remembered that Barsarbe had been particularly cool towards Azhure, even after her efforts had saved countless Avar at Yuletide. "Gorgrael will not come at you with words," Axis snapped, his tone harsh. "Already he has murdered your people. Would you spend the rest of your lives fleeing, or hiding under the pretty leaves of the Earth Tree?"

Barsarbe's eyes flashed furiously and she opened her mouth to speak, but Axis had not finished. "I promised the Icarii I would lead them back into Tencendor. I promise you the same. Do you want to replant your trees across the barren plains of Skarabost? Would you like to walk in shade all the way to the Mother? Or would you prefer to seek comfort in the legends and memories of the past, and condemn future generations of the Avar to skulking at night in order to reach the Mother? Do *you* want to regain your heritage, or have you lost your heart for such an adventure?"

Axis had not meant to be so forthright or so challenging, but he found the Avar's studied aversion to violence intensely irritating. How did they think they were going to rid themselves of the threat of Gorgrael? Throw flowers? Shout "Peace!"?

"We wait for Tree Friend," Raum said gently. "We have always believed that Tree Friend will lead us back into our homelands rather than the StarMan. It is Faraday who must lead us to you."

Axis forced himself to relax. Anger would get him nowhere.

"It is our understanding," Barsarbe said, "that you intend to war against the Acharites before you turn against Gorgrael."

"There are those among the Acharites, principally Duke Borneheld and the Seneschal itself, who will oppose any moves to unite the three races against Gorgrael. I must . . . persuade . . . them, by any means I find necessary, that such an attitude is foolish. If that means war, as I believe, then so be it."

Barsarbe glanced at Raum, then turned and looked at the Avar. "We will not help you in your war against Borneheld," she said, turning back to Axis.

"Damn it!" Axis snapped, "Faraday Tree Friend is with Borneheld. Don't you want to free her?"

"Why didn't *you* bring her out of Gorkenfort?" Brode shouted, stepping forward aggressively. "Why is she not here with you now?"

"We had to battle our way out of Gorkenfort," Axis said, fighting to keep his voice steady. "I judged her chances to be better if she remained with Borneheld. And there was no way I could seize her from Borneheld without risking her life."

"The fact remains," Barsarbe said, tilting her chin to look Axis in the eye, "that we will wait for her. Tree Friend will lead us home, not the StarMan. If she says we will unite with the Icarii and the Acharites, then we will do it. But only then."

Anger made a muscle in Axis' cheek flicker. The Avar had decided this well before he'd stepped inside the circle of stone.

"Axis," Raum stepped up and addressed him directly. "You must understand the Avar. We are a reclusive people. We understand the Prophecy and we understand the threat of

Gorgrael. We understand who you are and what your role is. But we are a people deeply scarred by the violence meted out to us during the Wars of the Axe. We are a people decimated by loss. We are not numerous, and we are not warlike. How could we fight for you? We have no Strike Force like our friends the Icarii. We have no weapons. So we wait for Tree Friend, and when she comes, then we will follow her. Faraday is a woman of gentleness and she is a woman bonded to the Mother. You are a warrior and you follow the way of the Stars. We mean you no disrespect nor do we mean to anger you, but we prefer to wait for Faraday."

"I understand, my friend," Axis said, placing a hand on Raum's shoulder. He turned to the assembled Avar. "I apologise if my words have caused you hurt. Sometimes I am too impatient. I understand your reluctance to act and I will accept your decision to wait for Tree Friend – Faraday. It will make my desire to reach her even deeper."

The entire assemblage of Avar visibly relaxed. None had been too sure how he would react to their decision. They knew that the Prophecy walked among them, but they would wait for the one who had been promised them. Faraday.

"Then we welcome you to Beltide, Axis SunSoar, Star-Man," Barsarbe smiled. "Beltide is the most joyous time of the year for us, a night when we put to one side all that troubles us, when we celebrate love and life and birth and renewal. Share with us that joy."

Whereas the Yuletide rites were closely tied to the sun and the sun god Narcis, and the Icarii male Enchanters and Avar Banes dominated, Beltide celebrated the rebirth of the earth after the death of winter, and, in rites that celebrated renewal, the females had long dominated. Tonight Barsarbe, assisted by MorningStar, would lead the rites. StarDrifter, as all other male Enchanters and Banes, was relegated to the audience.

None of them minded a bit. This was a night when the audience had as much fun as those leading the rites.

Azhure gathered with the Avar and Icarii as dusk fell. She had spent the afternoon with Fleat and Shra of the Ghost-Tree Clan. Shra had squealed with delight when she saw Azhure, throwing herself into the woman's arms, and Fleat had smiled with genuine pleasure, inviting Azhure and Rivkah to sit at the GhostTree fire for the afternoon. They had caught up on news and renewed their friendship. Azhure was relieved to find that neither Fleat nor her husband Grindle laid any blame at Azhure's feet for Pease's death.

"Pease would not have wanted you to grieve overlong," Fleat had said. "And tonight is Beltide, when wounds will be healed and new bonds will be forged. Tonight will be a joyous affair. We should not spoil Beltide with sorrowing for the dead. Pease would not want it."

Now Rivkah and Azhure threaded their way through the growing crowds of Icarii and Avar in the Earth Tree Grove.

"Where are we going?" Azhure asked.

"We will sit with the SunSoars, Azhure. At least, we will *start* the night with them. Who knows with whom we will finish the night," Rivkah replied, concentrating on finding her way through the throng of people.

Azhure was more than a little nervous about the Beltide celebrations. Over the past months there had been so many hints dropped about the excesses of a night when the normal ties and promises of unions were forgotten, a night when adventures could be explored without risk. When Avar and Icarii indulged curiosities and appetites otherwise forbidden.

And what would be offered her tonight? Azhure remembered the feel of StarDrifter's arms about her in the training chamber, the taste of his mouth. She wondered if she would be able to deny StarDrifter a second time, now that he and Rivkah had parted. Would she let him sate her curiosity tonight?

The SunSoars sat at the foot of the black cliff face that bordered the western edge of the grove. To one side of them the Avarinheim forest stood dark and wrapped in shadows. RavenCrest sat a little to one side, reserved and aloof, his wife several paces away, a dreamy expression on her face. Were they both planning their Beltide games? Azhure wondered. Did even the Talon and his wife indulge their desires as they pleased?

"Where's EvenSong?" she asked Axis as she sank down beside him, smoothing out her crimson robe. Her hair tumbled loose about her shoulders and down her back.

"She offered to serve with the patrols tonight," Axis explained. "She said that without FreeFall she had no interest in Beltide."

"Are we safe?" Azhure asked.

"We are safe," Axis said, his eyes on the circle of stone. "The Strike Force has a strong presence in the sky and in the surrounding forest. There is not a Skraeling within fifty leagues."

Several paces away StarDrifter sat in the shadow of a slight cleft in the cliff face. Tonight he was determined to have Azhure. Over the past months his desire for her had grown to the point where it dominated his every waking thought and drove him to dream of her constantly. He had never wanted another woman – Icarii, Acharite or Avar – like this. On the night before they had flown out to the Avarinheim he had dreamt that they were both tumbling entwined through the sky, their wings tangled and useless as they fell towards the ground, their thoughts only on assuaging their savage needs. In that dream Azhure had the wings and the features of an Icarii.

Tonight he would take her. Possess her, finally. He had told Axis that Azhure would bear powerful Enchanters, and tonight he meant to get one on her. But the night was long, and it was not yet time.

Avar Banes stepped through the crowds, quiet now as the rites neared. They carried deep bowls of dark liquid which glinted ruby red whenever a stray moonbeam caught them.

The young Bane who served their section stepped in front of RavenCrest first, murmured to him, then offered him the bowl. RavenCrest drank, then the Bane turned to Bright-Feather, then to Rivkah. He stepped carefully through the rocks and offered StarDrifter the blessed wine, then he turned to Axis.

"Drink well and deep, Axis SunSoar, and may the sacred wine of Beltide remind you of the joy and the steps of the Star Dance as you celebrate the renewal of life tonight."

Axis took the bowl in both hands and drank the wine deeply. He raised his head only with reluctance and Azhure, watching him, noticed that the wine clung in heavy, red drops to his beard. Two of the drops ran together, trickling down through the short golden hairs. She stared at them, fascinated. The wine was so thick and heavy it reminded her of blood.

The Bane paused briefly before Azhure, then bowed his head in regret. "You have not been accepted among us, Azhure. I am afraid that I cannot offer you the —"

He stopped, shocked, as Axis stood and took the bowl from his hands. "I take the responsibility," Axis said. "The wine is almost gone and you are needed before the circle of stone. I will take responsibility for what remains of the sacred wine."

After a moment the Bane bowed stiffly. "The bowl and its contents are your responsibility, Axis SunSoar," he said, then turned and marched away, every step stiff with displeasure.

Axis turned to Azhure.

"Stand, Azhure," he said, and Azhure slowly stood, her eyes on his face.

"Drink well and deep, Azhure," Axis said softly. "And may the sacred wine of Beltide remind you of the joy and the steps of the Star Dance as you celebrate the renewal of life tonight. Celebrate."

Azhure hesitated, aware that every eye within twenty paces' radius was on her.

"Drink," Axis repeated, his voice insistent.

Azhure reached for the bowl. As her hands wrapped themselves about the bowl, Axis, instead of dropping his own hands, slid them around the bowl to cover hers.

"Drink," he whispered.

The moment the warm, viscous liquid filled her mouth Azhure understood why all those she'd watched had been reluctant to relinquish the bowl. The wine felt alive and seemed to speak to her, sing to her as it filled her mouth. It tasted of earth and salt, birth and death, wisdom and sadness beyond knowing. As the warm, coppery liquid slid down her throat and warmed her belly, Azhure thought she could hear music. Wild music, as if the stars themselves were reeling naked and crazed with lust through the night sky.

Azhure took another great mouthful. There was not much left.

"Thank you, Axis," she said from the depths of her heart. "Thank you for making me a part of this night. I would that you drink the last mouthful."

Their hands still locked together about the bowl, Axis raised it to his lips and drained it. Now the trail of wine through his beard looked more like blood than ever and Azhure was vividly reminded of the magnificent Stag sacrificed in this grove at Yuletide.

"His life, his blood, he gave to us to celebrate tonight," Axis said, and placed the bowl carefully to one side of a boulder. Azhure wondered how he knew what she'd been thinking. As she turned she found every SunSoar eye riveted on her. Let them think what they like, she told herself, and sat down in one graceful movement. Already Azhure could feel the effects of the wine racing through her blood.

A light flared behind the torch-lit stone archways and all eyes turned away from Azhure and towards the circle.

Azhure blinked, her vision blurring, but her eyes cleared and she stared at the circle.

Figures dimly moved behind the archways, and wild music erupted violently into the night. This music was nothing like that Azhure had heard at Yuletide, or in Talon Spike. The Icarii generally sang unaccompanied, or used harps to make their music. But this music was the music of wild pipes. Avar music as Azhure had never heard it before.

The music reeled through the night and twisted down among the crowds until groups of the watchers stood to dance, gyrating wildly. Azhure longed to be with them, but, just as she was about to leap up, the music abruptly stopped.

Azhure's blood throbbed in her ears and her heart beat madly. Was it the music or the fermented stag's blood?

Someone nudged her elbow. It was Rivkah, smiling a little secretively as she held out a gourd of wine. "It is not as good as that you have just drunk, Azhure, but it is good never-theless. Drink, and pass it on."

Azhure took the wine and drank deeply, then handed the gourd to Axis. His face was intense. Perhaps he waits for the music to begin again, thought Azhure, and as she passed the wine over she touched the blood where it still lingered within his beard and at the corner of his mouth.

A movement at the edge of Azhure's vision caught her attention, and she looked back to the circle.

A figure walked through one of the archways, and a murmur ran through the watching crowd. It was Barsarbe, small, delicate, and completely, utterly naked. She had painted spiral designs over her body, emphasising her breasts and her belly, although what paint she had used Azhure could not see.

"It is what remains of the stag's blood," said Axis quietly at her side. "Can you not see its redness? Smell its warmth?"

"I have not the senses of an Enchanter," Azhure muttered, unable to drag her eyes away from Barsarbe.

Another woman walked through the archways. It was MorningStar, similarly naked, similarly painted, although this time the paint was some golden substance that highlighted the beautiful pale sheen of her skin.

By Azhure's side Axis stirred uncomfortably.

Both women started to dance. The pipe music had begun again, but it was softer this time, less insistent, and there was an accompaniment of drums that mirrored the beating of Azhure's heart.

The beat made her think, momentarily, of the insistent tug of the waves against a distant shoreline, and of the dip and sway of the moon.

As StarDrifter used his voice to speak and persuade, to relive memories and to tell stories, so the slow, sensuous dance of these two women spoke of many things to the watching eyes. They spoke of the gradual reawakening of the earth under the soft and sensual touch of the sun; of the seeds of life that lay buried under cover of darkness for long months but were now stimulated into life; of the green shoots that burst through the soil and grew to feed the mouths of man and beast. They spoke of the continual renewal of life, whether in the earth or in the belly of a doe or a woman; of the joy that was granted each time a child drew breath for the first time; and they spoke of love, its delights, its place in the continual renewal of the earth and of life.

Barsarbe danced with passion, but it was MorningStar who stirred Azhure the most. She not only used her long limbs and lithe body, but also her wings, using them one moment to hide and tantalise, the next to invite and demand.

The dance of the two women was building to its zenith, their movements slower but more intense. A man stood to dance with MorningStar, and with a start Azhure saw that it was Grindle, leader of the GhostTree Clan. MorningStar orientated her dance to Grindle alone, while another man now rose and danced with Barsarbe. Azhure swallowed as their movements became more intense, more intimate. Many Avar and Icarii were now engaged in their own private dances, while inside the stone circle, dimly visible frantic figures were writhing in pairs on the ground. Azhure did not need an Enchanter's vision to know what they were doing.

The wine sang through her blood.

Without conscious thought, Azhure stood and walked through the boulders into the surrounding forest.

Azhure walked until she no longer heard the music of the pipes or the drums. The grass was soft and cool under her feet, and the Earth Tree sang soft and seductive over her head. The night mist thickened around her, until it seemed that she was moving through a drifting sea of soft silver. Azhure had no sense of confinement, for the silvery mist created an atmosphere of light and space.

The wine sang through her blood, and somewhere, deep within her, she thought she could feel the faint pull of an answering Song. She slowed her steps. Her hands drifted to the emerald sash that bound her crimson robe, and she undid it, letting it fall gently to the ground, rejoicing in the feel of the material floating free to wrap and fold itself against her body in the soft, damp air of the Avarinheim.

The Earth Tree sang sweet and gentle, and Azhure closed her eyes and took a deep breath, letting the Avarinheim wrap her in its loveliness, giving herself completely to the Song surging through her blood.

The sense that another answered it was stronger now, more insistent, and Azhure opened her eyes.

StarDrifter stood some ten or fifteen paces away, holding out his hand and smiling. Slowly his fingers curled, beckoning, once, twice, a third time, and Azhure rocked as the Song roared through her blood in response.

A twig cracked behind her.

Azhure turned her head. The Song of her blood was now almost deafening; she could no longer hear the Earth Tree.

Distant, still distant, another figure was walking through the mist towards her. Axis.

"Azhure!" StarDrifter's voice cracked across her consciousness and Azhure blinked, tears springing to her eyes at the anger and tension in his voice. "Azhure! To me! Your blood calls to *me*, for *me*. Answer it. *Now!*"

But now a deep, gentle Song surged through her, intermingling with her own blood, and this Song she knew was Axis calling to her.

She moaned, her hands clenching by her side, knowing that her blood demanded of her that she choose, hating herself, knowing that she could not walk away.

The mist clung thick and loving to both forms, so that both StarDrifter and Axis, equal distances from her now, seemed ethereal, wraithlike, in the forest. Each now beckoned, demanding.

Without conscious thought or decision, Azhure turned to StarDrifter. His eyes widened in triumph and his fingers flared towards her.

"Sorry," she whispered, then walked towards Axis.

Behind her StarDrifter screamed.

Axis had thought his heart would tear itself apart with victory and craving when Azhure turned to walk towards him, her eyes downcast. His entire body had vibrated with every beat of his heart, his blood as wild and as febrile as the pulse of the feral pipe music.

"Dance with me," he'd whispered, and Azhure had raised her eyes to his. Neither had cared if StarDrifter still watched.

Now she rested, heavy and warm along the length of his body, sleeping. They lay underneath a stand of giant featherback ferns, encased in green tracery, warm and safe.

Axis shifted slightly, tensing a little as Azhure mumbled in her sleep, then relaxing with her as she slipped deeper into her dreams.

Did she dream of him? He knew *he* would dream of her for many long nights to come. No other had ever made him feel this way. She had sent him reeling among the stars, until his entire vision had been filled with the myriad blur of the stars as they rushed by, seizing him up in their mad dance through the heavens, until he could feel his very soul tear itself loose from its moorings and crash free about the firmament itself. Wonder and madness, exultation and pain, all had consumed him. He had withheld nothing, could withhold nothing, from this woman.

Perhaps it was her virginity, perhaps it was Beltide night, perhaps it was the wine they had both consumed. Axis did not know. Perhaps it was because this was the first time he had coupled with a woman since coming into his full powers as an Enchanter.

Slowly his touch grew firmer, and his hand moved further down her arm. How long, Axis wondered, did his body need to recover before he could make love to her again? His hand drifted to her back, and his touch softened. He remembered holding her as he lost himself among the surging waves of the Star Dance, feeling the terrible ridged scars that ran the length of her back. Only the single smooth strip of skin over her spine had escaped the cruel hand that had inflicted these scars. *Why?* What spirit of cruelty had driven Hagen to inflict this pain on Azhure?

"Azhure," he whispered, wishing the circle of his arms could protect her from any further hurt. He leaned his body towards her, stroking her gently awake.

She woke slowly, opening her smoky eyes into his pale ones. "Axis? Did we . . ." She hesitated.

"Did we celebrate Beltide together, my lady? Do you not remember?"

Azhure laughed a little, her cheeks colouring. "Yes. I remember."

Axis smiled, and kissed her very slowly, refreshing her memory. His hand moved down over her hips.

"And tell me, Azhure, did you ever think, when you were a small child growing up in Smyrton, that you would lose your virginity to an Icarii Enchanter on the hard ground of the Avarinheim forest?"

Azhure did not hesitate in her reply. "I swore that I would never give myself to anyone less than a hero, Axis SunSoar. That I should love him so deeply makes this night the more sweet."

Axis' hand stilled. "Azhure," he stumbled. "Do not love me. I cannot, I . . . Faraday . . ." His voice trailed off. It was the first time he had thought about Faraday this night, and the guilt struck deep.

Azhure flinched at the expression on his face. "I know, Axis," she whispered. "I know. I did not expect to be loved in return."

Now Axis winced. Who had he betrayed here tonight? Faraday — or Azhure? He leaned down and kissed Azhure again, shifting his body against hers, allowing his desire to swamp him. The night was yet young, and Faraday was very far away.

Neither knew that somewhere, sitting in front of his lonely fire, the Prophet laughed at the man and woman entwined beneath the ferns. He was pleased. Well pleased. Azhure had served the Prophecy well this night.

16

A Parting of Ways

Azhure, dressed in her Avar tunic and leggings, packed the crimson robe carefully into the base of her pack. Last night seemed a dream. But every aching muscle in her body told her otherwise.

"Rivkah, where will you be going from here?" she asked.

"Back to Achar, Azhure. Do you think to join me? Why not go back to Talon Spike with the Icarii?"

Azhure hesitated. "I –"

"I know what happened last night," Rivkah said gently. "I saw both StarDrifter and Axis follow you into the forest, and I saw StarDrifter return alone."

Azhure busied herself thrusting the last of her belongings into the pack. "It would be hard to go back to Talon Spike, Rivkah. StarDrifter would be . . . well –"

"Impossible," Rivkah said. "Yes, Azhure, I understand that. Do you want to follow Axis?"

"*That* would be impossible, Rivkah. No, I thought I might follow you. I am heartily sick of this Prophecy, and I do not want to get in Axis' way. It would be best if I left whatever we had last night here. As quickly as possible."

Rivkah nodded. She understood that Azhure wanted to walk away from Axis before he had the chance to tear her soul apart as StarDrifter had torn Rivkah's. Mortal women had no place beside Icarii Enchanters.

Axis stood conferring with several of the Crest-Leaders. Those of the Icarii who had not indulged too freely in the wine of Beltide were making preparations to return to Talon Spike. The groves about him were filled with the rush of feathers and shouted goodbyes.

"We have further reports of Sigholt, Strike-Leader," FarSight said.

Axis glanced his way sharply. He had sent three different patrols on long-range missions over Ichtar and the Urqhart Hills – he desperately awaited news of both Belial and Borneheld. "Well?" he snapped.

FarSight raised a black eyebrow. For a man who had, according to common gossip, thoroughly enjoyed his first Beltide, Axis had a ferocious temper this morning.

"Belial is well and has settled comfortably into Sigholt, Axis. Sigholt is secure and Belial is establishing supply routes into northern Ichtar. They currently have enough supplies for several months. Before we join him, Belial still wants to secure the area surrounding Sigholt, as well as the WildDog Plains."

"But Sigholt itself is secure?"

"Yes, Strike-Leader. The threat from the Skraelings is almost non-existent. None dare approach the waters –"

"The waters?" Axis broke in. "What waters?" To one side Ogden and Veremund, hovering about trying to look inconspicuous, gave up all pretence of indifference and stepped closer.

"Belial has somehow managed to reflood the lake and Sigholt not only has the waters of the lake to protect it, but is also surrounded by a deep and wide moat. Skraelings do not like water."

"Especially *magic* water!" Ogden cried, his white hair standing even more on end than usual. "It is a sacred Lake, Axis. One of the four magic sacred Lakes. I wonder how Belial managed it?"

"Jack!" Veremund whispered, tugging on Ogden's sleeve. "It must be Jack!"

"Well," Axis said, "Sigholt seems to be a good site for a base in more ways than one. I must get word to Belial."

"We can send more farflight scouts, Axis," FarSight began, but Ogden and Veremund broke in, speaking as one.

"We'll go, Axis!"

Axis laughed. "What? You expect me to entrust a message to two such rascals? Even if I did, would Belial believe a word that came out of your mouths?"

Ogden's and Veremund's faces fell and Axis relented. "I will entrust messages to both farflight scouts *and* to you two gentlemen," he said, then turned back to FarSight. "And Borneheld? What news of Borneheld?"

"Not much, Axis. Borneheld has encamped at Jervois Landing, where you expected."

Axis nodded.

FarSight continued. "Jervois Landing is too far for the farflight scouts to fly – and too dangerous. West of Sigholt Ichtar seethes with Skraelings, and Borneheld's archers would as soon shoot at Icarii as they would at the Skraelings. Belial intends to send human scouts on foot, disguised as peasants, to scout Borneheld and his encampment and learn what they can. At the moment, however, Belial knows little and we know even less."

"Then it would be best for the Strike Force to return to Talon Spike for the moment," Axis said, thinking aloud. "Continue training there until Belial has established a supply route strong enough to feed both his men and the Strike Force. Once supplies are guaranteed, you can move the Strike Force south to Sigholt. Whatever happens, they must be there by early autumn to ensure enough time to prepare for the winter campaigns. Gorgrael will use the summer to regroup, and he will strike again with the first of the northerly winds of Bone-month, if not earlier. Ideally, I'd want you to start moving down to Sigholt in no less than twelve weeks' time, by DeadLeaf-month. That would give you time not only to settle in before the winter campaigns, but also to train intensively with Belial's forces. I want you welded into one force."

"And who will command that one force?" FarSight asked.

"*I* will, FarSight," Axis said, "when I arrive in Sigholt. You will command the Strike Force in Talon Spike until you arrive in Sigholt. Then Belial commands until I return. Perhaps," he said carefully, "it *is* best that I send this message with two groups of messengers."

"You have no need to fear, Strike-Leader," said FarSight. "The Strike Force is yours to dispose of as you will. If you think Belial is best to command until you return then I will obey." He paused. "Do you think you *will* be gone months?"

"I truly do not know, FarSight," replied Axis. "Ogden and Veremund tell me that time passes in strange ways in the waterways. Perhaps I will be gone only days, perhaps months. Whatever the case, I need to learn what secrets the Charonites can teach me . . . and I have a promise to fulfil while I drift the waterways."

Ogden and Veremund wandered off, discussing the reflooding of the Lake of Life in excited whispers. Had Jack found Zeherah? They gripped hands, their eyes bright with barely suppressed excitement – oh, to see Zeherah again!

"Gentlemen?"

Startled, they whirled around at the sound of Rivkah's voice. Both Rivkah and Azhure approached.

"My dear," Ogden said, pleased to see Rivkah. The Sentinels treasured Rivkah for her role as Axis' mother. Azhure . . . well, Azhure was a puzzle which both Ogden and Veremund were determined to solve, especially after StarDrifter and Axis had, according to gossip, vied over her last night.

"Ogden, Veremund. I could not help but overhear your conversation with Axis and the Crest-Leaders. Are you travelling to Sigholt?"

Ogden nodded. "As soon as we can, Rivkah. Why? Would you like to join us?"

Rivkah relaxed. "Azhure and I would both like to travel with you. And we would be no trouble."

"We would be honoured," Veremund said. "It will be a trip into your past, will it not Rivkah, to see Sigholt again?"

"In more ways than one," Rivkah remarked. "Will we travel down through the Avarinheim to where the Nordra escapes the Fortress Ranges?"

Azhure visibly tensed. That meant they would have to pass very close to Smyrton – and Azhure would be loathe to get that close to her old village again.

Veremund patted Azhure reassuringly on the arm as he answered Rivkah. "No, my dear, we will not travel that way."

"Then which way?" Rivkah asked, confused. It would surely be the most direct route.

Ogden and Veremund smiled conspiratorially. "No," Ogden said. "We would prefer one of the lesser-known paths. We will travel through the Avarinheim for a few days, certainly, but we will strike west towards the Fortress Ranges immediately."

"But I thought they were impossible to cross," Azhure said. "Isn't the only route through the Forbidden Valley?"

"No, sweet lady," said Veremund. "There are other ways, and it will be our pleasure to show you one of them. But once through we will have to travel south through the WildDog Plains to HoldHard Pass. It is a long and lonely trip, so Ogden and I are relieved that we will have such charming company to keep us amused."

Rivkah smiled at them. "When will we leave?"

"This afternoon, Rivkah. Soon." Ogden paused. "If you have goodbyes to say then say them now."

The light died in Rivkah's face. For weeks she had talked about leaving the Icarii, but now that her departure was imminent the reality of leaving a marriage and a people with whom she had spent the majority of the past thirty years struck. She looked at the flights of Icarii lifting off from the groves, tears glinting in her eyes. Was she doing the right thing?

StarDrifter stepped up from nowhere and placed a hand on Rivkah's waist. "You look upset, Rivkah. What is it?"

Rivkah forced a smile to her lips. She wished that StarDrifter had not touched her, not when he really wanted the woman who stood beside her. "I am leaving this afternoon with Ogden and Veremund. And Azhure comes with us. We travel for Sigholt."

StarDrifter looked stunned. Azhure was leaving for *Sigholt*? He'd thought she would return to Talon Spike. StarDrifter had hoped that with Axis out of the way, Azhure might reconsider her choice. But now she would be escaping even further away and he might not see her for months.

The tension among the group deepened as Axis joined them. He had seen StarDrifter approach the group and had quickly made his excuses to the Crest-Leaders and hurried over. His eyes were all for Azhure. She had left his side sometime during the early hours of the morning and had been avoiding him ever since. It was too much that Star-Drifter should have the chance to speak with her, and not himself.

"Rivkah," he smiled, kissing his mother, then turned to kiss Azhure. It was a provocative action, meant to irritate StarDrifter.

Azhure quickly side-stepped, leaving Axis hanging awkwardly in the air. StarDrifter smiled, and Azhure caught his look of satisfaction. By the heavens, what wedge had she driven between these two men? she thought frantically. More than ever, Azhure knew she had to leave as soon as possible.

The Prophecy could not afford to have Axis and StarDrifter torn apart by their jealousy over her. What had possessed her last night? Why couldn't she have walked away from both of them?

Rivkah linked her arm comfortably through Azhure's. "Azhure and I travel to Sigholt with Ogden and Veremund," she said. "Both of us have had quite enough of the complications that Enchanters cause in our lives."

StarDrifter recovered first and leaned forward to kiss Rivkah. "Undoubtedly I will see you there again," he said softly. "Watch for me from the roof."

"Are you sure it is *me* you want to watch from the roof, StarDrifter?" she replied.

StarDrifter's smile faded fractionally, then he turned to Azhure, who offered him her hand before he could kiss her mouth. "Until we meet again, Azhure."

Azhure nodded, not trusting herself to speak. She did not want to alienate StarDrifter by ill-considered words now.

StarDrifter dropped her hand and turned to Axis. "Beltide sometimes brings out hidden desires and dreams, Axis. Unfortunately we've both discovered that we are more alike than we hitherto realised." His eyes sparkled. "I have never before had to compete with a son who has, apparently, inherited all of my charms and more. Azhure made her choice last night, and she has made her choice today. I harbour no grudges and I bear no ill will. I don't want this to come between us."

Axis hesitated, then embraced his father as Azhure and Rivkah watched with more than a little cynicism.

Once Azhure and Rivkah said their goodbyes to both Icarii and Avar, they waited at the edge of one of the lesser groves for the Sentinels.

"It is going to be a hard journey," Rivkah sighed. "And I am no longer such a young woman."

Azhure fingered her pack. Axis had given her the golden tunic to take down to Sigholt, and it was stowed, together with her crimson robe, at the bottom of the pack.

She raised her head. "Here they come now. I can hear them arguing about something."

Ogden and Veremund stepped into the grove, each leading a fat white donkey loaded with well-stuffed packs.

"I've heard about these two donkeys," Azhure said. "Where on earth did they find them this time?"

"What?" Veremund said as they drew level with the two women. "What? Find them? Why, they were in camp, weren't they, Ogden?"

"Yes, indeed," Ogden replied cheerfully. "Waiting for us. Veremund must have put them there."

"Oh no," Veremund disagreed, his face darkening. "*You* must have put them there. *I* had nothing to do with it."

"Well," Rivkah said, "at least we'll have something to sit on when we get too footsore."

As the Sentinels continued to squabble about who had procured the donkeys, Rivkah began to laugh. It would be all right. Leaving for Sigholt was the best decision that either she or Azhure could have made. For the first time in many, many years, Rivkah began to feel positive about the future.

In one of the northern groves Axis gave last instructions to FarSight. "As soon as Belial has established supplies then join him. I will join you in Sigholt as soon as I have learned what I can from the Charonites. Tell Belial that he must do what is right, but that above all he should consolidate."

"Do not be gone too long. Both Belial and I will need you there by late autumn," FarSight said, then saluted and lifted into the air.

Axis turned to his father, and they embraced again. "Thank you," he murmured, and StarDrifter knew it was for far more than the training he had given his son.

"Axis," MorningStar said, giving her grandson a quick peck on the cheek. Beltide had not turned out quite the way she had hoped, and StarDrifter was not the only SunSoar regretting Axis' choice of Beltide partner. "Learn well from the Charonites. And ask them if they have any idea about . . ."

She hesitated to put her thoughts into words, but Axis knew what she meant. Since their discussion many weeks earlier about the possibility – reality, really – that both Gorgrael and Axis had been trained by an unknown SunSoar Enchanter, powerful enough to use the Dark Music of the Stars, no-one had wanted to discuss it again. Nevertheless, the worry about who and where the Enchanter was marred their unguarded moments.

"If anyone will know, they will," StarDrifter said.

Axis watched the worry carve lines into his father's face. "I will find out what I can from the Charonites, StarDrifter, but somehow I think that this rogue Enchanter will keep himself well hidden until he wants to reveal himself."

"And what," MorningStar said in a toneless voice, "if he is someone you already know, Axis? What if he is someone close to you? An Enchanter this powerful could choose any disguise he – or she – wanted to."

Axis picked his way down the path that StarDrifter had directed him to, pushing through the overgrown oldenberry bushes to the mouth of the cavern. It was just as StarDrifter had described. Hesitating only slightly, Axis walked down to the back of the cavern and squatted by the wall, remembering the Song that StarDrifter had told him to use. He hummed it underneath his breath, tapping the wall gently with his fingers. Unlike StarDrifter, Axis was gentle with the Song and, after only a few moments, a small portion of the grey rock splintered and slid gently to the floor of the cavern, revealing a gleaming bronze door. Axis pushed it open and began the journey into the UnderWorld.

Hours later, when he reached the cavern far beneath, he found the Ferryman waiting for him. Great violet eyes, stunningly youthful among the Ferryman's otherwise cadaverous features, regarded Axis serenely. Behind the Ferryman bobbed his flat-bottomed boat.

Axis stopped two paces away and the Ferryman bowed. "Greetings, Axis SunSoar, StarMan," he said in his deep voice. "Welcome to the UnderWorld. What is it you desire?"

"Greetings, Ferryman," Axis said. "I understand that my mother won a boon from you."

The Ferryman inclined his head. "She did."

"That you would grant me assistance, in whatever manner I asked?"

Again the Ferryman inclined his head.

"Then teach me," Axis said softly. "Teach me the secrets of the waterways. Teach me the secrets you have unravelled over the ages."

The Ferryman's eyes were steady. "It is all I have ever wanted to do and it is why I have lived so long winding these waterways," he said finally. "Only to teach."

17

The Audience

She saw Borneheld, stepping down from the throne, Axis stepping to meet him. The two men circled, swords drawn, their faces twisted into snarling masks of rage fed by long-held hatreds. They fought until both were bleeding and stumbling with weariness. About them the Chamber rang with shouted accusations of murder and treachery. Blood. Why was there so much blood? A scream — hers. "No!"

The vision faded, but Faraday's stomach sickened and turned over. She closed her eyes momentarily, trying to regain her equilibrium. Ever since she had stepped into the Chamber of the Moons half an hour ago she had slid in and out of the vision the trees had given her so long ago outside the Silent Woman Woods. She was glad Priam had only addressed her briefly before turning his full attention to her husband.

They had arrived in Carlon four days ago, and Priam had made Borneheld wait until this morning before granting him an audience. Borneheld had fumed, but there was nothing he could do.

Now he stood before the royal dais, his body so tense it was almost quivering.

About him the packed Chamber was breathless with shock. Scribes scribbled furiously, nobles locked stunned eyes, servants crowded doorways, and Jayme, Moryson and

Gilbert, standing to the left of the dais, were ashen and sweating. The only relaxed person in the Chamber was Priam, sitting nonchalantly on his throne, his fingers tapping his royal displeasure.

Faraday blinked, trying to concentrate. She did not know Priam very well, but she had heard enough to realise that this hard-voiced, flint-eyed man was showing more backbone than he'd ever done previously.

"I made you WarLord," Priam snapped, "and for that you lost me Ichtar. No doubt these Destroyer-driven wraiths now mass to eat the rest of my realm while you lounge about my court!"

Borneheld's face flushed an even deeper red, and Faraday bit her lip, worried.

Borneheld restrained himself. "I was betrayed," he began, but Priam did not let him finish.

"I hear tell you escaped only through Axis' bravery."

Faraday could see the massive effort it took Borneheld to stay calm. His fists clenched by his sides, only very gradually relaxing.

"He has allied himself with the Forbidden, Majesty. 'Tis no wonder we lost Ichtar against such an unholy alliance."

"I hear tell," Priam said very deliberately, his eyes locked with Borneheld's, "that my nephew believes we should contract an alliance with the, ah, Icarii and Avar."

Faraday, as everyone else in the room, took a huge, incredulous breath. Priam had *never* publicly acknowledged Axis as his nephew previously!

"This prophecy I have heard," Priam continued, ignoring the reactions about him, "states that an alliance with those we once feared is vital to defeat this Gorgrael."

Faraday averted her eyes, terrified that Borneheld would see their sudden leap of joy. She took another breath, but this time one of sheer hope. An alliance with Axis would bring him down from his icy mountain and back to her. *Oh*

Mother! she thought, *please let Priam have the courage to embrace the truth! Bring Axis home to me!*

A movement to one side caught her attention. Gilbert, whispering frantically behind a hand to his Brother-Leader. Well may you whisper, thought Faraday contemptuously. A thousand years ago your beloved Seneschal orchestrated the Wars of the Axe to drive the Icarii and Avar from their homelands. And for a thousand years your Brotherhood has equated only evil and darkness with the so-called Forbidden. Now a King of Achar plans to ally himself with them. Faraday could not stop a small smile lifting the corners of her mouth. Do you wonder, Jayme, if the moment the *Forbidden* set foot in this land again the lies of the past thousand years will be exposed? Can you see your beloved Seneschal losing its insidious control over the Acharites as the Mother and the Star Gods once more spread their joy over this wondrous land?

Priam took a studied sip of water from the begemmed chalice by his side. "I am wondering," he said very softly but very clearly, "if I made the wrong choice in WarLord."

The gasp about the Chamber was audible this time. Scribes scribbled even more furiously. Faraday closed her eyes briefly again. Priam *would* ally himself with Axis. Civil war would be averted, Gorgrael defeated, and her love kept safe. Her vision was a lie, after all.

Jayme was now openly agitated, but restrained from speaking by Moryson's grip on his sleeve.

No-one held back Borneheld. "By Artor!" he shouted, taking an ill-considered step forward, "have you gone mad?"

He got no further. Furious himself, Priam leapt to his feet. "You are dismissed, Duke of nothing!" he seethed. "I will speak no more with you! I have made up my mind on this issue, and if you remain stubbornly persistent in your refusal to accept the obvious then *I will have to reconsider my choice of both WarLord and heir!*"

The Chamber took one gigantic breath and held it; the scribes could not believe what their pens recorded.

Borneheld visibly reeled. "I —"

"You have proved useless to me," Priam continued, his voice even once more as he sat down. "Get out of my sight, Borneheld."

Borneheld's face was pale now, but his grey eyes burned furiously. He did not move.

"Out," Priam repeated, then turned to chat quietly with his wife, Judith, sitting serenely by his side.

Ignored by his King, but aware that every other person in the room watched him, Borneheld only just remembered to offer Faraday his arm as he stalked from the Chamber. As they reached the doorway, Priam called after them.

"Duchess, the Queen has talked kindly of you. Perhaps you would join her for her midday meal on the morrow."

Faraday inclined her head graciously, feeling happier than she had for many months.

Borneheld's temper erupted the moment their apartment doors closed behind them. "He is mad! Crazed!" he hissed, his face flushed and perspiring.

"He thinks only of saving his people, husband," Faraday said, moving to sit at a small table by the window.

"Curse you, Faraday!" Borneheld took a threatening step towards her. "No doubt you revelled in my humiliation!"

Faraday raised her eyes, not in the least intimidated. "I, like Priam, care only for this land, Borneheld. Not for titles, nor for wealth, nor for the power you crave."

Borneheld flung himself away before he gave into his growing desire to hit her as she deserved. "Does not the chance to sit by my side as Queen tempt you, my sweet?"

Faraday's gaze was direct and truthful. "Neither the title nor the place by your side tempt me, husband." There, the words were said.

"Nevertheless, you sanctimonious *bitch*, you are tied to both, no matter what Priam says and no matter how much you lust after my brother! I —"

He was cut off by a knock at the door. It opened before either Borneheld or Faraday could say anything.

Gilbert stepped through the door. He smirked at the obvious tension in the room, then half bowed to Borneheld. "My Lord, the Brother-Leader requests an audience."

"An audience, Gilbert?"

"He, ah, thinks it best if we further discussed those possibilities I raised in Jervois Landing, Lord."

Borneheld took a sharp breath. "Of course, Brother Gilbert," he said smoothly. "My dear, if you will excuse us."

Faraday frowned at the door as it closed behind him. Why had Borneheld's mood changed so abruptly?

No matter. She stood and looked out the window, gazing sightlessly at the crowds in the streets below. Priam had done what she never thought he would — publicly allied himself with Axis, and publicly considered him as heir to the throne.

Faraday's eyes filled with tears, but they were tears of hope, not despair.

18

Through the Fortress Ranges

For two days Ogden and Veremund led Rivkah and Azhure south-west through the Avarinheim. The paths were narrow and overgrown in this part of the forest – the Avar tended to stay away from the range of mountains dividing their homelands from Achar. "They prefer to have a healthy buffer of forest between them and the Acharites," Veremund explained to Azhure.

But even overgrown as they were, the trails were beautiful. The lofty forest canopy sheltered them from the northern winds and let in a delicate soft golden light. As they walked the forest spoke to them in endless music – the secretive sounds of the wind as it moved through the trees and bushes, the soft drip of moisture from leaves, the cascades of streams as they rushed towards the Nordra River and the ever changing song of the forest birds. And weaving its way through both light and music came the wondrous sound of the Earth Tree Song, binding all under her mystery.

Veremund and Ogden enjoyed the two women's company. They were serene and restful companions, and walking with them through the Avarinheim over the past two days had proved a gentle joy. It had been some two thousand years since either Sentinel had walked the forest paths, and then the Avarinheim had stretched over most of the lands east of the Nordra River. Now, only the forest protected by the Fortress

Ranges remained inviolate – from either Seneschal or Gorgrael.

"Veremund?" Rivkah caught up to Veremund and Azhure. "Ogden has a problem with his donkey. Her off fore foot has a small stone in it and Ogden wants you to hold her head while he removes it."

Veremund nodded his thanks and turned back.

Rivkah took Azhure's arm as the two women drew away from the Sentinels. About them the filtered light was alive with butterflies and birdsong.

"Azhure," Rivkah said. "I am glad we finally have a chance to speak." She could feel Azhure tense a little under her hand. "I am not speaking of wrong or right, Azhure, only of what you feel. After all," she smiled wryly, "I am the last to apportion blame to women who find themselves the target of an Enchanter's attentions."

"I did not intend to do it," Azhure said, her tone slightly defiant. "I do not mean to get in the way."

Rivkah let her arm go and gave Azhure a brief hug. "Azhure, it is very hard to love an Enchanter. That is all I want to say. If ever you need to talk, then I will be here."

"I know, Rivkah." Azhure paused. "Axis loves Faraday. I know that, and I can accept it. But . . ."

"But . . . ?" Rivkah thought she knew what Azhure would ask.

"But, noble or not, Faraday is a woman like me. Wouldn't she and Axis have the same problems as you and StarDrifter did? As Axis and I would? Wouldn't she age and die well before he?"

"Azhure." Rivkah's tone was very gentle. "From what we have heard of Faraday and the Mother, she is no longer quite as human as either you or I. Perhaps she will live as long as Axis. Perhaps she will be able to hold him, to satisfy him where a human woman could not."

"It was one night. Do not fear for me. I can walk away."

"I hope you can, Azhure," Rivkah said. "Axis has his father's blood coursing through his veins. He is a powerful Icarii Enchanter. He will be back one day — can you walk far enough before then?"

Behind them Ogden and Veremund bent over the patient donkey's foot, finally letting the unblemished hoof drop to the ground.

"He spent Beltide night with her," Ogden said quietly.

"He has spent nights with many women," Veremund replied.

"This was different. *She* is different."

"Yes," Veremund finally, grudgingly, said. "Yes, she is. What does this mean for the Prophecy?"

Ogden sighed and gazed up the forest path where the women walked. "Who knows, dear one? Who knows? There is so much we don't know. So much the Prophet left unsaid."

"She is a complication."

"Yes," Ogden agreed.

"But I like her, Ogden. I like her."

"Yes," Ogden agreed again. He knew what Veremund meant. Neither could help liking Azhure because both felt intuitively that she was *already* an old friend. But how?

"She has a power about her, dear one," Veremund said. "But it is covered with a thick blanket of fear."

Ogden looked at his brother sharply. "You are very perceptive, Veremund. I had not noticed that, but now that you mention it . . . Yes, you are right. Is she a danger?"

"A danger? I had not thought of her that way. A danger? Perhaps, but I do not know who to."

"What do we do?" Veremund said eventually. "I do not know what to do about her."

Ogden clucked to his donkey. "What do we do? We do nothing, dear one, but watch. Wait. Serve, in whatever manner presents itself."

"She has the qualities of a hero, dear one," Veremund murmured. "One day she will overcome that blanket of fear and step forward to demand her birthright."

Both remained silent and introspective until they had caught up with Rivkah and Azhure. Then, smiling mischievously, Ogden started to tell the two women of a tale he had once heard of two shepherds, a goat and a saucepan.

The next morning they came to the foot of the Fortress Ranges.

"Well?" Rivkah demanded. "Where is this secret way of yours, Ogden? Veremund?"

"A little way from here. But it will take most of the morning to climb down into the tunnel."

"Tunnel?" Azhure echoed doubtfully, but the two Sentinels had already started down a barely marked trail.

The Sentinels led the two women into a crevice at the base of the nearest of the hills. For two or three hours they scrambled down, descending deeper and deeper into the gloom. After some time the soft light of the Avarinheim forest disappeared altogether, and Ogden produced a small oil lamp from his donkey's pack.

"We shall not need it for long," he remarked, and both women glanced at each other in concern. Neither liked the idea of climbing any further into this crevice. Where were the Sentinels leading them? If the way grew any steeper then they would not be able to take the donkeys any further.

"The worst is behind us, my sweet ladies," called Ogden. "We are almost there."

"I am not so sure that I wish to know where 'there' is," Azhure grumbled. Her limbs were stiff and sore and she had pulled a muscle in her left leg.

The next moment she breathed in relief as the slope eased.

"Where are we?" Rivkah asked breathlessly as they stepped onto a smooth gravel path. Ogden's lamp showed very little apart from the nearest rocks in what appeared to be a narrow crevice. Even though they knew it was only midday, it appeared darkest night. "Where will this lead us?"

"Into a mystery, dear lady," Ogden said.

Veremund stepped back and placed a reassuring hand on each woman's shoulder. "It is quite safe, and will be clean and dry and light soon. Bear with Ogden. He *does* like a mystery."

Ogden led the party behind a jumble of rocks. Before them, beyond the comforting glow of the lamp, stretched total darkness. Then stunningly, Ogden doused his lamp and complete darkness enveloped the group.

"Watch, dear ones!" he cried. "Watch!" and the two women sensed him moving forward.

There was a soft click, and suddenly a soft yellow light glowed at ankle level. Both Rivkah and Azhure gasped. Ogden was stepping forth onto a smooth, black metallic roadway. With every fourth or fifth step he took another light clicked softly on. Some at ankle level, some over his head. As Ogden skipped ahead in delight, a long straight tunnel was revealed, stretching forward until it was lost in the darkness. Yellow lines ran down the centre of the tunnel roadway.

Ogden's donkey patiently followed her master.

"What is it?" Rivkah asked Veremund, her arms wrapped about herself protectively.

"Who built it?" Azhure demanded. "When? How do the lights work? What is this tunnel doing here? What is this black shiny stuff that coats the surface of the floor?"

"All Ogden and I know," Veremund replied, "is that this tunnel exists, and others like it in various parts of Tencendor — we use them from time to time. They are old, very old, and we do not know who built them. Come." He stepped after the fast disappearing Ogden, and, after only a moment's hesitation, the women followed.

Behind them, precisely ten minutes after they had passed, the lights clicked off one by one.

The tunnel ran deep into the earth. For the rest of the day they descended a gentle gradient before the roadway finally levelled out. There Ogden announced they would rest briefly before continuing.

"We have no comfortable mats and no Enchanter to create magical mattresses of air for us," explained Ogden to the tired women, who protested they needed longer to rest. "Within only a few hours you will become so uncomfortable on this hard surface that you will be only too pleased to move again."

"Besides," Veremund added. "I admit that I yearn for the night sky and the fresh air again. Safe and convenient this tunnel may be, but it is monotonous and sterile and it gives my soul no joy."

"Where does this tunnel go?" Azhure asked, slipping the Wolven off her shoulders and putting it carefully down. "How long will it take us to walk through?"

"It travels completely underneath the Fortress Ranges," Ogden said, rummaging around in one of his donkey's packs. He pulled out a platter of raisin cookies with a flourish. "How long to walk through? Well, if we manage to keep moving with only brief rests, we should emerge into daylight in two days' time."

"Well," Rivkah said, helping Veremund ease the packs from the donkeys' backs, "I suppose I can put up with it if it gets us to Sigholt quicker."

Azhure sat down and accepted a cookie from Ogden. She could tolerate the stifling atmosphere of the tunnel if it kept her from having to travel close to Smyrton.

Veremund sat down cross-legged and looked hopefully at his brother. "Ogden, did you happen to find any apples in your pack?"

The Sentinels were right. After only two or three hours both women were tossing and turning, their hips, elbows and shoulders sore and cold from the hard, metalled surface beneath them. They rose gratefully when Ogden called them. Even walking half asleep would be better than another minute spent prone on this floor.

Over the next two days and nights they walked five or six hours until feet started to shuffle and tempers snap, then they'd rest three, perhaps four, hours until no-one could stand the cold hard roadway any longer. Nothing about the tunnel changed. It was an eerie feeling, trapped in a small bubble of light in what seemed to be an eternity of darkness. All hungered for open spaces and fresh air so badly they could physically taste their need.

On the morning of the third day the roadway rose gently, and everyone's spirits lifted with it. Even the tired donkeys pricked their ears and brayed as they leaned into the rise.

They emerged, every muscle in their bodies sore and weary after an eight-hour climb into a dark and cold afternoon. They scrambled over rocks and down a steep and treacherous ravine before they stepped onto flat ground, all shivering in the biting wind that blew down from the north. At Talon Spike and in the Avarinheim they had been largely protected from Gorgrael's malicious weather, but here, at the edge of the Fortress Ranges and the WildDog Plains, the northerly wind screamed down on the little group as they huddled among a tumble of boulders.

Rivkah looked at the bleak landscape ahead. "Should we rest the night here, Ogden, before we attempt to move south? These boulders might give us the only degree of shelter we're going to get for a long time."

Ogden shook his head. "No, lovely lady. We will move south some hours before camping for the night. We need to move as soon as we can." He paused. "I do not like the bite in this wind and I fear that it will sap our energies if we stay in one place too long. Best we keep moving. But, look, see what I have here."

Ogden pulled two cloaks from his donkey's packs and handed them to the women, who wasted no time wrapping themselves as close as they could. Veremund had similarly unpacked two cloaks from his donkey's packs and the two Sentinels rugged up as well. Then, to the surprise of both Azhure and Rivkah, the Sentinels insisted that they each ride a donkey.

Comfortable and relatively warm atop the donkeys, neither woman complained any further.

The wind had died a little by the time they made camp for the night in the inadequate shelter afforded by a small, dry creek bed. The remains of a few dead skeleton bushes made a tiny, cheerless fire. Ogden produced some hot soup and crusty bread from one of the packs and, after they had eaten, Veremund persuaded the donkeys to lie down close to the fire. Between the donkeys and the fire, the four spent a passable night, the dry creek bed feeling like the finest feather bed to muscles still aching from the tunnel floor.

Thus they travelled for three days, slowly wending their way southwards against whatever protection the sharp cliffs of the Fortress Ranges could give them. To the women, spring seemed to have hardly touched this land yet, but to the Sentinels who had survived the siege of Gorkenfort and who knew to what extremes Gorgrael could drive winter, the lack of snow gave them some hope that spring had broken through more strongly in the lands south of the Nordra. Nevertheless, the frigid wind at their backs reminded them all that Gorgrael sat to the north, rallying his forces, waiting to build his army of Ghostmen to invasion force again.

Wrapped in lonely silence atop her donkey, Rivkah wondered what her son could do to counter Gorgrael's powerful enchantments. What could he do against a half-brother who could manipulate the very weather itself?

19

The Alaunt

On the third day after the group left the Fortress Ranges tunnel, fluid white shapes started to nose about the rocks where the women and the Sentinels had briefly sheltered.

Suddenly one halted, and buried his nose in the remains of a scuff mark. An instant later his head lifted into the sky and an eerie howl washed over the rest of his pack. Soon all were baying, low and clear, as the pack shuffled around the remaining traces of scent. Then they moved as one past the boulders and took the faint trail south. Occasionally one or two of them lifted their snouts long enough to send another low bay winding plaintively across the empty plain before them.

The small, yellow native wild dogs after whom the plains were named, and who lived out their lives hunting mice and small birds, huddled deep into their burrows, terrified beyond reason.

They knew the Alaunt ran.

It was late in the afternoon of the fourth day when the Sentinels heard the sound of the pack baying to the north. Neither woman saw the look of deep alarm that passed between Ogden and Veremund as they urged the donkeys on a little bit faster.

Both Sentinels knew they had no hope of outrunning the Alaunt. Yet if they could delay the inevitable confrontation an hour or more they might find a more defensible position.

Azhure was the first to become aware of the tension between the two Sentinels. "What is it?" she asked, raising her voice against the wind. "Why are you worried?"

Ogden glanced at Veremund, and the two came to a swift decision. Azhure and Rivkah would hear the hounds soon enough, anyway. They were closing rapidly.

"We are being followed," Veremund said, his voice strained.

"Followed? Who by?" Azhure reached automatically for the Wolven. "Skraelings?"

Veremund shook his head. "No. Creatures far older, far deadlier."

"*What*?" Azhure hissed. Her blood ran hot with desire for action and her hand gripped an arrow. The Wolven quivered in her hand. "*What*?"

"Alaunt hounds," Ogden said shortly, casting his eyes about the terrain before them.

Azhure swung her leg over the donkey's wither and slid to the ground. "What are Alaunt hounds?"

It was Rivkah who answered, her eyes wide with fear. "I heard tales of them when I was small. My nurse said the Alaunt were a pack of enchanted hounds who hunted down humans. She said they neither breathed nor ate, but could run for weeks only on the scent of blood. She said," Rivkah's voice quavered, "that once they caught the scent of their prey they would never let go."

"The Alaunt have not run for many thousands of years, not since WolfStar died," Ogden said tightly, hurrying the group along, "and I do not know why they run now."

"Can they die, Veremund? Can they be killed?" Azhure asked.

Veremund shrugged. "Who knows?"

"Well," Azhure said, "either they will die or we will. Ogden, is that a stand of rocks ahead?"

By the time they reached the pitifully inadequate tumble of boulders near the foot of a sheer cliff face they could all hear the low, clear cries of the hounds. As the others scrambled for shelter, Azhure slapped the donkeys' rumps, hoping that they would gallop off and perhaps draw the Alaunt away.

Suddenly the cries of the hounds changed, doubling their efforts so that their howls filled the night.

"We are lost!" Veremund cried. "Hear, they clamour!"

Azhure, an arrow already notched in the Wolven, turned and slapped the Sentinel across the face. "Be quiet, Veremund," she hissed, her eyes hard and angry. "Get as far behind the rocks as you can."

Rivkah huddled with the two Sentinels behind the rocks. She desperately wished that she had not left StarDrifter, that she was huddled in his arms rather than cold and terrified behind these rocks where she would surely die. StarDrifter's casual infidelities seemed laughably inconsequential in the face of imminent death. How would it feel to die with your throat hanging open?

Azhure knelt against the rocks, the Wolven drawn and ready to cast the first arrow. She peered as closely as she could into the thickening dusk; was that movement ahead of her? To her left? Her right?

"Curses!" she breathed as pale shapes flickered at the edge of her vision. "They have surrounded us!"

Suddenly one of the shapes ceased its circling and paced stiff-legged towards the rocks. It was the largest dog Azhure had ever seen, almost as big as one of Ogden and Veremund's donkeys. Its lips were drawn back into a snarl, great growls rumbling from its throat. As Azhure's fingers tightened about the Wolven, the hound's eyes, dark gold flecked with silver, fixed into hers, almost daring her to shoot.

Azhure took a deep breath, held it for a heartbeat, then loosed the arrow, notching another one almost as soon as the first had left the bow.

In the instant before the arrow struck, the Alaunt twisted and leaped, snatching the arrow out of the air in his teeth. Instantly the clamour of the other hounds stopped.

Azhure's hands suddenly slicked with sweat and the Wolven slipped fractionally in her grasp.

The Alaunt stalked closer, the arrow held between its jaws. Its eyes were still fixed on Azhure, and it growled threateningly.

Azhure's heart thudded painfully in her chest as the Alaunt suddenly reared its forepaws on the rock and stood for a moment. Then, amazingly, it dropped the arrow at Azhure's feet and began to grin happily.

"By the Stars," Rivkah croaked, "it's returning your arrow."

The hound gave a small yip of greeting, then heaved itself entirely over the rock and into the small space occupied by the two women and the Sentinels. It sank down on its stomach in the dirt, its head on its forepaws, its eyes fixed on Azhure.

Ogden and Veremund stared at the hound, stared at Azhure, then turned to stare at each other.

Azhure warily reached out a hand and touched the Alaunt on its massive forehead. It quivered and closed its eyes. She pulled her hand back, clenching her fingers to stop their sudden trembling.

"Arise," she said very quietly.

The hound rose to his feet, towering over Azhure as she squatted on the ground. She reached out again and rubbed her hand along the hound's shoulder. "Good dog," she said.

Later they all sat, quiet and introspective, about a fire. Azhure, Rivkah, Ogden, Veremund and three of the fifteen Alaunt crowded into the space between the rocks. The rest of the hounds lay curled into tight wedges in a pack outside the rocks. The two donkeys had wandered back to the rocks an hour or so previously, their eyes wide and uncertain, but the hounds had taken no notice of them, and finally the donkeys had let Ogden and Veremund soothe them and divest them of their packs.

Azhure studied the three Alaunt close by her. Their bodies were heavy but sleek and shaped for both speed and endurance. Their heads were square, massive, but finely shaped, their muzzles long and strong. Their coats were short and a uniform pale cream, darkening to gold about their paws and muzzles. The lead hound lay with his head in Azhure's lap.

Azhure raised her eyes to the two Sentinels. "These are WolfStar's hounds?" she asked.

Ogden paused, then he nodded briefly. "Yes. He bred them for their intelligence as well as their speed and strength, for their loyalty as for their reckless savagery. Their leader's name is Sicarius – the cunning assassin." He paused. "The two were parted only by death."

"WolfStar," Azhure said. "Why does his name keep returning to haunt me? First his bow, and now his hounds. What else of his will find its way into my possession?"

Ogden and Veremund watched her, wondering exactly the same thing. The bow might have been coincidence, but the hounds as well? No. That was design and plan, not anonymous chance.

"Who was WolfStar?" Azhure finally asked.

Veremund hesitated, then decided the bare facts would not hurt. "WolfStar SunSoar was the most powerful Enchanter the Icarii have ever known. Perhaps potentially far more powerful than Axis."

"The Icarii do not like to speak of him," Rivkah said from one side. She knew WolfStar's story, but to speak of WolfStar's misdeeds would need the permission of the Icarii.

"I will say only that WolfStar died young," Ogden said. "He was not yet one hundred."

"How?" Azhure asked, noting Ogden's hesitation over the word "died". "Why did he die so young?"

"He was assassinated, Azhure. By another member of the SunSoar family."

"Assassinated?" It was, Azhure thought, a delicate word for what must have been a foul deed.

"He was murdered by his brother," Veremund said bluntly, and the three Alaunt about the fire stirred uncomfortably, their dreams disturbed with dark memories. "Murdered in Assembly, before all the Icarii, a knife plunged into his heart and none, none, none of the Icarii moving to assist him. He died, alone and unloved, in a pool of blood in the centre of the speaker's circle of the ancient Assembly Chamber on the Island of Mist and Memory — with the entire Icarii nation looking on impassively."

Azhure's eyes filled with tears. WolfStar had been alone and unloved? She knew how that felt.

20

Arrival at Sigholt

The next morning the Alaunt were still there, Sicarius sleeping curled against Azhure's back. The other fourteen hounds sat in a precise circle about the rocks, facing outwards, their eyes staring into the distance.

"They are keeping guard," Veremund said as Azhure rose and saw them. "Even the Skraelings would keep away from such as these. You have won yourself some powerful and loyal companions, Azhure."

Azhure patted Sicarius on the head and fingered the Wolven. "Could they have simply come to the bow, Veremund? If the bow once belonged to WolfStar, was made by him, then perhaps they simply come to the person who carries the bow?"

Veremund raised his eyebrows at Ogden. The woman had a point. After all, the Alaunt were hunting hounds and their master had wielded the Wolven. And who knew what magic the bow itself contained?

"We will easily find out, Azhure," said Ogden. "Give the bow to Rivkah – but make sure Sicarius knows you hand it over willingly!"

"Rivkah, will you mind the Wolven for me?" Azhure asked formally, and handed Rivkah the bow.

Sicarius shifted his hindquarters on the ground a little, bored.

"Now, Azhure," Ogden said, "walk beyond the boulders, as if you are leaving us."

Azhure walked briskly away from the rocks. As one, the Alaunt rose from their positions and padded silently after her.

Ogden and Veremund looked at each other. No doubt. They had come to Azhure, not the Wolven.

They travelled south for a further week, then turned southwest, looking for the HoldHard Pass. The Urqhart Hills were still a purple smudge on the western horizon.

The travelling was relatively easy, although it remained bitterly cold and all four shivered within their thick cloaks. The women continued to ride the donkeys, which remained placidly uncomplaining about the extra weight. Neither woman had sturdy enough boots to cope with the rough pebbly surface of the WildDog Plains.

Ogden and Veremund's magical hampers continued to provide food. Each evening as they made camp, the hounds waited patiently in line until Ogden found time to riffle through his packs and toss them jöints of meat. But such tame food bored the Alaunt. Sometimes during the day, and often at night, groups of three or four of them would lope off into the distance, returning later with blood-stained muzzles.

In return for the food and the company, the hounds lent their warmth to the group, and the women and Sentinels became used to curling up for the night with a hound at their back. One morning Azhure awakened early enough to see that a group of five or six had even curled around the donkeys. The nights were frosty on the exposed plain.

Two days after they had turned south-west across the WildDog Plains the small group saw a band of horsemen approaching. There were perhaps ten or twelve of them, and they approached cautiously, obviously wary of the Alaunt.

Azhure reached for the Wolven as soon as she saw the horsemen in the distance, and notched an arrow.

"Can you see who they are?" she asked the Sentinels. "Are they Belial's men, or Borneheld's?"

Ogden and Veremund peered towards the horsemen, who had now spaced themselves out into a wide line, directly in front of the setting sun. The Alaunt whined, tensing, ready for a fight.

But as the men rode closer, the group of hounds suddenly relaxed and Sicarius gave a short, gruff bark of greeting. He knew these men.

The horsemen were much closer now, perhaps no more than fifty paces away, but their forms and faces were still in shadow.

"Well, the Alaunt like them," Veremund observed, his hand to his eyes, trying to shade them from the light. "But I'm still not sure that −"

He was cut off by a shout from the leading horseman who had kicked his rangy roan into a canter. "Ogden, Veremund? Old men? Is that you?"

"Why," Ogden beamed happily, "it's Arne!"

A knot of nervousness formed in Azhure's belly. Arne was one of the senior commanders from Axis' Axe-Wielders − a man who had been in Smyrton when she cracked Belial over the head in order to help Raum and Shra escape. Would he remember her? And, if so, what would he think? Hurriedly she unnotched the arrow, sliding it into her quiver and slinging the Wolven over her shoulder.

Arne pulled his gelding to a halt beside Veremund and slid down from the saddle, glancing apprehensively towards the hounds. "Ogden, Veremund, it is good to see you again." He shook their hands. "Icarii farflight scouts sent word that you would be travelling across the WildDog Plains." He looked back at the hounds. "Where did you find these hounds, Ogden?"

"Ah, well," Ogden began, "they found us, really, but that is a long story. Um, Arne, you might not remember Azhure. She comes from —"

"I remember Azhure well enough," Arne broke in, his face hardening. "I also remember how many weeks it took before Belial's headaches faded."

Azhure's face flamed and the thought that she still had to confront Belial only made her feel worse. What had she been thinking of to club him so badly?

Arne stared at her, then turned to the other woman.

"The Princess Rivkah," Veremund mumbled at his side.

Arne's demeanour changed instantly. His face became respectful, and he bowed deeply, a gesture courtly even in this incongruous setting. "Princess, I am your servant to order as you will."

Rivkah smiled and held out her hand. Arne took it and pressed his lips briefly to its back. Ogden and Veremund stared at the man. The dour and uncommunicative Arne was showing a side they had not suspected previously.

"And my Lord Axis?" Arne asked, only reluctantly relinquishing Rivkah's hand. "He is well?"

Rivkah nodded. She liked this man. He had a good heart and honest intentions. "He is well, Arne, and has embraced his heritage."

Relief crossed Arne's face. "The farflight scouts had told us so, but to hear it from the woman who gave him birth is more than I had hoped for."

He gave Azhure one more hard stare, noting the handsome bow across her back, then whistled his men closer.

"Our camp is nearby," he said. "And we have spare horses there. Tomorrow morning we will ride for Sigholt."

As they turned the last bend in the HoldHard Pass and Sigholt came into view, Ogden and Veremund reined in their donkeys, astonished.

"Changed, hasn't it?" Arne remarked.

Rivkah kneed her horse beside the Sentinels' donkeys. Once she had hated Sigholt as the symbol of her loathed marriage to Searlas, Duke of Ichtar and father of her eldest son, Borneheld. Even though StarDrifter had come to her there, even though Axis had been conceived on its roof, Rivkah had never wanted to come back.

But the Sigholt that stood less than half a league down the pass was a very different Sigholt to the one she had known.

"The farflight scouts said that Sigholt had come alive," Veremund said, his voice full of awe, "but I had not realised how much the Keep had regained its vigour."

Ogden sat silently, tears of joy streaming down his face.

The most obvious difference was the Lake. It stretched away into the distance, ruby tints reflecting in the occasional shaft of sunlight that broke through the clouds. Steam gently rose from its surface, wafting towards them as it was caught by the northerly wind. In the month or more since the spring had been unblocked, the Urqhart Hills immediately surrounding the Lake had come alive. Red and purple gorse flowered across the mid- to high slopes, while in the lower slopes close to the heat and life of the water, ferns and rockflowers were starting to spread. The stone Keep itself, once a uniform and depressing leaden hue, had lightened so that it was now a pale silvery and welcoming grey. Colourful pennants fluttered from its parapets. In the following months, as the greenery and the flowers spread across the nearby hills, Sigholt would become a paradise. Even now it was close to being the most beautiful place Rivkah had ever seen.

"The air is warm," Azhure remarked. Ever since Arne had found them Azhure had been uncharacteristically quiet. Rivkah smiled reassuringly at her, knowing she was nervous about meeting Belial again.

Arne glanced at Azhure. Two days ago he had challenged her to demonstrate her skill with the bow she carried – Arne had thought that perhaps it was simply a gaudy toy. But she had won his grudging respect with her skill. Even Belial, one of the best archers Arne had ever known, would find it hard to match her. Then, of course, there were the hounds. The Alaunt were a well-trained, well-disciplined pack, and answered instantly whenever Azhure spoke to them. Arne had worked with hunting dogs before, but he had never seen such as these. They followed close behind Azhure day after day, the leading dog, Sicarius, loping by her side.

"The water is hot," Arne finally said, turning to face Azhure, "and it warms the air. Gorgrael cannot touch us here with his icemen. Sigholt is a haven."

As they rode closer, the sparkling moat surrounding Sigholt became obvious.

"It looks so different," Rivkah said to Azhure as they rode up to the bridge. "*This* Sigholt lives and laughs."

"Stop," Arne ordered as they neared the bridge. "Ogden, Veremund, you go across first, then Princess Rivkah and Azhure."

Ogden and Veremund, smiling broadly, dismounted from their donkeys so they could step across the bridge personally.

"Welcome, Ogden. Welcome, Veremund," the bridge said, joy obvious in her melodious voice. "It is long since I felt your steps across my back."

Rivkah's and Azhure's eyes opened wide in surprise.

"The bridge lives, Princess," said Arne, "and she guards against all who are not true."

Ogden and Veremund prattled happily to the bridge as they crossed, then embraced Jack who waited in Sigholt's open gate for them. They greeted him cheerfully, but their faces fell as they heard Zeherah had not been refound.

"Princess." Arne motioned with his head towards the bridge. "You next."

Rivkah heeled her horse's flanks. Just before the horse stepped onto the bridge, the bridge spoke. "Are you true?"

"Yes, I am true," Rivkah said in a clear voice.

"Then cross, Princess Rivkah, and I will see if you speak the truth."

Rivkah urged her horse forward. What did the bridge mean?

When she was halfway across the bridge spoke again. "You were once Duchess of Ichtar, Princess Rivkah." The beautiful voice was now toneless.

Rivkah was suddenly all too aware of the waters rushing underneath the bridge. Huddled in the shadows of the gate of Sigholt she could see a group of men waiting for her. Ogden and Veremund, as the man beside them, had fearful expressions on their faces. "Yes," she whispered. "I was."

Her horse abruptly stopped and Rivkah could not make it move forward. Perspiration began to bead her forehead.

"You were not true to your husband, Rivkah. You were not true to the Duke of Ichtar, Searlas. You betrayed him with another."

Rivkah swallowed. "No," she finally forced out. "No, I was not true to Searlas." Somehow she could not lie to this bridge. "I betrayed him atop this very Keep."

There was silence as the bridge contemplated this. Then, shockingly, it laughed, a peal of sheer merriment. "Then you have my heart, Princess Rivkah, for I do not like the Dukes of Ichtar! You and I will be friends!"

Rivkah grinned weakly, and her horse moved forward once more. "Thank you, bridge," she said. "Thank you."

Watching from the far side Azhure breathed a sigh of relief. For a moment she had thought the bridge would reject Rivkah. She glanced at Arne, who nodded at her, then she kneed her horse forward.

"Are you true?" the bridge asked as she approached.

"Yes, I am true," Azhure answered confidently.

"Then cross, Azhure, and I will see if you speak the truth."

The bridge accepted Azhure almost as soon as her horse had stepped onto the red-veined silvery-grey masonry.

"You spoke the truth, Azhure. Welcome to my heart."

"Thank you, bridge," Azhure said, looking to where Rivkah had halted her horse just the other side, waiting for her so that they could enter Sigholt together.

But the bridge was not yet finished. "I have not felt your father's step for many a long year, Azhure. Where is he?"

Azhure stared, open-mouthed. Hagen had crossed this bridge?

"Er, he is dead," she finally managed to say.

"Ah," the bridge said sorrowfully. "I am sad. I loved your father, although many did not. We passed many a night deep in conversation."

Rivkah frowned at Azhure as she rode up to her. "What was that about?"

"I don't know, Rivkah. Perhaps the bridge confused me with someone else. Hagen never crossed this bridge."

As they kicked their horses forward, two men stepped out from the shadows of the fortified gateway. Azhure tensed. One was Belial, although the other man she did not know.

"Belial," she whispered.

But Belial spoke to Rivkah first. "Welcome to Sigholt, Princess. I am Belial, once lieutenant to your son in the Axe-Wielders, now commander of his base here in Sigholt." He smiled, his pleasant face relaxing under sandy hair, his hazel eyes crinkling at Rivkah. "Welcome home, Rivkah."

Rivkah greeted him warmly. Axis had told her so much about this man. "I can think of no better man to welcome me back to Sigholt than the man whose friendship has meant so much to my son. I am pleased and deeply honoured to meet you, Belial."

Belial inclined his head, then turned to Azhure.

"Azhure." He held out his hands. "Come down from your horse."

Azhure hesitated, then leaned down, placing her hands on Belial's shoulders, feeling his hands grasp her about the waist as she swung down from her horse.

Rather than letting her go once her feet were on the ground, Belial's hands tightened. "I should throw you in the moat for what you did to me," he said, his face expressionless. "I trusted you, yet you did not repay my trust well."

Azhure's entire body tensed, and her eyes glinted with tears of shame and regret. She could not say anything to this man she had treated so poorly.

Belial's eyes flickered over her face. He had thought her beautiful in Smyrton, but since then she seemed to have not only grown more mature, but to have gained an aura of wildness that made her even more fascinating. And now here she was standing before him in Sigholt. Could life get any better? He dropped his hands from her waist reluctantly.

"As much as you might deserve a ducking, Azhure, I will merely welcome you to Sigholt instead. We will discuss the issue of recompense later." Azhure managed a small smile.

"Magariz?" Belial said, beckoning to his friend. "May I introduce you to the Princess Rivkah and to Azhure?"

The man Azhure had noticed earlier now stepped forward. In late middle-age, his black hair thickly lined with silver, his limp and the raised scar running down his left cheek only accentuated his handsomeness and appeal.

As Belial had helped Azhure from her horse, so now Magariz held out his hands for Rivkah.

"Welcome, Princess," Magariz said quietly. "It has been a long time. We are both considerably greyer than when we last met, but at least we meet in happier circumstances."

Rivkah held out her hand for Magariz to kiss. "But I am the greyer, I see, my Lord Magariz."

"But just as beautiful," he grinned, raising his eyes from her hand.

"You know each other?" Azhure asked. "How?"

Rivkah laughed at the puzzlement on both Belial's and Azhure's faces. "You forget that I was a child of the Carlon court, Azhure. When I was growing up Magariz was a youthful page, waiting at high table."

She turned back to Magariz, who still had not let her hand go. "And now you are a commander, Magariz. It is more than the grey in our heads which tells me how many years have passed."

Magariz finally let Rivkah's hand go, stepping back a pace. "I grew heartily sick of waiting at tables, Princess. Sometime after your marriage to Searlas I persuaded my father to let me join the palace guard. After many years, Priam assigned me to Borneheld's service when he became Duke and eventually Borneheld gave me the command at Gorkenfort. There I mouldered for over ten years before the events of the past eight months propelled me into a greater adventure than I had ever dreamed." He shrugged a little. "Thirty years in so few sentences, Rivkah. But that is my life since last we spoke."

"And from Gorkenfort you joined Axis' cause," Rivkah said. "You always did make reckless choices, didn't you?"

Magariz's mouth twitched. "Some of my choices have been a little impetuous, Princess, but there is not one that I have regretted."

Rivkah smiled and she turned away slightly, loosening her cloak in the warm air of Sigholt. "I know so little of Borneheld, Magariz. You must spend some time with me, tell me of him."

Grave now, Magariz bowed slightly from the waist. "Anything, my Princess."

"And Faraday, the current Duchess of Ichtar," Rivkah went on. "I know so little of her. You must speak to me of her as well."

Azhure had a fixed and overly bright smile on her face. Well, thought Rivkah, she must accept that Axis will ride across Achar into Faraday's arms. She must accept that she has no future with Axis.

Then Rivkah gasped in utter delight as Reinald stepped forth. She hugged him fiercely. When she'd lived here as Duchess of Ichtar, Reinald had been one of her only friends.

Belial introduced Magariz to Azhure, then all were interrupted by the sound of barking, and they turned to watch the Alaunt hounds pacing solemnly across the bridge. The bridge barked at them and Sicarius barked gruffly back.

Belial turned to Azhure. "Where did these hounds come from?"

"They, ah, seem to belong to me, Belial. I hope you will not mind their presence. They are well trained and will cause no trouble. I will tell you their story once I have changed into some clean clothes."

Belial belatedly realised that he had kept the two women standing in the gateway for far too long, but, just as he was about to usher them into Sigholt, Jack stepped up. Jack had recognised the hounds instantly, and a look of understanding had passed between himself and Sicarius.

"You are Azhure?" Jack asked, and Belial hastened to introduce them.

Azhure shook the hand that Jack offered, and the Sentinel smiled at her genially, thinking he understood her. Unlike the other Sentinels, all of whom had hardly ever conversed with the Prophet who had recruited them, Jack knew the Prophet well and had been entrusted with many secrets.

But there were yet deeper secrets to the Prophecy, and Azhure was one of them.

21

Long Live the King!

Faraday's hopes were dying as fast as the man before her. She stood behind Judith as the Queen leaned over the prone form of her husband, trying to lend the woman the strength of her presence and friendship. Beside her stood Embeth, now Judith's senior lady-in-waiting. Faraday exchanged a glance with Embeth. Neither could do anything to ease Judith's grief.

Priam's bedchamber was quiet and lit only by a few tapers. Incense smouldered out of sight on a high shelf. On the other side of the bed Jayme, assisted as always by Moryson, stood quietly. The Brother-Leader was wearing his full ceremonial vestments of office to mark this sombre occasion. Behind Jayme stood Borneheld, and Faraday's eyes met his briefly before she looked away, disgusted at what she could see in their depths. To the rear of the ornate gold and pink chamber stood several servants and courtiers, uselessly weeping, and one or two helpless physicians.

Faraday looked back at the King. Three weeks ago to the day Priam, ordinarily so hale and hearty, had begun to show evidence of madness. For three days he strode down the corridors of the palace, seeing demons and sorcerers in every shadow. Judith and sundry servants had followed him, pleading with Priam to let the physicians see him, pleading with him to rest, sleep. Perhaps it was simply stress, overwork.

But Priam had continued to pace the corridors, scarcely ever sleeping, spittle caking his stubbly chin.

His *illness* was crazy, thought Faraday despairingly. She had spent most of the past few weeks with Judith, supporting her as much as she could. Forcing her to sleep when she would wander after Priam. Trying to reassure her. Trying.

The physicians pronounced that the King was suffering from a severe form of brain heat which caused madness as the King's noddle sizzled. "It has been building awhile," they suggested, "and has only now boiled to the surface." They applied icepack after icepack to the King's brow, and leeches to his limbs and groin to drain away excess hot blood. They even considered wrapping the King in brandy-soaked bandages and leaving him in a dark room – but they had discarded that idea. The last nobleman to be treated with that particular remedy had died after a careless servant dropped his candle onto the spirit-soaked bandages. Nothing they'd suggested had worked, and the physicians were now forced to admit that they could do little.

Everyone shook their heads and sorrowed. Carlon and the surrounding districts mourned Priam's decline. And amidst all this sorrow and public shaking of heads came the despicable, rumours. If Priam had considered an alliance with the Forbidden, then it was because his mind was already addled. If Priam so thoughtlessly berated Borneheld, it was because he no longer knew right from wrong, friend from foe.

Jayme had been quick to seize these rumours and make them his own – Faraday wondered if they had been his all along.

"He has been struck by a miasma of the Forbidden," Jayme had ventured, and many had listened. "Their evil presence has stretched right into the heart of Carlon to implant the noxious notion of an alliance with them into Priam's mind." He shook his head sorrowfully. "Now all can see how the Forbidden work, now all can see the wickedness of their actions. Has not the Seneschal been teaching this for many hundreds of years? Is this not why we drove the Forbidden from our fair land in the first instance?"

And with the rumours and the King's increasing madness, Faraday's hopes died. Borneheld would take the throne and throw all Achar's resources against Axis. Now the brothers would tear Achar apart in their hatred for each other, tear it apart until finally they stood sword to sword in the Chamber of the Moons. As the vision had foretold.

Faraday bowed her head, trying to rub away her tears.

Borneheld had stayed with Priam constantly, and all remarked on the devotion that he showed his uncle. Day after day Borneheld had followed Priam about the corridors, offering him comfort, and holding his chalice for him so that Priam could wet his throat whenever he became thirsty. And when Priam had finally collapsed into his bed, Borneheld had helped care for him. Holding his head as Priam drank from the chalice, wiping his lips as he lowered his uncle's head to the pillow.

Faraday did not believe the charade of devotion for an instant. In those hours when he was not at Priam's side, Borneheld whispered with Jayme or one of his advisers. Gilbert hung about their apartments like an evil shadow, and Moryson glided along the corridors, the hood of his robe pulled close about his face.

Solicitous during the day, at night Borneheld slept badly, tossing at Faraday's side, his hands gripping the sheets. He muttered in his dreams, but Faraday could not catch his words, and the one night she had awoken him to save him from his nightmares and offer him a drink of water, he had screamed and struck the goblet from her hands.

After that Borneheld slept in another room, saying Faraday no longer pleased him and her presence disturbed his sleep. Grateful for her empty bed, Faraday nevertheless wondered.

Judith leaned back, and Faraday gave her a fresh cloth.

"I thank you," Judith murmured, then leant back to her husband's dying.

Four days ago, when Faraday had sent Judith to snatch some sleep, she had sat by Priam's bedside and laid her hands on the man. She had reached for the power of the Mother so she could heal Priam as she had healed Axis.

But Faraday had reeled back from the King's prone form almost instantly. What she had felt underneath her hands had been no natural illness. Dark enchantments had writhed beneath the King's skin. For long minutes Faraday had sat shaking, waving away a servant's murmured concerns. *Enchantments*? But how? By whom?

She had no dearth of suspects for the murder of Priam. Borneheld, obviously, but the whole Brotherhood of the Seneschal would doubtless fight for the privilege of slipping a knife into Priam's back, and Faraday also wondered if some of the nobles thought they might have too much to lose if the King concluded an alliance with the Icarii and Avar.

And yet who among all those could wield dark enchantments? Faraday had *felt* the power, but she could not understand it. It was like and yet totally unlike what she had felt from Axis.

Priam was in the final grips of a murder, and a murder effected by enchantment.

Embeth put a hand on Faraday's arm, bringing the woman back into the present. Faraday nodded her thanks, and realised that Jayme had reached across the bed and touched Judith's hand.

"I am sorry, my Queen, but I must commence the Service soon. Priam, well, he has only a small amount of time left."

Judith took a great gulping breath, her fragile shoulders heaving, then nodded. "Begin, Brother-Leader."

Jayme began intoning the Service of Passage, the age-old service meant to ease the soul of the dying into the next world. The words were beautiful and comforting, exhorting not only the dying to meet his maker with joy and thankfulness, but exhorting all those who grieved to remember that on the other side of death Artor waited to receive Priam into His eternal care. It was the duty of the dying to make a good death, to remember his faults and his sins so that Artor would accept him into His care, and it was the duty of those witnessing the death to make sure that the dying made their death the best one possible.

Faraday watched Jayme carefully, trying to discern the slightest note of satisfaction in his voice, the faintest gleam of triumph in his eyes. But if Jayme felt any of these emotions, he hid them well.

"Priam," he asked very softly, resting his three middle fingers on the King's waxen forehead, "listen to me. You must bind yourself to Artor's care, but you must remember that He will only receive you into His care once you have confessed your faults, flaws and sins. Priam, confess your sins now, that Artor may receive you with love."

Priam's eyelids opened. His cracked lips moved soundlessly, and Jayme motioned to Borneheld for the chalice.

"Drink, my King," Jayme whispered, "drink so that you may confess your sins."

Faraday stared at the chalice for a moment, disturbed. She took a deep breath, trying to calm her stomach. The more she stared at the chalice, the more she realised that there was something evil, shadowed, about it. Dark letters hovered about its rim, and Faraday felt her marrow chill. *It* was the source of the dark enchantment that killed Priam!

Nonetheless, Priam seemed to have been revived by the sip of water. He started to mumble, and Judith's eyes filled with tears – he was remembering the early years of their marriage, when all had seemed so bright, so full of life, when they were still convinced that healthy children lay only a year or two into the future. Unusually for a court-arranged union, Judith and Priam had enjoyed a marriage filled with love, even when disappointment at their childlessness sometimes threatened to overwhelm them.

"Yes, yes," Jayme encouraged Priam, his eyes gleaming strangely, "confess all, confess all that Artor may receive you."

Faraday stared at Jayme. He and Borneheld had handled the chalice. How was it they stayed healthy and Priam sickened? She averted her eyes, but her gaze was instantly caught by Moryson. What was the man *doing*? He was standing behind Jayme and Borneheld, the hood of his robe pulled close, but Faraday could see his lips moving silently and his eyes riveted on the chalice.

As Faraday stared Moryson suddenly lifted his eyes to hers . . . and grinned.

Faraday shuddered. The man's eyes were as ice, and they bore relentlessly into her own.

"Faraday?" Embeth murmured at her side, and Faraday finally tore her eyes away from Moryson.

When next she looked Moryson had his eyes back on the King, his face a mask of sorrow.

A spasm crossed Priam's face, and his entire body convulsed. Judith gave a soft cry of distress and grasped Priam's hand as tightly as she could. A trickle of bloodied froth issued from Priam's gaping mouth, and Embeth leaned over and wiped it away. The King's eyes now stared sightlessly at the canopy of his bed and his breath came in great uneven gasps.

Judith's mouth trembled, but she whispered to her husband words of love and farewell.

Then Priam rallied, and reached out a quavering hand. He pulled Judith's head close to his mouth. He whispered into her ear. Faraday saw Judith's entire body stiffen in reaction.

Finally Judith sat back, her face impassive. Priam's head sank down onto the pillow, his fingers trailed down Judith's face one last time, and then he died.

There was silence. After Priam's incoherent madness of the past weeks, his end had been surprisingly peaceful.

Finally it was Moryson who spoke. "The King is dead," he said, and turned to Borneheld. "Long live the King."

A strange expression crossed Borneheld's face, then Jayme pulled the amethyst ring of office from Priam's finger and slipped it onto Borneheld's thick digit. "Long live the King," Jayme intoned. "King Borneheld."

Faraday, watching, experienced a feeling of unreality.

Borneheld's eyes, burning with naked triumph, met hers above the bed. "My Queen," he said.

Faraday slipped quietly into Judith's chambers. She had spent the past three hours helping Judith and Embeth lay Priam's body out. The passing of a King required formal ceremonies, prayers, rituals, and the washing and preparing of Priam's body to lie in state. As Priam's widow, Judith had overseen all of this, her fragile face calm, emotionless. Her demeanour, as always, gracious and regal. But Faraday had seen that Judith was close to collapse, and now wanted to make sure she was resting as comfortably as her grief would allow.

Judith sat on a sofa by the fire, Embeth's arm about her shoulder. Both women had glasses of brandy in their hands.

Embeth smiled wryly as Faraday sank down beside Judith. "There can be no better time to get slightly drunk," she said, "than in the hours just after your husband has died."

Faraday knew she must be remembering her own husband Ganelon's death.

Judith sniffed her tears back and put her glass down. Her porcelain skin was smudged and bruised under her eyes, evidence that she had not slept for many nights, and her golden hair was streaked and disordered. Poor Judith, Faraday thought, stroking the woman's hair back into some semblance of order. What will you do with your life now Priam is dead?

"Thank you, Faraday," Judith managed, then cleared her throat and said, her voice stronger, "Priam and I both thank you for your kindness and support over the past three weeks."

Faraday smiled, but did not say anything. She hoped that she could be as gracious if ever faced with a comparable loss.

They sat in silence for some time, then Judith stirred and took Faraday's hand.

"My dear, I hope you will forgive me for what I now say . . . but say it I must and, having seen you with Borneheld over the past weeks, I think I can trust you to hear it."

Faraday met Embeth's eyes over Judith's head.

Judith abruptly picked up her glass and swallowed the last of her brandy. "Priam told me to name Axis his heir," she said. "He did not want Borneheld to succeed him."

Faraday's breathing stilled. What good would that do Axis now?

"Artor save us!" Embeth whispered. "You cannot stand up in *Borneheld's* court and say that Priam named *Axis* his heir!"

Judith smiled bitterly and straightened her back. "I know, Embeth. I have no death wish. I believe Priam's death was planned the instant he announced in audience that he wanted to seek an alliance with Axis."

Faraday stared at Judith, but decided against saying anything about the chalice. She had no idea who had ensorcelled the chalice, and the knowledge that it *was* ensorcelled would only distress Judith. She took Judith's hand. "Why did Priam change his mind?"

"Over past months," Judith said, "Priam realised how mistaken he'd been never to accept Axis for the man he was — a brilliant war leader and a better prince than Borneheld ever would be." She hesitated, glancing at Embeth. "I have told you this because Embeth has told me something of your feelings for Axis and that she encouraged you to marry Borneheld when you were racked with doubts."

"And for that I can never apologise enough," said Embeth.

Faraday bowed her head and thought for a moment. When she raised her eyes again they were brilliant with power.

Judith and Embeth both gasped.

"Let me tell you something about myself and about Axis," she said, her voice as powerful as her eyes.

She talked for over an hour, Embeth shakily pouring the three of them more brandy when she was halfway through.

"Now that Borneheld is King, Axis is going to need all the help he can get," Faraday finished. "Will *you* help?"

Judith nodded her head, her eyes thoughtful. "Yes, I will, Faraday. It is what Priam would have wanted me to do . . . and it is what *I* want to do." She paused. "And I think I know someone who may tip the balance in Axis' favour."

Borneheld's coronation was held the day after Priam was laid to rest. Clouds of war hung over Achar, and in times such as these, haste was called for.

A public holiday was proclaimed, and colourful bunting hung out. Flags and pennants were hastily raised to honour the new King the next. A public feast would have been appropriate and appreciated, but there was no time to arrange it, so Borneheld simply ordered that barrels of wine and ale be available on every street corner so that the good citizens of Carlon could simply get drunk without the food.

While the Carlonites partied in the streets, the actual coronation took place in the Chamber of the Moons. The entire court was present, every man, woman or child of noble blood crowded into the Chamber. The ceremony itself was officiated over by Jayme, who lowered the heavy gold circlet of office onto Borneheld's head. As the trumpeting of horns far above them announced to the outside world that a new King had been crowned, Borneheld stood to receive the pledges of homage and fealty from his nobles.

Beside him, Faraday sat on a smaller throne, a simple coronet on her head, remembering the night she had first seen Axis in this chamber. One day, she prayed to the Mother, I will sit with Axis on this dais.

The most important nobles approached the dais first. Duke Roland of Aldeni and Earl Jorge of Avonsdale, both down from Jervois Landing for the coronation; Baron Ysgryff of Nor, his exotic features fixed in an expression of the sincerest loyalty as he pledged himself to Borneheld; Earl Burdel of Arcness, Borneheld's friend and ally and now, no doubt, expecting handsome rewards for having supported Borneheld in the past; Baron Greville of Tarantaise, as volubly sincere as Baron Ysgryff had been; and, finally among the higher nobles, the lords of the provinces, came Faraday's father, Earl Isend of Skarabost – now, Faraday noted with some dismay, taken up with a blowsy young noblewoman from Rhaetia who had rouged her nipples so heavily that they had stained the sheer material of her bodice.

After the nobles came sundry dignitaries and ambassadors. As the Corolean ambassador bowed low over his hand, Borneheld made a mental note to request the ambassador to come and see him at the first possible opportunity. Borneheld wanted to conclude a military alliance with the Coroleans as soon as he could.

Before the minor nobles could step forward to pay Borneheld homage, Judith, former Queen, and her lady-in-waiting, Lady Embeth of Tare, stepped forward.

Borneheld frowned, but Faraday inclined her head slightly.

"Yes?" Borneheld asked, as Judith rose from her curtsey. The woman, so confident in her graciousness, had always made him feel clumsy.

"Sire," Judith began, "please accept my congratulations on your coronation and my sincere hopes for a long and bountiful reign. I pledge myself to you as your most loyal subject and hope that you know that if you need anything at all, I shall be only too willing to provide it for you."

"Sire." Judith's voice changed slightly, and Borneheld suppressed a grimace. He knew that tone of voice. The bitch was going to ask him for something.

"Sire, I would ask a boon."

No doubt a substantial annuity or country estate, Borneheld sighed inwardly. Dowager Queens ever were a nuisance.

"I am still prostrate with grief, Sire, and I would ask that you excuse me from court. You have your own court, and a beautiful wife to grace it." Judith inclined her head to Faraday and smiled slightly. She turned back to Borneheld. "Embeth, the Lady of Tare, has offered me the sanctuary of her home. I would ask that you excuse both of us from court and from Carlon, so that we may retire to the quieter life of Tare."

Borneheld was surprised. What? No money? No jewels? Just permission to retire from court? Easy enough. He waved a magnanimous hand. "You have my permission, Judith."

"I leave this afternoon, if it pleases you, Sire," Judith said humbly. In truth, she and Embeth had their carriages waiting outside.

"Then I wish you well, Judith, Embeth. Perhaps I will visit one day. Once the Forbidden have been put in their place, of course."

"I will look forward to it with pleasure, Sire," Judith said sweetly.

She curtsied deeply again, caught Faraday's eye for an instant, then she and Embeth swiftly left the Chamber of the Moons.

Faraday stared after them sadly. She wished she rode with them. They had gone, not only to recuperate, but also to wait for Axis. If Axis was alive and if he led an army against Borneheld, there was every likelihood that he would pass by Tare. And if he did, then there waited Judith to inform both Axis and all who would listen that Priam had named Axis his rightful heir. Faraday smiled to herself. Judith hoped to have another, equally substantial surprise waiting for Axis as well.

22

Azhure's Dilemma

Azhure lay under the light wraps and listened to Rivkah breathe. The women had shared an apartment since their arrival in Sigholt six weeks previously, and their friendship had deepened and broadened since their time in Sigholt.

For Azhure the past six weeks had been the happiest of her life. She had enjoyed her time in Talon Spike, and revelled in her acceptance by the Icarii, but she had found her true niche here in Sigholt. Belial, astounded by her skill with the Wolven and impressed by her determination to be useful, had given her a squad of thirty-six archers to train.

To his surprise and to the astonishment of everyone else, Azhure had proved a natural leader. The squad quickly became the most disciplined, ordered and happy in Sigholt, and, to Belial and Magariz's constant amazement, none of her thirty-six men complained about being put under the command of a woman. Life in a garrison filled with three thousand men and exactly two women could have been awkward, but Azhure was no prude and, despite her good looks, within a week most of the men had simply accepted her for her abilities and seemed not to notice her sex overmuch. She was more noted for her skill at archery and the constant shadows of three or more of the Alaunt hounds at her heels.

But Belial had not remained impervious to Azhure's femininity, and therein lay Azhure's dilemma. She sighed and carefully slid out of bed. She waited for her stomach to settle, then swiftly dressed in a pair of man's breeches, riding boots and a light shirt. She snatched a jacket as she slipped quietly from the room. Sicarius, who slept at the foot of the bed, pushed out in front of her.

As the door closed behind Azhure, Rivkah opened her eyes and wondered when the woman would confide in her.

Azhure hurried down the stairs of the Keep, nodded to the guard at the main entrance, and walked briskly across the main courtyard towards the stables. This was the time of day when Azhure loved to ride, before dawn, when the day was fresh and young, and her best thinking could be done without the distractions of the bustling Sigholt community about her. Two of the other Alaunt hounds joined her, but she waved the rest back. She did not want the entire pack to disturb her thoughts this morning.

Azhure walked down to Belaguez's stall, whistling as she approached. Much to Belial and Magariz's horror she had started to ride the stallion several weeks ago. Belial, knowing how difficult the stallion was to control, could not believe that Azhure would manage to stay on more than five minutes. But Belaguez had responded to something in the woman, and although he sometimes pulled too hard, he otherwise behaved himself for her. Watching from the edges of the courtyard the first time Azhure had put the stallion through his paces, Belial had looked at Magariz, and then simply shrugged. Well, someone had to exercise the horse, and if Azhure could manage, then she could have the job.

Azhure rubbed a brush over the grey stallion's coat, then slipped a light saddle on his back. She cinched the girth tightly, waiting for the horse to blow himself out, then tightened the girth one more notch. The bridle took only an instant to buckle, and then Azhure opened the stall door and led Belaguez out into the dark courtyard. The three Alaunt were waiting patiently by the gateway to the Keep, and Azhure swung into the saddle.

She nodded to the three guards on sentry-duty – they were used to her early morning rides – and then greeted the bridge cheerfully.

Once across, Azhure touched her heels lightly to the stallion's flanks and they were off, racing the sun to see which could top the crest of the Urqhart Hills first.

The view from the peak was superb. Azhure could see in a complete circle for many leagues. Directly below them stood Sigholt, gleaming in the pre-dawn light, the Lake steaming gently beyond. Azhure slid from the horse's back and sat on a nearby rock to watch the sun rise over the far distant Avarinheim. At the precise moment the sun crested the distant forest Azhure could almost have sworn the top of the forest canopy waved at her. But Azhure did not fool herself. The Avarinheim and the Avar were too concerned with their own problems to worry much about her. Besides, both Avarinheim and Avar waited for Faraday, no-one else.

Azhure looked back down at the Keep, preoccupied with Belial. She and Belial had soon overcome their initial awkwardness on her arrival, and he had made it plain he harboured no ill feelings towards her rather savage assault on his person in Smyrton.

"You can work your guilt off by proving your worth here," Belial had said, and that was exactly what Azhure had set out to do, working herself and her squad of archers to the best of her ability. She had seen the appreciation in Belial's eyes and basked in his words of praise. She enjoyed his company and his friendship. Belial was a large part of the reason why these last six weeks had been so good.

But, over the past ten days or so, Belial had indicated he wanted to develop their relationship to a more intimate level.

Last night he had come upon her in the stable as she groomed Belaguez, and had laughingly seized and kissed her. What had at first simply been a light-hearted kiss had deepened until Azhure had pulled back, afraid not of Belial, but of her own enjoyment. He had asked her, then, into his bed and into his life. But Azhure's eyes had filled with tears and Belial had been instantly contrite. Reassuring him, Azhure had kissed him gently, asking for a night to think.

And, oh, by the heavens, how tempting it would be to accept such a proposal! Azhure was sure she could develop a loving for Belial. He would be a man with whom she could easily spend a lifetime. And he loved her. That was a remarkable experience for Azhure, for, apart from Rivkah, Azhure had never before been loved. The entire village of Smyrton, as Hagen, had regarded her with disdain for her Nors features and beauty, and for her temper and independent spirit. The young men of the village had sought only the use of her body, and when she had consistently refused their attentions, they had spread rumours of her willing cooperation.

On all counts, Belial's obvious regard and love presented Azhure with every reason to accept his proposal. But there were complications. She loved Axis, yet that alone would not stop her from accepting Belial's proposal. Azhure well knew that Axis planned and hungered for the day when he would be by Faraday's side again. She harboured no childish visions about Axis asking for her hand in marriage. Azhure had already seen the disastrous effects of an attempted marriage between an Icarii Enchanter and a human woman, and Azhure knew, *knew*, that a life with Axis was denied her.

In that case, why not leap for the life that Belial offered her?

Azhure's hands fluttered over her stomach. Because she was pregnant with Axis' child, and that changed everything. She remembered that on the night she had fled Smyrton she'd dreamed that one day she would find a hero to father her children, and . . . well . . . now she had her wish. And though Belial might well accept Axis' child, Azhure simply could *not* go to his bed not only loving another man, but bearing his child as well. Besides, Axis had grown to maturity never knowing his own father, always doubting that he loved him, and it would tear him apart to know that a child of his would suffer a similar fate.

Azhure could not deny Axis his child.

What should she do?

Explain to Belial. Confide in him. Belial deserved to know. Then? Wait for Axis. Axis would surely return to Sigholt shortly.

Beyond that Azhure did not want to think. She was terrified that Axis might take the child from her completely.

"Never," Azhure muttered. "No-one will take this child from me." She would not deny *her* child its mother. Her eyes filled with tears. Azhure had loved her mother deeply, had pined whenever she could not see her, whenever she could not hear her mother's footfall or hear her sweet voice as she cleaned the house or tended the garden and poultry. Azhure had believed that her mother was the most beautiful woman in existence. Her desertion had scarred Azhure irreparably — scarred her with a guilt that constantly gnawed at her. Had she not loved her mother well enough? Had her mother thought her a bad daughter?

"Why?" Azhure whispered, "why did you not take me with you, Mama? I loved you, Mama, I *loved* you!"

Of all her sins, Azhure constantly berated herself that she could not remember her mother's name; that single loss had festered at Azhure's conscience day and night for more than twenty years. She struggled, fought through sleepless nights. As a growing girl Azhure had once asked Hagen what her mother's name had been, but Hagen had lost his temper in a frightening display of anger and had badly beaten Azhure, and the girl had never asked from that day forth. Not only her mother, but her mother's name was lost to her. Azhure took a deep breath. She would be there for *her* baby, and *her* baby would never have occasion to forget Azhure's name.

Her mind drifted, wondering what it would feel like to hold her baby for the first time, what it would feel like to have a child love and trust her and come to her for comfort and laughter. Axis' child would surely be wondrous. She smiled. Would it be golden-haired like Axis? Or would it inherit her dark hair and pale skin? How Icarii would it be, and how human?

She looked about her, and quickly realised that the sun was already well above the horizon. If she did not hurry, the entire garrison might come searching for her. Azhure shot to her feet and grabbed Belaguez's reins, making the horse toss his head in alarm.

"Damn," Azhure muttered feelingly as she mounted the restless stallion. He would have to forgo his run down HoldHard Pass this morning. Was Belial already waiting for her in the stable?

He was.

Belial smiled at Azhure and took the stallion's reins from her. Azhure busied herself with unsaddling Belaguez.

As she undid the girth, Belial stepped up behind her and touched the back of her neck with his fingers. "Azhure, I hope you did not misunderstand me last night. I meant marriage, not simply a casual affair. I do not want you simply for a night, but for my life."

"I know," Azhure whispered, then closed her eyes as he gently kissed her neck, then her cheek, and then slipped his arms about her. He would make a good father for my children, thought Azhure. My dreams of heroes were so childish. What woman could ask for anything more than a good, solid man to support her?

"And your answer?" he said, his mouth in her hair now.

"Belial," she took his hands where they rested against her waist and slid them gently over her stomach. "Belial, I am pregnant. I cannot accept."

She felt his breathing falter and closed her eyes as she felt his pain. He did not deserve this.

"Axis," he said woodenly.

Azhure hesitated, then nodded. "Yes."

"Do you love him?"

"Yes," she said, and at her answer Belial tore himself away from her and thumped the stable wall in frustration and anger. Belaguez jumped sideways, startled, his ears laid back along his skull.

"Damn him," Belial seethed. "I have never, *never*, envied him his women until now!" He turned to face Azhure again. "Azhure, I love you. I want you whether you are pregnant or not. Whether you love Axis or not. You *know* that you have no life with him! You *know* that we could build a good life together!" Why couldn't Axis have left her alone? Had the man no conscience? No self control? What of Faraday?

Azhure started to cry silently. "Belial. You must know more than anyone how it would hurt Axis to know that a child of his would be raised without true knowledge of its parentage. Do I know that I have no future with him? Yes, I do, Belial. But until Axis returns and the child is born I can make no decisions. None."

Belial looked away again, his eyes dull now. "When?"

"Early Raven-month next year. The child was conceived at Beltide. The first day of Flower-month." She looked down at her hands. "It was just that once."

Belial laughed sourly. "Once? That was all he needed?"

Azhure nodded, knowing that Belial was angry at Axis rather than at her. She wiped away some of her tears.

Belial shook his head in disbelief. "Axis should have bastards littered across half of Achar if once was all he needed to get a woman with his child. Why you, Azhure? Why you?"

He reached out and cradled Azhure against his body, certain that this would be the last time he held her. He could not compete with Axis. "Azhure, if you had not been pregnant, would you have come to me?"

Azhure did not hesitate. "Yes, I would have been honoured to do so."

For a long time they stood there quietly in the stable, listening to Sigholt wake up about them.

Rivkah had been up an hour when Azhure came back to change. Rivkah knew immediately she saw her that something was very wrong.

"Azhure? What is it?"

Azhure could say nothing as tears streamed down her face, and Rivkah hurried across the room and folded her in her arms. She hugged the younger woman and rocked her a little.

"Azhure, I know that you are pregnant." She smiled, trying to cheer Azhure up. "This will be my first grandchild."

"Belial asked me to marry him last night, and I cannot. Not carrying Axis' child."

"Ah." Rivkah began to see. Azhure had wanted to walk away from the inevitable pain of Axis. Belial would have provided the perfect escape for her. But Azhure had not walked far enough nor quickly enough. And Axis was not likely to let a child of his go, especially if it was an Enchanter.

Rivkah led Azhure to the bed and held her while the woman cried herself out. Like Belial, Rivkah wondered at the fact that Axis had left no children behind him to this day, despite a string of lovers. Azhure's child would be his first.

Unlike Belial, Rivkah knew the reason why. Male Enchanters – indeed, Icarii birdmen generally – found it difficult to father children. And once they had managed it with one woman, they were as reluctant to let that woman go as they were to let the child go. In fact, Icarii often did not formally marry until the couple were expecting their first child – and sometimes a marriage would never take place if a child was not conceived. The couple would simply separate and reform partnerships with other people. A large part of the reason StarDrifter had been so fascinated with Rivkah, a large part of his love for her, had been her ability to bear him children. Now she was too old for a pregnancy, and StarDrifter still had the majority of his life to find another woman to bear him more children.

Rivkah rocked Azhure in her arms. After only one night, Azhure had fallen pregnant to Axis. No matter what the bond between Axis and Faraday, Azhure's simple fecundity would weld him tightly to her. Had Azhure left it too late to walk? Yes. Azhure could run as far as she liked now, but Axis would hunt her down. He would be unable to help himself.

23

The Enchantress' Ring

They sat in a flat-bottomed boat in the centre of a vast violet lake. Above them soared a massive domed roof of multifaceted crystals.

The Ferryman's eyes reflected the violet of the lake. "Your mother won for you the right to ask me for assistance. You ask to be taught. I will do that. But I have a condition."

"What?" Axis' voice was wary. Both StarDrifter and Rivkah had warned him that the Ferryman was a cunning bargainer – and one who spoke in riddles.

"I will teach you whatever you ask. But of you I will ask one thing. Whatever I teach you is for your use and the use of your issue only. When you return to the OverWorld, you will not teach StarDrifter, or any other Icarji Enchanter, what you have learned down here. My teaching is for you and your children only. Do you agree?"

"Why?"

The Ferryman's eyes glinted. "My purpose is not your concern. Do you agree? Or would you like me to return you to the OverWorld?"

"Agreed. I will teach none but my children."

"Good. What do you wish to know?"

"Your name."

"My name was once Orr, and you may call me that. What next?"

Axis looked about him. The massive lake was completely deserted except for the boat they sat in, and Axis had seen no-one else in the waterways they had travelled. "Where are the other Charonites?"

"*I* am the Charonites, Axis SunSoar. Not simply the last one left alive, but I am myself the complete race. We all reside in here." Orr tapped himself on the chest.

Axis looked at him strangely, but decided to let it pass. "Orr, what are the waterways?"

Orr actually chuckled, surprising Axis. "The waterways are far less mysterious than most suppose. It is simply that they are hidden so far from sight and so deep in memory, that whenever anyone from the OverWorld thinks of them, they think of them in shadows of mystery."

"Then tell me."

"You are impatient, Axis. That is your father in you."

Axis had already learned that Orr did not think very much of StarDrifter. "Don't waste my time in riddles, Orr."

Orr sighed and meticulously adjusted his ruby-red cloak. "You have learned of the Star Dance?"

"Yes. I hear it about me every moment I am awake, and at night it rustles through my dreams."

"Axis, as you know the Icarii Enchanters use music to mirror the patterns of the Star Dance. The waterways do the same thing, except the pattern is laid down in a physical form. To travel the waterways is literally to move through the patterns of the particular 'Song' you wish."

"So for each Song there is a corresponding waterway?"

"Yes," the Ferryman said, a little hesitantly.

"As an Enchanter I have learned Songs, melodies, each with a specific purpose. I use each Song to manipulate the power of the Star Dance, the Songs serve as a conduit to weave the power of the Star Dance to my particular purpose."

"Yes, yes. All know that."

"But the waterways act as a different conduit for the power of the Star Dance? Instead of singing a Song, I simply travel the particular waterway that suits my purpose? Each of the waterways has its own purpose?"

"Yes. The waterways are just another way of manipulating the power of the Star Dance. Icarii Enchanters use music. The Charonites travel a particular waterway. It is a, ah, slightly more cumbersome way."

"In Talon Spike StarDrifter and MorningStar taught me all the Songs they knew. It is a finite number," said Axis.

Orr's great violet eyes sparkled. "A finite number? Really? How many?"

"Perhaps a thousand. It is what I find most restricting. If I have a purpose but no Song to suit, I cannot use my powers."

"They only know about a thousand Songs?" Orr said, his mouth twitching. "Have they forgotten so much?"

Axis leaned forward, his excitement growing. He *had* been right to come down here. "How many do you know?" he asked, his voice tight. "How many waterways do you have?"

Orr fought to control his humour. "Let me answer that by asking you another question, boy. Did StarDrifter teach you how to use your ring?"

Axis frowned and looked at the ring on the middle finger of his right hand. Made of red gold and encrusted with diamond chips in star patterns, it was the SunSoar ring. Each House only had one ring, passed down through the generations, and StarDrifter had been happy to let Axis wear it.

"It is simply a symbol of my status as an Enchanter," Axis said finally. Use it? What for? "The senior Enchanters of each House wear them. It has no use . . . does it?"

Orr covered his face with his hands and rocked back and forth with silent merriment. Axis frowned in exasperation. What had he said now?

"My dear young man," Orr said finally, patting Axis affectionately on the knee. "My dear young man. I had not realised that the Icarii Enchanters had forgotten so much, had slipped so deep into ineptitude. How can they still call themselves Enchanters?"

Axis almost shouted in his impatience. "*What is it?*"

"Axis," Orr said, "there is almost no limit to the Songs you can sing, just as there is almost no limit to the waterways you can travel. You can wield the power of the Stars virtually any way you wish. How is it that the Icarii have forgotten this? Look at your ring."

Axis dropped his eyes.

"Is the pattern uniform?" Orr asked.

"No. The same pattern never seems to be repeated."

"Quite. Now, think of a Song you know, think of the music, and look again at the ring."

Axis thought of the Song of Harmony. As the music ran through his head, his eyes widened. The pattern of the stars on his ring had shifted to match the Song.

"Now, Axis," Orr whispered, "think of a purpose for which you have no Song. Something simple. I do not want you to blow us out of the water. Think of the purpose, and then look at the ring."

Axis thought, and the colour of the Ferryman's cloak caught his eye. A Song to change the colour of Orr's cloak to silvery grey, he thought to himself, then glanced at the ring.

The pattern of the stars on his ring had shifted again – into a configuration that he did not know. He translated the pattern the ring showed him into a melody in his mind and instantly the Ferryman's cloak altered colour from ruby red into silvery grey.

Orr smiled. "Such a simple thing, eh? Yet the Icarii Enchanters have forgotten how to use their rings. The number of Songs that can be sung are limited only by the number of purposes you have."

"Do you mean," Axis said, hardly believing it could be this simple, "that all I have to do is to think of the purpose, watch the ring show me the pattern of the melody, and then I have the Song for the purpose?"

Orr nodded. "In the same way I use the waterways. There are relatively few physical waterways. If I have a purpose, or a place to go for which there is not a physical waterway, I simply think of the purpose, and the waterway is created."

"Can I use the power of the Star Dance for any purpose?"

"No. You can't. Certainly there is a Song for most purposes, and all you need to do to learn the Song is to watch the patterns that the ring forms for you. But some Songs, some melodies, would be too dangerous for you. They would allow too much of the power of the Star Dance through – and you would die. A great deal of your learning as you grow in power, Axis SunSoar, is going to be knowing what patterns, what Songs, are too dangerous for you to attempt to use. That is why I asked you to think of a simple purpose. Generally, the more complex the purpose, the more you need to do, and the more power of the Star Dance you will be required to manipulate through Song. Having learned to use your ring, Axis, you must be very, very careful. Otherwise you will die as you attempt to use it."

Axis looked at the ring with new-found respect. For what purposes would the ring show him Songs that were too dangerous to use?

"You will learn, Axis," Orr said. "You may scorch yourself now and again, but you will learn. There *are* purposes for which no Song exists. Only a few, and they are mostly to do with healing. Rarely will you be able to use the music of the Star Dance to heal. Strange, because you can manipulate the Star Dance to recreate the dying, but a simple cut or bruise? At that the Star Dance baulks. I do not know why."

"For what you have told me I thank you, Orr," Axis said finally. "It is a great gift you have given me."

Orr inclined his head. "And you have given me a gift in return, Axis SunSoar. I had not realised to what depths of stupidity the Icarii had sunk, but your revelations have been most informative. Forgotten how to use their rings, indeed!"

"Orr. MorningStar has told me some disturbing news," Axis said, cutting through the Ferryman's laughter.

"What is it?"

"She believes I was taught many Songs as a baby. She tells me no Enchanter knows a Song intuitively, yet I already knew many before I began training with her and StarDrifter."

"She is right. You did not have that ring as a baby?"

"No. I only received it some eight months ago."

"An Enchanter needs a ring, or someone else of their family, to teach him or her what Songs to sing. What were the Songs you already knew?"

"The Song of Recreation, and the Song of Recall."

"Both are powerful and complex Songs!"

"Yes. Orr, is there another SunSoar Enchanter about? StarDrifter believes the same Enchanter has taught Gorgrael."

Orr hissed in surprise. "I had never wondered who taught Gorgrael. It was remiss of me."

"And Gorgrael uses the Dark Music of the Stars," said Axis. "So whoever taught him knows how to use that music as well?"

Orr nodded, obviously troubled.

"Orr, can I use the Dark Music with this ring?"

"No. The rings are only designed to draw on the power of the Star Dance itself. Gorgrael has no ring in any case, and what Icarii Enchanter knows the use of the Dark Music? None that I know of. Axis, your words trouble me. I will have to think on them further."

After a long while Axis spoke again. "Orr. I have seen some of Gorgrael's creatures fade from view. They seem to be able to use their magic to move through space, perhaps time. Can I do that?"

Orr nodded. "Obviously they use the Dark Music to do that, and that you cannot touch. But it is possible for you to travel across vast distances in a fraction of a heartbeat using your ring. Nevertheless, there are limits," he said quickly as he saw excitement on Axis' face. "Although you can travel *from* anywhere, there are only a few sites you can travel *to*."

"What do you mean?"

The Ferryman's fingers tapped the side of the boat. "Only certain sites in Tencendor can pull you to them. If you try to use the Song of Movement to travel to some other place, you will simply disintegrate into thin air. *Do I make myself clear?*"

"Yes. What sites can pull me to them?"

"Sites with enough inherent magic to act as beacons, as it were, for the Song of Movement. The magical Keeps – Sigholt, the Silent Woman Keep, Spiredore –"

"Spiredore?"

"What you know as the Tower of the Seneschal. Yes," Orr said wryly, noting the stunned look on Axis' face, "the Seneschal has taken up residence in one of the ancient and certainly the most magical of the Keeps of Tencendor. But be wary of trying to use that as a base for travel, Axis, because Spiredore's magic currently lies slumbering under the weight of the Seneschal's lies. Until it is awakened, like Sigholt has recently been, then you cannot use it."

"I understand. Are there any other sites?"

"Yes. The Earth Tree now that she sings. The Star Gate –"

"I have heard of the Star Gate," Axis broke in, "but I have not seen it."

"Be patient," Orr snapped. "I will take you there eventually. The Island of Mist and Memory is another, but, like Spiredore, its Temple needs to be relit before you can use it."

"So, when you have finished teaching me, all I have to do to travel to Sigholt is to think of the Keep, note the pattern of stars on my ring, and sing the melody it depicts?"

Orr nodded. "Yes. That is all. But remember, Axis, only those sites that I have mentioned – and only those among them that are currently awake – are strong enough to pull you towards them. Try the Song of Movement with any other site and you will die."

Sobered, Axis studied his ring. In only a few minutes he had learned more from the Ferryman than he had learned in months from StarDrifter.

Orr stared at the water, a strange urge building in him. He had been waiting a very long time for this. So this was the man? He trailed his fingers in the violet water, then abruptly snatched something from beneath the water's surface.

Axis jumped. "What?" he began, then the Ferryman held his dripping hand palm up for Axis' inspection.

Lying in the very centre of Orr's palm was the most exquisite ring Axis had ever seen. It was an Enchanter's ring, he could see that at once, but unlike his or any other. The entire ring appeared to be crafted from sapphire, although the deep blue was far more translucent than any sapphire Axis had ever seen. On Axis' ring, as on the others he had seen, the stars were represented by tiny diamond chips embedded into the ring's surface. But, as he picked this ring up, Axis saw that golden stars actually danced and weaved from *within* this ring. It was a tiny ring, obviously crafted for a woman's finger.

"It is very beautiful," he whispered.

"Yes," Orr replied. "It is. Axis, this is the original ring from which all other Enchanter rings were copied. It first appeared in the custody of the original Enchantress, the common ancestor and mother of both the Icarii and Charonite races who first discovered how to use the power of the Stars. She lived some fifteen thousand years ago. A very long time." He paused. "I do not know how she came by it."

"She did not make it herself?" Axis asked, unable to tear his eyes away from the beauty of the ring.

"No. She was merely its custodian. The ring seeks its true owner. It *will* come home, but only when the Circle is complete."

Axis glanced up. "The Circle?"

The Ferryman's face closed over, and Axis understood that this was one mystery he was not yet prepared to divulge.

"And you have kept it since she died?" tried Axis.

"No. When the Enchantress died, she passed custody of the ring to the Icarii. They kept it and revered it for many thousands of years. It was their most precious relic."

"Then how did you come to get it?"

"It was brought to us by one of the Enchanter-Talons, some four thousand years ago, just before he died. His name was WolfStar SunSoar."

WolfStar's name again. "Why did he give it to you?"

"He said that patterns were altering. WolfStar was powerful, and promised far more great power. He died an untimely death – which in itself was not too unfortunate. I believe that he would have led the Icarii to disaster with his strange ideas and experiments. But that is neither here nor there. WolfStar handed it to me for safe-keeping. He told me that I would know to whom to pass it. I feel that person is you."

"What am I supposed to do with it? Can I use it?"

"No. You cannot. The Enchantress' ring does not work in the same manner as the ring you now wear – not even the Enchantress understood its full mysteries. All WolfStar told me was that I would know who to give it to, and that when I handed it over, I was to tell that person the same thing."

"What? What do you mean?"

"That you, in time, will also know who to hand the ring to. Believe me in this, Axis. The feeling will be overwhelming. You *will* know when and to whom the Enchantress' ring must be handed. Until then you must keep the ring safe. Do not show it to anyone. Understand?"

"Yes. I understand. I will keep it safe," Axis reluctantly slid the ring into a small pocket, "and I will show it to no-one."

Who would the Enchantress' Ring pick? Who would complete this mysterious circle?

24

The Patrol

"**Y**our squads do well, Azhure," Belial remarked, standing at the window of the map-room and watching the bands of mounted archers at practice. "You have done remarkable work with them."

Azhure accepted the compliment. Belial had given her a further two squads to train four weeks previously and Azhure had turned her three squads of mounted archers into a mobile and deadly force that would complement any army. Although none of the archers came close to demonstrating Azhure's level of ability, they had all increased their skill twofold. There was not an archer in Achar who could better them now, Belial mused, as he watched them practise hitting moving targets while at the gallop.

His eyes met Azhure's and they moved back to where Magariz and Arne sat at the table in the centre of the room. In the five weeks since Azhure had told Belial of her pregnancy they had overcome their initial awkwardness and established an easy, friendly relationship of mutual respect. Belial buried his feelings for Azhure as deep as he could.

All four in the room were garbed similarly in simple grey tunics over white breeches, each with the blazing blood-red sun on their left breasts. Azhure had argued persistently that the force in Sigholt would have to wear a common uniform, emblemised so that all would know for whom they fought.

"We are ready to fight, Belial," Azhure said as they sat down. "*I* am ready to fight. Do not think that I'm going to stay at home and knit. Use me, use my command."

Belial caught Magariz's eye. Azhure had a familiar determined tone in her voice, but neither man felt comfortable using a woman in battle. Arne studied the flecks on the ceiling of the chamber. If the woman could fight, then he saw no reason why she shouldn't be allowed to do so.

"When the Icarii Strike Force arrives," Azhure pointed out, "you will see that *they* allow their women to fight. Axis has no qualms about using me."

"That was before you, ah, um . . ." Belial's voice drifted into an awkward silence.

Azhure laughed. All in the room knew she was pregnant and that Axis was the father. "Before I fell pregnant? Well, maybe so. But my pregnancy has not stopped me thus far, has it? My sickness has gone now and I feel fitter, stronger than I ever have before. And see," she pressed her hands against her belly. "Still flat. Rivkah says that Icarii babes are small, that I won't grow too large. So, the fact is, I refuse to stay home. Until I grow too cumbersome to ride, I will be there, leading my command. Why give me three squads of archers? Do you want me to command them from my couch?"

Belial laughed and raised his hands in surrender. "All right, Azhure, if there is action and I think your command would be useful then it – and you – will be used. But," his tone and eyes became serious, "I will not allow you to ride if I think you will prove a risk to yourself, to your baby, or to your command. Do I make myself clear?"

Azhure wiped the smile from her face. "Perfectly, Commander."

"Well then," Belial said briskly. "Shall we get down to business? Magariz. What news of the Skraelings?"

"Not enough to ease my mind, Belial." Magariz looked tired and drawn, and the scar on his cheek was even more prominent than usual. "We know the Skraelings run through most of Ichtar and that they are slowly moving south – our patrols are now encountering small numbers of them in the hills below Sigholt. But how many all told? And where do they gather? I don't know. All I do know is that we're only weeks away from autumn and Gorgrael has had months in which to build his forces. He must surely be massing for an attack . . . somewhere."

Belial studied the map before him. "Their most direct route into Achar is past Jervois Landing."

"What about the WildDog Plains?" Arne queried. "That route would give them straight run through to Skarabost."

Belial leaned back and looked at Arne. "We'll have to plan for that eventuality, but I don't think Gorgrael will send his main force that way. The River Nordra is a natural barrier between the WildDog Plains and Skarabost. Remember how the River Andakilsa funnelled them through the Gorken Pass."

"Is there any chance they can isolate us from our supply routes, Belial?" Azhure largely had responsibility for the garrison's stores.

Belial started to say "No", then looked at the map again. "If they *do* push down the WildDog Plains they could cut off HoldHard Pass."

"If, if, if." Magariz's voice was tight with strain. "Always *if*. Must we sit here and wait for their first move?"

"There isn't much else we *can* do, Magariz," Belial replied shortly. "Our force is currently too small to scout any further than the southern and eastern Urqhart Hills. And Axis . . ."

There was silence. When *would* Axis get back? Azhure briefly laid a hand on her belly.

"We need Axis," Belial finished. "*And* we need the Strike Force's scouting abilities. Magariz, is there no more news regarding the Strike Force?"

"No, Belial. The last intelligence we had from their farflight scouts was that they'd arrive in three weeks' time."

Belial sighed. "Well, whatever our problems, Borneheld undoubtedly faces far worse. Last night I received word from the scouts I'd sent into Jervois Landing. The news is good *and* bad, my friends. Borneheld has ordered a series of canals be constructed between the Nordra and Azle rivers to create a barrier of running water. Borneheld has enough men that, with the aid of the canals, he *may* have a chance of holding Gorgrael's Skraelings to Ichtar this winter."

"And the bad news," Arne put in, "must be that if Borneheld manages to blunt the Skraeling danger he'll have a battle-hardened army to throw at us. Borneheld will indulge his hatred of Axis with everything he's got."

"Well, we must have roughly the same number of forces," said Magariz carefully, watching Belial. "And as good."

Belial was silent.

"How many forces *does* Borneheld command at Jervois Landing, Belial?" Azhure asked finally.

Belial took a deep breath. "At best estimate, almost twenty thousand."

All three started forward, and Arne swore viciously.

"*Twenty thousand*?" Magariz repeated. "But where could he have got so many? At the most we had fourteen thousand at Gorkenfort – and Borneheld had almost stripped Achar bare to get those. We lost some six thousand in the fighting, three thousand left with us to follow Axis . . . why, Borneheld would have left Gorkenfort with only some five thousand men. Belial, your information must be wrong!"

Belial shook his head. "I wish it were, my friend, I wish it were. No, Borneheld has at least twenty thousand in Jervois Landing. My spies tell me that the Ravensbund chief, one Ho'Demi, brought at least eleven thousand men to Borneheld's cause. And Borneheld also has the use of all the refugees who fled Ichtar before the Skraelings, plus the soldiers who fled Sigholt itself. At the least twenty thousand. Probably more."

There was silence. With the Icarii they would number at best five thousand. It would be a fierce and bloody fight for control of Achar.

Azhure tapped the table, thinking aloud. "But Borneheld will have to fight on two fronts. He will always have to keep an army at Jervois Landing to keep the Skraelings back, and once Axis takes command here he will undoubtedly move down through Skarabost before he swings west towards Carlon. Borneheld will have to split his force."

Belial studied her. "You're right, Azhure. But Axis will have to do the same thing. If he moves down into Achar with his main force, then he will still have to leave a good force here in Sigholt to guard the WildDog Plains. The last thing Axis will want is to have Gorgrael attack him from his rear while he's trying to defeat Borneheld."

"Well, don't forget you also have my pack of fifteen Alaunt." Azhure grinned. "They might well tip the balance in our favour."

The men stared at her for a moment, then they guffawed with laughter.

"Enough of Borneheld and the Skraelings," Belial said, grateful to Azhure for breaking the tension. "At the moment the influx of refugees into Sigholt is almost as worrying."

When Belial had first occupied Sigholt he had sent small bands of men down into Skarabost to scout out possible supply routes and spread word of the Prophecy. The organisation of supply routes was going well, but news of the Prophecy was now attracting so many people to Sigholt that it was rapidly representing a major new problem. Small groups – sometimes only four or five, sometimes twenty or thirty – had started to arrive some four weeks ago and the numbers had grown steadily ever since.

"Belial, I am sure there is no need to look so worried," Azhure said. "You should be pleased that so many see fit to flock to Axis' cause."

"Don't lecture me!" Belial snapped, "just tell me what you've done with them." As well as training her three squads of mounted archers, Azhure had also assumed responsibility for feeding, accommodating and generally organising the new arrivals.

"I've managed to accommodate them in tents on the north-eastern shores of the Lake. We have enough food for the moment, and many of them have brought their own. And soon we'll have additional food to supplement what we get via our supply routes."

"Really? How so?" asked Magariz.

Azhure glanced out the window. "Since the Lake has sprung to life, so have the Urqhart Hills. I set the larger number of refugees to clearing and digging vegetable gardens. They were planted some two weeks ago, and the first vegetables are nearing maturity now. It is the waters, apparently, that encourage new life."

"Good." Belial nodded, then looked to Arne. "Any fighters among them?"

Arne shrugged. "Most are peasants, driven to hunger by the extremity of the previous winter, and clinging to any story or rumour that promises them a better life. But many of the younger men are strong, many are eager. They can wield a stave with the best of them."

"Do they *want* to fight for Axis," Belial asked, "or are they just streaming into Sigholt because it promises some refuge from Gorgrael's icy winds?"

"A bit of both, I think," Magariz answered. "Many Acharites have been scared by the news of the fall of Gorkenfort and the loss of Ichtar. They wonder if the Star-Man the Prophecy speaks of might be the one to save them, rather than Borneheld. And you know the reputation Axis enjoyed as BattleAxe. Still, from what I can gather, it is only a tiny fraction of the population of Skarabost that seeks to wend its way north. Most either prefer to stay with their homes, with what they know, or are scared by the idea that the Prophecy speaks of an alliance with the Forbidden."

Belial sighed and rubbed his eyes. "Well, I hope they won't jump too much when the Strike Force drops out of the sky."

Magariz reined in his horse, waving at the patrol behind him to stay out of sight. He turned in the saddle and looked for Azhure. They were on an extended patrol in the southern Urqhart Hills, the River Nordra only half a league away to the south. This was dangerous territory. Not only were there Skraelings about, but Borneheld's forces had been increasing their patrols here as well. The last patrol Belial sent into this area had encountered a well-armed band of twenty men from Jervois Landing. In the skirmish that followed both sides lost almost half their men. Thus the presence of Azhure and two squads of her archers on this patrol – they had already proved their worth.

Magariz motioned Azhure forward. They had been out some eight days, scouting the southern hills to test the strength of both Skraelings and Borneheld's forces. Already they'd encountered small bands of Skraelings, and Azhure had proved as calm and reliable in battle as she was around the conference table. Her archers had conducted themselves as well as their leader, and when they returned Magariz would recommend to Belial that Azhure be given several more squads. The Alaunt were also showing themselves to be useful in battle. The day before yesterday they had encountered a band of about two hundred Skraelings, braver and better organised than most. Azhure had directed her archers, then motioned to the hounds, sending them in among the Skraelings. Magariz had been horrified, thinking that if the Alaunt survived the Skraelings then they'd be murdered by the arrows raining down among them. But the Alaunt weaved and ducked, knowing instinctively when an arrow sped their way, and they pulled down as many Skraelings as

Azhure's archers. Both archers and hounds had kept the patrol's injuries minimal.

"What do you think of the valley ahead?" he asked as Azhure reined in Belaguez by his side.

"There's a camp site about a third of the way down the valley," she said. "Perhaps some fifteen men and their horses. They have a camp fire, but they use long-dead wood so that it burns bright with no smoke."

Magariz nodded. "Good. If you were their commander, would you allow all your men to sit about the fire and sing cheerful songs in territory that is distinctly unfriendly?"

"No. No. There are, ah," Azhure strained her eyes, "about fifteen men around the fire, but considerably more horses. He has sentries posted. Perhaps six or seven."

"Very well, what do you suggest?"

She turned to look at him. His face was dark and inscrutable beneath the hood of his black cloak. "Attack?"

Magariz considered. "Perhaps. Twenty or so less men for Borneheld would help us, but I do not know where the patrol commander has his sentries, and I hardly think it worthwhile to risk an attack for just twenty or so men."

"And if we could dispose of the sentries — could we capture those about the fire? Wring what information we could from them before we kill them?"

"Ideally. But how do we dispose of unseen sentries?"

Azhure's eyes were cold. "I send in the Alaunt. They can track them. Kill them in silence. They will be dead in half an hour at the most. The main group about the fire will never know we are there until we have them surrounded."

"Then send in the hounds, Azhure, and we will see how silently they can track and kill."

They killed both silently and well, and were back at Azhure's side in less than twenty minutes, their muzzles flecked with red. "Well?" she asked Magariz.

"We go in on foot for added silence. The band about the fire will suspect nothing. Come, bring your archers."

It was dusk by the time they surrounded the fifteen men relaxing about the fire. Azhure had kept the Alaunt close by her side and had approached downwind in order not to frighten the men's horses, hobbled some distance away down the stream. Five men flanked the patrol about the camp fire and moved to cut the horses free. Magariz moved the rest, both archers and ordinary soldiers, into position with hand signals, then indicated that Azhure should stay close to him. Azhure notched an arrow into the Wolven.

They crouched in the tree line just outside the range of the firelight, listening to the men talk. They were from Jervois Landing, and, like Magariz's patrol, almost at the end of their duty and relieved they had avoided the desperate armed bandits they'd heard were in these hills.

Azhure felt Magariz tense and glanced at him. He pointed to a soldier relaxing against a rock and whispered, "Nevelon. Lieutenant to Duke Roland. A good man."

Azhure looked at the man. He was young and fit, with thick brown hair and a short-cropped beard. Not good enough, she thought, if he still owed his loyalty to Borneheld rather than Axis.

Magariz placed a hand on Azhure's shoulder and whispered into her ear. "Back me up on this, Azhure. I want to speak to them. Nevelon is a sensible man. If he knows his command is surrounded by archers he will not try to fight his way free. Can your archers put a ring of arrows about them?"

Azhure nodded, signalled to her men, then raised her eyebrows at Magariz. She had the Wolven ready to fire. "Now?"

"Now," he nodded.

At Azhure's signal a vicious rustle of arrows filled the air, and an instant later the men about the camp fire leapt to their feet and gazed horrified, at the arrows ringing them in a perfect circle.

"Nevelon." Magariz stepped into the firelight. "Do not consider your weapons. At my signal, or at the first handspan of steel that you or any one of your men draw, you are dead."

Nevelon nodded curtly and motioned to his men to drop their hands from their sword hilts.

"Magariz," he said. "I thought you were dead."

"Alas, no." Magariz's entire posture was relaxed and confident. In the firelight his scarred face looked demonic. "It seems we both escaped Gorkenfort safely. Tell me, how is your Duke, Roland?"

A muscle in Nevelon's cheek twitched. By Artor, the man was as cool as if he trod the court in Carlon. Did he intend to kill them? "Roland still lives – although these last months have seen him lose considerable weight."

"And Borneheld. Fit and well? I would hate to hear he had succumbed to a cold on the flight from Gorkenfort."

"The King is well," Nevelon said carefully.

Magariz rocked in surprise. *Borneheld* was King? He almost tripped as his wounded leg slipped on a loose rock underfoot.

Nevelon grinned, and reached for the dagger in his belt. He was widely renowned for his skill at throwing the blade, and he could easily kill Magariz before the man had time to signal to his archers. If they all died in a hail of arrows after that – well, Magariz surely intended to kill them anyway. His hand whipped the knife out of his belt, but before he let it fly Nevelon gave a cry of pain and dropped the knife. Bristling from the back of his hand was an arrow fletched with beautiful blue feathers.

"The next one goes in your left eye, Nevelon," a woman's voice said, "and I will personally be the one to twist it all the way through to your brain. Do you understand me?"

Nevelon nodded, clutching his hand to his chest.

"Then I would appreciate my arrow back, Lieutenant," the voice continued. "Would you mind twisting it out and throwing it behind Magariz?"

Nevelon couldn't believe what he'd just heard. Twist it out? The arrowhead had penetrated so deeply it was halfway through the palm of his hand.

"*Now!*" the voice demanded.

Magariz laughed sardonically. "Nevelon, hear her. She has a special attachment to those arrows, and will not mind killing you with another to get the first back."

Nevelon abruptly took hold of the shaft of the arrow and twisted it free. He gave a harsh grunt of pain, then, ashen-faced, tossed the arrow behind Magariz.

"Thank you," the voice said, and from the darkness emerged the largest hound Nevelon had ever seen, pale cream and gold. It paced carefully to the arrow, its eyes on Nevelon's throat, then picked it up and disappeared back into the night.

"Thank you, Azhure," Magariz called softly. "I think you saved my life."

Nevelon heard the name. Azhure?

Magariz shifted his black eyes back to Nevelon. "Borneheld is King? Priam is dead?"

Nevelon nodded warily. He could just make out the woman now. Raven-haired, she had a magnificent bow drawn tight in her hands. He noticed that two of his men, Ravensbundmen, were staring at the bow fixedly. "Yes. Priam died some weeks ago. He developed a fatal brain fever and died crazed."

"Well," Magariz said. "The message remains the same."

Message? Would he live after all?

"As you can see, Nevelon, Azhure and myself wear the emblem of the blazing blood-red sun. Do you know it?"

Nevelon shook his head.

"Well, Nevelon, then you must remember it. It is the emblem of the StarMan. You must remember the Prophecy that so many spoke of in Gorkenfort."

"It was a lie." Nevelon's voice did not sound very sure.

"No," Magariz said, wiping his face free of any expression of artfulness. "The Prophecy does not lie. We wait for the StarMan to lead us — and Achar — to victory against Gorgrael."

"Axis!" Nevelon spat, remembering Magariz naming Axis as the StarMan at Gorkenfort as he revealed his treacherous nature and deserted Borneheld. "You *both* betrayed us at Gorkenfort."

Magariz's face hardened. "No, Nevelon. Axis and I, as others, did the best we could in a situation that was unwinnable. Now listen, for I have a message for Borneheld. Tell him that if he does not ally himself with the cause of the StarMan he will die. Only Axis can lead Achar to victory. Tell him that if he persists in denying the Prophecy then the Prophecy will tear him apart. If he has won a kingdom, then he will not long enjoy it. Tell him Axis comes, and he comes with the power of the Prophecy behind him."

"And allied with the Forbidden?" Nevelon asked harshly.

"Allied with our *friends*, Nevelon," Magariz said. "We have an alliance built on trust and friendship. Tell me, how well does Borneheld trust those around him? News of the Prophecy spreads throughout Achar. The past is crumbling beneath our feet. Reach forward and embrace the future, Nevelon."

Nevelon spat at Magariz's feet.

"A brave, but somewhat foolish action, Nevelon. What will it accomplish? Remember my message for Borneheld. Now, I must go. Do not think to follow us. Your horses have been scattered and it will take you hours to find them. I would take your weapons, but if I did that you would be easy prey for the Skraelings, and I want my message to reach Borneheld. Your sentries are dead, killed by these hounds. Azhure?"

Azhure whistled softly and the fifteen Alaunt stepped forward from the shadows to encircle Nevelon and his men.

"They will stand guard while we move away," said Magariz. "If you make one move they will kill you. Azhure?"

She nodded and murmured to Sicarius who stood with his golden eyes fixed on Nevelon's face. He could smell the man's blood.

Magariz stepped back and put his hand on Azhure's shoulder. An instant later they were gone in the shadows.

Nevelon stood and stared at the hounds.

"I would believe what he said, Lieutenant Nevelon," one of the Ravensbundmen said softly. "They are the legendary Alaunt."

Nevelon looked at the Ravensbundman, startled. He swallowed and stood perfectly still, clutching his crippled hand against his chest, until the ghost hounds eventually melted back into the night.

Even then, no-one moved for almost an hour.

25

Star Gate

T hey sat in the flat-bottomed boat in the centre of the violet lake underneath the light of the crystals. The Star Dance drifted about them. Sometimes they talked, mostly they sat in silence.

"Explain about the Star Gods," Axis asked, "for StarDrifter and MorningStar's teaching confused me."

"In what manner?" Orr prompted.

"There are nine Star Gods," Axis said, and Orr inclined his head. "Yet I know only seven names: Adamon and Xanon, the two senior Gods of the Firmament; Silton, God of Fire; Pors, God of Air; Zest, Goddess of Earth; Flulia, Goddess of Water; and Narcis, God of the Sun. Yet the gods of Moon and Song have no names. Why is that?"

"Over many thousands of years seven of the Nine of the Star Gods have revealed themselves," Orr replied. "Only Moon and Song are yet to grace us with their names. In time, perhaps in thousands of years, we will be enlightened of all."

Axis frowned slightly. "But these Gods seem very distant, Orr. When I lived as BattleAxe, and followed Artor, I could often feel his presence in prayer or moments of contemplation. Yet I cannot sense that when I pray to the Star Gods."

"They live, StarMan, but they have been trapped."

"Trapped?"

Orr shook his head sorrowfully. "There is nothing you or I can do, StarMan. Nothing. The battle between Artor and the Star Gods concerns neither of us."

"Battle?"

But to that Orr would say no more, and they sat in silence for hours (days?) more as the Star Dance drifted about them.

Later Axis asked Orr about the Sacred Lakes. "Where did they come from? What makes them so sacred? So magical?"

Orr shifted a little uncomfortably. "Many thousands of years ago, Axis, before my time, the Ancient Gods – those who came before even the Star Gods – wrapped Tencendor in a fire-storm which lasted many days and almost blasted all life from the face of this earth. Only those who could find shelter in deep caves survived.

"The fire-storm and the Lakes the storm bequeathed us were a gift to remind us of the power of the Ancient Gods and of the paucity of our own being. Some say that the Ancient Gods never returned to the Sky but lay down to sleep under the waters of the Sacred Lakes." Orr smiled. "But that I do not believe. I have never seen or heard them, and I have been here, silent, watching, some considerable time."

Axis rested his chin in his hand thoughtfully. Orr had given him vivid imagery but not much else. He opened his mouth to ask further about the fire-storm, but Orr deflected his question.

"The time has come for you to show me how well you have learned, Axis. Take us to the Star Gate."

The Star Gate! Axis looked down at his ring. He thought of the purpose, and the purpose was to glide the boat to the legendary Star Gate, most sacred site of the Icarii people.

The stars on his ring re-formed themselves and Axis noted the pattern they created. He reached for the power of the Star Dance and hummed the melody softly.

They glided down tunnels, under strange bridges, and through strange caverns. Some caverns yawned empty, some had the skeletons of entire cities huddled about the water, some contained forests frozen in stone, some were so encased in grey mist that Axis could not see an arm's length beyond the boat.

"Note," the Ferryman said, "that the pattern of the waterway we travel reflects the pattern of the melody you sing."

"And if I were in the OverWorld," Axis asked, keeping the melody running through his head, "how would I travel?"

"I do not know, Axis SunSoar. That will be your adventure to discover."

Eventually they reached a small cavern and the boat glided to a halt in front of a set of stone steps which rose from the water. Axis moored the boat to a small stone pillar.

"Come," the Ferryman said, and stepped out of the boat, gathering his cloak about him.

Orr led Axis along a narrow passage which sloped gently upwards. As they walked Axis became aware of the sound of rushing wind and of a blue light that pulsed through the air.

"What is that sound, that light?" Axis asked, breathing hard in his attempt to keep up with the Ferryman.

"It is the sound and the light of the Star Gate," Orr replied. "Come."

The next moment they stepped through into the Chamber of the Star Gate.

Axis was as awe-struck as Faraday had been. The Chamber was exquisitely beautiful. And whereas Faraday had thought it resembled the Chamber of the Moons in the palace at Carlon, Axis knew instantly that the Icarii Assembly Chamber had been modelled on the Chamber of the Star Gate. Perfectly circular, it was surrounded by pillars and archways. Each pillar was carved from translucent white stone in the shape of a naked winged man. Most of the winged men stood with their heads bowed and arms folded across their chests, their wings outstretched to touch those of their neighbours, thus forming the apex of the archways. But Axis noticed that an entire section of pillars across the far side of the chamber were different. These winged men had their heads up and their eyes wide open, their golden orbs staring towards the centre of the chamber, their arms uplifted in joy with their wings.

"They represent the twenty-six Enchanter-Talons who were buried above in the Barrows," the Ferryman said, and Axis abruptly realised they were directly below the Ancient Barrows where Gorgrael's storm had killed so many of his men. And where he had lost Faraday.

Orr moved forwards, gesturing for Axis to follow. What appeared to be a circular pool, surrounded by a low rim, occupied the centre of the Chamber, above it blue shadows chased each other across the domed ceiling. Both the pulsing blue light and the sound of the gale emanated from that pool.

As he peered into the Star Gate Axis observed, as had Faraday, that it was the gateway into the universe. The real universe, not the poor imitation that lit the night skies. The sound of the Star Dance was strong here, and Axis could see why. Stars reeled and danced, suns chased each other across entire galaxies, moons dipped and swayed through planetary systems, luminous comets threaded through the cosmos.

Its beauty was unimaginable, its allure almost irresistible. The Star Dance called to Axis, pleaded with him, begged him. It wanted a lover, and it had chosen Axis. Come! it pleaded, Come! Step through the Gate. Come to me!

"Resist the call," Orr whispered. "Resist."

Hardening himself against the lure of the Star Dance, Axis let the beauty of the universe wash through him. The colours amazed him; when he looked into the night sky from the OverWorld all he could see were the silvery stars, sometimes touched with a hint of gold or red. But as he gazed into the Star Gate Axis could see entire galaxies of emerald or gold or lilac, solar systems of cornflower and crimson, while the colours of individual stars were every imaginable shade of the rainbow.

"When you stand in the outer world and look at the night sky," Orr explained, "you look at the universe through a veil of air and wind and indistinct cloud and sound. To see the true universe you must either die, or stand at the lip of the Star Gate."

They stared into the Star Gate for an indeterminate length of time, until finally Axis shuddered and turned away. The call of the Star Dance was becoming too much to bear. If he did not step back now he might well be unable to resist.

Axis stared about the Chamber, then he wandered past the first of the twenty-six Enchanter-Talon statues, all obviously the work of master craftsmen. Axis could not resist the urge to reach out and gently touch the fourth statue he passed. The stone felt cold and unforgiving beneath his fingers.

"Do not do that, Axis," Orr said. "It is disrespectful of those gone to touch their statues."

"They are dead and long gone, Orr. I do not think they will mind. Besides," he had reached the eighth in the line and ran his hand over its outstretched wings, "I will one day stand among them."

"Axis." Orr's tone was firmer now. "There is a long-standing tradition that to touch these statues is bad luck, and I think you should stand back."

Axis reached the ninth and touched it briefly, ready to stop, but instead of his fingers feeling cold hard stone, they went straight through the statue.

Axis gasped in shock and stepped back, then leaned forward and tentatively touched the statue again. It shimmered, wavered, then disappeared entirely, and Axis and Orr were left staring at nothingness.

"It was an illusion," Orr finally managed to say. "An illusion!"

Axis dropped his hand. "What does this mean, Orr?"

Orr wrapped the cloak about himself protectively. "I never thought to see this," he whispered. "Never."

"See *what*?" Axis snapped.

"The ninth of the Enchanter-Talons has returned," Orr said in a very weak voice. "WolfStar SunSoar has come back through the Gate."

Axis took a shocked breath. "When?"

"I do not know," Orr said. "He died some four thousand years ago, but he could have come back at any time since then."

"Is *he* the SunSoar Enchanter who trained me? Who trained Gorgrael?"

"He could be wearing any disguise," said Orr. "Any at all. A babe, an aged man, a pretty young woman. WolfStar was already powerful when he died and went through the Star Gate. If he had the power to come *back* then he is now powerful beyond imagination."

"But why, Orr? Why did he come back? Why hasn't he revealed himself?"

Orr shrugged.

Axis quickly ran his hand over the remaining statues. All were solid. He turned back to Orr. "Where could he be?"

Orr laughed harshly. "I wish I knew, Axis SunSoar, because then I would know the safest place to hide."

"Why say that?" Axis could not hide his concern.

"Because WolfStar was a terrible, terrible Enchanter-Talon. His power was *virulent*!" Orr said. "He was so horrifying that he was eventually murdered by his own brother."

Virulent? Axis thought to himself, remembering how loath MorningStar and StarDrifter were to talk of their ancestor.

"Who is more terrible, Orr, WolfStar or Gorgrael?"

Orr replied without hesitation. "WolfStar has the potential to be far more terrible, Axis."

"But why would WolfStar train us both?" Axis said. "Why?"

"Because he is already manipulating both of you, Axis. For whatever foul purpose he has."

But *what* purpose? Orr asked himself. Revenge? Is that why WolfStar has come back to haunt us?

"Orr," Axis asked, "what is the connection between WolfStar and the Prophecy of the Destroyer? If WolfStar is manipulating both Gorgrael and myself, then is he also manipulating the Prophecy? Or is he being manipulated by the Prophecy?"

Is *WolfStar* the traitor the third verse of the Prophecy warns me about? Axis wondered.

"Orr, this is news that I must take back to MorningStar and StarDrifter. Perhaps, somehow, we can discover where he is. Why he has come back. But there is one more thing I must do within the waterways. One more thing. I made a promise."

"What?"

"I must return FreeFall SunSoar from the dead," Axis said, staring the Ferryman in the eyes. "And you are going to help me."

26

···

Gorgrael Makes a New Friend

Gorgrael stared at the frozen grey sludge. It was the remains of the SkraeBold Belial had killed outside Gorkenfort and Gorgrael was determined to do something with it.

He had his Skraelings and he had his IceWorms, but Gorgrael wanted to create something special for his drive south. He was rapidly building his forces for the winter push south through Jervois Landing, or even, perhaps, the WildDog Plains.

What Gorgrael wanted was something that could fly. Something that would turn Axis' face grey with worry. Something that could destroy the Icarii in the air.

Now, let me see, Gorgrael thought, surveying the grey matter before him. Dragons? When he was but a child, his Skraeling nursemaids had whispered stories to him about great dragons that had once flown the sky. Beautiful dragons, vicious dragons, dragons that had carried off creatures as large as whales. But dragons were too gaudy, and far too large to make from what he had before him.

What, then? Gorgrael shifted from foot to foot, his claws clicking sharply on the floor.

"Gorgrael," the loved voice said behind him.

"Dear Man!" he cried in delight. Two visits in such quick succession – he was blessed!

The Dark Man emerged from a darkened corner unlit by the failing fire, his heavily cowled head and figure almost indistinguishable from the shadows about him.

"You are going to recreate?" the Dark Man asked.

"Yes," Gorgrael said, and indicated the grey sludge in front of him. "It was the SkraeBold who failed me. I had thought to cast his remains to the crows, but that –"

"Would have been a waste of such good building material," the Dark Man finished thoughtfully.

"Precisely," Gorgrael said, suppressing the edge of triumph in his voice.

"And what did you think you would make from this, Gorgrael?" the Dark Man asked. "What creature would you make to work your will?"

Gorgrael couldn't answer. He glared at the grey sludge as if it were at fault in this.

"Demon-winged," the Dark Man suggested, sliding his gloved hands into the deep sleeves of his cloak.

"Demon-winged," Gorgrael repeated. Yes, that was good.

"Ogre-bellied." Now the Dark Man's voice was louder.

"Ogre-bellied." Gorgrael nodded. "Yes. Yes, I like that."

"Grave-jawed."

"What creature is this, Dear Man?"

The Dear Man tipped his head to one side and regarded his protégé. "Can you not yet recognise it, Gorgrael?"

Gorgrael shook his head in frustration.

"Dragon-clawed," the Dark Man prompted.

A dim memory of ancient nightmares stirred. "Blight-eyed!" Gorgrael cried.

Underneath his cowl the Dark Man smiled. "It will cry with the voice of despair."

"Gryphon!" Gorgrael shrieked, triumphantly.

They waited, each on edge, unsure of how their enchantments had worked. The Gryphon was to be a creature that could thrive, not only in the snow and ice of Gorgrael's homeland, but in the warmer climes of southern Achar. It would have to soar in the air thermals above Grail Lake, and penetrate to the very heart of Axis' command. It would be a creature brave and committed, single-purposed.

"You will be my vanguard," Gorgrael said. "My herald. Your voice shall be mine, and it shall be the voice that the forces of the StarMan shall hear as they die. Despair."

The working of the Gryphon had been fraught with worry. The Song of Recreation was hard and dangerous when worked with the Dark Music. The power of the Dance of Death had flooded through both Gorgrael and the Dark Man as they wrestled with the Song. But the Dark Man, Dear Man, was a master, and he had managed to control the Dark Music as it threatened to rope out of control through their bodies and about the room.

They had both sung, both waited as the grey sludge firmed and warmed and writhed beneath their touch. As the Song had wound to a close, Gorgrael, almost in ecstasy, plunged his hands into the all-but-dead fire in the fireplace and seized two coals, still smouldering bright. Ignoring his own burning flesh Gorgrael had carried the coals to the writhing grey sludge on the floor and plunged them deep into its mass. As he withdrew his clawed hands the Song finally died, and the Dear Man pulled him back a safe distance.

"Now we must wait, Gorgrael," he said.

The grey sludge darkened, became even more ill-defined, until Gorgrael could see only a quivering, black mound that absorbed what little light the room held. Deep within glowed two spots of red. Every so often it jerked, and every time it jerked it doubled its size. Soon both the Dark Man and Gorgrael had to step back to avoid being absorbed by the growing creature.

"Something is wrong," Gorgrael suddenly hissed. "We did not sing the appropriate music. We missed a phrase, a beat.

We did not twist enough power through for a successful making."

"Patience, Gorgrael!" the Dark Man barked. "You were ever too impatient!"

Gorgrael subsided at the criticism, his contorted face coiling into a frown, wondering if it was past time he asserted his own power over the Dark Man.

"Ah!" the Dark Man gasped. "It will be born!"

His moment of rebellion gone, Gorgrael dropped his eyes. The round black mass, now the size of a small boulder, had a dark membrane stretched over it. Something roiled within, as if it struggled to be free.

A slight perforation suddenly appeared in the membrane and, an instant later, the membrane split down one entire side. A sleek head emerged, twin eyes glowing with the promise of death. It blinked, looked about briefly, then it opened its beak and shrieked with the victory of birth.

It had the head of a massive eagle.

Gorgrael whimpered in glee. They *had* sung aright!

The creature turned its head and ripped viciously at the rest of the membrane, freeing itself in only three or four movements. It stepped forward, regarding both the Dark Man and Gorgrael curiously, then it sank into a crouch before Gorgrael, resting its head on its front paws in a spontaneous act of submission.

Gorgrael bent down and stroked the Gryphon's gleaming brown head feathers. The Gryphon closed its eyes and grunted with gratification. It knew its master. Gorgrael ran his hands over the rest of its body. From the shoulder blades and spine extended graceful wings, feathered in the same glossy brown of its head. But the Gryphon's resemblance to a bird stopped with its feathers. It had the muscular body of a great cat, its tawny coat short and thick and designed to stay the claws or arrows of enemies. A long, tufted tail swung behind. It rested on short but thickly muscled legs that ended in massive paws. At each stroke of Gorgrael's hands, the Gryphon sheathed then unsheathed its dreadful claws.

It was, overall, a frightful beast.

The Dark Man was also well pleased with the Gryphon, and, indeed, with Gorgrael. Gorgrael had worked hard to rebuild his forces, and even now the Dark Man knew that the Skraelings and the IceWorms, under the leadership of SkraeBolds determined not to fail their master again, massed just south and west of Hsingard. It would not be long before an offensive could begin again.

No stranger to death himself, the Dark Man looked forward to the fighting and the slaughter that would ensue.

It gave him satisfaction.

"Gorgrael, my friend. I wove something extra into the Song of Recreation. Thrust a little more meaning into the Dark Music as we folded and directed it to our purpose. Gorgrael, the Gryphon is female. Feel her belly."

Gorgrael slid his clawed hands either side of the Gryphon's body and felt her belly. He frowned.

"My friend. The Gryphon draws close to birthing nine pups, exact replicas of herself. In a day or so, perhaps less, you will have ten of the creatures. In a few months, as they grow and mature, you will have a pack to rival no other. And the nine will breed as well, Gorgrael. All will be born female – and all will be born pregnant."

The Dark Man thought he had done well. He *thought* he had woven the music of the Gryphon's making so that the breeding would stop when the nine whelped. Unfortunately, he was wrong.

"She will be a good creature. Obedient, like the best hound," the Dear Man said, stepping back. "But deadlier, far deadlier."

Gorgrael stroked the Gryphon for a moment longer, then abruptly strode over to his chair by the fire. "Come," he said, and snapped his fingers.

The Gryphon rose obediently and padded over to the chair, sinking down at Gorgrael's feet. Gorgrael looked back to the Dear Man with shining eyes. "Will you sit with me a moment?" he inquired, indicating the empty chair across the other side of the hearth.

"A moment only, Gorgrael. I am required elsewhere shortly." The Dark Man sat in the empty chair, and waved his hand impatiently at the fire so that it flared bright.

Where else shortly? Gorgrael thought to himself. He had never discovered where the Dark Man lived, how he lived, in what form he lived, once he left Gorgrael's presence. Perhaps he simply faded into nothingness until he was required again.

The Dark Man grunted in amusement. "Oh, I live elsewhere, Gorgrael. I have work to do, tasks to perform, music to sing."

"Have you heard of Axis lately, Dear Man?" Gorgrael asked. "How goes my brother?"

"I have not seen him, heard of him, for some time," the Dark Man finally said. "It is as if he has disappeared from creation." He grinned underneath his hood.

"Dead?" Gorgrael asked, although the thought caused him disappointment. He looked forward to tearing his brother into shreds.

The Dark Man laughed. "No, not dead, Gorgrael. Very much alive – his death I would have felt . . . as would you. But I do have news of Borneheld . . . and Faraday."

Gorgrael sat up. "What?"

"Borneheld is now King," the Dark Man said reflectively. "It is said that Priam died a crazed death. And if Borneheld is King in Carlon, then Faraday sits by his side as Queen. A tastier morsel than ever now, Gorgrael, a much tastier morsel."

"Tastier," Gorgrael echoed, his thoughts on the woman so far to the south. Queen. Faraday.

27

The Strike Force Lands

The last of the Icarii bound for Sigholt left Talon Spike on the third to last day of DeadLeaf-month. The Crests and Wings of the Strike Force had been gone some ten days and the last of them would have arrived in Sigholt. Small groups of Enchanters had left each day since.

The final group included MorningStar and StarDrifter. RavenCrest was reluctant to leave the security of Talon Spike for an unknown world; until Axis had won Tencendor back the majority of the Icarii would stay in Talon Spike. As he stood on the flight balcony watching his mother and brother disappear over the southern Icescarp Alps, RavenCrest had to fight a wave of depression from swamping him. The fate of the Icarii had been taken from his hands. Was this the beginning of their long-hoped-for pilgrimage back to their homelands or a journey towards the death of all their dreams?

"By the Stars, Axis," said RavenCrest, the wind ruffling his black neck feathers, "do not squander the hopes of the Icarii in your battles with Borneheld and Gorgrael. You promised to lead us back into Tencendor. Make sure you do it."

No-one who had just left Talon Spike missed the significance of their flight south. For the first time in a thousand years the Icarii flew for Tencendor rather than just winging their way about the Icescarp Alps or the Avarinheim. None thought the path would be easy, and all understood that some would die in the attempt. But Icarii spirit had been rekindled. They were finally taking active steps to regain their heritage.

Several hours after they left Talon Spike the group found a thermal which lifted them high into the atmosphere, and for more than an hour they spiralled upwards, only very slowly moving south. The view was stunning. Far below, the Icescarp Alps ridged and plunged their way south towards the Icescarp Barren and east towards the Avarinheim forest. To the east the Widowmaker Sea glinted in sunlight. As she tilted a little in the thermal MorningStar caught a glimpse of the Nordra, silver from this height, as it wound its serpentine way through the Avarinheim. The river was a life-giver, both to the Avarinheim and to the bare plains of Achar, and the Avar worshipped the Nordra almost as fervently as the sacred Earth Tree. MorningStar smiled a little as she half closed her eyes against the glare of the sun. How fortunate that Gorgrael's clouds did not cover the Avarinheim. The forest canopy waved green and black, almost like a sea itself, and Morning-Star hoped that she would live long enough to see the first trees replanted in the plains beyond the Fortress Ranges.

Above her, StarDrifter waved the group further east. The flight would take three or four days and they would rest each night within the Avarinheim. The Avar had established three camps just inside the protecting walls of the Fortress Ranges, keeping the Icarii who used them supplied with food and fire at night. Willing enough to help the Icarii, the Avar waited for Faraday before they would actively move to help Axis.

As they flew further south, MorningStar remembered her mother speaking of the sacred sites lost to the Icarii. Would she live to see Fernbrake Lake, the Mother, and the Island of Mist and Memory? She let herself dream a little, hope a little.

Azhure approached the circle of Icarii and Acharite warriors quietly, so as not to disturb them, especially those who fought in the centre. The majority of the Icarii Strike Force had been here almost three weeks now, and their intensive combat training with Belial's soldiers continued apace.

FarSight CutSpur, true to his word to Axis, had surrendered the Strike Force to Belial's overall control. He had no regrets in doing so. Any decision Belial took regarding the Icarii he made sure to discuss with FarSight and his Crest-Leaders. Indeed, FarSight and his two senior Crest-Leaders – HoverEye BlackWing and SpreadWing RavenCry – had been included in Belial's inner circle on an equal footing with Magariz, Arne and Azhure. FarSight respected Belial greatly. He was a good man, and a capable commander; Axis had chosen well in his second-in-command.

The Icarii had been dismayed by their lack of combat skills when compared to the Groundwalkers, despite Axis' earlier warning. Over the past three weeks they had done almost nothing but work on their hand-to-hand skills with Belial's soldiers. To begin with, the Groundwalkers had been able to best the Icarii easily, and many an Icarii Strike Force member had spent long hours of the night rubbing soothing salve into abrasions and bruises or soaking in the rejuvenating hot waters of the Lake of Life. But, driven by their deep-seated pride, the Icarii had learned quickly. In fact, so determined were they to put a stop to their embarrassing losses, that over the past few days a growing number of Icarii had come out victorious from their combat bouts with Belial's men. SpikeFeather, in particular, had earned their respect.

Azhure crept around the edge of the circle of watching warriors until a gap appeared in the tightly packed bodies. She shouldered her way through.

EvenSong was battling with a soldier from Arne's unit, a brawny, ginger-haired, experienced campaigner from Aldeni called Edowes. The Acharite soldiers had quickly learned that the female members of the Icarii Strike Force were just as determined as the male. Now, as the two grappled in the centre of the circle, it was obvious that Edowes was giving no quarter.

Ever since SpikeFeather had shamed her in front of Azhure and the other members of her Wing, EvenSong had put all her efforts into becoming an asset to the Strike Force. Today was the first time she felt she had a good chance of besting her practice partner, but the actual "kill" was proving frustratingly difficult.

Azhure glanced about the circle. Arne stood to one side, his arms folded, his posture relaxed, his emotions hidden behind his usual expressionless mask. Only the jerky movements of the twig he was chewing showed he felt any concern about the outcome of this bout. A few paces from him stood SpikeFeather TrueSong, commander of Even-Song's Wing. His wings were held tense and tight against his back, and his fingers convulsively flexed at his side, as if he wanted to leap into the ring and help EvenSong.

EvenSong and Edowes both wore light armour, but both had collected more than their fair share of bruises during the bout. Suddenly EvenSong grunted and fell to her knees, caught by a particularly heavy blow to the ribs by Edowes, her stave slipping from her fingers. Azhure's stomach twisted, and she only just managed to stop herself from leaping forward and pulling Edowes back.

Edowes raised his stave to shoulder height for the final blow. But he had badly misjudged his opponent. EvenSong's fingers tightened and shifted on the stave and, her face twisting with determination, she brought the stave upwards with all her might. Straight between Edowes' legs.

Every male within the circle of watchers whimpered in sympathy as they heard the sickening crunch. Edowes howled, dropping his stave and falling to the ground, clutching at his abused manhood.

Azhure clapped to her mouth to hide her grin, and her eyes met those of a jubilant EvenSong. The Icarii woman's eyes glittered with pride, and she did not look the least bit sorry that she had destroyed Edowes' hopes of enjoying the young Skarabost woman he had been courting for several weeks to come.

SpikeFeather slapped EvenSong on the back before offering her his hand. "I am heartily glad you never thought of that manoeuvre while practising with me, EvenSong," he laughed. He turned to Arne. "You owe me a jug of Reinald's spiced wine, I believe, Arne. I look forward to enjoying it with my evening meal."

As the watchers gradually dissipated, Azhure and Even-Song walked slowly across the practice field bordering the Lake of Life. The Keep glistened silvery grey in the sun, for the warmth of the Lake of Life kept Sigholt and its immediate environs free of Gorgrael's clouds.

"Well done," Azhure congratulated EvenSong. "Did you notice how all the men blanched as you struck home?"

EvenSong laughed breathlessly, still winded after her exertions. "I hope I have not wounded him permanently."

"Oh, I am sure he will recover to father his share of children," Azhure said lightly. Azhure was now well into her pregnancy and her abdomen protruded gently beneath her tunic. Belial had forbidden her to take part in hand-to-hand combat sessions, although Azhure still trained with her archers – six squads now, over two hundred men – and occasionally went out on patrol. She had returned only last night from leading a four-day patrol into the northern Urqhart Hills. Azhure was well respected among both Icarii and Acharites, and only rarely was her womanhood or her pregnancy commented upon.

As Azhure lapsed into silence, EvenSong sensed there was something troubling her and slid her arm about Azhure's shoulders. "What is it?" she asked.

Azhure took a deep and shaky breath, placing both her hands over her belly. "The baby has hardly moved, EvenSong.

Sometimes I lie a-bed at night and all I feel is this weight in my belly, and I wonder if the baby is still alive. I should have felt it move weeks ago."

"You are a silly!" EvenSong laughed, relieved. "If you had asked either Rivkah or myself we could have told you what the problem is."

Azhure stopped. "You know what's wrong?"

"Azhure. The child you carry is part Icarii. All Icarii babes sleep in the womb until their father awakens them. Azhure, your baby is perfectly all right – awake or not, it will grow and develop normally. Once Axis arrives he can awaken it. Apparently it is the most exquisite feeling, to feel the babe awaken at the sound of its father's voice."

Azhure's shoulders relaxed under EvenSong's arm. "I was so worried," she said, her voice cracking with emotion. "I thought that perhaps I had harmed it." A frown creased her forehead again. "But already I am five months pregnant. When should Icarii fathers sing to their children? Is it too late? And what if Axis *doesn't* arrive before it is born?"

"Azhure, calm down," EvenSong said. "It is best that Axis be here for the baby's birth. But it has been known for a baby to be born without being awakened by its father, and even then, the baby was perfectly normal."

Azhure's shoulders relaxed totally and she dropped her hands from her belly. Embarrassed by her show of vulnerability, she turned the conversation to combat and commands. "How are the Icarii coping with their quarters?" No-one had been too sure what the Icarii – used to the luxury of Talon Spike – would think of the tents they were housed in.

"The Icarii would sleep wrapped in their wings on the cold ground if they thought it was needed to win themselves Tencendor again," EvenSong reassured her. "We are fine. Do not worry about us."

The other worry Azhure, Belial and Magariz had harboured was the reception of the Icarii by the Skarabost villagers at Sigholt. But this had proved no problem at all. For the Acharites camped in tents and rudimentary huts about the shores of the Lake of Life, the arrival of the magical Icarii simply reinforced their belief that they had done the right thing in following the call of the Prophecy. Obviously the StarMan, if not actually here himself yet, would prove a hero of legend if these mythical creatures had left their mountain home to follow him. The teachings of the Seneschal seemed to be rapidly fading from their minds.

Dominating everyone's thoughts was the anxious wait for Axis. Azhure, though sure she had made the right decision in refusing Belial's proposal, increasingly worried about what she could expect from Axis. She still sometimes had the lingering fear that he would take the baby from her and give it to Faraday. Although consciously she realised it was a groundless fear – Axis would never do such a thing – at night it sometimes caused her nightmares.

"Azhure!" EvenSong cried at her side. "Look! My father and grandmother arrive!"

Azhure squinted in the direction EvenSong pointed, but she could see nothing save some black spots in the clouds far to the north.

"Come," EvenSong caught at Azhure's arm and dragged her around the moat of Sigholt towards the bridge, "they'll land on the roof. Come! *Hurry!*"

Magariz had been alerted to the Icarii arrival and now stood on the roof of the Keep. He heard a movement behind him and Rivkah stepped to his side. He smiled at her, delighted. He remembered how beautiful she had been as a teenager in Carlon. Then her hair was deep auburn, her face always mischievous, always alive with humour and love of life.

That had been before her father had arranged her marriage to Searlas, Duke of Ichtar, which had almost broken Rivkah's spirit. Still handsome more than thirty years on, Rivkah was more introspective. Her humour was still there, but more restrained. How strange, thought Magariz, that they should be here now in these circumstances.

Busy as both were, Magariz had not yet had a chance to speak to Rivkah privately since her arrival at Sigholt.

Now Rivkah noticed him looking at her. She reached out and touched his hand where it lay on the grey stonework.

Magariz turned his eyes back to the approaching Icarii. Among them would be Rivkah's former husband, the man for whom she had betrayed Searlas.

"Did he ever know?" Magariz asked very quietly, so that the other Icarii waiting on the roof might not hear. He was not referring to StarDrifter but to Searlas, Rivkah's previous husband.

"No," Rivkah whispered. "No. He never suspected."

Magariz's hands relaxed on the stones. "I worried for you," he said, and tears sprang to Rivkah's eyes.

"And I for you." She blinked back her tears and noticed FarSight had just arrived on the roof. "I am glad this will be the last flight for a while," Rivkah said brightly, "for I do not know where we would have put any more. As it is, we shall have to share apartments."

FarSight's perceptive black eyes picked up Rivkah's discomposure, but assumed it was because StarDrifter was arriving. It must be hard for them, he surmised, to be constantly thrown together this way before they have learned to rebuild their lives apart.

As the approaching Icarii closed, the bridge threw out her challenge. All of the Acharites had been stunned to learn that the bridge not only challenged those on foot, but also those who approached Sigholt from the air. "What would she do if one of the approaching Icarii failed the test?" Belial had asked Veremund when he heard the bridge challenge the first Icarii flight. "Well, Belial," Veremund had answered, "if any fail the test then I guess we will find out, won't we?"

But none had ever failed the test, and none failed now. StarDrifter, his mother and the other Icarii with them landed on the roof of Sigholt, all obviously excited by the Lake and the change in the Keep.

"It's wondrous!" MorningStar cried, as she kissed Rivkah in welcome. "It is so beautiful!" Indeed, in the months since the Lake had refilled, the greenery had spread over all the hills closest to Sigholt, and the Keep and its environs were like an oasis. Now tree ferns as tall as a man grew down most of the closest slopes, and flowers, creeping shrubs, wild roses and gorse bushes covered the hills further away. Sigholt was turning into a garden.

"One day all Tencendor will reawaken like this," said StarDrifter, his eyes on Rivkah. As they kissed briefly, dispassionately, both could not help but remember those days when it seemed as if the world were theirs.

Magariz's mouth twisted as he watched StarDrifter greet Rivkah, then he stepped forward to formally welcome the Icarii. So this was the Icarii Enchanter who had stolen Rivkah from Searlas, and now, so carelessly, had let go. Well, you ageing fool, he thought, you let her go thirty-two years ago. Do not think to criticise StarDrifter for failings you are guilty of yourself.

Magariz's courtly greeting and gracious manners impressed the Icarii, and StarDrifter wondered – as so many others had – how this man had come to serve Borneheld for so long.

As Rivkah started to explain the increasingly crowded living arrangements in Sigholt, EvenSong burst through the staircase doorway, dragging Azhure with her.

"Father!" she cried, delighted, and StarDrifter stepped forward to hug her. EvenSong looked happier than he had seen her at any time since FreeFall's death. "Greet your grandmother," he said, his eyes hunting Azhure. He had not ceased thinking about her in the months they had been apart.

The instant he saw her the world stilled about him.

"Welcome, StarDrifter," Azhure said awkwardly, aware of StarDrifter's face as he stared at her rounded stomach.

Rivkah stepped forward and took StarDrifter by the elbow. "Look, StarDrifter, isn't it wonderful?" she exclaimed, a little too artificially. "Azhure and Axis are going to make us grandparents."

MorningStar brushed past them. "Well," she said, her voice studiously casual, "a Beltide baby, StarDrifter. What do you make of that?"

She reached out for Azhure's arm, but Azhure took several rapid steps backwards. She knew the ancient tradition of both Icarii and Avar peoples – a baby conceived of Wing and Horn at Beltide should never be carried to term. One year an Avar woman had ignored that ancient tradition, and the baby she had conceived with StarDrifter was Gorgrael.

"I am not Avar!" Azhure said, determined to fight for her baby's life if she had to. "Do not try to take this baby from me!"

"Do not fear," MorningStar said. "I merely wanted to . . ."

She got no further. At Azhure's cry, a huge hound leapt from the shadows of the doorwell and seized MorningStar by the wrist, breaking her skin but not crushing the bone.

"The Stars save me!" she cried, "it is an Alaunt!"

A savage growl rumbling deep in his throat, Sicarius twisted his head a little and MorningStar whimpered in pain and sank to her knees.

"*Azhure!*" StarDrifter shouted. "Call the Alaunt off!"

Azhure hesitated, then motioned with her hand. Sicarius dropped MorningStar's wrist and backed off to stand by Azhure's side. He continued to snarl at both MorningStar and StarDrifter, his hackles stiff and aggressive.

"No-one harms my baby," Azhure said into the shocked silence of the rooftop. "No-one."

"I did not mean to harm your baby," MorningStar grated, clutching her bloody wrist to her breast. "Not only is that your baby, but it is a SunSoar, possibly an Enchanter, *and it is my great-grandchild*! I would not harm it!"

StarDrifter helped his mother to her feet, but his eyes were on Azhure. "Neither MorningStar nor myself wish the baby harm. On the contrary."

Azhure nodded stiffly. "MorningStar, I apologise for Sicarius' actions." Both MorningStar and StarDrifter winced at the naming of the hound. "He only wanted to protect me." She stepped forward and took MorningStar's wrist. "Come below and I will wash and bind it for you. These marks will scab in a day and be gone in a week."

As she led MorningStar and StarDrifter below, Magariz and the other Icarii on the rooftop let loose a collective sigh of relief. FarSight raised his eyebrows at Magariz. "A poor welcome for MorningStar."

"If you knew how much Azhure wants that baby then you would only be surprised she did not set Sicarius to Morning-Star's throat," Magariz said quietly.

Azhure washed and bandaged MorningStar's wrist as Star-Drifter sat on the side of the bed. His eyes lingered on Azhure's belly. He had no doubts she carried an Enchanter. Who would sing to the unborn baby if Axis didn't get here in time? His fingers twitched.

At their feet Sicarius stirred, and StarDrifter blinked.

"Where did the Alaunt come from, Azhure?" he asked.

Azhure paused in her bandaging. "The Alaunt? When Ogden, Veremund, Rivkah and I crossed the WildDog Plains they surrounded us one night. We thought they would attack, but instead they bound themselves to me. They have proved good companions."

MorningStar and StarDrifter glanced at each other. WolfStar's hounds? To the woman who carried his bow?

MorningStar also knew the attraction Azhure had for both StarDrifter and Axis, and wondered further.

28

The GateKeeper

"No-one returns from the dead!" cried Orr.

"WolfStar did!" Axis retorted. "Will you help me with this or not?"

"You could kill yourself if you attempt to do this," Orr said, regaining composure. "You do not know the ways."

"I can read the ring," Axis said quietly. "The ring will show me the way. I have a purpose. It will show me the Song."

Orr shook his head. "There is not a Song for *every* purpose, I told you that. You said you promised FreeFall you would bring him back. When? Under what circumstances?"

Axis related how FreeFall had died on the rooftop of the Keep at Gorkenfort, killed by Borneheld's traitorous sword. "As he collapsed in my arms, FreeFall told me to seek out StarDrifter. Then he said something strange. He said, 'The Ferryman owes you, Axis. Learn the secrets and the mysteries of the waterways and bring me home! I will wait at the Gate. Bring me home to EvenSong! Promise!' "

"EvenSong?" Orr queried.

"FreeFall's cousin and lover. And my sister. They were to have married."

Orr repressed a smile. "Ah yes, I had forgotten the SunSoar attraction each to the other. And you promised to do this?"

Axis nodded. "He was dying, and he was dying on my account."

"Did you know to what he referred?"

"No. I had not met my father then, and I was only groping at the very edges of my powers. I had no idea what the Gate was, or the waterways." He paused. "Even now I do not quite know what FreeFall meant by 'the Gate'. Did he mean the Star Gate here?"

Axis and Orr stood close to one of the archways of the Chamber of the Star Gate, near where they had originally entered.

Orr folded his arms inside his cloak and stood deep in thought for long minutes. Just as Axis was about to speak again, Orr raised his head. His violet eyes were almost completely drained of colour and were now dead, soulless. "FreeFall should not have known of the Gate. No Icarii, Enchanter or not, knows of the Gate. No-one. Explain, Axis, how FreeFall could have known about it." His voice was as cold and colourless as his eyes.

Axis was unsure what to say. Why was Orr so upset? "FreeFall spoke those words with his last breath, Orr." Axis' own voice slowed and he returned the Ferryman's stare without blinking. "Perhaps his soul already stood before this 'Gate'. If you want an explanation then that is the only one I can give you. FreeFall knew what the Gate was because he already stood before it."

Orr nodded. "It is the only explanation." He sighed, and the violet slowly started to filter back into his eyes. "And you promised, not knowing what it was you promised. Axis," Orr took Axis' arm, and led him through the archway and down the dim corridor towards the boat. "The Gate is one of the deepest mysteries that the Charonites know of, if not the deepest. If I take you there, you must promise never, *never*," he almost spat the word, "to tell another living soul, not even family."

Axis steadied the boat as Orr stepped in. "I promise," he said, and climbed in behind Orr, settling himself in the prow of the boat.

"Hmm." The Ferryman raised his hood, something Axis had never seen him do. "Are you sure you want to do this?"

"Yes."

Orr arranged his cloak neatly. "Well, I can take you to the Gate, Axis SunSoar, and well might FreeFall wait there for you. But you will have to convince the GateKeeper. She is the only one who can free a soul back to life – and I have never known her to do it yet. Now, speak only when I tell you to, and touch nothing."

The boat slowly started to move, and for a while they passed along normal waterways. The stars sparkled within the green water, and the smooth tunnel walls alternated with great grey caverns as they floated along. But suddenly, so suddenly he was not aware of the transition, Axis realised that they were moving across a vast expanse of dull black water – no stars shone within its depths. There were no walls, no roof at all that Axis could see. They just drifted through a vast sea of blackness, above and below, only the sound of the boat skimming through the water reassuring Axis that they still sailed rather than flew.

A strange pale shape off one side of the boat caught Axis' eye. It was a weeping young woman, carrying a tiny baby. Both the woman and the baby were mist-like, insubstantial, gliding only a handspan above the water. Behind the woman came another shape, but Axis could not see whether it was male or female.

"We travel the River of Death," Orr said. "If you touch the water, you will die."

Startled, Axis placed his hands firmly in his lap. He looked again at the woman and baby.

"She died in birth," Orr said, "and she cries for the life that was denied her and her baby." He paused. "On the night

Gorkentown fell and Yuletide was attacked, the river was crowded with souls – Icarii, Avar, and Acharites."

Axis raised his eyes in unspoken query.

"Yes, Axis. All travel the River of Death, even Skraelings. Death makes brothers and comrades of all."

Orr's eyes brightened, and he leaned forward. "Look behind you, Axis SunSoar. We approach the Gate."

Axis swivelled on his seat. They were rapidly approaching what appeared to be a large island, slightly raised towards its centre. On the top of the rise was a large rectangle of pure light, slightly wider than a normal door and twice as tall.

The next moment the boat rasped across the gravel of the shore and came to a complete halt. Beside them the woman and baby continued to glide towards the rectangle of pure light. "You must go on alone, Axis. By the Gate you will find the GateKeeper. Ask of her what you wish, but do not ask what lies through the Gate. If you do – alive or not – you will be forced through."

"Thank you, Orr. Will you wait here for me?"

"*If* you come back," Orr said comfortingly, "then I will be here for you."

The surface of the island was covered with loose grey gravel, and Axis had to fight to keep from losing his footing. The air was thick and heavy about him, but all he could see was the rectangle of light atop the hill, throbbing with a hypnotic power. Ahead of him the woman and baby reached the rectangle, paused briefly, then stepped through. The light pulsed for an instant, then was calm again – but still it seemed to call, hungry for more.

As he neared the crest of the hill Axis saw that a thin, dark figure sat at a table to one side of the Gate. As he drew closer the figure lifted its head from its contemplation of two shallow bowls, a faint glow emanating from each, and spoke.

"I hear footsteps."

Axis crunched to within five paces of the table and stopped. In the reflected light from the Gate he saw it was a woman who sat there, gaunt, with pale luminous skin, great black eyes sunk into her skull, and black hair left free to flow down her back. White hands rested on the table before her.

She reminded Axis of Veremund.

"I . . ." Axis' voice faltered and he had to clear his throat. It was very hard to speak in this place and before this woman. She did not look very pleased to see him. "I seek the GateKeeper," he finally managed, relieved that his voice emerged calm and steady despite his inner turmoil.

She considered him with her great unblinking eyes. Another soul drifted up to the Gate, paused as it looked at the woman, then passed through. As the Gate pulsed the woman lifted a small metallic ball from one of the bowls and dropped it into the other bowl. It made a soft clink as it fell.

"I am the GateKeeper," the woman replied, her voice toneless. "I keep tally. Have you come to be counted? Why? You are yet alive." She smiled, and Axis wished she hadn't. Her smile had the appeal of a four-day dead corpse and the malevolence of a nightmare.

"I have come with a request."

Another soul drifted into the Gate and the GateKeeper dropped another metal ball from one bowl to the other. She looked up at him again. "Yes? A request? How unusual. Rarely am I asked for requests."

Before Axis could answer, a stream of souls approached. The GateKeeper slowly and deliberately transferred the balls from one bowl to the other as each soul passed through the Gate. The continual and deliberate clicking of the balls as they dropped into the second bowl began to irritate Axis intensely. He tried to stop himself from shuffling.

Finally the stream of souls subsided and the GateKeeper looked up again. "A tavern fire," she explained listlessly. "Thirty-four dead."

"Do all who approach pass through?" Axis asked, wondering what she would do if one of the souls refused to pass through.

The GateKeeper pursed her lips. "No," she finally said, and waved at a small pile of some fifty dull black balls that lay on the extreme right side of the table. "These refuse to go through."

Axis glanced at them, about to ask if FreeFall was among them, then he noticed that there were two other, smaller, piles of balls on the table. One pile of seven balls, sparkling like the stars, lay at the front centre, while a larger pile of some thirty or forty softly glowing golden balls, lay to the extreme left of the table. He pointed at the two extra piles. "And those?"

"Those?" The GateKeeper raised her eyebrows, and in that moment Axis realised she was the most impossibly beautiful woman he had ever seen. "You *see* those?"

"Yes," Axis replied. "Both piles glow, perhaps with the reflected light of the Gate. Are these souls who also refuse to go through?"

"No. These," she pointed at the pile of seven sparkling balls, "are the Greater, and they have no need of me or my Gate." She pursed her lips. "They are incomplete. They await Song and Moon."

Axis frowned, then his face relaxed as he remembered Orr's words. "The Star Gods."

"Yes. You *are* good. And these . . ." The GateKeeper pointed at the larger pile of golden balls, then waved at the Ferryman waiting in his boat far below them. "These," she said with a hint of amusement in her voice, "are the Lesser. They also do not have to go through my Gate."

Axis frowned. The Lesser? What did she mean? He opened his mouth to ask, but the GateKeeper forestalled him.

"Why are you here?" she asked, calm and inscrutable again. All appearance of beauty had vanished.

"I have come to bring FreeFall SunSoar back from the dead," Axis said, realising how ridiculous it sounded. "He said he would wait at the Gate. Perhaps," he indicated the small pile of balls that represented those who would not go through, "he waits among those."

"How amusing that you should think you could bring someone back. No-one ever comes *back* from the dead."

"WolfStar has!"

The woman took a harsh intake of breath, but retained her composure almost instantly.

"WolfStar left through a different Gate," she said, reverting to her expressionless tone. "And thus he would have come back through a different Gate. No-one comes back through this Gate. This is *my* Gate."

Axis glanced at the Gate, curious about what lay on the other side of Death – the greatest mystery of all, and the opportunity to solve it lay only paces away. If WolfStar could come back through the Star Gate then perhaps he could somehow come back through this Gate if he walked through.

"If you wish, you can walk through, Axis SunSoar," the woman said, and Axis noticed a ball in her hand. "But you will never come back. Never." Her hand hovered over the second bowl.

"No." Axis swung her hand away from the bowl. To his surprise her flesh was warm and soft. Was that his life she held in his hand? "I do not wish to go through."

"Well," the GateKeeper smiled and replaced the ball in the first bowl, "as you will. Now, tell me. Why do you think you can return this soul to life?"

Axis told her the story of FreeFall's murder, of the promise the birdman had extracted from Axis as he lay dying. "FreeFall must wait among those souls who refuse to go through. Release him to me."

"Ah," the GateKeeper sighed melodramatically, her face softening into beauty once again, "it is a touching story you tell." Her face hardened. "But no. No. No. No. No-one goes back once they are dead. Now, go away and leave me. FreeFall SunSoar will not return to the land of the living."

"Damn you!" Axis gave in to his anger and disappointment. "Don't you understand anything? FreeFall died well before his time. Murdered. I *promised*! He believed me and now he waits for me! I cannot go back on my promise!"

Far below the Ferryman stirred restlessly.

"No," the GateKeeper said again.

Axis tried one last time. "I was unable to save him from Borneheld, GateKeeper, please give me the chance to save him now!"

The GateKeeper's lips formed the word "No", then stopped at the last moment as the name Axis had mentioned sank in. "Borneheld? Is this Borneheld the one who is also Duke of Ichtar?" she inquired placidly, but Axis could see that her fingers trembled on the table.

"Yes, he is the Duke of Ichtar."

"Ah," the GateKeeper breathed. "I do not like the Dukes of Ichtar."

Now her agitation was evident. She sat silently, deep in the memory of some wrong the Dukes of Ichtar had done her, her fingers shuffling up and down the table like wary spiders. Finally she spoke again, but now her voice quivered with repressed excitement.

"You have it in your power to right an injustice," she said.

"As do you. Release FreeFall."

"And you will help me to right the injustice done to me and mine?" the GateKeeper asked.

"What is it you want me to do?"

"Promise first."

Axis hesitated, then nodded. "I agree. What is it I have to do to bring FreeFall back?"

The GateKeeper's face collapsed in on itself until she resembled nothing more than a skull covered with a thin parchment of skin and a wig of stiff horsehair. "Listen," she rasped.

Axis listened.

When she was done, Axis looked almost as cadaverous as she did. "Even Borneheld does not deserve that," he whispered. "That is horrific. Barbarous."

"You promised," she hissed, "and even now I can exterminate FreeFall's soul so that he will never know the existence that waits for him on the other side of the Gate."

Axis had no choice. "Then you have a bargain, Gate-Keeper."

"Remember, the conditions of the contract must be met within a year and a day of your returning to the OverWorld."

"Yes, I remember. GateKeeper . . ."

"Yes?"

"Why do you request such a bargain?"

"It is required," she said, calm once more.

Axis took a deep breath. "And FreeFall?"

"As I promised, StarMan, but you must keep your bargain, or the transformation will not complete itself and FreeFall will wither and die again."

Suddenly Axis wanted to escape these worlds beneath the surface of the earth into warmth and life again.

"Well," he finally said, "until we meet again, GateKeeper," and he sketched a salute and marched back down the gravel-coated hill towards the Ferryman.

"Oh," the GateKeeper smiled to herself, her face that of a beautiful young girl. "And that will be far sooner than you wish, StarMan."

Her thoughts drifted as she tallied the never-ending shuffle of souls through the Gate. She hated and loathed the Dukes of Ichtar even more than Sigholt did. Zeherah was her daughter.

29

Caelum

Azhure twisted over to her side in the bed, hoping she had not woken Rivkah. She desperately needed her sleep for she had trained her archers hard today and was tired and sore, but no matter what she did she could not drift off. And tonight the baby lay heavy and uncomfortable in her womb. Despite the reassurances from EvenSong, Rivkah and MorningStar, Azhure still worried that for a six-months babe, the child was small and rarely moved.

Azhure sighed and eased herself out of the bed carefully, then padded silently across the floor to the door. She hesitated as she considered whether or not to take a wrap with her, but the Sigholt nights were so temperate that the linen of her nightgown would keep her warm enough.

Sicarius rose and followed his mistress out the door.

Leaving the silent corridors behind her, Azhure climbed the narrow staircase to the roof. A few minutes in the night air usually calmed her.

She sighed happily as she reached the deserted roof. A warm breeze blew off the Lake, and Azhure unbound her hair and shook it out. She gazed at the Lake of Life – a long soak in the steaming waters would be the perfect relaxant. But she could not be bothered with the walk. A stroll around the roof should do. Sicarius settled down by the doorway; there was little danger on the roof of Sigholt.

Azhure leaned over the waist-high wall and surveyed the sleeping camps. Around the northern shore of the Lake stretched the tents of the Skarabost refugees, now numbering several thousand. Azhure sighed as her eyes drifted over the faint lights of the camps. Vegetable gardens, although they helped, would not be enough if Sigholt were forced to live off its own resources.

She took a deep breath and held it. The wild gorse was flowering across the hills; already the HoldHard Pass was blossoming with new life as both plant and animal life crept along its length.

"Sigholt will prove the heart of the new Tencendor," she whispered, closing her eyes. "I am so glad that I am a part of this reawakening."

Still with her eyes closed, Azhure turned and leaned her back against the waist-high wall. When she finally opened her eyes Axis was standing in the centre of the roof, staring at her.

He had said his goodbyes to Orr in the centre of the violet lake of the crystal cave as they bobbed gently in the flat-bottomed boat and then he'd transferred almost immediately, feeling the surge of the Star Dance through his body, revelling in its power. What would it be like to one day manipulate the entire Star Dance rather than the minute portion needed for this Song? Axis forced his thoughts back to Sigholt. How long had he been gone? Was all well?

He felt himself being drawn across a vast distance as if by an unseen hand. The closer he got to Sigholt, the faster he travelled, and Axis feared he would be slammed into its roof with such force that his bones would be crushed.

But just as that horrifying thought crossed his mind, his stomach lurched and he found himself standing on Sigholt's roof, surrounded by darkness, the stars wheeling in their perpetual dance in the heavens above his head.

Confused, Axis thought he must have somehow transferred back in time to the vision he had seen of Rivkah, young, lovely and pregnant.

But the woman who turned to him was Azhure, not his mother. But like Rivkah, her waist was thickened with midterm pregnancy.

She opened her eyes, and they widened as she caught sight of him.

Axis opened his mouth, unsure what to say, when a deep and musical voice boomed about him. "Are you true?"

"Yes, dammit!" Axis snapped without thinking, and the bridge, offended, muttered grumpily to herself.

"Azhure? Azhure?" He took one step forward, then just stood and held out his hand.

Azhure stood motionless, still too shocked to move or speak. Somehow she had always thought Axis would stride in across the bridge, and Azhure would meet him serenely, invulnerable behind her uniform and her position as commander in his army. They would talk about the baby sensibly, adults discussing the unexpected outcome of their Beltide excess. They would come to a civilised and utterly mature arrangement whereby Axis would still love and teach his child but neither it nor Azhure would stand between him and Faraday. Indeed, Azhure could tell him about Belial's proposal, which would solve all their problems, and Axis would be comforted that Belial could relieve him of this small embarrassment.

But here she stood, her hair down, barefoot and only a thin nightgown between her and Axis. There he stood, his face looking tired and strained, his entire body slumping with weariness, but holding his hand out to her as he had on Beltide night, and, oh, curse him! she could feel her blood surge as strongly as it had that night. All she wanted to do was to run light-footed across the space between them and let him hold her and comfort her and tell her that he loved her.

But he did not love her, and that thought alone managed to keep Azhure at a reasonably safe distance.

"Axis," she said in a voice considerably calmer than she felt. "Welcome to Sigholt."

Axis stood there, his hand extended, then strode the distance between them and hugged her tight.

Sicarius, watching from the door, sat up, but otherwise made no move towards the pair. He could feel the pull of their blood each to the other.

"Azhure," Axis whispered. "What have I done to you?" His hand, trembling, gently passed over her rounded abdomen, feeling the tug of the baby's blood.

"What any man will do to any woman when he lies with her at the right moment," she said, too lightly.

"Azhure," Axis asked, "what's wrong?"

"Oh, Axis." Azhure's voice was artificially cheerful as she disentangled herself. "I am sorry that I have presented you with this complication. I can assure you that I won't try to tie you down. Perhaps," Azhure's voice broke a little under the strain, "we can talk about this slight embarrassment in the morning, when you are rested."

Complication? Embarrassment? Axis couldn't believe what he was hearing. Did she think she was any of these things? But he could see her discomfort, and was scared that she would dart away any moment.

"You're right, Azhure. It would be better if we could talk about this in more congenial surroundings. Do you know if there are quarters prepared for me?"

Azhure relaxed. "Yes, of course. Belial has kept the main apartment complex prepared, awaiting you. Axis, you cannot know how pleased all will be at your return. And there is so much to tell you!"

"Then show me these quarters, Azhure. I am sure that Belial will keep me busy in the morning. And I, as well, have news to share."

Azhure led him down the stairs, Axis raising his eyebrows at the huge hound which clattered after them, but making no other comment. Azhure chatted brightly, telling Axis some of what had been going on in the Keep in his absence. Axis answered in monosyllables, his eyes drifting every few steps to her thickened body. She was going to make him a father! Axis felt light-headed – no other woman had ever done this for him. A father. The thought sobered him. He would not fail this child. This child would know its father. It would have no cause for doubts. No cause for nightmares.

The corridors were quiet, deserted at this time of the night, and no-one was there to see Azhure let Axis into the main apartment complex.

"Come in, Azhure," Axis said easily, "and help me light the lamps. Besides, there is something I have to say to you."

The main apartment suite consisted of several chambers grouped about a central one, where Axis and Azhure now stood. It was richly furnished with warm, mellowed woods and draped and cushioned in yellow and crimson damask. To one side a door to an equally opulent bedchamber stood ajar.

The hound settled quietly by the door, his golden eyes on his mistress.

"Azhure?"

She turned from the lamp she was lighting and smiled. "Yes?"

"How long have I been gone? Or should I," he grinned, "hazard a guess from the roundness of your belly?"

Azhure coloured. "It is the first week of Bone-month, Axis."

He sighed and turned away, rubbing his face tiredly. "Late. I had not thought to be gone so long. There is so much to be done."

"You will need your rest," Azhure said, putting down the lamp she was carrying and starting to edge for the door. The sooner she was gone from here the better.

Axis toyed with the fringe of a lampshade. "Azhure, there is one more thing I would ask of you," he said.

"Yes?"

Axis raised his pale eyes. "Stay with me. Be my lover."

Her whole body stiffened. "No, I cannot," she whispered. Why had she let herself be caught like this?

Axis walked over, his eyes locked in Azhure's. She went rigid as he approached, but he walked straight past her, his arm brushing hers, closed the door, and turned back. "And why is that? Why can you not stay?"

Azhure had spent months putting her arguments together for this moment. Where were they now? Increasingly desperate, she blurted, "Because I am a simple peasant girl and you are an Icarii Enchanter."

Axis took a step closer to Azhure. "The simple peasant girl stayed behind in Smyrton," he said, "and before me is the woman who has mastered the Wolven." And the woman who sent me reeling among the Stars at Beltide. Would he feel the Star Dance through her body again when he lay with her? "Stay with me. Dance with me."

Azhure swallowed. "I am mortal, short-lived, and you will live for hundreds of years. You have seen how StarDrifter and Rivkah's marriage foundered on this. There is no hope for us. No hope."

Axis stepped yet closer. "I may be dead in a year or less, Azhure. What does a five-hundred-year lifespan count for when events of such magnitude threaten to envelop us all? And we are not StarDrifter and Rivkah. Stay with me." He smoothed a tendril of hair back from her cheek.

Azhure took a deep breath and closed her eyes, balling her hands into fists as she tried to ignore the soft stroking of his fingers. "Faraday," she said tightly.

Axis kissed the tender spot at the junction of her jaw and neck. "Faraday is many months and many leagues away. Stay with me."

"Faraday loves you!" She felt his teeth against her skin, and it brought memories and desires flooding back.

"Faraday's love for me does not stop her sharing her bed with Borneheld. Stay with me."

"Faraday loves you, and you her!"

Axis laughed softly and untied the laces of her nightgown. "What is love, Azhure? Can you tell me? Stay with me. Dance with me."

He tilted Azhure's head and kissed her mouth. "It is too late to be talking of remaining true when you stand here heavy with my child. Besides, Faraday is a noblewoman, a lady of court. She accepted my previous lover and she will accept you. Stay with me."

"Axis, do not ask this of me!"

"Azhure." He leaned back slightly, his hands slowly pulling the nightgown down over her shoulders and breasts, his fingers stroking. "What reason is there for you to go? You are my friend and my helpmeet, my ally. You fill my eyes and my thoughts. You carry my child. And you love me – you cannot deny that. Would you deny me my child, deny the child its father? What reason is there to go? Stay with me. Feel the power of the Star Dance through my fingers, through my hands, through my body. Be my lover."

Azhure could not resist. She had fought as best she could. Axis was right, Faraday was far away, and Azhure would deal with it when she had to.

"Yes," she whispered, and in his darkened corner of existence the Prophet laughed loud and merrily.

They lay still and quiet on the bed, both awake, both unwilling to slip into sleep and waste the night in unconsciousness. After a while Azhure felt Axis' hand caress her belly again, and she finally spoke.

"Axis, the baby hardly moves. They say that you must sing to it, awaken it, teach it."

Axis kissed her cheek. "Our child is a boy. I can feel it."

"You can? A boy?" Azhure laughed, and her own hand stole down to her belly. "A son."

Axis smiled at her excitement. "What would you like to call him? If I am to sing to him, awaken him, we should really grace him with his name."

Azhure rolled over a little so that she faced Axis. "You would let *me* name him? Don't you want to name him yourself?"

Axis gently ran his hand around her back, slowly stroking her skin, feeling the ridged scars. She had endured so much pain already in life, so much rejection, so much uncertainty. And now she had carried his child for over six months without any support from him. "Tell me what you would like to name him."

Azhure did not have to think about it. "Caelum."

"Why Caelum?"

"When I was a small girl, after my mother had left me," Azhure said, "there was a blacksmith who would come to Smyrton every two weeks to ply his trade. A big man. Dark. He called himself Alayne and he was kind to me. He told me stories, and for many years he was the only friend I had. Caelum . . . Caelum was the hero of his favourite story. The name is appropriate, surely. It means . . ."

"Stars in heaven, Azhure, I know what it means," Axis murmured. He had thought he'd led a lonely life, but his loneliness was nothing compared to the misery of Azhure's childhood. He had enjoyed the love and support of so many Brothers within the Seneschal, not the least Jayme himself. All Azhure had were the fortnightly visits of a blacksmith who was occasionally kind to her and who told her stories of mythical heroes.

"Caelum is a fine name," he said finally.

"Axis," Azhure suddenly said. "Promise me you will never steal this baby to give to Faraday to raise!"

Axis sat up on his elbow, appalled. How could she think that he would do such a thing? Unbidden, StarDrifter's words from many months ago in Talon Spike echoed through his mind, "In ages gone past Icarii birdmen simply took the babies of human–Icarii unions and never spared a thought for the women who had struggled to birth their children." Did Azhure fear he would do that to her?

"Listen to me," he said, his voice rough with emotion. "I will never take our son from you. Both of us have suffered because our parents were torn from us. Do you think that I would perpetuate the same pain on our son? Azhure, hear me, I swear on everything I hold dear that I will never, *never*, take our son from you. Believe me!"

Azhure finally let go of her fears. She reached up and cupped Axis' face in her hands. "Then awaken our son, Axis, and tell him that his parents love him dearly and will never desert him."

Axis sat up and pulled Azhure against him. He put his arms around her and placed his splayed hands over her belly.

"Awake, Caelum," he said clearly, and began to sing.

Azhure closed her eyes and let his Song envelop her, feeling their baby – Caelum – stir to wakefulness in her womb. He twisted and turned so his entire body pressed against the outer wall of her womb, as close to Axis' hands as possible. The sensation was so exquisite it went way beyond the description of words.

How could she ever have considered Belial's proposal? Azhure wondered. How could she ever have believed she could walk away from Axis? Beltide had been a point beyond which there was no turning back. No longer would she attempt to deny her love for this Enchanter who held her now.

Rivkah had told Azhure that it was a tragedy for a human woman to love an Icarii Enchanter, to be entrapped in a love which would cause only pain, but Azhure hoped these months with Axis and their son in Sigholt would somehow store up enough love and happiness to see her through the inevitable suffering. Azhure's body relaxed completely against Axis', letting the rhythm of the Song he was singing wash through her, feeling her baby respond to his father.

After a long while Axis stopped, and he smiled and whispered into Azhure's ear. "You have grown a wonderful son within your body, Azhure. Speak to him. Speak to your son. He loves you and would hear your voice."

"Me? But I thought it was only the Icarii father who could speak to babes still in the womb. Me? Why would he want to listen to me?"

"He loves you," Axis repeated, smiling against her ear. "You are his hero. He will hear you. He is awake."

Azhure slid her hands down over her belly, and Axis' covered hers. What would she say? Slowly, hesitantly, then with more confidence and joy, Azhure spoke to her son.

30

"Let Fly the Standard!"

R ivkah hurried along the corridors of Sigholt, increasingly fretful. She had woken early to find Azhure gone, her side of the bed stone cold. Her clothes were still lying draped casually across the chair – Azhure was still in her nightgown. Had she gone for a midnight stroll through Sigholt and suffered some mishap – a fall perhaps? Was Azhure now lying injured some place?

Rivkah turned down the main corridor and hurried towards the stairwell that led to the roof. She halted by the door to the main apartment. The door was closed and nothing seemed amiss. But there was something . . . different.

Rivkah suddenly realised what it was as the faint odour of lamp oil registered. Had Azhure gone in there? Was she now asleep – injured, perhaps – on the floor? Rivkah gripped the door handle and stepped into the central chamber.

Lamps had indeed been lit, but had now burned down. Rivkah glanced about the chamber and took a deep breath. She had not been in these apartments since returning to Sigholt, and they brought back a flood of memories. Searlas is long dead, she told herself firmly, and stepped further into the room – and saw Azhure's nightgown lying in a pale puddle in the centre of the floor. She turned her head towards the open door to the bedchamber, then walked slowly over and stepped through.

Azhure and Axis lay asleep on the bed, Axis' arms wrapped protectively around Azhure. Well, thought Rivkah, a curious stillness in her mind, you did not run far enough or fast enough, did you Azhure?

Axis opened his eyes and stared at Rivkah standing just inside the doorway. He gently disentangled himself from Azhure; who murmured a little as he left the bed. He paused to pull the sheets over her before he hugged his mother.

"Welcome home to Sigholt," Rivkah whispered, holding her son tightly to her. "Did the Ferryman teach you well? Did you learn his secrets?"

"The Ferryman still plies his boat along the waterways, Rivkah. He is well." Axis brushed some stray silver wisps of hair back from his mother's forehead. "Does anyone else know I am here?" he asked.

"No." Rivkah paused and glanced at Azhure, still asleep.

"She carries a beautiful son, Rivkah."

"She was very worried. Have you sung to him?"

"Yes," Axis replied softly, remembering.

"Rivkah?" Azhure murmured sleepily behind them. "Is that you?"

Rivkah let her son go and sat down on the bed beside Azhure, stroking her hair.

Azhure knew exactly what she was thinking. "I will be happy, Rivkah. Do not fret for me."

Rivkah's face hardened. They were both so young and both so sure that life would work out exactly as they hoped. Well, already plans and vows lay shattered across the floor. Could they not see that?

"Azhure, it grows late, and Belial has called a meeting of his commanders in the map-room. You must dress. I'll bring your clothes here.

"Axis," Rivkah turned to him, "Belial would be more than pleased to see you. He has long fretted about your absence."

Axis nodded. "Then shall we surprise him, Azhure? Let me see what Belial has done with my command over the past eight months."

"And while you are in conference I will tell StarDrifter and MorningStar you have arrived," Rivkah said, rising from the bed.

"They are here?" Axis asked sharply.

"Yes. They arrived some time ago."

"Good," he nodded, "for I must talk with them."

Belial paced about the map-room. Where *was* she? Magariz, Arne, FarSight and two of his Crest-Leaders had been here almost a quarter of an hour, chatting about inconsequential matters. Well, Belial fumed, if her pregnancy was going to make her sleep in during the mornings, then perhaps . . .

The door opened and Azhure stepped into the room.

"You're late," Belial snapped. "I . . ."

Axis stepped into the room behind Azhure. "I am afraid that was my fault, Belial."

Belial gaped at Axis, then he strode across the chamber and enveloped his friend in a great hug. "Axis!

"Eight months' absence is too long, my friend," Belial said, finally stepping back. "I am glad to have you back."

Axis turned to Magariz. "Magariz!" They gripped hands. Axis' warmth for this man who had abandoned lifelong loyalties to follow his cause was only slightly less than for Belial. Without Belial and Magariz Axis' cause would be almost hopeless. Axis touched the blood-red blazing sun on Magariz's chest. "Azhure has been wrapping you in her designs, I see."

Axis greeted Arne, then FarSight and the two other Crest-Leaders. Their black uniforms, although similarly emblazoned with the blood-red blazing sun, made them look forbidding and dangerous and Axis wondered how their training was going.

After all the greetings were done, Axis gestured to the others to take their places about the table; it was clear that Axis had assumed full command the instant he'd walked into the chamber.

Axis placed his hands on the table, stared about the table, then said quietly to Belial, "Tell me."

Talking in confident tones, Belial informed Axis of the status of Sigholt and of his command, now a combined one of Acharites and Icarii, ground and air combatants.

Axis nodded occasionally, raised his eyebrows in silent query at other times. Belial had worked wonders, and Axis was impressed – and grateful. The Icarii were doing well, learning the skills they would need in battle. The Lake had awakened both Keep and hills. When Belial described Azhure's work with the archers, her abilities as a fighter and as a commander, Axis was not surprised. As Axis and Azhure shared a look, Belial quickly moved on to the growing number of refugees who flocked to Sigholt. Word of the Prophecy was spreading, and proving potent.

"I could not have asked for a more capable or a more courageous group of commanders than the seven of you," Axis said. "I thank you with all my heart for what you have done here in Sigholt and for what you have done for me personally. If I emerge victorious then it will be your victory as much as mine. Belial." He looked at his friend. "To you I owe the greatest debt. You accepted me for what I was when I was consumed with self-doubt about my heritage. You saved my life from Borneheld and engineered not only my escape from Gorkenfort, but the escape of an army as well. You took that force and built me a base here in Sigholt which nothing my enemies enjoy can rival. Belial, my friend," he reached across the table and gripped Belial's hand, "I thank you.

"Now." Axis leaned back and spoke to the rest of the group. "What do we control? What is the state of the Skraelings? Borneheld's men? What do you know?"

Magariz lifted a map from the rack behind him and unrolled it across the table. His hand swept over the Urqhart Hills in an arc from north to south. "We control most of the Urqhart Hills, except the extreme north and north-west, which the Skraelings occupy. We also dare not approach too close to Hsingard, which the Skraelings have destroyed. The HoldHard Pass is ours, as is the territory spreading south from the Pass to the Nordra. Below the Nordra we can move fairly easily in the northernmost parts of Skarabost, but we do occasionally skirmish with the outer patrols from Jervois Landing in the north-western parts of the Seagrass Plains. We have supply routes stretching into Skarabost, which should remain open unless our access to the Nordra is cut off."

"A good start," said Axis. "And the rest?"

"We face problems from both Gorgrael and Borneheld," Magariz said slowly. "Intelligence from the farflight scouts shows that Gorgrael builds his forces. We hurt them badly above Gorkenfort, and for months the Skraeling masses were scattered all over Ichtar, too disorganised to push further south. But now Gorgrael has regained control and rebuilt his forces. Skraelings, under firm direction now, mass below Hsingard in an effort to break through Borneheld's defences at Jervois Landing. A smaller force also builds in the northern WildDog Plains. Gorgrael obviously plans a two-pronged attack into Achar this winter. Not only past Jervois Landing, but also through the WildDog Plains. I only hope Borneheld can hold them at Jervois Landing, because I suspect most of our efforts this winter will be directed at keeping the Skraelings from pushing south through the WildDog Plains."

This was bitter news for Axis. He had hoped to move his own forces into southern Achar during the winter while Borneheld was occupied at Jervois Landing. But now it appeared that if Borneheld was going to be occupied with the Skraelings, so was he. Axis knew he could not let Gorgrael succeed in his push through the WildDog Plains.

But his agreement with the GateKeeper would last only a year and a day before it lapsed and FreeFall would never be reborn. He had to be in Carlon before then.

"And Borneheld?" he asked. "What has he done at Jervois Landing? How has he equipped his forces? What is his strength?"

"Axis, Borneheld now commands over twenty thousand men in Jervois Landing, and . . . he controls the force as *King*. Priam died some months ago."

Axis went rigid with shock. "*King?*" He took a deep breath. "I can just imagine how Borneheld seized the throne," he muttered bleakly. Now Borneheld would be immeasurably more dangerous. "But how did he manage to find a force of twenty thousand? How?"

Magariz explained about the Ravensbundmen and the extra forces that Borneheld had scavenged from about Achar. Then, as Axis' shoulders slumped, he briefly explained about the system of canals Borneheld had ordered built between the Nordra and Azle rivers.

There was silence about the table. After a moment Axis shook his head. "Well, FarSight, your Strike Force should be worth five men each. At least Borneheld has not taken to the air yet – unless there is still more bad news, Magariz?"

Magariz laughed, relieving some of the tension in the room. "No, Axis, Borneheld is still ground-bound. The Strike Force will go far towards evening out our chances."

Axis nodded. "Then I had better announce my arrival. Shall I stand from atop Sigholt and shout it for all to hear?"

"No," Azhure said softly. "I have a better way."

Axis met StarDrifter and MorningStar outside the map-room. As Azhure brushed past, StarDrifter raised his eyebrows.

"A son," Axis said. "And an Enchanter."

StarDrifter's eyes glinted. "I knew she would breed powerful Enchanters, Axis."

"I do not think of her as a brood mare, StarDrifter," Axis snapped. "She is Azhure, and I value her as much in her own right as I do for being the mother of my son." He wheeled away and followed Azhure down the corridor.

StarDrifter watched them go, still bitter and resentful that Azhure had chosen Axis that night, then hurried after them.

As the SunSoars and a group of commanders gathered on the roof of the Keep, Rivkah handed a bundle to Azhure.

"Axis," Azhure said, "over the past months Rivkah and myself have worked on this whenever we had time. Arne?"

Arne, obviously forewarned, took the bundle from Azhure and walked over to the empty flagpole.

"Now you are here in residence," Azhure said, "let all know it," and she turned to Arne.

Axis watched Arne unfold the deep gold material, then his eyes caught Azhure's. "Thank you," he whispered.

As Arne raised Axis SunSoar's standard, the breeze caught the fabric and it unfurled in a shimmer of light. As the golden tunic Azhure had wrought for Axis, so his standard – the deep gold field with the blood-red sun blazing in the centre. All stood and watched it whip and crack in the sun.

"The command is yours, Axis," Belial said formally. "I have done my best. Now it is yours to do your best with."

Trying to control his emotions, Axis strode to the wall and gazed over the valley. He could hardly reconcile what he saw there with the Sigholt of before. The Lake of Life had truly lived up to her name, and now new life bloomed all about the Lake and Keep. Late summer roses were even starting to crawl up the silvery walls of the Keep. Sigholt was truly alive.

He looked closely at the camps spreading around the edge of the Lake, then at the practice fields where units were engaged in their mid-morning combat training. Eventually, more and more of them noticed the standard high above their heads, and eventually they fell still. Axis raised a hand, and a faint cheer reached his ears.

"I cannot wait to begin, my friends, but there is one more thing I must do before I rejoin my command." Axis gave a single sharp whistle, and stared into the sun.

"What are you doing?" asked StarDrifter.

"I await my wings," Axis replied, motioning for silence.

All eyes turned to the sun.

Very slowly – and the Icarii with their extraordinary vision were the first to see it – a black spot spiralled out of the sun.

He spiralled down out of the sun, escaping its blazing fury. He was alive and he rejoiced in that life, although he had no memory of the state of death or of his previous life. He simply rejoiced in the freedom of the unlimited sky and the heat of the sun on his wingbacks as he plummeted further and further down to the green and blue earth below him.

Gradually he realised he had to go somewhere, meet someone. He pulled himself out of his crazy dive and scanned the earth below. The glint of the Lake and silver grey of the Keep caught his eye, and he soared in a gigantic loop above them. An exultant scream left his throat.

All below heard the eagle's cry and watched as it tipped its wings and drifted towards Axis. He laughed in sheer delight and extended his left arm, whistling once more.

In a flurry of white and silver feathers the eagle landed on his arm, both fighting for a moment to keep their balance.

StarDrifter stared in amazement. No-one had ever tamed a snow eagle previously. And this was half as large again as most snow eagles, though coloured like all its kind with white and silver feathers, and black eyes, beak and talons.

"Axis?" MorningStar finally managed to ask.

"He is my eyes in the sky, my wings, my voice as I need a voice," said Axis, explaining nothing at all. "He is a gift from the UnderWorld."

Everyone looked at each other in confusion.

31

WolfStar's Story

As the eagle preened itself on the parapet wall, Axis asked for time to speak to MorningStar and his parents privately. He touched Azhure's cheek as she turned to go; the gesture was lost on none.

"Gather the unit and Wing commanders in the courtyard after noon," Axis told Belial, "and I will address them there. Arne. A word?"

Arne paused, listened to Axis, and nodded briefly.

Soon the rooftop was empty save for the three Icarii Enchanters and Rivkah.

"And what secrets did you learn from the Ferryman?" StarDrifter asked eagerly.

"Many secrets, StarDrifter, and most I have promised not to reveal."

StarDrifter's mouth hardened into a thin line. "Are they so terrible?"

"No. They are quite simple. But I vowed not to reveal them, and I will not. However," Axis paused and scratched the eagle under its beak, "what I can tell you is terrible enough."

MorningStar walked over to her grandson. "What?"

Axis sighed, and all noted how tight and tense the skin was under his eyes. "In Talon Spike, MorningStar, you theorised that there was another SunSoar Enchanter, an Enchanter who, for his or her own purposes, had taught both myself and Gorgrael."

MorningStar nodded. "Yes?"

"I can now tell you who it is."

Both StarDrifter and his mother visibly tensed. *Who?*

"It is WolfStar SunSoar, come back through the Star Gate."

StarDrifter and MorningStar paled in shock, unable to say anything. Rivkah shook her head. Of all Enchanter-Talons to step back through the Star Gate, it had to be WolfStar. What had the Icarii done to deserve this?

Steps sounded in the stairwell and MorningStar and StarDrifter jumped nervously.

"I asked Arne to send the Sentinels up," Axis explained. "Perhaps they can help explain what WolfStar might want, why he came back."

"Axis? What is it?" Ogden asked, noting the tension.

Briefly Axis told the Sentinels about WolfStar's return.

"WolfStar!" Veremund muttered. "But Axis, why are you so sure?"

Axis related how he had discovered the illusion of WolfStar's statue in the Chamber of the Star Gate, and how the Ferryman – Axis did not give them his name – had realised WolfStar had come back through the Star Gate. He paused and looked around. "It is more than time you told me WolfStar's story, and explained why you fear WolfStar so much. I need to know why he has come back."

"It would sicken me to tell the entire tale," MorningStar said. "Veremund? Will you speak of WolfStar?"

Veremund nodded. "WolfStar's story belongs to a lost world, Axis, a world of four thousand years ago. WolfStar was a remarkable Icarii Enchanter who, at the extraordinary age of only ninety-one, succeeded as Talon of Tencendor."

"There was always rumour about his succession at such an early age," Ogden interrupted. "His father was young and fit, only some two hundred years old, and should have lived hundreds more years. But . . ."

"He fell out of the sky one fine afternoon," MorningStar finished for him. "And no-one claimed the arrow that feathered from his chest."

"Murder, or accident?" Veremund mused. "Who knows? WolfStar had an alibi – he was in council with several of the Crest-Leaders at the time – but it was rumoured and is now generally believed that he planned, if not executed, the murder of his own father."

"He wanted the throne. Badly," Jack said, gazing out across the Urqhart Hills so none could see his face.

"Yes. He wanted the throne badly, Jack." Veremund sounded annoyed at the constant interruptions. "WolfStar, ever since he was a flightless child, had been fascinated by the Star Gate. Access to the Star Gate was much more open then, although only a Talon and his heir were allowed completely free use of it. WolfStar would spend hours, sometimes days, simply staring into the Gate. He was consumed with the idea that the universe contained other worlds."

Axis looked up in surprise. Other worlds? The thought had never occurred to him, but now he felt a tug of curiosity.

"Other worlds," Veremund repeated. "WolfStar surmised that each sun was paired with a world, perhaps like ours, that circled it, as ours does. He looked at the multitude of stars in the universe, and surmised that a multitude of worlds also existed."

"Crazy," StarDrifter muttered.

"For years WolfStar had lived with his obsession, and then, suddenly, he was Talon. Now he felt he could do something about it. The Icarii had long talked about the possibility that someone could step through the Star Gate, and survive to step back through it." Veremund laughed quietly. "But who would be the first to try? One day WolfStar approached the Assembly and asked permission to send an Icarii child, one with Enchanter talent, through the Gate. He claimed it was better to waste the life of a child, if waste it would be, than the life of a fully trained Enchanter."

There was horrified silence around the rooftop, as there had been in the Icarii Assembly that long-distant day.

"The Assembly, as you might expect, refused WolfStar permission to so sacrifice one of their children." Now Veremund was almost whispering. "But WolfStar's obsession was consuming him, and perhaps now he *was* slightly mad. He was determined to step through the Star Gate and explore other worlds, but he also wanted to be able to step back into this one. And he needed to *know* he could step back. One day a young Icarii child, only fourteen years, went out flying and never returned. He was mourned; it was believed that perhaps he had suffered a fatal wing cramp while flying. But then, a few weeks later, another child disappeared, and then another. Then someone realised that all three had possessed Enchanter powers. And then someone accused WolfStar of child murder."

Veremund paused for breath. "WolfStar, defiant and very sure of his own powers, said that it was not murder, but necessary experiment. The secrets of the Star Gate *must* be solved. He asked what would happen if one day a race from another world wanted to invade our world through the Star Gate? What would happen if someone else, some*thing* else, discovered the secrets of the Star Gate, and Gates like it, before he did?"

Axis rocked on his feet at the idea. WolfStar's methods may have been appalling, but were his concerns so crazy as the others seemed to think? He started to speak, but Veremund continued.

"WolfStar claimed it would only be a matter of time before one *did* come back. Dear ones, WolfStar was an Enchanter-Talon, and he was very powerful. Far from feeling remorse for the three children he had murdered to this point,

WolfStar produced a roster of children, all with Enchanter powers, whom he proposed to send through the Star Gate one by one until he found one who could come back."

Bile rose in Axis' throat as he thought of his own son growing safe in Azhure's womb. How would *he* have felt, sitting among the Icarii, listening to his child's name read out by WolfStar as the fifth, or sixth, or twenty-sixth child to be sacrificed to the Enchanter-Talon's mad obsession?

"As I said, WolfStar was powerful, very powerful, and by now none dared challenge him. All, I suppose, hoped that a child before theirs would be the one to come back."

"I don't believe it," Axis whispered. "They let their children be murdered? How *could* they? How *many*?"

"He sent a further two hundred and seven children tumbling to their deaths in the Star Gate, Axis," said Veremund. "Some only as old as three or four, the oldest about sixteen. He sent his own niece, daughter of his younger brother. He sent," and Veremund almost did not say this, knowing how much it would pain those listening, "he toppled his own wife, heavy with child, through the Gate."

Axis went as white as the snow eagle. "Why?"

"Because WolfStar thought his wife's body might serve as some protection for the child within. WolfStar knew his wife carried an extraordinarily talented child, and he hoped the unborn child might be able to succeed where other children had failed. It was a procession of death, Axis. The Icarii parents wept and grieved and lamented, but still they brought their children to the Star Gate as WolfStar demanded."

"Part of the reason why the Icarii are so sensitive about WolfStar," MorningStar explained brokenly, "was that our ancestors did not try to stop him. Virtually an entire generation of Enchanters was lost."

Veremund was glad the tale was almost at its end. "WolfStar almost crippled the Icarii race with his obsession. So many died, and those left were emotionally and mentally scarred. Many parents who had lost children threw themselves from high rocks in their grief, dashing themselves to death on the hard earth."

"And did WolfStar discover the secret, Veremund? Was all this sacrifice worth it?" Axis asked, his voice hoarse with emotion. *He* was descended of such mad blood?

"No. None ever came back. WolfStar would stand on the lip of the Star Gate and scream abuse at the children who had gone through, scream at them to take their courage in their hands and make the effort to come back."

"Why didn't someone push the murderer through the Star Gate himself?" Axis demanded.

"It took WolfStar's younger brother, CloudBurst SunSoar, who had watched his own daughter scream as WolfStar hurled her into the Star Gate, to put an end to his brother's murderous ways," said Veremund. "One day in Assembly, CloudBurst simply walked up behind his brother, and stabbed him. Just once, but it was a fatal blow."

"That was the only way the SunSoars managed to salvage their self-respect, Axis," MorningStar said. Her face was pale and lined. "CloudBurst managed to save both the SunSoars and the Icarii people. He took the Talon throne and stopped the murders, but the scars remain."

"We so rarely speak of WolfStar," StarDrifter explained, "because of our deep shame."

MorningStar's mouth twisted. "The murder of so many children was not WolfStar's only crime. He was guilty of many other crimes against the Icarii People . . ."

"He stole the Enchantress' ring," interrupted StarDrifter, and Axis jumped a little guiltily. He fingered the pocket where he'd secreted the ring.

". . . but the children's murder was one that the Icarii have never, never forgotten," MorningStar finished. "What is an ancient ring, even one so precious, when compared to so many wasted lives?"

"And now WolfStar is back," Axis mused. No wonder the Ferryman had reacted with such horror. "*He* learned the secrets of the Star Gate, and now he has stepped back through. All right. Why? Jack? Do you have any idea why WolfStar has come back?"

Jack had been very quiet as the horrific tale unfolded. Now he faced Axis, composed, his green eyes tranquil and steady. "No. I have no idea."

Axis looked inquiringly at the other two Sentinels, and then to his father and grandmother. "Anyone?"

All shook their heads.

Axis studied the blank faces carefully. Why did he feel as though someone on this rooftop knew *precisely* why WolfStar had come back through the Star Gate?

"Well then, if we cannot know precisely the reason *why* WolfStar has come back, does anyone know how long he has been back?"

Again everyone shook their heads. Axis gestured with impatience. Someone must know *something*! "If WolfStar has been back some time, he would have to protect himself against discovery. He would not want people to know. And yet the Icarii, as others, perhaps," he glanced at Jack, "were still using the Star Gate until a thousand years ago. MorningStar, Veremund, how long has the tradition of not touching any of the statues been around?"

It was Jack who answered. "Three thousand years."

Axis took a horrified step backwards. "Three thousand years? He has been back three thousand years? What mischief could WolfStar have got up to in three thousand years?"

"Surely," StarDrifter said irritably, "the more pertinent point is, where is WolfStar now? And what disguise does he wear?"

"What disguise does WolfStar wear?" Axis said. "I don't know. I know *I* am not WolfStar, but any of you here could be. How can I know? WolfStar must be a master of disguise."

Eyes and mouths opened in horror and indignation. "Us?" Ogden spluttered. "But we are the Sentinels! It cannot be *us*!"

Ogden's indignation was nothing to MorningStar's and StarDrifter's angry and resentful denials. Harsh words were shouted.

"Peace!" Axis said, holding up his hands. "Do you think if I seriously thought any of you might be WolfStar I would have actually approached you with what I know? But I cannot know for sure. It could be anyone, and," he stumbled, "and the third verse of the Prophecy warns me that I have a traitor within my camp, someone who will betray me to Gorgrael. Who else could that be except WolfStar? Where is he? *Where*?"

"I fear I might know," MorningStar said very, very quietly, almost too afraid to speak.

Axis whipped around. "Who?"

"Too much of WolfStar is resurfacing, Axis, and it is resurfacing about one person. Azhure."

"No!" Axis and StarDrifter exclaimed together, and Rivkah cried out softly in denial as well. "No! It cannot be!"

"*Think!*" MorningStar hissed. "The scars on her back, as if someone has ripped out Icarii wings."

"No," StarDrifter said. "If WolfStar assumed the form of a woman – and a woman who can fall pregnant – then he would be able to assume the form of a smooth-backed woman. Mother, be sensible."

"WolfStar's bow, and WolfStar's hounds," MorningStar continued. "Both came to Azhure. Would Sicarius answer to anyone *but* WolfStar?"

Jack watched MorningStar very, very carefully.

"You cannot be right, MorningStar. You *cannot*," Axis insisted.

"Of course," said MorningStar. "I am not surprised that both you and your father defend her. If she was WolfStar then she would be of SunSoar blood, and both of you lust after her as if she were SunSoar bred and blooded."

Axis and StarDrifter stared at each other. Both remembered how their blood had sung for her.

"No!" Axis cried. MorningStar *must* be wrong. "If she were SunSoar, MorningStar, you would feel it too. Am I right?"

"Not necessarily, Axis. The sexual tug is always the strongest." She arched an eyebrow. "And perhaps WolfStar did not *want* to conceal it."

By the Stars! Axis thought, trying to control his anger. "MorningStar," he said, "WolfStar is going to extraordinary lengths of disguise if he assumes the form of a woman who can fall pregnant. That extreme is surely not necessary. Besides, Azhure cannot sing, as Rivkah, Ogden and Veremund can vouch," the three nodded vigorously, "and, most important, she grew up in Smyrton, younger than me. What opportunity did she have to creep into Carlon to teach me as a baby? What?"

"Axis is right," Rivkah said evenly. MorningStar was a cold-hearted bitch on occasion. "You forget that I have known Azhure since she was about fourteen. I have watched her grow. Azhure may be a mystery but I stand with Axis and StarDrifter in denying that she is WolfStar SunSoar."

"Nevertheless, Axis," said MorningStar, not ready to concede. "It might be a good idea to send for word to Smyrton. Make sure that people remember her being born, remember her growing from a small child."

Axis nodded curtly. "If that will ease your mind, MorningStar. But I am already convinced." He stepped forward and caught MorningStar's chin between his fingers, and his voice took on the menace of threat. "Do not think to attack her again, MorningStar, or move against her in any way. I value Azhure more than most about me. Do I make myself clear?"

Rivkah smiled to herself. She had waited thirty years to see MorningStar finally put in her place.

"Above all," Axis said, stepping back from MorningStar and looking about him, "there is one thing that convinces me beyond doubt that Azhure cannot be WolfStar. No compassionate man, whatever the cause, could send hundreds of children as well as his own pregnant wife to the deaths that he did. But Azhure overruns with compassion and love – for me, for her child, and indeed, for all those who she calls her friends. All this despite nearly a lifetime of rejection. That alone convinces me that she cannot be WolfStar. Leave her alone."

He stared unblinking at the silent group watching him, then turned on his heel and stalked down the stairwell.

32

Winter Approaches

Winter approached, and with the arrival of Frost-month swarmed a dark, writhing mass of Skraelings above Jervois Landing. Gautier had stopped sending patrols northwards over the past few weeks – patrols had become a pointless waste of life. Gorgrael did not even bother to disguise his intention of storming into Achar through the defences of Jervois Landing.

On the third day of Frost-month, Borneheld's determination to hold Jervois Landing and redeem his performance at Gorkenfort was almost fanatical. He had returned from Carlon the previous evening, leaving behind a grateful Faraday (and a furious Timozel to guard her), and was now gathered with most of his commanders in the Tired Seagull.

"And," Nevelon stuttered, painfully aware of Borneheld's expression, "Magariz said, and I quote, 'Tell Borneheld that if he does not ally himself with the cause of the StarMan he will die. Tell him that only Axis can lead Achar to victory. Tell him that if he persists in denying the Prophecy then the Prophecy will tear him apart. If he has won a kingdom, then he will not long enjoy it. Tell him Axis comes, and he comes with the power of the Prophecy behind him.'" Nevelon stopped, awaiting the inevitable outburst.

Yet Borneheld did not explode instantly into fury. He narrowed his eyes and stared at Nevelon, his lips thinning.

What could Roland have been thinking of to pick this man as his second-in-command? Borneheld looked at Gautier. "Well?" he barked.

"Axis must be alive, Sire," Gautier said finally. "Magariz's words, foolish and demented as they are, are full of confidence. He must know Axis is alive."

Borneheld grunted. He'd hoped that Axis had died amid a gnashing of Skraeling teeth above Gorkenfort, but deep down he wasn't surprised to discover his traitorous brother had managed to survive. "And?"

"And," Gautier said, rubbing his chin thoughtfully, "he must have a force somewhere. Who knows how many of the three thousand who fled with him lived? Some must have died. Perhaps a thousand. Even the best commander, and Axis is not the best," he hastened to add for Borneheld's benefit, "would have lost a significant number to the Skraeling host which followed them out of Gorkenfort."

Borneheld stared back at Nevelon. "Well fed and uniformed, you say?" he snapped.

"Yes, Sire, at least the two I saw were. Both were fit, and their uniforms clean and well made."

"And the emblem of the blood-red blazing sun," Gautier murmured. "Axis has found a new mark, it seems."

Borneheld frowned. Where was his bastard brother? Over the past two months the men Gautier had sent into the southern Urqhart Hills had met with increasing resistance from patrols of a well-trained and well-supplied force. All wore the blazing sun emblem and one or two were led, it appeared, by this same woman who had struck Nevelon. It was now unsafe for Borneheld's men to ride anywhere close to the Urqhart Hills, and even the eastern reaches of the Nordra were becoming dangerous. Not only did Axis have a force somewhere, it was growing stronger and extending its influence.

"Where are they?" Borneheld asked.

Nevelon cleared his throat nervously. "Uh, Sire, I've been thinking about this. It must be Sigholt. The garrison there deserted when they heard the Skraelings were moving eastwards. It has to be where Axis has based his force."

Borneheld jerked up, shocked, sending a goblet of wine spinning to the floor. "Sigholt!" he cried. Curse the commander who had panicked and abandoned one of the best garrisons in the country!

"If Axis has a rebel force based in Sigholt, then he has the power to hurt you," said Earl Jorge. Though he and Roland were sadly out of favour with the King, it would not stop Jorge speaking his mind when he felt it was needed. "And there are rumours that many of the peasants from Skarabost are moving north of the Nordra river to join him."

Borneheld swore, his temper smouldering dangerously. "*Why*?" he seethed. "Why do they move to join one who has allied himself with the Forbidden?"

Roland considered Borneheld warily. "Axis still has a powerful reputation in Achar, Sire. As BattleAxe he was revered. That is what draws them."

Roland had lost considerable weight since the fall of Gorkenfort — his skin now hung in great folds from his cheeks and neck where the fat had dissolved. In past months he'd felt his mortality keenly, and without thinking he rubbed the spot on his abdomen where he could feel the great hard canker deep in his belly.

Borneheld battled to hold his temper. Would he never be free of his hated half-brother? *Why* did so many rally to Axis' name and not to his? Why revere Axis' name and not his? Borneheld could not understand it. "We must stop him," he muttered finally. "Attack Sigholt."

Everyone present, from Gautier and Roland to the anonymous guards, started in horror. Attack the rebels in Sigholt? Now? When the Skraelings could attack Jervois Landing any day? Madness!

"Sire," Gautier said carefully. "The Skraeling host masses to our north. Obviously they plan to attack soon. And Sigholt is an easily defensible fort. It would be, ah," Gautier hesitated, "inadvisable to split our forces right now."

"So we leave him free to take Skarabost?" Borneheld spat.

Gautier glanced at Jorge and Roland. "Majesty, Axis will face the same problems from the Skraelings as we do. Doubtless Gorgrael will attack through the WildDog Plains as well. Neither we, nor Axis, are going to be able to move very far from where we are encamped this winter. Axis must only have a small force, a few thousand at most. As *we* cannot move, neither can he." He paused, summoning his courage. "Sire, we must seek a truce with them for this winter."

"*What!*" Borneheld exploded out of his chair.

"Think of how we could use this to our advantage, Majesty," Gautier said urgently, desperate to deflect Borneheld's anger. "First of all, Axis is as keen as you are not to let the Skraelings further south into Achar. Whatever our differences, Axis hates the Skraelings as much as us. *If* he is at Sigholt, then his forces can do much of the work – and dying – to keep our north-western flank covered. And if we arrange a formal truce, we can get some idea of what force Axis commands. What do we know now? Magariz, some dark-haired woman who can use a bow, and a pack of vicious hounds!"

"He is right," said Jorge, his voice low and intense. "Not only do we not have the forces spare to attack Axis, we do not have the forces spare to defend Skarabost from the Skraelings if they come down through the WildDog Plains. Let Axis' force do the work and the dying in defending our north-western flank. A truce would keep Skarabost free from both Skraelings and Axis."

Borneheld abhorred the idea of a truce with Axis, but he knew he couldn't afford to fight on two fronts over the winter. He sat down again, deep in thought. He was desperately aware of just how important this coming winter campaign would be. If he lost Jervois Landing, then he would lose all. Hate Axis he might, but Borneheld knew when to compromise. He could not afford to move against him this winter, and if he could not afford to, then best he make sure that Axis was tied by his word to Sigholt. Axis' death would have to be delayed until spring next year.

He nodded curtly. "Very well. Gautier, can you make some initial contact with Axis' force?"

Gautier's face relaxed. "If I send a patrol into the southern Urqhart Hills, then yes, I believe so. When do we want to meet them? Where?"

Borneheld looked at Jorge. "What do you think?"

Jorge thought quickly, surprised to have been asked. "We must have this arranged before Snow-month commences, Sire. That is only three and a half weeks away. Time? Last week in Frost-month at the latest. Where? On the Nordra south of the Urqhart Hills – perhaps Gundealga Ford. We do not want to be trapped within the Urqhart Hills, and if we state the Nordra, then that will draw Axis out of wherever he is based. He will have to come with a significant force to protect himself, and we will gain some idea of his strength."

"Good," Borneheld said brusquely. "If I can't flush Axis from Sigholt before next spring, then at least I can do something about these weak-minded fools who rush to join him from the backward villages of Skarabost, and cut off some of his supply routes as well. Nevelon! Fetch me pen and parchment. I must write to Earl Burdel in Arcness. I have a task for him. One he will enjoy."

He turned to Jorge, Roland and Gautier. "If I am to meet Axis then I need him to know what he faces. Contact Brother-Leader Jayme as well, and tell him that I want a senior member of the Seneschal present when I face this evil-bred brother of mine. Perhaps one of his advisers. Surely he could spare one from his side."

Borneheld sat back in his chair, a smirk spreading over his face. "I think I will enjoy meeting my brother over the treaty table, gentlemen. I want to see if he has grown any lizard features."

Absent from the deliberations, the Ravensbund Chief sat in his tent in the camp outside Jervois Landing. His wife, Sa'Kuya, prepared him a pot of Tekawai, the traditional tea of the Ravensbund people. The ritual was almost as old as the Ravensbund race, and the pot and cups Sa'Kuya used had been handed down over countless generations.

Picking up a tiny cup, she handed it to Ho'Demi, carefully turning it so that the design emblazoned on the side of the vessel faced him.

It was the blood-red blazing sun.

Unsmiling now, for this was a serious ritual, Ho'Demi took the cup from his wife, bowing slightly as she handed it to him, then took a tiny sip.

Sa'Kuya served the other four men in the circle about the brazier, then she bowed gracefully and retreated to the shadows further back in the tent. Ho'Demi glanced at his four fellow Ravensbundmen. Ho'Demi had been grateful to be left out of Borneheld's discussion tonight because he wanted to speak again with the two Ravensbundmen who had accompanied Nevelon on patrol. He inclined his head at the two other Ravensbundmen present, elders whose advice Ho'Demi respected, but spoke to the two warriors.

"Izanagi, Inari, I am grateful that you consented to sip Tekawai with me on such short notice."

Izanagi and Inari, both highly regarded warriors within the Ravensbund force – though Gautier had yet to acknowledge their value – lowered their eyes in reply and bowed slightly. It was always an honour to sit in Ho'Demi's tent.

For some time the five men sipped their tea in silence, their movements slow and graceful, contemplating the complications that night raid on Nevelon's patrol had wrought among the Ravensbundmen.

It was Ho'Demi, as was his right, who eventually spoke again. "Both the Wolven and the Alaunt hounds walk the night," he sighed. "And they walk with those who wear the emblem of the bloodied sun."

"Both the Wolven and the Alaunt walk with the black-haired woman," Inari said. "She who would be so beautiful if only her face were not so naked."

As the Ravensbundmen had passed on the Prophecy for thousands of years, so too had they passed on the story of WolfStar. The Icarii might think that none but they knew of WolfStar's story, but the Ravensbundmen had heard of WolfStar many, many generations ago. And they knew enough to recognise WolfStar's bow and his hounds.

"I wish Borneheld's wife, Faraday, and her companion, the SentinelYr, were here to discuss this with us," said Ho'Demi. "But they are far away in Carlon, and this is a decision that I must make on my own."

"Must we make a decision so soon?" asked Tanabata, one of the elders, inclining his head in deference to Ho'Demi. His face was so aged and wrinkled that the swirling blue lines on his face had lost their symmetry.

"I cannot ignore the signs, Elder Tanabata. Both this man, Magariz?" Ho'Demi raised his eyebrows at the two warriors for confirmation of the name, and they nodded. "And the woman, Azhure, wore the badge of the bloodied sun."

All present glanced at the designs emblazoned on their cups as Ho'Demi spoke.

"The woman carries WolfStar's bow, and his hounds trot by her side. Magariz spoke the name of the StarMan as if he were this Axis. 'Axis comes with the power of the Prophecy behind him'," Ho'Demi recited, repeating Magariz's message for Borneheld. He looked at the others. "Is *he* the one who will forge the alliance to defeat Gorgrael?"

Ho'Demi was worried. He had committed his people to fight for Borneheld – the Ravensbundmen hated Gorgrael and his Skraelings and, if Borneheld was committed to fighting the Skraelings, the Ravensbundmen would help him. But they owed their first allegiance to the Prophecy – and thus to the StarMan. But what were the marks of *WolfStar* doing marching with the StarMan? Ho'Demi did not understand it, and it made him reluctant to act. Where best did his people belong? With Borneheld, or with this unknown Axis?

For an hour, their cups empty and cold in their hands, the Ravensbundmen debated back and forth what they should do. Ho'Demi hesitated to commit himself to Axis, not only because of the Wolven and the Alaunt, but also because none had seen Axis or his army. The patrols of the force Gautier's men had engaged within the southern Urqhart Hills had been small . . . but they had also been highly skilled and disciplined.

"It is not an easy age in which to make decisions," Ho'Demi finally said, feeling his uncertainty keenly.

"The decision should not be rushed, Ho'Demi," the other elder present, Hamori, reassured. "You cannot hurry what may be the last remnants of your people into the unknown."

Ho'Demi, about to speak, was interrupted by a cough at the tent flap. "Come," he called.

One of the Ravensbund warriors entered. He bowed deeply, then knelt. "My Chief. A message from Gautier. You are to meet with him in the morning. The King intends to meet with the rebel force and their commander in three weeks' time to offer a truce for the winter while we battle the Skraelings. You are to attend."

Ho'Demi glanced at the other four men, his eyes gleaming. "The gods have heard my prayers, my people. My questions may be answered after all."

33

Forgotten Vows

Axis stared into the fire, letting the crackling flames and the soft melody of the Star Dance relax him. He was still tired from the patrol he had led home last night. Driven by one of Gorgrael's SkraeBolds, small bands of Skraelings were drifting south through the WildDog Plains, testing Axis' strength. If the bands of Skraelings were relatively small, the wraiths were vicious and the fighting bitter, and his patrol had come home smaller than it had left. Soon he would have to move a sizeable force into the Plains.

Damn it! All he wanted to do was lead his army south . . . south to wrest control of Achar away from Borneheld.

"King!" Axis snorted, and took a sip of wine from the goblet he held. "I cannot imagine that Borneheld would make an impressive King."

Rivkah looked up from her embroidery. One son King, the other longed to be King. She shivered and blamed the cool air. Even by the steaming waters of the Lake of Life, winter chills were starting to penetrate Sigholt, especially once the sun went down. She looked about the rest of the group sitting before the fire in the Great Hall of Sigholt. Previously no-one had felt comfortable sitting in the vast Hall. Now, with Axis here, it somehow felt right.

Axis had worked tirelessly over the past five weeks and Sigholt had rapidly been turned from a slightly disorganised rebel base composed of disparate elements, into the seeds of a unified kingdom. And at the heart of that kingdom strode Axis and over its head flew the blood-red blazing sun. Rivkah wished this magical time would never, never end. Icarii and Acharite worked as one for the first time in a thousand years and they all worked for Axis.

Rivkah's eyes drifted about the group. MorningStar and StarDrifter were absent, visiting friends among the Strike Force. Ogden and Veremund sat, exclaiming over a book they had discovered underneath a flour bucket in the kitchens. Beside them Reinald snored softly, asleep even though he was sitting ramrod-straight in his chair. Whatever Veremund and Ogden found so exciting in the book had sent him into a deep slumber. It was probably Reinald who had found the book boring enough to shove it under a wobbly flour bucket in the first instance. Jack was nowhere to be seen. Probably off on one of his silent wanders through the corridors of Sigholt. Still looking for Zeherah, still hoping to snatch a trace of her scent or a lingering of her passing.

Rivkah's eyes softened as she watched Azhure sitting cross-legged at Axis' feet. The woman's pregnancy was now well advanced, but still she rode and trained, although on a quieter nag now that Axis had reclaimed Belaguez. Tonight she spent her leisure hours cleaning the Wolven and her arrows – rags and a small bowl of wax lay to one side. Every so often Axis' hand would steal down and touch her hair. If Axis ever worried about her continuing to work with her archers, he never showed it. The only concession to her pregnancy he'd forced her to make was to stop riding out on patrol these last few weeks; Axis did not want her giving birth under a bush somewhere in the Urqhart Hills. Azhure had been indignant, and the two had fought, but eventually Axis had prevailed.

Five of the Alaunt hounds were stretched out in front of Azhure, soaking up the warmth of the fire. The Alaunt followed Azhure about like silent shadows; there were always a few close by, and the others not far away. When Azhure had still been riding patrol the entire pack had run with her, capable of killing as silently and efficiently as Azhure's arrows. Rivkah shook her head. If Azhure had always had a latent talent for violence, as the Avar had accused, then it had found a suitable outlet in fighting for Axis.

In a chair the other side of the hearth Belial sat slumped, his shadowed eyes on both Axis and Azhure. Rivkah had watched him wilt slightly since Azhure had moved into Axis' quarters. He had a sense of deep sadness about him that he never quite shook, even in more light-hearted moments.

Above Rivkah heard a rustle of feathers. The snow eagle spent the nights perched in the rafters of the Great Hall, but in the days it soared far above the Urqhart Hills, catching mice and rabbits, sometimes winging south and west on strange errands for Axis. Axis had consistently refused to answer any questions about the bird, but on many an occasion Rivkah had watched him talking soft and low to the eagle as it perched on his arm. There was a bond there, but Rivkah did not know what it was.

In a chair close by her side sat the man Rivkah had consciously avoided looking at all evening. Magariz. Now she spoke, although her grey eyes remained on her stitching.

"My Lord Magariz."

"Princess. What can I do for you?"

"My Lord Magariz, when I first arrived here you promised that you would talk to me of my eldest, Borneheld. Will you do so now?"

Axis turned his gaze from the fire to Magariz's face, his blue eyes cold. Azhure laid down her bow and Belial also watched Magariz carefully. Even Ogden and Veremund ceased their chattering.

Magariz, uncertain, glanced at Axis, but Axis waved his hand languidly. "You do not have to hold your tongue on my account."

"Princess," Magariz sighed, hesitating. How to talk about Borneheld?

"After I served my time with the palace guard, Priam sent me to serve with Borneheld soon after he became Duke. Borneheld gave me the command of Gorkenfort, a lonely and wearying place, some ten years ago –"

"You were in the palace guard at Carlon?" Axis interrupted.

Magariz laughed. "And led it the last two years I was in Carlon, Axis. Why? Do you find me familiar?"

Axis only just managed to resist swearing in surprise. Magariz must have been in Carlon when Axis was a child growing up in the Seneschal. Axis had often played in the back corridors of the palace when Jayme was there. Magariz *must* have had access to him as a child! Could *he* be the traitor in his camp? Could *he* be WolfStar? Axis took a hasty mouthful of wine. The thought was almost as unsettling as the notion that it might be Azhure.

Magariz smiled at Axis, misunderstanding the reasons for his stare. "You were a mischievous child, Axis. I once found you in the stable, tying all the horses' legs together with a long ball of twine."

Axis forced a light-hearted grin to his face. *If* Magariz was WolfStar, then he would possibly have had access to the northern wastes above Gorkenfort. Access to the northern wastes and to Gorgrael. No! He had to stop this! Had to stop staring every friend in the face, trying to see the traitor lying beneath.

Magariz, still unaware of Axis' inner turmoil, touched Rivkah gently on the arm. "Rivkah, I am sorry. You wanted to know about Borneheld. Well, he is a complex man. Though often harsh, he does try to be fair. He is organised, disciplined, and has a strong sense of right and wrong. When I knew him he always tried to do what he thought was right, *always*. He is too narrow-minded, but that is the way he was brought up. He does not know how to love, but that is because he was never loved."

Rivkah put her embroidery down, her face blank.

"He is crazed in his jealousy of Axis, true, and for several reasons. Rivkah, you loved Axis' father, not his, and he believes you abandoned him for StarDrifter." Rivkah opened her mouth to deny that, but Magariz forged on. "As far as Borneheld is concerned, your death while giving birth to your unknown lover's child constituted abandonment."

Blinded by the tears in her eyes, Rivkah winced and cried out softly as a pin stuck deep into her thumb. Was Magariz talking of Borneheld . . . or of himself?

"Borneheld is also jealous of Axis because Axis has the charm that Borneheld never had and will never have, and Borneheld has always been aware of his sad lack of charisma." Magariz paused. "And Borneheld suspects that Axis is the better war leader than he is – and fighting is the *one* thing Borneheld feels he is reasonably good at. At Gorkenfort Borneheld watched Axis daily earn the adulation of his soldiers, and that cut deep, very, very deep. Now Borneheld is probably consumed with jealousy that Axis, his hated half-brother, is the fabled StarMan, the one who is prophesied to save Achar."

Aware of the emotions he had already sparked, Magariz wondered if he should go on. "And then there is Faraday," he said very, very quietly. Both Axis and Azhure stilled. "Does Borneheld realise that Faraday loves Axis? If so, then it will deepen Borneheld's anger and jealousy . . . perhaps beyond reason." Magariz hastily drained his wine glass, wishing he'd kept quiet.

"If Borneheld has one serious flaw, Magariz, one thing we might exploit, what would you say that to be?" asked Belial.

"Besides his consuming resentment of Axis? Borneheld's major fault is that he is too set in his ways, too rigid. He will not, *cannot*, change his attitudes. The Forbidden will always remain the Forbidden, never potential allies. He is a sad man and will feel abandoned by a world that changes about him."

"A sad man, Magariz?" Axis' voice was harsh. "Misunderstood? Tell that to FreeFall SunSoar who felt Borneheld's sword slice open his heart. You witnessed that murder, and by your own confession it was what decided you to turn to my cause. Borneheld is marked by death, do not try to turn him into a martyr to a lost world now!"

"Enough!" Rivkah cried, and abruptly stood from her chair, the silks and material tumbling from her lap in a bright flood to the floor. "Enough! I wish I had never asked about Borneheld!"

She turned on her heel and hurried towards the door. Both Axis and Azhure made as if to go after her, but Magariz waved them back. "It was my fault," he said quietly, and limped after Rivkah.

He caught her just outside the door and took her hands. "Rivkah, I am sorry. I did not think too carefully on what I said. If I appeared judgemental, then I did not mean to be. These past years were —"

"I am such an inconstant woman, and such a bad woman," Rivkah whispered, distraught. "You were right to speak of abandonment to me. I deserved no less."

"Rivkah —"

"I never loved Searlas, you know that."

"Yes, I know it."

"I never wanted to marry him."

"Yes, I know that, but —"

"I was not untrue to Searlas at all when StarDrifter landed on that roof, was I, Magariz?"

He was silent, his eyes dark.

"I was untrue to you. You have never remarried, Magariz, and yet I have betrayed you twice, once with Searlas and once with StarDrifter. The two sons and the daughter I bore should have been yours."

"Rivkah. You know that I would not have expected you to remain true to our vows. Not after what happened."

Rivkah blinked the tears from her eyes. Too late to cry now about the mistakes of over thirty years ago.

"I wonder how people would react, Magariz, if they knew that you are my legal husband, not Searlas, not StarDrifter." There. The words were said.

For the first time in many years Magariz let his mind drift back to that long-ago night in Carlon. Rivkah was an impetuous fifteen year old, and he an equally impetuous seventeen. Rivkah had rushed down to his room, furious that her father, King Karel, had just promised her to Searlas, Duke of Ichtar. Determined to defy her father and Searlas, Rivkah had whispered her plan to her friend. They had fled via poorly lit passageways and unguarded doors to a small Worship Hall in the seamier quarter of Carlon. There a Brother, old and careless, had accepted the gold Rivkah thrust into his hand and married them. Magariz remembered how he'd taken Rivkah back to his bare room in the lower regions of the palace where, awkward and shy, they had both lost their virginity.

But the next day Karel had unexpectedly spirited Rivkah northwards and forced her into marriage with Searlas. What to do? If Magariz spoke out he could endanger both their lives and if he kept quiet he would lose Rivkah forever. So young, Magariz could do nothing but grieve for the brief love he had lost. Two years later, when Rivkah had died in childbed of her second son, Magariz had taken to his room and wept, swearing that his single night with Rivkah would last him a lifetime. When her foundling bastard son had arrived in Carlon under the care of Jayme, Magariz had taken every opportunity he could to play with the child. And he had always wondered, until he had actually set eyes on Borneheld, whether her eldest son was his or not. But Borneheld was the image of Searlas, and Magariz was grateful that he did not have the guilt of Borneheld on his conscience as well.

Rivkah pulled her hands from his, interrupting the memories. "We can never recapture the past, Magariz, or strive for what might have been. We cannot prove our marriage – if indeed we would want to now after so many years. But there is always the future, and," she smiled, "there is always the fact that since Azhure moved to Axis' bed, I have lain cold and lonely at night. No-one, in this crowded Keep, has come to share my quarters. My chamber lies in an isolated corridor, my Lord Magariz, and should you decide to wander down it one night, I doubt that you shall find the door to my chamber locked."

Then she was gone.

34

Parley

They stood in the central map-room of the Keep of Sigholt – Axis, his senior commanders and his father and grandmother. All stared at Arne, standing grey and haggard after riding for three days for Sigholt.

Four days ago a band of eight soldiers from Jervois Landing had made contact with Arne's patrol in the southern Urqhart Hills. They'd been led by Nevelon, and Roland's lieutenant had a message for Axis that had astounded Arne.

"A parley? What do you think?" Axis asked Belial.

"He thinks to use us," Belial surmised. "He is weak on his north-eastern front, and hopes we'll keep the Skraelings back in the WildDog Plains."

Axis grimaced. "As do I, my friend. As do I. Daily those wraiths increase their nibbles at our patrols." The fear that the Skraelings might cut off HoldHard Pass and his supply routes south gave Axis nightmares.

Forcing the problem of the WildDog Plains from his mind, Axis turned to Magariz. "You know Borneheld better than any of us. What do *you* think?"

"That he is doing the sensible thing," Magariz said without hesitation. "I would do the same in his position. Neither of you can afford to fight on two fronts, Axis. Better that we effect a truce this winter than fight each other and let Gorgrael slip south through our ranks."

"I had wanted to move south this winter," Axis muttered, though he had always known a move south into Achar before next spring would be all but impossible. "And I do not want to speak to Borneheld without having the opportunity of running him through with my sword." He glanced at the snow eagle on the windowsill. How long would he have to wait? How long? The days were turning and fading, and the GateKeeper was counting.

Axis strode to the window and stared out. A thin layer of grey clouds skimmed across Sigholt despite the Lake of Life's warmth. Axis chewed his lip, thinking, thankful that none in the map-room could see his worried face. Could he avoid a lengthy and damaging civil war by defeating Borneheld in single combat when he met him at the Nordra? But Axis could not challenge Borneheld without Faraday present. Borneheld could not die without Faraday there as witness.

"Arne? Did Nevelon say anything about Faraday? Do you know if she is still in Jervois Landing?"

There was a stunned silence in the room and Azhure turned away, her eyes downcast. Did Faraday fill his thoughts? When they lay curled together at night, edging towards sleep, did he imagine that it was Faraday his arms encircled? When he caressed her, did his hands feel another woman's body?

Her baby, Caelum, shifted in sympathy as he caught some of his mother's misery.

Arne frowned. "Nevelon said nothing, but she is Queen, my Lord Axis. She would hardly be in Jervois Landing."

"Yes, you are right. Well, never mind." Axis looked at Far-Sight, Belial and Magariz. "So, my friends. Borneheld wants to meet with us at the border of the Urqhart Hills and the Nordra, a halfway point between Sigholt and Jervois Landing. Should we go? Should we parley? Should I smell a trap?"

Magariz shrugged. "We have the advantage, Axis, with the Strike Force. We will be able to scout for a trap long before he could spring it. And we also have the advantage of approaching through the hills. He must approach through flat plains. What trap could he spring?"

"While Borneheld engages Axis in parley far south of Sigholt, Magariz, a force from Jervois Landing could swing north and attack the Keep." Azhure's voice was flat, and MorningStar eyed her speculatively. She still deeply distrusted Azhure – what better disguise could WolfStar adopt than one who would ensnare every male SunSoar Enchanter within lusting distance?

Axis ignored Azhure's tone. "No. I don't think Borneheld would be able to get a large force close to Sigholt. There are so many Skraelings packed into the ruins of Hsingard now that any force riding by would be eaten before they had time to spur their horses into a gallop. All other approaches to Sigholt through the Urqhart Hills are commanded by my men, and patrolled by both air and ground forces. Sigholt will remain safe for the time being, I think. No," he said slowly, "I think I will attend this little parley my brother asks for. As he undoubtedly wants to survey my forces, so I wish to survey his."

He smiled suddenly, illuminating the entire room. "Somehow, my friends, I do not think that Borneheld's commanders will stand as strong behind his back as I know mine will behind me. Azhure?"

She looked up. "Yes?"

"I will leave you in charge of Sigholt and the main part of my army. I –" He halted at the flare of anger across her face.

"Axis! I do not want to stay here!" Azhure began, but then stopped equally abruptly. Her pregnancy was too far advanced for her to ride south . . . and she knew if she protested against Axis' orders he would reprimand her without hesitation and as severely as any other commander who dared argue with him – even if he did share his bed with this one. Anyway, Azhure thought bitterly, all he can think about is Faraday.

"Yes, my Lord Axis," she replied very formally. "As you wish." She relaxed slightly. "But I will cede you my pack of Alaunt for the venture. Take them . . . please."

Axis smiled. "I will take four couples, Azhure. The others I will leave for your own company."

Azhure felt the gossamer touch of his power. *And to keep you and our son safe and warm at night, Azhure, while I am away.*

"Magariz, Belial," Axis' tone was now brisk as he spoke to his two most senior commanders. "We need to discuss who we will take with us, which route to take and, most important, what terms we will demand. Perhaps we can yet twist this to our advantage.

"MorningStar, StarDrifter? You may be interested to know," he said off-handedly, "that my messengers have come back from Smyrton. Their report has confirmed what I already knew. Do you understand?"

Both MorningStar and StarDrifter knew exactly to what Axis referred. Axis had sent to Smyrton for confirmation that Azhure had indeed been born and spent her childhood in the northern Skarabost village.

StarDrifter smiled at his son, relieved, but MorningStar's expression did not change, and Axis knew that the news had done nothing to ease her suspicions.

If I come home from meeting with Borneheld and find Azhure dead at the foot of Sigholt's main staircase, MorningStar, I swear that you, too, will die.

MorningStar's face blanched. No-one threatened her like that! But Axis held her eyes with his, and kept her wrapped in his power, and eventually MorningStar was forced to concede with a curt nod.

Axis looked at Sicarius, sitting attentively at Azhure's side. *Make sure that no harm comes to her while I am gone.*

Sicarius whined, and shifted slightly.

Azhure looked about the room, bemused. Why was Axis interested in Smyrton?

35

Carlon and Beyond

Faraday opened her eyes to the early morning light. Since Borneheld had returned to Jervois Landing she had recovered much of her zest for life.

"Pleasant dreams, dear one?"

Faraday rolled over and smiled at Yr, sitting scrubbed and dressed for the day on the silken edge of the Queen's mammoth bed. "I dreamed of Axis, Yr. I dreamed he was here with me . . . loving me."

Yr pretended genteel distaste. "Does the Queen dream of a lover?"

"Every night, Yr, every night." Faraday propped herself up on an elbow. "Does he lie in his bed and dream of me? Does he hunger for me as much as I for him?"

She laughed shortly and sat up, trying to dismiss Axis from her mind. "So tell me, Principal Maid, what duties do I have to look forward to today?"

Faraday's life as Queen was not one of idle indolence. Most days she had to receive guests, flatter diplomats, listen to endless trade missions, attend lengthy and stupefyingly boring ceremonies celebrating obscure alliances and treaties, and listen to either Jayme or Moryson as they detailed their future plans for the Seneschal and the Way of the Plough. The last she hated especially, and she would sit, her face expressionless and her eyes veiled, thinking of the Mother and of the beauty and serenity of the Sacred Grove. Occasionally she amused herself by wondering what Jayme would look like with a pair of antlers sprouting from his forehead.

And Faraday had to sit through all these onerous duties and obligations swathed in jewel-encrusted gowns, scarves, bracelets, crowns, necklets and shoes that together weighed as much as she did and that made sweat trickle down her back.

Yr grinned. She knew how much Faraday hated her duties, and yet she also knew that Faraday carried them out scrupulously. As Queen, Faraday had a job to do, and regardless of what eventually happened, she was determined to serve the people of Achar properly. The entire part of northern Achar might be a battle zone, but here in Carlon ritual and tradition went on as if nothing had changed.

"You have a remarkably free morning, my sweet. The Ambassador for the Barrow Islands has come down with stomach cramps and cannot leave his privy closet. He sends his apologies. At least that is what I think he mumbled through the door."

Faraday laughed, and inched her way towards the far side of the bed.

"The Baroness of Tarantaise, Fleurian, has a pimple on her chin and is so embarrassed she has declined your kind invitation to share breakfast. Finally, to conclude this list of woes, the Master of the Butcher's Guild, who had an appointment to meet with you in the hour before lunch, last night sliced off his thumb into the lamb chop casserole he was preparing for his wife's dinner." Yr grinned. "The apprentice who brought me his Master's apologies assured me the casserole was served regardless."

Faraday could not believe it. Ever since she had become Queen it felt as if each moment of each day was accounted for. Now, finally, she had a free morning.

"What would your majesty like to do with her spare hours? Read? Sleep? Chew sweetmeats? Have one of the lesser nobles demonstrate that the touch of a man's hand can be a wondrous thing?"

"Do not even jest about it. You know I hate sweetmeats."

Yr laughed delightedly. Faraday had not joked in months. "The morning is yours, pretty woman. Use it as you wish."

"Yr," Faraday said. "I think I feel stomach cramps approaching. I think it would be best if you told the court that I am indisposed this morning and will not make an appearance before lunch." Her face darkened. "And tell Timozel as well."

When Borneheld had told Timozel that, as Faraday's Champion, he must remain in Carlon with her, Timozel had lost his temper and shouted at Borneheld.

"I care not what your visions show you!" Borneheld's eyes were bright with anger. "Your place is with Faraday."

Despite his obvious frustration at being left in Carlon, Timozel had taken note of Borneheld's orders and guarded Faraday every waking moment. In fact, it was as much as she could do to keep him from standing guard by her pillow as she slept. Faraday knew Borneheld had left orders that her every movement was to be watched and reported on. No doubt he had his own fears about the ambitious intentions of some of the more handsome courtiers. Whatever his motive, Borneheld's orders or the twisted devotion of his Championship, Timozel's dark and brooding presence shadowed her shoulder virtually every hour of the day.

"The Sacred Grove?" Yr whispered.

"Yes," Faraday said. "The Sacred Grove. I need to be renewed, infused once more with peace and joy."

The emerald light bathed her and power pulsed through her body. Faraday tipped her head back and shook her long hair loose, skipping through the light towards the Sacred Grove. It had been months, many months, since she had managed to find her way here, and she had forgotten how good it felt to let the power flood through her, let the love and the peace and the serenity wash away her doubts and fears. The light changed about her, resolving into shapes and shadows, and she stepped onto the grassy paths that led to the Sacred Grove. The trees formed about her and above her head the stars whirled in their god-driven interstellar dance. Faraday never wanted to leave this place. Exultation filled her.

She stepped into the Sacred Grove. Whispers of wind cradled her body as she walked. Shapes shifted and slipped through the deep shadows behind the trees. She felt no fear at the power of the Grove or the eyes that watched her from the shadows. They did not mean harm, but only wished her strength so that she could find harmony in her troubled life.

Five Sacred Horned Ones stepped forth. The silver pelt who had greeted Faraday on her previous journeys to the Sacred Grove rested his hands gently on her shoulders, and he leaned his stag's head forward to nuzzle her cheek lovingly.

"Faraday, Tree Friend. We have been so worried. We have seen the pain you suffer, and we suffer with you."

Emotion almost overwhelmed Faraday. Simply to know that someone besides Yr watched over her filled her with comfort. "Thank you," she said, and stepped forward to greet the other Horned Ones.

She turned back to the silver pelt. "Have you seen Axis in your visions, Sacred One?"

The silver pelt threw back his head and shook his antlers slightly, his stance noticeably stiffening. Faraday was afraid she had offended him. The other four Horned Ones muttered quickly, then fell silent.

"I have seen him only as he has touched the Avarinheim," the Horned One said eventually, "for I have not sought him out deliberately."

"He is well?" Faraday asked.

"He is well," the Horned One confirmed. "He celebrated Beltide in the Earth Tree Grove with the Icarii and the Avar."

He hesitated. "He has come into his powers as an Icarii Enchanter, Tree Friend. He asked the Avar to pledge to his cause, as the Icarii already have, but the Avar refused him."

"Oh!" Faraday cried, her eyes wide with shock.

"They wait for you," the Horned One said softly. "They will not move without you, Faraday Tree Friend. You will be the only one who can lead them to Axis SunSoar's cause. If you wish to."

What a silly thing to say, Faraday thought, of course she wished to lead the Avar to Axis' cause. "Does he think of me?" she asked, hating to ask, but desperate to know.

"He thinks of you daily, and speaks of you to his friends."

And betrays you with his body, and perhaps even with his heart, the fairy creature thought. Should I tell you that he has given another woman the heir which should have been yours by right, Faraday Tree Friend? No, how can I?

"Thank you. Sacred One . . ." Faraday hesitated, and the creature stepped forward and rested his hand on her shoulder.

"Never hesitate to ask for anything from me, Tree Friend. If I can grant it, I will."

"Sacred One, you exist in a magical and enchanted world. Does it extend beyond this Grove and these trees here?"

One of the younger Horned Ones stepped forward. "It extends as far as your world does, Faraday Tree Friend, and contains as many, if not more, wonders." His voice was low and musical, but resonated with power and mystery.

Faraday's eyes widened.

The silver pelt stepped back and waved. "It is all free to you, Tree Friend. Wander as you will. When you wish to return home, just think of this Grove and you will return. From here you can find your way back to your own world."

With that he and the other four Horned Ones vanished.

For a long time Faraday stood in the Grove. The stars spun overhead, reminding her of Axis. He had regained his heritage. And he still thought of her! She extended her arms, and danced about the Grove, wishing that he were here with her now. Soon, perhaps, he would share her bed in reality rather than dream.

After some time, Faraday wandered among the trees – and halted in wonder. From the Grove the trees looked dense and closely packed, but once beneath their sheltering branches, she saw that the trees were widely spaced, their branches so high that the trunks looked like the smooth pillars of some sacred hall, lifting the eye to a green-vaulted canopy so distant that it almost became a sky in itself. Her reaction to this enchanted forest was much the same as Azhure's when she had first wandered into the Avarinheim – she was overcome with the space and the light and the music around her.

Faraday finally dropped her eyes and gazed about her. Small shrubs of exquisite beauty flowered about the feet of the great trees, and between the trees wandered some of the strangest creatures Faraday could ever have imagined in her most fevered dreams. Hedgehogs with horns? Horses with wings? Bulls of pure gold and diamond-eyed birds? Small multi-coloured dragons gambolled along the lowest of the branches and a family of blue and orange-splotched panthers disported themselves in a nearby stream. Dryads and sprites drifted shyly between trees and silver-finned fish flashed beneath the crystal waters of the stream.

As Faraday wandered the sights shimmered and changed, but never became less wondrous. Glades and mountain ranges, oceans and gardens, caves and rolling dunes, this world contained them all. And at the next step always the forest, holding and loving her.

"What can I do for you?" she eventually whispered. "What is it I must do for you?"

The light shimmered about her and Faraday found herself entering a small glade. In the centre of the glade was an immensely cheerful hut, white-walled, golden-thatched and red-doored. Completely surrounding the hut was a spreading garden, enclosed by a white picket fence. There was something a little strange about the garden, but before Faraday could turn her mind to the problem the red door of the hut opened and an incredibly ancient woman emerged.

She wore a cloak as red as the door, but had thrown back the hood to reveal her bald cadaverous head, the papery skin was drawn tight over her cheek and skull bones splotched here and there with wisdom and experience. The woman's face was saved from outright ugliness by her eyes. They were immense pools of violet, almost childlike in their expression.

She stretched out a wavering hand. "Welcome, child of the trees. Welcome to my garden. Will you stay awhile?"

Faraday started to say yes, but suddenly the light around her darkened into emerald, and before Faraday could say or do anything she had spiralled out of the enchanted world and back into the painful one of the palace court of Carlon.

"I'm sorry I had to summon you back, Faraday," Yr said brusquely, "but it is gone noon, and the Queen is needed."

As the power faded from Faraday, Raum whimpered and slowly uncurled from the foetal position he had been rolled into for the past five or six hours.

The two Sentinels had been right about Faraday's power touching him, but Raum had never felt it this strongly before. Each step she had taken into the forests beyond the Grove had increased the pain within Raum until the forest about him reverberated with his screams.

He knew what was happening to him. But it should not be this powerful, not this painful.

And he was so young, so young to be transforming now. So much to do here. So much.

"Faraday," he whispered. "Faraday. Where are you? What do you do? Where do you go? Faraday?"

36

Gundealga Ford

They were to meet on the last day of Frost-month at Gundealga Ford on the Nordra. Once it surged out of the Forbidden Valley the Nordra widened and slowed, and by the time it approached Tailem Bend it was shallow enough to be forded by a man on horseback.

Axis camped his force just inside the southern Urqhart Hills, about half a league from Gundealga Ford. He had some thousand mounted soldiers with him, swordsmen as well as three of Azhure's squads of archers, and two Crest of the Icarii Strike Force. The majority of his command remained behind in Sigholt, although several units currently patrolled the HoldHard Pass and Urqhart Hills. Axis had brought only enough soldiers to convince Borneheld he would be a formidable opponent without giving away his true strength. The sight of his mounted force plus several hundred Icarii wheeling about the sky should be enough to convince Borneheld to think twice about his own strengths. The parley would be as much a mental game as a verbal one.

Axis glanced up as Belial approached through the gloom.

"Borneheld must be close now. How do you feel?"

"As though I have an appointment with a toothdrawer," Axis grimaced. "I do not look forward to meeting with my brother over the parley table. I don't think I can cope with the social niceties."

Belial laughed. He knew Axis would rather face Borneheld with a sword in his hand, and he knew few polite phrases would be traded tomorrow.

"The Icarii scouts have returned," he said.

Axis' head jerked up. "And?" His voice was tense.

"Borneheld's force has camped about the same distance south of Gundealga Ford as we have camped north. If we both leave at dawn tomorrow we should meet at the Ford mid-morning."

"I do not want the travel details!" Axis snapped. "What force does Borneheld bring with him?"

"About five thousand," Belial replied quickly. "Mounted men, mostly swordsmen, although the scouts could see a few units of archers among them."

"Were the Icarii scouts spotted?"

"No, Axis. They are almost impossible to spot at night, with their black uniforms and wings. Their presence will still come as a surprise."

As if to confirm Belial's words, FarSight CutSpur suddenly dropped down out of the darkened sky and smiled at the surprise on both men's faces. That Axis was as startled as Belial was an indication of just how preoccupied he was about his meeting with Borneheld.

"Strike-Leader." FarSight saluted formally. "Azhure has sent two farflight scouts down with messages from Sigholt. They await at your tent."

Azhure? Axis glanced at Belial. Both men turned and hurried back to Axis' tent.

Axis, lifted the flap of his tent back and ushered the two scouts inside.

"Well?" he demanded.

"Strike-Leader," Wing-Leader FeatherFlight BrightWing saluted, her face hollow and exhausted. "I bring two pieces of news, neither good. Six days after you left one of the patrols returned from the eastern Urqhart Hills. Strike-Leader, the mass of Skraelings at the top of the WildDog Plains have begun to drift south. Azhure has sent six Crest of the Strike Force and a large mounted force through the HoldHard Pass to meet them."

Axis' worried eyes met with those of Belial and FarSight. "Azhure has not gone herself?" he asked FeatherFlight.

"No, Strike-Leader. Azhure knows she is too far gone in her pregnancy to go a-fighting. She sent Arne in her place."

Axis sighed, relieved. But the news was grim, and it tied his hands regarding the negotiations. Now he needed the truce as much as Borneheld. Both were going to be facing such threats from Skraelings this winter that neither would want to be fighting on a second front. Well, best he know this now than find out after he had met with Borneheld.

Magariz entered, breathless, and Belial quickly informed him of the news. "Should one of us go to meet Arne in the HoldHard Pass?" Magariz asked, turning back to face Axis. "The fighting will be bloody."

Axis hesitated. "Arne has sufficient subcommand to support him – any one of the Crest-Leaders I left in Sigholt will do well. Once we are free of this place I'll lead this force east to meet up with Arne's command, and FarSight can fly his two Crest there within only a day or so." He turned back to FeatherFlight. "And the other news?"

"Another band of peasants from upper Skarabost arrived just before I left, dirty, tired and scared. They had fled north, terrified about rumours sweeping Skarabost that an Earl . . . Burdel?"

"Yes, yes," Axis said. "Burdel is the Earl of Arcness."

"Well, this Earl Burdel is apparently sweeping through southern Skarabost with a large force. He is putting to the stake or the cross any whom he finds repeating the Prophecy of the Destroyer. He is supposed to have put an entire village and its inhabitants to the torch where he found the Prophecy to be particularly entrenched. Anyone who mentions your name dies. Anyone who mentions the 'Forbidden'," her face twisted in distaste at the name, "with any sense of goodwill also dies. Any that Burdel finds fleeing northwards to join your cause at Sigholt dies. Fear and death sweep Skarabost, Strike-Leader."

Axis paled. Burdel would not be doing this on his own; it must be on Borneheld's orders and with the encouragement of the Seneschal. "Damn them!" he whispered.

"What can we do, Axis?" asked Belial.

"Nothing," Axis muttered wretchedly. "Nothing. We are tied to Sigholt, Belial, by the Skraelings moving south through the WildDog Plains. And I fear that Borneheld and Burdel know it. *Damn* them!"

Axis forced his face to relax, and addressed FeatherFlight again. "And Azhure is well?"

Since he'd left Sigholt, Axis found he missed Azhure so badly that even the melody of the Star Dance seemed tarnished without her.

Borneheld sat his glossy bay stallion and shaded his eyes against the glare. They had ridden out from their camp before dawn, and now sat their horses some one hundred paces from Gundealga Ford itself. Where was Axis? *Was* he still alive? Where was this rebel force?

Five horsemen formed a line immediately behind Borneheld, then, in ordered units, sat the five thousand horsemen Borneheld had brought with him.

Of the five leading horsemen, only Ho'Demi and Brother Moryson appeared unperturbed and relaxed. Gilbert sat his horse with ill-disguised bad temper, Gautier was tense and anxious, and Duke Roland of Aldeni shifted uncomfortably, trying to ease the canker in his belly.

A shout from behind caused everyone to jump, and Borneheld wheeled his horse about irritably. "What . . . ?" he began, then looked up to where one of the men in the first rank of soldiers was pointing frantically. Borneheld cursed the glare in the high layer of light grey clouds, then stilled as he saw what his man had been pointing at.

Far, far above them, circled hundreds of flying creatures, as black as Borneheld's darkest nightmares. He knew what they were – more of those cursed creatures who had parleyed with his traitorous brother Axis on the roof of Gorkenfort.

Now everyone craned their heads skyward. Ho'Demi's eyes narrowed. He knew the creatures were Icarii – though he had never met one of them and had only occasionally seen them as they soared above the plains of Ravensbund near the Icescarp Alps. The Icarii soared with this Axis? Ho'Demi dropped his eyes and caught those of Inari and Izanagi, sitting their horses in the first rank of soldiers. Axis was powerful indeed if he had the backing of the Icarii. Ho'Demi felt a small knot of excitement harden in his belly. Perhaps this man *was* the StarMan.

Beside Ho'Demi, Gilbert muttered under his breath. The Forbidden flew over Achar once more! May Artor himself condemn Axis to the worm-ridden pits of the After Life, Gilbert prayed, for he deserves eternal torment for his cursed alliance with these filth. And we . . . we should have moved sooner. Who knew what damage Priam's wretched obsession with the Prophecy had caused?

Moryson was as riveted by the sight of the Icarii as anyone else, but his thoughts were hidden behind a bland mask.

Finally Ho'Demi looked ahead, and his mouth dropped open as his eyes swung across the Nordra. A force of about a thousand men were fanned out across the plains some fifty paces from the opposite bank of the Nordra. From the centre of the line of men rose a magnificent standard, a deep golden field with the blazing blood-red sun in its centre.

"Borneheld!" he croaked.

Borneheld followed Ho'Demi's shocked eyes, then barked an order to his troops.

Two men were now almost halfway across the river, the water splashing about their horses' chests.

Borneheld squinted, trying to identify them before they reached him. Both were dressed in black, both rode black horses side by side. As suits such evil men, thought Borneheld grimly, keeping his hand from his sword only with a supreme effort. Behind him he could hear his men drawing their weapons. He pushed his horse forward a little to meet the two horsemen, waving the five behind him to follow.

As the two men rode their horses out of the Nordra, Borneheld finally recognised them, and his lip curled. So, both Axis' lieutenants had survived the battle above Gorkenfort. But where was Axis?

Magariz and Belial reined their horses to a halt some ten paces from where Borneheld sat his horse. Both were uniformed identically in black, their chests emblazoned with the blood-red blazing sun outlined by a tracery of gold and a circle of small golden stars.

"Borneheld," Belial said flatly. "We received your message and here we are. What do you want?"

"Where is he?" Borneheld demanded. "Where is my misbegotten brother? Or did he die above Gorkenfort?" He shifted his gaze to Magariz. "I am glad to see you survived, Magariz. I shall take pleasure in killing you myself."

"I would return the compliment," Magariz replied, "except that another has already claimed your life." Far above them a lone eagle screamed.

"Enough, Borneheld," Belial said. "Do you wish to parley or not? The longer you sit here the longer the Skraelings can nibble at your defences in Jervois Landing. I doubt you can afford to lose as many as you lost at Gorkenfort."

Borneheld snarled. The number of men *he* had lost? All the men lost were due to the treachery of Axis and the betrayal of these two men before him. "If Axis lives I will parley with him alone. Not any of his minions."

"My Commander stays behind until *I* am satisfied that you plan no treachery here," Belial responded. "Why do your men have their weapons drawn?" He waved at himself and Magariz, neither carried any weapons. "Borneheld, I understand you feel so vulnerable that you must have five thousand armed men to face two unarmed men, but I ask you to summon your courage. I do not intend to leap on you and force you into a wrestling match on this damp turf."

Borneheld's face reddened at this slur on his courage. "Gautier," he snapped, "order the men sheathe their weapons and retreat two hundred paces. Perhaps that will make my lizard-begotten brother feel safer."

Borneheld waved at the Icarii circling far above as Gautier wheeled his horse away. "But what of your flying lizards above? If I am so courteous as to pull my men back, then please do me the same honour."

Belial signalled to the Icarii and they began to tilt and wheel away towards the closest hill. Two, however, spiralled down to the small group left on the flat ground by the ford.

"What?" Borneheld growled, his fingers fidgeting nervously about the reins of his horse.

"I am only evening numbers," Belial said mildly. "And another will join us from beyond the river. See?"

Indeed, a pale silver creature had lifted from behind the line of mounted men and was winging its way towards them. Within moments Belial and Magariz were joined by two black-uniformed Icarii, one female, one wearing the same markings on his chest as Belial and Magariz, and the silver-winged male from beyond the river.

Before Borneheld could say anything, Gautier had returned to his side. "Sire," he whispered urgently, "look!"

Borneheld looked back to the force across the river. It had opened in its centre where the golden standard flew, and a man rode forth on a silvery-grey horse. He wore a tunic as golden as the field of the banner, and Borneheld could clearly see the blood-red blazing sun in the centre of his chest. Axis.

Axis spurred Belaguez into a gallop, two great hounds racing after him. As the stallion plunged into the river both horse and rider were lost in a plume of water. A heartbeat later they reappeared out of the spray, the horse surging through the river. One day, thought Borneheld, I will seize that horse for my own.

Behind Axis the hounds bounded through the water with as much ease as Belaguez. Overhead a lone snow eagle dipped and soared.

Ho'Demi watched them come, and his heart gladdened. The man who now crossed the river was a King, of that he had no doubt. The Alaunt served, as did the eagle which flew overhead. The Icarii had donned their ebony of war for him, and the man flew the banner of the bloodied sun above his force. He could be none other than the StarMan.

Axis slowed Belaguez to a walk. "Borneheld," he said tonelessly, finally reining Belaguez to a head-tossing halt. "Have you come to ally yourself to my cause as the Prophecy demands? I see you wear the coronet of King of Achar. It is within your power, then, to save Achar from unnecessary bloodshed. Will you fight under my banner to drive Gorgrael back and proclaim Tencendor once more?"

Borneheld snarled, intimidated. Axis had the presence of a burning sun and the aura of power to match. *I am King!* Borneheld seethed to himself, legitimate and rightful born! *I* hold all power here, not this pitiful refugee from justice. But even as he tried to bolster his own courage and respect, his hate and resentment grew. Why had Artor favoured Axis with so much, when it was Borneheld who had the birthright?

Before Borneheld could speak, Axis nudged Belaguez past him to the five men who sat their horses behind their King.

"Gautier." Axis briefly acknowledged Borneheld's lieutenant, then rode straight past.

"Duke Roland." Axis could not keep the shock out of his voice. He had always liked and respected Roland, and was appalled by this ashen and haggard man sitting his horse before him. He leaned forward to offer Roland his hand. Behind him Borneheld swung his horse around.

"Forgive me, Axis," Roland said, "but I cannot."

Axis dropped his hand. "I hope you find peace, my friend," he said softly, then he nudged Belaguez forward.

"Gilbert." Axis' voice was now hard. "I'd have thought all this riding about the countryside in the fresh air would have cleared your complexion. I can only assume it is the foulness of your thoughts that reflect in the pattern of your skin."

Gilbert's scarred face mottled in embarrassment, and Axis rode on.

The next man Axis did not know. He was a Ravensbundman, and a chieftain by the markings on his face. Axis reached out to him with his power rather than his voice.

Who are you?

"Ho'Demi," the Ravensbundman replied. "Chief of the Ravensbundmen."

You ride with Borneheld?

This time, shockingly, Ho'Demi replied in kind. *I, as my people, live to serve the Prophecy. You are the StarMan?*

Stunned, Axis only stared at him. *Yes. I am the StarMan. But, if you serve the Prophecy, then why do you ride with Borneheld?*

Until now I – we – did not know where you were, who you were. Now I know. I will return to Jervois Landing and lead my people to you.

Axis' eyes blazed. *Be careful. Very, very careful. If he suspects that you are going to ride to my cause . . .*

Ho'Demi's eyes crinkled. *I know. I will be careful.*

Then welcome, Ho'Demi.

The rest watched Axis and Ho'Demi stare at each other, confused. Then, seemingly put out by the inscrutable savage's stare, Axis dropped his eyes and kicked Belaguez to the last man in line.

"Moryson." Axis hesitated. Next to Jayme, here sat the man who Axis had once loved more than any other. Now he loathed them both and feared their tricks.

Moryson spoke, his eyes calm. "Axis. I have a message from the Brother-Leader for you."

Axis raised his eyebrows. He doubted it would be a message of love and support.

"Axis, Brother-Leader Jayme bids me tell you that you are cast out of Artor's House and out of His care. The Seneschal declares you excommunicate, and informs you that your soul is doomed to wander through darkness eternally unless you recant your sins. Forswear your dark alliance with the Forbidden now, Axis, and Artor may yet be prepared to forgive you."

"Artor is a god of lies and deception, Moryson," Axis replied, "and the Seneschal takes those lies and deceptions and magnifies them a hundredfold in order to control the hearts and minds of the poor folk of Achar." He paused. "Tell Jayme that Rivkah lives. Tell Jayme that one day I will give him — and you — to Rivkah to do with as she amuses. Your murder did not succeed, Moryson. She *lives*!"

"She *lives*?" Borneheld cried. "My mother lives? Moryson, what does Axis mean? What did you do?" Murder? What did Axis mean?

"He lies!" Moryson hissed. "Do not listen to him, Borneheld. Your mother died screaming as she gave birth to this bastard. Do not listen to his lies."

Axis turned his horse to face Borneheld again. "She lived, Borneheld, and lived to give birth again. Behold, your sister EvenSong."

Borneheld, appalled, looked at the creature Axis indicated. *Sister?* The creature had great violet eyes, narrow features like the other two of her kind, and massive black wings.

Borneheld forced a derisive smile to his face. "You are not my sister."

"Believe me," the creature snapped, "I would that were so. You murdered my lover, Borneheld, and for that my brother," her eyes flickered towards Axis, "says he will kill you. It will not be soon enough for my liking."

"She has the Icarii temper and lust for revenge," said Axis. "If I am not quick about your murder, then I fear EvenSong might slip into your chamber late one night. I hope you have guards posted who look into the night sky as well as the shadows hovering at the edges of corridors and chambers.

"And this," Axis indicated the black male, "is FarSight CutSpur, commander of the Icarii Strike Force under my control. They were the ones, Borneheld, who greeted you on your arrival this morning."

Borneheld felt the meeting slipping entirely from his control. "Axis —" he began belligerently.

But Axis went on as if he had not spoken. "Belial you know, as you do Magariz — although I feel bound to point out that you did not know Magariz as well as you might have thought. He has a far deeper sense of honour and justice than you ever gave him credit for.

"And," now Axis indicated the final flying creature, watching Borneheld's face as he spoke, "this is my father, StarDrifter. You might remember him, perhaps. You were there, StarDrifter tells me, when he seduced Rivkah atop Sigholt, although you were only a babe at the time."

Borneheld almost gagged in disgust. His mother had let herself be seduced by one such as this? It must have been rape, for how could *his* mother have allowed such as this to touch her so intimately?

"You were a tiresome baby," the creature said conversationally, and Borneheld realised with horror that Axis had its eyes and features, "and it does not surprise me to find that you have grown into such a tiresome man. Axis, I have had enough of this. I will talk with you later." Abruptly he spread his wings and lifted out of the group.

"I, too, am growing tired," Axis said. "Brother. I understand that you face threats from the Skraelings this winter and would prefer that I did not complete your humiliation until next summer."

Axis' taunting words pushed Borneheld over the edge into fury. "I have more than enough men to burn you and yours to the ground with Sigholt *and* break the Skraeling attack!" he shouted, shaking a clenched fist at Axis.

Alarmed, both Roland and Belial pulled the brothers back, speaking to them urgently.

Unconcerned by the ruckus, Moryson's eyes flickered over the two hounds which had accompanied Axis. Both sat well back from the fray, and both were staring fixedly at him.

Axis cursed himself as Belial reminded him that Sigholt, nay, Achar, could not survive if both brothers went to war against each other while the Skraeling threat was so bad. What had he been thinking of? But, face to face with his hated brother, Axis had not been able to resist taunting him.

Roland, and then Gautier, spoke as urgently to Borneheld, reinforcing that he could not attack Sigholt without leaving Jervois Landing fatally crippled.

It was, eventually, Axis who spoke. "Borneheld. Our ill tempers will have to wait until spring of next year."

He paused, and finally, grudgingly, Borneheld replied. "The winter advantage belongs to Gorgrael. We both want the same thing, Axis. Achar. And neither of us wants Gorgrael to have it. Very well. I will not destroy you until spring. You have winter to prepare."

Axis remained calm. "We agree on a truce for winter, brother, while we both fight back these Skraelings?"

Borneheld nodded. "Until Thaw-month. I should have defeated Gorgrael by spring, Axis, and then I will come after you."

Both men rode forward and gripped the other's hand, both tightening their grip until they could feel the other's bones shift. Neither let a spasm of discomfort cross his face.

"A truce until Thaw-month, Borneheld. My word on it."

"A truce until Thaw-month, Axis. *My* word on it."

"Burdel burns and pillages his way across southern Skarabost," Axis said, his hand still gripped by Borneheld's. "Call him off."

Borneheld smiled coldly. "I am King, Axis. Not you. And Burdel merely keeps order in a disorderly province. What he does in Skarabost is none of your concern." He let Axis' hand go.

"It concerns me that Burdel kills innocent people," Axis insisted. "Perhaps you might like to inform Burdel that I will eventually hold him responsible for each life lost, for each home burned, for each chicken carried away. Oh, and as for being King, Borneheld, I was surprised to hear of your sudden elevation to the crown. Priam was so well when last I saw him."

A shadow briefly flared behind Borneheld's eyes. So, Axis thought, there *is* something amiss here. Well, it will wait, and for all of your murders, Borneheld, you will pay.

"Until spring, brother." Axis sketched a salute, then turned to those behind Borneheld. "Roland." This time the salute was more formal. "Moryson, Gilbert, as I come for Borneheld in the spring, so I will also come for the Seneschal." Gilbert managed a sneer, but Moryson simply looked bored. Axis stared at Ho'Demi. *I hope I will not have to wait until spring to see you and yours, Ravensbundman.*

Ho'Demi held his eyes. *When the winter snows arrive, watch for us.*

Axis reined Belaguez back and whistled for the hounds. "Gentlemen," he said, then spurred his mount back across the Nordra, Belial and Magariz close behind him as FarSight and EvenSong lifted into the sky.

37

Yuletide

Still as tired and cold and dirty as he'd been when he'd lain down to sleep, Axis struggled up from the make-shift bed. He sat on its edge and took the bowl of vegetable broth Belial handed him. It seemed as if he'd been campaigning, fighting, these cursed wraiths for an eternity.

Mindful of Azhure's warning, Axis had not returned to Sigholt from Gundealga Ford. Instead, he had led the thousand mounted men and the two Crest of Icarii Strike Force through the south-eastern corner of the Urqhart Hills into the WildDog Plains and into hell.

The Skraeling mass had penetrated deep into the WildDog Plains and, for the four days it took Axis to reach the fighting, it had been the command that Azhure had sent into the Plains via the HoldHard Pass which had held the Skraelings back. Now Axis' command had been fighting virtually non-stop for nearly three weeks, and only slowly driving the Skraelings back towards the central Plains. Sigholt was left with only one squad of archers and one hundred men to protect it. Every single Icarii Strike Force member was with Axis — it had been a baptism of fire as far as the Strike Force had been concerned.

But they had done well. Gorgrael had only sent one SkraeBold with the Skraelings down the WildDog Plains, and it stayed well behind the Skraeling lines. There were no

IceWorms. The Icarii had been left almost unhindered in the air, raining death on the Skraelings. But they still had to be careful. The clouds swung down so far that the Icarii also had to fly low, and the Skraelings were perfectly capable of suddenly leaping from the ground to seize a careless wingtip. Axis grimaced. Over a dozen Icarii had been lost that way.

The mounted soldiers had not done so well, despite their bravery and skill. The Skraelings had massed down through the WildDog Plains in huge numbers, and without the Icarii Axis knew they would have suffered as badly as at Gorkenfort. But Arne had fought bravely, rallying his men, and after Axis' thousand had reinforced him, they'd gradually begun to force the Skraelings back.

Azhure's mounted archers had been almost as useful as the Icarii. Axis used them wherever the front line was weakest. Each archer could shoot over twelve arrows a minute, proving over two thousand arrows a minute in flight, and all with pinpoint accuracy. Their only handicap had been recovering enough arrows each night to be effective the next day. The SkraeBold got his Skraelings to haul back as many arrows as they could find on the ground whenever they retreated, and sometimes the hand-to-hand fighting was as much over the possession of arrows as about the taking of lives.

At Gorkenfort the Skraelings had been fearsome, but only if things went to plan. If caught unawares by a tactical manoeuvre, they were likely to retreat in confusion and whispering fear rather than stay and fight. But now they were more resolute, more courageous. Axis feared that, given enough time, Gorgrael could make his creatures unstoppable.

But they could yet be killed, although Stars knew what Borneheld faced at Jervois Landing if this was, as Axis suspected, only a minor force sent on the off-chance that he could break through into Skarabost via the WildDog Plains.

Axis tossed the empty bowl back to Belial. They sat in a too-thin tent in a makeshift camp at the foot of the eastern

Urqhart Hills, about five leagues above the entrance to HoldHard Pass.

"I wonder how Gorgrael thought the Skraelings were going to cross the Nordra if they had managed to push that far, Belial," he said. "Does the SkraeBold carry a purse full of coppers to pay the ferryman?"

Belial grinned at the thought, but it faded quickly. "The good folk of Smyrton would have abruptly found there were worse things to fear in the night than the Forbidden," he said quietly. Neither he nor Axis had much time for the stolid villagers of Smyrton. A great number of the refugees making their way to Sigholt travelled via the ferry at Smyrton, and the villagers lost no time in telling as many as they could that only darkness could be found at a place like Sigholt where – so it was rumoured – the Forbidden swarmed in large numbers. For some reason the village of Smyrton remained a stronghold of the Seneschal, and the villagers would have nothing to do with the Prophecy, or those named in the Prophecy. Axis had not gone back there since he had ridden through on his way to Gorkenfort over a year ago.

So much has happened since then, Axis thought. So much. The engaging girl who stared so rudely at me in the Chamber of the Moons is now Queen. Once . . . once I thought I loved her, but was it half of what I now feel for Azhure? Oh Stars, what am I going to *do* . . . what am I going to *say* to Faraday when finally I stand before her again?

Axis forced Faraday to the back of his mind. She was a problem many months away.

Perhaps now that they were finally holding against the Skraelings he might find an excuse to return to Sigholt briefly. It would be good to hold Azhure, talk to her, let her soothe away his doubts and fears.

Axis had not managed to use his powers as well as he'd hoped against the Skraeling mass. The ring could show him Songs that could kill or maim, but most were so potent and required so much power of the Star Dance that their use threatened to cripple Axis. Orr had warned him that some Songs were still too dangerous for Axis to use – he would have to grow in power and experience before he could handle them well enough to avoid being killed himself. Now Axis knew what he meant. The effort for a Song that killed some forty or fifty Skraelings left him so drained he could do nothing for hours afterwards. Stars help him, he had thought one day, if ever I am forced to use more power than I do now against Gorgrael's creatures.

In the end, Axis used his powers only sparingly. In times of crisis, when a push by a section of the Skraeling line threatened his own lines, or when some of his own command pushed too far and were in danger of being cut off.

"Will our line hold, Belial?" Axis asked. He sat on the makeshift bed, watching his second-in-command clean and oil his sword. The sight reassured Axis. During the first week of fighting there had been no time to clean anything.

Belial shrugged, not looking up from his task. "Probably. I don't think Gorgrael is sending any more Skraelings down through the Icescarp Barren. This was only ever a secondary attack anyway. If it succeeded, well and good. If not, well, I don't think Gorgrael will worry too much. His main attack will be on Jervois Landing. If no more Skraelings appear, then I think we can hold with what we have here."

There was silence as Axis contemplated Gorgrael and the attack on Jervois Landing and Belial contemplated the bed, wondering how he could ease Axis off it.

"Do you think Gorgrael knows I am here?" Axis asked, his thoughts obviously far away.

"Undoubtedly, Axis, since you have been using some of your Enchanter powers on his pet creatures. If nothing else, I'm sure the SkraeBold has reported your presence."

Axis wondered if there was any implied criticism in the man's comments about his Enchanter powers. He was sensitive to the fact that his powers were relatively useless against the Skraelings.

Belial, noting the sudden interest in Axis' face, but mistaking the reason for it, continued. "If Gorgrael does know you're here, I doubt he has much interest in the knowledge."

"What do you mean?" Why shouldn't Gorgrael take an active interest in his activities? Wasn't Axis the StarMan, the one the Prophecy said would destroy Gorgrael?

"Axis." Belial's voice was tired, and all he could do now was stare at the bed that Axis continued obstinately to sit on. "If you were a real threat to Gorgrael at the moment you would be beating down the front door to whatever fortress Gorgrael has secreted himself in. All Gorgrael wants right now is to overrun Achar before you have a chance to unite the country behind you. He knows he doesn't have much to fear from you at present."

"I am never in danger of falling into complacency and self-congratulation about you, am I, Belial? You always manage to remind me where I am and who I am."

"Well," Belial said, "can I remind you that you are still on that bed, yet it is my turn to sleep? Perhaps you could —"

He was cut off by a sudden, agonised groan from Axis, who clutched at his head. "StarDrifter," he muttered. "I *hear* you! I *hear* you! Calm down!"

Belial started and watched Axis carefully as he communicated with his father. StarDrifter had returned to Sigholt after Gundealga Ford, so . . . what was wrong at Sigholt? Was the Keep under attack? Was it . . . oh Mother, was it something wrong with *Azhure*? Belial sat forward on his stool, anxiety etching deep lines into his face.

"Stars!" Axis leapt to his feet, his face paling underneath its layer of grime. "Belial, the bed is yours. Can you hold this line against the Skraelings if I leave you?"

"What is it, Axis?" asked Belial, grabbing Axis by the arms. "What's wrong at Sigholt?"

"It's Azhure. She's gone into labour."

Belial's face went grey. "But it's too early. She's only just into her eighth month."

"I know." Axis' face was, if anything, even more anxious than Belial's. "I know. Belial, *can* you hold this line if I leave you? You have Magariz, and Arne, as well as FarSight and the Strike Force."

"Yes, yes," Belial muttered impatiently, dropping Axis' arms. "Yes, I can hold. But it's going to take you days, even if you ride at a flat-out gallop. You can't possibly get there before –"

"I have a faster means. Look after Belaguez."

A hint of music brushed the air, and then suddenly, shockingly, Axis wasn't there any more. Belial stared at the space where Axis had been standing, astonished.

"Why do I always get to look after the horse?" he muttered, then sat down on the bed, his face in his hands, suddenly too worried to sleep.

Would Azhure be all right?

The first contractions had caught Azhure while, of all things, she was returning from an early morning walk. She had gasped and clutched her protruding belly as she neared the Keep, and the bridge, alarmed, had hallooed so loudly that everyone in the garrison had been awakened and had hastened out, half dressed, clutching swords and bows, expecting to find Sigholt under attack.

Azhure, grim-faced with embarrassment, had marched back to her apartments with as much dignity as she could muster, half the Keep flustering at her heels.

Now Rivkah sat quietly in a chair while Azhure, still in the early stages of labour, paced nearby, Sicarius shadowing her every step. The rest of the Alaunt had been relegated to the kitchens while both MorningStar and StarDrifter fretted outside in the corridor.

The early onset of labour in itself was not a trouble. First children were often early. The problem was that Axis was not here, and Icarii children needed at least one Icarii parent there to talk them through the birth.

Icarii children were always far more aware than human babies were, and high-strung as well. Labour, the feel of the womb relentlessly contracting about them, usually frightened and confused them, and any sense that the mother was in pain or frightened only increased the child's terror. They needed an Icarii to talk to them, reassure them, convince them not to fight the birth, but to flow with it. If the Icarii parent wasn't there, then the child, struggling for life, often panicked and twisted, fighting against the pressure of the womb. Rivkah repressed a shudder. Axis' birth had gone so terribly wrong because StarDrifter had not been there to reassure Axis. Terrified by his mother's pain, Axis had twisted himself so badly that she'd almost died in giving him birth.

Rivkah did not want Azhure to go through that. How long would it take Axis to get here? Would Azhure have to undergo days of agony, days when the life drained from her, as she waited for him to arrive?

Theoretically, either MorningStar or StarDrifter could talk to the child, try to reassure him, but since Azhure had let neither of them talk to Caelum before this, he would not trust them, and would, in all likelihood, be so terrified by the time Azhure let either of the Enchanters near her that it would be too late anyway.

Rivkah bit her lip, watching Azhure pace slowly backwards and forwards in her loose linen nightgown, her hands kneading at the small of her back. She was in discomfort now, and Caelum surely was, but it would be nothing compared to what would come. But the last time Rivkah had mentioned either MorningStar or StarDrifter's name in front of her Azhure had snapped at Rivkah to keep them out.

Suddenly the door burst open and Axis strode in.

"Azhure!" Axis took three huge strides over to Azhure and wrapped her in his arms. Both laughed and cried at the same time and Rivkah gave in to her relief and let some tears slide down her cheeks. She wiped them away with the backs of her hands, standing to embrace Axis herself, patting him on the back and pushing his too-long hair out of his eyes.

Axis leaned back from Azhure, his face creased in some puzzlement. "I heard you were in labour, but –" He looked at Rivkah, as if she could explain why Azhure wasn't writhing about on a bed working with every breath she had to birth her child.

Both women laughed at his expression. "Labour takes some time, Axis," Rivkah explained, "and Azhure is still only in the early stages."

Then her smile died as she took a deep breath and started to explain to her son about Icarii births.

Eleven hours later in the dark hour before dawn, the time for levity had long passed. Azhure lay on the bed in a half-sitting position, leaning against Axis. Her eyes closed, her hair clinging to her forehead, she waited for the next contraction to rack her body. Axis whispered encouragement in her ear, his hand resting on her belly, feeling Caelum's fear and anxiety. Mother and child were now deeply frightened, and it was all Axis could do to reassure both of them.

He kissed Azhure's cheek again and whispered to her, then turned his mind to the child.

Caelum, I know you are frightened, but you must not fight your mother. Soon you will be born, and you will have escaped from this pain and this fright.

Afraid. Hurt. It was all Axis could sense from the baby; just the two emotions, fear and pain.

He lifted his eyes and met those of Rivkah. She tried to smile reassuringly at him. "It is going well, Axis, truly. The baby is in a good position and Azhure is bearing up well."

MorningStar had finally worked her way into the birthing chamber. Azhure no longer had the strength to complain, and Rivkah was glad. She needed the help, and MorningStar was an experienced Icarii midwife.

"Azhure *is* doing well, Axis, and you are doing well with the baby," MorningStar agreed.

"He's frightened," Axis muttered, remembering how Rivkah had suffered in his birth. Had he felt like Caelum? He must have.

Azhure grunted as another contraction twisted her body, and Axis winced as he heard the baby wail in fear.

Axis stroked Azhure's belly again. Somehow, Caelum could feel it and the touch of his father's hand reassured him.

Caelum, you must not fight what is happening. You are being born and your mother struggles for you. Go where she tells you. Trust.

Trust. Caelum's thoughts picked up that word and kept repeating it. *Trust.*

"Trust," Azhure whispered and groped for Axis' hand, then cried out again as another contraction seized her.

Rivkah rubbed the woman's leg. "He comes, Azhure. Now is the time to start to push with your pains. Now!"

The baby was silent now, and Axis grabbed both of Azhure's hands in his own. Surely, he thought frantically, there must be a better way than this! His ring could show him no Songs to relieve Azhure's suffering and now, as Azhure hung on to his hands as if her life depended on it, Axis remembered the times that men in the Axe-Wielders had appeared haggard-faced at his door, asking for some days off to arrange both the funeral of a wife who died in childbed and the futures of their motherless children.

No, he thought, don't let Azhure die now, not like this.

"Again," Rivkah grunted, "push," and Azhure's body again twisted next to his.

Axis heard MorningStar say something, but it sounded as if she were a thousand leagues away. All he could see was

Azhure's face below his, her smoky eyes opening wide in pain and astonishment as she felt the baby move within and through her.

"Push!" Rivkah's voice commanded from somewhere. Axis pulled Azhure as close to his own body as he dared. "Azhure," he whispered, "stay with me. Stay with me. Do not leave me. What would I do without you? Stay with me."

Rivkah looked at her son, then glanced down again. "His head comes. Your son is almost born. Two more contractions, three at the most, and you will have your son in your arms."

"Hear her, Azhure. You have almost finished. Your struggle is almost done." If possible, Axis held Azhure even tighter.

Azhure struggled once, twice, then gave a great gasp of relief. "Rivkah?" she asked feebly, scrabbling to sit up. Axis slipped an arm about her and lifted her, supporting her against his chest. He peered as anxiously as Azhure did.

A ray of light, the first of the day, glittered across the chamber and struck Azhure's face. She blinked in its radiance.

Rivkah wiped the baby's face with a towel, clearing his mouth and nose, then, smiling broadly, hoisted the baby onto Azhure's belly. Still attached to his mother by his umbilical cord, the baby squirmed weakly, his eyes blinking open, his tiny mouth in a round "O" of astonishment.

"Look what a beautiful son we have made," Axis whispered. "Thank you, Azhure, for this baby." He turned and kissed her gently on the forehead, and then on the cheek.

"I enjoyed the making more than the birthing," Azhure replied, but she smiled and her eyes were soft as she gazed at her son wriggling gently on her body. "He's so tiny."

Rivkah bound and cut the cord, then gently pulled MorningStar back from the bed. "Give them these few minutes together, MorningStar," she whispered. "You will see your great-grandson soon enough."

Azhure lifted the baby to her breast, and now she laughed delightedly as the baby began to suckle.

"Do you still think she is WolfStar?" whispered Rivkah.

MorningStar was silent for a time, watching Axis and Azhure absorbed in their new son. "She is not what she seems," she said finally.

Later Axis sat on the bed cradling the baby as Azhure, tired but determined not to slip into sleep yet, watched proudly. He had held Caelum and sung to him as Rivkah and MorningStar washed and attended to Azhure. Now Azhure lay clean and comfortable, although desperately tired, and StarDrifter had finally been allowed in.

"You must stay awake for this," Rivkah whispered. "It is rare, rare indeed, that three generations of Icarii Enchanters get to welcome a fourth generation into their family."

StarDrifter was entranced by the baby and, after asking Axis and Azhure for permission, took the baby into his own arms, rocking him gently and singing to him. The baby was still awake, and stared at StarDrifter curiously.

"Icarii babes can focus and see within only a few minutes of birth, Azhure. He will recognise and remember faces from this point on," said Rivkah.

StarDrifter smiled at the baby, then raised his head and smiled at Azhure. "He is a wonder," he said softly and turned his eyes back to the baby again. "Who would think that he is half human! His SunSoar blood sings so strongly."

Axis' and MorningStar's eyes met and caught.

"Just like EvenSong's," Rivkah said over-brightly. "Don't you remember, MorningStar, when EvenSong was born? StarDrifter said exactly the same thing then."

But everyone save Azhure knew exactly what had crossed MorningStar's mind as StarDrifter spoke. Of course the baby's SunSoar blood would be strong if Azhure were WolfStar.

StarDrifter spoke into the silence. "A name, Axis. What name will you give him?"

Axis smiled at Azhure. "Azhure has named him."

Both StarDrifter and his mother looked startled.

"Caelum," Azhure said. "We will call him Caelum."

"Impossible!" MorningStar cried. "He needs a Star name! He is an Icarii Enchanter."

"*I* am an Icarii Enchanter and I do not have a Star name," Axis said. "Azhure wants to call him Caelum, and I think it is a fine name. And suitable, if you think about it. The world is changing, MorningStar, and we cannot linger among the traditions of the past. Welcome Caelum into the House of SunSoar."

MorningStar dropped her eyes and her objections, although all could see by the stiffness of her shoulders that she was still displeased. She bent over the baby in StarDrifter's arms and kissed him gently on the forehead. "Welcome, Caelum, into the House of SunSoar. I am MorningStar, your great-grandmother. Sing well and fly high, and may your father win you Tencendor to grow in."

Now StarDrifter leaned down and kissed the baby softly. "Welcome, Caelum, into the House of SunSoar. I am Star-Drifter, your grandfather. Sing well and fly high, and may you always hear the beat of the Star Dance." He handed the baby to Rivkah.

She kissed the baby on his other cheek. "Welcome, Caelum, into this world of strife. I am Rivkah, your grandmother, mother to your father. Never forget that through my blood you also carry the hopes and heritage of a people who will never sing well or fly high, but who can love and cherish the better because of it."

She handed the baby to his father, then stood straight and stared defiantly at MorningStar and StarDrifter.

"Welcome, Caelum Azhurson SunSoar," Axis said softly. "I am your father, Axis Rivkahson SunSoar, and know that I love you well. Remember your grandmother's words, and never forget your human heritage or your human compassion. Both will be more important to you than your Icarii enchantments." He handed the baby to Azhure.

"Welcome to my heart, Caelum Azhurson SunSoar," Azhure said, "for you already know how much I love you. Never forget that you were born amid the death of Yuletide night and that you took your first breath as the sun crested the horizon. You are truly a child of the sun, Caelum. Live long and bright."

There was a stunned silence in the room as Azhure's words sank in. Everyone had forgotten she had laboured through the Yuletide night and given birth as the sun rose the next morning. StarDrifter muttered to himself. How could he have forgotten Yuletide? Had the rites gone as planned at the Earth Tree Grove? This was the first time he'd missed the Yuletide rites since he had been fourteen and old enough for the long and difficult flight to the Avarinheim. He had sent the larger number of Icarii Enchanters back to the Avarinheim two weeks previously in readiness for the rites, but had then completely forgotten them himself. Well, perhaps Azhure had supplied them with a rite which achieved exactly the same thing. Both the child and the sun had been reborn at exactly the same moment. What did that mean? Was Caelum a child of the gods?

"Behold the child," Axis whispered, stroking Azhure's hair from her forehead. "Caelum was conceived at Beltide and born at Yuletide," he paused again and kissed the crown of Azhure's head gently, "of the most remarkable mother."

Watching Azhure smile at Axis, StarDrifter finally realised how hard it would be to steal her from Axis.

"But your first daughter is mine, Azhure," he whispered, only to himself, "for surely she will be as remarkable as her mother."

Yet would the conquest of the daughter ever compensate for failing to achieve the mother?

38

The Nursery

Faraday had managed to keep the third week of Snow-month virtually free of court engagements – easy enough to do when the social life of court and city quieted under the oppressing certainty of war in the north. Most citizens had a husband or brother or son at the front, and all were well aware of what winter heralded. Yuletide was not celebrated or marked in any way in Achar, but Faraday and Yr had their own small celebration in the Queen's apartments. The two women had drawn very close, leaning on each other for company and for emotional support. Both felt trapped in Carlon, both were trapped within the Prophecy. Yr now spent most of her time with Faraday, even to the point of sharing her bed at night. It was a large bed, almost four paces across, and two bodies could get lost quite easily in it, but neither Faraday or Yr ever seemed to lose each other. In circumstances that sometimes seemed as hopeless as Faraday found hers, she took what comfort was offered, and Yr offered the girl a virtually bottomless well of comfort.

Faraday took a sip of water from a pewter goblet, thinking of the royal chalice. Borneheld had never used it, stating loudly to all who would hear that such a cup was too gaudy for a man of steel. His actions firmed Faraday's suspicions about Priam's murder into near certainty. And when Borne-held had given the chalice to Jayme and Moryson for safe-keeping, he announced to her who his accomplices were. The poisoned chalice was too subtle for Borneheld. It must have been suggested, planned and ensorcelled by someone else.

Ensorcelled. That the chalice *had* been ensorcelled was beyond doubt. But by *whom*? *How*?

Faraday shook her head slightly, and put the goblet down. "Yr? Can you keep Timozel away for the rest of this afternoon? I want to step the paths of the Sacred Grove again."

Yr nodded. "I will tell him that you sleep. That you need to rest before the New Year celebrations."

Faraday removed the bowl of enchanted wood from the chest where she had secreted it. "Yr, do you know why Timozel has changed? Why he has turned from a loving, cheerful youth into the dark and brooding man he is today?"

"No, sweet girl. I have thought long and hard on the matter. Perhaps he has a canker in his soul that eats away at his peace of mind." She shrugged. "I do not know what it is."

"I heard him speak of visions to Borneheld, Yr. Has he never spoken of them to you?"

"No." Visions? From who? "And he's never shared them with you?"

"No." Faraday sighed and began to prepare the bowl for her ritual embracement of the Mother's power. "We are not as close as once we were. He prefers to serve Borneheld now."

Timozel was her Champion, but these days always supported Borneheld against his wife. Nevertheless, Faraday was as yet loath to break the bonds of his oath of Championship to her. Perhaps Timozel needed her help. Perhaps one day she could help him as he had sworn to help her.

But now the Mother's power and the Sacred Grove awaited, and next to them, nothing else seemed important.

The power, the Grove and the Horned Ones awaited her. Once she had greeted the Horned Ones, Faraday wandered past the Grove and into the enchanted forest. Again she delighted in watching the strange beasts cavorting through glades and trees, but this time she was anxious to reach the small hut she'd been dragged away from so precipitously before.

Responding to her wish, the forest helped her feet onto the paths to the old lady's hut.

It was as she remembered; the grove with the tiny hut in its centre, surrounded by a picket-fenced garden. Just as Faraday focused on the plants the garden contained, the glossy red door of the hut opened and the old lady issued forth, dressed again in her red cloak with the hood thrown back from her cadaverous head. Her child-like eyes glowed with vitality and humour, and she held out her age-spotted hands to Faraday.

"Welcome, Faraday, child of the trees. Welcome to my garden. Will you stay awhile?"

"Yes, I'd like to stay. Very much. Thank you, Mother."

"Oh, no, no, no," the old woman clucked, limping down the garden path and opening the green gate into her garden. "No, no, I am not the Mother. But she allows me this little plot to tend my seedlings, and I, as they, are grateful for that."

Faraday stepped through the gate, closing it behind her. "Then what am I to call you?"

"Name? Oh, you may call me Ur." She rolled the "r" so that the name stretched over a breath and became almost a melody. "Now, dear girl, do you see my garden?"

Faraday looked carefully, and after a moment saw why this garden was different to most she had seen. "Why! It's a nursery!" she exclaimed.

"Good girl! *Good* girl!" Ur cried, and Faraday had to steady the old woman as she tottered alarmingly on her feet.

Instead of flowers and shrubs planted in the earth, Ur's garden was filled with thousands upon thousands of tiny terracotta pots, each filled with rich, damp black earth, and each supporting a single, slender seedling.

"I tend," Ur said, her violet eyes misting, "those who have entrusted themselves to me."

Faraday sensed that there was far more to these seedlings than was apparent. "Tell me," she pleaded. "Tell me."

The old woman motioned to a garden seat, warm and inviting in the sun, and Faraday helped her over, sitting down beside her and lifting her eyes to the sky for a moment. She did not think it strange that the sun could shine so ebulliently while the stars still reeled overhead in their tens of thousands.

"There is so much about the Prophecy that is not yet understood," Ur said, "and these seedlings are part of it. I doubt if even the Prophet was quite aware of what he meant when he wrote of the age-old souls locked into their cribs."

She halted and stared at the seedlings waving gently in the breeze. "Each will one day become a great tree in the re-planted forests of Tencendor, Faraday Tree Friend. You know that the Avarinheim has been slaughtered, cut down by the Axes of the Plough-fearing idiots of the Seneschal?"

"Yes," Faraday replied, feeling guilty she was of their race.

Ur's mouth thinned. "The Avarinheim as it stands today is but a fraction of what it once was. Yet, if you succeed, then the forests will one day stretch south like a vast sea into the lower reaches of Tencendor. They will one day resemble the enchanted woods that you see about you here.

"And here wait the seedlings of that great and enchanted sea, Faraday. Not only will they recreate the ancient forests, but they are also the only things that can wipe completely the filth of Gorgrael's armies from the face of Tencendor. You are the only one who can replant them. The only one who can remove them from the Sacred Grove."

Tears sprang to Faraday's eyes. In recent months she had sometimes felt bitter, trapped by the Prophecy in a role that held only pain, trapped in a spreading darkness that seemed to hold no light. But now Faraday felt overwhelmed at her good fortune. She would reawaken the greatness of the ancient forests, replant the enchanted seedlings across Achar. "Thank you," she whispered, squeezing Ur's hand.

"Enough," Ur grumped. "There is more you should know, more beauty."

She leaned forward, her joints creaking, and picked up one of the nearest seedlings. It was tinier and more fragile than most, having only just sprung from the earth of its nursery pot. "Here," the old woman said, and handed the seedling to Faraday. "Take it, feel it."

The pot was warm, and Faraday could feel a faint tingling running through her fingers. The seedling was so fragile that Faraday could see the tiny veins in each of the almost transparent leaves, each throbbing with new life, each throbbing with newly awakened potential.

"Her name is Mirbolt," Ur said.

"Mirbolt," Faraday murmured. "Do all the seedlings have a name?"

"Indeed they do, Faraday. And you must learn them all."

"Why?" The woman must be doting, Faraday thought, if she thinks I can learn the names of these thousands of seedlings about me.

"Have you not noticed the Horned Ones are all male?"

"Yes," Faraday answered hesitantly.

"And yet," Ur smiled, "the Avar have both male and female Banes. Where do the female Banes go when they die, Faraday? When they transform?"

"Oh!" Faraday gasped, nearly dropping the seedling pot as she realised she held the life of a female Bane in her hand.

"Mirbolt died in the attack on the Earth Tree Grove at Yuletide a year ago. She has only just transformed. Here she waits, with her almost forty-two thousand sisters, for the moment when they can be replanted across Tencendor. You have just learned a secret which only the female Banes know. Not even your friend Raum knows these seedlings exist."

"Forty-two thousand?" Faraday repeated.

"The female Avar Banes have been transforming for well over fifteen thousand years, Faraday Tree Friend. As have the male Banes — who, I should point out, often retransform into the fairy creatures you saw about you in the forest. The Avar are the most ancient race of Tencendor, and their Banes have been transforming for a very long time."

"And I must learn *all* their names?"

"Indeed you must, Faraday. They cannot be transplanted if you do not know each and every name. And just think, now you have learned one. Mirbolt."

In his den of tree branches and shrubs, Raum whimpered in agony. His bones were gradually stretching and altering, and he knew that he would shortly have to leave his people. He knew his transformation was not as it should be, not as it normally was for male Banes. Somehow Faraday held the key to his successful transformation. He would have to find her.

"Faraday," he whispered, then shrieked as his bones began to pull apart again.

Faraday straightened her skirt and turned to Yr. "Am I presentable?"

"Very. Now go down to the Chamber of the Moons and conduct Audience. It will be the last one before New Year."

"Thank the Mother for that," Faraday muttered, and patted her hair into place. Audience seemed so insignificant after what she had just learned from Ur.

"Timozel waits outside to escort you, Faraday."

"And what will you do with your free afternoon, Yr?"

Yr grinned. "I shall stay here and watch the Palace guard at exercise from your private balcony. That should keep me entertained."

Faraday laughed. Yr would no doubt manage to inveigle one of them into the stable for some further exercise once their courtyard callisthenics were done. She winked and walked through her chamber door into the outer chamber of her apartment complex, closing the door carefully behind her.

39

Skraelings and SkraeBolds

Two nights after Yuletide Gorgrael's Skraelings struck Jervois Landing with their full force. If it had not been for the canals, Ho'Demi mused, crouched in his muddied trench, Borneheld and all who fought for them would surely have been eaten by now.

By his side Inari hefted his spear in his hand. "They will strike soon, Ho'Demi. Already the mist begins to seethe."

Ho'Demi did not bother to reply. He was a courageous man, but every Skraeling charge caused a hard ball of cold fear to roll about his belly. He glanced along the trench. After six days of heavy fighting the weaker and less experienced among them were dead – many of the peasants Borneheld had pressed into fighting had proved all but useless – but those who'd survived were the better tempered for their experience.

There were many Acharites as well as a unit of Corolean mercenaries among the Ravensbundmen in Ho'Demi's section of the line. Borneheld had hired thousands of the dark-eyed and fair-haired soldiers to bolster Jervois Landing's defences. Ho'Demi nodded at their unit commander. They had proved silent and efficient killers, and the Ravensbund Chief was pleased to have their support.

A soft sound behind him made Ho'Demi's heart lurch in fear – had the Skraelings somehow circled behind them?

But it was only Borneheld. He jumped down beside Ho'Demi and stared into the mist before them.

"Soon," he said, his voice tight, hefting his sword in his hand.

Yes, very soon, Ho'Demi thought. Borneheld had earned his grudging respect over the past week. He did not hesitate to fight among his command, but he bolstered courage with harsh words and a hard hand where Ho'Demi thought encouragement would have worked better.

Gautier had an even harder hand, and many grew to fear his visits to their section of the trenches.

"There!" Inari called, pointing, and Ho'Demi signalled his men as he caught side of the wraiths seething through the mists towards them.

Teeth gaping, eyes gleaming, gibbering with delight, the Skraelings poured over the lip of the trench. Ho'Demi barely had time to skewer the first with his pike before another took its place, and then another. Beside him Borneheld grunted and seized a Skraeling by its stringy hair, twisting its head to one side as he manoeuvred his blade for a killing stroke.

Up and down the trench the predominant sound was of the harsh breathing of the defenders intermixed with the excited whisperings of the wraiths – interspersed occasionally with an agonised cry as a man fell victim to the hungry teeth of a Skraeling.

After twenty minutes Ho'Demi stuck the Skraeling currently reaching for his throat, then looked up to see clear space before him.

By his side Borneheld was struggling to best a particularly large Skraeling, and Ho'Demi seized its hair and pulled its head back, giving Borneheld the chance to puncture its great silver eye.

Blood spattered over the three of them.

Borneheld nodded his thanks to Ho'Demi, then glanced along the line. "They falter."

Yes, Ho'Demi thought, exhausted after a long day fighting, they falter. Many had cursed Borneheld as they had struggled for months to dig the system of trenches and canals that stretched between the Azle and Nordra rivers, but now all could see their brilliance. The Skraelings could not attack in mass as they had at Gorkentown. The canals forced them to splinter into small bands as they wound their way around and between the waterways. Instead of attacking as they preferred, in a great mass of writhing, nibbling teeth and claws that panicked and overwhelmed most opponents, the wraiths were forced into pits and traps. There the defenders were able to deal with them more easily than if they had been forced to meet a mass charge.

But they were still vicious and deadly and Ho'Demi wondered how Borneheld's forces would cope with the full weight of the Skraelings massed in southern Ichtar if Gorgrael managed to breach the canals.

Several hundred paces to the west came the faint cries of battle, and Borneheld climbed wearily out of the trench and strode silently towards the sound.

Ho'Demi looked at Inari. "I need to speak with the elders this night, Inari. Can you hold for a few hours?"

Inari's teeth gleamed. "I shall stick your share of Skraelings as well as mine, Ho'Demi."

"Make sure the men get something to eat, Inari. That was the fifth attack in as many hours."

And with that Ho'Demi was gone.

Behind him men slumped wearily, snatching what rest they could. Many took the opportunity to pray, the Ravensbundmen to their ice gods, the Coroleans to the bronze deities that hung at their belts, and the Acharites to Artor.

But not all the Acharites mumbled Artor's name under their breath. A small yet increasing number of soldiers muttered Axis' name. Rumours of his survival were spreading, and those among the five thousand who had accompanied

Borneheld to Gundealga Ford told of the golden man who rode out to meet their own dour and singularly unmajestic King. The Forbidden circling in the sky had been black and ominous, certainly, but they had done them no harm, though it was clear they could have rained death down from the skies had they a mind to.

And with rumours of Axis' survival spread word of the Prophecy.

Too weary and worried to waste the night in sleep, Ho'Demi called a secret Gathering of the Ravensbund elders and advisers in his tent.

After Sa'Kuya had served Tekawai to those gathered in the circle, she sat down by Ho'Demi's side.

Ho'Demi opened the Gathering with ancient formalised and ritual words, then spoke what was on his mind. "You know I spoke with the StarMan, Axis SunSoar, at Gundealga Ford four weeks past," he said bluntly, and the assembled Ravensbundmen nodded solemnly. The Prophecy swirled about them all.

"I have wrestled with my conscience every waking moment since then," Ho'Demi continued. "My soul and heart cry out for me to lead my people to Axis SunSoar's side where we belong, but my mind and conscience know that to do this now would be to leave Jervois Landing so vulnerable that Gorgrael would break through and claim Achar."

"Yes," Elder Tanabata said. "I am glad it is your choice and not ours. But tell us, have you reached a decision?"

Why else call us here? their faces seemed to say as they watched Ho'Demi drain the last of his Tekawai from the tiny cup emblazoned with the blood-red sun.

Ho'Demi nodded slowly. "I yearn for the StarMan, but I am also committed to fighting Gorgrael. We stay here until it appears that Borneheld can hold without us."

The others nodded. It was the decision they had expected.

"But," Ho'Demi's eyes were dark with worry, "I told Axis SunSoar we would join him when the first winter snows fell. We have now been blanketed with snows for three weeks and I worry that Axis will think we have abandoned him."

"He must be fighting as heavily as we are," observed Elder Hamori.

Ho'Demi considered Hamori's words. "Sa'Kuya will lead a party to Sigholt to tell Axis what is happening."

All nodded. It was a sensible plan.

"Over the next weeks I want to send small parties, mainly of women and children, to Sigholt. Borneheld and Gautier will never notice they are gone."

No-one was concerned at the thought of their wives and children making the dangerous journey to Sigholt. The Ravensbund women could fight as well as the men, and despite the bells the Ravensbund wore, all possessed the almost supernatural power of moving completely silently and invisibly when they needed to.

"If the fighting lessens, if Borneheld's own forces are strengthened by the arrival of more fresh Corolean mercenaries, then I will order the complete withdrawal of Ravensbund assistance to Sigholt."

"Borneheld will never let us go," a warrior remarked.

"No," Ho'Demi replied. "Borneheld will not want to see us go. Nevertheless, I intend that by spring I and the Ravensbund people will fight by Axis SunSoar's side. I will not remain allied to Borneheld if he wars against his brother."

All nodded, relieved.

"I will leave tonight," Sa'Kuya said, "and I hope to be at Sigholt in less than two weeks' time. Which of your wives and children will come with me?"

Axis left for his command in the WildDog Plains four days after Caelum's birth. He hated leaving, but he was needed, and Azhure and Caelum had recovered well.

Since he could not use the Song of Movement to travel to the camp site he had left, Axis rode with a small unit of reinforcements. It had been years since he had ridden any horse but Belaguez, and it exasperated him that his current mount did not respond to his every wish. He had formed such a bond with Belaguez over the years that he now found it hard to ride another horse.

Riding at their limits, they arrived in the makeshift camp in just over four days. Both Belial and Magariz had heard the news of Caelum's birth from an Icarii who had flown in earlier that day, and both were there to congratulate Axis. Axis was all broad smiles as he explained how remarkable the baby was, and only halted when he realised that both Belial and Magariz were staring at him with fixed expressions on their faces that unsuccessfully hid their boredom.

"Well," Axis subsided, remembering how he had reacted with similar boredom in past years to tales of newborn babes. FarSight pushed through the tent flap to join them, his wings crowding what spare space there was. Axis greeted him, accepted FarSight's congratulations on Caelum's birth, then moved on to more pressing problems. "Enough of women and babies. What news of the Skraelings? Has the SkraeBold managed to push them to new efforts?"

"We have held them back along this line." Belial's finger traced along a map of the WildDog Plains. "Gorgrael seems to have infused new purpose into both SkraeBolds and wraiths this year. The SkraeBold is cunning. He directs the Skraeling attack here, and here, and here," Belial's finger jabbed at several spots on the map, "where our line is weakest. Two nights ago he almost succeeded in breaking through. He learns from experience. No longer does he direct mass attacks against the length of our defences, but concentrated attacks against the weakest points."

Axis looked at him sharply, his earlier excitement forgotten. The SkraeBolds had been deadly last year – one had all but killed him – but they were inconsistent and easily diverted. The three that attacked the Yuletide rites at the Earth Tree Grove had failed to push home their advantage and had eventually suffered a devastating failure of purpose and loss of Skraeling lives. The SkraeBolds at Gorkenfort had won through the town to the fort, true enough, but they had then let themselves be taunted into sending their entire force northwards after Axis and his men, leaving those inside the fort free to flee south to Jervois Landing.

"How does he deal with the Icarii?" Axis asked FarSight.

"He was the one who thought of removing spent arrows from the ground, and of sending the wraiths leaping to seize the low-flying Icarii," FarSight replied. "He rarely shows himself. Do you think he is frightened of the Strike Force?"

Axis shook his head. "Not for himself, although you are obviously hurting his Skraelings. He is just being wary, I suspect. With his powers – Gorgrael has taught his Skrae-Bolds limited use of the Dark Music – he would probably come out the victor in any skirmish with members of the Strike Force, even if there were Enchanters with them. Belial, what do you make of him?"

"He is the mind behind this push south through the Wild-Dog Plains," Belial replied without hesitation. "Without him I am certain the Skraeling attack would fall apart and we could clear the plains relatively easily. However much Gorgrael has infused the Skraelings with new vigour and purpose, I believe they still rely on the SkraeBold for directions and encouragement. They are incapable of coordinating any attack themselves."

Axis' fingers slowly tapped the map as he thought. "I don't think Gorgrael really expected to break through here, he's just keeping us occupied . . ."

"While he directs his main attack against Jervois Landing," Belial finished.

Axis nodded. "Yes. And he *has* succeeded in tying us up. If we continue the way we are then we'll spend further weeks stuck out here in this wilderness picking off wraiths one by one." He paused. "I suspect Gorgrael has something special to throw at Jervois Landing and would prefer that I and the Icarii Strike Force waste our time fighting back this Skraeling push through the WildDog Plains." He studied Belial, considering. "Your assessment of the situation is a good one, Belial. I think the SkraeBold is our key to a quick and decisive victory. Destroy him and we destroy the Skraeling attack."

He looked at his three senior commanders. "Do any of you know where the SkraeBold nests at night? From where he directs his Skraelings?"

FarSight indicated a spot on the map. "This ridge overlooks much of the area we have been fighting in and is relatively isolated. He could be there. Do you want me to send farflight scouts to have a look?"

Axis shook his head. "No. I have a better idea."

The eagle soared above the WildDog Plains, his sharp black eyes scanning the country below him.

Far below him Axis sat alone on the plains, the cold wind blowing his hair about his face. He saw only what the eagle saw. He did not feel the hard dirt and pebbles beneath his buttocks, but only the sweep of air beneath the eagle's wings. West, his mind directed, and the eagle tipped his balance towards the Urqhart Hills.

Over the past weeks the eagle had spent a great deal of time watching the creature. The eagle considered the creature particularly ill-formed, worse even than carrion vultures. It was leathery and lizard-like, silver-eyed and fierce-clawed, and even though it had wings to fly and a beak to cry with, the eagle felt very little affinity with the creature. It soared, but it did not enjoy it.

But now the man needed to know where it was, and the eagle undertook to take the man to the SkraeBold.

The SkraeBold sat on a ledge high on the rocky ridge that FarSight had indicated to Axis. His leathery wings encased his body entirely from his jaw down. To a casual eye, or even to the gaze of someone who looked for him, the SkraeBold simply looked like one more grey and featureless rock on the ridge. Only his narrowed silver eyes moved as they surveyed the WildDog Plains before him.

The SkraeBold was pleased with his efforts so far. Gorgrael had sent him down the WildDog Plains with instructions to keep Axis busy. The less support Borneheld had at Jervois Landing, the better. He had numerous thousands of Skraelings to work with, and he had learned early that it was better to use the wraiths in concentrated attacks than mass surges down the entire width of the WildDog Plains. If it had not been for the Icarii Strike Force, the SkraeBold thought he might actually have been able to break through to the Nordra. The Icarii were far too good at decimating any surge or probe the SkraeBold sent southwards. Their cunning arrows floated from the sky, rarely failing to strike a wraith in the eye, and the SkraeBold blinked in painful sympathy. And there had been those nasty, agile archers on horseback too.

So, despite his relative success at keeping Axis' force occupied, the SkraeBold was learning to loathe arrows. His wraiths had orders to retrieve any arrows and bring them back to the SkraeBold. Now several thousand of the vile feathered implements lay in a deep crevice at his feet.

But the arrows were not the SkraeBold's only concern. Where was Axis SunSoar? He had not seen the man for a week or more now. He had not left his camp, of that the SkraeBold was sure, because his wraith-grey horse was still tied up in the horse lines. So why had he not seen him, when Axis was usually at the forefront of any action?

He noticed the eagle as it drifted overhead, but did not think to give it a second glance. Then, unexpectedly, it swooped down and landed on a rock just out of the Skrae-Bold's reach.

"SkraeBold," it said, and it spoke with Axis SunSoar's voice. "I greet you well. You are proving a worthy opponent."

The SkraeBold was so shocked he could not move.

"My forces cannot move against you, my arrows are numbered, and one of your late-night Skraeling attacks has left me terribly injured." The voice faltered a little, as if he who spoke was gasping for breath.

The SkraeBold hissed as he thought quickly. *Axis had been injured!* No wonder he'd not seen him!

"I am tired of this impasse," the Axis-voice said. "Why do we fight back and forth, back and forth, when we could so easily settle this once and for all?"

The SkraeBold tilted his head to one side, his eyes bright as he regarded the eagle.

The eagle hopped judiciously to a rock a little further away. "I have a proposal for you," the Axis-voice continued. "We could settle this once and for all, you and I, just you and I. Why don't we meet honourably? One on one. Fight."

The SkraeBold considered. Gorgrael had been so very angry whenever one of the SkraeBolds had countermanded his orders. SkraeFear had paid dearly for attacking StarDrifter at Yuletide.

"The victor claims the field," the voice continued. "The loser . . . well, the loser loses all."

But, the SkraeBold thought, what if he brought Axis down for Gorgrael? He briefly imagined himself dropping Axis' torn body at Gorgrael's feet.

"One on one?" he asked suddenly. "No helpers? No assistance? No nasty feathered things?"

"You have my word," the voice said, and the SkraeBold fancied he could hear a fatal weakness creep into the man's voice. Imagine the triumph if the SkraeBold could not only break through to the Nordra, but kill Gorgrael's nemesis at the same time! The SkraeBolds had been sadly out of favour with Gorgrael since the disaster above Gorkenfort, but this . . . well, this might restore Gorgrael's faith in his SkraeBolds. Convince him they were more worthy than the Gryphon.

The SkraeBold launched himself at the snow eagle.

The eagle, even wary as it was, was still only just agile enough to evade the creature's attack. It twisted and wheeled out into the open sky, the SkraeBold, ominously silent, twisting after it.

Far below, both Skraeling and human stood watching as the SkraeBold hunted the eagle through the sky. The Icarii, warned of Axis' tactics, had positioned themselves along the cliff faces of the nearby Urqhart Hills, but they watched as silently as those below.

The snow eagle led the SkraeBold high into the sky, always just out of reach, always managing to twist its way out of the SkraeBold's claws just as it appeared the creature was about to strike. Both eagle and SkraeBold disappeared into the clouds, and for a few agonising moments none below could see what was happening. But then the snow eagle plummeted out of the clouds, wings loose, tumbling over and over. The SkraeBold dropped through as well, but his descent, even though fast and furious, was controlled where the eagle's was totally wild and unrestrained.

The eagle dropped like a rock through the air, plummeting to a point on the plain where stood a man alone.

Axis.

At the last possible moment the eagle pulled out of its mad dive. It checked and pulled its wings back, its claws extended, and, still travelling far too fast, careened onto the man's waiting arm. Rocked by the force of the eagle's landing, the man stumbled and took a quick step back, but he recovered just as the SkraeBold shrieked out of the sky above them.

He did not even hesitate. He knew who the man was, and hungered for his blood. He went straight in for the attack, the claws of his hands and feet extended, razor-sharp beak open to tear at the man's flesh.

He hit nothing but hard ground.

The man had been an illusion. A trickery.

Half stunned, but knowing he was dead if he remained on the ground, the SkraeBold stumbled to his feet, one wing hanging brokenly behind him. Axis stood some five or six paces away, the eagle still on his arm. As the SkraeBold blinked in confusion and pain, Axis launched the eagle to soar free into the sky, then looked at the SkraeBold and laughed.

"Did you like my mirage, SkraeBold? It is one of my new tricks."

The SkraeBold shook his head, trying to clear his mind, then screeched with fury as he realised that one wing was broken.

"Have you hurt yourself, SkraeBold?" asked Axis, taking a step forward.

The SkraeBold stepped back, hissing softly. He had no intention now of trying to battle it out with this fully fit man. He reached inside for the small well of power Gorgrael had given all of his SkraeBolds, preparing to fade from view.

But Axis was ready for him. He reached out with the power of the Star Dance, using a Song of Muddlement that wrapped the SkraeBold's mind in shadows, reflections and dead ends. Flustered by his inability to touch his power, the SkraeBold launched himself at the cause of his confusion and misery.

But as his mind was full of confusion, so his physical reactions were similarly befuddled, and Axis nimbly side-stepped. A sword suddenly gleamed in his hand, and as the SkraeBold blundered past he struck him underneath the SkraeBold's right arm, sliding it deep into the soft flesh of his armpit. The SkraeBold screamed and wrenched himself off the blade, twisting away from Axis.

"It bleeds," Axis observed, "as red a blood as do the Skraelings."

The SkraeBold, agonised by the wound underneath his arm and by the useless flapping of his broken wing, finally started to think a little more clearly. He pretended mortal hurt, gave a single sobbing sigh, and, hugging his arm to himself, crouched down as if he were preparing to die.

Axis was not fooled, but he let the creature think he had been. He stepped close, over-confidently, his whole body apparently relaxed and off guard.

The instant he was close enough the SkraeBold leapt to his feet and swung out with his injured arm.

But Axis was quicker and far more agile than the heavily muscled SkraeBold. He ducked underneath the arm and sank his sword deep into the creature's belly. The SkraeBold caught him with his uninjured arm, hurt too deep this time to cry out, but Axis was prepared for that as well and, as the SkraeBold clutched him to his chest, punctured the creature's left eye with a knife.

The SkraeBold convulsed, and Axis felt his claws tear through the black wool of his tunic and into his back. He grunted and grabbed at the hilt of his sword, still buried deep in the SkraeBold's belly. As he stepped back Axis placed his booted foot to one side of the SkraeBold's belly, using it as a lever to pull his sword free, twisting it as viciously as he could as it started to slide free.

The SkraeBold collapsed on the ground, his remaining eye staring at Axis in horror. "You tricked me," he hiccupped softly, then he died.

Axis stood there, wondering at the ease of his kill, when he heard a horseman behind him.

"Axis."

He turned. Belial rode up on his stallion, leading Belaguez. Both horses laid back their ears and tossed their heads at the sight and smell of the dead SkraeBold.

"Look!" cried Belial, and Axis turned back to the Skrae-Bold. It was slowly fading from view.

"Returning to its master," Axis said tiredly, "for him to do with as he will." Exhaustion threatened to overcome him, and he swung into Belaguez's saddle before he slipped to the ground.

Belial gazed worriedly at him. He could see the reddened tears in the back of Axis' tunic, but Axis' exhaustion concerned him more.

By morning the majority of the Skraelings had disappeared from the WildDog Plains. They drifted back through the Icescarp Barren and down towards southern Ichtar, where they could hear their comrades whispering and crying softly to each other. Their orders had been clear. If, for whatever reason, they were forced to abandon the push south through WildDog Plains, they were to rejoin their companions at Jervois Landing.

Gorgrael himself, faced with another pile of grey sludge on the cold floor of his chamber, was not overly distressed. He had not expected any of his SkraeBolds to do well against Axis. Not with what Axis had undoubtedly learned. And this SkraeBold's death had provided Gorgrael with what he needed most. Building material. Already his first pack of Gryphon were approaching maturity and once they had whelped Gorgrael would throw them against Jervois Landing. Now he had the materials to make more.

Axis pulled his troops out of the WildDog Plains, leaving but one unlucky unit to patrol (with the assurance that they would be relieved soon) the wind-swept and increasingly snow-bound plains. A Wing of the Strike Force was also left in the northern Urqhart Hills to provide an early warning if Gorgrael sent his Skraelings through the WildDog Plains again. Somehow, Axis did not think he would.

The Strike Force already winging its way over the Urqhart Hills towards Sigholt, Axis led the mounted section of his command south towards the entrance to HoldHard Pass. Nosing ahead ran the four couples of Alaunt which had proved as valuable as Azhure's mounted archers. Well, now both archers and Alaunt were heading back to their mistress.

As am I, thought Axis. As am I.

At the mouth to HoldHard Pass, Axis' command found a small group of refugees from Skarabost just about to enter. They were a ragged bunch, having spent some weeks fleeing northwards into the worsening weather. Their trust must have been great, thought Axis, as he rode forward to meet them, to keep on moving northwards even though the weather worsened with each step north they took.

The leader of about forty-five men, women and children, was a middle-aged, plump and grey-haired trader called Dru-Beorh. He was beside himself with pleasure to learn that the golden-haired man who sat the magnificent grey stallion before him was Axis himself.

"Great Lord," he breathed, abasing himself in the dirt before Belaguez. "To meet you like this is an added boon. I have travelled from Nor to join your cause." Axis, as Belial and Magariz behind him, raised his eyebrows in some surprise. News of the Prophecy had spread as far as Nor? "And I have brought you a gift for you to do with as you will. Behold!" he cried, waving his hand towards the back of his small column.

Axis drew in a quick breath of surprise as he saw what Dru-Beorh indicated. He knew exactly what he was going to do with it.

40

"Woe! Woe!"

"Azhure."

Azhure turned at the sound of Axis' voice, wiping the sweat out of her eyes. She had resumed training two weeks ago, and had spent the morning at archery practice in a small field just outside the Keep.

"What is it?" she asked, wondering if something was wrong with Caelum, only four weeks old. She had left him in their apartment with his grandmother and Sicarius watching over him.

"Relax. Nothing is wrong, Azhure. I simply came out to watch my archery commander at weapon practice. So, tell me, Azhure, are you fully fit now? Ready for any action your StarMan might demand of you?"

"I *would* be fully fit if I had a decent horse to ride," Azhure said tartly. "As it is I have to trail behind the slowest of my command on a nag that should have been retired five years ago. I might as well ride one of Veremund or Ogden's donkeys."

Axis couldn't believe she'd given him such a perfect opening.

"I expect you think I should give you Belaguez back," he said, making his voice as terse as hers.

Azhure's back tensed as she sighted down the shaft of an arrow, then loosed the arrow and swung round to Axis in one fluid movement. "Are you going to tax me about exercising your horse after all this time? Why didn't you say something earlier?"

"Oh, I'm not upset, Azhure. You did well with Belaguez. Even now when he greets me in the stable I do not know if he welcomes *me* with his soft nose, or searches for scent of you. No," Axis waved to one of the guards standing in the shadows under Sigholt's main gates, "I'm not upset at all. Impressed, rather. So impressed, in fact," he paused, "that I have decided to give you your own war-horse."

A plump grey-haired man, whom Azhure recognised as one of the refugees Axis had returned with from the WildDog Plains, stepped out from the shadows of the gateway. He led a finely boned chestnut Corolean stallion, fully outfitted with saddle and bridle. Dru-Beorh hesitated as the stallion skittered in the sudden light, then led the horse across the bridge towards Azhure.

Axis took the Wolven and the quiver from Azhure and laid them carefully to one side. "Do you like him, Azhure? He is fully trained, but young, and so he will take to a new rider well. He has not been exercised for some time though, so he will be a bumpy ride for the next few days."

The sheer delight on Azhure's face was enough thanks for Axis. He took her arm and led her tó meet Dru-Beorh and the horse. "He is an inadequate gift to thank you for Caelum, Azhure. Inadequate, because nothing I could do in this life could be thanks enough. Here, stroke him. Do you like him?"

Azhure reached out a hand and touched the horse's silken coat. It gleamed a dark bronzed red in the sunlight and twitched under her fingers. "He is a wonderful gift, Axis," she said, her eyes bright with tears.

Dru-Beorh shuffled a little in embarrassment. He did not mind in the least that the Great Lord had elected to pass on his gift to this beautiful lady, for Dru had heard of her exploits and her courage. "His name is Venator, my Lady,"

Dru muttered. "In the language of the Coroleans the name means 'One Who Hunts'."

"Venator," Azhure repeated. "What a beautiful name. And you gave him to Axis?"

Dru nodded and explained briefly how he'd seized Venator as recompense for a bad debt from a Nors nobleman who had only just purchased him from a Corolean unit passing through Nor.

"A *Corolean* unit was passing through Nor?" Axis asked sharply. "How many, and where to?"

The trader felt the shift in mood. "Over the past several months Corolean troops have been moving through Nor and catching river transports for Jervois Landing, Great Lord. Many of them. How many?" He shrugged. "I do not know. Several dozen units, at the least."

Axis' eyes caught Azhure's and she turned to Dru. "I thank you for bringing us the horse, Dru-Beorh."

Dru bowed, recognising the dismissal, and led the horse back into the Keep.

Azhure turned to Axis. "Borneheld has Coroleans fighting for him?"

Axis watched the horse disappear back into Sigholt, but his thoughts were far away. "Apparently so. Has he concluded a treaty with them? A military alliance?" He did not have to go on. If Borneheld had the weight of the Corolean military behind him, Axis would find it all but impossible to defeat Borneheld.

Beside him, Azhure started. "Axis!"

Alarmed by her tone, Axis snapped out of his reverie and looked to where she pointed. Walking slowly up the road that led to HoldHard Pass was a group of several hundred women and children, but the oddest women and children Azhure had ever seen. All of their faces were so heavily tattooed that they seemed dark blue from this distance, and their black hair was oiled and plaited into tiny braids. Many of them rode ugly and stunted yellow-haired small horses, almost ponies. The sound of myriad soft bells and chimes drifted to meet them.

"They are Ravensbund!" Axis cried, and Azhure wondered at the gladness in his voice.

The next day, after Sa'Kuya had sufficiently rested, Axis invited her to attend the daily conference he held with his commanders in the map-room.

Sa'Kuya had taken almost three weeks to lead her party northwards to Sigholt. They had evaded discovery leaving Jervois Landing, and had met none of Borneheld's patrols south of the Nordra.

"We crossed the Nordra at Gundealga Ford," she said to Axis, "where you met with my husband, Ho'Demi."

Axis inclined his head.

"Then we travelled the southern Urqhart Hills, joining HoldHard Pass just before its final bend towards Sigholt." She shook her head a little, the beads and bells jingling merrily, and looked to Magariz and FarSight. "We passed two of your mounted patrols," she said, "and sighted five of your winged people in the skies. But we remained silent and unseen."

"Then I am glad you came as friends and not to cut our throats in the night," Axis said, with a sharp glance at his commanders.

"If we had come to cut your throats in the night, you would already be dead," said Sa'Kuya tartly.

"Your husband said he would be here with the first winter snows," Axis said, changing the topic. He waved out the window, "Though the Lake of Life keeps Sigholt and its surrounding hills free of snow, the rest of northern Achar is thigh-deep in it. Where is Ho'Demi?"

And why can he speak to me with the mind voice? Axis thought. *What is he?*

Sa'Kuya explained Ho'Demi's dilemma. "He wants with his heart and soul to join you, but he knows that to do so would leave Jervois Landing so stripped of soldiers that Gorgrael would almost certainly win through. No-one wants to see that happen."

Belial spoke up. "Sa'Kuya, my intelligence told me that your husband brought some eleven thousand men into Jervois Landing. Is that correct?"

Sa'Kuya nodded. "Eleven thousand, save those already dead at Skraeling hands. Plus a further nine or ten thousand women and children. All will join you as soon as possible."

Axis caught Belial's glance. Twenty thousand? Where would they put them all?

"Azhure," he said finally, "have you seen to the Ravensbund already arrived?"

She nodded, knowing what Axis was thinking. Eleven thousand fighters would be welcome indeed, but with many thousands of refugees already, how would they feed them and their families?

Axis sighed, and turned back to Sa'Kuya. "I hear that Corolean forces join Borneheld at Jervois Landing. What can you tell me of them? Has Borneheld forged an alliance with the Corolean Empire?"

"No, he has not managed to forge an alliance with them, although he would like to do so. He hires mercenaries from the Coroleans. He has perhaps some three or four thousand with him at the moment, and more are on the way."

Axis' shoulders slumped with relief.

"Corolean mercenaries are expensive," noted Magariz. "For that many Borneheld must be draining his treasury."

Axis nodded, then spoke to Sa'Kuya again. "Tell me about the Skraeling attacks on Jervois Landing, and of the defences Borneheld has constructed there."

Sa'Kuya described the viciousness of the Skraeling attacks, how they were deflected only by the system of canals Borneheld had built. "The Skraelings, hating open water as they do, are herded like cattle in a run. Wherever the Skraelings attack along the line between the Azle and the Nordra, they meet these canals, and their attack is splintered and fragmented by the twists and turns they are forced to make. Gorgrael throws hundreds of thousands of Skraelings at the defences, but at the moment they hold."

"No IceWorms yet?"

"No. Only Skraelings."

Axis looked at Belial and Magariz. If the IceWorms arrived, *when* they arrived, would they be able to bypass the traps by vomiting their repulsive cargo completely over the canals? He turned his gaze back to Sa'Kuya. "When will Ho'Demi join me, Sa'Kuya?"

"By spring at the latest, Great Lord." She had picked up the title from Dru-Beorh last night. "Borneheld will not have the use of the Ravensbund people if he moves against you."

"Thank the Stars for that," Axis began, but the next instant everyone was on their feet as the bridge screamed.

"To the roof! To the roof! Woe! Woe!"

"*Stay still!*" Axis yelled, as everyone headed for the door. "Belial, FarSight, you come with me. Azhure, send for your archers. Magariz, Arne, prepare Sigholt for attack as we planned. SpearWing, get the Strike Force in the air. Sa'Kuya, stay here."

SpearWing went straight out the window, while the others let Axis and the three he had named through the door first, then hurried to their tasks. Axis had long planned the defence of Sigholt – now it appeared that they were going to stand in good need of the countless drills they had practised.

"Woe! Woe!" the bridge wailed. "To the roof! To the roof!"

"It can hardly be an attack," Azhure said as she scurried up the stairs after Axis, the Wolven already unslung and an arrow notched, "if the bridge is screaming for us to go to the roof."

"Nevertheless," Axis grunted, "the bridge is hardly screaming for us to come and look at the view. Something is wrong, very wrong."

SpikeFeather TrueSong spiralled out of the sky towards the roof of Sigholt, only barely managing to hold on to life. By his side flew EvenSong, calling out encouragement even as she wept. Beside them, almost wingtip to wingtip with EvenSong, flew the snow eagle.

The rest of their Wing was dead.

The group watching from the roof of Sigholt realised how badly SpikeFeather was injured the instant his blood spattered down in great drops about them.

Hurriedly, FarSight launched into the air.

"SpikeFeather," Azhure whispered as she lowered the Wolven, "EvenSong." They were her closest friends among the Icarii.

A group of archers clattered out of the doorway to the stairwell, closely followed by StarDrifter and the three Sentinels.

SpikeFeather lost consciousness some five wingspans from the roof, and FarSight and EvenSong could not contain his fall. He landed with a sickening crunch, his form apparently lifeless, dreadful injuries marking his wings and torso. Blood pooled about him.

Azhure took one look and almost vomited with shock. His belly had been ripped open, and ropes of bowel glistened in the sun; his left arm had been torn almost completely off, and now hung only by tendons and blood vessels.

Axis dropped to his knees by SpikeFeather. The Wing-Leader was a close friend.

Then EvenSong landed, and Azhure rushed to her side. She had obviously also been attacked by whatever had all but killed SpikeFeather; one cheek lay open, and both arms and hands were cut horribly. But she was not dying.

Axis was determined not to lose SpikeFeather like he had FreeFall. This time he would not fail. He gathered the birdman into his arms, spreading his wings to either side.

StarDrifter started to step forward, but Veremund held him back. "Behold your son, StarDrifter."

All three Sentinels were very calm amid the cries of horror about them. They moved about the roof quickly, pulling everyone save EvenSong and Axis back from SpikeFeather.

Ogden put an arm about Azhure. "Watch, pretty mother," he whispered in her ear. "Believe in Axis."

Of all present, it was StarDrifter who appreciated the power of the Song of Recreation that Axis sang most of all. This was a Song so powerful, so extraordinarily hard to sing, so difficult to control the power of the Star Dance as it flooded through the music, that few Enchanters had ever been able to wield it properly.

As Axis cradled SpikeFeather close, he sang the Song of Recreation for him. It was a strange Song, with little melody, filled with breathy catches and lilts, but extraordinarily compelling and beautiful. As he sang, Axis ran his hands gently over SpikeFeather's body, smoothing the blood away.

Belial and Magariz glanced at each other. They had seen Faraday heal Axis, but it had been nothing like this. She had worked hard, her hands buried deep in his body, compelling and persuading broken flesh and blood vessels to repair themselves. But Axis was far more relaxed, and his hands far more gentle. They ran over grossly torn flesh, leaving it whole and healthy. For a moment both hands hovered over SpikeFeather's open belly, the Song intensifying slightly, and when they moved on the birdman's entire abdomen looked as if it had seen nothing more violent than the touch of the sun. His left arm, hanging by fragile tendons one minute, was clean and whole the next.

Axis moved his hands to the birdman's face, and cradled it between his palms, the Song dwindling to a close.

SpikeFeather slowly opened his eyes into Axis'.

"Welcome home," Axis said simply, and by his side EvenSong burst into great sobs. Azhure knelt down by her side and put her arms about her.

"Hush," she whispered, and wondered if EvenSong were crying for SpikeFeather, for herself, or for FreeFall.

Axis raised his eyes from SpikeFeather. "EvenSong."

EvenSong gulped her tears down and looked at her brother.

"EvenSong. Where is the rest of your Wing?" Axis had sent them to scout over Hsingard and Jervois Landing three days ago.

"Dead."

There was a shocked murmur among the group huddled about.

"What attacked you, EvenSong?" Axis' eyes bored into his sister's.

"Gryphon," she whispered, and far below the bridge wailed again.

"Woe! Woe!"

"We were attacked by Gryphon."

41

EvenSong's Memory

Recreated, SpikeFeather remembered nothing of the attack. He could vaguely recall leading his Wing west for a reconnaissance flight over southern Ichtar, but retained no memory either of the patrol itself or of his Wing's destruction to the east of Hsingard. Now, as he stood in Rivkah's apartment, he struggled to recall any memory, any emotion he might have that could help EvenSong.

Rivkah sat on the other side of the bed from Axis and held her daughter's hand. Through all the traumas of her own life, she had somehow managed to convince herself that EvenSong would live the peaceful, contented existence that Rivkah had been denied. But not only had EvenSong lost her lover, but here she lay torn and battered on Rivkah's bed, her wings folded flat and lengthways underneath her body, her great violet eyes closed, her breasts barely rising with her breath. EvenSong would live, would recover physically from the wounds given her, but her soul seemed fatally stricken.

Gryphon. Rivkah shuddered and looked about the room. Azhure stood close by Axis' side, her hand on his shoulder, her eyes on EvenSong. Axis had been unable to heal his sister; his powers gave him the ability to recreate the dying, but he could not use the power of the Star Dance to heal ordinary wounds. To one side, packing her herbs and potions, was an Icarii Healer famed for her wisdom and patience and steeped in common sense and practised in natural healing. She had done her best for EvenSong, now it was up to the birdwoman to find the courage to take a stronger hold on life. Further away, close by the door, stood Magariz. His eyes caught with Rivkah's for a moment, and Rivkah understood that his concern was for her own pain for her daughter.

Rivkah felt a hand on her own shoulder, and knew it was StarDrifter. Behind StarDrifter was MorningStar, and behind her the three Sentinels, Belial and FarSight CutSpur. At the foot of the bed lay a hound, although which one Rivkah knew not, and outside she could vaguely hear the scream of the eagle as it cartwheeled through the sky.

"EvenSong." Axis spoke softly, but was desperate to know of the attack that had destroyed SpikeFeather's Wing. It was one of the more experienced within the Strike Force, and each of the twelve members had won Axis' respect. He would have trusted his back to any of them. But something had attacked them. Something that had torn ten lifeless from the sky, left SpikeFeather for dead and EvenSong barely able to support SpikeFeather home.

What had EvenSong said? Gryphon. What was a Gryphon? And why had it caused so much distress on the faces of those Icarii present? Axis reached for his sister's hand, wincing at how cold it was, and gently squeezed.

"EvenSong," he repeated. "Please, I – we – need to talk to you about what happened."

EvenSong sighed and opened her eyes, looking over those grouped about her bed. "You returned safely, SpikeFeather. I was so afraid that you would remain lost."

"I still have a life to live," SpikeFeather said lamely, but EvenSong seemed satisfied. She turned her pale face, scarred almost identically to Magariz's now, back to her brother.

"Thank you, Axis, for what you did. I fought for many hours to bring SpikeFeather home. To have lost him in the final few minutes would have been hard to bear."

Axis let her hand go and stroked her forehead. "I did not save him, EvenSong. You were the one who brought him home."

EvenSong's eyes filled with tears. No-one would ever know what she had gone through to bring SpikeFeather home. To fly beside him, pleading with him not to die, pleading with him to keep his wings beating, pleading with him not to give up, not to succumb to the pain and the shock and the horror before he could reach Sigholt. And all the while watching the life seep from his ghastly wounds.

"Share it, EvenSong," Axis said. "Tell us what happened. Share the memory."

"We had been out three days," EvenSong said finally, closing her eyes again, drawing her strength from the touch of her brother's fingers and the pressure of her mother's hand, "and were returning home. We had scouted the reaches of Ichtar above Jervois Landing – the Skraelings are massing, Axis, bearing down on Jervois Landing. Tens, hundreds of thousands of them. So far the defences are holding, but . . ."

"Later," Axis said. "For now, tell me what attacked you."

EvenSong sighed again. "We were flying home, skirting the passage between Hsingard and the western Urqhart Hills. Normally there are few Skraelings there, and certainly no-one with arrows to take aim. It was dawn . . . yesterday?" EvenSong was a little disorientated, how long had she been lying here?

Axis grasped her hand again. "Yes, EvenSong, you arrived yesterday morning."

Her hand turned in Rivkah's. "Dawn. The best time of the day. And the most dangerous." How many times had Axis told them dawn and sunset were the worst times of the day for flyers – and how did *he* know that? "We were almost blinded by the sun rising far to the east. We were attacked from the north-east. I think they must have seen us approaching from far away and circled high above us so they attacked from out of the dawning sun. They were a pack of Gryphon, although I did not realise it at first. It was later, I think, much later during the dreadful flight home, when I had a chance to go over what happened, that I realised what they were."

Azhure, looking about the room, wondered why the Icarii and Sentinels looked so grey. What were these Gryphon? And why did the bridge cry "Woe!" when EvenSong had first uttered the name?

"They dropped out of the sun," EvenSong finally continued. Her eyes were unfocused now, staring at the ceiling, her hands lying limp in Axis' and Rivkah's. "They dropped out of the sun and onto our backs. I was one of the first attacked, but I twisted and the creature fell away. Others were not so lucky. There were about eight of them, perhaps nine. The other Gryphon clung to . . . to . . ." Her voice almost broke, but she took a deep breath and continued. "Clung to my comrades' backs, wrapping their legs about and underneath their wings, using their claws to . . . to rip and tear. Once a Gryphon had its grip, nothing could dislodge it. Those not attacked in the first flurry died when the Gryphon attacked again. They now outnumbered us."

"SpikeFeather and yourself – how did you manage to escape?" asked Axis.

"We were lucky. A single Gryphon landed on Spike-Feather's back, but before it had managed to kill him outright I managed to pull it off. I landed on its back and gouged at its eyes with my fingers."

Axis blinked. It must have been an appalling sight. The three winged bodies entwined and twisting through the air, wings beating frantically, each fighting for life.

"It was all I could think to do at the time, Axis." Even-Song's eyes were bright with unshed and guilty tears. "I didn't think to use an arrow. If I had reached for an arrow I might have been able to kill it, stop it from harming SpikeFeather so badly. I . . ."

"You saved SpikeFeather's life, EvenSong, at the risk of your own. And you brought him home." Axis' voice was firm.

"It fell off SpikeFeather, but I nearly crashed to the ground with it. I had to fight to free myself. But I did, eventually. Both of us pulled out of our dives with heartbeats to spare."

"And they didn't attack again?"

EvenSong shook her head. "No. Ten of the Wing were dead. SpikeFeather was crippled. I was no use. No. They did not stop to attack us again. They flew south. South to Jervois Landing." Her whole body trembled. "They must have believed that SpikeFeather and I were close to death."

Axis finally let her hand go, and bent down to kiss her forehead. "Thank you, EvenSong. That is a terrible memory to live with, but I am afraid we all will face as terrible, if not more, in the months and years to come."

He sat back and looked at StarDrifter and MorningStar. Both were noticeably ashen and gaunt.

"StarDrifter," he said. "What are these Gryphon?"

It was not StarDrifter who answered, but Veremund, standing tall and spare at the very back of the room.

"No-one has seen a Gryphon for over six thousand years," he said. "But the Icarii remember them still. EvenSong, describe for us the creatures that attacked you."

"Winged, and the size of one of Azhure's hounds," she said. "But not shaped like one at all. An eagle's head, visciously beaked, bronzed feathered wings, and the tawny body of a great cat, clawed for death. Its eyes were red-bright, glowing."

"Dragon-clawed," Ogden put in hollowly.

"Blight-eyed," Jack said.

"It cried —" EvenSong began.

"With the voice of despair," her father finished, and EvenSong nodded and burst into tears.

"Ogre-bellied," Veremund said, "and grave-jawed. A Gryphon. MorningStar, tell Axis what became of the Gryphon, and why."

"The Gryphon," said MorningStar, "once haunted the high places, as the Icarii now do. They were hunters – agile, intelligent, able. They fed off the living. But they also hated." She took a deep breath. "They particularly hated the Icarii. We loved to fly, but feared to as well. Anywhere we went, we were vulnerable to Gryphon attack. Finally, we fought back."

Now FarSight CutSpur spoke. "It was the moment, some six and a half thousand years ago, Axis, when the Strike Force was first formed. The Icarii were braver, more warlike than now, and eventually they cleared the skies and high places in Tencendor of Gryphon. We destroyed them. We destroyed their dens, their young, their breeding grounds. We left nothing. We thought we had swept them from the skies and the minds and hearts of the Icarii – of all Tencendorans – for ever. We were wrong."

"Gorgrael has recreated them," Axis said, then stopped. Did Gorgrael *recreate* in the same way – or in a twisted way – as Axis recreated?

"Gorgrael must be powerful, very powerful," Ogden said, his plump face ashen and concerned, "to have recreated such as these Gryphon."

"Then tell me how you can evade them, FarSight," Axis asked. "I do not want to lose my Strike Force to these creatures as SpikeFeather and EvenSong lost their comrades."

FarSight shrugged. "It depends."

"Depends on what?"

"On how many of these Gryphon have reappeared."

"How many can a Wing protect itself against?"

"Obviously not eight or nine, although SpikeFeather's Wing were not expecting attack from Gryphon. Now that we are aware of the danger, then perhaps more would survive. But from what I can remember of legend, the Gryphon would never attack when they were outnumbered. They will only attack when they feel they have an advantage – a single Wing, obviously. But any stray Icarii will be a target."

"Then no member of the Strike Force goes out in anything less than a Crest," Axis said, "until we know more certainly how many of these creatures Gorgrael has to loose on us. I must speak to the bridge, find out whether or not she can protect Sigholt from attack by such as these, but until then, Magariz, Belial," they both stepped forward, "post guards with eyes turned skywards. I do not want to wake to find one of these clutching at my back one morning."

Azhure shuddered. "How will Jervois Landing fare? Will we help them?"

Axis, grey-faced, took a long time to answer. "I fear we will have no choice," he answered, finally. "If we wish to stop Gorgrael from taking Achar as well as Ichtar. We cannot stand by and watch Jervois Landing fall."

That night, as Axis and Azhure sat before the fire in their chambers, Caelum wriggling naked and cheerful on a rug between them, Azhure asked Axis how he felt about aiding Borneheld.

"How do I feel? If any other man led the defences at Jervois Landing I would not hesitate, I would not doubt. But it is Borneheld who fights there. Azhure," he leaned down and picked Caelum up, "I sometimes forget that Borneheld and I fight for the same thing – to save this beautiful land and its people from Gorgrael."

Caelum wriggled in Axis' arms, and Azhure smiled as she watched them. Caelum loved his father deeply, and was miserable when Axis could not spare time each day to be with him. Although he had Azhure's colouring – raven-black curly locks, pale skin and smoky blue eyes – Caelum nevertheless had Icarii features, even in his chubby early baby months. Azhure hoped she had planted something of herself besides her colouring in her son.

"Here," Axis handed Caelum over to Azhure. "He wants to be fed."

Constantly amazed by the depth of communication between father and son, Azhure hugged Caelum to her, murmuring softly. She unbuttoned her tunic and nestled her son against her breast. Well, this was something that Axis could not do for their son.

Axis sat and watched Azhure nurse Caelum, listening to the magical melody of the Star Dance as it danced about and between them, then he spoke as if nothing had interrupted their conversation. "Perhaps Borneheld and I do not fight for quite the same thing. He fights for the Acharites and Achar, and the continuation of a world that is safe and known. I fight for three peoples, Acharite, Icarii and Avar, and the recreation of an old world. But . . . both of us fight against Gorgrael."

Azhure looked up. "Do you want to recreate an old world, Axis, or create a new one?"

"A new one," Axis admitted finally. "A new one. Tencendor was not the land of myth and glory that the Icarii would have us believe. Tencendor will live again, but I mean to make it a fairer place for all races."

As Axis watched his son suckle at Azhure's breast, the Gryphon attacked Jervois Landing. Nothing that the men lining the trenches and defences of Jervois Landing could have expected matched the fury of their assault.

Borneheld was riding the lines when the Gryphon swooped. It was sheer luck that they carried off Nevelon, riding directly beside him.

Borneheld hauled his terrified horse to a standstill, watching as Nevelon's screaming form disappeared into the night sky. Great drops of blood splattered across his upturned face and the neck of his horse.

"Artor's blow-hole!" he cursed. "It's the Forbidden!"

"No." Ho'Demi said close behind him, his shaggy yellow-haired horse unperturbed even by the attack from above. "Worse than that. Far, far worse."

42

In the Bleak Mid-Winter . . .

Ho'Demi kicked his shaggy yellow horse into a trot — the best it could manage in the muddied slush of the battle lines — and worked his way slowly back towards the Ravensbund camp. It was an hour past dawn and the worst of the night attacks were over. Now he needed sleep badly. It had been three days since he had last found the leisure to lie down in his furs.

He glanced up to the clouds. Heavy and grey with snow and ice, they bore down from the north. Even before the end of Frost-month, Gorgrael had swept southern Ichtar and the defences of Jervois Landing with sleet. Now the sleet had turned to ice and Borneheld's forces had to fight the battle of Jervois Landing in conditions which had travelled beyond the miserable into the appalling. Snow and ice turned to knee-deep mud in those areas heavily travelled by the feet of men and horses, and both feet and hooves had to be carefully cleaned and dried each night in case the mud froze to flesh. Yet in battle conditions, especially when Gorgrael's forces struck at night, it was difficult to find the time or the opportunity to dry and tend the extremities, and they were losing almost as many men to frostbite and gangrene as to the Skraelings.

The snow and ice had a more sinister function than simply creating appalling fighting conditions for the humans. The

Skraelings had found the system of canals a sufficient deterrent for Gorgrael to attempt to freeze them with the frost and ice that rained down at night. Gangs of men who Borneheld could ill-afford to lose from the battle lines had to be kept at work throughout the night, breaking up the thick sheets of ice that formed across the canals before the Skraelings could rush across. Three times over the past weeks they had not been fast enough, and then men died in their hundreds before the ice could be broken and the Skraeling rush halted.

Ho'Demi's horse floundered a little in the mud, and Ho'Demi leaned forward and gave him a reassuring pat on the neck. After a moment the horse found his footing again and staggered wearily on.

Ho'Demi could dimly hear the sound of battle going on some five hundred paces behind him, but he was now so tired he simply did not care. The battle to defend Jervois Landing — and thus Achar — from the forces of Gorgrael had now been going on continuously for some six weeks. The Skraeling wraiths, massing in southern Ichtar since autumn, had finally begun their push south during Snow-month, but their efforts and determination had increased dramatically in the past three weeks. Ho'Demi's men spent their waking hours pushing swords, pikes, daggers and even sharpened cooking irons into the eyes of Skraelings that scuttled and whispered their way into the trenches.

The Skraelings had grown and changed since their attack on Gorkenfort a year ago. They were far more solid, their torsos showing hard flesh and muscles, their heads and limbs swathed in more bone-like armour. As their flesh grew more solid, so did their courage, their resolve and their cunning.

Ho'Demi hoped Inari would be able to keep his section of the defence lines clear of the IceWorms. A week ago the IceWorms, which the veterans of Gorkenfort regarded with horror, had writhed their cumbersome way out of the mists of southern Ichtar, the wraiths making way for their massive and obscenely bulging bodies. Having been the crucial factor in the collapse of Gorkentown, vomiting their loads of Skraeling wraiths over the fortified walls, the IceWorms were again proving devastating here in Jervois Landing. The IceWorms floated, despite their loads, and they were not overly afraid of water. They writhed through the canals as efficiently as they writhed across land.

And the IceWorms were far, far harder to kill. They were huge, rearing fifty, sixty paces above a man, their twisted, horse-like, tooth-crowded heads too far above the defenders to attack with sword or pike. The defenders needed skilled archers to stop the IceWorms, for the only way to kill them was to shoot an arrow through one of their silvery eyes. But Borneheld's archers died as easily as did his swordsmen or his pikemen, and there were not enough archers to spread along the lines to counter an IceWorm attack on any one section.

Ho'Demi knew that the defences of Jervois Landing would eventually collapse. The defences rested on the system of canals siphoning the Skraelings into narrow areas where the wraiths could be more easily attacked and killed than if men had been forced to fight them in open spaces. But the IceWorms simply bore straight across the canals, often creeping silently behind Borneheld's lines and vomiting forth their wraiths before the men knew they were there.

And every day more and more of the IceWorms lurched their way out of the northern mists.

Borneheld had his men so thinly spread along the system of canals that a break through anywhere could well prove fatal for the entire system. Ho'Demi knew that Borneheld fought as gallantly and as long as any of his soldiers. But Borneheld had given orders that men could only be relieved one day in five. What would happen when the men were so tired they simply slept where they stood, leaning on their staves and pikes?

At least most of the Ravensbund women and children had been sent to Sigholt. They had left secretly at night, when all attention was on the battles for the canals. If he and his men died, then at least the children had been saved. Ho'Demi had also sent small units of his fighters northwards to Sigholt. All he thought he could spare from the front lines – although that was precious little. Ho'Demi was desperate to join Axis, but knew that to pull his entire army out now would mean disaster, not only for Borneheld, but ultimately for Axis. So he sent small numbers east and north to Sigholt, and hoped for the day when he could strike camp completely and ride for the StarMan.

High above a snow eagle circled, almost invisible against the low clouds, watching the lone horseman approach the Ravensbund camp. As the rider's shoulders slumped, the eagle folded its wings and hurtled towards the man.

Ho'Demi! Wake up! Your arm, extend your arm!

Ho'Demi sat up straight so fast he almost fell off his horse. *Your arm!* the voice sounded again in his mind, and unthinkingly Ho'Demi extended his left arm. Almost instantly a large snow eagle dropped out of the sky and onto Ho'Demi's arm, the sudden weight so upsetting the exhausted Ravensbundman he had to fight to keep his balance.

"I could have been a Gryphon, Ho'Demi," the eagle said with Axis' voice. "You should not ride alone and so vulnerable."

Ho'Demi shifted in the saddle, trying to adjust to the eagle's not inconsiderable weight on his arm. "Had a Gryphon snatched me from my horse this past moment, my Lord Axis, then he would have had a tired and tough meal. Besides, Gorgrael does not like to risk them to the arrows of the daylight."

After their initial, horrific attack when they had carried off Nevelon as well as some lower-ranked soldiers, every man along the Jervois Landing defence line had kept as wary an eye on the sky as on the trenches and canals before him. Especially at night. Especially then. Although the Gryphon did not attack often, they attacked well, reserving their cruelly taloned attentions for obvious commanders.

"The defences are holding?" Axis' voice asked. The eagle flapped its wings a little as Ho'Demi's horse stumbled slightly again, and Ho'Demi had to lean back to avoid being hit in the face.

"Only just," Ho'Demi said. "The IceWorms now appear, and they threaten to break through in a dozen places. They float, my Lord, and they vomit."

"You need not tell *me* of their abilities, Ho'Demi." Axis' voice was harsh. "I know them well."

"Does Gorgrael attack Sigholt as well?" asked Ho'Demi.

"No. Gorgrael sent a Skraeling force through the Wild-Dog Plains, but we managed to beat it back and destroy its SkraeBold. Sigholt is well, and most of the Urqhart Hills peaceful, although the Gryphon decimated an Icarii Wing."

"They took Nevelon," Ho'Demi said, pulling his horse back to a slow walk as they approached the camp.

"Ah." Axis' voice was sad. "I liked Nevelon. We spent many fine hours together before these current troubles began." The eagle closed its beak, and tilted its head to one side, eyeing Ho'Demi. "Ho'Demi, how many Coroleans does Borneheld have fighting for him now?"

"Some six thousand, my Lord. More wait in Nordmuth for river transports north."

"Mercenaries? Or does the Corolean Emperor now officially extend military aid to Borneheld?"

"Mercenaries still. Borneheld pushes for a military alliance – his ambassadors wait upon the Corolean Emperor at this moment, but the Emperor still hesitates."

"Yet even with these six thousand the defences of Jervois Landing falter? Borneheld must have a force nearing thirty thousand now."

"The defences are long, Lord Axis, and the Skraelings seemingly unending. However many we kill, they simply keep on massing and pushing south."

The eagle was silent as Ho'Demi rode through the outskirts of the camp. The soft chimes of bells hung from poles and cooking tripods drifted from most tents, but few people were about.

"I speak with you for a reason," the eagle finally resumed. "I will send aid, aid for Achar rather than for Borneheld."

Ho'Demi smiled cynically. Axis was splitting hairs here, but at least he was not going to let his hatred of, and rivalry with, Borneheld prevent him from aiding Jervois Landing.

"I will not send mounted men. I do not trust Borneheld enough to send units that would be many days from the protection of Sigholt. Besides, whatever I could send in terms of mounted men or foot soldiers would not make an appreciable difference to the saving of Jervois Landing."

"You will send the Icarii," Ho'Demi said. It was the only thing Axis could do.

"Yes. I will send the Strike Force. But I will concentrate their attacks well behind the Skraeling lines in southern Ichtar – for two reasons."

Ho'Demi reined his horse in at his tent and dismounted – carefully, lest he dislodge the eagle. "I can guess at least one, my Lord. You do not trust Borneheld to stay the order to shoot them if they fly over the defences of Jervois Landing."

"Do I misjudge my brother?"

"No." Ho'Demi stood sheltered from wind and prying eyes between his tent and the protecting body of his horse. "No, you do not misjudge him. Borneheld somehow thinks that all flying creatures fly in league. He is incapable of telling the difference between Gorgrael's Gryphon and SkraeBolds and the Icarii. They are all targets. All evil."

"There is an added reason I will direct them behind Skraeling lines, Ho'Demi. I can do more for you if I can stem the tide of Skraelings and IceWorms before they actually reach Jervois Landing's defences. The Strike Force is good. They were winning the battle in the WildDog Plains for me and I hope that they can turn the tide of wraiths at Jervois Landing." The voice paused. "The Icarii will arrive soon. Persevere. Tell all who will listen that the Icarii Strike Force will arrive to fight for Achar, as it once did thousands of years ago. Let people know that only a united effort will save Achar from Gorgrael. Spread word of the Prophecy. Serve the Prophecy, Ho'Demi, as you tell me you are bound to do."

"It is what every Ravensbund man, woman and child lives for. I will do what I can for you."

"By turning the tide at Jervois Landing I hope you will be freed the sooner to come to me, Ho'Demi. I need you."

The eagle abruptly lurched into the air, and Ho'Demi staggered as it beat its wings momentarily in his face.

Farewell, Axis SunSoar.

Farewell, Chief Ho'Demi.

As the eagle soared into the clouds above the Ravensbund camp, Ho'Demi quickly unsaddled his horse, brushed him down, and gave him some oats. He lifted the tent flap and slipped inside. He was asleep even before he had finished pulling his outer bed furs about him.

Borneheld leaned out the window of the Tired Seagull and peered at a cluster of soldiers talking and gesturing animatedly in the street. He frowned, then ordered Gautier to bring their sergeant up to explain the excitement.

"Creatures!" the sergeant exclaimed. "Flying." He was so terrified he could say no more.

Their hearts pounding, Borneheld and Gautier called for their horses and rode to where they could get an unobstructed view. Both clearly saw that the black shapes whirling and diving north of the town were attacking, not reinforcing, Gorgrael's Skraelings.

"What?" Gautier asked, confused, trying to shade his eyes against the glare of sunlight on the clouds. "What are they?"

"They are Icarii," Ho'Demi said behind them, and they whirled around. "The Strike Force of the birdmen of Talon Spike. They accompanied Axis to Gundealga Landing."

"The Forbidden," Borneheld said. "Cursed and forsaken by Artor. No better than lizards."

"It would appear that Axis," Ho'Demi carefully did not call Axis "Lord" in front of Borneheld, "has sent them to aid us. See — they attack the Skraelings. There must be more than five hundred of them, shooting arrows into the Skraeling masses. The Icarii are fine archers."

Borneheld glared at Ho'Demi then turned back to the sight before him. As much as he hated to admit it, it did appear that the flying lizards were attacking the Skraelings.

"And when do you think that Axis will send them to attack *us*, Ho'Demi?" Gautier said, hiding his fear behind a sneer.

"You have a truce between you, Gautier," Ho'Demi replied. "I have no doubt that, as a man of honour, Axis will honour the truce." He paused. "As will yourself and King Borneheld."

Borneheld wheeled his horse about and kicked it towards the town. "Order the men not to watch the lizards," he snapped to Gautier, then caught Ho'Demi's eye as his horse pushed by the Ravensbundman's. "That order goes for your men, too, Ho'Demi. No-one watches the Forbidden. No-one discusses them. As far as I am concerned, they are not there."

But even before the words were out of Borneheld's mouth it was too late. Along the entire front line, men wearied and despondent turned unbelieving eyes to the sky.

Inari stood in a section of trench with a dozen Coroleans and several Acharites. Inexplicably the tide of Skraelings had lessened slightly an hour ago. Now they could all see why.

The Acharite men murmured fearfully to themselves, but the Coroleans were curious.

"Who are they?" asked their lieutenant.

Inari said nothing, considering.

"*Damn*, they're good!" the Corolean muttered as he peered into the sky, and his subcommander punched the trench wall before him in his excitement.

"See how fast they shoot their arrows!"

The lieutenant dropped his eyes to Inari. Of all the men in the trench, his were the only ones which showed no surprise.

"*Tell me!*" the Corolean demanded.

Inari finally spoke. "They are the Icarii Strike Force," he said, "and they are sent by the StarMan of Prophecy to aid us and to save Achar."

"Do you speak of Axis?" one of the Acharites asked cautiously, his curiosity finally overcoming his fear.

"None other," Inari replied. "Listen."

The Skraeling mass panicked under the unexpected attack, and the SkraeBolds found the assault on the trenches faltered.

Above them four Crest of Icarii warriors screamed battle cries not heard in a thousand years, their excitement controlled and directed into the deadly rain of arrows they sent hurtling into Gorgrael's creatures. Every one found a mark.

Further above them soared several dozen scouts, their eyes and senses attuned exclusively to the possible presence of Gryphon.

Hovering over the battlefield, FarSight turned his extraordinary vision to the north, and his nostrils flared in excitement.

"HoverEye! SharpEye!" he screamed. "Turn your Crests to the north. *IceWorms!*"

Within minutes, two of the twelve IceWorms that were hunching their way towards the canals toppled to the ground, their silver eyes dulled with the weight of countless feathered arrows.

Only nine of the remaining IceWorms managed to get close to the canals, and only seven of those completed the swim across the water.

Infuriated by the Icarii attack and the loss of so many IceWorms, the SkraeBolds used threats and violence to reinfuse their Skraelings with determination and the lust for blood. Within an hour the relentless attack on the trenches behind the canals had resumed.

But as the IceWorm attack had been blunted, so too had the Skraelings'.

It was not a rout, nor even a small victory, for Gorgrael had so many Skraelings packed into the territory above Jervois Landing that the mass largely absorbed the arrows without fatal damage. But it was a start, and it lessened the pressure on the trenches at a moment when they were close to collapse.

Over the next few days the Icarii attack strengthened from above as word of who they were and who had sent them spread along the front line. Borneheld's orders not to watch the Icarii or speak of them were ignored the instant he and Gautier were out of sight and hearing. The Coroleans were the most curious, and they learned quickly that the Ravens-bundmen had the answers they craved. And, gradually, the Coroleans shared their new-found knowledge with their Acharite companions.

Soon whispered word of the Prophecy and the StarMan swept the length of the trenches. Stories of the pride and beauty of Icarii culture, and of the legendary skills of the Strike Force followed; this news, at least, the watchers from below could confirm with their own eyes. Within a week, the men huddled in the mud had heard it all, from the depravity of WolfStar SunSoar to the wonders of the Star Dance and the Icarii Enchanters.

The Ravensbundmen served the Prophecy and the StarMan well.

At any given time Axis had four Crest flying above the Skraeling forces, while four more waited in the south-west Urqhart Hills, some fifteen to twenty leagues from the fighting, and the final four Crest of the Strike Force waited at Sigholt. Every five or six days one of the groups would be relieved by a fresh force of four Crest from Sigholt.

Even as highly trained as they now were, the Icarii found the constant fighting hard. They faced the threat of Gryphon attack, and, mindful of the disaster that befell SpikeFeather's Wing, they kept together as much as possible. Four Crest contained almost six hundred Icarii, far too many for Gorgrael's pack of nine Gryphon to attack. But even so, stragglers would sometimes fall to the fearsome creatures.

To the eyes of the scouts, Axis added the eyes of the eagle, and the solitary figure of the eagle floating high above them became almost a talisman for those Crest fighting the Skraelings below. Peculiarly attuned to the presence of Gryphon, both EvenSong and SpikeFeather spent more than their fair share of hours flying sentinel to the Crests fighting the Skraelings.

One of the main problems facing the Icarii was, again, the replenishing of their arrows. The four Crest soaring above the battlefield on any one day could shoot tens of thousands of arrows – how to ensure enough arrows to fight a full and useful day?

No Icarii could carry enough arrows for a full day's fighting, and they faced constant danger trying to retrieve arrows from the field of battle.

The Icarii concentrated their attacks on one section of the Skraeling mass, shooting dead as many – if not all – as they could. Then, as the remaining Skraelings fled the area, the Icarii swept to the ground, retrieving as many of their arrows as they could, then soared skywards before the Skraelings could regroup. But this was dangerous, very dangerous, for both SkraeBolds and Gryphon learned quickly to await that moment when a significant number of the Icarii had landed, their eyes to the ground searching for arrows among the disintegrating Skraeling wraiths, and then launch an attack. The Icarii had to divide their number between those on the ground and those remaining in the air, protecting their comrades below.

Ho'Demi did what he could to supply the Icarii with new arrows. The stores in Jervois Landing had good supplies which weren't used much because of the lack of archers there. Increasingly, the Ravensbundmen stole from Borneheld to supply the Icarii. Through the eagle, Ho'Demi would let the Icarii know when he could supply them with more arrows and a clandestine meeting would take place perhaps a half a league to the east of Jervois Landing. Again, when and if Borneheld discovered what was going on, Ho'Demi and his men would risk death.

While it sometimes seemed to the Icarii they made little appreciable difference — for every Skraeling shot another three crawled into view — it only took a few days for the men on the ground to realise how much they owed the Strike Force. After ten days of the Icarii presence, not even Borneheld could deny that the Icarii were making a difference. The Skraeling pressure on the defence lines eased and then noticeably weakened. The number of IceWorms reaching the canals was halved, and then halved again and, unbelievably by the third week, halved once more. Soon only a handful per day were creeping across the canals. They dropped from being a certain disaster to being a worrisome nuisance.

Unit commanders along the lines were finally able to relieve their men, sending them back to the town for a day or two of rest. Those left on the lines still had to fight, for the

Icarii could not stop thousands of Skraelings whispering their way to meet the swords and pikes of the defenders, but they did not have to fight so hard or so long.

And, in the longer and more frequent rest breaks, men continued to talk – although all were wary of talking about the birdmen before unit commanders.

Over several weeks the Acharites not only learned of the Icarii, they had the time to observe them as well. Some of the Acharites began to wonder if the Forbidden were quite as forbidding as the Seneschal had always claimed. Could Artor match anything that the Star Dance had to offer? And what of the Wars of the Axe, that had so cruelly driven the Icarii from these lands? Why should the Icarii help Jervois Landing when the Acharites had treated them so poorly in the past?

As the year stretched into Raven-month, men dared to believe that Jervois Landing would hold. Slowly, achingly slowly, the tide of the Skraelings was lessening as their numbers were decimated by Icarii arrows. Most Acharites who were prepared to be honest with themselves knew that they owed their lives to the Icarii.

After a thousand years, and despite the lingering hatreds of the Wars of the Axe, Icarii and Acharite again shared common purpose.

During the weeks the Strike Force spent fighting above Jervois Landing, life in Sigholt was almost entirely geared about supporting them. A significant number of the people who had fled Skarabost to Sigholt put themselves at the disposal of the Icarii, cleaning their gear and weapons, refletching worn arrows and fletching new ones, cooking and carrying for the Strike Force so that the Icarii could simply rest while they were in Sigholt.

The Icarii were grateful, and they showed it. Many among the Strike Force spent hours each day playing with the young children of the Acharites, letting them finger and exclaim over their Icarii wings and telling them stories of old Tencendor and of Icarii legends. On several occasions when a parent, heart in mouth, permitted it, one of the Icarii would take a small child for a short flight over Sigholt and the Lake of Life.

Soon children prattled to their parents at night about such remarkable places as the Star Gate or even the lost Island of Mist and Memory. The singing of the Icarii generally, and of the Enchanters especially, fascinated all, and at least once or twice a week an Icarii Enchanter would be invited to eat with a group of the Acharites in return for an hour of Song about the fire in the evening. At that Axis had to smile. He had never thought the Icarii would enjoy eating and sharing their evenings with Acharite peasants, but apparently the Icarii were finding that many of their age-old beliefs about the Acharites were as false as the Acharites' beliefs about them. It gave Axis hope for the Tencendor he wanted to create. The music of the Star Dance filtered through and about all at Sigholt and sometimes when Axis lay half asleep in his bed he could hear in the Star Dance the faint echoes of the thousands of heartbeats of those in and about Sigholt.

The Urqhart Hills were relatively safe now. No more Skraelings had appeared in the WildDog Plains, and none ventured near the western extremities of the hills. The mounted force at Sigholt still trained, as well as continuing its patrols. Azhure began to take a more active role in the force, leading several two- and three-day patrols through the Hills. She simply secured Caelum in a sling on her back next to her quiver of arrows, and rode Venator out of Sigholt. Belial had opened his mouth to remonstrate with her the first morning he'd seen her, but she just stared at him with cold, flat eyes, and he'd subsided.

Azhure was delighted with her new horse. Venator was smaller than Belaguez, and more finely boned, but faster and more manoeuvrable because of it. He also had intelligence, courage and spirit, and Azhure found it very easy to train him to her specific needs. He responded to voice and knee commands alone, as Azhure needed when she had to fight with the Wolven, and had a graceful and fluid gait that allowed Azhure to shoot without worrying about being jolted.

On the first day when Azhure took a patrol out, leading a supply train into the south-western Urqhart Hills to the Icarii Strike Force camp there, Axis stood on the roof of Sigholt watching her go and trying to suppress qualms about Caelum's safety. Azhure kicked Venator into a canter as they left the bridge, Caelum and the Wolven secured to her back and the pack of Alaunt surrounding her dancing red stallion. Despite his lingering worries, a small smile lifted the corners of Axis' mouth. Azhure was not only a highly competent commander, but an extraordinarily unusual woman. Just a year and some few months ago she had been the outcast peasant daughter of the Plough-Keeper of the village of Smyrton. Now here she was, the mother of his son, a commander within his army, riding patrol with the Wolven and the Alaunt.

With WolfStar's bow and with WolfStar's hounds.

Axis shook himself. He could almost feel MorningStar by his side. Azhure *could* not be WolfStar, *could* not be the traitor within his camp.

But doubt niggled at him. Was it just a coincidence that the Gryphon had found SpikeFeather's Wing? Azhure had known about that flight, would have known where they could be found.

"Dammit!" Axis cursed as he turned away from the parapets. Any one of two dozen people close to the inner command of his force would have known where that Wing was.

And it could have simply been coincidence. The Gryphon were flying south to attack Jervois Landing. Had, unfortunately for the Icarii, come across SpikeFeather's Wing flying home into the sun, blinded and unaware.

As Axis thought on the Gryphon attack a memory crashed through his consciousness. Azhure, smiling, easy and graceful, wandering along the narrow rock ledge of Talon Spike. Surely only one of Icarii blood could have walked that ledge, a thousand pace drop at her feet, with such ease and confidence?

It could not be her, *could* not be. Stars! Didn't she have the perfect opportunity each and every night to slip a knife into his back if she wanted to? No. Axis knew that it could not be Azhure. She had too much compassion and love within her to be WolfStar. And she had been born and had grown to maturity in Smyrton. She had no opportunity to teach either Axis or Gorgrael.

His good humour gone now, Axis stared at the spreading town about the Lake of Life. Many of the Acharites who had journeyed to his cause had been here almost seven months now. Originally they'd camped in tents about the Lake, but over the past months they had organised gangs to reopen an old quarry half a league into the northern Urqhart Hills, and now well-constructed stone buildings were beginning to appear — with a singular lack of imagination, the inhabitants had named the town Lakesview. Axis, when he realised that the Acharites were building in stone, had insisted upon proper planning, and from his vantage point Axis could see the well-laid-out blocks of buildings, with large gardens for each house, and the straight and wide streets. They were, Axis realised, building a new life here. Most of the refugees he had talked to in recent weeks had shown no interest in returning to Skarabost. Why, they had queried, when these hills are blooming about this warm lake even in the depths of winter and we can grow enough food and raise enough stock to feed ourselves and our children. Axis wondered if, in centuries past, Sigholt had previously had a town about the skirts of the Lake. Many of the builders had dug up old foundations. Perhaps they were simply rebuilding another part of Sigholt which had died when the Lake was drained.

Calmed by his contemplation of the growing town, Axis rested his hands on the parapets and turned his mind to the snow eagle, far away, soaring above Jervois Landing. What did Ho'Demi have to report this day?

When Borneheld finally found out how far knowledge of the Icarii had spread through Jervois Landing, he lost control of himself so badly that Gautier and Roland thought he would strangle the soldier he'd overheard talking about the Icarii.

"Who told you of these foul creatures!" he roared, shaking the man so badly his helmet fell off.

"The Coroleans, Sire," the man stammered.

Borneheld eventually let him go, and the man scrambled out of reach.

"How would the Corolean soldiers know of the cursed Forbidden?" Borneheld growled to Gautier and Roland.

Roland, tired, ill and dispirited, simply shrugged. He hardly cared any more. All he wanted was to die honourably, somewhere far away from Jervois Landing. He did not like it here. And he no longer respected Borneheld. He was not a King who Roland wanted to lay down his life for. He often wondered if he should have left with Magariz, back at Gorkenfort. Surely Magariz had made the right choice.

"Ho'Demi seemed to know of these, ah, Forbidden," Gautier said. His own ambitions kept Gautier completely loyal to Borneheld. "Sire, the Ravensbundmen come from a land that borders with the Icescarp Alps. I would lay ten to one they are the source of these rumours and lies which sweep Jervois Landing."

Borneheld stared at Gautier. By Artor, the man was right! "Then I rest responsibility for the suppression of these lies in your hands, Gautier. Flush out the traitors within our midst who spread these lies. Then we can deal with them appropriately. Report back to me this afternoon – with results."

"Yes, Sire." Gautier bowed deeply, saluted, and, turning on his heel, stalked off. Both Roland and Borneheld watched him go, but both were thinking very different thoughts.

Gautier had not reached his present position without a good deal of cunning. Disguising himself in the thick cloak and scarf of a peasant, and moving from camp fire to camp fire on the pretence of looking for a loose horse, it did not take Gautier very long to discover a traitor or two. At the fifth camp fire he visited, Gautier discovered three Ravensbundmen talking animatedly about the Prophecy of the Destroyer and the StarMan to a group of wide-eyed Acharite and Corolean soldiers.

They were arrested, disarmed and bound before being marched back to the town of Jervois Landing to face the King.

The three Ravensbundmen stared silently at Borneheld. None of them showed any emotion, nor, for that matter, any discomfort at their tight bonds. They simply stared, hostile black eyes in blue-lined faces, each with the naked circle in the centre of his forehead.

"Do you speak of my bastard brother as the StarMan?" Borneheld finally asked.

Arhat, the oldest of the Ravensbund warriors present, nodded curtly. "We do, King Borneheld."

Borneheld took a deep breath. These men would die for their insolence and their treachery. "And you spread lies about the flying filth that drives the Skraelings down to slaughter the good people of Achar?"

"The Icarii have turned the tide of the Skraelings," Arhat replied. "Jervois Landing would have fallen and the Skraelings flooded through Achar now but for the Icarii Strike Force."

"They are filth!" Borneheld shouted, stamping about the room. "How dare you refer to the cursed lizards as though they deserved honour!"

"They do deserve honour, Borneheld," said Funado, the youngest Ravensbund warrior present, "for they have saved your kingdom. Once more the Icarii fly to aid the Acharites. Whether they deserve it or not."

All three knew they were dead. But they would die serving the Prophecy, and with that knowledge all the pride of their ancient race shone from their faces.

It was that as much as Funado's words which pushed Borneheld over the edge of anger into outright fury.

"Gautier!" he screamed. "Erect three crosses on the edge of town and crucify them! Then fetch me their traitorous leader. We shall see where his loyalty to the Forbidden gets him now!"

"It will be my pleasure," Gautier said, "to make an example of these three."

Ho'Demi sat his horse before the three crosses, his face masked as if with stone.

He had been summoned from the forward lines where he was supervising the defence against a particularly nasty Skraeling attack. He had cursed as the soldier gave him Borneheld's message, "Meet me on the western edge of Jervois Landing. Now." Did the King think Ho'Demi was simply enjoying a late afternoon stroll out here among the canals?

But he had gone, and now he saw the fruits of Borneheld's suspicion. Three of his men hung dead from crosses, and it was evident that they had not died easily or fast.

"They spread treacheries," Borneheld seethed atop his horse at Ho'Demi's side. "Lies! About the Forbidden! I will not have it."

"No," Ho'Demi whispered, not shifting his eyes from the sight in front of him.

"Their infections spread about Jervois Landing. Soon all will believe the lie that the Forbidden fly to our aid instead of flying to seek our destruction."

"No," Ho'Demi said again, but Borneheld did not hear him. At the foot of the crosses Gautier strolled, a pike in his hands, prodding the naked bodies to see if any spark of life remained within them. Frustrated, Gautier used the iron tip of the pike to slice open the last warrior's gut.

"No," Ho'Demi said yet again, very, very softly.

"Dead," Gautier announced, "and not before time." He tossed the pike to one side and remounted his horse.

By the great Icebear herself, Ho'Demi swore silently, I will have your life for this treachery against the Prophecy and against the lives of three true men.

"I suspect treachery in this, Ho'Demi!" Borneheld suddenly hissed by his side. "I suspect *you* of treason, Ho'Demi."

Ho'Demi dragged his stare away from the three dead and looked at Borneheld. "I have committed no treachery, Borneheld."

Borneheld's lips thinned and the heavy features of his face reddened. "You *promised* me, Ravensbund savage, that you would be true. You swore that you would not prove traitorous!"

"And I *have* remained true, Borneheld. I have not proved a traitor to my oath." And my oath and my loyalty was always to the Prophecy, Borneheld, and only to you so long as you acted to serve the Prophecy. With this action, you have shown *your*self the traitor.

Borneheld could not believe what he was hearing. Would this barbarian continue to lie? "Order your men back from the lines of defence, Ho'Demi. Order them back to your camp. I no longer need your 'help' in defending Achar!"

And that at least is true, thought Ho'Demi cynically, now that the Icarii have stemmed the flood of the wraiths for you.

You can hold this line with your own men and your mercenaries. You no longer need us.

But he inclined his head politely. "As you wish, Borneheld. The Ravensbundmen will return to our camp."

He glanced once more at the bodies hanging from their crosses, then turned his horse and nudged it into a canter.

Roland, sitting his horse behind Borneheld and Gautier, swung after Ho'Demi. "I will make sure he does it, Sire," he called as he spurred his horse after the Ravensbund chief.

Gautier looked at Borneheld anxiously. "Sire, what can we do about the Ravensbundmen? Even though many have died fighting the Skraelings, they are still too many for us to either guard or otherwise dispose of."

"This evening, late, eight river transports of Corolean soldiers land, Gautier. Their first duty? To surround and attack the Ravensbund camp at dawn tomorrow. The Ravensbundmen will not move against us before then, for they be hampered by the number of women and children in their camp. Soon we will be rid once and for all of these savages."

Borneheld woke before dawn the next morning, intending to lead the raid and slaughter of the Ravensbund people himself. As he rolled out of his bed and struggled into his armour in the dark, cursing when he caught his thick fingers in the buckles, Borneheld suddenly realised that there was something strange about the morning. Something missing.

He paused, half dressed, and angrily shushed the young girl in his bed as she muttered sleepily. He stood for a long moment, then, suddenly, horrifyingly, realised what was wrong.

The morning was completely silent. There were no bells, no chimes.

When he reached the Ravensbund camp site a half-hour later it was to discover that the newly arrived Corolean mercenaries had the site completely ringed. Completely, uselessly ringed, for the site was utterly bare. Everything had gone. The tents and their chimes. The horses and *their* chimes. Every last one of the Ravensbund people and *their Artor-forsaken chimes*! Even, as Borneheld would shortly discover, the three bodies from the crosses had gone.

"What?" he spluttered, turning to an equally wan-faced Gautier. "How?"

Gautier simply stood and shook his head slowly, unable to speak for several minutes. "The Coroleans ringed the camp late last night, Sire. It – and the Ravensbund people – was there then. But this morning, when we moved in . . . gone . . ." He shook his head again. *How* could they have disappeared so silently, so completely?

Back in Jervois Landing Jorge, as he did every morning, checked his friend's bed to make sure he was still alive.

Roland had disappeared.

43

The Skraeling Nest

"It will work! I know it can!" Azhure's eyes were bright with conviction. "You have heard the Icarii flight reports!"

Axis glanced at Belial and Magariz – FarSight was still with the final Crests in the southern Urqhart Hills and would not be back at Sigholt for a week or more.

Since the Ravensbundmen had disappeared from Jervois Landing Axis had cut back on the Icarii support for Borneheld. They had done enough. The Skraelings had been severely curtailed and most of the IceWorms destroyed. With his Corolean mercenaries, Borneheld still had almost eighteen thousand at Jervois Landing to man his defences. Axis believed Gorgrael had reached his limits for this winter campaign. It was the first week in Hungry-month, the last month of winter. Spring would shortly be here, and with it, promises would have to be fulfilled further south in Achar. But now Azhure had conceived of a final strike against the Skraelings.

"I'm not sure, Axis," Belial said, avoiding Azhure's stare. "Is it worth the effort?"

"Worth the effort?" Azhure cried. "What do you mean, worth the effort? You have heard the Icarii reports, Belial. This would be our best chance yet to attack Hsingard."

Over the past several weeks, as Crests of Icarii had flown between Jervois Landing and Sigholt, many of them had passed over the ruins of the former capital of Ichtar, Hsingard. Once-proud Hsingard now lay in ruins, torn to rubble by the wraiths and the IceWorms. The Skraelings were using its rubble as shelter, possibly even as their base.

Azhure turned back to Axis. "We might even find a SkraeBold there, Axis. Or the nest of the Gryphon pack. It *is* worth the effort!"

"Azhure." Magariz, quiet until now, stepped forward. "Hsingard is a large place. There is no way that a small force like ours could cover the entire city – and the place is now nothing but rubble! It would be a trap! Axis, I beg of you, remember Gorkentown."

Axis' face froze. "But this time *we* would be the attacking force, and the Skraelings would not be expecting us. We *could* do some damage."

"We could ride there in a day," Azhure argued. Hsingard was only some two leagues beyond the furthest reaches of the Lake of Life, but they would need a day for the attack because of the need to approach carefully and circumspectly, through the Urqhart Hills, instead of directly across the plain. "A day to attack, then less home. We could do it."

"There are not the numbers of Skraelings in Hsingard that there used to be," Axis said slowly, thinking it through. "Most of the Skraelings are further south, making a last push against Jervois Landing. The Icarii have seen very little activity among the ruins, even at night when the Skraelings are usually the most active. This could be our last chance to hit the main Skraeling base in Ichtar while both Borneheld and Skraelings are busy in Jervois Landing. I have to admit a fancy to see what it is the Skraelings have been doing in Hsingard."

"We have the Alaunt," Azhure added. "They can both warn of impending attack and track within the rubble. Icarii scouts can keep watch overhead."

"Axis," Belial pleaded, "you cannot think of doing this! Leave well enough alone."

Axis looked up from the map in front of him. "I have sat on the rooftop of this Keep for the past month, Belial, and watched through the eyes of the eagle as the Icarii Strike Force saved Jervois Landing. I have done nothing but sit. *I* want to see some action, and this could be a good preparation for the mounted soldiers and archers before the summer campaign against Borneheld."

"They are already hardened," Belial snapped. "They do not have to be sent on some foolish mission to Hsingard to harden them further."

Azhure's mouth dropped open. Foolish? An opportunity to attack what could be the Skraeling main base while it was almost empty?

"Azhure," Axis said. "What force would you take?"

She didn't even have to think about it. "All six of my squads of archers, and two hundred mounted men – just over four hundred on the ground altogether. One Crest of Icarii – I don't need that many for scouting purposes, but they need the safety of the numbers in case we rouse the Gryphon. And I take the Alaunt. They can scout out the hiding places of the Skraelings among the rubble, and with four hundred men we can do some damage. We would strike during the day, when the Skraelings are the least active."

"Good," Axis said, before Belial objected again. "Azhure, you have command."

"*What*!" Belial and Magariz exploded together.

A muscle in Axis' jaw jumped, the only sign that he was angry, and he looked past Belial at Azhure. "Of course, Azhure, if you don't‑feel that you are capable of it, I will assume command myself."

"I can do it," she said, meeting Axis' eyes steadily. She had not even allowed herself to think that Axis might give her command, but she knew she could lead this mission.

Belial spun about. "You don't know what you are doing, Azhure."

"I can do it, Belial," she said softly. "Do not worry for me or for the men I lead."

Axis watched Belial and Azhure carefully. He thought he understood why Belial had lost his temper. Axis suspected that Belial felt more for Azhure than simple comradeship, and that made him wonder what had happened in Sigholt in those months before he had arrived.

"Belial," Axis forced a light tone into his voice. "Do not concern yourself too much. I intend to ride along as support. Azhure should enjoy giving me orders for a change. You have overall command here in Sigholt. Magariz can back you up."

"You are mad, Axis," Belial said tonelessly, "to risk yourself and your command for what is nothing more than a fool-hardy adventure."

"Belial, I want to see what the Skraelings have been doing among the rubble of Hsingard. And I want the opportunity to skewer a few more of the wraiths."

Axis had sent the eagle over Hsingard on several occasions over the past weeks, and something strange was going on in the rubble. Axis glanced at Azhure. This mission would be a good test of her abilities.

"You leave Caelum behind, Azhure. This is no gentle patrol through the Urqhart Hills. He has Imibe to care for him." Imibe was one of the younger Ravensbundwomen. She had a baby herself and plenty of milk, and already helped Rivkah with the task of caring for Caelum when Azhure and Axis were both busy.

Although the sun had just risen, the clouds were so thick overhead that the light was grey and insubstantial. "Well?" Azhure demanded, her voice low. Her hair was pulled back from her face and braided tightly about the crown of her head. She wore the usual outfit of the SunSoar command, grey wool tunic with the blood-red sun, buttoned to her neck against the cold, and white breeches. The Wolven was slung over her shoulder and two quivers of arrows hung down her back. Axis suspected she also had several knives secreted about her body.

Axis blinked and his eyes refocused. "There is no activity, Azhure," he replied. "The eagle sees nothing."

Azhure had kept the Icarii back from Hsingard, not wanting to give the Skraelings any hint of impending action.

"They must be buried in the rubble, gone to their nests," Azhure said. About her the Alaunt lay silent and watchful.

Axis watched her, waiting to see what she would do next. The force was hunched among the tumbled and deserted masonry of a once large and proud Retreat of the Seneschal near the outer ruins of Hsingard.

"They would surely be well within the ruins of the city," Azhure thought aloud. "Where they felt safe." She squinted, checking the piles of masonry that marked the fallen walls of Hsingard. "Axis use your Enchanter eyes or those of your eagle. Is that the roadway the map showed us to the north? Is it blocked with rubble, or will we be able to move down it?"

Few among the SunSoar command had ever been to Hsingard, and Azhure had been forced to rely on maps to learn the layout of the city and the position of its main buildings and squares. According to the map, this road should be one of the main avenues leading to the heart of the city.

Axis looked where she pointed, then communed with the eagle. "The road is strewn with rubble, especially as it nears the centre of Hsingard, but it will still be passable on foot."

Azhure nodded. "Good." She bent down and patted Sicarius, speaking to him quietly. The great beast rose, four of his companions with him, and padded out of the ruins of the Retreat towards Hsingard.

Axis raised his eyebrows at Azhure.

"They go to sniff out the first few blocks and the road-way," she said. "If they are clear, then I move the force across this open space."

After about ten minutes Axis spotted Sicarius trotting a short distance back out of the ruins. He sat down some five or six paces from the entrance to the roadway. Axis touched Azhure's shoulder and indicated the hound.

"Good," she whispered. "It is clear. Come."

She moved the force across to the outer ruins of Hsingard in groups of one hundred, waiting until each had reached the ruins safely and disappeared before sending the next group out.

Azhure led them quietly and as carefully as she could along the street. Most of the buildings were completely destroyed, occasional walls standing desolate and lonely against the grey sky, like the sad ruin of an old man's mouth. Great blocks of masonry lay tumbled and piled higgledy-piggledy, some strewn across the roadway, where Azhure's command had to climb over or around them.

Hsingard appeared completely deserted and for the first half an hour of their silent penetration of the city they saw no-one. But Azhure took no chances. She kept all the members of the force to the side of the roadway, as much as she could among the shadows of the ruins. At regular intervals she signalled small groups of archers and swordsmen to wait crouched among the ruins, ready to guard their retreat.

The hounds ranged before and beside them, silent, heads to the ground or deep among the tumbled piles of masonry, serving – together with the eagle that still soared overhead – as an advance warning of attack.

Axis knew Azhure was on edge, worried that they had not yet found any Skraelings, concerned about where they could be. But her anxiety was not making her impatient, or, conversely, too confident. Axis was impressed. She was doing well. He followed some ten or fifteen paces behind her, his sword drawn, his entire body ready to fight.

Suddenly the nearest Alaunt gave a gruff bark and Skraelings swarmed out of ground-level cracks. Almost before they could draw breath, Azhure and her command were engaged with the wraiths.

Because the Skraelings had wriggled out of cracks virtually underneath the feet of Azhure's force, the archers among them had no chance to loose a volley of arrows before both swordsmen and Skraelings were so intermixed that the archers risked killing their comrades as much as the Skraelings. But Azhure shouted to the archers to watch the ground, watch the cracks, and after the initial surprise, the archers were able to prevent larger numbers of the Skraelings from emerging from their underground holes.

The archers' rapid response gave the swordsmen the chance to deal with the initial rush of Skraelings without having to worry about being overwhelmed. Perhaps some fifty or sixty managed to escape to attack the men, and that was not enough to cause them serious concern. With the help of the hounds, it took only a few short, sharp minutes of fighting before the Skraelings lay dead about the roadway. None of the swordsmen had been killed, although two were injured, and Azhure sent them back to wait at the edge of the ruins with the men she had stationed there.

"Different," Azhure remarked, bending to inspect one of the bodies of the Skraelings. The Skraelings had almost completely abandoned their wraith-like forms once they came through the cracks. They were fully fleshed, well muscled, and standing as a man. Their naked grey bodies were covered with tough leathery skin which had hardened over shoulders, joints and back into a bony armour, virtually impervious to a sword thrust. Their heads were encased in the same substance – their silvery eyes, once so huge and vulnerable, were now simply narrow slits behind bony protuberances.

As they watched, the Skraeling's body disintegrated into grey sludge.

"They're changing," Axis said. "Gorgrael is building himself a more solid force."

Azhure stood up. "We outnumbered these seven to one. But what if, next winter, we have to meet an army of hundreds of thousand of bone-armoured Skraelings, almost completely impervious to sword or even arrow?"

Axis shook his head. The thought horrified him.

"Then perhaps we ought to find out where these came from," Azhure said. "Let's call the Icarii in. There is no point holding them back now. The Skraelings know we are here. Theod," she called to one of the unit leaders among the swordsmen, "tell the men to keep their eyes sharp as we move along the road. If there is an entrance to below ground, then I want to know about it."

Theod nodded and turned to the men.

They were attacked three more times as they moved along the road to the city centre, but now the men knew what to look for most kept their eyes to the ground-level cracks in the tumbled masonry and the Skraelings were unable to surprise them as they had at first. But each time they emerged, Azhure and her force had a sharp battle on their hands. Before leaving the Urqhart Hills Azhure had ordered that each man construct himself a brand from the low gorse bushes, and now she directed that two of the squads of archers sling their bows over their shoulders and light their brands.

When the Skraelings attacked again, Azhure led the two squads of archers, wielding their flaming brands now rather than bows, into battle alongside the swordsmen. Behind her the four remaining squads of archers kept their arrows trained on the ground-level cracks where the Skraelings emerged, making sure that as few of them escaped from their underground holes as possible.

Azhure found herself fighting alongside Axis. She laughed exultantly as she rammed the brand she carried into the face of a Skraeling as Axis seized another and thrust his sword deep into one of its eye cavities. He pulled his sword free and stuck Azhure's Skraeling as it lay writhing on the ground.

"A service," he cried, grinning at her exultation, then abruptly leaned forward, unmindful of the battle going on, and kissed her fiercely. The next instant they were fighting back to back as more Skraelings lunged at them with their teeth and claws, leaning against each other, still laughing, more aware of each other than of the creatures they fought. Both felt invulnerable and immortal. Nothing could harm them while they stood back to back, leaning each against the other.

Once the Skraeling attack had finally diminished, Axis turned and seized Azhure. "I love you," he whispered. "Never doubt that." Then he was gone to help the swordsmen kill the final few Skraelings left standing.

Azhure gazed after him, unable to believe what she had just heard, then she lowered her eyes to stare at the flaming brand she carried. What did it mean, that he loved her? What did *he* mean? Love her or not, Axis would still go to Faraday. She was his future, not Azhure.

The insistent barking of one of the Alaunt broke Azhure's reverie and she looked over to where a hound was scrabbling at a shadowed pile of masonry a little further down the road.

"Cover me," she said to her archers, and walked down the road to the Alaunt. She squatted beside him, her hand on the hound's back, and peered into the jumble of stone blocks. There was a solid blackness behind the fissure that the hound had his nose jammed into, and Azhure pulled his head back and thrust her brand into the crack. A flight of steps, still looking remarkably intact, led below.

Excited, Azhure waved over several men and set them to clearing the entrance to the steps.

She felt Axis at her back, and she glanced at him. "What do you think?"

"Dangerous, but your decision."

"Then we go down. Carefully." She looked at the men behind her. "I will take one squad of archers and thirty swordsmen only. And the pack of Alaunt – they will be more useful than a hundred men if it comes to a fight within this dark corridor. The rest of you stay here. If we are not back by," she glanced at the sky, "mid-afternoon, then leave without us. But until then, watch this entrance. Do not let any Skraelings creep down after us. I want only to worry about what lies before us, not what creeps at our backs."

"And me?" Axis asked.

"I am in command here, and I cannot risk you down this hole. You have a greater chance of survival out here in the open than you would cramped below. You stay."

"No," Axis said. "On this I override your orders. I come down with you. I need to see what is down there – and my powers will be more useful to you below ground than above."

"As you decide," she said shortly. "But make yourself useful. Light the way."

Axis stepped down onto the first of the stairs. He held out his hand, and a soft ball of light began to glow in its palm. As it grew stronger, he let it slide from his hand and roll down the stairs. It stopped about a third of the way down a straight and wide corridor, well built from solid stone. There was nothing to be seen.

"Good," Azhure said, and pushed past Axis. She motioned to Sicarius. "Sicarius. Scout."

The hound leapt down the stairs and trotted cautiously, nose to floor, down the corridor. He disappeared from sight into the blackness. Azhure waved her men forward.

They walked slowly down the corridor, Azhure in the lead, Axis directly behind her shoulder. All had weapons drawn or carried burning brands ready in their hands. As they walked forward, so the ball of light rolled forward slowly, always keeping the same distance in front of them.

After perhaps fifty paces the corridor bent to their left and as Azhure peered cautiously about she saw another flight of steps leading down. She could dimly see Sicarius sitting at the bottom of them, tense and alert.

"Come," she said again, and trotted down the stairs to the hound. She bent to touch Sicarius' head for an instant, then straightened and looked before her.

The steps had led them into a large, low-vaulted chamber, the stone pillars that supported the ceiling casting long shadows across the floor of the chamber. There were some broken and empty wooden boxes and kegs to one side, but otherwise the chamber was empty. In the far wall a heavy, arched wooden door stood ajar a fingerspace.

"What do you think?" Azhure asked as Axis joined her.

"We're reasonably close to the heart of Hsingard. I would think that we are in the underground chambers of one of the main civic buildings."

"It's cold," Azhure observed, and pulled the collar of her tunic a little higher about her throat.

Indeed it was cold, much colder than the air above, and that had been icy enough. Their breath frosted about them, and Azhure could see that thin tendrils of ice ran around the stone pillars. She glanced at the far door, then bent down and murmured quietly to the hound. Her fingers ran through the thick, creamy hairs of Sicarius' head, and the hound's golden eyes gazed steadily into hers, his mouth open, panting a little.

Azhure rose. "He has not been through that door," she said quietly. "He wanted to wait for us. He does not like it."

Axis stared at her, and then at the Alaunt. He hesitated, then extended his hand and motioned with his fingers. The ball of light floated placidly back to nestle in the palm of his hand. "Azhure. Be careful."

Azhure hefted the burning brand in her hand and motioned the others to follow her. She walked unhesitatingly over to the door, waving her men to either side, then, seizing the door, hauled it open.

Nothing issued forth from the door save a gust of air far colder than that of the vaulted chamber.

Azhure met Axis' eyes, then she looked at the ball of light he held in his hand and motioned into the blackness beyond the door with her head. He stepped forward and threw the ball through the door, humming a phrase of music. As the ball of light lobbed into the chamber it flared into brilliance, and a dismayed whispering and muttering arose from within.

Axis paled and took an involuntary step backwards at what he saw. Azhure took one look, turned away in horror, then forced herself to look again.

There was a vast chamber beyond the door, perhaps once the grain store of the city. But now it had been converted by the Skraelings into a hatchery. Azhure felt Axis slide his arm about her waist and pull her back from the door.

Across the floor of the chamber before them undulated a seething mass of Skraeling young among the broken shells of thousands upon thousands of eggs. They were almost white, with slimy, transparent bodies that had not yet hardened into the flesh which their parents had attained. Their silver eyes were huge, and their mouths, already complete with sharp and hungry fangs, yawned wide as they mewed and cried. They did not like the light.

"Stars," Axis whispered, "they've probably got these hatcheries in every cavern underneath this rubble."

"They are next winter's troubles," Azhure said. "At least, they were." She tossed her burning brand into the chamber and where it fell among the writhing Skraeling young it burst into flame, and the mews and whispers rose to a clamour.

"Quick," she said urgently, "before their parents come back. Toss in your brands, and then let's get out of here."

The broken husks of the shells caught fire first, then the extremities of the nearest hatchlings. Those that caught fire scampered screaming about the chamber, climbing over their fellows, and setting fire to further shells and hatchlings. As the flames spread, Azhure slammed the door shut and Axis grabbed her hand.

"Let's go," he said, pulling Azhure after him. "*Fast!*"

Where they had crept slowly down the stairs and the corridor, now they fled at a run. No-one wanted to be trapped underground when the cries of the hatchlings caught their parents' ears.

They reached the surface safely, but by that time the screams of the now rapidly burning hatchlings had roused what seemed like every Skraeling in Hsingard. They seethed out of cracks and fissures from both sides of the roadway, and Azhure and her command had to fight their way free of the city in a bloody battle that left many of them wounded to some degree; Azhure herself gained a nasty cut over her left ribs. That they escaped at all – and with few fatalities – was due to the Crest of the Icarii Strike Force above them, for now that the Skraelings had emerged from their rubble they were vulnerable to arrows from above.

When they reached their horses, Axis pushed her onto Venator. "Can you ride?" he asked anxiously, his eyes drifting to her blood-stained tunic.

"Yes," she gasped. "I'm fine. Get to Belaguez."

About her men scrambled atop their horses, protected from the Skraelings by the arrows of the Strike Force, and Azhure kept Venator on a tight rein until all were mounted.

"Ride!" she screamed, turning Venator's head and urging him forwards with her heels, "Ride!"

As they galloped for the Urqhart Hills, leaving the Skraelings well behind them, Azhure began to laugh.

They halted as soon as they were deep within the Urqhart Hills and protected by the arrival of the Icarii above.

Axis leapt from Belaguez and hauled Azhure from her horse.

"I'm all right," she gasped, still smiling with the excitement of the battle and the mad ride from Hsingard to the hills, but Axis tore her tunic open and pulled her shirt out of the waistband of her breeches. It was soaked with blood, and Axis' heart clenched as he felt how warm and wet the shirt was.

A Skraeling claw had scraped a deep gash along one of Azhure's lower ribs. It had bled profusely, but the bone of the rib had stopped any major damage.

"It needs to be stitched," Axis muttered, accepting the bandage that one of the archers thrust forward. He bound her ribs tightly, then pulled her shirt down.

"It's nothing," Azhure said softly. "Others are hurt far worse. Let me go. I should see to them. They are my responsibility."

She stood up, pulling her tunic on, and went to see to her command, bending to talk briefly with those wounded, proud that she too had blood staining her tunic. At her heels trotted Sicarius, scratched and bleeding from a dozen small wounds like most of his pack.

Behind Azhure Axis stood straight and tall, watching her, his eyes veiled.

The next morning at dawn they rode into Sigholt. Warned by the Icarii, who had arrived the previous evening, comrades and servants stood ready to tend the wounded and feed the rest.

"The Icarii told us what happened," Belial said, stepping forward, his eyes riveted to Azhure's blood-stained tunic. "Are you all right?"

Azhure smiled. "A mere scratch, Belial. Isn't that what all good warriors say when they ride home to fretting families?"

Axis stepped up and slipped his arm around her waist. Now they were home he could act more like the concerned lover than her second-in-command. "She is not wounded badly, Belial." He glanced about the courtyard of the Keep. "Ravensbundmen?"

"Yes. They arrived yesterday morning. Most are quartered in camps about the Lake, but I have put the senior command in Sigholt itself."

"Stars knows where," Azhure muttered, looking anxiously about her and then relaxing into a smile as she saw Rivkah hurrying across the courtyard with Caelum in her arms. As she took Caelum from Rivkah's arms, a tall, black-haired man stepped forth from the shadows.

"Ho'Demi," Axis said, staring at the man's tattooed face. When he had seen Ho'Demi at Gundealga Ford and, through the eagle's eyes, at Jervois Landing, the man had a naked circle in the centre of his head.

Now from the centre of his forehead, as from the centre of the foreheads of each and every Ravensbund man, woman and child in Sigholt, blazed forth the bloodied sun.

44

"It is Time to Reforge Tencendor"

The young Ravensbundwoman slipped the final pin into Azhure's hair and then stood back, holding a mirror so Azhure could see her hairstyle from all angles.

"Thank you, Imibe, you have dressed my hair beautifully."

Over the past several weeks Imibe's duties had grown from minding and nursing Caelum to acting almost as a full-time maid to Azhure. And though Azhure found it strange to have the attentions of a maid, she was so busy she had little choice. From three thousand men, three Sentinels, two women and one retired cook, now Sigholt and Lakesview reverberated with the noisy activities and enthusiasms of almost thirty thousand people. Not only were there Acharite, Ravensbund and Icarii soldiers, but also townspeople, traders, servants, cooks, stablehands, secretaries, messengers, hangers-on and myriad other people. A week ago a historian had even arrived, declaring he'd come to take notes and keep records of Axis SunSoar's journey through Prophecy.

Even more than the attentions of a maid, Azhure found the deference shown to her by the people of Sigholt and Lakesview unnerving. Now, if she walked down the streets of

Lakesview, with or without Caelum in her arms, the people made way for her with smiles, bows and bobbing curtsies. Azhure had to consciously force herself not to curtsey back.

"Come," Axis said, walking into the room. "Stand up and show me your finery."

Azhure took his outstretched hand, and let him guide her across the room to where a full-length mirror stood against the wall. Azhure stopped before the mirror, and Axis stood behind her, his hands resting lightly on her shoulders. Axis wore his golden tunic over blood-red breeches that matched the blazing sun on his chest. In total contrast, Azhure was dressed in a simple black gown, cut in stark lines that both emphasised her tall, lithe figure and directed attention to the fine bone structure of her face and her unusual smoky eyes. Her hair, as black as the gown, was piled on top of her head in a complex knot.

Axis smiled at Azhure's reflection and reached into a pocket. "Dru-Beorh always gives me gifts, Azhure, that I find myself passing on to you."

He clipped a pair of heavy, twisted dark-gold drop earrings onto Azhure's ears. They were beautiful, and they created a perfect frame for her lovely face.

"We make an elegant pair, don't we," Axis said, and kissed the top of her head. Suddenly he realised that Azhure's eyes were swimming with tears. "What's wrong?" he said. "Why so melancholy?"

"Because I do not belong here with you," she whispered. "Soon you will lead your command south, and then to Carlon. There your Queen awaits."

Axis' entire body stiffened. He and Azhure avoided mentioning Faraday – nevertheless she lay between them constantly.

"I know you have been talking about her to Duke Roland and Ho'Demi," Azhure continued, determined to speak her mind. "This," she waved at their reflections, "is simply make believe. What we have together is as insubstantial as a reflection across water and will shatter as easily as this mirror."

Axis' hands tightened on Azhure's shoulders, and she knew she had angered him. "I meant what I said in Hsingard, Azhure," he said. "I love you. You are not simply some makeshift bedwarmer to keep me amused until I reach Faraday. Do *you* love *me*? Or is this some roundabout way of saying you want to leave?"

"You know I love you." Azhure fought to keep her voice steady. "But I will have to walk away when we reach Carlon. The guilt I feel about Faraday gnaws at me each day. Surely your conscience troubles you?"

"Does my conscience trouble me?" he repeated. "Yes, I suppose that it does. Do I think about Faraday? Yes, I do. And, in a way, I still love her, but every day my love for you undermines what I feel for Faraday. All three of us are in the unforgiving grips of this damned Prophecy, Azhure. Manipulated beyond our own free will. But you and I cannot deny the magic of Beltide night . . . or the continuing magic that each night brings. Neither can we deny the child we have made between us." His voice hardened. "But I will not let you go, nor lose you nor forget you." Axis slipped his hands down to wrap her waist and cradle her back against his body.

Azhure took a deep breath. "But you will marry Faraday."

"I have to, Azhure. As the Prophecy bound Faraday to marry Borneheld, so it binds me to marry Faraday. Does not the Prophecy state that she will lie with the man who kills her husband? Besides, I need her goodwill to bring the trees behind me."

"Then I must go —"

"No," Axis said sharply, and his arms tightened. "I will *not* let you go, Azhure. Faraday is a sophisticated woman of the court. No doubt Borneheld has kept lovers —"

"No!" Azhure cried, and tried to twist out of Axis' arms, but his grip tightened still further.

"Stay with me. Dance with me. Be my Lover. Faraday will accept you."

Azhure closed her eyes. Mistress, courtesan, concubine. There was no delicate way of dressing up the word. But poor Faraday. Azhure knew she would not accept what Axis proposed without deep hurt.

"Can you walk away from me, Azhure?" Axis asked. "*Can* you?"

"No," Azhure said, her eyes still closed, feeling nothing but Axis' warmth against her body. "No, I cannot."

"And as you cannot walk from me, so I cannot walk away from you," Axis said. "I thought that I might be able to. I thought perhaps I could insist that you and Caelum stay here when I rode south. But I cannot bear to be parted from either of you. You have woven my soul so tightly with enchantments, Azhure, that I will never be free from you. Stay by my side. Please . . . I beg you."

A terrifying image filled Azhure's mind. Axis and Caelum, three hundred years from now, both still young and vital. They were sitting on the rock ledge in Talon Spike, and they were both, unsuccessfully, trying to remember her name. They laughed and joked, and eventually gave up. Mistress and mother, long dead and long gone from their thoughts.

"Please," he whispered into her hair.

"Yes," and she hated herself for the word.

"Then come," Axis said, his hands loosening about her body. "Open your eyes, collect our son, and come below. Sigholt awaits."

Azhure picked Caelum up from his crib, and cradled his head close to her mouth. She whispered something, so low that Axis, curious, could not catch it.

"If you do one thing for me in your long, long life, Caelum, do not forget your mother's name as I have forgotten the name of my mother. My name is Azhure, Caelum. Azhure. Azhure."

This, the twenty-third day of Hungry-month, was Rivkah's nameday, and Axis had planned a reception for her in the Great Hall of Sigholt. But the reception was far more than a simple celebration of Rivkah's birth. Over the past weeks, fighting with Gorgrael's forces had come to a halt, and almost all of Axis' command was now back in Sigholt. The reception was also Axis' way of thanking his forces. Tonight all of the unit commanders, as the more senior commanders, were gathered in the Great Hall, together with the most important townspeople, the Ravensbund commanders, the Sentinels, most of the Icarii Enchanters currently in Sigholt and sundry guests.

The reception was the first gathering of what would eventually become Axis' royal court. It was time for Axis to assume the mantle of claimant to the throne of Achar, and heir to the Icarii Talon throne. Powerful and glorious, Axis now needed a court to reflect his power and glory. Present tonight were several traders from Tarantaise and Nor, and Axis wanted them to spread the word south that Axis, StarMan, was a fit claimant to the throne of Achar. If Borneheld did not provide Achar with the Sun-King who so many craved, then Axis would.

Several of the Icarii Enchanters willingly provided the music for the occasion, lolling about the rafters of the Great Hall and letting the music of their harps and voices fall upon the gathering below. Among the guests, all dressed in their finest, hurried servants, refilling goblets and wine glasses or carrying platters of food. Reinald had exceeded himself in the kitchens, overseeing the scrambling activities below stairs. Now he was content to watch the reception from the gallery, seated in a comfortably cushioned chair, a large decanter of his favourite spiced wine on a small table to one side. Never, he mused, in either Searlas' or Borneheld's tenures as Duke of Ichtar, had Sigholt come alive with so much merriment and beauty.

The Hall fell silent the instant Axis and Azhure stepped into view on the main staircase. They were a magnificent pair, both handsome, young and confident, the man golden and scarlet, drawing every glimmer of light in the Hall towards him, the woman tall and dark, moving so gracefully down the flight of stairs she seemed to glide rather than walk. Azhure held Caelum in her arms, and he gazed at the gathering below with the serene blue eyes his mother had bequeathed him. Though his hair was starting to grow out into an unruly tangle of black curls, Reinald's rheumy eyes could see that the boy had inherited the Icarii bone structure from his father.

Axis moved to the great fireplace, letting the leaping firelight further enhance his already golden aura, letting all who wished to talk with him come to him. Rivkah stood by him, smiling and laughing. Azhure, however, baby tucked in one arm and a glass of wine in the other, moved among the guests. She was calm and relaxed now, none of the emotion and doubt she had felt earlier showing on her face. As they had walked down into the Great Hall, she'd realised that all the eyes raised to her and Axis contained respect, a great deal of admiration, a trace of envy, and even a little love. She had searched anxiously for traces of derision, but found none. These people accepted her. Axis had smiled at her from the corner of his eyes as his voice spoke in her head. *You could command them as easily as I, Azhure, and as easily as you do me. Never underestimate either your power or your abilities.*

She had felt both his love and that of her son wash through her at that moment, and then, stunningly, Caelum spoke in her mind as well, something he had never done before. *Azhure. That is your name. I know that.* Both father and son lent her strength, and Azhure suddenly realised that whatever troubles the future held she would somehow survive. So she smiled, laughed, and stepped down into the throng.

"Roland." Azhure paused to talk with the sick Duke of Aldeni.

When he had arrived with the Ravensbundmen, Roland had been close to death. Already weakened by his wasting sickness, the hard ride north to Sigholt from Jervois Landing had debilitated him to the point where he'd spent some four days in bed, unable to move. When Roland had recovered a little, Axis had asked him why he had decided to desert Borneheld now, after fighting with him so long. Roland had replied simply that he was dying, and wanted to die with his heart and his conscience at peace. "I stayed with what I thought was right for a very long time," Roland had said, "but when Borneheld ordered Gautier to crucify the three Ravensbundmen, I knew that I had been wrong. I want to die honourably, Axis. Let me stay. Please." And Axis had let him stay.

Reinald had persuaded Roland to make the effort to stumble down to the Lake of Life. "The Lake has helped my arthritis," Reinald told him, and the Lake had also helped Roland, shrinking the growth in his belly and invigorating him with new life.

But Axis had told Azhure that death still lingered in the corners of Roland's vision, and while it might not catch the man this month, or even this year, he doubted that Roland would live longer than two more years.

Roland stared curiously at Azhure as they chatted. She looked Nors, but there was an indefinable quality about her that Roland could not place. No wonder Axis has set thoughts of Faraday aside, Roland thought, smiling at Azhure's witty remarks about the Icarii musicians, when he has this to tempt him here. And she has given him a son. The baby was unusually alert, even perceptive, for such a young babe, watching all about him with his wide blue eyes. Roland wondered if it was his fairy blood that made him so sharp-witted. His eyes flitted down to the hound at Azhure's side. Nevelon had told him of this woman and her skill with the bow and her pack of killer ghost hounds. Perhaps the baby had inherited as much fairy blood from his mother as from his father.

"Poor Nevelon," Azhure said, abruptly changing the topic of her conversation. "I heard he was seized by a Gryphon."

Startled, Roland could only nod. She *must* have fairy blood, he thought, to read my mind thus.

"We lost some of our own close friends to the Gryphon pack," Azhure continued. "They are truly frightful creatures. I am sorry that I wounded Nevelon, Duke Roland. Magariz told me that he was a good man."

"He was confused by the changes about him, my Lady Azhure. As so many of us have been."

Azhure accepted the title without comment and sipped her wine. The light and the music and the conversation hummed about her and her son clung close to her side.

"It takes courage to accept what strange turns life provides," she said eventually, realising this piece of advice applied as much to her as it did to Roland. Have courage, and accept. Yes, that was good advice. She would simply accept the direction in which life had thrown her. Mistress? Courtesan? Perhaps. Loved? Yes, and yes twice over.

"Do you know," Roland said casually, "that about three years ago I advised Axis never to marry, or let himself love too much? I told him a dedicated fighting man could never devote enough time to both a sword and a woman. Of the two, I advised, the sword would give him the more loyal service."

Azhure's eyes widened and Roland smiled. "I was wrong, Azhure, and I am glad Axis has ignored my foolish advice. He could never have achieved this," he waved his hand about the Great Hall of Sigholt, "without you by his side. What I am trying to say is that no matter how hard we try to manipulate life, oftentimes life manipulates us – and oftentimes for the better, even though we might not realise or acknowledge it at the time. Axis has been fortunate that you walked into his life, my Lady Azhure. About Sigholt, your name is almost as legendary as his."

Tears sprang into Azhure's eyes. Caelum wriggled in her arms, and reached out his hands for Roland. Laughing, the dying man lifted Caelum into his own. "If Axis succeeds, then one day this one will be a King," he said and Caelum gurgled contentedly.

"Azhure, Roland." Belial stepped up and greeted them both, EvenSong by his side. EvenSong had reverted to her natural wing colours of gold and violet for this evening's reception and wore a silken ivory gown.

A servant came by with a decanter of Romsdale gold, and refilled glasses with the dry, fruity wine.

"Axis' supply routes are better than I could have believed," Roland remarked, bouncing Caelum expertly in one arm, "if he drinks Romsdale gold while Borneheld and his closest commanders sip rough red."

"This wine was laid down in the cellars of Sigholt years ago, Roland," Belial said. "Even this crowd would find it hard to drink their way through the stocks in under three years. Supply routes? Not as good as they were." Belial suddenly looked decidedly worried. "Earl Burdel has been wreaking havoc in Skarabost. Our supplies have been cut in half over the past few weeks, and look like dropping further. Luckily, Sigholt is already well supplied by its gardens and the game in the green hills about the Lake of Life."

"But not enough to keep the Keep and the growing town fed indefinitely?" Roland said.

"No. We will have to do something about Burdel soon. It is not only the supply routes that he decimates, but much of the population of Skarabost as well. Roland, did Borneheld order this?"

Roland nodded unhappily. "Yes. Yes, he did. He thought it would annoy Axis. Cause him some problems."

"Well, it's working," Belial said. "Axis will have to move south soon anyway, but the sooner because of Burdel."

South? Faraday lay south. Azhure abruptly reached forward and lifted Caelum back into her own arms. "I see Ogden and Veremund," she said.

Then she was gone.

Belial raised his eyebrows at Roland and EvenSong. "What did I say?"

By the fireplace Axis was trying desperately to keep an interested expression on his face as a pair of traders from Tarantaise stood beaming enthusiastically in front of him. One of them had been talking nonstop for what seemed like an hour, trying to sell Axis a cartload of fine linen thread.

"Rivkah!" Axis murmured in a plea for help.

Rivkah stepped forward. "Gentlemen." Her eyes moved over both men. "We are flattered by your offer. In other circumstances, I would have pleaded with my son to purchase your cartload of threads, but," her face fell in a good imitation of woe, "we are at war, and my son refuses to buy such luxuries for his mother."

Axis glared at her, but the traders took the hint. They bowed low at Rivkah, exceptionally handsome tonight in a gown as black and as revealing as Azhure's, and murmured their farewells. But just as they started to move, one of them slipped a sealed letter into Axis' hand. "For your eyes only," he whispered, and then disappeared into the throng.

Axis' heart thudded as he saw the seal. It was Priam's personal seal, and could be from only one person. Judith.

Axis slipped a finger under the seal and flicked the parchment open.

Axis,

Our relationship has hardly been cordial thus far, and for that I blame myself and Priam. As you have no doubt heard, Priam is dead, and his death was hardly blameless. Before he died Priam was considering allying himself with you. He had heard of the Prophecy, and it made sense to him.

Axis' eyebrows shot up. Priam had been considering allying Achar with himself? No wonder the man's life had been cut short.

Axis, I consider you the rightful heir to the throne of Achar, and I will do everything in my power to support your claim. But I am a widowed woman, marginalised and ostracised, and far from the centre of power. Nevertheless, I will do what I can. I have one lady-in-waiting left for my comfort — Embeth, Lady of Tare. I rest quietly and comfortably at her house, and should you decide to visit, I do not doubt that we shall both welcome you warmly.

I hope that I can further your cause, and already I speak to two men whose names I dare not commit to paper. Your name and your fame spread. Many that you may have thought turned against you now think to join you.

Take heart.

J.

With a quick flick of his wrist Axis threw the letter into the fire and watched it blacken and burst into flames. Rivkah was looking at him anxiously, but Axis did not dare tell her what the letter contained, or who it was from. Judith had risked a lot sending the missive on a journey hundreds of leagues north into Ichtar. Axis' eyes flickered through the crowd before him, but the trader had long gone, and was probably on a horse and well into the road down HoldHard Pass by now.

At the bridge, a dark man limped forward, holding a tattered cloak tight about him.

"Are you true?" the bridge asked, distracted by the revelry in the Great Hall.

"Yes, I am true," the figure replied.

"Then pass, and I will see if you speak the truth," the bridge replied perfunctorily.

"As you wish," the dark man replied, and stepped onto the bridge.

The Icarii Enchanters had moved from light background music into songs and revels that invited the feet to skip and dance and the body to sway in rhythm. Seven or eight couples danced the Hey-de-Gie, a merry dance between two opposing lines of males and females, and the rest of the crowd had stood back to make room for them, laughing and clapping as the dancers bent and swayed to the music floating down from above.

Rivkah turned at a touch on her shoulder.

"It has been a long time, Princess," Magariz said, "but I wonder if you still remember?"

"My memory remains clear on the important issues, my Lord Magariz, and the Hey-de-Gie remains, after all, one of the more important issues of life."

Magariz laughed and held out his hand. "Then, Princess, I wonder if you would do me the honour of accompanying my halting footsteps one more time through the dance."

Rivkah took his hand. "It would be my pleasure, Lord Magariz."

Axis took a healthy mouthful of wine, and watched his mother dance with Magariz. For a man with a pronounced limp, he managed to manoeuvre his way through the intricate dance with particular grace. Where was Azhure? He looked about the crowd, and finally spied her moving towards him, Caelum in her arms.

Axis kissed her cheek as she joined him, then lifted his eyes. "Ah, here are Belial and EvenSong." Axis smiled companionably at Belial, then narrowed his eyes at his sister. EvenSong blushed, and both Axis and Azhure smiled knowingly.

"Axis," Belial said. "I was talking to Roland about Burdel. It reminded me that we must move soon."

Axis instantly sobered. Yes, it was time they moved. Gorgrael still waited, and the GateKeeper would be counting the days off on her thin-fingered hands, waiting for Axis to fulfil his side of their contract before the year and a day expired. How long had he spent here at Sigholt? Axis quickly calculated. Five months?

"Soon," he agreed, and pushed the GateKeeper's contract into the back of his mind. Gorgrael was the more pressing problem. "My friends, I fear greatly the prospect of Gorgrael pushing further south while I am mired down in Arcness or Tarantaise. He could reach Carlon before me."

Axis stopped abruptly. Gorgrael reach Carlon before I? Reach Faraday before I? For the very first time Axis wondered about the identity of the Lover mentioned in the third verse of the Prophecy – Faraday or Azhure? Which one?

"Neither is the news from Jervois Landing good, Great Lord." Ho'Demi had joined their circle, and the four stared at him.

"No. No, it is not," Axis conceded.

Spies, both Icarii farflight scouts and ground spies, had reported in the past few days that Borneheld was building his forces at Jervois Landing. With the Skraeling attack deflected, Borneheld appeared to be concentrating his forces for an attack on Sigholt. Not only had further reinforcements from Coroleas arrived, but Borneheld had apparently conscripted every able-bodied man within fifty leagues of Jervois Landing.

"It would be best to move before Borneheld does, Axis," Belial remarked quietly.

"*And* before Gorgrael has bred up an army of these newly armoured and fleshed Skraelings," Axis said.

The dark man reached the Keep. He was cold, despite the balmy air surrounding the Lake of Life, and he missed his shadowed habitat. Would he ever see it again?

The guard at the entrance to the Keep eyed the approaching cloaked figure warily, not liking the closely drawn hood, nor the strange gait of the man. "Your business?" he demanded, as the figure stepped closer.

The man threw back the hood of his cloak, and the guard stiffened in surprise and more than a little shock.

"I have come to join Axis SunSoar and Azhure, the woman who carries the Wolven," the man said. "I need to travel south with them."

Though the man had managed to cross the bridge, the guard was still wary. But, just as he was about to bar the entrance and turn the man away, he heard a step behind him.

"I will vouch for this man," Ogden said softly. "He is true, and he is a friend to both Axis and Azhure."

"And *I* will vouch for this man," Veremund echoed. "He is a good man, and vital to the cause of Axis SunSoar and the Prophecy." So, it had begun.

Axis waited until the dance was over, then motioned Rivkah to his side. She was breathless, her cheeks red and her eyes sparkling.

"I have not danced the Hey-de-Gie for over thirty years, Axis. I could hardly remember the steps." She laughed at Magariz as he joined her. "And neither has my Lord Magariz, if his fumbles were any indication."

"A fighting man soon loses courtly skills, madam," Magariz said. "I claim my stiff leg as adequate explanation for my lack of skill here tonight."

Axis regarded them dryly. Their words regarding Magariz's fumbles were artificial – he had clearly been the best dancer on the floor, and Rivkah seemed to have no trouble remembering any of the steps.

Axis refilled his glass, then signalled to the Icarii musicians. They stopped instantly, and conversation in the Hall ceased with the music. All knew that Axis had called them together tonight to speak to them. Most thought they knew what he wanted to announce.

Axis stepped forward. He made an imposing figure, golden and blood-red, and as he halted at the front of the dais he turned and held out his hand for Azhure. He wanted all to know that she stood at his side as his equal. Azhure hesitated a moment, then stepped forward to take his hand. He smiled at her before addressing the Hall.

"Tonight is a special occasion," he said clearly. "We have come together to celebrate several events. It is my mother Rivkah's nameday, and I would like to use this occasion to welcome the Princess Rivkah back home to Achar after so long in exile. Welcome home, Rivkah."

Rivkah inclined her head gracefully at his words.

"Princess Rivkah," the crowd murmured politely, raising their glasses.

"I would also like to thank you, my friends," Axis said, "for your work on my and on Achar's behalf, this past winter. If Achar owes its current liberty from Gorgrael's creatures of frost and ice, then a large part of the reason why rests with the commanders in this room, particularly with the Icarii Strike Force. I thank you."

He paused, and ran his eyes over the crowd. They were tense, waiting.

By the door, the dark man hesitated, suddenly shy within this company. He squinted to the front of the Hall and saw Axis and Azhure standing side by side on the platform. They looked like the sun and the moon standing there, Axis golden and vibrant, Azhure dark and pale and serene by the StarMan's side. The dark man's eyes filled with tears as he watched them. Then his black eyes widened in shock as he saw the baby which Azhure held.

"As you can see," Axis continued, "this gathering is unusual for we have among us Acharites, but we also have Ravensbund men and women, the Sentinels of the Prophecy, and the Icarii. We stand in Sigholt, a Keep revitalised and reborn into the magic of the past. Perhaps it is no longer so correct to speak of this land as Achar, my people."

The Hall was completely silent. Axis' eyes caught those of StarDrifter, standing twelve or thirteen paces back from the dais. For once his eyes were on his son, rather than Azhure.

"We have done what we can here. It is time to move on." Axis paused and ran his eyes around the Hall. "It is time to move south, my friends. It is time to reforge Tencendor."

The Hall erupted. The Icarii, always excitable, whooped and screamed with joy. They were taking the next step on the long road home! South! *South* towards those high places so long denied them and towards the lost Icarii sacred sites! StarDrifter's face was tight with excitement. Lead us home, Axis, he prayed silently, lead us home.

The dark man started to shoulder his way through the crowd towards the dais. In the general hubbub, few noticed the strange man who passed through their midst.

The Acharites among them, particularly the newer arrivals, looked a little discomfited. They were unsure of the Icarii, unsure of the new order. Most had worked well with the Icarii at Sigholt, fought side by side with them. But what would happen when the war was won? Would they lose their homes to the Icarii? Would the greater number of the Icarii, still in Talon Spike, seek to revenge themselves on the Acharites for the Wars of the Axe and their thousand-year exile?

"It will not be the old Tencendor but a new one," Axis shouted above the Icarii jubilation. "A *new* Tencendor! One where all races will live side by side."

Azhure caught a slight movement at the front of the crowd, and she gasped in shock. Axis followed her startled eyes.

The dark man stepped to the edge of the dais and stared intently, almost feverishly, at Axis and Azhure.

"Will you take me south? South to Faraday?"

"Raum!" Azhure gasped. "*What has happened to you?*"

A week later, the beginning of Thaw-month, Axis' army moved out of Sigholt and down through the HoldHard Pass. They stayed in the Pass only a league before swinging south through the Urqhart Hills towards Gundealga Ford. It was a calculated risk, but Axis didn't want to be delayed at the Smyrton ferry crossing as the army units were slowly ferried across. At least they could cross Gundealga Ford in a day, then swing east again to relative safety. And, unlike Borneheld, Axis had the advantage of the Icarii Strike Force who could both warn and protect should Axis' force be threatened by another.

Axis could hardly believe how large his command had grown. He had led some three thousand men out of Gorkenfort before going into the Icescarp Alps alone. Now, fifteen months after Gorkenfort, his force numbered almost seventeen thousand.

Trundling along behind the mounted and winged force was the supply train, perhaps a thousand packhorses, several dozen sturdy wagons, and sundry cooks, physicians, servants and, no doubt, Axis thought, a dozen or so whores as well. A large number of the Ravensbund women also rode with the supply column, although the majority of the women and children had remained behind in Sigholt and Lakesview. Riding the wagons much of the day were also those Icarii, mainly Enchanters, who had chosen to go south with Axis, StarDrifter and MorningStar among them. Axis was still concerned about the Gryphon. If the Strike Force was not about, either flying ahead to scout the terrain before them, or lagging leagues behind to cover the rear of the army and supply column, then the Enchanters were grounded, complaining, to the supply wagons. Two of Azhure's squads of archers and several units of mounted soldiers travelled with the supply column for protection.

Leading the supply column were the Sentinels, Ogden and Veremund atop their ever-placid white donkeys, Jack riding a quiet brown mare. In the wagon immediately behind them rode Raum, feverish and distraught much of the time. He was transforming into a Horned One, Ogden and Veremund had explained to a concerned Axis and Azhure, and his transformation was connected in some as yet ill-defined way with Faraday. Normally Raum would not have dared to leave the Avarinheim in the middle of transforming, but he was desperate to reach Faraday. Somehow she held the key to his successful transformation.

Raum's entire head looked as though a giant had grasped it in his hands and forcibly rearranged the bones. His forehead bulged unevenly and was covered with transparent down. Just above his hair line what appeared to be nubs of bone glistened whenever he turned his head. His nose was broad and long, his mouth twisted, and his teeth grown yellowed and square. Despite his frightening appearance, Raum's eyes still glistened black and friendly underneath his heavy brows. The Raum inside, Azhure realised, was no different despite his external appearance.

Azhure usually rode with her archers in the main column of Axis' army, although she sometimes reined Venator back to wait for the supply column. Caelum was always with her, generally securely fastened in a sling about her back. Over her shoulder was slung the Wolven, and at her side ran the Alaunt hounds, pleased beyond measure to be out of the confining Keep and running free across the plains. They could almost smell blood on the wind.

Axis spent most of the day at the head of his force. Belial and Magariz sometimes rode with him, at times further back in the column of soldiers, sometimes further back still with Ho'Demi and his ten thousand, all mounted on the sturdy, shaggy yellow horses of the northern ice plains. Despite their bells and chimes, the Ravensbundmen moved silently.

Sigholt and the people of Lakesview had been left protected with a token force of five hundred men. Roland, sick but cheerful, was put in overall control, promising Axis that he would remain alive until Axis could reclaim his home. Axis had spent a day and a night wrapping Sigholt in enchantments with the help of the bridge, collapsing exhausted in his bed to sleep two days and nights at the end of it. A thick blue mist surrounded Sigholt and its environs, leaving the Keep itself, the town, the Lake and the immediate hills in clear and sunny air. The mist had been created using various Songs of Moisture and Muddlement. Any stranger looking for Sigholt would ride about in circles for hours, confused and bewildered. Only those the bridge knew could find their way through.

Sigholt was safe, and Axis was on the move. Finally, he breathed, I am moving. He had to have gained control of Achar by the first day of Bone-month, six months away, or else all would be lost.

Far overhead, the eagle soared, also glad to be moving, but unable to understand why.

Once past Gundealga Ford, Axis swung his column east and south through Skarabost, bypassing Smyrton completely. Somewhere south Earl Burdel waited with an unknown force. Axis signalled to the farflight scouts far above. Find Burdel. He had been burning and murdering in Borneheld's name for months, and now it was time to stop him. Burdel would be the first obstacle Axis had to counter in his bid to reforge Tencendor.

45

Bad News

"*hat?*" Borneheld whispered, appalled. "What did you say?"

The Corolean soldier licked his lips, uneasy. "The peasants living in the scattered hamlets to the east of the Nordra, Sire, report that two weeks ago a massive force crossed the Gundealga Ford from the Urqhart Hills and swung east into Skarabost. It was so large that it took many hours to pass, even though the force was moving swiftly."

The soldier paused. "The peasants said that the force moved with ghostly silence, but it was composed of men and horses, not wraiths. They said a golden-haired man on a grey horse led the force –"

"Axis!" Borneheld swore.

"– and that both Acharites and strange dark men on yellow horses made up his army."

"Ravensbundmen!" Borneheld's face darkened in fury, and Gautier hurriedly waved the Corolean scout away.

"Two *weeks*!" Borneheld snarled, and flung a pile of dispatches to the floor. "He could be anywhere!"

Jorge prudently waited for Gautier to say something first. The King had gone into such a fury after the desertion of both the Ravensbundmen and Duke Roland that Jorge had believed he was on the verge of an apoplectic fit. Now Borneheld trusted no-one about him save Gilbert and

Gautier, and spent much of the time he wasn't actively involved in fighting muttering about treachery. Yet Jorge was still in Jervois Landing; much as Borneheld might wish to, the Earl was still too valuable to dispose of in a fit of temper.

Why *am* I still here? Jorge asked himself, watching Borneheld pacing the room. Why haven't I just rolled out of bed one dark night, got on my horse, and ridden for Sigholt? Because Jorge believed Achar still needed a voice of sanity about Borneheld, and he wasn't completely sure Gautier and Gilbert always gave Borneheld the soundest advice. Gautier sometimes advised only for his own advancement, while Gilbert doubtless made sure Borneheld's decisions were the best for the Seneschal . . . but not always the best for Achar.

If Jorge was unsure of Borneheld's fitness to rule, he was still not completely sure about Axis, either. Jorge found it hard to set a lifetime's prejudices and teachings aside. For almost seventy years he had believed that the Forbidden were foul and polluted beasts whose only thought was the destruction of Achar. He had grown up with the legends of the times before the Wars of the Axe when the Forbidden had made life miserable for Artor-fearing people. Yet now this Prophecy demanded that Acharites accept the Forbidden back into their homelands and form an alliance with them so that, united, they could defeat the invader from the north. For weeks Jorge had struggled with himself, yet every dawn brought further uncertainties. He wished Roland were still here.

"We go after them!" Borneheld snapped.

"Sire! No!" Gautier and Jorge cried in unison.

Gautier stood, extending his hand in appeal. "It would be too dangerous for us to try and follow Axis into Skarabost."

"Do you think that I cannot deal with the few scattered communities of peasants we are likely to find, Gautier?"

Gautier paled. "That is not what I meant, Sire!"

"I think what Commander Gautier meant, Majesty," Jorge said, "was that Axis has two weeks' start on us. He could be anywhere. Skarabost is a large province. We could ride around there for months and not find him."

"So you want me to simply sit back and let Axis have the eastern half of Achar!"

"Sire," Gautier said, battling to stay calm, "Earl Burdel has a force of almost six thousand in southern Skarabost. Perhaps it is not as large as Axis' force, but it is, at worst, enough to severely damage Axis. At best Burdel might be able to stop Axis altogether, especially if he manages to trap him as he crosses the Bracken Ranges into Arcness."

"We could still ride into Skarabost," Borneheld retorted, his temper barely restrained, "and help Burdel. Catch Axis in a pincer movement."

"Skarabost is so big," Gautier argued, "and we do not have any reliable information on where Burdel is. Our communications with him are poor. In all likelihood we would miss both Axis and Burdel, and ride about in circles in Skarabost."

"Tiring your army, Sire, when it badly needs rest and reprovisioning," Jorge added.

"And if Burdel doesn't stop him?" Borneheld grumbled.

"Then there is still Baron Greville of Tarantaise and Baron Ysgryff of Nor, Sire. Axis would still have to fight his way through both Tarantaise and Nor."

Borneheld stared at Gautier. "Those two are about as trustworthy as Ysbadd's famous whores. And neither is much of a fighting man. Anyway, how do you know where Axis is heading? Have you perchance seen his itinerary?"

"Sire," Gautier said. "There can be only one place Axis is heading. Carlon."

There was deathly silence in the room.

Gilbert's eyes widened, appalled. Axis and his Artor-forsaken force were heading for Carlon? There was only one cohort of the Axe-Wielders left to protect the Tower of the Seneschal! And how loyal would those Axe-Wielders prove, when confronted with their former BattleAxe?

"Carlon," Borneheld breathed. Somehow he'd never contemplated that Axis would be so daring. *Carlon*?

"He has to be heading there," Gautier said. "He would expect you to have your forces tied to Jervois Landing. If he captures Carlon, then he has us as good as defeated. But to reach Carlon Axis will have to ride in a wide sweep through Skarabost, Arcness, Tarantaise and Nor. He will have to subdue eastern Achar before he can capture Carlon – no commander in his right mind would want to leave problems at his back that could attack him later."

"But if you chase Axis through Skarabost you risk losing him altogether." Jorge spoke strongly now. "He will almost certainly reach Carlon first. And once you have lost Carlon you have lost Achar. Your best course of action would be to ride for Carlon. Better to secure your capital than gamble on finding Axis somewhere in the wastes of Skarabost." Dammit! Borneheld *had* to see the sense behind that! Carlon was too important a prize – Artor! but it was the key to Achar itself!

"Artor," Borneheld whispered, his face grey. "You're advising me on a course of action that could see me lose the entire east to Axis? What would that leave me? Western Achar? Have you forgotten that treachery and ill-luck already cost me Ichtar? A third gone to the wraiths, and you tell me that I would be better off losing another third to Axis?"

No-one spoke. Who was brave enough to remind Borneheld he was now in the weakest position he had ever been in? Who was foolhardy enough to remind him that Axis probably not only had a strong force behind him, but possibly now held the upper hand? Lose eastern Achar to Axis? Better that than Carlon. But it would leave Borneheld with only a tiny proportion of his kingdom. Less than a third, perhaps even only a fifth. Gautier and Jorge wished they were anywhere rather than in this room. Both wished they were three years into the past, when all was as it should be and no-one had heard of Gorgrael, wraiths, or the Artor-cursed Prophecy.

Gilbert stepped from his shadowed corner, his face sallow in the late afternoon light. "Borneheld, you have no choice. I add my voice to those of Gautier and Jorge. Carlon is vital. *Vital*! If Carlon falls to Axis, then the Seneschal also falls. I do not have to remind you what that might mean."

Indeed Borneheld did not have to be reminded. The Seneschal was one of his main supporters. Indeed, he would not *be* King if . . . if . . .

Borneheld forced his mind away from the guilt. "And you would be content to let the Forbidden crawl over eastern Achar, Gilbert? What would your Brother-Leader say to this?"

"He would say that united the King and the Seneschal will have a good chance of winning Achar back, from Axis *and* Gorgrael. Have you forgotten the lesson of the Wars of the Axe? We drove the Forbidden out of Achar once, we can do it again. These are dark days, Borneheld, no-one denies that. What we need is a King who can lead us out of them."

Gilbert's words infused Borneheld with determination. "Yes, these *are* dark days, gentlemen. And I am the one to lead us out of them." He laughed, the sound harsh in the room. "Imagine what would have happened if that lily-livered Priam had still sat the throne of Achar, gentlemen! Artor must have indeed meant me to lead Achar out of the shadows and into glory if he struck Priam down in the prime of life."

Yes, that *was* the message of Timozel's visions, wasn't it?

Borneheld's mind was now made up. The Skraelings had all but retreated into Ichtar, and only a token force could man the defences. Yes. He would ride for Carlon with the majority of his army. He would wait for Axis to ride into the Plains of Tare and meet him there. Borneheld's mouth curled. He would finally enjoy meeting his brother on the battlefield. They had waited all their lives for this confrontation.

"We ride for Carlon within the week, gentlemen. There we will make our stand. From there we will begin our march into victory over both Gorgrael and Axis."

46

Contemplations of a Rag Doll

In the eight weeks since they'd left Sigholt Axis' forces had swung east through northern Skarabost, then south in an almost direct line through the centre of the province. Axis had to curb his impatience to move faster. He was determined not to wear his army out on a march that left them facing battle weakened and tired.

Frustratingly, Burdel's force retreated before them. There had been some minor skirmishes with the rearguard of his men, but they had not managed to push Burdel himself to battle. He no doubt intended to make a stand either in one of the passes of the Bracken Ranges, where the defending force would have the advantage, or in his home province of Arcness, probably in the heavily fortified city of Arcen itself.

Burdel also had another very good reason for riding out of Skarabost before Axis' invading force. For at least six months Burdel had been running a campaign of retribution in Skarabost. Determined to stop the spread of the Prophecy, and equally determined to stop local villagers drifting north to join Axis' rebel base at Sigholt, Borneheld had given Burdel a free hand. "Do whatever you need to stop those village idiots who wish to join Axis," Borneheld's orders to Burdel had stated. "Do whatever you have to do to kill word of the Prophecy. And do more than you have to in order to cut Axis' supply routes into northern Skarabost."

For the past five months, as groups of refugees drifted into Sigholt, Axis had been hearing horrific tales of Burdel's campaign of terror through the province. Now, as he rode through the Seagrass Plains, the winter-sown crops just starting to shoot their heads above the last of the spring snow, Axis had a chance to see Burdel's handiwork for himself. Village after village had been razed to the ground, sometimes only on vague rumour that someone there had recited the Prophecy. In other villages, the houses had been left standing and the majority of the villagers left alive, but crosses lined the approaches to the village, and crow-picked cadavers hung from ropes and nails. It was sickening. Wherever they found villages where people remained Axis spent a few days, his army helping to rebuild houses and the confidence of those left alive.

It helped that Axis' name had been well-known and widely praised as BattleAxe. Now he commanded a vastly different force, but he received as much – if not more – respect. Not only was his force numerically superior to the Axe-Wielders, but Axis had grown immeasurably in assurance and authority. With his stunning red cloak, the outline of the blazing sun stitched in gold across its back, Axis looked like a King as he walked among the villagers, talking to them quietly, and most remembered that he was the son of the Princess Rivkah and would have been a prince in his own right, save for the stain of bastardy. This man did not look like the skulking rebel or the desperate felon they'd been warned against.

Unlike Burdel's loose command, Axis kept his army under strict control. They always camped well away from the villages they came to, careful not to trample growing grain crops, and they moved into a village only to help rebuild homes and barns. Axis could not rebuild the lives of those rotting on crosses, but he did have them cut down and buried. It was a thankless and stomach-turning task.

As each village slowly began to take shape again, Axis often had Rivkah come and talk to the villagers about her life among the Icarii. The Princess Rivkah's name was well remembered, and her presence generally overawed the local peasants, but Rivkah spoke well and persuasively, letting these people know that the Icarii were hardly the gruesome creatures of legend at all, but living breathing creatures as the peasants were, who shared many of the same problems, and who laughed at many of the same things. Depending on how well a particular village had reacted to Rivkah's words, Axis would often call in several of the less intimidating Icarii to talk to the villagers too.

Whatever village they were in, the villagers always reacted the same. There would be a few moments of shocked silence as the first Icarii landed into the square before them. EvenSong was usually among them, for she was good with the peasants of the Seagrass Plains, and would alight among them, all gold and violet, laughter and smiles. It would invariably be the children who approached the Icarii first, crying out to be allowed to touch their wings. Reassured by the Icarii reaction to the children, perhaps a few of the elderly women, braver than most, would come forward, and then, finally, the entire village would flock about the Icarii, listening in awe as one or more of the Icarii started to sing, stroking their soft wing-backs, exclaiming over their beautiful and alien faces.

Slowly, slowly, and not *always* successfully, Axis tried to re-educate the people of Skarabost about the Forbidden. Resistance to the idea that the Forbidden were acceptable people rather than demon-spawned horrors was strongest in those villagers which still had a resident Plough-Keeper, the Brother assigned to a village by the Seneschal to instruct them in the Way of the Plough. Generally these Brothers warned the villagers back from both Axis and any Icarii who happened to be about.

Axis well knew that the military campaign to win Achar would probably be the easiest part of his campaign to reunite Tencendor. Much harder would be persuading a reluctant people to accept those who they had been taught from the cradle to loathe. The Seneschal had over a thousand years' head start on Axis, and a tight grip in the poorer rural areas of Achar. Sometimes worry about how he would be able to persuade the Acharites to accept first the Icarii and then the Avar kept Axis awake well into the night.

Axis was happiest, as were the Icarii, when they camped alone under the night skies among the endless grasses of the Seagrass Plains. Most camps were of one night's duration only, and instead of erecting tents they would sleep rolled into blankets or wings on the hard earth, the stars reeling above them. The skies were clearing the further south and the further into spring that Axis rode, and by mid-Flower-month, when they were approaching southern Skarabost, the skies were invariably clear day and night. As he had when riding at the head of the Axe-Wielders, Axis would often pull out his small travelling harp about the camp fire at night. Axis' voice had improved even more with his training as an Icarii Enchanter, and his camp fire was one that many vied with each other for the privilege of sitting around. Azhure, her son at her breast, would sit and smile as she watched Axis over the flames of the fire. Her love for him increased daily, and she put aside any thought of where they were headed. She did not know that once Faraday had sat across a camp fire and listened to Axis sing, loving him as Azhure now loved him.

There was one night when Axis made sure that his army was well clear of any village. The first day of Flower-month. Beltide. For the first time in a thousand years, Beltide was celebrated in Achar. The Icarii, two thousand strong, built large bonfires and the Ravensbund people, who also celebrated Beltide, cooked for an entire day. The Acharites, puzzled by this celebration but infected with the suppressed air of excitement that both the Icarii and the Ravensbund people exhibited, accepted StarDrifter's invitation to partake of this most sacred rite. The night was long, and filled with beauty and music. MorningStar led the rites, assisted by one of the younger Enchanter Icarii women travelling with the SunSoar command, and their sensual and haunting dance celebrating the resurrection of the earth after the death of winter brought Icarii, Ravensbund and Acharite to their feet in union, dancing with them, seeking partners among the throng.

It was a special night for Axis and Azhure. They distanced themselves from the main revelry, taking their son and a blanket to a small hollow where they lay and recreated the magic of that night a year ago, while their son slept. Their blood sang strong and clear each to the other, as it had Beltide a year past, and as it had every other night since, when they made love. Axis wondered again at the extraordinary way Azhure made him feel, at how close he came to the Star Dance as he moved deep and certain within her body.

What Axis did not realise was that Azhure could hear and feel the Star Dance too. It was one of the reasons she had not been able to resist him when Axis had returned from the UnderWorld, one of the reasons she would find it all but impossible to walk away from him, why she would accept any role, no matter how demeaning, if it kept him returning to her bed. The music consumed her, making her blood surge as wildly as the moon-driven tides against strange coasts. But Azhure never mentioned how she felt to Axis. Having known no other man, Azhure simply assumed that all women felt as she did when they lay with a man they loved.

On a night like Beltide, when the magic of the earth was strong in the air about them, and the stars spun closer to them than they did on more ordinary nights, the Dance sounded so loud and so clear in Azhure's mind that she lost herself among it, revelling in the ecstasy and power of the Dance and the beat of distant tides. She grasped at Axis' back and shoulders and stared into his eyes, and all she could see were the Stars within them, stretching back into infinity, and all she could hear was the beat, beat, beat of the waves.

She did not know that her eyes contained as many Stars as did Axis', nor that Axis was as lost in her eyes as she in his.

And she most certainly did not know of the waves that wept and cried and called her name along the coasts of Tencendor even as she cried and called Axis' name.

That night they conceived their second and third children, but that night the Prophet, watching, did not laugh at all.

In the last week of Flower-month Axis sat Belaguez atop a small rise and frowned at the sprawling manor house below him. It was the handsomest residence that he had yet come across in Skarabost, and he had come out of his way to see it. Behind him, and surrounding the manor house at a distance of three or four hundred paces, his army lay encamped.

Belonging to Isend, Earl of Skarabost, Faraday's father, the manor house was not defended, only having a head-high brick wall about the building itself. Isend was not a fighting man, and Axis knew he would always retreat rather than stay and defend his home.

Behind Axis, some dozen or so paces, Azhure sat Venator, her eyes on Axis' back.

Axis turned and stared at Azhure, then signalled her and the commanders about him that he would ride down to the house alone.

He cantered Belaguez down the slope, then slowed him to a walk as he rode through the gardens. The spring flowers and shrubs were blooming among miniature trees, pruned so that they grew no more than shoulder height. The gravel of the paths was neatly raked, as if the gardeners had been out only this morning. Axis rode through the ornate black iron gates, dismounted, and tied Belaguez to the railings. Then he continued on foot, his blood-red cloak billowing out behind him.

As he stepped onto the shaded verandah, his boot heels loud on the terracotta tiling, the front door swung slowly open. A woman in her late twenties stood there, waiting calmly for Axis to approach. She was very much like Faraday, with the same green eyes and chestnut hair.

Axis stopped as he reached the door, groping for words. He had not thought what he would say when he got here – or even what he actually wanted.

The woman smiled at him, and it was Faraday's smile. Axis' heart lurched in his chest. How could he have forgotten the beauty of her smile?

"You are Axis, I presume," she said, her voice low and confident. "Once BattleAxe, now something a little more strange, I think." She looked at his cloak and the emblem blazing across his chest. "And far more colourful than once you were."

She held out her hand. "Welcome to Ilfracombe, Axis. My name is Annwin, daughter to Earl Isend, wife to Lord Osmary. I do hope you have not come to burn my home to the ground."

Axis took her fingers and kissed her hand. "I thank you for your welcome Annwin, and I assure you that I have not come to burn Ilfracombe to the ground. Is your father home?"

How strange, Axis thought, that we should both be acting as if this is nothing more than a polite social visit. Please, madam, ignore my army. I take it everywhere.

Annwin stepped back and motioned Axis inside. She led him down a dim and cool corridor into a reception room, waving Axis into a chair and taking one opposite.

"I regret my father is not home, Lord Axis. Earl Isend is in Carlon." Her eyes gazed steadily into his. "With my sister."

Axis was glad that Isend was not here. He did not think he could deal with that simpering fop now. Isend had arranged and then pushed Faraday's marriage with Borneheld with no thought but his own gain.

"Do you know her?" Annwin's face remained coolly polite. "The Queen?"

"I met Faraday in Carlon some eighteen months ago. She accompanied myself and the Axe-Wielders some distance into Tarantaise where, through some misfortune, she became separated from my command."

"You were careless, Axis." Now Annwin's voice and eyes were hard. "Faraday is a precious gem, beloved of her entire family and of most in Skarabost. You are not the man rumour touts if you could so easily have lost Faraday to misfortune."

Axis' face tightened. "There are forces moving beyond the walls of this peaceful house, Annwin, that perhaps you do not understand. Both Faraday and myself have been caught up by the Prophecy to use much as it pleases."

Annwin inclined her head in a show of civility.

"I met her again in Gorkenfort," he continued. "It was a hard place, but she made it beautiful simply by her presence. It was only with her help that so many escaped the horrors of the Skraeling army that lay in wait outside the fort's walls."

"I have heard the story of the fall of Gorkenfort," Annwin said slowly. "It is said that the fort was betrayed by treachery within. By *your* treachery, Axis."

"We all fought for the same thing, Annwin – to keep the Skraelings from Achar. But we were too weak. No-one could have saved Gorkenfort, and yet no-one betrayed it either. We simply went our different ways once we had escaped."

"You to the shadowed mountains of the Forbidden."

"To Talon Spike, yes. It is the mountain home of the Icarii. Do you know of the Prophecy of the Destroyer?"

Annwin dropped her eyes. "Yes," she admitted.

"I am the StarMan mentioned by the Prophecy, as I am sure rumour has bruted it about Skarabost by now. I currently ride with my army to unite the three races of Tencendor. Only then can we defeat Gorgrael."

Annwin's eyes glittered with anger. "Child's lies, I do not –"

Axis broke in. "And Faraday also has her part to play. She is beloved of the Sentinels, and of Avar, the People of the Horn. The Horned Ones who wander the Sacred Groves, the magical glades of the Avar, consider her their Friend."

Annwin's eyes widened. "Faraday?" she stuttered. "Faraday is caught up in this?"

"Yes, but don't tell Borneheld. I don't think he would take it very well."

Annwin was quiet a very long time. "Faraday is Queen," she said finally, "in Carlon. She is not happy married to Borneheld. Do you march to Carlon?"

Axis nodded.

"Will you free her from Borneheld, Axis?"

"I will marry her, Annwin, when I take the throne of Achar," he said. "It is all I have ever wanted." And the Stars forgive me for that lie, he thought to himself. But for so many months it *was* all I thought that I would ever want.

"Ah," Annwin breathed, her eyes glistening. "So."

"Annwin, I wonder if I might sit awhile in Faraday's room."

Surprised by the request, Annwin simply nodded. "Come. I will show you."

Axis sat a long time in the simple room which had been Faraday's as a child. Here, surrounded by her memories, he could finally think about her without the deep guilt over his betrayal of her love making him shove all thought of her to one side.

He hummed the Song of Recall, and watched as glimpses of Faraday as a young child, growing to maturity and beauty, flickered before his eyes. He smiled. She had been an awkward child, her hair carroty, her face long and freckled. But she had been joyous and giving, qualities she had not lost as she transformed through girlhood into the beauty she was now. There were numerous childish disappointments and frustrations. The loss of a beloved cat. A storm that ruined a picnic. Her mother's gentle chidings at selfish tempers. But happy memories predominated. Faraday had grown to womanhood in this room contented and loved.

Axis had not lied when he told Azhure he loved her. But did his love for Azhure undermine what he felt for Faraday?

Or did the two simply exist side by side? Was he, poor fool, in love with two women? Both so different that he could love one of them without compromising his love for the other?

"Yet I have never told Faraday that I loved her," Axis said aloud, seeking excuses for his behaviour. "So perhaps she assumes too much in thinking that I do."

He *had* never told Faraday he loved her. That was true. He had said many things to Faraday, he had *intimated* that perhaps he loved her, but he had never actually spoken the words.

"And *she* was the one who chose to run away at the Ancient Barrows, fleeing to Borneheld's side and marrying him," Axis reasoned aloud. "How then could she expect me to wander chaste and desolate through the rest of my life?"

Axis sat on Faraday's virginal bed a long time, voicing soft excuses for his behaviour through the room, until finally his eyes fell on a soft rag doll, lying legs and arms akimbo on the floor. It reminded him of everything Faraday had gone through. She had been pushed and manipulated by so many — by Isend, by the Sentinels, by the Prophecy itself, even by Raum, and certainly by himself, that she had almost no control over her own life. Like the rag doll, Faraday lay lost and forgotten in Carlon, waiting only for some other force to come along and fling her about according to its will.

"You bastard," Axis whispered to himself. "How *can* you try to justify the way you have betrayed Faraday?"

But the fact remained; Axis could not right the wrong he had done Faraday by removing Azhure from his life. He loved both, in totally different ways, and he would have both.

And both would have to learn to accept it.

He sighed and stood up. Perhaps coming here had not been such a good idea after all. It had only gnawed at his conscience, and Axis had so many things to worry about now he did not need a wounded conscience to cope with as well.

"Faraday," he murmured as he picked up the rag doll and sat it straight and comfortable on a chair.

47

Carlon

Borneheld stared out the window of his private apartments in the palace at Carlon, refusing to look Jayme in the face.

The Brother-Leader was furious and did not bother to hide it. What was the use of assisting this . . . this *oaf* to the throne if all he could do was sit still and lose almost half the nation to Axis?

"He has captured Skarabost," Jayme fumed, his normally implacable face strained and lined with anger. "And is moving down towards the Bracken Ranges. Arcness and Tarantaise will fall next. And you just *sit* there and say 'let him'?"

Borneheld took a deep breath and watched a crow circle high above the walls of Carlon. If he ignored Jayme for long enough the man might simply go away. Borneheld was beginning to get very, very irritated with this bothersome priest. He had been King almost a year now, and the Seneschal's dark manipulations which had seen him gain the throne seemed very far in the past. The world had changed. Power had shifted away from the Seneschal. Perhaps Jayme did not yet realise that.

"I sit here and say 'let him'," Borneheld suddenly snapped, "because I have no other Artor-forsaken choice!

"I have been fighting across Ichtar and the north of Aldeni for more months than I care to remember, Jayme, while you have sat here like a spider in your web, pulling people each and every way you want them to go. You think you understand what lies at risk here? What issues are at stake? Forgive me, Brother-Leader, but I did not see *you* walking the battlements of Gorkenfort as Ichtar collapsed about me. I have not seen *you* trudging ankle-deep through mud and sludge in the trenches at Jervois Landing as Skraelings surged down from the north. *You have NO idea of what it is like to command an army that is half dead from fatigue and sad-heartedness!*"

Jayme did not flinch as Borneheld surged from his chair and shouted in his face. The old man stood straight and tall, his robes of office hanging in thick blue folds about him, a jewelled sign of the Plough hanging from a heavy golden chain about his neck. "No, I was not there to watch you lose Gorkenfort," Jayme said, "and I was not there to watch you let the Forbidden chase the Skraelings back from Jervois Landing. I understand you lost close to half your army when the Ravensbund savages packed up and left one night, Borneheld? Forgive me, but *I* would have made sure that ample watch was kept over such savages."

Borneheld's hands clenched at his sides and he kept himself from hitting the Brother-Leader only through a supreme effort. "The Ravensbundmen accounted for only a third of my forces," he hissed, "and I *had* posted a guard. But the Ravensbund have lived too close to the Forbidden for too many years, and undoubtedly used enchantments to slip past the encircling troops."

"Then if you still have some twenty thousand men, Borneheld, it does not explain to me why you keep them fat and idle in Carlon while Axis swings south and west. Surely an army is to be used. Or do you enjoy watching the Forbidden swarm back over the territories that the *Seneschal* won for you a thousand years ago?"

Now Jayme's temper was re-emerging. What was Borneheld thinking of to let Axis get away with so much? Jayme didn't care that Gilbert had counselled Borneheld to move his army to Carlon. All he wanted was Axis stopped.

"I cannot risk abandoning Carlon to Axis," Borneheld said, "which is exactly what I will do if I ride off to the east without a clear idea of where the bastard is. Axis will come here eventually. He has to, if he still thinks to seize the throne from me. So," Borneheld lowered himself back into his chair, "I shall sit here and wait for him. When Axis arrives, his troops shall be tired and battle-wearied, nursing blisters on their feet and a dozen small wounds each from the battles they have fought to win their way this far. I, meantime, will await them with troops rested and refreshed."

Jayme slowly shook his head, staring at Borneheld. He had thought, as had Moryson, that Borneheld represented the Seneschal's best chance of survival. How was the Seneschal going to survive if Axis thundered at the head of an army across the Plains of Tare towards the Tower of the Seneschal?

"Need I remind you, Borneheld, that the Tower of the Seneschal rests on the far side of the Grail Lake? Axis will decimate the Brotherhood before you can rally your army to the front gates of the city."

"Well, it shouldn't worry *you*," Borneheld said. "You spend most of your time here in the palace, anyway. You and your two advisers. But rest easy. I shall meet Axis on the Plains of Tare well before he approaches your white-walled tower."

Jayme tried to collect his thoughts. Everything was going so badly. He remembered the time, so long ago now, it seemed, when he had first heard rumours of trouble to the north, of strange ghost-like creatures who nibbled and chewed fully armoured men to death in minutes. How could he have foretold then the disasters that would envelop Achar? Ichtar was gone, lost to Gorgrael. Soon everything east of the Nordra would be gone, lost to the Forbidden and the one who led them. And what did that leave? A relatively narrow strip of land to the west of the Nordra? A pink and gold city?

"At night, Borneheld," Jayme said softly, "I can hear the weeping souls of those poor tormented wretches who have been overwhelmed by Axis and the hordes of Forbidden that he directs. Do you know what he does to them, Borneheld? Do you know the pain the poor wretches of Skarabost have suffered as that wretched army overwhelms village after village? Children are sacrificed for the plunders of those flying vermin he calls friends. Women are forced to yield their bodies, then their lives. Men watch their families die, then are gutted and strung up from poles and doorframes by their bowels, to die themselves from pain and shock and loss. Does that not concern you, Borneheld? How can you sit here and say 'Let him come'? Artor alone will judge you on this."

Borneheld fidgeted nervously. He'd been having nightmares since he returned to Carlon. He dreamed that anonymous, pale hands held out the ensorcelled chalice for him, whispering entreaties to him to drink. He dreamed of wandering the halls and chambers of the palace, the whispers and laughter of the court following him.

And he dreamed of a stern-faced woman, black-haired and raven-eyed, who sat at a counting table, two bowls before her, a gleaming rectangle of light behind her. She raised her eyes as he approached, laughing as she recognised him. "I await your presence before my table, Borneheld, Duke of Ichtar."

In vain would he protest that he was Duke of Ichtar no longer, but King of Achar.

"Your blood names you a Duke of Ichtar, Borneheld," she whispered. "And your blood condemns you. Your death approaches from the east. Watch for it."

Borneheld fidgeted and looked out the window, fancying he could see Artor staring at him from the massed clouds sliding down from the north.

Faraday sat, half asleep, as Yr brushed her hair out. Unlike Borneheld and Jayme, Faraday regarded the slow approach of

Axis and his army as a gift. A gift from the Mother, for Faraday had long since abandoned Artor and his cruel and shallow ways. Each day brought fresh rumours from the streets of Carlon. Axis had won through to Arcness in a battle deserving of the gods in the Bracken Ranges. Axis and his army had been penned up in an isolated glen high in the Bracken Ranges and had fallen into a mighty lake and drowned – Faraday had smiled when she heard that one. Axis and his army had proclaimed a new land and a new nation in Skarabost. Had he proclaimed Tencendor so soon? Faraday had thought Axis would wait until he reached Carlon, until he reached her, before he would do that. Yr heard most of the rumours from the captain of the guards, a darkly virile man. She also heard most of the facts – or as much of facts as anyone in Carlon could get – about Axis' drive south through Skarabost.

"And of what do you think, my sweet?" Yr murmured as she brushed Faraday's burnished gold hair out with long and languid strokes.

"You know perfectly well that I think of Axis, Yr. It is rare that I think of anything else these days."

Borneheld had returned to Carlon a month ago. On his arrival he had granted Faraday an audience, relieved her of most of her court duties, completely disregarding the fact that Faraday had virtually run Achar while he had been ensconced in Jervois Landing fighting the Skraelings, briefly inquired after her health, and then dismissed her. He had not required Faraday's presence in his bed, and Faraday had heard that he had taken a mistress – none other than the blowsy woman who had accompanied her father, Isend, to court.

Freed from most of her onerous court duties and Borneheld's attentions, Faraday now had her time almost exclusively to herself, and she used it to good purpose, spending the larger part of most days in the glorious garden of Ur or wandering entranced through the enchanted forests that spiralled out from the Sacred Grove. Each time she wandered them she found different things – a new glade she had not seen previously, a creature that was more impossibly beautiful than any other she had met before, a mountain more mysterious and fascinating than the rest. But always she ended up at the gate to Ur's garden, and the woman would emerge from her cottage, or wave at her from her sunny garden seat, and Faraday would smile and enter and begin another lesson.

Lessons with Ur mainly consisted of learning the names and histories of the tens of thousands of Banes represented by the tree seedlings gently swaying in their tiny terracotta pots. Ur would pick up a pot, hand it to Faraday, and tell her of the Bane who had transformed into this tree.

Faraday found that as she listened to Ur speak, as she murmured the Bane's name to herself, she formed a bond, a friendship, with the seedling. As she would never forget the name or the history of a friend, Faraday knew she would never forget the name and the past of each of these seedlings as she heard them from Ur's lips. It did not matter that there were some forty-two thousand of them.

They were magical hours, the hours spent with Ur in the garden nursery of the enchanted woods, hours when Faraday was healed of so much of the pain that she had suffered, and given the strength to survive so much of the pain she had yet to endure.

Raum whimpered behind his hood as he rode his wagon south with Axis. It was all he could do not to cry out loud, and that he managed to keep even mildly sane was due to the support of the three Sentinels who often sat by his side. Each bent what power he had to aid Raum through this transformation that it seemed would take months instead of weeks.

And it was taking place so far from the Avarinheim. What would happen, Raum worried, if he transformed completely while so far from the shaded walks of the trees? So far from the Mother, from Fernbrake Lake? Would he wither and die under the unremitting sun and wind of the Seagrass Plains?

"Why me?" he had whispered one day when the pain had finally ceased, when Faraday had finally left the Sacred Grove. "Why am I tied to her like this? Why do I transform only when she uses her power?"

It was Jack who answered. "You were the one who bonded her to the Mother, Raum. And she was the one who renewed your bonds with the Mother. Perhaps that is what binds you, why you are so tied to her power."

Raum shrugged inside his cloak. His face was now so misshapen that he kept it hidden. Axis often sat by his side at night, soothing him to sleep with his harp and his enchanted music. But very little could soothe Raum through this dreadful transformation.

Faraday was not unaware of Raum's pain. She sensed it every time she used her power to enter the Sacred Grove and the enchanted forests that surrounded it.

Sometimes Faraday wandered the enchanted forest, feeling Raum's pain, knowing that he was transforming, wishing she could help him. She asked the Horned Ones what would happen to Raum, what she could do to help.

"Nothing," the silver pelt answered. "Nothing. Raum's transformation is different because of the bond between you, and because your grasp of the power of the Mother and of these woods is so great. What can you do to help? Wait until Raum manages to find the Avarinheim again, or one of the surviving remnants beyond what remains of the forest. Wait until Raum is ready to step into the Sacred Grove, wait until he is ready to complete the transformation – then pull him here with all your power, help him with every ounce of your strength. Raum cannot reach you until he reaches the power of the trees, and he is currently far from any trees that can help him. Wait. Watch."

Faraday turned away, grieving for Raum, but knowing there was not much she could do for him. She knew he was trying to find her, and she hoped for his sake that he would not take too long.

Faraday did not now need the enchanted bowl to move between this world and the Sacred Grove. Her command of her power had increased to the point where she could simply will herself into the emerald light that led to the Sacred Grove. She did not know what to do with the bowl. She had suggested to the Horned Ones that she give it back to them.

"You will find a use for it, Faraday," they had counselled. "Keep it."

So she had kept it, pleased that she did not have to give it back, and it now sat on the dresser in her chamber. To any ordinary eye it simply looked like a rather plain wooden bowl, hardly fit for a Queen, but it daily reminded Faraday not only of the enormous task that awaited her, but of the comfort the bowl and the Mother had given her in days past.

She smiled at Yr as she put the brush down. "Axis comes, Yr. I can feel it. In a few short months he will be here. Oh, Yr, I can hardly wait until we are together!"

48

Axis' Salutary Lesson

In the dark hours before dawn the Icarii Strike Force had lifted off. Burdel's men were entrenched themselves in the steep, rocky passes of the Bracken Ranges, and nothing save an airborne force could dislodge them without massive loss of life.

But this was a battle Axis was highly uneasy over. It was too likely to reopen old wounds and old hatreds. Axis loathed having to set the Icarii Strike Force on humans. He had wanted to use them as little as he could, hoping that the Acharites would the more easily accept the Icarii if they did not perceive them as an invading force. This battle was a risk, but it was a risk Axis had been forced to take. The Icarii were the only ones who could effectively clear the slopes of the Bracken Ranges with minimal losses.

Now Axis paced back and forth, his blood-red cloak wrapped about him. Every three or four strides he looked up at the Bracken Ranges rising in the rapidly lightening sky. He knew what was happening in the narrow passes of the Ranges, for the eagle circled high overhead.

"Well?" Belial's face was almost as strained as Axis'.

Axis blinked, cleared his vision, and stared at Belial. "It goes well. Burdel's force had no idea what was attacking them when the Icarii sent down their first volley of arrows. They could not see, and simply shot blindly into the sky."

"Casualties?" Magariz asked.

"Five Icarii have taken arrows in the wings and are limping their way home or are safe among the ridges. The others evaded well. The casualties are all on Burdel's side. I think," Axis' eyes assumed a dreamy quality, and Belial and Magariz knew he was seeing through the eagle's eyes again, "that Burdel is pulling his men out as fast as he can. The passes will be clear for us by noon."

"Pulling back to Arcen?" Belial queried.

"Undoubtedly." Axis shrugged. "We will not be able to catch them. It will take at least a day to get this army moving into the lower Ranges, and several days to get through. What remains of Burdel's force is more lightly armoured and much more mobile. He will be able to race to Arcen and slam the gates shut well before we're through the Ranges."

Arcen was Burdel's capital in Arcness. It lay some ten leagues south of the Ranges, surrounded by the grazing lands of the province.

"A siege then," Magariz remarked.

Axis sighed. "Yes, a siege." Axis had ridden through Arcen on his way north to Smyrton almost two years earlier. The city had high walls, thick battlements and a good militia.

Axis knew he had to be very, very careful with Arcen. Sieges always tended to drag out over months, and Axis could not afford to encamp himself and his army outside Arcen for the next six months. Neither could he afford to ride by and open his rear to possible attack from Burdel sometime in the future. Arcen would have to be conquered.

Azhure walked up. "Can you send the Strike Force after Burdel as he flees across the plains towards Arcen?"

Axis glanced at her. Azhure had left Caelum with Rivkah in the camp and walked only with Sicarius as company. She looked slim and fit in her grey and white uniform, the Wolven slung over her shoulder, her hair tied back into a plait rolled in the nape of her neck.

In the two weeks since Axis had visited Faraday's childhood home relations between him and Azhure had been, if not cool, then slightly businesslike. Even their lovemaking, on those few nights when there had been the time or the privacy, had lacked the usual laughter and had become intense, almost fierce. Both felt Faraday's closing presence keenly.

"No." Axis turned back to the Ranges. "Most of the Strike Force are too tired. They have been on the wing for close to five hours now, and I want them to remain above the passes to watch for stray remnants of Burdel's force. To send them flying after Burdel as he flees across the plains towards his home base would drive them dangerously close to exhaustion." And expose them to the watching eyes and itchy tongues of countless peasants and townsfolk, Axis thought. The last thing he wanted was to have half the population of Arcness watch as the Icarii rained death down on Burdel. It would simply confirm their worst fears about the Forbidden and the Seneschal's teachings.

"No," he repeated, contemplating the siege ahead. "Let's go. By the time we get this army on the move the Strike Force should have cleared the passes."

He forced the problem of the siege to the back of his mind and smiled at Azhure.

"Come," he took her hand, "we have a pleasant ride through the hills before us."

"You did well, FarSight," Axis said, reining Belaguez to a halt before the exhausted birdman.

Most of the Strike Force were now on the ground in the passes, although several dozen circled far overhead, keeping a watch over Burdel's retreat. It was early afternoon, and the Icarii had been flying and fighting for almost twelve hours.

FarSight looked up. His dark face was lined and there were pouches of weariness under his eyes, but the expression on his face was one of quiet pride. His force had done a fine job, and he knew it. That dark day in Talon Spike when Axis had painfully outlined each and every flaw within the Icarii Strike Force seemed several lifetimes ago. FarSight now headed an elite fighting force. "Burdel's men did not fight well, but they fought tenaciously. It took an hour longer than I had calculated to flush them out of their rocks."

Axis dismounted and sat down beside FarSight. "And those of the Strike Force who were struck by arrows?"

FarSight shook his head with relief. "Two will not fly for some time, but the other three were only slightly hurt. A week's rest and they will be fighting fit again."

"EvenSong?" Axis' sister had returned to the Strike Force for fighting duty for this attack.

"Fought well, as did SpikeFeather. I think, when the opportunity arises, I shall give him a Crest to command. He is too valuable now to waste on a Wing. His experience with the Gryphon, and his somewhat unconventional recovery, seems to have hardened him."

"Axis!"

Axis jerked his head up. It was StarDrifter, alighting on a nearby rock. His face was flushed with excitement, and his great silver and white wings fluttered behind him. He hopped down and strode over. "Axis, I know I should not be here, but I could not help myself. Do you know how close we are to Fernbrake Lake from here? Only several hours' flight, if that!"

"No," Axis said. "We can't afford to have *any* Icarii flying about the Bracken Ranges without any protection and vulnerable to whatever stray forces Burdel or Borneheld has in these hills."

StarDrifter's face coloured in anger and his body stiffened. "The Icarii have waited a thousand years to return to their homeland and the sacred sites lost to them, Axis," he said.

"Then another few weeks or months won't make any difference," Axis snapped. "Curse your impulsive nature, Star-

Drifter. It is too dangerous for you to fly off on a whim to view Fernbrake Lake. I cannot afford the Icarii to guard you. Don't you realise how exhausted FarSight and his Strike Force are? They need days to recover, and in a few days' time we will be long gone from the Bracken Ranges. *Think*, Star-Drifter, damn you!"

StarDrifter stared at his son, then FarSight, seeing clearly how fatigued the birdman was.

"StarDrifter," Axis continued, "we head south. We will undoubtedly ride straight through the Ancient Barrows and by the Silent Woman Woods. You cannot see every sacred site you have lost in a week. You have your lifetime ahead of you to recover your heritage. Have patience. First I have to win this land for you."

StarDrifter hesitated, then nodded. "I apologise Axis, Far-Sight. I did not think. Two years ago I never thought that one day I would have the opportunity to see the lost sites of Tencendor again. Now that we are so close . . ." His voice drifted away.

Axis relaxed, knowing what StarDrifter was trying to say. StarDrifter and MorningStar, as all other Enchanters, were beginning the arduous task of recovering the lost sites of the Icarii people – the Ancient Barrows, tombs of the twenty-six Enchanter-Talons, Star Gate, buried beneath the barrows, the Silent Woman Woods, their Keep and the Cauldron Lake, Spiredore and the Island of Mist and Memory. That last Axis knew the Icarii yearned after almost as much as the Star Gate, yet it might well prove the hardest to win for them. In any case, they had some bitter fighting to conduct before the Icarii could recover it. As StarDrifter wandered off, Axis watched as the first units of his army wound their way through the passes.

Burdel succeeded in retreating to his capital, and by the time Axis and his army reached the city of Arcen, it was shuttered and bolted tightly.

Axis focused on the eagle soaring above the battlements of the city a league away. People scurried back and forth atop the walls, pointing nervously at the approaching army. Axis thought he even saw Burdel himself, a tall and spare man, almost ascetic, standing still and silent as he shaded his eyes against the sun and stared at the approaching black stain across the Plains of Arcness. Axis had taken pains to keep the Icarii well back, and most were still resting in the lower reaches of the Bracken Ranges. The main part of the Strike Force would join Axis' army later that night, when the people of Arcen would be blinded by the darkness.

Belaguez stamped impatiently and rattled the bit in his mouth. Axis smiled and patted the horse's neck, then turned and waved Belial, Magariz and Ho'Demi forward.

"Well?" he demanded as they drew their horses to either side of Belaguez. "How would you solve this problem?"

"I have no experience in sieges," Ho'Demi said. "The closest I have come is waiting for an icebear to emerge from his snow cavern in the morning. Me? I would sit cross-legged before the gates, spear in my lap, and simply wait for someone to come out." He waved the problem over to Magariz.

Magariz shrugged. "It is difficult, Axis. You have no siege engines and Burdel has, in all probability, planned and provisioned for a siege."

"We could sit here and simply wait them out," Belial said, then winced at the expression on Axis' face. "And wait, and wait, and wait. We could be here for years."

You do not know the extent of it, Axis thought, his eyes tracing the flight of the eagle overhead. We are now past mid-Rose-month and I have only three and a half months left to fulfil my contract to the GateKeeper. I can waste but a week or two here at the longest.

Axis was silent, his eyes focused on the tiny figure of Burdel. I shall have to rely on some sweet words to open those gates, he thought. That and a little enchantment.

Axis swung his gaze back to his three most senior commanders. "Here is what I want you to do."

By evening Axis' entire army, supply column included, had surrounded Arcen outside the striking range of arrows shot from the city's walls. The army set up camp as though it intended a long and patient wait, and Axis ordered his own command tent to be erected opposite the main gates into the city. Above the tent floated his golden standard, the blood-red sun blazing in its centre. Axis strode about in the evening light, wearing the golden tunic under the red cloak, loose and relaxed, laughing and joking with those of his commanders who talked with him, one or two of the Alaunt constantly by his side. He was unarmed.

From the walls of their city the people of Arcen watched. Axis' every movement, as that of his army, was noted and remarked upon. Most had admired Axis as BattleAxe, and many had met and liked him when he had stayed in Arcen briefly two years previously. Two or three Arcen-based traders, who had traded with Axis and his force while they were still in Sigholt, were questioned again and again about the man and his army who now besieged Arcen. Three of the men Belial had sent out from Sigholt some fifteen months previously to spread the word of the Prophecy were also in the city. For the past two months they had resided in Arcen, spending most of that time drinking quietly in the city's various inns and taverns and spreading word of the Prophecy among the townsfolk.

Axis spent a pleasant evening about camp. Azhure, Rivkah, Ho'Demi and his wife, Sa'Kuya, and Belial and Magariz joined him for dinner, the Acharite women wearing brightly coloured gowns and Azhure bouncing a laughing Caelum on her lap throughout the meal. To all intents and purposes Axis was relaxed, confident, and prepared for a long wait.

When they rose in the morning, Axis surprised Azhure by asking her to wear the long black gown she'd worn on the night of the reception in Sigholt.

"You brought it with you?" he queried, and Azhure nodded, puzzled. "Then wear it, Azhure. And leave your hair loose."

He strode out of the tent and Azhure rose, washed, and dressed as requested. She smoothed the elegant black gown over her hips and rested one hand briefly on her belly. She suspected she was pregnant again, but she had not told Axis. Azhure smiled humourlessly to herself. Undoubtedly she would find herself face to face with Faraday sooner or later, and Azhure wished desperately that she did not have to do it with her belly bulging again with Axis' child. Faraday would find the idea of a lover hard to accept; a lover pregnant with her husband's child would be even worse.

Azhure emerged from the tent eventually, feeling slightly silly dressed in the elegant gown, and saw Rivkah standing to one side. Axis had obviously given Rivkah similar instructions, for his mother stood wearing a gown almost identical to Azhure's, looking every inch the Princess of Achar.

"Azhure," Axis' voice sounded behind her and Azhure jumped. "Your bow." He handed her the Wolven and her quiver of arrows, and Azhure slung them over her shoulder, feeling even more ridiculous. The ring of soldiers, Acharite and Ravensbund, encircling the town stood ready, their weapons hanging loose from their hands, their eyes fixed on the walls before them. Axis spoke quietly to Belial, Magariz and Ho'Demi, then motioned Rivkah and Azhure close.

"You and I are going to talk to the good people of Arcen," he said. "Rivkah, I want you to address them – take your lead from what I say."

Rivkah, puzzled, nevertheless nodded in agreement.

"Azhure, notch one of those blue-fletched arrows in the Wolven and try your best to look like a fairy creature yourself. Few within Arcen will have seen such a beautiful woman approach their gates to threaten them with bow and arrow before. Come," he waved both women to his side. "Let us go and talk to the people of Arcen. Do not fear for your safety, I can protect us from anything they might throw our way."

There was a stir on the walls as the three figures approached on foot. Here was Axis, looking like a sun god in his tunic and cloak, with him walk two black-clothed women, both handsome, both queenly. What did it mean?

Burdel stood atop the wall close to the bolted gates. He was unnerved, both by the extent of Axis' army, and by the approach of these three figures. He straightened his back, refusing to let his nervousness show. Axis' army had no siege engines and Arcen was provisioned to wait out a year-long siege, should that be necessary. Burdel was reasonably sure he was in a stronger position than Axis.

Axis halted some fifty paces from the walls, noting the eagle's position.

"Greetings, Burdel," he called cheerfully, and his enchanted voice carried magically about the entire walls and drifted down into the city itself. "It is a fine morning, and a good one to talk."

Burdel opened his mouth to call down insults but Axis continued before he had a chance to speak. "And greetings to you, Culpepper Fenwicke," he called, naming the mayor of the city. "I see you standing inside the gates and I would have words with you. Please, would you climb the walls so I can the more clearly meet your eyes?"

There was a collective gasp from the people of Arcen. How could the man see straight through iron-reinforced wood?

Culpepper Fenwicke, a stout grey-haired man of middle years, slowly climbed the ladders to the top of the walls, moving to stand next to Burdel. He had met Axis when he'd ridden his Axe-Wielders through Arcen on his way to Gorkenfort and had formed an instant respect for the man. His respect now deepened tenfold. How could Arcen withstand a man such as this? "It is good to see you again, Axis."

Burdel muttered an expletive under his breath. What was the fool thinking of to say such a thing?

Axis called back as if he had simply run into Fenwicke in the streets of Arcen on a fair day. "It *is* good to see you again, Culpepper. How is your lovely wife? Igren?"

"She is well, Axis," Fenwicke muttered as Earl Burdel shifted angrily by his side.

"I am pleased to hear that. She entertained myself and my lieutenant Belial, who waits behind me, very hospitably on our journey through here the year before last. Now, Fenwicke, I have not much time to spend on further pleasantries and you and I find ourselves in a somewhat awkward situation here."

Fenwicke spread his hands helplessly. Awkward wasn't the word for it!

"Culpepper Fenwicke, I speak to you not as my friend, but as the mayor of this fine city. It saddens me to say this, but it appears that you harbour dangerous criminals within."

The mayor cleared his throat. "Criminals, Axis?"

"Criminals, Culpepper Fenwicke, who may have persuaded you that myself and my army represent something of a threat. Culpepper, I do not want to threaten you or yours. I simply want Burdel. I have pursued him through most of Skarabost and now I finally have him cornered in your fair city. Do not make me destroy your city, Culpepper Fenwicke, for the sake of one criminal and his henchmen."

Burdel's hands clenched on the stone battlements. "*You* are the criminal, Axis," he shouted. "*You* are the misbegotten son of the Forbidden! You seek to destroy Achar and the peaceful life we lead within it."

Axis ignored him. "Culpepper Fenwicke, and you good people of Arcen. I have standing by my side my mother, the Princess Rivkah of Achar. Perhaps she can clarify some of your misapprehensions."

Axis' words caused a stir within the city. Rivkah? Alive?

Rivkah, cool and calm, stepped forward. As she spoke, Axis wrapped her voice with enchantments so all could hear.

"Culpepper Fenwicke, I greet you and your good people well. I speak on behalf of my son, Axis SunSoar. Many of you will know of the myths and rumours that surrounded his birth. Many will be surprised to find that I am alive. I did not die in Axis' birth, as you were led to believe, but was left to die on the slopes of the Icescarp Alps by none other than Brother-Leader Jayme and his adviser, Moryson. They stole my son, and they tried their best to murder me."

The city stood still, mute with astonishment. The Brother-Leader of the Seneschal? Party to attempted murder?

None disbelieved Rivkah, because Axis had quietly run the Song of Truth-Seeing through the city. The Song forced people to see what was true, not what was false. It was a powerful Song, requiring its user to manipulate a significant proportion of the Star Dance, and it had weakened Axis badly.

"Axis is the StarMan, good people of Arcen. Perhaps you have heard of the Prophecy of the Destroyer?" Most had, because both northern traders and Belial's men had ensured that the Prophecy was quietly spread about the city. "He is the son of myself and one of the great Princes of the Icarii people – the people who rescued me from certain death. If I stand before you now, it is only through the goodwill of the Icarii people. They do not bring death and destruction, good people, but hope and joy for the future. Axis is no criminal. He acts only for the truth. He is incapable of anything less. He does not seek to destroy Achar and your peaceful lives. He seeks to unite those who have been riven apart. He seeks to create a new land of unity and of lasting peace. A land built on truth, and not on the lies of the Seneschal. Listen to him, for he is the only one who can save you."

She finished and bowed her head, then smiled at her son and stepped back.

"Good people of Arcen," Axis resumed. "Earl Burdel is the one who is guilty of trying to destroy the peace of this land. He has ridden his force through Skarabost and has tortured, burned and murdered all those who sought to follow the way of truth. Truth-seekers have ever been persecuted, and none more cruelly than those in Skarabost. Burdel has acted, it is true, under the orders of your King, Borneheld – but his own spite and cruelty have driven him to extremes even beyond those his master called for. Good people of Arcen, doubt not that I speak the truth. See."

The air in the open space between Axis' encircling soldiers and the walls of the city shimmered and shifted. Culpepper Fenwicke, as all who stood on the walls, save Burdel, cried and muttered in horror.

Arcen was now ringed by a ghostly circle of crosses and wooden frames. Hanging from each were the torn and twisted bodies of those whom Burdel had ordered murdered. Some had been nailed to their frames, others hung from ropes slung under armpits and around necks, their eyes and tongues bulging as they had slowly suffocated to death.

"See," Axis whispered, his own eyes gaunt with the frightfulness of it, and his whisper reached into the heart of every man, woman and child within Arcen. Even those within the city who could not see over the walls experienced ghastly visions of their northern neighbours' dreadful deaths.

Burdel had been responsible for this?

"No," Burdel tried to shout, but his voice did not rise above a hoarse whisper.

"Listen," Axis whispered, battling to control the power that was needed to produce these visions, trying to stop it from consuming him completely.

Then, in a nightmare that surpassed even the vision of the bodies strung to die, each of the ghostly images spoke, spoke whatever had last crossed his or her mind as they slipped towards a grateful death.

One whispered the name of his sweetheart, raped and strung up on the cross next to his, dead an hour before him and already eyeless from the attentions of the crows. Another murmured Burdel's name, a curse before dying. Yet another cried out for his children, burned to death within his home. Another cried Burdel's name and wished on him the same death as she suffered. One old woman wondered what she had done in her life to die in this manner. A child whimpered and wondered at the gaping hole in her chest where a soldier had thrust a careless spear. Another man whispered Axis' name and called on him to save him. The woman next to him took up the cry, and soon the entire circle of murdered souls about Arcen were crying Axis' name, crying out to him to save them, crying out to him to avenge their death.

Axis swayed on his feet, not only from the power that he struggled to control, but also from the horrors that the murdered souls revealed. He had no control over what they said, he could only release what they had actually been thinking at the moment of their deaths. And that flood of thought was horrifying to listen to. Azhure and Rivkah stepped close to Axis, each taking his arm, each supporting him.

"I can stand no more!" Axis rasped, and he let go the enchantment. Abruptly the circle of bodies strung up about the city of Arcen vanished, but their cries and laments seemed to linger in the air and in the memories of the people listening for hours – and in some cases, for years – to come.

Men and women broke down and wept in the streets of Arcen, and more than one of the militiamen standing on the walls had to put his spear or bow aside and turn aside to lean for comfort on his neighbour.

Axis took a deep breath and stood straight. "I am all right," he said to Azhure and Rivkah, and reluctantly they let his arms go. "Azhure," he said, "I rely on you now, do not fail me. Take your bow."

Azhure nodded, and Axis raised his head and spoke again. "Culpepper Fenwicke. You harbour a criminal within your ranks. I ask that you give him and his senior commanders to me. You heard the souls of the people as they died. They cry out to me to avenge their deaths. I can do no less."

"No!" Burdel shouted, amazing even himself with the strength of his voice. "No! Fenwicke, I am your Earl and overlord. You must listen to me. I *order* you to listen to me! He," Burdel pointed a shaking finger at Axis, "can do nothing to us. We are all safe behind these walls. Eventually he will simply go away. Fenwicke, I order you not to listen to him."

"You are wrong, Earl Burdel," Axis called. "I have asked Culpepper Fenwicke and the citizens of Arcen to cooperate with me, for my fight and my grievance is not with them. Indeed, I wish all of them well. I do not want to fight them. But know this, Fenwicke, if I am forced to fight I can decimate your fair city."

Axis indicated Azhure. "I command a force of archers such as you have never seen before. They could mark every man, woman and child within your fair walls. We do not need vision or an unobstructed view to mark with deadly certainty. In the streets behind you there is a cart piled high with baskets of fruit. At the top of the pile is a basket full of overripe melons. The topmost melon has been marked. Watch."

Azhure, watch with me. See? This is what the eagle sees.

A vision of the interior of Arcen flooded Azhure's mind.

Trust in me, Azhure, and trust in what the eagle sees. The cart is directly behind the gates. Do you see?

"Yes, I see."

Then aim.

Almost in a trance, Azhure raised the Wolven. She sighted along the arrow, but she did not see the walls before her. Instead she saw the great fat overripe melon sitting atop the cart of fruit as if the walls did not exist.

Trust in me. Trust in yourself.

Azhure let fly the arrow, and every man along the walls traced its arc with their eyes. It flew high above the walls, then dropped straight and true into the melon, exploding it in a shower of juice and bright red pulp.

"And so might every head in Arcen be marked, Culpepper Fenwicke. I do want to threaten you, for, as I said, my quarrel is not with you but with the man who stands by your side. Give him to me."

I thank you, Azhure.

Burdel struggled and shouted, but Fenwicke was adamant. It had not been the arrow that persuaded him, but the cries of those that Burdel had murdered. If Burdel could do that to the poor people of Skarabost, how long would it be before he turned on the people of Arcen? Best hand him over to Axis SunSoar now. Those few soldiers who came to Burdel's aid were tied and bundled outside the city gates with Burdel, his two sons and his three surviving commanders.

Axis would let none of them live — not after what he had witnessed. The soldiers were killed instantly with quick blades to the back of the necks. But Burdel, his sons — both of whom had ridden with their father in Skarabost — and the three commanders did not escape so lightly.

"Culpepper," Axis said, turning away from Burdel for a moment. "You know what I must do."

Culpepper Fenwicke nodded. "I know. I accept it."

"Good. Belial, have cause to erect six crosses. These men will die as the people of Skarabost died."

Belial, his face pale but determined, nodded and walked away. Within moments the sound of saws and hammering could be heard.

Axis turned back to Burdel, who stood stiff and defiant. "Perhaps I should ask you if you have anything to say, Burdel."

Burdel hawked and spat at Axis. "I hope that Borneheld gut-knifes you and leaves you to linger at death's door for days as the juices of your bowels slowly poison the rest of your body."

Axis ran slow eyes over the Earl. "I hope that thought comforts you as you hang a-dying, Burdel," he said and turned away.

Axis glanced at Burdel's sons as he walked away a few paces. They were Burdel's only children. That was good. In the new nation of Tencendor he would have no place for the aggrieved sons of nobles whose fathers had died in Borneheld's cause. Axis was deeply thankful that Isend had no sons. He would not have liked to kill Faraday's brother, but he would not have hesitated to do so.

The six men were strung up naked to the splintery crosses, held by ropes underneath their arms and about their necks. Lead weights were tied to their feet and then they were left with only their consciences for company.

They took several hours to die as the weight of their bodies augmented by the lead weights pulled their chests apart, their lungs slowly filling with blood, and they did not die quietly or prettily. Axis stood there the entire time, his face expressionless. He wondered what, if anything, the GateKeeper would say to them as they approached. Perhaps, knowing their crimes, they went through a different Gate to the one Axis had seen.

"A salutary lesson," he whispered as the last of the men gurgled and died.

49

Baron Ysgryff's Surprise

From Arcen, Axis moved his army towards the Ancient Barrows at the boundary of Tarantaise and Arcness. Though exhausted by the exercise of so much power at Arcen, Axis had not wanted to delay. Time was slipping through his grasp, and day after day as they rode south Axis' eyes would drift to the eagle soaring above.

It would be a long time before the people of Arcen would forget the sight of the ghostly souls crying out Burdel's name in accusation, and five thousand of Arcen's militiamen had begged Axis for permission to join his force. Let them make what restitution they could for Burdel, they argued, and Axis had reluctantly accepted their offer.

For the first two days after Arcen, Azhure rode silently by Axis' side. She had been physically nauseated by Burdel's death and Axis was concerned for her. But Azhure had kissed him and told him that she would be well, and had stayed close to Axis because she was so worried about his health. Both she and Rivkah had seen how damaging the power of the Star Dance had been on his body and how injurious the sight of the dead souls crying out his name had been on his spirit. Axis had felt responsible for so many of those who had died, and his conscience troubled him sorely. If he'd moved south faster, could he have saved a few of those who'd cried out his name?

No wonder he had been so harsh on Burdel, Azhure reflected, hoping he'd never turn on her with such cold anger.

A day out of the Ancient Barrows two of the Icarii farflight scouts returned with appalling news.

"An army awaits you the other side of the Ancient Barrows, Axis SunSoar," one of the scouts reported, his wings trailing dismally in the grass behind him. "Perhaps some eight thousand, maybe nine thousand, in strength . . ."

"Mounted men," the other scout broke in. "Fully armoured, both riders and horses. Equipped with lances, pikes, swords. They stand like a wall of steel, waiting for you to emerge from the Barrows."

"Who?" Axis asked sharply.

The two scouts described the pennants that the army flew, and Axis glanced at Belial and Magariz to his side.

"Barons Ysgryff of Nor and Greville of Tarantaise," Magariz said. "Borneheld must have positioned them there to delay our passage across Tarantaise and the Plains of Tare."

Axis nodded and sat back in his saddle. Nine thousand men? Axis' force now numbered over twenty-two thousand, but a heavily armoured force of nine thousand would be more than a nuisance. This time, he thought bleakly, I'll have no choice but to use the Icarii Strike Force.

"Most of the men must be from Nor," Magariz continued. "Greville's Tarantaise is so sparsely populated he would struggle to raise a hunting party, let alone an army. Nor, on the other hand . . ."

"Is one of the most densely populated regions of Achar," Axis said slowly, continuing Magariz's train of thought. "Ysgryff has decided to put aside his dancing boys, it seems, and take up the arts of war." Well, at least he had finally come to Borneheld's aid, Axis thought sourly. Borneheld could have used those men a lot sooner.

Azhure had ridden up to the group as Magariz and Axis had been talking. An army of Nors men awaiting the other side of the Ancient Barrows? They would be her mother's people, the people who had bequeathed Azhure her exotic face and hair. She felt suddenly queasy.

"We camp a half a league out of the Barrows," Axis said quietly, "and prepare for battle on the morrow."

But on the morrow, as they advanced towards the Barrows, Axis called the column to a halt, surprised. A single horseman rode slowly out of the Barrows, and as the figure drew closer Axis could see that it was not a man at all, but a woman, riding graceful side-saddle.

"By all the gods," Axis muttered, stunned, as the woman drew closer. It was Embeth, Lady of Tare.

She reined her horse in a few paces away and she and Axis stared at each other. They'd been lovers once, and friends for longer. As he stared at her, Axis realised how close he was to a final confrontation with Borneheld. Carlon lay just weeks away . . . beyond the army on the other side of the Barrows.

Embeth finally smiled. It had been almost two years since she'd seen Axis. Two years, she thought, and look what changes those years have wrought.

The horse was the same, and the blond hair and the beard, but so much else seemed to have changed. His eyes were colder, harder, older. The black of the BattleAxe was gone, as were the twin crossed axes. Now he dressed in a fawn tunic and breeches, a blood-red sun blazing across his chest, a cloak of the same shade draped about his shoulders. He had ridden out of her life across Tarantaise, and now he would ride back into it from out of the dawning sun.

Her smile faltered slightly. The sight of Axis reawoke many emotions she had thought dead. "Axis. It is good to see you."

Axis nodded, his eyes boring into Embeth's deep blue ones. "And good to see you, Embeth. But a surprise."

"Nor and Tarantaise await beyond the Barrows," Embeth said, her voice, gratefully, remaining steady and cool.

"I know."

"Yes. We saw your, ah . . ." How was she to refer to the strange and hauntingly lovely creatures she had seen in the sky yesterday?

"They are Icarii, Embeth. You saw some of the Icarii farflight scouts yesterday."

Embeth considered that for a moment. Faraday had told her much about Axis' heritage, but until now it had never really sunk in. "Yes," she repeated. "We saw some of your Icarii farflight scouts yesterday."

"We?" Axis said softly. "Do you ride with Nor and Tarantaise against me?"

Embeth sensed the danger seeping across the space between them. "I ride with Nor and Tarantaise, Axis, but we ride to join you, not oppose you."

Axis was so stunned his mouth hung open until he recovered and closed it with a snap.

"Of course," Embeth continued, her voice deep with amusement, "both Baron Ysgryff and Baron Greville have some conditions."

Axis' mouth twisted wryly. "Why am I not surprised to hear that?"

"I rode out alone because we felt that you were less likely to send an arrow through me than if either Ysgryff or Greville rode out. Will you meet with them?"

"Belial, Magariz, what do you think?" Axis asked. "Should I meet with these two Barons, or should I decide that it's a trap and attack anyway?"

"I would not trap you," Embeth retorted. "We have meant too much to each other for me to do that."

A black-haired Nors woman suddenly rode up, accompanied by the most extraordinary man Embeth had ever seen. He had blue lines tattooed across his face, a red blazing sun in the centre of his forehead, and rode the ugliest horse this side of the gates of the AfterLife. Embeth glanced again at the woman. Only the fact that she carried a bow slung across her shoulder made her reconsider her first thought that she must be one of the Nors whores who inevitably attached themselves to wandering armies.

"We have no choice," Belial said after a pause. What would those two women find to say to each other? "We parley. I admit I'm tempted by the thought of nine thousand heavily armoured horsemen."

Axis nodded. "Magariz?"

"I concur," Magariz replied. "I find myself grateful that Nor and Tarantaise wait to talk rather than fight." As with most of Axis' army, he had spent an unsettled night, tossing and turning in his sleeping roll. Magariz was a trained man of war, but even so, he disliked the idea of fighting against men he had once called friends. He knew that many within Axis' force felt the same. They would fight, but it would be hard and dispiriting.

Axis nodded. "Ho'Demi?"

Embeth swung her eyes to the blue-lined savage. Was he a Ravensbundman?

"I will brew and serve the Tekawai tea myself," he said solemnly. "Tekawai is a sacred drink vital to the success of any parley."

"I shall look forward to sipping Tekawai with you and with my potential allies," Axis replied, and looked at Azhure. "Well, Azhure-heart? Do you agree with your fellow commanders?"

The use of the endearment surprised everyone present. Axis' personal relationship with Azhure normally never intruded upon their relationship as army commander and subordinate. Axis used the endearment deliberately to inform Embeth of the relationship between Azhure and himself, and to let all know that he was not going to hide his love for Azhure. She would stand by his side, both as a respected commander in her own right and as his Lover.

Embeth was stunned. Lover *and* commander in his army? Axis turned his cold stare back her way, watching her reaction. Drawing on all her experience as a lady of court, Embeth calmed her face and squared her shoulders. Damn him! What about Faraday?

"I have no desire to fight if I do not have to," Azhure said, hiding the turmoil in her own heart. He had acknowledged her in front of this woman and her fellow commanders! "I say we parley."

"Then we parley," Axis said to Embeth. He straightened in the saddle. "We meet in the cleared space of the Ancient Barrows."

"They already await you there," Embeth replied, her eyes drifting back to the woman. She had not thought Axis' tastes to run to Nors women, at least not to the extent that he would publicly acknowledge this one. Well, Embeth had heard tales of the abilities of Nors women and she supposed this one must be better than most. Without another word she swung her horse around and dug her heel into its flank.

They met that afternoon within the semicircle of Icarii tombs. The waiting army had erected a huge tent in the centre of the space, a gaudy arrangement of multicoloured layers and silken tassels. A typical piece of Nors finery, Axis thought as he reined Belaguez to a halt before it, but he heard Ho'Demi sigh in admiration. He had brought a number of both Acharite and Ravensbundmen with him and, as he dismounted, StarDrifter, FarSight CutSpur and EvenSong lifted down from the sky, to the astonished whispers of the Nors and Tarantaise men present.

"We will save your Tekawai for later," Axis murmured to the Ravensbund chief as they entered the tent. "Perhaps we can celebrate a new alliance with it this evening."

The interior of the tent was cool and dim, and Axis had to blink several times to adjust his vision. Ysgryff, dark and handsome and some fifteen years older than Axis, stood to one side in a silken brocade tunic and breeches. Well, at least he's not dressed for war, Axis thought as he bowed slightly. Greville stood by Ysgryff's left hand, a man approaching old age, paunchy and sallow-skinned, but with clear blue eyes that missed nothing. He matched Axis' bow with exactly the same degree of coolness Axis had afforded him. Embeth stood a little further into the tent, together with what Axis guessed by their attire to be several of the Barons' military commanders.

As Axis stepped further in a woman emerged from the shadows at the back of the tent. She was frail and ethereal, with light golden hair and porcelain skin. She wore a gown stiff and black with mourning.

"Judith!" Axis bowed with a little more respect this time. Were Nor and Tarantaise the two whom Judith had intimated in her letter would turn to Axis' cause?

"Axis." She smiled coolly, inclining her head.

Baron Ysgryff stepped forward. Ye gods, but Axis looked the part, he thought, noting the tunic and cloak admiringly. His eyes caught those of the dark-haired woman at Axis' back and Ysgryff smiled and winked at her. Well! The man had taste. His countrywoman, no less! Ysgryff stared at her a moment longer. Why did her face seem familiar? Why did her eyes recall so many memories of his childhood? So much laughter?

"Axis," he said smoothly, turning away from the Nors woman and running his eyes curiously over the Icarii. He had never thought to see the Icarii before he died – and one of them an Enchanter! "Please, be seated." Ysgryff waved at cushions spread about the canvas floor of the tent, and the group spent a minute or two settling themselves comfortably.

"So," Axis finally said. "You have come to join with my cause."

"Well," Ysgryff said. "Perhaps that is taking it a little too far, Axis. We have come to, ah, negotiate. Let me be frank with you. Greville and I have no wish to back the loser in this conflict between you and your brother. Judith has persuaded us that yours is the cause not only most just, but most likely to succeed."

There lay the nub of the matter, Axis thought wryly. Justness had little to do with it. Ysgryff merely wanted to make sure he backed the winner.

"So," Ysgryff continued. "I wonder what you could offer Greville and myself should we decide to ally ourselves with your cause."

Axis stared at him coldly. "Apart from your lives?"

Ysgryff rocked back, angered by Axis' words. "Our lives? You go too far, Axis!"

"Perhaps you have not heard of Earl Burdel's fate, Ysgryff. Burdel thought to oppose me. This is what happened to him." Axis waved his hand, and an image formed in the space between them of Burdel, his sons to either side of him, hung naked and dying on the cross outside Arcen.

Ysgryff paled, not only at the sight of Burdel's death, but also at the evidence of Axis' power.

"Think not that I conjure lies, Ysgryff," Axis said softly. "I am sure you have contacts who can confirm the truth of what you have just witnessed."

"You broke Arcen?" Ysgryff asked. His fingers toyed with the tassels of his cushion. Axis was stronger than he had realised. Well, that was nothing but good. He, as so many others, had waited a long, long time for this moment and this man.

"Arcen ceded itself to me without a fight, Ysgryff. Skarabost and Arcness are mine. If you force me to ride through your shiny soldiers behind you then I will do it. You may delay me a few days, but that is all you will do." Axis' tone hardened. "I have not come here to bargain with you, Ysgryff, Greville. I have come simply to accept your aid. It is your decision whether to ride with me or against me."

Ysgryff dropped his eyes, but Greville stared at Axis. He had expected Axis to fall over himself with gratitude that he and Ysgryff had offered to parley with him. He had expected to wring considerable concessions out of the man – perhaps trade concessions, perhaps even more territory for the two of them to divide between themselves. They had not counted on the self-confidence of the man, nor on his undoubted power. Already Icarii and Ravensbund rode with him. And if Axis could seize Skarabost and Arcness then he would undoubtedly be able to seize both Tarantaise and Nor.

"Gentlemen," Judith said softly into the silence as Greville joined Ysgryff in dropping his eyes to the floor. "I have some information that may make the decision easier." She and Embeth had not yet told anyone save Faraday of Priam's death-bed wish, nor, indeed, had they told anyone of what they suspected about his death. "I have no proof, but I believe Priam was murdered, probably by Borneheld in concert with the Seneschal."

Eyes about the room widened and breathing stilled. Borneheld had murdered his uncle? Axis was the least surprised. He had seen Borneheld murder FreeFall.

"As he died, Axis," Judith took a breath, "Priam named you his heir. Axis, you have a rightful claim to the throne of Achar, and I will be prepared to swear to the truth of that statement on any sacred relic presented to me."

"Axis," said Embeth. "You *are* the rightful King of Achar. It is Borneheld who is the pretender. Not only pretender, but murderer. The present Queen, Faraday, will also be prepared to swear that Borneheld murdered Priam."

If Judith had thought Axis would be gratified that Priam had finally recognised him, she was as disillusioned as Greville.

"Priam refused to acknowledge me for thirty years," Axis said harshly. "He left it late indeed to acknowledge my worth and my blood. And for that he paid the price."

Judith bowed her head. Axis had a right to be bitter.

"Nevertheless," Axis continued in a softer tone. "I thank you for your words and for your support here today. I grieve for you that you had to lose your husband in such a cruel manner." Axis knew that Priam and Judith had loved each other, and now was no time to tell Judith that Axis would have as cheerfully waged war on Priam if he had obstructed his purpose as he was now doing on Borneheld.

Axis turned back to Ysgryff and Greville. "Well?"

Ysgryff shrugged expressively at Greville and turned his smoky blue eyes towards Axis. They were, Axis realised, precisely the same shade as Azhure's. "Then we are here to aid you, Axis."

"Then I welcome you to my cause, gentlemen," Axis said. "Of the lands of the two earls that I have passed through thus far, one of them has been completely dispossessed, and the other I executed. It gives me a pleasant feeling to be able to speak to the lords of the next two provinces and know that I will leave them both their lands and their lives."

Ysgryff and Greville recognised the underlying threat. Do not think to betray me, for then both your lands and your lives will be forfeit.

Axis watched the impact of his words sink in. Good. They understood him.

"But the negotiations are not yet concluded," he said, surprising Ysgryff and Greville. "I am willing to cede you some concessions. Exclusive rights to control Achar's trade with Coroleas, Ysgryff?"

Ysgryff's face brightened. He and his province would be richer than he could have ever dreamed. "I thank you, Sire," he said, giving Axis the benefit of the regal title.

Axis' mouth twitched. Who said that respect could not be purchased? "Greville, I imagine that you would appreciate exclusive fishing rights to Widewall Bay? As well as rights to control the grain trade of eastern Achar?"

It was as rich an offer as that made to Ysgryff, even though Greville had less to offer Axis in terms of arms and men. "It is generous, Sire," Greville said carefully. "Perhaps overly so. Sire, do not take my words amiss, but I wonder why you are so generous when, as you have made explicitly clear, you could have had Ysgryff's and my lives without overly troubling yourself."

Axis nodded. "Perhaps you are right to be suspicious, Greville. Gentlemen, you must know that I aim not only for the throne of Achar, but to unite the three races of Acharite, Icarii and Avar?"

"We have heard as much," Greville said, even more cautiously. Judith and Embeth, who had heard it from Faraday, had told both Barons of the Prophecy and its implications.

Ysgryff simply stared at Axis, his hands now still.

"I aim to recreate the ancient land of Tencendor, a land where the three races can once again live in harmony. The Icarii and the Avar will move back down into parts of what is now Achar, and, gentlemen, I am afraid that both of you stand to lose much of your territory."

Both Barons narrowed their eyes and Axis went on quickly. "I remind you of the trade, fishing and grain concessions I have granted you," he said. "Those concessions will make both of you, as your people, rich. You can well afford to lose a little territory – and I assure you, I only want to take the barren and troublesome bits that you have little use for."

"Tell us, Axis," Greville said, leaning forward, his blue eyes sharp. "What exactly will we lose . . . and to what?"

"Thus far I have done all the talking," Axis said. "Now, perhaps, it time for me to introduce my father, StarDrifter SunSoar, Enchanter and Prince of the Icarii people."

"Prince" was not a title the Icarii normally used, but it was one that the Barons would understand, and it roughly described StarDrifter's royal connection.

Eyebrows shot up as Axis introduced StarDrifter as his father. So this was the lover whom Rivkah had taken? This is who had cuckolded Searlas into becoming the laughing stock of Achar?

StarDrifter watched the curiosity blossom across the faces before him and inclined his head. These were the ones who had trampled roughshod over the Icarii and Avar sacred lands for so many generations?

"Both the Icarii and the Avar have deep attachments to some parts of the land you now call Achar," he began, shifting his gaze slowly from one to another. "The Avar forest, the Avarinheim, once stretched as far as the Widewall Sea, and my people lived scattered over most of southern and eastern Achar. But we do not expect that you will give us all the land you have cultivated, nor would we wish to demand it."

Axis knew that StarDrifter had spent much time consulting carefully with Raum over this matter, and he knew that the pair had come to a workable arrangement which should not alienate too many of the Acharites.

"The Avar would wish to replant the forests in certain areas," StarDrifter continued. Axis repressed a smile. Despite his heavy-handedness at it, StarDrifter was threading a little of the Song of Harmony into his voice. MorningStar would be proud of you, Axis thought, for using the water music so effectively when you find it so hard.

"Parts of eastern Skarabost, eastern Arcness and," StarDrifter paused a little, "the larger part of Tarantaise."

Ah, Greville nodded, no wonder Axis is willing to grant me so many concessions. Well, Axis was also right when he said that he only wanted the barren and troublesome bits. And what was the majority of Tarantaise, if not broad and useless grass plains? Perhaps the fishing and grain rights would be worth the loss of so much territory.

"We would also want the Bracken Ranges, but that is neither here nor there as far as you two are concerned."

StarDrifter looked about him and smiled, and both Embeth and Judith gaped at the sudden beauty and virility of his face. No wonder Rivkah, may she rest in peace, had succumbed to him.

StarDrifter's smile widened until even the two Barons were affected by it. "And here we sit among some of the tombs of our most revered Enchanter-Talons, or Kings. This is also a deeply holy site for us, and we would want to regain control of the Ancient Barrows and the swathe of territory that stretches down to and surrounds the Silent Woman Woods. Greville, will you agree to the loss of some two-thirds of your territories for the concessions that my son is willing to grant you?" StarDrifter did not mention Star Gate. There was no need for the Baron to know what lay beneath their feet.

Greville thought about it. The fishing and grain rights would more than adequately compensate for the land that this StarDrifter requested on behalf of his people and the Avar. And so few people lived in the northern and eastern parts of Tarantaise that hardly any would be displaced. Most of his people lived closer to Tare and to the south-western border of Tarantaise and Nor. He took a deep breath. Besides, Axis did not have to offer him anything at all. He could simply have taken it.

"I agree and I accept," he said firmly, and leaned forward and offered StarDrifter his hand. "You are welcome to the areas you have requested."

StarDrifter shook Greville's hand, relieved. Like Axis, he wanted the Acharites to cede their land willingly rather than have it forced from them.

"And for control of trade with the Corolean Empire," Ysgryff said dryly and with evident concern, "I suppose you want the majority of Nor?" Nor was a much richer and more densely peopled province than Tarantaise, and Ysgryff was not sure that he wanted to hard over the larger part of *his* province to these Icarii or Avar.

StarDrifter's smile faded a little. "I would ask for only one thing from Nor, Ysgryff."

Ysgryff raised his eyebrows inquiringly.

"Pirates' Nest."

Ysgryff only managed to keep his mouth shut with a supreme effort. Axis was prepared to allow Ysgryff rich trading concessions for that sea-lapped rock infested with pirates? What secret treasures did Axis think the island hid? What did he *know* of the island?

"No hidden treasures, Ysgryff," Axis said softly, and Ysgryff allowed an expression of excitement to filter across his face at this further exhibition of power and ability. By the sacred gods themselves! The time *was* here!

"No hidden treasures, but simply one of the most sacred sites of the Icarii People. StarDrifter?"

"We know the island as the Island of Mist and Memory, Ysgryff. We had our Temple of the Stars on the island, and we believe that, beneath the pirates' filth, its ruins must still be there. We would like to reclaim the island and rebuild the temple."

Ysgryff's face had gone white and he was having obvious difficulty breathing. Both StarDrifter and Axis wondered if it was the sudden revelation that Pirate's Nest held an ancient Icarii temple.

They were both wrong.

Ysgryff took a deep breath and squared his shoulders. Courage, Ysgryff, he thought to himself, it is time to step forth from the shadows. It is time for a thousand years of deception and secrecy to end. This *is* the time, and this *is* the man.

"The Temple still stands," he said, and now it was both StarDrifter and his son's turn to look stunned.

"The Temple still stands. The pirates have left it alone." Until StarDrifter had mentioned it himself, Ysgryff had been determined not to break the code of silence that protected the Temple of the Stars. He had first heard of it when a baby, and first visited it when a young boy. This was the first time in his life he had spoken of it to an outsider.

StarDrifter's eyes filled with tears. This was more, far more than he could have hoped for, but Ysgryff was not yet done.

"Nor has supplied the nine priestesses for the past thousand years, StarDrifter. The nine still wander the walks and paths of Temple Mount. The Library still contains its ancient scrolls and parchments. The Dome of the Stars still protects the First Priestess –"

Forgotten in the shadows behind Axis, Azhure shuddered as if the cold fingers of memory gripped her soul. She thought she heard the crash of waves against towering cliffs.

The Dome . . . the Dome!

Azhure? Azhure? Is that you?

What had happened in the Dome? Tears filled her eyes, and she turned her head aside.

"– and the Avenue still stretches straight and shaded towards the Temple of the Stars. The Star Dance still lingers among the orchards and the vines and fills the otherwise empty Assembly of the Icarii."

StarDrifter could not believe what he was hearing. Did the entire Temple complex still stand unviolated? And Ysgryff? By the Stars themselves, StarDrifter breathed, Ysgryff – indeed, perhaps the entire Nors people – knew far more about the Icarii than the Seneschal had ever known.

Not only StarDrifter, but all the Icarii present had been stunned by Ysgryff's intimate knowledge of the complex on Temple Mount and particularly of the nine priestesses. The Icarii themselves rarely ever mentioned the nine priestesses of the Order of the Stars. Even Axis had barely heard of them. Yet here was the Baron of Nor prattling on as if he were well acquainted with Icarii mysteries.

"Do not think *all* the Acharites have forgotten the ancient ways. Even my elder sister took her turn as one of the priestesses. StarDrifter, had you asked for the Island of Mist and Memory for nothing I would willingly have ceded it to you. As it is," Ysgrff grinned at Axis, "I now have control of the richest trading routes in Achar."

Axis smiled weakly back. Never underestimate your enemies, Axis, he told himself. And never underestimate your allies, either.

"However, I am willing to be generous." Ysgryff was enjoying himself hugely. "For the trading rights I am willing to beg the pirates to permit the Icarii to land on their island."

And yet, Ysgryff thought to himself, looking Axis in the eye and hoping the man was still reading his every thought, I still have the last laugh, because the pirates' occupation of the Island of Mist and Memory was only ever intended to protect the Temple of the Stars from the Seneschal. No Brother of the Seneschal would ever have stepped foot on the island knowing that he was likely to end up in some pirate's cooking pot.

"I'm sure the Icarii will not mind granting some of the island to the pirates, Ysgryff," Axis said, the smile now completely gone. He had underestimated this man badly, and the man's obvious service to the Icarii sacred site humbled him. "Seeing how they have done the Icarii such a great service."

StarDrifter turned and looked at his son strangely.

That evening was one of the happier occasions of the march south. Extra tents were hastily erected in the open space and several bullocks – purchased from a passing herdsman – were slaughtered and roasted whole over spits. The Barons and Axis invited their commanders and sundry guests to the feast and to witness the signing of the treaty between them, a treaty that also gave so many of the Icarii and Avar sacred lands back to them.

It was, Axis thought as he bent to add his signature to the treaty, a most auspicious occasion. With one simple signature, in his twin role as heir to both the Acharite and the Icarii thrones, so much of the bitterness and hatred of the Wars of the Axe and the subsequent thousand-year period had been undone. The Icarii were free to start moving south again, and, hopefully, the Avar would follow. Once they had Tree Friend to lead them, of course.

All I have to do now, Axis sighed, handing the pen over to a hooded Raum, is defeat both Borneheld and Gorgrael.

Axis had asked that Raum co-sign against his name on behalf of the Avar. Raum had cried with relief when StarDrifter and Axis told him that the Avar would be allowed to replant so much of the ancient forests. The forests had once stretched to the Nordra as well, but Raum had known that it would be unrealistic to expect the Acharites to give up so many of their rich grain lands, and so he had proposed a compromise. The forests would one day stretch down the eastern side of Achar to Widewall Bay, extending westwards only to include the Bracken Ranges and the Silent Woman Woods. It was enough, Raum thought, as he made his sign as a Bane, a leaping deer, and his sign as a member of the GhostTree Clan, a pair of entwined branches.

The Barons stepped up next to add their signatures. Ysgryff took the pen from Raum and signed his name with a flourish. He then handed the pen to Greville, who did not hesitate to add his signature to a document that would make himself and his people rich on grain and fishing concessions.

As soon as the treaty and its copy was signed, Ho'Demi solemnly helped his wife, Sa'Kuya, to serve Tekawai.

Once Sa'Kuya had picked up her own cup, Axis raised his Tekawai in a toast. "To Tencendor," he said. "May all the trials ahead be as simply and amicably solved as this treaty was parleyed."

"To Tencendor," the gathered crowd chorused, draining their Tekawai at a gulp, then reaching with somewhat indelicate haste for more alcoholic sustenance.

Both Ho'Demi and Sa'Kuya smiled as they retrieved their cups. What a crowd of savages they found themselves among.

And then they set about enjoying themselves.

If Embeth and Judith thought they had received all the shocks they were going to get, then they were in for yet more surprises. As they chatted quietly in a corner of the main tent, a handsome middle-aged woman approached them, a young baby of some six or seven months in her arms.

Judith looked at her in some puzzlement. The woman's face seemed somewhat familiar.

"Judith." The woman smiled, and Judith frowned. This stranger was addressing her with a little too much familiarity!

"Do you not remember me, Judith?" the woman asked. "Do you not remember how we used to steal peaches from the cooks in the kitchens of the palace in Carlon when we were children? How we used to chase the pigeons from the courtyard at dawn?"

"Rivkah!" Judith breathed, unable to believe that her closest girlhood friend, whom she had thought dead some thirty years, now stood before her.

Rivkah smiled and embraced Judith briefly. Then she stood back and took her first good look at the woman. Judith looked wan and fragile, her skin papery and translucent. She had always been delicate, but now she looked like a dream-image which would be shattered by a simple puff of breeze.

Judith, overwhelmed to find Rivkah standing here before her, began to cry silently, reaching out her hands for Rivkah, almost as if she would not be able to believe that she was really there until she could touch her.

"Shush," Rivkah said. "Axis should have said something. It was remiss of him. Judith, I am sorry beyond telling to hear of Priam's death."

"He was your brother as well as my husband," Judith said through her tears. "We have both suffered loss through his death."

Rivkah said nothing for a moment, but when she spoke her voice was hard. "Axis tells me that you blame Borneheld for Priam's death."

Judith reached out a trembling hand. "Oh, Rivkah, I forget so easily that Borneheld was your son. I . . . I do not mean . . ."

Rivkah was instantly contrite. "Judith, I do not chide you for blaming Borneheld. I disassociated myself from my eldest son the instant he slipped from my body. I have no intention of bonding with him now, or of acknowledging him. Knowing his father, I can well believe that Borneheld murdered to gain the throne. He murdered my brother as well as your husband, Judith, and I cannot forgive him that. Do not fret that you accuse him."

As Judith and Rivkah's conversation turned from Borneheld to mutual friends, Embeth let her eyes slip about the room. It was so strange, being here in this company. The Icarii dominated the room, their extraordinary beauty and grace, as well as their wings, catching Embeth's eyes at every turn. It was the men among them who commanded her attention, however. Men like StarDrifter, who, when he caught her looking at him, had such a knowing look on his face that Embeth felt her legs weaken. It was easy to see who Axis had inherited his magnetism from. She hastily looked away, but found her eyes being dragged back to the Icarii Enchanter. He was still looking at her.

Embeth closed her eyes, clenching her fists by her sides, trying to break the spell he had woven about her. By Artor, she breathed, these Icarii will wreak havoc among the loose morals of court. When she opened her eyes again StarDrifter had turned away, and Embeth breathed a little more easily. She saw Belial, smiling gently at a young Nors girl, perhaps seventeen or eighteen, who chatted animatedly to him. She wore a bright red dress of fine wool that highlighted her pale skin and blue eyes and contrasted with her black hair. When

Magariz stopped momentarily to catch at Belial's arm and indicate a group of soldiers and Crest-Leaders a little further away, Belial shook his head and pulled his arm free, moving a little closer to the girl. Embeth raised her eyebrows. So he preferred the company of a young girl to that of fighting and drinking comrades?

The soft chiming of bells caught Embeth's attention. Many of the Ravensbundmen, some with wives, were also present, and Embeth watched them, fascinated, for a long while. Each had different patterns tattooed into his or her face, but all had the blazing sun emblazoned across their foreheads. Embeth wondered at the Ravensbund devotion, that they would mark themselves so for Axis. Their black hair glistened blue and green as the lamp light caught the glass among their braids, and they marked their passage through the throng with soft chimes and whispers. Behind the Ravensbundmen were a group of three men who, someone had whispered to Embeth, were the Sentinels mentioned in the Prophecy. Embeth regarded them curiously as they chatted to Baron Ysgryff, almost as if they were old friends.

Axis caught Embeth's eye, and she watched him move among the crowd for a while. The Nors woman was by his side again, laughing and chatting familiarly, not only with Axis, but with most of those he spoke to. She was wearing a black gown, startling in its simplicity, cut low over her breasts and clinging to her slim form. Her hair hung loose down her back. She looked stunning. A true Nors woman, Embeth thought, refusing to admit to herself that she was bitterly jealous.

She did not realise that, to one side, Belial had turned from the lovely young Nors girl and was watching her with some concern. Whispering an excuse to the Nors girl, Belial slowly began to move through the crowd towards Embeth. The girl stared after him, her face losing much of its radiance as she watched Belial move away.

At the same moment Azhure turned and saw Embeth staring at her. Smiling and touching Axis' arm for a moment, murmuring a word or two of excuse, Azhure also began to make her way through the crowd towards Embeth.

"But, Rivkah, explain this baby," Judith asked finally, and Embeth turned back towards the two women. The baby was very handsome, chubby pale cheeks beneath a loose mop of black curls. Smoky blue eyes regarded the women solemnly.

Rivkah smiled. "Judith, Embeth, I would like you to meet my grandson, Caelum."

Embeth's heart thudded painfully. She did not need mystic vision to know who had bred this child.

Azhure joined them in a rustle of silk, and Rivkah turned and handed Caelum across as he wriggled and laughed at the sight of his mother. "And this is the woman I regard as my daughter, Azhure."

Embeth's ill feeling only increased. Wormed her way into both Axis' *and* his mother's hearts.

"How nice to meet you, Azhure," Judith said.

"And you are Axis' wife?" Embeth asked.

"No. No, I am not. But we *are* lovers," Azhure said coolly. She knew who Embeth was, and who she once had been. "And Axis does not hesitate to acknowledge *me*."

Embeth took a sharp breath at the woman's emphasis on the last word. Her eyes glittered angrily, but before she could respond, Belial stepped up to the group and put a restraining hand on her arm.

"Azhure," he said, "I'm sure Axis would appreciate both you and Caelum back at his side as he speaks to Baron Ysgryff."

Azhure nodded stiffly. "I am sorry, Embeth," she said. "My remark was uncalled for." Then she was gone.

"Do not be fooled by her Nors looks, Embeth," Belial said in an undertone. "She means far more to Axis than you give her credit for."

Embeth dropped her eyes as Azhure rejoined Axis. He had turned and smiled at the woman with such love that she had felt a painful jolt of memory. Ganelon had once smiled at her with love, but never Axis. Axis had offered her friendship, no more.

"I have been a fool, Belial. Come, talk to me of some of your exploits over the past two years."

Baron Ysgryff bowed low over Azhure's hand and smiled at her.

"You are my countrywoman, Azhure," he said. "I knew when you walked into the treaty tent earlier this afternoon beside Axis that I would be able to refuse him nothing. I am but wet clay when faced with such beauty." He turned a little to Axis, although he kept his grip on Azhure's hand. "She is your most dangerous weapon, Axis. Use her well and your enemies will all fall at your feet."

Axis laughed. "You are quite the courtier, Ysgryff."

Azhure smiled graciously. "My mother was a Nors woman, Baron, but I was born and bred in northern Skarabost."

"Your mother?" Ysgryff raised his eyebrows. "Lost to us in northern Skarabost? Please, tell me her name. I might have known her."

A look of deep distress crossed Azhure's face and she snatched her hand from Ysgryff's fingers. "She died when I was very young," she stammered, white-faced. "I cannot remember her name."

Axis slipped a hand about her waist, concerned at Azhure's reaction. Why did she say her mother had died? Had she heard something of her mother's fate after she had run away with the pedlar?

"Azhure, I apologise if my remark caused you distress," Ysgryff said hastily. "Please, accept my belated condolences. Your mother must have been very beautiful if I can judge anything by her daughter's beauty."

Azhure relaxed slightly and her face regained some colour. "Yes," she said, "she was very beautiful." Her eyes became dreamy. "She would talk to me of many things."

"Of strange and faraway lands, perhaps? Of seas and tides and long pale beaches?" Ysgryff's voice was curiously insistent.

"Yes. Yes, she had seen many wonders."

"And what did she tell you about these strange lands, Azhure? What did she show you?"

"Flowers," Azhure said, her voice curiously dull. "Many flowers. Moonwildflowers. Yes. She liked those. And hunting . . . and . . . moonlight . . . and . . . the *Dome* . . ." she whispered. "The Dome. I remember the Dome."

Axis glanced at Ysgryff, puzzled, and he tightened his arm about Azhure's waist. Had she had too much wine?

Azhure blinked at the pressure of Axis' arm. "Oh, Ysgryff, it was so long ago. I cannot remember. Her tales are lost in the mists of memory."

As is her name, Ysgryff thought. As is her name. All the priestesses lost their names the day they took their final vows. But what was one of the nine doing in northern Skarabost? *And which one was it?* The first opportunity Ysgryff got he would be making some very specific inquiries at the Temple of the Stars. Meanwhile he had a Sacred Daughter standing before him. He must determine her age — that would make his inquiries the easier.

"Then, Azhure, if such things are lost to you, perhaps you will let me tell you of your mother's homeland?"

"I would be delighted," Azhure said. "Please, tell me about Nor. I have often wondered what my mother's people are like."

No wonder, Ysgryff thought, Axis had taken up with this woman. Did he know what he had won for himself? Did he know what the gods had given him?

Apparently not, for otherwise the man would not have hesitated to marry her.

Every so often Ysgryff's eyes would drift to the child in Azhure's arms, equally fascinated by the baby as he was by his mother. This was a magical line indeed.

In Carlon, Borneheld was enjoying himself immensely. Before him sat the Corolean Ambassador, almost as thin as the pen he held poised in one hand. The man's dark eyes skimmed over the page before him.

"Where do I sign, Sire?"

"Here," Borneheld pointed with his finger. "And here."

The Ambassador signed perfunctorily, then handed the pen to Borneheld, watching as the King of Achar signed the document as well. The man was almost obscene in his haste.

As soon as he had finished Borneheld sat back, feeling a deep sense of peace and security. Let Axis come for me now, he thought, let him come and see what a surprise I have in store for him. "When will the Emperor begin to send the troops, Ambassador?"

"Most of the troops are waiting to embark, Sire," the Ambassador said. "They should be here within two weeks."

Not before time, Borneheld thought. Not before time. He had worked hard to conclude this treaty with the Corolean Ambassador – and the troops which the Emperor had promised him would win him back his country.

"Some more wine?" he inquired politely, although he disliked having to waste such good wine on this constipated vegetable. "It is of the finest quality."

50

The Silent Woman Dream

It was the last week of Harvest-month, only eight weeks before Axis had to fulfil his side of the contract with the GateKeeper. Axis' temper grew shorter day by day as he realised how little time he had before his bargain died. But his army had now grown so vast it could not possibly move at the same speed as Axis' former Axe-Wielders had been able to. As tents were erected at a site just south of the Silent Woman Woods, Axis remembered how his Axe-Wielders had taken three days to traverse the distance between the Silent Woman Woods and the Ancient Barrows. His thirty-one thousand had taken just on nine days to travel the same distance.

Axis sighed and stared at the Silent Woman Woods. He had not objected when his father, grandmother and sundry other Icarii Enchanters had flown into the woods earlier that morning. There was little of danger within the Silent Woman Woods to harm the Icarii, and much to fascinate them, though three Wing of the Icarii Strike Force had accompanied them. Surprisingly, both Ogden and Veremund had shrugged when Axis had asked them if they wanted to ride in, saying that they would return to the Silent Woman Keep one day, but not this one. Raum, beside them, had stood staring longingly at the Woods from beneath the deep overhang of his hood, but had turned away shaking his head when Axis asked him if he would walk among the trees. "Later" was all he had said.

Axis walked slowly towards his tent, preoccupied. His relationship with Azhure was becoming more strained the closer they came to Carlon and to Faraday. Every night between the Ancient Barrows and the Silent Woman Woods Azhure rolled herself and Caelum into her bedroll and turned her back on him. One night Axis had laid his hand on Azhure's shoulder and murmured into her ear. "Do not lock me out of your life, Azhure, I do not intend to let you go."

She had been silent for a long minute, and Axis had thought she was pretending to be asleep. But she had finally spoken. "You and I have lived together almost a year, and every day I have fallen a little more deeply in love with you. Do not blame me if, now that you draw closer to Faraday, I try to reconcile myself to losing you."

"You will not lose me –" Axis started, but Azhure rolled over and stared him in the eye.

"I will lose you the moment Borneheld dies, Axis. No matter how much you protest that you love me, I know that one day you will let me go entirely for Faraday. Forgive me, Great Lord, if occasionally I allow myself a little self-pity."

At that she had rolled back towards Caelum and deter-minedly shut her eyes, refusing to respond as Axis stroked her and whispered protestations of love for her.

Damn her! Axis swore as he stepped carefully around ropes and tent stakes, perhaps it would be better if I just let her go! But even as the thought crossed his mind, Axis knew he could not do it. Not now that she had bitten so deeply into his soul.

As the night thickened about the Silent Woman Woods, the Cauldron Lake slowly began to boil. A deep golden mist rose from the Lake's surface and drifted through the trees towards the camp site of Axis SunSoar's army.

Deep into the night, Axis opened his eyes. For a long time he lay on his back, staring at the dark canvas stretched above him, listening to Azhure breathe deeply by his side.

He was not sure if he dreamed or if he was awake.

Finally Axis rolled out of his blankets and stood up. He considered waking Azhure — for something strange seemed to be about to happen — but decided against it. She had been looking tired and drawn of late and needed her sleep.

Axis ducked his head low and pushed the tent flap back. The camp was shrouded in a thick golden mist. Strange. Perhaps this *was* a dream. He stepped outside the tent and straightened up. A glint of gold caught his eyes as he dropped his arm from the tent flap. How strange! He was dressed in his golden tunic with its blazing blood-red sun. The one Azhure had stitched for him so long ago in Talon Spike. But why was he wearing it now?

Axis contemplated his appearance, then shrugged. This was a dream, and anything could happen in a dream.

He walked through the camp. About him the camp fires had burned down to glowing coals — no flames leaped to challenge the intruding mist. The Alaunt lay in a sleeping circle about the tent Axis shared with Azhure. None stirred as he walked past, though their sides fell up and down as they breathed deep in their own dreams. Guards, both within the camp and at its perimeter, gazed straight ahead as if in a trance. They did not challenge Axis as he walked slowly past.

None of this troubled Axis. It was a dream, after all.

Slowly, very slowly, Axis moved on, pausing at Belial's tent and glancing in. Belial lay deep in sleep, twisted into his bedroll beside a dark-haired young girl who travelled with Ysgryff's retinue. A red wool dress lay thrown carelessly across the foot of the blankets. Axis' mouth twitched. Had Belial found a woman who could take his mind off Azhure?

Axis let the tent flap drop and went to the next tent. Like Belial, Magariz also lay twisted with a woman, but this one Axis knew. Rivkah. His mother.

Axis stood a long time staring at the outline of their entwined bodies beneath the blankets. Was this simply a figment of his sleeping mind? He told himself this was only a vision, and, even if it did speak of truth, why should he speak out against this? But something, deep inside him, told Axis this was a development that should – *must* – concern him. It bespoke danger, although Axis could not see what kind.

Axis let the canvas of the tent flap slip from his fingers, and he resumed his slow walk through the tents and camp fires, winding his way past sleeping forms towards the perimeter of the camp. Nothing moved. Even time seemed not to breathe within this mist.

Beyond the camp Axis turned towards the Silent Woman Woods, perhaps a hundred paces away. When he had camped here on his journey towards Gorkenfort, he had kept his Axe-Wielders as far from the trees as practicable. Then he and his had feared the trees. But as fear of the Forbidden had lessened and died among those who rode with Axis SunSoar, so also dread of trees and shadowed places had been replaced with acceptance, and even a mild curiosity. When the forests were slowly replanted within eastern Achar – Tencendor – Axis had no doubt that Acharite men and women would walk its paths along with the Avar and the Icarii.

A movement in the mist ahead caught his eye. Movement? In this, the most motionless of dreams? A figure walked ahead, almost totally obscured by golden tendrils of mist. Axis tried to walk faster, but the mist clung heavy to his limbs, weighing them down, and it felt as though he were striding through thigh-deep water.

As he gained on the figure ahead of him, Axis could finally see that it was Raum. He was naked and now Axis could see how his body had twisted almost completely out of shape. Great misshapen growths humped out of his back and chest, and his limbs were twisted and malformed. His face, when he turned, was so warped it was almost unrecognisable, and he lurched rather than walked, rolling from one leg to another, his pace so unsteady that Axis feared he would fall at any moment. He quickened his own pace as much as he was able, thinking to aid Raum.

But before Axis could catch Raum the Bane abruptly halted and bent down. Axis saw the flash of a knife, then Raum lifted something in his hand. It was the body of a hare. The Bane dipped the fingers of his hand into the open cavity of the hare's chest, then lifted his fingers to his face and chest.

Axis finally caught up with the Bane and stepped to his side. Raum had drawn thick lines of blood down his face, the middle line centred on his nose, the two companion lines running down either cheek. Three more lines ran down his chest, ending at his nipples. The thick blood had clotted among the hairs of the Bane's chest and its warm coppery freshness clung to Axis' nostrils.

Raum's eyes widened. "Have you been called also?" he whispered.

Have I been called? Axis wondered sluggishly, unable to collect his thoughts. "I do not know why I am here."

"You are here to witness, Axis SunSoar," a voice said behind him, and Axis swivelled around as if in slow motion. The three Sentinels, Jack, Ogden and Veremund, stood three or four paces away, each dressed in a plain white robe that hung down to bare feet.

"Have you been called?" Ogden wondered aloud. "You must have been, else you would not be here. Tread carefully where you go, Axis SunSoar, and do or say nothing that will offend your hosts."

Ogden stepped forward and kissed Raum softly on the cheek, slightly smearing one of the lines of blood. "Be well, dear one," he said. "Find peace where you go."

Jack and Veremund also stepped forward, kissing Raum on the cheek and repeating Ogden's blessing. "Find peace," Veremund muttered a second time, tears glistening in his eyes, and Axis noticed with some surprise that Raum's eyes also glittered with tears. What was going on?

"Raum finds his home and his peace tonight, Axis SunSoar," Veremund said, "and you have been called to witness. You have walked the Sacred Grove once before and tonight you will re-enter. By invitation, this time."

Axis remembered the dream that had visited him the previous time he had slept outside the Silent Woman Woods. Then he had found himself in a dark grove peopled by frightening and dangerous creatures. The Horned Ones. Axis felt a small tremor of anxiety, but he had grown since that night two years ago. He knew more, and he was more.

Axis nodded. "Will you come with us?"

"No," Jack replied. "This is for Raum and yourself alone. Be at peace."

Impatient now, Raum turned to the opening among the trees. "Come," he said, and Axis followed him into the forest.

They walked slowly through the dark trees, the mist dissipating as they moved into the Silent Woman Woods. Colours shifted about them until Axis breathed deep in excitement – the light among the trees had lightened and brightened until they were walking through a tunnel of emerald light. Even the forest floor beneath their feet had disappeared so they were completely suspended in the emerald glow.

"We walk through the Mother," Raum muttered hoarsely, his eyes bright, almost feverish.

Axis could feel the power floating about him, and he shivered. It was good that this was a dream, he thought, for otherwise this power would perturb him. This was the source of the power that Faraday had used to give Axis and his three thousand the means to escape and then destroy much of the Skraeling force surrounding Gorkenfort. Axis remembered the emerald flame he had summoned to destroy the Skraelings and he took a deep breath of awe – Faraday must be powerful indeed to handle such forces as drifted through this emerald light!

They walked until Axis suddenly realised that he could feel leaves and twigs under his feet again. At exactly that moment the emerald light started to mottle and shadow about him, resolving itself into close, dark trees. Stars whirled across the dark velvety sky above them.

"The Sacred Grove," Raum whispered beside him, and Axis realised with a start that this was the first time in months he'd heard Raum speak in a voice that held no shadow of underlying pain.

Before them the trees opened into the circle of the Sacred Grove, and both Raum and Axis slowed. Power drifted among the trees. Unseen eyes watched. It no longer felt like a dream. All traces of the mist had disappeared long before in the brilliance of the emerald light, and Axis understood that he stood here in the Sacred Grove in reality.

He felt gaudy and overly conspicuous in his gold and red. For the first time since he had accepted the golden tunic from Azhure, Axis felt slightly uncomfortable in it.

"*You* will never feel comfortable here, Axis my heart," a woman's voice said quietly beside him, "because your power is tied to the stars, and this power emanates from the earth. From the Mother."

Faraday walked slowly out of the trees to one side, wearing a loosely draped robe of peculiar shifting greens, purples and browns. Her long chestnut hair lay thick and loose over her shoulders and down her back.

"Faraday?" Axis whispered, completely forgetting Raum on his other side. "Faraday?"

She smiled and touched his arm gently. "How long, Axis? Twenty months? Too long, my love. But wait. I must greet Raum."

She stepped past Axis and wrapped her arms about Raum, laughing and crying at the same time, murmuring to him as she hugged him close, softly stroking his face as if she could soothe away the bumps and lesions that marred it.

Axis stared at her. Faraday seemed different from when he had last seen her. No longer was she the innocent girl who first caught his eye at Priam's nameday feast in the Chamber of the Moons. Nor was she the beautiful but sad woman he remembered as Borneheld's wife. There were lines of pain about her eyes that Axis did not remember, and lines of humour at the corners of her mouth. Both experience and power had changed her. Would this Faraday accept Azhure?

Axis hastily clouded his thoughts – Faraday had demonstrated only a moment ago that she was as capable as he at reading the mind of another, and Axis did not want her finding out about Azhure from his unguarded thoughts. What would be the best way of telling her?

"Why do you frown, Axis? This is the first time we have seen each other for a very long while, and this is a very special moment that I have asked you here to witness. It is one of the few occasions that I could invite you here and the Horned Ones would accept your presence. You are almost as closely linked to Raum as I am."

"You asked me? You were responsible for pulling me into this dream?"

Faraday smiled and slipped her hand about Axis' arm, entwining her fingers through his. "No dream, Axis. The dream is the husk of your body which awaits you in your camp beyond the Silent Woman Woods. Now, be silent. We are both here only to witness – for the moment, at least."

Raum stumbled into the centre of the Grove, moaning again, as if his pain had returned. Faraday's hand tightened around Axis', warning him to keep silent. Raum dropped to his knees, his head twisted to one side, his hands held out as if in supplication.

Nothing moved, save the stars that whirled overhead and the watching eyes that shifted among the trees.

Raum screamed, and Axis' entire body jerked. Be silent, Faraday's stare said, then she shifted her eyes back to Raum.

Now he twisted about on the grass, caught in the throes of a dreadful suffering. Another scream rent the Grove, then another, and Axis realised that a dark stain was spreading about Raum's twisting body. Blood! Axis shuddered at Raum's agony. By the Stars! he thought, Azhure was right about these people. They preach a life of non-violence, but their very lives and culture exude violence.

Azhure? a voice asked in his head, and Axis jumped guiltily, screening his thoughts again.

A woman who lived with the Avar for a while. Now she earns her keep as an archer in my army.

Faraday smiled. A woman archer – indeed!

Raum screamed again. His voice had lost its earlier pain-purified clarity and was now harsh and guttural. The blood about him was spreading, and now Axis could see that it seeped from every orifice in his body and, in places, from tears in the skin stretched over painfully tight joints.

All Banes, whether male or female, must die to transform, Axis. What we witness here is both Raum's death and his renewal. All witness. But Raum must do this on his own. None can help him.

Axis wept silently. He liked Raum, had felt a special bond with the Bane. He remembered the moment his eyes had locked with Raum's in the cell beneath the Smyrton Worship Hall. Remembered the understanding that had passed between them. That was the day he had not only met Raum for the first time, but had also met . . . Axis blanked out his thoughts only just in time.

Who? Faraday asked in his mind.

Shra, Axis replied. *The Avar girl.*

Faraday's eyes misted. She had also met Shra at Fernbrake Lake, the Mother. Raum had bonded both her and Shra at the same time.

Raum had not the breath to scream now, although agony still gripped his body. His breath came in harsh gasps that reached Axis and Faraday clearly across the Grove. They stilled, as every eye watching did. After a few minutes Raum's breathing all but ceased, although his body still jerked convulsively. His head had twisted about so that his great dark eyes, streaming tears of pure blood, stared directly into Axis'. Axis felt as though they somehow accused. He saw himself as Raum must see him. Standing close to Faraday, while Raum knew well that Axis had taken . . . Stars! Axis gave a great groan.

Shush! The moment of transformation is close now, Axis. Be still. Do not fear for him.

Axis shielded his eyes from Raum's unblinking stare and screened his thoughts from Faraday, guilt consuming him. Guilt, but determination also. He would not suffer like this once Faraday knew about and had accepted Azhure.

Faraday gasped as Raum sickeningly, appallingly, exploded.

Axis could not stop himself from crying out in horror as a fine spray of blood and tissue arced through the Grove.

By his side Faraday flinched, although she managed not to cry out. Instead, a look of utter amazement spread across her face. "Mother!" she cried in shock. She had known Raum would transform, but not like this. Not into this!

Axis raised his eyes and stared at the spot where Raum had, but a moment before, lain convulsing in pain. All traces of blood had gone. Instead, a magnificent white stag lay there, its head drooped so that its nose rested on the ground.

Axis' head jerked, his eye caught by a movement at the edges of the grove. One of the half-man half-stag creatures he remembered from his dream – a Horned One with a magnificent silver pelt – had stepped forth and was walking over to where what-had-been-Raum lay curled in the soft grass. He bent down, extending a hand to touch the stag's forehead, and for an instant the stag bowed its handsomely antlered head under the Horned One's touch.

As the Horned One stepped back a great cry erupted from the watchers among the trees. The Horned One threw his head back and screamed, the cry turning into myriad exultations.

"Raum," Faraday muttered brokenly by Axis' side. Raum had not transformed into a Horned One at all, but into the Sacred Stag of the Enchanted Woods. "Oh Raum," she breathed. "I always knew you were special, and I have been blessed beyond measure to witness this."

She did not yet fully realise that it had been her own use of the power of the Mother and the Sacred Grove that had effected this transformation.

"I don't understand," Axis said.

Faraday paused before she answered, recalling some of Ur's teachings. "Occasionally," she said, "once every hundred generations, there is a Bane of such purity and goodness who, when he transforms, does not transform into a Horned One but into a Sacred Stag – the most magical and fey of the creatures of the Sacred Grove."

"The Avar revere the stag," Axis said softly, recalling his own teaching in Talon Spike. "The stag plays a central, pivotal role in the Yuletide celebrations. It is his sacrifice, his blood, that gives the sun the strength to be reborn. All Banes identify with the stag."

Faraday nodded. "Yes. The leaping deer, or stag, is the emblem of all Banes." She paused, and when she resumed her voice was choked with emotion. "I am so glad that Raum's purity of heart and soul have been rewarded in this manner. Now the Sacred Stag will run through the Enchanted Wood again. Mother, you have blessed *all* of your children."

Slowly the Raum–Stag rose to his feet, rocking a little as he got used to balancing on four legs instead of two. Gradually other Horned Ones drifted from the tree line, reverentially moving to greet the Sacred Stag.

For a long time Axis and Faraday stood silently, observing the acceptance of the Sacred Stag into the holy community of the Sacred Grove.

Eventually Faraday's hand tightened once more about Axis' arm. "Come," she whispered, and Axis reluctantly let her lead him into the centre of the Grove where the Horned Ones milled about the Stag.

As they drew close the Horned Ones regarded Axis with ill-concealed hostility.

So, they still dislike me, Axis thought. I will ever have trouble with the trees.

Do not fear, beloved, Faraday reassured him. *They will learn to accept you.*

"Who are you?" the whisper rose around Axis. "How did your feet find the paths? Why do you stand so close to Tree Friend?"

His feet followed mine along the paths. The Stag's mind-voice echoed through the Grove as he stepped forward and tipped his antlers in greeting.

"I am Axis Rivkahson SunSoar," Axis said eventually. "Once BattleAxe —"

The Grove was filled with hisses.

"— but now released from the lies that bound me. I am Axis SunSoar, StarMan. I reforge Tencendor to stand against Gorgrael."

"What do you do here?" a voice asked from deep among the group of Horned Ones.

"He is here because *I* invited him," Faraday said firmly. "And you should greet him well. He is the StarMan, and I brought him here this night to meet you. One day you will work on his behalf against Gorgrael. Both his efforts and mine will see the forests replanted into Tencendor."

The silver pelt nodded and spoke. "We have been watching you, Axis SunSoar. We have watched and observed." He stared into Axis' eyes, and, though Axis stared defiantly back, he wondered how much the Horned Ones had observed.

The silver pelt bared his teeth, and Axis hoped that it was the Horned One's equivalent of a grin. "You have already

• 528 •

won for Tree Friend the right to replant most of the ancient forests."

By Axis' side Faraday gasped in surprised pleasure. She did not know, as the Horned Ones obviously did, of Axis' treaty with the Barons Ysgryff and Greville.

"For that we thank you," the silver pelt finished, swinging his eyes to Faraday. "But much pain lies ahead." There was too much knowledge in those eyes for Axis' liking.

"Forgive us if we do not yet welcome you into the Grove with open hearts," the silver Horned One said, "but perhaps one day your wife can bring you back. She will always be welcome."

He turned and placed his hand lightly on the Stag's shoulder. "Welcome to our community, Holy One," he said. "Come. We have the secret forest paths that your hooves crave."

Axis blinked, startled. The Horned Ones had completely vanished, and with them had gone the Stag – Raum.

Faraday smiled into Axis' eyes and, consumed with guilt, he bent to kiss her.

"No," she said, drawing back. "Not while I am still married and vowed to Borneheld. Will you come to free me soon?"

"Yes," Axis whispered.

She took a step back from him. "Free me soon, Axis. I have waited so long for you. Too long." Her smile died. "I have hungered so long, and yet you look so different. Not the same man who left me in Gorkenfort. What have you done since then, Axis SunSoar? Who have you become? Do you still love me?"

Axis opened his mouth, desperately searching for words. Instead of speaking, he simply stretched out his hands towards her. Mist began to drift about the Grove.

"Do you still *want* me?" Faraday whispered. Why did her voice sound so frightened?

"Yes," Axis replied. Yes, he did still desire her – she was a beautiful woman, and her power called to him. Well, perhaps desire would be enough for her.

"Then hurry," Faraday said. "Hurry!"

The mist thickened and congealed about them, and in the space of only two heartbeats both Faraday and the Grove were completely obscured.

He closed his eyes and strained desperately forward.

"Faraday!" he called, and opened his eyes straight into Azhure's stare, leaning over him as he twisted about in the blankets.

"You have been dreaming," Azhure said flatly, "but now it is morning."

She turned away and began hurriedly to dress, keeping her back to him as she pulled her tunic over her head. The scars down her back ridged and bunched as Azhure twisted into the tunic, and Axis watched her silently, the emotions of his dream lingering still. What was he going to do?

Azhure stood and picked up her son. "Breakfast cooks on the fire outside," she said, avoiding Axis' eyes. "If you continue to lie there it will spoil."

Then she pushed aside the tent flap and was gone.

"I'm sorry," he whispered, too late.

51

Then it is War, Brother?

He kept Belaguez to a walk as he rode through the ranks of his army. On their right flank Grail Lake glittered in the distance, the pink walls and the silver and gold rooftops of Carlon rising like a fairytale backdrop behind it. On its shores waited the Tower of the Seneschal – Spiredore.

It was the third week of Weed-month. Over the past month Axis had painstakingly marched his army slowly from the Silent Woman Woods across the Plains of Tare. Borneheld had sent nothing to stop them.

Ahead of him Magariz and Belial sat their horses patiently, their mail coats gleaming as brightly as Grail Lake itself, and for a moment Axis' eye lingered on Magariz. The vision of his mother sleeping in Magariz's arms still returned to bother Axis at odd moments. He had observed Rivkah and Magariz carefully over the past weeks. If they did spend the occasional night together then there was little hint of it in their daytime relations.

Axis hastily averted both his eye and his thoughts. Rivkah could choose as she wished. Why should a dalliance with Magariz bother him?

Belaguez had almost reached the front ranks now, and Axis saw Azhure. She sat Venator slightly to one side of Magariz, as beautiful in her weapons and mail as she was naked in his blankets. Yet over the past five or six weeks the most Axis had seen of Azhure's body had been her naked, scarred back. Ever since Axis had awoken calling Faraday's name Azhure had grown ever more distant and silent with him. She still lay by his side at night, but remained stiff and unyielding.

Axis burned for her, more than he could have ever imagined burning for any woman. She occupied his thoughts almost constantly, and the deepening distance between them was slowly driving him mad. No woman he had wanted before had denied him like this. To have her breathing softly by his side night after night, completely untouchable, drove him to distraction.

As Axis passed Azhure turned her head slightly, refusing to look him in the eye.

Axis' mouth thinned and he reined Belaguez to a halt some four or five paces beyond his commanders. He forced Azhure from his mind and lifted his eyes.

Borneheld sat at the head of his army five hundred paces away as it lay huddled about Bedwyr Fort and the sharp elbow of the Nordra where it turned south towards its mouth into the Sea of Tyrre.

Today Axis would give Borneheld his last chance to back down, to agree to join Axis in fighting against Gorgrael. Of course, Axis sincerely hoped that Borneheld would elect to fight him instead, for Borneheld still had to die, and Axis preferred it to be as a result of battle rather than cold-blooded murder. Yet . . . yet . . . Borneheld could not die here on the field. If Faraday wasn't present then the GateKeeper's contract could not be fulfilled.

"Come," he said to Belial and Magariz, and spurred Belaguez forward. Behind them rode Arne, carrying the golden standard, the wind whipping and crackling the material so that the blazing sun actually seemed to spit and hiss like an angry fire.

None of the men were armed, and all were unhelmeted.

As Axis and the three who accompanied him rode across the open field between the two armies, a small group of horsemen broke away from Borneheld's army and rode to meet them.

As the two small groups of horsemen approached each other Rivkah kicked her horse forward and joined Azhure. Their eyes were glued to Axis' retreating form.

"Have you told him yet?" she asked.

Azhure shook her head. "He does not need to know, Rivkah. He has too much to worry him at the moment for me to add to his concerns."

"He has *every* right to know, Azhure. How can you deny him this knowledge?"

Azhure turned to Rivkah, angry now. "I understand your concern, Rivkah, but this a problem for myself and Axis. After the battle for Tencendor has been won, then I will tell him."

Rivkah shook her head, her face lined with worry. What was *Axis* planning to do about Azhure and Faraday? He was as touchy on the subject as Azhure was about her pregnancy.

Slowly the two groups of horsemen converged. It is Gundealga Ford all over again, thought Belial as he reined his horse back to a trot, except the purpose of this meeting is to declare the truce null and void — and to make sure everyone understands this fight will be to the death. Finally Axis and Borneheld's bitter feud would reach its bloody conclusion.

Axis and Borneheld halted some seven or eight paces apart and stared into each other's eyes. Axis' blood-red cloak flapped about his golden tunic, Borneheld wore a regal golden circlet above his gleaming bronzed WarLord's armour. What would this world have been like, Belial wondered suddenly, if only one and not the other had been born? Both were largely what they were because of the rivalry between them. Would Borneheld have been so hostile to the Forbidden if Axis had not led them? So full of doubts if he did not have the golden rivalry of his brother to overshadow him? Would Axis have been so willing to subject Achar to civil war if Borneheld had not been King? So desperate to reach Faraday if she had not been Borneheld's wife?

"Well, brother," Axis said, "it seems the time for treaties and truces has well and truly died."

"Have you made your peace with your dark and male-volent gods, Axis?" Borneheld sneered. "Shortly you will meet with them face to face."

Axis forced a smile to his face, and watched as Borneheld's own face darkened in anger. "Brother, I have asked to meet you this one last time to offer to you again the chance to fight under my command so that we may both repel the invader."

"*You* are the invader, Axis," Borneheld sputtered angrily. "And *I* am here to repel you."

"Then it is war, brother? You would prefer that I now move to complete your humiliation?" Axis broadened his smile. "Borneheld, surely you realise that I now control more of Achar than you do?"

"I see the standards of the traitors Ysgryff and Greville flying in the ranks behind you, Axis. What did you offer them to make them renege on their duty to their King and to their god?" Borneheld snarled.

Each new example of traitorous activity drove Borneheld close to despair, and none so much as Ysgryff and Greville's defection. Why was Artor betraying him like this? Artor? Artor? Do you still listen, Artor? Are you still *there*?

Over the past weeks Borneheld's nightmares had got so bad that he hardly dared lay his head down at night. The evil-eyed black-haired witch, a-waiting at her counting table, appeared night after night, beckoning to him with her long white fingers.

Sometimes she held out a begemmed chalice, brimming with water.

During the day Jayme, as his advisers, bolstered Borneheld's conviction and his belief in himself, but Borneheld
wondered if their consciences troubled them late into the
night too. And well might they desperately try to bolster my
courage and belief, Borneheld thought cynically, because I
am all that now stands between them and disaster. My army is
the only thing that stands between Axis and the Tower of the
Seneschal. Even Jayme has laid aside his ill-temper in the face
of Axis' army.

"Ysgryff and Greville came willingly to my cause," Axis
said, noting the dark shadows under Borneheld's grey eyes.
"As did all my army. Every one at my back loves me,
Borneheld, and loves my cause. Can you say the same? *I* do
not have to hire men to fight for me."

Borneheld relaxed on his horse. At least this Axis did not
know. "I have concluded an alliance with the Corolean
Emperor, Axis. Hourly there arrive ships from Coroleas
bringing me reinforcements. If you think to attack me, Axis,
then delay not. Each day, each hour you wait, adds to my
strength."

The only indication of Axis' surprise was a slight
tightening of his hands about Belaguez's reins. An alliance
with Coroleas? Axis had long feared this. The Corolean
Empire had massive resources in both gold and manpower –
if Axis did not defeat Borneheld quickly and decisively, then
he could be bogged down in southern Achar in a disastrous
war of attrition for months to come. Not only was there the
GateKeeper's contract to fulfil, but Axis also worried deeply
about Gorgrael and his continuing development of the
Skraelings. Every day Axis wasted in southern Achar brought
the likelihood of disaster in the north closer. Axis glanced
behind Borneheld. Jorge and Gautier had accompanied him
to meet with Axis – but if Jorge and Gautier were in Carlon,
who was left to effectively command the defences at Jervois
Landing?

And what had Borneheld offered the Emperor for a military alliance?

Borneheld could read the query on Axis' face as soon as it crossed his mind.

"Nor, brother. I offered him Nor."

"Well, I hope the Emperor does not lust too badly for Nor. He shall not have it." Axis' smile had gone completely now.

"I doubt we have much else to say to each other, Axis," Borneheld said, and wheeled his horse away.

"Wait!" Axis' voice was sharp. "There is someone waiting behind who wants to speak with you."

Borneheld pulled his horse up and turned as a lone figure spurred its horse forward from the front ranks of Axis' army.

"Someone you have wanted to meet for a very long time," Axis added.

A silver-haired woman drew close, slowing her horse. She was very handsome, fine-boned. Borneheld's frown deepened.

"Rivkah," Axis said, smiling at her, and Borneheld literally lurched in his saddle with shock. "Our mother wants to speak with you, Borneheld. She wants to see you once more before you die."

Rivkah walked her horse over to Borneheld and slowly reached out and touched his cheek. Her face was impassive.

"*Mother?*" Borneheld whispered. Now she was closer he did not doubt that this was his mother. She had Priam's eyes, and her face was an older version of the portrait of her he had in his apartments. Her memory was almost as important to him as was his devotion to Artor. And now here she sat before him, her fingers running gently down his cheek, her face expressionless, her grey eyes cool.

"Borneheld," Rivkah said. "I had wondered what my eldest had made of himself. Now here he sits before me." He was the image of Searlas, she thought, and abruptly she shivered.

As Rivkah remembered how much she loathed his father, her fingers, once gentle, now pinched Borneheld's cheek sharply, and he pulled away in shock. Rivkah's eyes had hardened and narrowed so that her gaze was now flinty and angry.

"You murdered my brother, Borneheld!"

"You abandoned me to a cruel and heartless childhood, Mother," he retorted, trying to turn the accusations against her. "How could you have done that?"

"Easily," Rivkah said. "*I* was the one trapped in cruelty and heartlessness. I never cared for you or your father and I revelled in the chance to make a life for myself, a new family, among others."

"Then be not surprised that I have turned out to be the man I am," Borneheld said, gaunt and shadowed. "Be not surprised that I have done the things I have done."

Everyone listening stiffened in shock. Was this an admission of guilt regarding Priam's death?

"If you do not like what you see before me, then blame yourself. I was not the one who ran away to let me grow unrestrained and unloved in a cold household."

"I did not abandon you in quite the way you seem to think, Borneheld," Rivkah said finally. "I was forced from your side to give birth to Axis in a cold and cheerless room. Then my newborn son was hurried from my side and my ears filled with the lie that he was dead. I was dragged, desperate and bleeding, to die on the slopes of the Icescarp mountains. Borneheld, why don't you ask Jayme and Moryson how I got there? And Borneheld, please pass on to them my wish that we soon meet. There is a small matter of attempted murder that must surely weigh heavily on their minds. Perhaps, before they die, they might wish to confess to both me and their god." Her face was cold.

"No," Borneheld whispered. He did not want to be forced to believe the lie that Axis had told him at Gundealga Ford. He did *not* want to believe that Jayme and Moryson were guilty of trying to murder his mother. But they had planned other murders with ease, had they not?

"I have no doubt that they are men easy with murder, Borneheld," Axis said. "Are *you* safe from their plots?"

Borneheld gave a wordless cry and wrenched the head of his horse about. "You ask if it is war, brother? It has *always* been war between us, and I long for the moment when your death puts an end to our rivalry and hatred!"

For a long agonising moment he stared at Rivkah, then he booted his horse and galloped back towards his army.

Gautier turned after him, but Jorge hesitated.

"Princess Rivkah," he said, bowing slightly in his saddle. "I am well pleased to see that you survive and look so well." He turned back to Axis and spoke but one word. "Roland?"

"Roland is as well as can be expected. He rests easily at Sigholt."

"Ah," Jorge said, his eyes far away, then they refocused on Axis. "Axis, if I do not survive this battle, will you tell him that I have valued his friendship above all else during the past few years?"

Axis stared at the Earl of Avonsdale. "Jorge, why don't you join me? You have heard Borneheld. The man is either mad or a murderer, and quite probably both."

Jorge thought of his family, his daughters and son and their children. If he spurred his horse to join Axis they would all be dead by morning.

"Ah," Axis said. "Does Borneheld now have to take hostages to ensure the support of his commanders?"

Jorge's eyes filled with tears. "I wish you well, Axis. That is a strange thing to say to the commander of an opposing force, is it not? But I do wish you well, Axis."

"And I you, Jorge," Axis said. "And I you."

52

Battle Eve

"All lies, Borneheld," Jayme said soothingly. "All lies. Axis probably now wields sorcerer's powers, certainly if he now reads minds as easily as you suggest. How much effort would it take for him to conjure a vision and attach it to some strange woman's face? Now, now, Borneheld. Be calm. Think rationally."

Jayme looked over at Moryson standing patiently across the room. Both men, as the larger number of the Brotherhood, had taken permanent refuge in the palace in Carlon. That Jayme had been forced to virtually abandon the Tower of the Seneschal to Axis' army appalled him. The remaining cohort of Axe-Wielders surrounded the Tower, but Jayme doubted they could hold out for long against the forces arrayed before them.

But that was not Jayme's current concern. Borneheld had come back from his foolish meeting with Axis in a dither about some woman who claimed to be Rivkah.

Jayme squared his shoulders and stared at Borneheld. The man had succumbed to an attack of conscience. Artor damn him! Jayme thought savagely. Why develop a conscience at this late stage of his life?

"Majesty," Moryson said, stepping forward from his corner. "I can only echo what Jayme has said. Why believe a man who is undoubtedly in league with demons? What has he done for you to trust him? Betray you at Gorkenfort? Send his flying monstrosities to worry you at Jervois Landing? Seduce away some of your most senior – if unreliable – commanders? Why trust a man like that?"

Borneheld looked at Moryson, desperate to believe him. Moryson's open face and clear blue eyes, his habitually mild expression and soft voice reassured him a little.

"Always before the dawn is the darkest hour," Moryson continued. "Now is your darkest hour, Borneheld. Artor waits to see if you are capable of leading Achar and the Seneschal through it. Borneheld." Moryson stepped close now and laid a calming hand on the King's shoulder. "I bless the luck which brought you to our aid at this moment. Who else could lead us through?"

Well, Borneheld, Jayme thought as he watched Moryson pat the man soothingly on the shoulder, you only live because we cannot find the man to replace you. As yet, my King, we still need you, although I fear that we made a grave mistake in elevating you to such a powerful position. Oh Artor, perhaps we should simply have continued with Priam? The man was a fool, but generally manageable.

A feeling of peace and tranquillity flooded through Borneheld. Yes, Moryson and Jayme were right. How could he have listened to Axis? The man was evil to the core.

Gautier, silent while Moryson and Jayme had reasoned with Borneheld, now stepped forward. "Sire. I have some thoughts regarding our plan of action on the morrow."

"Yes?" Borneheld asked. It was late, but he did not want to go to sleep. "A plan?"

"Let me explain . . ." Gautier began.

In another corner of the palace Faraday sat silent while Yr brushed out her hair.

"I can feel Jack, Ogden and Veremund," Yr said. "They are close. Soon we will be reunited." She put the brush down.

"Although what the four of us can do I do not know. With Zeherah absent, lost, the Prophecy will undoubtedly fail."

Faraday stood and walked over to the window overlooking Grail Lake. Far away, so far distant that she could almost not see it, she could discern the flickering points of light which marked the first ranks of Axis' camp.

Since she returned from the Grove Faraday had been consumed with worry about Axis' feelings for her. He had *hesitated* when she'd asked if he still loved her. Even then he had really only said he desired her. Faraday's eyes filled with tears. Borneheld had *desired* her, and that desire had brought only pain and hate. She wanted to be *loved* before anything else.

"I thought he loved me," she said, her eyes on the camp.

Yr put a comforting hand on Faraday's bare shoulder. "Faraday, sweet heart," Yr began softly. "He has been away a long time. You have both grown in different directions. Axis has become an Icarii Enchanter – no longer is he the Battle-Axe you fell in love with. And no longer are you the girl who stared at him so innocently in the Chamber of the Moons. I have no doubt Axis was astounded to find *you* so changed. Sweeting, perhaps all you both need is a little peace to get to know each other again. After all, what time have you ever managed to spend alone? What time *have* you had to get to know each other? Fear not, Faraday. Your time awaits you."

"Do you think so, Yr?" Faraday turned to the Sentinel, hope illuminating her green eyes. "Do you really think so?" What Yr said made sense. Both Axis and she had undergone their own transformations – but they could soon learn to re-love each other.

Another watched the distant camp fires that night as he paced the rooftops of the palace of Carlon. Timozel seethed with fury and resentment. Battle loomed on the morrow and Borneheld insisted he remain behind – *remain behind!* – to guard Faraday lest some feathered evil try to carry her off.

I am the man of vision, Timozel thought furiously, pacing back and forth across the rooftops, *I* am the one Artor has indicated should lead the battle on the morrow!

A great and glorious battle and the enemy's positions were overrun – to the man (and others stranger who fought shoulder to shoulder with them) the enemy died. Timozel lost not one soldier.

"Me!" Timozel muttered and stopped abruptly, his dark cloak swirling about him. "*Me!*"

Remarkable victories were his for the taking.

And yet thin-faced Gautier would ride at Borneheld's side, but not Timozel.

"You will lose if you do not let me fight for you," Timozel said, more calmly now. "Lose. Stay behind yourself, Borneheld, and let me command Gautier and your army. *I* am the man of vision. *I* am the man of victory!"

But were his visions wrong? Misleading? Had he misinterpreted them? Was Borneheld, the fool, not the Great Lord for whom he would win so many victories?

His name would live in legend forever.

"Yes!" Timozel muttered ecstatically.

Axis sat, smiling, before the dancing fire, bouncing Caelum on his knee. Every day his son grew more fascinating than the day before. He was talking in short sentences now, and crawling about whenever he got the chance. Only this morning Axis had been forced to rescue him from beneath Belaguez's agitated hooves.

"Caelum," Axis whispered into his son's ear, and brushed back the child's mop of unruly black curls.

"Papa!" Caelum cried, and then shrieked with laughter as Axis began to tickle his stomach and back.

Azhure, sitting to one side, looked on and couldn't help but smile. Axis, glancing up, reached across and took her hand. "Azhure, let us not go into battle distanced as we have been. Do you want to reconsider your decision to stay with me?"

"No," she said softly. "I do not want to reconsider my decision, Axis. But I fear it. I fear the future very much."

"Mama!" Caelum reached out both arms for Azhure. "Azhure!"

Caelum had never called Azhure by her given name previously, and Azhure laughed in sheer delight, dropping Axis' hand to lift their son into her arms. "Azhure!" Caelum cried again, and spoke to his mother with his mind as well. *I will never forget your name.*

Azhure's eyes filled with tears as she hugged Caelum.

"Why should he say that?" Axis asked. Caelum's words had sounded in a faint echo through his mind as well.

Caelum turned and regarded his father solemnly with his great blue eyes. *Because Azhure has forgotten her mother's name, she fears that one day I shall forget hers. She fears that as we both live on far past her own lifespan we will forget her name as her bones crumble into distant memory.*

Axis' mouth dropped open, astounded both by the length of his son's thought and by his perception, and he lifted his eyes to Azhure. Was that what was wrong?

"Faraday will live with you, Axis," Azhure said. "You will both live into legend, as will Caelum. Eventually you will forget me. Am I mentioned by the Prophecy? No. Yet Faraday is the wife who will hold her husband's slayer in joy at night."

"By all the gods that walk the distant paths of the stars, Azhure, *I will never forget you! I swear it!*"

Nor will I forget, Caelum whispered into her mind. *Nor I.*

"It is why I fear the future with you, Axis," Azhure said. "Because, in the end, I will not share the future of either you or my son. Faraday will, but I will not."

Caelum turned an accusing eye on his father. *Who is this Faraday?*

"You may say now that you love me, Axis, and that Faraday must share you with me. But in short years she will have you all to herself. Will she accept me? Why not? She knows she will probably outlive me by hundreds of years. She controls almost as much power as you do. And if I have learned one thing over these past two years, it is that use of such power extends life far beyond what is considered usual in Achar."

A step behind Axis made them all start. Belial squatted by Axis, knowing as he did so that he was intruding. "Axis, Ho'Demi wants to speak with you, as does FarSight. Can you join us? Azhure? We need to speak about tomorrow."

"You go ahead, Axis," Azhure said flatly. "I'll give Caelum to Rivkah and then join you."

Axis caught her hand as she rose. "We'll talk later, Azhure."

"Yes," Azhure said, knowing that there would be no time later. Not this battle eve. "Yes, we'll talk later."

Far to the south, eight massive Corolean transport ships, carrying almost five thousand men, approached the mouth of the Nordra River at Nordmuth.

"From Nordmuth we'll be able to row to Bedwyr Fort by dawn," the first mate of the lead ship remarked to his captain.

"Good," the captain grunted. "Borneheld has promised me a fat bonus if we reach him two hours before dawn. I suggest if you want your slice of it you go down to the oarsmen and make sure that they understand it's *certain* death for them if they do not put their backs into it."

The first mate chuckled with his master and patted the pilot on the back as he prepared to go below deck. "Make sure you do not run us atop any sandbars, my friend. I have gambling debts that need resolving."

The pilot grimaced. "My eyes shall not leave the waters before us. I have no wish to be stuck atop a sandbar with yourself and your captain for company."

Of course, it might have been helpful if the Corolean transports had posted guards at the stern of the ships as well, for there was more in the dark of the night at their backs than they had bargained for.

53

The Battle of Bedwyr Fort

They stood around the camp fire in the dark hours before dawn, sipping hot tea sweetened to calm nervous stomachs.

"How do you feel, about to go into battle against your own countrymen?" FarSight CutSpur asked Belial and Magariz.

"None of us like it, FarSight, but what can we do? Besides," Magariz's dark face relaxed a little, "most of my countrymen stand with Axis, not Borneheld. Of Borneheld's forces, some half, perhaps even more, are Coroleans."

Belial nodded and sipped his tea. "At least. It's some consolation that Borneheld must bolster his forces with foreign troops. Axis, do you know if the remaining cohort of Axe-Wielders fight with Borneheld?"

That was what Belial most feared, coming face to face with a friend on the battle-field.

"They are still at the tower," Axis said. He was dressed, as were all about the camp fire, in light armour over tunic and breeches. The blood-red sun blazed from his chest plate. "The eagle flew over the tower late yesterday evening and the Axe-Wielders were still there then. I doubt Borneheld will use them. No doubt the Brother-Leader will want to hold on to what remains of his Axe-Wielders for his own defence."

He looked about the camp fire. All the major commanders had joined him, and they represented the variety of races and beliefs who had, over the past twenty months, swung behind his standard. Belial and Magariz, his most senior commanders – the men who'd brought him the core of his army. FarSight CutSpur, senior commander of the Icarii Strike Force, with two of his Crest-Leaders, HoverEye BlackWing and Spread-Wing RavenCry. Ho'Demi, looking alien and exotic with his tattooed face, a collection of knives and swords bristling from his leather armour. He had tied his long black braids back today so that an enemy could not use them as a hand-hold, but they were as full of blue and green glass and chimes as ever. Ho'Demi stood close to Baron Ysgryff, who had abandoned his silks and damasks for the full armour of his force of mounted knights. His helmet was still lying on the ground to one side, but otherwise Ysgryff was fully capari-soned in metal armour, burnished and bright, and bearing the baronial crest of his family. The Baron looked both comfortable and dangerous in his armour.

Azhure stood with a light coat of chain mail over her tunic. Her hair, too, was tightly bound back, and covered with a close leather cap. The Wolven and a quiver of arrows were slung over her back, and at her feet lay Sicarius, the rest of the Alaunt lying a few paces beyond the light of the fire. Even the dogs wore light chain mail. Axis hoped they would be one of his most potent weapons this day. A surprise for Borneheld.

Axis' eyes flickered back to Azhure, trying to catch her eye. They had not found the time to resolve their problems last night. Axis had stayed late talking with senior and unit commanders, and Azhure had been busy with her archers. When he'd returned to their bedrolls, he'd found her asleep.

Caelum was with Rivkah, safe with the supply wagons far to the rear and with several reserve units to guard them. If the battle went badly, their orders were to take the wagons and flee to the Silent Woman Woods – the Woods would protect the remnants of Axis' family and force against any-thing Borneheld could throw at them.

Azhure, I love you.

And for how long?

Axis flinched a little. *Stay safe today.*

And you, Axis. And you.

"Borneheld has his forces grouped about Bedwyr Fort," Axis said to the group. "He will not come to us, but will wait for us to attack him."

"Will Borneheld conduct the battle from the fort?" Ho'Demi asked.

"No," Axis answered. "No, I do not think so. Bedwyr Fort is old and full of holes. It was once vital for the protection of Achar, guarding the approaches to Carlon and Grail Lake, but over the past several generations it has been left to decay. Its main defences and fortifications face the river, not the plains, and it will be vulnerable to Icarii attack. No, I think Borneheld will fight with his men. My friends . . ." Axis paused, and the group about the fire looked at him.

"I have a request. No. An order." He looked up and all could see that his eyes burned strangely. "Borneheld must *not* die on the battlefield today."

"*What?*" Ysgryff exclaimed. Axis had told him about Borneheld's promise to the Coroleans and he was appalled. Borneheld meant to give the Corolean Emperor the province of Nor?

"I cannot say much, but I have certain obligations, both towards the Prophecy and towards other . . . allies . . . who have given me aid. Borneheld can only die with Faraday present."

Azhure stiffened. Kill Borneheld before Faraday? What could Axis be thinking of?

"I cannot say why," Axis said, aware of Azhure's shock. "But believe me when I say it is important. Faraday must still be in Carlon – even Borneheld would not haul her out to the battlefield, so I have no doubt that eventually I must chase Borneheld back to the royal palace in Carlon itself. Understand?"

Axis was clearly ordering, not requesting, and all nodded stiffly.

Belial broke the awkward silence that had descended. "Borneheld has chosen badly to fight about Bedwyr Fort. He will have himself and his army trapped in the triangle of land between the Lake, the river and our army."

"Perhaps, perhaps not," Axis replied. "If extra Corolean transports sail up the river – and I believe that late last night there were some eight approaching Nordmuth – then they can easily disgorge their load behind *our* lines once we move in to attack Borneheld. We will have to be careful. Watchful. Far-Sight, are your farflight scouts keeping an eye on the river?"

FarSight nodded. "They are already in the air, Strike-Leader."

"Then today we reforge Tencendor. After today, I hope, Gorgrael will be my only enemy."

And WolfStar? he thought. Where are you? What do you plan this day? What surprises will *you* spring?

FarSight nodded. "Today we fight to restore Tencendor. It will be a great day, Axis. A great day."

Axis stared at the Senior Crest-Leader. "Then perhaps it is time to launch your strike, FarSight. Time to loose the Icarii Strike Force on Borneheld of Achar."

Axis intended to use the Strike Force on Borneheld's army as he had used it in the passes of the Bracken Ranges against Burdel. But Borneheld's army had a large number of soldiers who had seen battle at Jervois Landing – and who had seen the Icarii Strike Force in action against the Skraelings. Watch had been kept for the Icarii Strike Force, and even though they were not spotted until they were virtually upon the army, as soon as the cry went up, "Ware! Above!", men reached for shields in a well-practised manoeuvre and raised them above their heads, creating a ceiling of steel over the tightly grouped ranks of Borneheld's army.

Some were not fast enough and some did not keep their shields close enough together, but overall the Icarii strike did not have the same devastating effect on Borneheld's army as it had had on Burdel's force.

Borneheld had arranged his army in much the same manner as he had his defences at Jervois Landing. Most units were well dug into trenches that would, Borneheld hoped, direct the flow of Axis' army into traps and trenches that would break the legs of their horses and, eventually, the hearts of their riders. Numerically his army was some five to eight thousand less than Axis' army, but Borneheld knew he had the advantage of being the defender.

Borneheld, relatively safe in a hastily erected command tent (well protected from above with several layers of thick canvas) surveyed the maps of his defences one more time.

"The transports?" he asked Gautier. Both men, as all within the command tent, were heavily armoured and weaponed.

"They sailed through Nordmuth late last night, Sire," Gautier replied instantly. "And they are currently anchored on the Nordra midway between Bedwyr Fort and Nordmuth awaiting your orders."

"And the smaller boats?" Borneheld said

"Ready to sail, Sire," Gautier replied. "Axis will die today, along with his malformed crew."

"I surely hope so," Borneheld began, then stopped and listened, his entire body tense. "What is that?"

A sound like heavy rain permeated the command tent.

Gautier listened. "It is the sound of the Forbidden's arrows raining uselessly down on the shield ceiling covering your troops."

Borneheld clenched his fists and pumped them into the air. "It has begun!" he shouted, his eyes bright.

All he felt was relief. At last, the end to his rivalry with his brother.

The Battle of Bedwyr Fort began with the Icarii Strike Force attack on Borneheld's army and dragged its bloody way through the day. For hours men – and women – fought and died until the western Plains of Tare were stained bright with the blood of the dead and the dying.

Axis had been disappointed but not overly surprised by the relative failure of the Icarii Strike Force to cripple Borneheld's army. Borneheld was a far superior commander to Burdel and he also had the benefit of having watched the Icarii Strike Force in action above Jervois Landing. As the Strike Force flew back over Axis' lines – there were no casualties apart from one birdman who had suffered a crippling wing cramp and had fallen to his death among the Corolean soldiers – Axis began to move his mounted units forward. He already knew about Borneheld's trenches and traps, and was wary of moving his mounted units too deep into the lines of trenches; Ysgryff's mounted knights he kept to the rear to use only if he could tempt Borneheld's soldiers out of their trenches.

It would have to be a combination attack on the front trenches by mounted men, foot soldiers – both spearmen and pikemen – and the Icarii Strike Force. The entrenched soldiers would not be able to maintain their shield defences against the Icarii *and* repel a ground attack as well.

In the end Axis did as he had against the Skraelings in the WildDog Plains. Rather than move against the entire line of trenches, Axis made small, concentrated attacks from both ground and air forces. He chose his sites carefully, surveying the system of trenches from above through the eagle's eyes, and attacking those areas he thought would later provide vulnerable holes in Borneheld's front lines.

At those sites Axis selected, initially some nine, he sent the mounted archers in first, protected by the Strike Force. Both the mounted archers, whether those under Azhure's command or Ravensbund archers, and the Icarii archers let loose their arrows – and up would go the shield defences. As soon as the troops were committed to maintaining their shields above their heads – and the shields were so large and heavy it took two arms to do it – Axis would send in the spearmen and pikemen . . . and the Alaunt.

The Alaunt had been instructed by Azhure to go for the commanders. At each point of attack three or four Alaunt would spring into the trenches, unerringly leaping for the throats of the two or three senior commanders within the immediate area. They created confusion and sometimes hysteria; not only did they kill the commanders within moments of entering the trenches, but their snarling and snapping confused and terrified the soldiers. Shields dropped as men reached for swords to deal with the hounds, and as shields dropped arrows rained down from above, and spearmen and pikemen closed the gap between their ranks and the trenches and thrust their weapons into the muddle of leaderless soldiers.

Always the Alaunt leapt out of the trenches the instant before the arrows, spears and pikes flashed down. Always they leapt out unharmed.

They had the devil's own luck.

It was a slow and cumbersome method of attack, but by mid-morning Borneheld could clearly see that one by one, the front trenches were collapsing. It might take a day, even two, but Axis would eventually work his way through the entire trench system.

"We can't defend ourselves from simultaneous attack from above and ground-level," Borneheld growled. "Why doesn't the damn coward send his entire force to attack us?"

It was clear that Axis was determined to win this battle, and he wasn't going to win it by leading his army into a death trap.

"We have no choice," Borneheld finally said. "If Axis will not come to me, then I will have to go to him. I want this resolved today. Today." He turned to Gautier. "Send the orders, Gautier. Mount up. This battle will be fought one against one across the plains of Tare."

"The Icarii?" Gautier asked, so forgetting himself he gave the Forbidden their correct name.

Borneheld buckled his helmet on. "They will be dangerous only while we ride through the trenches to meet Axis. Once our forces meet and mingle, they will not dare to loose their arrows below. No, Gautier, this will be a one-on-one battle of attrition. The last one left standing wins." Borneheld paused. "And your reserves, Gautier?"

"Ready to go, Sire, as planned."

Borneheld's eyes were cold. "Then perhaps we *will* win, after all. Send a message to the Corolean transports to start to move a little closer to Bedwyr Fort – but not too close. I want them in position to loose their soldiers behind Axis' lines."

Gautier bowed. "Sire."

It was, as Borneheld predicted, a battle of attrition.

For hours the two armies melded and fought entwined, knights, foot soldiers, spearmen, pikemen, archers, swordsmen. It was the largest battle any present had ever been engaged in; some fifty-five thousand men and women, all determined their side should win the day. All sense of time fled for those engaged in the heat of the battle; it was simply strike, withdraw, take a deep breath, defend, strike, withdraw, take a deep breath, defend, strike – and kill or be killed.

Axis fought in the thick of the battle, Arne always close at his back, his golden standard flying high above the field. Sometimes Axis found himself fighting beside a common soldier whose name he did not know, sometimes beside Ysgryff, sometimes by the side of Ho'Demi, sitting his horse with ease and confidence, sometimes by the side of either Belial or Magariz, both fighting smoothly and efficiently, faces grim with concentration. All, even Axis, took small wounds.

Axis eventually let Belaguez's reins drop, guiding the horse by pressure of knee, by voice, and sometimes by thought. He wielded his sword with two hands, striking to the left and the right, and trusted Arne to cover his back. Above him Far-Sight had detailed two Wing to watch over Axis exclusively.

Azhure's mounted archers were largely engaged at the edges of the battle, moving quickly to where they were most needed, driving their arrows cleanly to where they would do most damage. Axis could feel her, feel her excitement at battle, and he tried not to worry too much for her. Azhure was perfectly capable of looking after herself.

Sometimes Axis caught a glimpse of Borneheld's standard, but he did not try to fight his way through to it. Their battle would not take place on this field.

It was a relatively evenly matched battle. Axis' army outnumbered Borneheld's, but they were also slightly travel-wearied. For hours they fought backwards and forwards, the tide shifting this way and then that – but always men died or were crippled to lie screaming under hooves steel-edged with terror. Above and about all stirred thick, choking dust.

By mid-afternoon every muscle in Axis' body ached. How long had they been fighting? He took a quick glance at the sun and almost paid for it with his life as a sword suddenly arced down from his left. It was stopped only inches from the juncture of his neck and shoulder by the quick action of Arne, and Axis heard him grunt in satisfaction as he sliced the Corolean swordsman's arm from his body. The man screamed and fell from his horse.

Axis took a moment to catch his breath. He knew almost nothing except what was happening in the small circle about him, and he desperately needed to know the overall state of battle.

"Arne, watch over me," he muttered, and his eyes drifted out of focus as he looked down over the field through the eagle's eyes.

What he saw appalled him. Countless men lay dead and dying. How many? Thousands, at the least, and they wore the emblems and uniforms of both Borneheld's men and his. As with men, so with horses. There were thousands of riderless horses, some dying and kicking out their life in great gouts on the ground, others running wild-eyed with fear through the chaos. Suddenly he spotted Azhure, Sicarius running at the heels of Venator, leading a squad of her archers into battle at the northern edge of the mass of seething soldiers. She was unharmed, although she swayed with exhaustion.

Be strong, Azhure, he whispered into her mind, *stay safe.*

She hesitated as his thought reached her, and Axis cursed himself for a fool. She could not afford to be distracted – for any distraction might easily kill her – but in the next instant an arrow flashed from the Wolven, and Sicarius leaped for the throat of a foot soldier who thought to thrust his spear into her side.

As he gazed across the field Axis thought he could see more of his men left standing than Borneheld's, and Borneheld's standard looked like it was being forced, step by step, back towards the trenches.

Is the day mine? he wondered. Will another hour or two see this bloody and senseless civil war finished once and for all?

But then the eagle drifted a little further out over the battlefield and Axis saw something that appalled him.

Eight massive Corolean transports were moving inexorably towards Bedwyr Fort. How many men did they carry, Axis wondered desperately, how many? Four or five thousand, at the least, and four or five thousand fresh men would swing the battle Borneheld's way. They had been fighting now since the break of dawn – nine hours – and many of his men were succumbing through exhaustion rather than lack of skill or lack of will to fight on. Five thousand fresh men?

"Stars save us," Axis muttered, and Arne glanced at him, worried.

Another movement caught Axis' eyes. As well as the transport ships, smaller barges, packed with Corolean soldiers, were moving along the southern edges of the Grail Lake and the Nordra above Bedwyr Fort, moving to outflank Axis' army, attack from the rear. There were perhaps fifteen, containing some two and a half thousand men – enough to prop up those areas where Borneheld's force was beginning to fail.

Azhure! Ho'Demi! Those two were the only commanders who Axis knew he could reach with his mind. *Look to the waters to the north! Stop those men before they can join the fray!*

Axis watched as gradually Azhure and Ho'Demi rallied their units, and directed them to the shoreline where the barges were disgorging their loads. Axis desperately looked about for the Strike Force. They had been hovering over the battlefield all day, doing what they could. Finally he spotted FarSight and sent the eagle reeling in his direction.

"Ware to the north!" the eagle screamed as it flashed past FarSight, and FarSight sent five Crest of Icarii winging to Azhure and Ho'Demi's aid.

That should stop the barges, Axis thought desperately, but what about the transports? If they manage to land their soldiers then I am finished!

Even though the battle had closed about him again, Axis continued to watch through the eagle's eyes, relying on Arne to protect him. He had to watch – for those transports meant the death of his hopes and the death of the Prophecy.

Bleeding from numerous small wounds, his sword hanging limp from his hand, Borneheld also watched the ships with worried eyes. What were they doing this close to Bedwyr Fort? He had sent clear instructions that they were to disgorge their soldiers much further south so that, together with the barges to the north, Borneheld could attack both flanks of the battlefield with fresh soldiers.

"By Artor!" Borneheld swore, "you'd think they were intent on attacking us rather than Axis."

An awful premonition gripped him, and his voice dropped to a horrified whisper. "Is this *more* infernal treachery? Has the Corolean Emperor forsaken our agreement and turned against me?"

Almost as one the Corolean transports dropped anchor by the banks of the Nordra and dropped their landing ramps. Each began to disgorge hundreds of men, hundreds and hundreds of them, running screaming with delight and battle-lust straight towards Borneheld's standard.

Every last one of them a dark-skinned, brightly scarved, gleaming-toothed, scimitar-waving pirate.

"Foul treachery!" Borneheld croaked, then leaped in surprise as Gautier's hand fell on his shoulder.

"Sire!" he gasped. "Treachery! Your safety is compromised. I have a barge waiting – we must seek refuge in Carlon."

"What?" Borneheld yelled. "Leave the field?"

"We have lost the day," Jorge shouted hoarsely, riding to join Borneheld. "If you wish to save yourself, then do so now. I will continue to lead your forces on this bloodied field – to the death if you so order."

Borneheld stared at Jorge and Gautier. The gleeful screams of the pirates were getting uncomfortably close. The next instant he dug his spurs deep into his horse's sides and was galloping towards safety.

All this Axis saw through the eyes of the eagle.

Azhure, Ho'Demi, he called, *Borneheld rides for one of the barges and for escape into Carlon. LET HIM GO! I need him in Carlon. It is VITAL that he escapes to Carlon!*

At the same time that Axis felt the agreement of their minds, the eagle screamed the same order to the Icarii Crests above the northern part of the battlefield: "Let Borneheld escape! It is *vital* that he escapes!"

As the pirates streamed down into the fray Axis turned to see Baron Ysgryff, helmetless now, grinning at him.

"Did you like my surprise, Axis SunSoar?"

Laughing with joy, Axis booted Belaguez next to Ysgryff's horse and, leaning over, seized the man by the top of his tunic as it peeked above the chest plate of his armour.

"I will make you a Prince for this!" he grinned, then, letting Ysgryff go, turned to the men still struggling about him.

"The day is mine!" he screamed, waving his sword in an arc about his head. "Tencendor is mine!"

In an hour it was over. Demoralised by Borneheld's desertion, his army slowly ground to a halt and, as the sun set over the Nordra, Axis took the army's surrender from Jorge, the most senior commander left on the field.

Jorge glanced about the battlefield and noticed as if for the first time the thousands of bodies and the reddened soil. A pointless waste of life, Jorge thought bleakly. Could it have been avoided if Roland and I had found the courage to follow Axis after Gorkenfort? Would our departure have weakened Borneheld to the extent that he would not have had the resources of command experience left to wield an army against Axis?

"He would still have fought," said Axis, and Jorge slowly raised his eyes.

The man's earlier excitement had died, and Jorge could see that exhaustion and sad-heartedness hung heavily over him.

"Jorge," Axis said softly, stepping forward and placing his hand on the man's shoulder. Jorge's eyes filled with tears at the gesture of support. "Jorge, where does Borneheld hold your family?"

Jorge named a small town to the north of Carlon and Axis beckoned to FarSight. "FarSight, can you detail the two Wings you held in reserve to fly to free Jorge's family?"

FarSight nodded and turned away.

Axis turned and stared at Jorge. "Welcome to Tencendor, Jorge."

Jorge nodded wearily. He did not expect to hold a place of high honour within the new order.

54

The Aftermath

The following hours were confusion and chaos.

After accepting the surrender of both Borneheld's army and Borneheld's kingdom, Axis' first priority was to fill the eight Corolean transports with as many of the remaining Coroleans as he could and get them home as quickly as possible. He had no intention of holding thousands of Coroleans prisoner. Let their Emperor take care of them.

"Tell your Emperor, or your Ambassador, or the first whore you come across in Coroleas for all I care," Axis said tiredly to the most senior Corolean he could find, "that I repudiate the treaty Borneheld made with your Empire and that I repudiate all conditions, payments and other varied promises Borneheld may have foolishly made. Go home. I bear you no personal ill will, but I will not stand for your continued presence in my realm."

It was a startling word, "realm"; Axis was mildly surprised at how easily it had slipped past his lips.

The Corolean captain gave a short bow. "May I inform my Emperor that you will be willing to receive his Ambassador at a future date when all," he looked briefly at the darkening carnage about him, "has settled down?"

"As long as he realises that I refuse to pay any of Borneheld's debts."

"I will be sure to tell him," the captain said shortly, then he sketched a salute and wheeled about, walking stiffly up the loading ramp into the nearest transport and wishing he were home already. Too many of his men had died in a cause not their own.

"Belial." Axis turned and leaned briefly on Belial's shoulder. "Belial, can I leave you in charge of the burial pits?" A thankless task, but it needed to be done and it needed to be done fast.

Axis snapped his fingers at the boy holding Belaguez and mounted the stallion when the boy led him over. He rode slowly across the battlefield, stopping now and again to speak to a group of soldiers, or to lend a word of support to one of the wounded being carried towards the physicians' tents. He saw Arne in the distance, detailing guards to watch over the remaining prisoners of Borneheld's army – and there seemed to be thousands of them. What was he going to do with them? Axis thought wearily. They are all Acharites, and all mostly good men who simply found themselves on the wrong side through no fault of their own.

Axis' depression deepened as he rode east across the field of battle. Soldiers were slowly starting to pile the dead – and the piles were both numerous and large. How many thousands had died?

And where was Azhure? Axis' mind was so tired that he could not feel her anywhere, and the eagle had roosted for the night. The darkness closed in about him as he rode, but he continued to peer through the gloom, asking all he came across if they had seen her. Each time a head shook wearily Axis pushed Belaguez further east, searching, until he reached the site where his army had camped the previous night.

He found Rivkah at his personal camp site, Caelum asleep in her arms.

"Azhure?" he asked anxiously, slipping from Belaguez's saddle.

Rivkah nodded towards a blanket-wrapped bundle at her feet and Axis fell to his knees and pulled the blanket back from Azhure's face. She was asleep, her face white, great circles of weariness under her eyes.

"Is she all right?" Axis asked his mother, his hand stroking back the tangled hair from Azhure's forehead.

Rivkah considered a moment. Should she tell him about Azhure's pregnancy? The woman had ridden into the camp an hour before and had simply collapsed in an exhausted heap at Rivkah's feet. It had taken the combined strength of Rivkah and a passing soldier to pull her chain mail off and wrap her in this blanket and Azhure had not stirred once during the procedure. Rivkah knew Azhure was finding this pregnancy a difficult one, and she feared that Azhure was so drained the baby would simply slip from her.

Rivkah finally shrugged. "She is exhausted, but she has no wounds. Perhaps sleep is all she needs."

Axis sat down and took Caelum from his mother's arms.

"He has been awake all day, Axis," Rivkah said quietly, "fretting and crying. He knew that both his parents were in battle, and he seemed to know how desperate the fighting was. He refused to eat or to be comforted until Azhure stumbled back into camp."

She paused. Dare she ask? "And Magariz? Is he well?"

"I have not heard if he is alive or dead, Rivkah," Axis said flatly after a long pause, "as I have not heard about most of my commanders or soldiers. With that you will have to be content."

A servant stepped forward and helped Axis unbuckle his armour. Axis passed the baby back to Rivkah and gratefully let the servant cart the armour away. He literally tore his sweat- and blood-stained tunic from his torso and threw it to one side.

Rivkah noted the wounds across his chest and back, but said nothing. They were not life-threatening and would heal quickly. "Sleep Axis. I will watch over you. You will be able to do nothing until you get some sleep."

Axis wrapped himself in the blanket and lay down beside Azhure. "Two hours, no more," he mumbled. "Wake me after two hours."

Both within and without the palace, Carlon was in confusion. Most of the city folk learnt the outcome of the battle, and many had stood in silence as Borneheld, Gautier and perhaps two dozen men had run through the city gates, ordering them locked and barred.

Two dozen men and one King to defend them? the Carlonese wondered. Carlon, as Achar, is lost.

Courtiers abandoned the palace for discrete townhouses hidden deep within Carlon's twisting streets. Borneheld's court was no place to stay a-visiting now. What would Axis' court be like? Would he find a place for them? Undoubtedly, most consoled themselves. Every King, new, usurped or borrowed, needed a court to keep him wrapped in happy flatteries.

In the streets eyes turned once again to the battlefield, where torches burned as soldiers carried on with the grim task of digging and filling the burial trenches. Of those watching from the city walls, many had lost sons, fathers or husbands – on both sides of the battle, for as many men from Carlon had fought for Axis as had fought for Borneheld.

All in all, the mood along the streets of Carlon was one of sadness and acceptance rather than anger or fright. Like Axis, most regretted that the battle had been fought at all – surely the brothers could have come to some compromise? Now it looked as if Borneheld had lost it all – for Carlon was not designed to withstand siege. It had walls, but virtually no militia to repel an attack or stores to withstand a siege. Carlon was normally a city of fun and laughter, money-making enterprises and sins, not a city destined for the grim realities of battle that now surrounded it.

If the good people of Carlon were resigned to Borneheld's defeat, then Jayme was close to hysteria.

"You have lost the kingdom and you have lost the Seneschal!" he screamed at Borneheld, his habit stained and dirty.

Borneheld sat on his throne in the Chamber of the Moons, drunk. All his dreams? Ambitions? Come to *this* end? What had gone wrong? A flagon of red hung empty and useless from one hand as it dangled over the armrest of the throne – the next moment it was flying through the air towards Jayme's head.

The Brother-Leader managed to duck the flagon and it smashed on the floor behind him.

"All gone," he whispered, appalled at the consequences of the day. "The work of a thousand years gone in one day!"

"I hear you lost, Borneheld," a light voice said from the doorway, and Faraday walked into the Chamber. Borneheld looked away from Jayme and towards his wife. She was resplendent in a deep-emerald velvet gown, her hair piled elegantly on top of her head, diamonds and pearls at her ears and throat. "You look unwell, Borneheld. Should I call the physician? Perhaps you are suffering from whatever ailed Priam."

Borneheld curled his lip; it was the best he could do. "Axis has won through treachery. It is his way. If my kingdom falls apart before me it is simply because I have been betrayed once too often. Nothing remains."

"If your kingdom falls apart around you, husband," Faraday retorted, feeling nothing but scorn for this man who sat before her, "it is because you were never meant to hold it. How long before Axis sits that throne, Borneheld? How long?"

Borneheld lurched forward on the throne, almost falling, he was so drunk. "Whore! How much of this treachery do I owe to you? How many men have you taken to your bed and turned against me? How many times have you betrayed me with Axis?"

Faraday's face twisted in contempt. "*I* have remained true to our vows, husband. Unlike you."

Without giving him the time to reply Faraday swung around and stared at Jayme. "You are a pitiful old man, Jayme. You have lost as much as Borneheld has out there on the battlefield today, you and your god. Do you know, Jayme, that once I believed in Artor fervently? Then I fell under the thrall of the Prophecy and I was introduced to new gods, new powers. Artor means as much to me as does my husband, Jayme. And that is not very much at all."

She turned on her heel and strode from the room.

Jayme trembled. He looked about uselessly for Moryson. But both Moryson and Gilbert had disappeared the moment they realised Borneheld had lost the day.

"Moryson?" Jayme muttered weakly, peering into the shadows. "Moryson?" Oh Artor, why wasn't his friend here *now*? "What are we going to do," he whispered. We? Me. Me, alone. I am alone, save for this drunken mule sitting on the throne of Achar.

Borneheld smiled at him. "What are we going to do, Jayme? Why, have another drink, Brother-Leader. I think you will find a flagon in the cabinet in the far wall."

Out in the corridor Faraday's show of bravado faltered and died.

Faraday knew well what would happen. Somehow, and Faraday did not care about the details for they were un-important, Axis would appear to challenge Borneheld in the Chamber of the Moons. And when he appeared Faraday knew that the dreadful, apocalyptic vision that the trees of the Silent Woman Woods had given her two years previously would be played out in real life.

Even though Faraday believed, desperately wished to believe, that Axis would win – that the trees had shown her only shattered and jumbled images – she clutched at the front of her gown, feeling again Axis' warm blood running down between her breasts.

"Win, Axis, *win!*" she whispered.

As the night passed Rivkah anxiously sat guard over Axis, Azhure and Caelum. Several hours before dawn her fears were finally allayed when Magariz walked into the circle of firelight. Rivkah stood and held him close, tears streaming silently from her eyes.

As tired and as sick at heart as Axis had been, Magariz sank down by the fire, Rivkah gently unbuckling his armour, and, his words stumbling through his exhaustion, he told Rivkah the story of the battle until he fell asleep mid-sentence. Rivkah lowered him gently to the ground and covered him with a blanket.

As she rose from Magariz's side Rivkah noticed a tall, dark Nors girl standing at the edge of the firelight, her bright red dress covered with a tightly clutched cloak. "Belial?" she whispered, her voice hoarse with fear, her blue eyes dark and enormous in the shadows.

Rivkah shook her head. "I have not heard," she said gently.

"Ah," the girl murmured, and turned away. Rivkah stared after her a long time, sorrowing.

As she sat by the fire to watch over the sleepers, heavy with weariness, Rivkah pondered the way of battle and the way of the world. Men fight, and women wait and weep. Rivkah was very, very tired of not having what she wanted. She quietly vowed not to let life or love escape from her again. She would spend the last half of her life in happier circumstances than the first half. This time no-one, not even her son, would keep her from the man she loved.

Finally Rivkah shook Axis awake as instructed, but he was so exhausted he fell straight back into a deep slumber again and she decided to let him sleep through to the dawn. There was nothing that could be done in the middle of the night.

In the cold hour after dawn Axis, Azhure and Magariz sat in silence about the fire, all still with great circles of weariness under their eyes, but all looking infinitely better than they had. Rivkah watched Azhure feed her son. The new baby was still safe, but Rivkah did not know what would have happened if Azhure had been forced to fight any longer.

Axis shared his mother's concern for Azhure. "You will stay in camp today, Azhure," he said quietly. "Tired as you are you will be no use to anyone, least of all your son, if you don't get more sleep."

It was a measure of Azhure's weariness, and her own concerns for her growing baby, that she nodded and cuddled Caelum a little closer. She had wondered, at critical moments during yesterday's battle, if she would ever see Caelum again and she was not yet ready to leave him now.

Magariz raised his head from his hand. "Axis? Where do we start?"

Axis grimaced. "Where do we start, Magariz? We simply stand up from this camp fire and we start walking . . . and then we start where we can. Come."

Axis stood and pulled Magariz to his feet. "Rivkah was worried for you last night," Axis said quietly. "I am glad, not only for her sake, but for mine also, that you are still alive."

It was a simple statement, but deep with meaning. Magariz managed a wan grin. "I am glad for *my* sake that I am still alive," he said, and Axis laughed.

"Come on," he said, pulling Magariz away from the women. "Let us see what sort of a victory we have won."

Somewhat of a hollow one, Axis thought two hours later as he finished receiving reports from his commanders. They had won, but at enormous cost. The Icarii Strike Force had fared best of all, with only minor casualties to stray arrows and three dead to sheer misfortune. Ho'Demi, his face white behind its blue lines, reported that almost fifteen hundred of his Ravensbundmen had lost their lives.

Ysgryff, out of his armour but still dressed for war, was similarly sombre. "A thousand," he said simply when Axis looked at him. "A thousand of my knights, and over three thousand of their horses."

"And the pirates?"

"None," Ysgryff grunted. "Pirates are protected by the gods, it seems, Axis. Besides, they came late into the fray, when their opponents were exhausted."

"Where are they now?"

Ysgryff waved vaguely towards the Nordra. "Waiting for ships to take them home, Axis."

"I cannot thank you enough for those pirates. If they had been Coroleans . . ." Axis shuddered, unable to go on.

"Then we would be counting our dead while awaiting death ourselves, Axis," Ysgryff said quietly. "The pirates will also fight for the Prophecy when it demands it of them, as will most of the people of Nor."

Axis lifted his head and stared at the trampled Plains of Tare. All of the bodies had been buried during the night, but the earth still retained a pinkish tinge. "The Prophecy has friends where I least expect to find them," Axis said slowly. "Nor and the pirates have proved among the greatest."

He sighed and dropped his eyes. Belial, his body stiff with weariness, had joined the group.

"Have you managed any sleep, Belial?"

Belial shrugged. "Two, perhaps three hours. Enough, Axis."

"And our dead?"

Belial knew what Axis meant. How many of the ordinary mounted soldiers had they lost? "Around eleven hundred, Axis. Mostly the inexperienced soldiers who joined us at Sigholt. Some of the militia from Arcen, and some of our own men. Some of our oldest friends among them."

Axis turned away.

"Axis," Belial continued. "Our total losses come to well under four thousand men; Borneheld lost twice that number, Coroleans and Acharites. And Axis, remember, we lost close to . . . what? Seven thousand at Gorkentown? We will recover from this."

"Oh, yes," Axis said, turning back. "We will recover. But what a senseless, useless loss, Belial, and I grieve for every one of the Acharites who lost their lives for Borneheld's cause as I grieve for those men who lost their lives for ours."

"These men fight for you knowing that you care for them," Belial said fiercely. "And I believe we have replacements from a somewhat unexpected source."

Axis frowned. "What do you mean?"

Belial beckoned a man forward. He wore the tattered and blood-stained uniform of Borneheld's army and he walked with a slight limp.

"Lieutenant Bradoke, my Lord," he said, his voice firm but respectful. "I am the most senior of the prisoners. My Lord, we fought for Borneheld because he was the King and because our oaths bound us to him. But none of us liked to see him flee the field yesterday afternoon, and many of us have been discussing the Prophecy around the privacy of our camp fires for weeks now. Last night we talked again. Great Lord, we are at your mercy, but we plead to be allowed to decide our own fate."

"And that is?" Axis asked.

Bradoke took a deep breath. "We would fight for the Prophecy too, Lord. We would join your force. Great Lord," he carried on as he saw Axis about to object. "I have stood to one side and watched you grieve for each and every man who died for you. Borneheld would never have done that for us. We want, *I* want, to be given the chance to fight for you."

Axis glanced at Belial and Belial nodded. Axis looked back at the lieutenant. He seemed sincere, but should Axis trust him? What else can I do, thought Axis, *but* trust him? I cannot afford the men to guard them and I desperately need forces to throw against Gorgrael. He sighed and nodded wearily. "Work out the details with Belial. How many men do you command, Bradoke?"

"Seven thousand, Great Lord."

"By the Stars," Axis said. "How are we going to feed you all?"

"Cheer up, Axis." Ysgryff slapped him heartily on the back. "Carlon will be ours soon, and I'm sure that Carlon can feed us all. Besides, I have supply ships sailing up the Nordra now."

"By the gods, Ysgryff," Axis said weakly, "I might as well just hand the kingdom over to you."

Ysgryff winked. "My ugly head would look ridiculous with a crown on top of it, Axis. Besides, like Ho'Demi, I am committed to the StarMan."

Apart from feeding and resting the troops, then moving his main camp site to the banks of Grail Lake, there was only one other thing that Axis wanted to do that day.

Late in the afternoon he rode with a small escort to the Tower of the Seneschal — Spiredore.

It had been two years since he last saw this tower, but it seemed like yesterday. For thirty years it had been his home and the home of the man he had regarded as his father, Jayme. For thirty years he had believed in the Seneschal and everything it had stood for and for thirty years he had believed that the Tower had stood as the outward manifestation of Artor's love and of the Seneschal's care for the people of Achar.

Now Axis saw the beautiful white tower differently. It was a shining example of the lies and the deceptions that the Seneschal had forced on the people of Achar, and of the cruelty that the Seneschal had plotted and conducted against the people of the Horn and the Wing — the Avar and the Icarii. Once, Axis knew, the Tower of the Seneschal had been Spiredore, one of the magical Keeps of Tencendor, one of the most powerful places in the ancient land.

Now Axis intended to rid the Spiredore of its jailers once and for all.

It rose, as it always had, pristine and white, soaring some one hundred paces into the air, its seven sides gleaming softly in the late afternoon sun. To one side the silver-blue waters of Grail Lake — one of the sacred lakes — twinkled merrily, as if it knew that its friend and companion of so many thousands of years would shortly be released.

What do you hide? Axis asked himself as he rode closer to the tower. What secrets do you have buried within you? What will I find when I throw the Seneschal out?

But of more immediate importance was what the cohort of Axe-Wielders ranged in neat formation before the tower meant to do. Axis waved his escort to a halt and reined Belaguez back to a walk, pulling him to a stop some ten paces from where Kenricke, the commander of this, the final cohort of the Axe-Wielders, sat his horse.

He was a greying man, tall and spare, and his face was unreadable. For a moment Axis' eyes flickered to the twin crossed axes on the man's tunic. How long had he worn that emblem with pride? Now he was dressed in his fawn tunic with the blazing sun. A different world, a different man.

"Kenricke," he said, by way of greeting. "It has been a long time."

Kenricke stared at Axis for a moment then, suddenly, shockingly, he saluted Axis in the manner of the Axe-Wielders, fist across the twin axes on his breast, bowing sharply and crisply from his waist. "Axis," he began, then paused, embarrassed. "I do not know by what title to honour you now."

"Just call me Axis. It is still my name," Axis said.

"Axis. Why are you here? For what purpose have you ridden back to the Tower of the Seneschal?"

"I intend to recreate the world that the Seneschal sought so long to destroy, Kenricke. The tower of Spiredore is an integral part of that world. I come here today to release Spiredore from the Seneschal."

"Many words for a simple purpose, Axis. You intend to throw the Seneschal out," Kenricke replied.

"You always did have a brutal way with words, Kenricke. Will you stand against me?"

Kenricke sat his horse a long time in silence, gazing at Axis, then abruptly he booted his horse forward, drawing his axe out of his belt. Axis tensed a little, but he did not move. Kenricke had been his first master of arms when he had joined the Axe-Wielders as a teenage boy – and he did not think the man would attempt to strike him down.

As his horse drew level with Axis, Kenricke hefted the axe in his hand so that he held it by the blade and presented it to Axis haft first. "I surrender my blade and my command into your hands, Axis. Since you left us we have been simply a sad memory waiting for our commander to return. Take my axe, Axis, and take my loyalty with it."

The significance of the moment was not lost on Axis. Kenricke was effectively ending over a thousand years of proud military history.

"I accept both axe and surrender, Kenricke, and welcome you to my force. Belial waits back in camp," Axis tilted his head towards the camp along the shores of the Lake, "and will redeploy you. But, Kenricke, you will all have to surrender your axes. In this new land there will be no place for them."

Kenricke nodded. "I understand."

Axis turned his eyes to Spiredore. "Jayme?"

Kenricke grinned sourly. "The Brother-Leader, his advisers and most of the senior Brothers fled to Carlon days past, Axis. The Tower of . . . Spiredore is inhabited by a few old men and young novices. They ask only that you leave them their lives."

Axis thought about it for a moment. "Can I speak to the most senior of them?"

Kenricke nodded and waved at one of the Axe-Wielders in the rear of the formation. The Axe-Wielder tapped on the white door set into the centre of the nearest side of the tower, and after a moment it opened, an elderly Brother scurrying out.

"Brother Boroleas," Axis said, recognising the man. As Kenricke had taught him skill in arms, Boroleas had largely taught him his letters. "I have come to reclaim Spiredore."

"I have come to plead with you for our lives," Boroleas said stiffly.

"You shall have them," Axis replied.

"And our freedom?" Boroleas asked.

"You shall have an escort of twenty armed men to Nordmuth, Boroleas, where you will board a ship for Coroleas."

"And our books?" Boroleas pressed, hardly daring to hope.

Axis killed the hope immediately. "I have granted you your lives, Boroleas. Do not ask for your books as well. You leave now, and you leave everything behind you. Kenricke, will you supervise the Brothers' evacuation?"

Kenricke nodded, and Axis turned back to Spiredore. It was his.

55

MorningStar

Three days after the Battle of Bedwyr Fort Axis' camp had spread along the eastern shore of Grail Lake. Tents, gaily pennoned with the standards of the individual commanders within Axis' combined force, or, increasingly, with miniature versions of Axis' personal golden standard, spread along virtually the entire shore. Men rested and recovered in the early autumn sunshine. Carlon was left alone as Axis' army concentrated on recovering its strength after the battle. Ships from Nor had resupplied the force, and the Carlonese, running out of fresh supplies, had to put up with watching Axis' men feast on new breads and freshly-picked fruits. They also watched the Ravensbundmen play a rough and sometimes deadly game of football from horseback, and the Icarii drift about the skies and camp in a flurry of wings.

MorningStar and StarDrifter shared a tent in the northern part of the camp, and on this third day Axis stood with them, going over some of the books the Icarii had recovered from Spiredore. All of the Brotherhood's works Axis and StarDrifter had ordered burned, but StarDrifter and MorningStar, to their delight, had discovered hundreds of ancient Icarii texts secreted away in locked cupboards and chests.

"What did the Seneschal *do* with them?" MorningStar muttered, her head bent over one of the latest finds. "Not read them, surely?"

Axis shrugged. "I have no idea why they kept them. Perhaps they simply did not understand what they had found. Perhaps when they moved into Spiredore they packed these books up, or stuffed them into back bookcases, and completely forgot they were there."

StarDrifter shared his mother's excitement. "Axis! So many of these texts we thought completely lost! And now to have recovered them! See, mother!" he pointed to a small book he had just unpacked from a crate, "*The History of the Lakes* – I thought this book was only legend!"

MorningStar gasped in astonishment and picked the book up. "*The History of the Lakes*," she breathed. "Oh, Axis, thank you for all you have done for the Icarii!"

Axis smiled. Now, with most of the sacred sites of the Icarii opened to her and her brethren, Axis was seeing a side of his grandmother he had not known existed. Only this morning Axis had seen her laughing and chatting with Azhure as she took Caelum for a walk in the morning sunshine. Apparently MorningStar had put her deep suspicion of Azhure to one side.

MorningStar reluctantly put down the book. There would be plenty of time to read these at her leisure. "Is there anything left in Spiredore?"

StarDrifter shook his head. "No. We have removed everything that belonged to the Seneschal – burned most of it. Underneath the wooden panelling on the walls we have found the original carvings in the white stone – very much like the carvings that encircled the well leading down to the UnderWorld, Axis."

Axis nodded, recalling the beautiful carvings of women and children dancing hand in hand in the UnderWorld. He could not wait to see what those in Spiredore looked like restored.

"When will you be able to reconsecrate Spiredore?" he asked his father.

"Tomorrow night, Axis. The moon will be full – Spiredore shares a special harmony with the moon."

"Oh," MorningStar muttered. "What is that girl doing?"

Axis and StarDrifter stared at her, but MorningStar was gazing out the open tent flap. "Imibe is supposed to be watching Caelum as he has his afternoon nap. Now, here she is running off to watch her husband at his horse games again. I'd better go and watch over the boy – Azhure is visiting some of the wounded in the physician's tents this afternoon."

"I'll go, MorningStar," Axis offered. "I know how much you want to examine these books, and *you* know how much I enjoy spending time with my son."

"But StarDrifter needs to talk with you about tomorrow night's ceremony, and I have many years ahead of me to enjoy these texts. And, Axis," she grinned, "*I* enjoy spending time with Caelum as much as you do."

Axis gave in without further argument. Later his decision would return to haunt his dreams. What would have happened if *he* had walked into his tent that fine afternoon to check on his son?

MorningStar smiled at her son and grandson – and walked out of the tent and into Prophecy.

MorningStar knew something was badly wrong the instant she walked into the tent that Axis shared with Azhure and Caelum. Caelum's cot was in the far corner, lost in shadows, and a darkly cloaked figure was bent over the cot, reaching down to the baby.

"Who are you?" MorningStar began, her voice hard, and the figure whipped about.

"Oh," MorningStar whispered, her hand creeping to her throat in horror, feeling the dark power seep across the space between them and encircle her.

Dark power. Dark Music. MorningStar could do nothing against it.

"WolfStar," she murmured. "I had always wondered what disguise you wore."

"MorningStar," WolfStar said, moving towards her, a hard smile across the face he wore. Then his disguise faltered and faded, and MorningStar saw the real person beneath.

WolfStar was incredibly beautiful underneath the hood of his black cloak. He had the violet eyes of so many of the Sun-Soars, but dark coppery hair. His entire face was alive with power, strange power that MorningStar assumed he had brought back from the universe beyond. How would Axis deal with this, she thought frantically as WolfStar stepped close to her and took her chin in his hand, *how will Axis deal with this?*

"Axis will deal with me when he finds me, my sweet," WolfStar said softly. "But I do not intend that he should find me yet. I still have much work to do in my current disguise."

"I will not tell," MorningStar whispered.

"Sweet MorningStar SunSoar. How could you not tell? Your knowledge will shine out of your eyes, and either Axis or StarDrifter will eventually force the knowledge from you. My sweet, you have seen me in my everyday disguise, and for that you must pay."

MorningStar whimpered.

"Ah," WolfStar said, "you are afraid." He wrapped both his hands about her head and pulled her to him, kissing her gently, kissing her goodbye.

MorningStar moaned, her hands and power hanging limp by her side.

WolfStar lifted his head. "Goodbye, my lovely," he whispered, then his hands abruptly tightened about her head, crushing it as easily as a child would an egg it held in its hands.

As WolfStar carefully lowered MorningStar's body to the ground, Caelum began to scream in terror.

Only at that point did the five Alaunt who had been resting quietly in the tent, and who had shown no signs of distress as WolfStar murdered MorningStar, rise to their feet and encircle the cot protectively.

"How strange," StarDrifter said, raising his head from the text he was showing Axis. "I feel a loss, an emptiness, but of what I cannot tell."

Axis looked at him, but after a moment StarDrifter shook himself and continued to explain the text to Axis.

WolfStar hurried through the ranks of tents, upset to have been discovered – and even a little upset that he had been forced to dispose of MorningStar. She was a SunSoar woman, and WolfStar had not liked to kill her.

WolfStar was so upset that for a crucial minute he forgot to recloak himself in his usual disguise.

Not even thinking to look where he was going, disturbed by Caelum's screams so close behind him, WolfStar turned a corner and walked straight into Jack.

Jack took a step back, stunned. "Master!" he whispered.

WolfStar placed a calming hand on Jack's shoulder. "Jack, listen to me. There has been some unpleasantness. Do not mention that you have seen me."

Jack stared at WolfStar a moment, then lowered his head in submission. "As you wish, Master."

The next instant WolfStar had gone.

"See here," StarDrifter said a few minutes later, pointing to an illustration in the book he held, "this is a representation of the fourth order of the . . ."

"*Axis!*"

Both StarDrifter and Axis' heads shot up. It was Azhure's voice, and she was screaming in terror.

"*Axis! Axis!*"

Both Enchanters dropped the books they were holding and ran outside.

Azhure ran through the tents towards them, Caelum screaming in her arms, five of the Alaunt hugging her heels.

"Axis!" She was so terrified that her breath came in great heaving sobs, unable to speak. All Axis could get from Caelum was a pure wail of terror.

"Azhure?" he demanded, seizing her shoulders. "What is it? *What is it?*"

"MorningStar," StarDrifter whispered, his eyes on Axis' tent some three or four away from where they were standing.

Azhure did not answer, but simply burst into tears.

Axis shared one frantic look with his father, then they were both racing as fast as they could for the tent.

Both Axis and StarDrifter stopped, horrified beyond words or emotion, a pace inside the tent. MorningStar's body lay just beyond the centre of the tent. Her arms were neatly arranged by her side, as if someone had taken care to lay her out neatly, but her head had disappeared in a disgusting mess of blood, bone fragments and brain tissue. It had been completely crushed. Even Axis, used to the wounds of the battlefield, felt physically sickened by the scene.

Azhure stumbled into the tent behind them, shielding Caelum's head from the sight of MorningStar's body. Slowly words started to fall out of her between sobs. "I was on my way back to our tent . . . then I heard Caelum start to scream . . . I hurried . . . ran . . . and found . . . I didn't know what to do . . . what could I do? . . . I grabbed Caelum and ran . . ."

Axis leaned back and put his arm about her just as Belial, Magariz, Rivkah, Ysgryff and Embeth all rushed into the tent. All stopped abruptly, their faces appalled at the sight of MorningStar's death.

His face hard and emotionless, Axis lifted Caelum from Azhure's arms. He cuddled the baby, soothing him both with Song and with power, reassuring him. Gradually the baby's screams began to lessen.

Caelum was the only witness.

My son. Shush. You are safe. Safe, safe, safe. Who did this to MorningStar?

For a moment he received nothing from his son.

A dark man.

Do you know his name?

Axis could feel his son's hesitation. *MorningStar called him WolfStar.*

Caelum. Did you see his face?

No. His cloak was drawn tight about his face.

"WolfStar?" StarDrifter said. "WolfStar did this?"

He touched me with his mind, Caelum thought reflectively. *Such a gentle touch. He said that he loved me.*

When StarDrifter finally returned, grief-stricken, to the tent he had shared with his mother, he found that *The History of the Lakes* had vanished. No matter how hard he or any others looked over the next weeks, they never found it again.

Much, much later, when the moon had risen and MorningStar's body had been removed and the tent cleared, Axis and StarDrifter sat together on the sandy shores of Grail Lake. Axis had given Caelum and Azhure a calming enchantment, and now both slept deeply in Rivkah's tent – the one she now openly shared with Magariz. Axis ordered his own tent burned; he could never use it again now.

For a long time both father and son sat in silence, watching the drift of the moon over the dark waters of the Lake.

Axis heard his father take a deep breath, and he reached over and took StarDrifter's hand. "I know how close to MorningStar you were," he said softly, hoping to get Star-Drifter to talk. StarDrifter and MorningStar had often argued, their temperaments and personalities were so similar, but there was a deep bond between them that both encompassed and went beyond love.

"I cannot believe she could have died like that," Star-Drifter whispered, his eyes on the small waves lapping at their feet. "She was always the one most concerned about WolfStar, always the one fretting about who he was, in what body he hid . . . perhaps she had a premonition that she would die by his hand."

"WolfStar." Axis did not want to think about him – or about MorningStar's thoughts on who WolfStar might be. Not Azhure.

"Not Azhure," StarDrifter said. "It could not be her."

"No," Axis replied. "She had no opportunity to teach me as a child, did she? She was born and raised in Smyrton while I grew in Carlon."

Both Enchanters clung to that, both so deeply in love with the woman that they would cling to any excuse not to consider her as WolfStar.

"Rivkah, Magariz, Belial, Ysgryff, Embeth," Axis said slowly, thinking aloud. "All were in the tent within moments of us. All must have been close."

"No," StarDrifter said. "Not Rivkah. She never had the opportunity to teach you as a child."

"Perhaps she did, StarDrifter. All those months and years she spent away from Talon Spike. How do you know that they were spent with the Avar?"

"Axis, you can't be serious," StarDrifter said. "*Not* Rivkah."

Axis sighed. "Not Azhure, not Rivkah."

"The others?" StarDrifter asked.

"The others. All older than me. All had access to me as a child. I lived with Embeth and Ganelon as a child from the age of eleven, and she would have seen me at an earlier age at court. Magariz has admitted himself that he knew me as a baby in Carlon when he was a member of the palace guard, and later its captain. He also possibly has had access to Gorgrael via Gorkenfort. Belial? Eight years older than I, and who knows if he ever saw me at an age earlier than fifteen or sixteen when I joined the Axe-Wielders and he was commander of my unit?"

"Ysgryff?" StarDrifter said quietly.

"Ysgryff," Axis mused. "Perhaps the perfect disguise. Over the past few weeks we have learned, to our mutual surprise, that the baronial family of Nor has kept the Temple of the Stars protected for the past thousand years. Ysgryff himself constantly refers to small parts of Icarii culture that should be unknown to any save the Icarii, and he knew that Raum was transforming."

"He did?" StarDrifter asked.

"I came across Ysgryff one night just before we reached the Silent Woman Woods, offering the Bane comfort. He knew what he was going through."

"What better place to hide yourself for thousands of years," StarDrifter said slowly, his eyes back on the water again, "but among the baronial family of Nor. Access to most of the holy sites, and especially the Island of Mist and Memory. You must admit, Axis, that Ysgryff is far more than he seems."

Axis gave a short laugh. "Listen to us, StarDrifter. All we know is that WolfStar is not me and he is not you. We both provide each other's alibi. Otherwise we have a smorgasbord of suspects. Most have had the opportunity, and who knows what motive WolfStar has for returning? And what was he doing with Caelum? *Why my son?*"

StarDrifter expelled a short breath in frustration. "Axis, you have never told me the third verse of the Prophecy."

"It was meant for my ears only. Anyone else who hears it simply forgets it within a moment or two."

"Tell me," StarDrifter urged. "Perhaps I will remember it. Perhaps there is some understanding I can cast upon it."

Axis raised his eyebrows, but he recited the third verse for his father.

StarMan, listen, for I know
That you can wield the sceptre
To bring Gorgrael to his knees
And break the ice asunder.
But even with the power in hand
Your pathway is not sure:
A Traitor from within your camp
Will seek and plot to harm you;
Let not your Lover's pain distract
For this will mean your death;
Destroyer's might lies in his hate
Yet you must never follow;
Forgiveness is the thing assured
To save Tencendor's soul.

StarDrifter frowned. Already the words were warping themselves in his mind. "I cannot . . ." he muttered, perplexed.

"The third verse tells me what I must do to defeat Gorgrael," Axis explained patiently. "But that is no of import to anyone save myself. But the verse also warns me that there is someone who pretends love for my cause, but who will eventually betray me to Gorgrael."

"WolfStar."

"It must be. But *who* is it? Which disguise does WolfStar wear? StarDrifter." Axis' voice almost broke with his frustration. "It could have been *anyone* within the camp, or even anyone from Carlon who had crept out during the night. How many suspects do we have within the immediate vicinity? Seventy thousand? Eighty? More?"

But what was he doing with Caelum? What? Did MorningStar die so that my son could live? Or was WolfStar simply visiting?

StarDrifter put his arm about Axis' shoulders. "We must trust only each other," he whispered. "Who else can we trust?"

"That is a terrible way to live, StarDrifter."

"MorningStar died a terrible death, Axis. Never forget it."

56

One Nors Woman Wins,
Another Loses

Faraday stood with her husband on the parapets of the palace in Carlon and stared across Grail Lake, Timozel lurking dark and brooding in the shadows behind them. Since Borneheld's loss at Bedwyr Fort Timozel had hardly spoken. His respect for Borneheld had been severely tested by the battle loss, and sometimes Faraday heard him muttering of strange visions and promises under his breath. His skin had begun to take on an unhealthy sheen, almost as if he had a slow-burning fever inside him. Bags of skin hung heavy under his eyes. Poor Timozel, Faraday thought briefly, you are not looking forward to seeing Axis again, are you?

Faraday did not know that Timozel hardly dared sleep now, lest Gorgrael appear to him, laughing and beckoning with his hand. Timozel no longer screamed, but he always woke wide-eyed with fear and horror, clutching at the sheets.

Faraday closed her eyes and leaned her face to the autumn sun, feeling its warmth. It would be soon, now, and both she and Borneheld knew it. They stood only two paces apart, but the gulf between them was immeasurable. If Axis died during the brothers' duel in the Chamber of the Moons, then Faraday would not wish to live. Darkness would close from the north as the Prophecy shattered, and Faraday had no intention of living in a world of ice and darkness that did not hold Axis.

She took a deep breath, savouring the faint scent of the final autumn flowers, and opened her eyes. The distant shore of Grail Lake was only just visible, but Faraday could see the rising height of the white tower that Yr had told her was rightfully called Spiredore. (What had the Icarii done inside Spiredore to make it glow as it had last night?) Axis' victorious army had been encamped about the Lake for almost a week now, recovering its strength after the dreadful battle about Bedwyr Fort, and it had not escaped Faraday's attention, as it had not escaped the attention of most of the people in Carlon, that those of Borneheld's army he had left to die as he fled the field had happily joined the ranks of the force they had fought against. Axis had taken no prisoners, only welcomed comrades.

Faraday leaned a little closer to the stone parapets, wishing she had a glass so that she might see the more clearly. Last night she had stood here and watched the great fire that had been lit on the eastern shore of the Lake. It had been a funeral pyre, Yr told her later, a funeral pyre for a great and loved Icarii, for only the best were farewelled in so lavish a manner.

But while the pyre blazed, Faraday had only seen the flames leaping high into the sky and the shadowy figures of thousands gathered about it – not only Icarii, but Acharite and Ravensbund men and women too. Had Axis been there? What about his father StarDrifter and mother Rivkah? Borneheld had told Faraday that a woman claiming to be Rivkah had talked to him before the Battle of Bedwyr Fort, and, despite Borneheld's disclaimers, Faraday had no doubts that it was indeed Rivkah, and she smiled for Axis' happiness.

As the flames had leapt for the stars torch-bearing Icarii had taken flight, spiralling higher and higher above the flames to slowly disappear into the night-sky, the flaming torches they carried fading to star-like pin-pricks of light in the blackness above. They had been escorting the released soul on its journey to the stars. It had been a sight so beautiful, so moving, that Faraday had wept and wondered who was being farewelled with such honour and ceremony.

Later, as the funeral pyre died down, the attention of the thousands across the Lake (as indeed, all the thousands within Carlon who watched) turned to Spiredore. Curious music, Song, had drifted across the Lake towards Carlon, and Faraday had glimpsed a silver and white figure atop the roof of the tower. StarDrifter she thought, sometimes on his feet, sometimes slowly spiralling into the air. After some time Spiredore itself had begun to glow as if a beacon, a gentle white light pulsing out from its walls, growing in strength until the entire structure seemed to throb. Faraday had been entranced by the sight of the pulsating white tower, and she had stood watching for hours. She and Yr had lain awake until dawn stained the sky, talking of the evening's events.

Now, only just risen from her bed, Faraday felt refreshed, alive. Even Borneheld's presence couldn't dampen her spirits. She could almost *feel* Axis' presence. Soon, she thought. Soon.

Footsteps sounded from behind her, and Faraday turned slightly.

Gautier approached, dressed in light armour, his sword rattling, and stepped to Borneheld's side, and both men stared silently at the far side of the Lake. Both had recovered some of their spirit, some of their bravado, in the past few days.

"When?" Gautier asked softly.

Borneheld paused, then answered just as softly. "Soon."

"What will you do, Sire?"

"Nothing," Borneheld answered, his eyes fixed on a tiny scarlet and gold figure across the Lake. "Axis will come to me. He must. We both want to end it. Just he and I. That is all it was ever meant to be."

Borneheld turned from the parapets. His face was shadowed with red beard; he had not shaved or washed in days.

"Our rivalry started the instant he was conceived," Borneheld said to Faraday. "And we have fought ever since he arrived as a baby in Carlon, one way or another. Do not deceive yourself, Faraday, that he will come across the waters of Grail Lake for love of you alone. Will he love you once I am gone?" He paused and eyed her coldly. "No. I doubt it. There will be no reason to, you see, once I am gone."

And with that he turned and walked away, Gautier at his side. The slap of their boots on the stone flagging sounded like dark bells tolling a death knell.

Faraday watched her husband go, a cold fear in her heart. Borneheld had simply assumed that he would lose, as if he had always known that he was fated to die at Axis' hands. Knowing that, it gave what he said about Axis' love for her, or lack of it, the fatal ring of prophecy.

Axis watched with his Enchanter's vision as first Borneheld then, after a long pause, Faraday turned and left the parapets of the castle.

"When?" Belial asked.

"Tonight. I have waited long enough. It will be tonight."

Belial nodded. "How?"

"Rivkah knows a way in. A secret way. We will approach across Grail Lake."

"Who?" Belial asked.

"Me. You, Ho'Demi and Magariz. Jorge. Rivkah."

"Rivkah?" Belial was stunned.

Axis' eyes were as cold as the water. "She must come. She must witness. One of her sons will die tonight. She must be there."

Belial shivered. "Who else?"

"The Sentinels. They will need to be there."

"To witness?"

Axis shook his head, his eyes far away. "They can serve to witness, yes, but they will be there primarily to wait."

Belial frowned. Axis was in a strange mood, very strange. "Wait? Wait for what?"

"A lost love, Belial. A lost love."

"And that is all you will take?"

Again Axis shook his head. "StarDrifter, I think, although he may get in the way. But he wants to come. EvenSong. She must come too. To wait, like the Sentinels. Arne, and perhaps some five or six men-at-arms. Ravensbundmen, I think."

"You'll need a merchant ship to carry that lot across," Belial muttered.

Axis clapped Belial on the back. "Seventeen, perhaps eighteen, my friend. A good rowboat will get us there."

"You're not going to take Azhure?"

Axis' face hardened. "Someone will need to stay in command of this camp, and I hardly think she will want to come."

"Axis," Belial hesitated. "Be careful you do not treat Azhure too badly in this. She loves you too deeply to be able to watch you sail across that Lake tonight with a calm and understanding heart."

Axis took a deep breath, fighting to control his temper.

"Be careful, Axis," Belial said, knowing that he was going too far, "Azhure is held in high regard by many within this camp. Hurt her, and you will hurt many."

"Including you?" Axis did not care if Belial saw his temper now. "How much do *you* love her, Belial?"

Belial held Axis' furious stare without flinching. "I will not deny that I loved her once. But there was no point feeding a love and a desire when Azhure could see none but you. It would have destroyed me, and I was not yet ready to die. But I still care for her, as does Magariz, and Rivkah, and Arne, and a thousand others I could name. Axis," Belial's voice was low, but steady. "We all care too much for her to watch her slowly die of wretchedness when you marry Faraday. Either let her go, or let Faraday go. You will destroy both of them if you continue in your desire to have them both."

"I will let neither go!" Axis seethed. "There is no need. They will both accept the other. It has been done before."

"But not with such women!" Belial's voice rose now. "Both are wondrous in their own right, but both will fade and die if forced to share you!"

"I hardly think . . ." Axis began, but both men were distracted by a shout from the line of tents.

Ysgryff, his face livid with fury, strode towards Axis and Belial as they stood on the shore of the Lake, dragging a slight Nors girl with him.

"Oh gods, no," Belial whispered. "Cazna!"

Ysgryff's handsome face was so twisted with anger that it was almost unrecognisable, while the girl, dressed in a bright red wool dress, was wearing an expression of sulky rebellion.

Ysgryff drew to a halt some four or five paces away from Axis and Belial, and started to shout at Belial.

"Do you realise what you have done, you low-born oaf? Did you not stop to think what you did when you ravaged my daughter's virtue?'

"Daughter?" Belial said. Cazna was Ysgryff's daughter?

"Daughter!" Ysgryff shouted. "Daughter! Did you think her some camp whore? Did she *act* like some camp whore? Did you not stop to consider what you did when you dragged her into your bed?"

"I –" Belial began but Ysgryff did not give him the chance to explain.

"Of what value is she now? None! What sort of marriage can I arrange for her now? None! Some hurried and secret-ive affair with a ploughman who has been paid to overlook her swollen belly?"

Again Belial tried to interrupt, appalled at the inference that he had got Cazna pregnant, but Cazna overrode her father.

"Father," she said, low but firm. Axis noticed that she had inherited her father's striking looks to the full. "Belial did not seduce me. I seduced him. The night of the treaty-signing in the Ancient Barrows I went to his tent and lay waiting for him in his bedroll."

Belial smiled slightly. *Will I ever forget what I felt when I entered my tent that night and saw her lying there, waiting for me?*

Ysgryff stared at his daughter in horror. "What did I raise," he said, "that she should treat me like this?"

Belial stepped forward and took Cazna's hand. "Ysgryff, there has been little harm done." He hurried on as Ysgryff opened his mouth in horror yet again. *Little harm done?* "I have already asked – your daughter – to marry me."

Axis raised his eyebrow. Belial had thought to castigate him over his treatment of Azhure when all the time he had been busily violating the Baron of Nor's daughter?

"Marriage? Do you think that will heal the hurt and the shame you have dealt my family?" Ysgryff shouted, although he was having a great deal of trouble maintaining the façade of his temper. If he played the part of the enraged father well enough, he would be able to get Belial to accept Cazna without a single gold piece as dowry.

"I have accepted," Cazna said, watching her father carefully. She already had her suspicions about her father's display of righteous rage. Her hand tightened about Belial's.

"Well," Ysgryff said, pretending to be slightly mollified. "How do I know that he means it? Was it just a ploy to bring you to his bed?"

"I hardly think you have behaved well, Belial," Axis said, speaking for the first time since Ysgryff had dragged his daughter forth to accuse Belial. "I think that perhaps you have treated Cazna rather badly, don't you?"

Belial glared at Axis. He knew perfectly well that Axis was referring to their previous conversation with that remark.

"Then find me two more witnesses, Axis," he retorted. "And I will wed Cazna here and now. *I* am not afraid to grace the woman I love with vows of lifelong love, partnership and honour."

Axis stared at Belial, standing calm and straight with the Nors girl close to him, then he spun on his heel and strode off.

"I cannot take you with me, so I will leave you in command of the camp and the army," Axis said carefully. "FarSight CutSpur will be your second-in-command."

"I understand," Azhure said, folding her cloak for the third time, then shaking it out and starting all over again.

They were in the tent that they now shared with Rivkah and Magariz, and this was the first time Axis had found a chance to talk with Azhure alone for many days. Caelum had gone with Rivkah for an evening stroll by the waters.

"Damn it," Axis swore softly, and strode over to Azhure, tearing the cloak from her hands and throwing it to the ground. "What is wrong, Azhure? What has come between us these past months?" How long since he had touched her, kissed her, lain with her? Not since the night he had signed the treaty with Ysgryff and Greville at the Ancient Barrows, and how many weeks was that?

"What has come between us? She sits in her pink and gold palace across the Lake. Faraday."

"Azhure," Axis said, taking her chin gently in his fingers and forcing her to meet his eyes. "Azhure, I love you, you know that. You will always be a part of my life."

She twisted away. "It is a hard thing you ask of me, Axis."

"What? To stay with me? To be my Lover? You love me, you can do no less."

"I wish I could have found the courage to walk away from you before this," she said.

"Walk away from me? Who to? Belial?"

Azhure whipped her head back, her eyes wide.

Axis seized her chin again. "If you try to leave me, I will track you down. *Believe it!* No-one will take you from me!"

Azhure stared at him. How could a man who could show so much compassion to strangers show such a face of cruelty to her?

"Azhure," Axis moderated his tone as he watched the effect his words had on her. "Do you love me?"

"Yes," she whispered, unable to deny it.

"Then you would be miserable away from me. Azhure, listen to me. Marriage to Borneheld's widow will further cement my claim to the throne of Achar. Besides, the Prophecy binds me to Faraday, and I need Faraday to bring the Avar and the trees to my cause. I cannot abandon her, Azhure, and I will not. Not when she has done so much for me, and will do so much more. But my heart belongs to you. Never belittle yourself, or your effect on me, Azhure. "

He bent down and kissed her lips softly. "If I was not already bound by vow to Faraday then I would not hesitate to marry you, Azhure. Believe it."

"Yes." Azhure believed it.

"Azhure, I will not hesitate to acknowledge you, my love for you, or your role in my success thus far. I love you, and your son will be my heir. Walk tall and proud."

"Go," Azhure whispered, "go to Faraday. I cannot fight the Prophecy."

After Axis had left her, and walked down to the shore of Grail Lake and the boat that waited to take him to Faraday, Azhure walked out of the tent, took Caelum from Rivkah, and wandered through the camp, pausing to chat now and then with a member of her command. She wore a cool, confident smile on her face and didn't let a single ray of her grief shine through. Sicarius trotted at her side, his eyes golden and seeing.

Once she had inspected the camp and made sure all was in order Azhure shared a meal with Cazna, and envied the young woman that she had captured her husband's heart intact.

57

The Chamber of the Moons

As twilight deepened into dark, people started to file into the Chamber of the Moons. Servants, guardsmen, courtiers, kitchen maids, stableboys – all were driven by the presentiment that something strange would take place this night in the Chamber of the Moons.

They moved silently, none speaking, none feeling the need to. As the night drew on perhaps two hundred stood, still and noiseless, circling the Chamber, leaving its centre free.

Borneheld sat on his throne atop the dais, his face expressionless, sword drawn and resting on his knees. On the stone edge of the dais sat Faraday, green skirts spread about her, shoulders square, face serene, hands folded smoothly in her lap. Like her husband, Faraday stared straight ahead. Waiting.

In a group of four to the left of the dais stood Timozel, morbid; Gautier, a thin sheen of sweat across his face betraying his inner fears; Jayme, pale; and Yr, as serene as her mistress, feeling the presence of the Prophecy strongly in the night.

The only light in the Chamber was an inadequate ring of blazing torches round the pillars. They threw more shadows than light, and those shadows provided the only movement.

Everyone waited.

On Grail Lake the boat moved through the smooth waters.

All on board were absorbed in their own thoughts.

Axis thought of Azhure one moment, Faraday the next. He thought of Borneheld, and the end they would make of it tonight. He thought of FreeFall and of Zeherah, and of the bargain with the GateKeeper.

Belial thought of the duel ahead and of his wife. He had wed Cazna there on the shores of Grail Lake this afternoon, and the pledges he made had tasted right in his mouth. He thought of the life they would make together when this Prophecy had ground itself to a close. Would they settle in his home province of Romsdale? Or in one of the three manors Cazna had had bestowed upon her? Belial's thoughts saddened. He prayed Cazna could be all he hoped.

Rivkah and Magariz thought of Axis, and of the duel that they would witness tonight. Rivkah had not wanted to be there, but knew that she had to be. She had brought both men into this world, and she would witness one of them out of it tonight. She hoped it would be Borneheld. She was glad she had Magariz with her tonight, glad that they no longer needed to hide their love for each other.

As the boat slid through the darkness Rivkah looked into the water. She snatched at Magariz's hand and indicated with her eyes. Far into the depths of the Lake a line of double lights glowed as if marking a road. The boat glided directly above. Every now and then the row of glowing lamps would diversify into circles and arrows, reminding Rivkah vaguely of the swirls and lines on the faces of the Ravensbund people. They glowed welcomingly, and Rivkah fought the urge to slip into the water and swim down to meet them. She had often sailed these waters at night when she was a girl, but she had never seen lights such as these before.

Jack, Ogden and Veremund had seen the lights as well, but none were puzzled. There it lies, thought Jack, and Ogden and Veremund silently agreed with him. Our fate.

All three knew what they would soon witness, and they hoped that tonight would provide the final stroke for the war between Axis and Borneheld, for the war which had riven Achar apart.

But why, thought Veremund, why go through with this, when the fifth is still lost? Ogden squeezed his brother's hand, and Jack placed his own hands on the shoulders of the two Sentinels. Trust, he thought, it is all we can do. Trust.

Arne thought of Axis and he thought of traitors. He thought of backs, and he thought of Axis' back. Sometimes when he looked at Axis he thought he could see a knife emerging from between his shoulder blades. Sometimes he thought he could see Axis' hands covered in blood, but he could not tell whose. Arne's eyes darted about the boat. Where the traitor's hand? Where? Who?

At the very stern of the boat sat StarDrifter and Even-Song, both a little uncomfortable, both trailing their wings slightly in the cool waters. StarDrifter thought of his mother, of her excitement at finding *The History of the Lakes*, of her death before she could read it. He thought of MorningStar's crushed head and of WolfStar who lurked somewhere among them. Who?

EvenSong thought of FreeFall. She had fought to put him out of her mind this past year, even to the extent of seducing Belial one night in Sigholt and again this Beltide night past. But nothing had worked, not even Belial's ardent love-making, and tonight the memories of FreeFall seemed closer than ever before. FreeFall, she thought, leave me to live the rest of my life without you. Let go my heart. Soar back to the stars where you belong.

Jorge sat shoulder to shoulder with the impassive Ravens-bund chief and the six Ravensbundmen who accompanied Axis. Over the past months Jorge had grown to respect the Ravensbund people where once he had only loathed them as savages. Nevertheless, Axis had picked a peculiar force to invade with, a strange one indeed. Magic and enchantments and alien vows with unseen faces have more to do with the selection for this mission than fighting skill. And why me? Why me? I am too old for this. Too tired.

The boat came to a small and forgotten postern door set low in Carlon's walls. It was a little-known gate that Rivkah remembered from her childhood. Once, many generations ago, it had been used for courtiers who wished to enter and leave the palace as secretly as they might. Rivkah had discovered it as a child, and had sometimes come down here late in summer evenings to sit with her feet dangling in the cool waters of Grail Lake. Was the gate still here, unblocked, unlocked? It opened into a stairwell and narrow corridor which eventually led to the main hallways of the palace. Perhaps, Rivkah pondered, it had been built hundreds of years ago for the very purposes of this Prophecy.

Axis lifted his head to the night sky and whistled softly. A sudden rush of wings signalled the arrival of the snow eagle on Axis' outstretched arm.

The boat rocked gently as it bumped against the stone wall and Arne crept forward and worked the latch on the gate.

It swung silently open, revealing a rectangle of darkness. Axis was suddenly, vividly reminded of the rectangle of light that sat behind the GateKeeper, and he pondered the similarities. This was a Gate into the Prophecy as surely as that golden Gate in the UnderWorld was a doorway into the world beyond.

Arne tied the boat to a ring to one side of the gate and disappeared into the darkness for some minutes. Everyone sat quietly, waiting. Axis gently stroked the eagle's feathers, calming it and himself. Earlier Belial had apologised to him for his ill-considered words about Azhure and they had grasped hands, friends once more. Axis had complimented Belial on his new bride. Both men were relieved that their friendship had been restored on this, the most critical of nights.

Arne reappeared. "The place is deserted," he said. "I scouted well ahead. Nothing. No-one."

"No guards?" Belial queried.

"They will all be in the Chamber of the Moons," said Axis quietly, and although he was not sure why he said it, he knew it to be true. "Waiting. Come."

They moved quickly and quietly through the lower corridors of the palace.

The eagle was becoming more and more restless the further they moved into the palace, and Axis soothed and stroked it. StarDrifter and EvenSong, as nervous about being trapped where they could not fly as the eagle, were grateful the instant they moved out of the tight and narrow lower passageways; their wings had scraped painfully in places against cold and damp stone.

As they moved further and higher into the palace the group passed small numbers of servants. As soon as the servants saw the party was headed by the golden man with the eagle, they slunk back against the walls, their eyes great and solemn. One or two bowed slightly as Axis, his eyes fixed straight ahead, passed them without comment or recognition.

There were no guards. No fighting. Borneheld was willing now that it should come down to the duel.

They reached corridors which were wide and spacious, decorated with bright lamps, silken banners and intermittent tapestries showing scenes from Achar's glorious past. Not a few depicted triumphant battles from the Wars of the Axe, which caused StarDrifter to grimace.

Axis finally came to the part of the palace he knew so well. How many times had he trod this very corridor, striding to an audience with Priam in the Chamber of the Moons? And how many times had he walked, not at the head of a party as he did now, but three paces behind the figure of the Brother-Leader Jayme? Walking as Jayme's right arm, his sword arm, the support of the Seneschal? Well, now he walked towards the Prophecy, and when he crossed swords with Borneheld he would be fighting the power of the Seneschal as much as the power of his brother.

"Wait," he called suddenly, holding out his free hand as they turned a corner. The others stopped behind him, looking down the straight and wide corridor. At the end, perhaps some fifty paces away, double doors stood wide. Beyond was a darkened chamber, lit only by the leaping light of torches.

"The Chamber of the Moons," Jack said, moving forward to step next to Axis. "Yr is there. I can feel her."

"And Faraday," Axis said, relieved. He could feel the slight tug of her power as well. "And Faraday."

He turned to look at those behind him, smiling as if realising for the first time what a strange group he had brought with him. Sentinels, Ravensbundmen, nobles, a Princess, a friend, a father and a sister.

"Let us go and strike the final blow for Tencendor," he said quietly. "Let us go and finish this."

When Axis strode into the Chamber of the Moons, the eagle hopping in agitation on his arm, the torchlight caught at his golden tunic and hair, making all who looked at him blink – some in wonder, some in fear, and at least one in love.

He is so different, so changed, so much more powerful than when I first saw him enter this Chamber, Faraday thought, rising to her feet as Axis stared across the Chamber of the Moons at her. He strides through the doors like a golden god and yet still he has my heart as helpless as that first night I saw him so long ago. Her eyes travelled over the golden tunic with its blood-red blazing sun and matching red breeches. And blinked.

A bloodied sun hanging over a golden field.

For an instant her hand hovered about her throat as the vision threatened to overwhelm her again. She managed to regain control, and dropped her hand, her eyes calm.

Axis stood a moment, glancing about the Chamber, his eyes finally coming to rest on Faraday standing tall and beautiful before the dais, Borneheld sitting motionless behind her. With a movement so abrupt it brought gasps from all who witnessed, Axis threw the eagle into the air. Eyes followed the silver and white bird as it soared into the dome of the Chamber, coming to rest on a ledge far above.

Faraday's eyes fluttered to the eagle. Feathers?

Feathers! She felt as if she were choking on feathers!

She took a deep breath, and dropped her eyes.

All eyes were now on the golden man standing in the centre of the Chamber before them.

"The traitors," Borneheld said calmly, evenly, by way of introduction. He had not risen from the throne. "Here they are, Jayme, all together in one room. All walking with their treachery open for all to see. Open for all to note."

Jayme stood some eight or nine paces behind the throne, virtually lost in the shadows. He looked gaunt and grey, and a palsy rippling rhythmically across his cheek gave him a slight air of insanity.

His eyes caught with Axis', and if Jayme had thought that Axis might still retain some measure of compassion, perhaps even love, for him, then Jayme quickly realised that all Axis now felt for him was loathing and contempt.

Jayme was so lost in Axis' eyes that he did not see Rivkah move quietly into the Chamber behind her son. For the first time in thirty-four years the Princess Rivkah had returned to the home of her youth. She took a deep breath, looked between her sons, then gazed about the Chamber. Prophecy. Her life and those of her sons had been manipulated by the Prophecy. Every time she thought she was free of its grips, she realised it continued to manipulate and use her as it willed.

Those entering with Axis moved quietly to join the watchers about the pillars of the Chamber, and even Faraday moved away from the dais so that the brothers could face each other. She gave Axis a smile, but his eyes only flickered quickly over her. His entire attention was reserved for his brother.

The Chamber rang with shouted accusations of murder and treachery.

"The traitor sits the throne," Axis' voice cried out. "Borneheld, I accuse you of FreeFall SunSoar's murder. I accuse you of our uncle's murder. I accuse you of ordering the murder of thousands of innocent men, women and children in Skarabost. You have murdered your last, Borneheld, and now it is time to let the gods pass judgement on your crimes."

Borneheld rose to his feet. "A fight, brother? Is that what you want?" he cried. "And yet you come to me surrounded with your tricks and your enchantments. I am an Artor-fearing man, Axis. A plain soldier. How can I compete with your enchantments? Your sorcery?"

"I stand before you as your brother, Borneheld. Tonight I will not be an Icarii Enchanter. I will come to you only with my sword. We will stand evenly matched for gods and for prophecies to choose which has the right to live, and which the right to die." With an abrupt motion Axis twisted the Enchanter's ring from his right hand and tossed it across the Chamber to StarDrifter.

When Faraday saw the ring glint through the air she cried out, her composure finally breaking. "No!" The thought that Axis would face Borneheld only with his sword appalled her – and again Faraday saw the blood dripping from Axis' hair and felt the soft trickle of blood down her breasts. She moved as if to run to Axis, but a strong arm caught her about the waist. Jorge.

"Let him be," he said. "Borneheld and Axis must end this. Here. Finally."

"No," Faraday wailed again, twisting against Jorge's arm. The vision of the trees overwhelmed her, and now she was afraid, dreadfully afraid, that what they had shown her (*were showing her*) had been (*was*) the truth. Axis would die here tonight, and there was nothing she could do to stop it.

"No," she whispered, as Axis glanced her way. "Axis, no."

She saw Borneheld, stepping down from the throne.

Borneheld took a step away from his throne, his sword raised before him.

Slowly Axis unbuttoned the golden tunic and threw it to Belial. It was a beautiful tunic, and he did not want it rent, or stained with blood. He rolled up the sleeves of his white linen shirt above his elbow, then, in a quick movement so fluid most could hardly follow it, drew his sword from the scabbard at his side.

"Borneheld," he said, and his brother leaped from the dais towards him and into fate and vision.

Time passed, and its passage was marked only by the ringing of steel through the Chamber of the Moons.

Dreadfully, inexorably, caught by fate, Axis and Borneheld fought as the vision of the Silent Woman Woods had foretold and Faraday's face crumpled in despair. Although she strained against Jorge's arms to be free, reaching into the centre of the Chamber, he was too strong for her. She wept, terrified by what she saw unfolding before her. In the centre of the Chamber the two men circled, each bloodied with small stinging wounds, swords drawn, faces twisted into snarling masks of rage fed by long-held hatreds. How long had they been fighting? How many blows had they traded? How many times had one slipped, the other lunging for the kill, only for the other to roll aside just in time to escape the sword thrust?

Faraday did not realise that she whispered Axis' name over and over as she continued to struggle feebly against Jorge's arm. Her slim fingers twisted the Ichtar ruby around the knuckle of her heart finger until the skin broke and bled.

Apart from Faraday's movements and whispers, there was no other movement or sound in the Chamber of the Moons save those of the men fighting. Magariz stood behind Rivkah, his hands on her shoulders, lending her support as she witnessed the death struggle between her two sons. No matter how much Rivkah had disowned Borneheld, no matter how much she claimed to despise him, Magariz knew that she would not be able to watch his death without pain.

Rivkah's attention was caught by the scene in front of her. Both her sons had grown to be skilful warriors. Borneheld fought with muscles and tactics honed by battle, Axis with the grace and fluidity bequeathed him by his Icarii father. Borneheld's size and the gold circlet about his brow lent him authority, Axis' white and scarlet-clad form imbued him with an almost ethereal beauty.

StarDrifter realised that the sound of the swords clashing and scraping along each other, the sounds of the men's heavy breathing and of their boots scuffing across the green marble floor, made a music unlike any he had ever heard before. It was a strange music, dark and foreboding, and StarDrifter's eyes widened as he realised he was listening to an echo of the Dance of Death, of the Dark Music of the Stars. Had this duel been choreographed by WolfStar? Was he *here*, watching? StarDrifter's eyes ran anxiously about the Chamber, but could see nothing beyond the dim figures of those who encircled the Chamber. Did WolfStar watch with the eyes of that courtier? Or perhaps the stableboy beyond? StarDrifter returned his eyes to Borneheld and Axis. That they fought to the sounds of the Dark Music worried him more than anything else – why was the Prophecy using Dark Music to work its will? Was there no place for the Star Dance tonight?

Time passed, and its passage was marked only by the ringing of steel and the scuff of the combatants' boots on the marble floor. Unknowingly, StarDrifter had begun to sway from side to side rhythmically, to sway from side to side with the beat of the Dance of Death.

Both Axis and Borneheld weaved with weariness now, and both began to slip every third or fourth step. Their breath was laboured, their faces and torsos wet with perspiration, while their arms looked as though they had invisible lead weights attached to them. Both men had sustained wounds, but Axis was bleeding a little more heavily than Borneheld. Borneheld was dressed in a thick leather jerkin and trousers, and the leather protected his skin more than Axis' thin linen shirt protected his.

At no point did either man drop his eyes from those of his opponent. They had waited all their lives for this, and every stroke, every thrust, was powered by long years of resentment and hate.

Everything that Faraday saw was shadowed by the vision the trees had shown her. It was as if there were four men out there; every time Axis raised his sword a ghost-like figure beside him raised his, every time Borneheld lunged so a ghost-like figure lunged with him.

Time passed, and the music danced on.

Axis staggered with weariness. How long had he been fighting? Borneheld allowed him no quarter, no time in which to catch his breath, no time in which to position himself to drive home a series of blows and thrusts that might serve to push Borneheld to his knees. His brother seemed to have the strength of a bull, fighting without pause, his eyes gleaming with madness.

In the end it was the eagle who proved Borneheld's undoing. Throughout the fight the bird had clung to its high ledge, bored yet distracted by the fighting going on so far below it.

Finally it began to preen itself, twisting its head to and fro among its feathers as it sought to clean itself of some imagined stain.

It tore a small downy feather from among its chest feathers and spat it out, irritated, then turned back to comb the flight feathers of its left wing.

The white feather slowly floated, this way and that, now rising, now falling, now wafting this way, now that. But always it drifted lower and lower until it began to jerk and sway as it was caught by the laboured breathing of the combatants just beneath it.

It almost lodged in Axis' hair, and Axis flicked his head, irritated by the feathery touch along his forehead, distracted enough that he only just managed to parry a blow close to his chest.

The feather, dislodged from Axis' hair, spiralled upwards a handspan or two, then, caught in a down draught, sank towards the floor. Borneheld had not noticed it, and Axis had forgotten it, as the brothers began a particularly bitter exchange, fighting so close now that they traded blows virtually on the hilts of their swords, taking the strain on their wrists, both their faces reddened and damp from effort and weariness and determination and hate.

The feather settled on the marble floor.

Axis suddenly lunged forward. Momentarily surprised, and caught slightly offguard, Borneheld took a single step backwards and . . . lost his balance as his boot heel slipped on the feather.

It was all Axis needed. As Borneheld swayed, a look of almost comical surprise on his face, Axis hooked his own foot about the inside of Borneheld's knee and pulled his leg out from under him.

Borneheld crashed to the floor, the sword slipping from his grasp, and Axis kicked it across the Chamber. Fear twisting his face, Borneheld scrabbled backwards, seeking space in which to rise. He risked a glance behind him – not two paces away Faraday stood held in Jorge's tight grasp, a look of utter horror on her face. Borneheld stared briefly at his wife, knowing it was all over, knowing he had lost, then he turned his face back towards Axis, wanting to see the blow that would kill him.

All Faraday could see was what the vision let her. Real figures were obscured by the ghostly, and Faraday was certain, *certain*, that it was Axis who had tripped, exhausted, and now lay waiting for death at her feet.

Axis placed his booted foot squarely in the centre of Borneheld's chest, raising his sword, but instead of bringing the blade down to sever the arteries of Borneheld's neck he twisted the sword in his hand and struck Borneheld a stunning blow to his skull with its haft, leaving the man writhing weakly, semiconscious. Then Axis threw the sword away.

Every eye in the Chamber watched, bewildered, as Axis' sword spun across the floor of the Chamber. What was he doing? Why did he not finish Borneheld with a quick, clean blow?

Axis sank to his knees, straddling Borneheld, and drew a knife from his boot. Then he tore open Borneheld's leather jerkin, pushing the flaps to one side, and slid the knife deep and long into the man's chest.

He used both hands wrapped about the haft of the knife to get enough leverage to split Borneheld's sternum in two and crack open his rib cage, grunting with the effort.

The sound of bone splitting open was horrifying. Rivkah, directly across the Chamber, doubled over and gagged at the sound, and Magariz seized her in his arms and held her tight against his chest.

Borneheld's eyes rolled back in his head, and his hands clenched by his sides. His entire body spasmed as Axis threw the knife to one side and took hold of Borneheld's exposed rib cage with both hands and tore it apart.

Under the pressure of Axis' fingers, Borneheld's aorta split asunder. A massive gout of his blood arced out of his chest and splattered across Faraday's neck and chest, running down between her breasts in warm rivulets. Driven to madness by the feel of the warm blood trickling down her body, Faraday screamed and screamed, twisting in Jorge's arms.

But no matter how much she writhed, Faraday could not escape Borneheld's dying stare. Or was it Axis' eyes she saw? Faraday still could not distinguish the real figures from the ghostly. Who was dying at her feet? Whose eyes stared into hers in mute appeal? Was it Axis? Oh Mother, pray that it was not Axis who lay on the floor dying!

His arms bloodied to the elbow, his entire shirt-front warm with his brother's heart blood, Axis reached into Borneheld's open chest cavity and seized his brother's frantically beating heart with his bare hands. Then he tore it out, spraying blood over all those within the immediate vicinity.

"*FreeFall!*" he screamed, leaning back from Borneheld's body and staring into the dome of the Chamber. "*FreeFall!*"

The eagle launched itself from its ledge, its shriek mingling with Axis' scream, and plummeted for the floor of the Chamber.

As the eagle dived, Axis threw Borneheld's still uselessly beating heart as high as he could, black blood spattering in great drops in his golden hair and across the floor of the Chamber. As the heart reached the peak of its arc, the eagle seized it in its talons and crashed to the floor in a tangle of wings, talons and beak, feeding frenziedly on the sweet meat offered it.

Everyone was so horrified by the sight of the eagle tearing Borneheld's heart apart in the centre of the Chamber floor that they were literally incapable of movement. Even Rivkah, held close against Magariz's chest, was mesmerised by the sight of the snow eagle feeding on her eldest son's heart.

Axis leapt to his feet, slipping slightly in the pool of blood about Borneheld's body.

Faraday stared at him, appalled. *He was covered in blood – it dripped from his body, it hung in congealing strings through his hair and beard. He reached out a hand . . .*

. . . and seized Faraday. Jorge let her go, sickened by the sight of the gore that dripped from both Faraday and Axis. Faraday twisted feebly as Axis seized her left wrist, frightened by the look in his eyes, gasping in pain as his warm and slippery fingers closed so tightly about the delicate bones of her wrist that they began to grind against each other.

Borneheld's blood trickled yet further between her breasts, and she gagged. *Everywhere, the blood. She could feel it, smell it, taste it.*

Axis wrenched the Ichtar ruby from her heart finger and half turned back to Borneheld's body. He still kept Faraday caught in his vice-like grip.

"*I have fulfilled my part of the bargain, GateKeeper!*" he screamed, "*Now fulfil yours!*"

He tossed the Ichtar ruby into Borneheld's chest cavity where it glinted momentarily before sinking beneath the pool of coagulating blood where Borneheld's heart had once been.

58

Transformations

For two thousand years she had been trapped in the hated ruby, trapped on the fingers of countless Duchesses of Ichtar. For two thousand years she had been trapped, listening to countless conversations, watching countless lives drift past through a ruby haze, weeping with the countless women forced to wear the ring and endure the cursed Dukes of Ichtar.

It had been the damming of the spring two thousand years ago which had bound Zeherah into this ruby, although what other dark enchantments had been used to trap her, she did not know. Which Duke had it been, so frustrated by the bridge's refusal to let him pass that he had decided to dam the spring and drain the Lake of Life? Zeherah could not remember and, in the end, it did not matter very much. All that mattered was that as the waters had dried up so Zeherah felt herself start to fade. As the sun dried the last muddied puddle in the moat, and the bridge sighed and disappeared, the watching Duke on the far bank had pointed into the moat and cried out at the magnificent ruby lying there in the mud. So Zeherah, the fifth Sentinel, had been condemned to eons trapped in this hated gem.

These last thirty-odd years had been the most frustrating of all. She had been on the finger of the previous Duchess of Ichtar when the Icarii Enchanter had spiralled out of the sky and got the StarMan on her. She had been on the finger of the previous Duchess of Ichtar when she had carried the prophesied babe and when she had gone into labour with him. But Searlas, most damned of men, had wrenched her from Rivkah's finger when she was in the throes of labour, and she had not known whether the babe had been born alive or dead.

For many years she had lain in a cold stone vault somewhere deep in the husk that had once been the extraordinary Sigholt. Wondering, weeping with frustration that the Prophecy walked and she knew nothing of it, she could not move from her ruby-red prison. Where were Ogden and Veremund and Yr? Were they walking now, too? Where was Jack? Jack! Zeherah could not feel any of her companions, but it was the feather-light touch of Jack's mind that she missed the most. Would she ever see him again?

Then one day Borneheld's hand had reached into the vault and grasped her. He had carried her to Carlon and placed her on the finger of the next Duchess. Zeherah had travelled with Faraday through all her adventures, painful and delightful, over the past two years, and with Faraday had watched the Prophecy unfold about her. She had seen the other four Sentinels through Faraday's eyes, but had not been able to communicate with them. She had watched as Faraday fell deeper and deeper in love with the StarMan – Axis, what an unusual name! She had endured Faraday's marriage to Borneheld and watched the fall of Gorkentown. She had aided Faraday in her determination not to fall pregnant to Borneheld – Mother knew she could not wait to see the end of the line of the Dukes who had cursed her. She had travelled with Faraday through the Sacred Grove and the Enchanted Wood.

And tonight Zeherah had watched the death of Borneheld both through Faraday's eyes and through the imprisoning walls of the ruby. And when the StarMan had seized the ruby Zeherah had screamed with delight. When Borneheld's warm blood had closed over the ruby, Zeherah could feel the knots of the curse finally unravel. The death of the last cursed Duke of Ichtar would give her back her life.

He tumbled, puzzled, out of the sun. Where had he been? What had gone wrong? Why was he so confused? There was a tremendous heat about him, and he fell further and further, trying to escape the fire of the sun, but never succeeding. It surrounded him, burned him, seared him, blinded him, and his mind unravelled with the pain and terror. Forgetting to even try to control his headlong fall through the sky he raised his hands to his face, trying to protect his eyes, and screamed.

The heat burst through the Chamber of the Moons in a massive blast that caused all present to throw hands and arms over their faces and turn away. All heard the eagle scream, a sound of pure terror, and those closest to Borneheld's corpse saw a searing red light burn through his body. Axis pulled Faraday to him, protecting her from the worst of the heat and light. When Faraday's vision cleared, she realised it was Axis who held her and Borneheld's bloody corpse that lay at her feet, a golden and white form slowly rising behind it.

"Axis!" she cried and buried her head against his chest.

When the light and the heat faded, people turned back to the heart of the Chamber. Where the eagle had been now crouched a naked Icarii male, white and silver wings, golden hair and violet eyes that stared wonderingly about him.

"FreeFall!" EvenSong cried. She pushed past her stunned father and rushed towards him.

"EvenSong," FreeFall said. "Where are we? What is going on? Who are all these people?"

EvenSong took his hand and raised her violet eyes to Axis, standing with Faraday clutched in his arms. "Thank you," she whispered, "thank you," then she turned back to FreeFall and wrapped arms and wings about him, cradling him gently, crooning with her voice, telling him how much she loved him.

Axis' attention was commanded by the woman who now stood before him. As naked as FreeFall, but with infinitely more presence and power. This must be Zeherah, the lost Sentinel. She was tall and slim, not beautiful but handsome, with her mother's black eyes and deep red hair, as red as the Ichtar ruby, that tumbled down her back.

"Thank you," she said as simply as EvenSong. "Thank you."

And then Jack was by her side.

Axis finally took a deep breath and kissed Faraday briefly.

"It seems I need a wife," he smiled, "and it has just occurred to me that you are now widowed. Will you marry me, Faraday?"

"Yes!" she said fiercely, hugging him tightly, unmindful of the fact that they were both covered in blood. "Yes!"

Jorge stared at them, still appalled by the way Borneheld had died.

"You did not murder to protect your world," Axis said softly, and Jorge started, realising that Axis had raised his eyes to stare at him over the top of Faraday's head. "Remember FreeFall's murder, Jorge. Remember Priam sickening and dying after he publicly announced that he would seek an alliance with me. Think of the thousands of people crucified and murdered in Skarabost because their hearts led them to follow the new way when Borneheld could not relinquish the old."

Jorge lowered his eyes and bowed his head.

"Think of the new life that Borneheld's death has wrought," Axis continued, determined to see that Jorge understood why Borneheld's death had been necessary. "FreeFall, brought back from the halls of the UnderWorld.

Brought back into the life he should never have been thrust from so violently. And Zeherah, trapped in her ruby for thousands of years by the line of the Dukes of Ichtar. Freed finally to take her place with the other Sentinels."

"I accept, Axis." Jorge's eyes flickered over what was left of Borneheld. "This new order demands to be accepted, does it not?"

"I will do whatever I have to," Axis said, "in order to see that it is."

Jorge stared at Axis a moment, then turned away. Axis squeezed Faraday's shoulders then let her go. "Yr, take her away from this. Wash her, and see that she gets some sleep."

Around the Chamber people were finally starting to move, murmur, talk. StarDrifter, bending down by FreeFall and EvenSong's side, looked up at his son and grinned.

"Your enchantments have proved powerful tonight, my son." He tossed Axis' ring towards him, and Axis caught it and slid it back onto his finger.

"I had help, StarDrifter. But I will tell you about it later. FreeFall?"

FreeFall looked up from the floor where he still sat bewildered, EvenSong weeping gently by his side. "Axis? What has been going on? Where am I?"

"You have been away, FreeFall, but now you are home. Rest tonight with EvenSong, and I will tell you of your adventures when we have a quieter moment."

"Tonight?" StarDrifter laughed. "Look, Axis, the dawn begins to lighten the Chamber!"

Axis looked up, startled, and stared at the tiny windows set into the domed roof. StarDrifter was right; the sky was pink with dawn. "Stars," he whispered, "how long did Borneheld and I battle?"

"Most of the night, my friend," Belial said behind him. "Most of the night. I do not know how you have the energy to even stand."

Axis embraced his friend, and took the sword that Belial handed him, sliding it into the empty scabbard at his side.

"Belial. Is the captain of the palace guard here?"

Belial nodded and indicated a tall dark man. The captain of the guard looked distinctly nervous.

"What is your name, Captain?" Axis did not recognise him from when he had been in Carlon two years earlier.

"Hesketh, ah . . ." Hesketh's voice trailed off. "Sire."

"Hesketh, I am now taking control of Carlon as I have taken control of Achar. Does that trouble you?"

"No, Sire." Hesketh glanced across at Yr, just about to step out of the Chamber with Faraday, and she nodded at her lover before disappearing through the doorway.

"Good," Axis said briskly. "You and your guard will now go with Belial and secure the palace. Once you have done that, you may march yourself down to the city gates and open them. Everyone within and without Carlon is free to come and go as they want. There will be no reprisals on my part to the palace guard, or to any remaining soldiers of Borneheld's army within Carlon. All I ask is your loyalty."

"Yes, Sire." Hesketh's voice was a little brisker. "You have it." Axis had fought for the crown of Achar with his brother in this Chamber and won it in fair fight. If all that Axis accused Borneheld of were true, then the gods themselves had judged Borneheld in trial by battle.

"Good," Axis repeated. "Belial? Go with Hesketh. Make sure the palace is secure. Take two of the Ravensbundmen with you – I'll need the other four."

Belial saluted and strode away.

Axis turned and looked for Gautier, Timozel and Jayme. All three were standing to one side, guarded closely by Ho'Demi and his remaining four men.

"Timozel," Axis said, walking over to the group. He honestly did not know what to say to this man. His once light-hearted and good-natured features were now overlain with a dark, brooding manner. His eyes gleamed, almost burned, with fanaticism. "Timozel. Do your vows to Faraday still stand?"

Timozel stared at Axis. He had watched the battle and its outcome with horror. Now Borneheld lay dead on the floor before him and his visions appeared about to crumble into lies. Where were the armies that undulated in leagues in every direction? Where were the tens of thousands who screamed his name? The victories? Where? Where? *Where*?

And what about Faraday? Her husband lies dead and butchered on the cold and unforgiving floor. Will she let Axis seize her?

"Yes. I am still Faraday's Champion. And I can see that she will need my advice and guidance more than ever, Axis, in case she should be tempted to make decisions she will ever regret."

Axis fought to keep his face expressionless. "Don't forget that you are bound to protect her and support her, Timozel, in *whatever* decisions she makes. You are not her lord."

"And I swear by whatever gods are listening, Axis, that I will do my utmost to make sure that you will not be her lord either!" Timozel hissed, then abruptly brushed past Axis and strode from the room.

"Let him go," Axis said as Ho'Demi made to follow. "None of us can do much to stop him. And he is Faraday's Champion; I will not harm him."

"He is dangerous," Ho'Demi observed. Something dark had taken possession of that young man's soul.

Axis ignored Ho'Demi and turned to Gautier. The man's face was gaunt and tired.

"You followed Borneheld too easily, Gautier," Axis said. "I cannot forget that. But," Axis paused and his eyes caught briefly with Ho'Demi's, "it is not I who has best reason to stand and accuse you, Gautier. You are a man hated by your own troops for your cruelties. How many men have you ordered slaughtered, because they could not crawl another step? Because they could not give any more of their strength than they had already given? But your worst crime, Gautier? Your worst crime? You crucified three brave Ravensbundmen, men whose only transgression was to speak well of me. Ho'Demi," Axis turned to address the Ravensbund chief. "He is yours to do with as you wish. All that I ask," Axis glanced at the high windows, "is that he be dead by nightfall."

"No!" Gautier shrieked, horrified, struggling as two grinning Ravensbundmen seized him by the arms. "Kill me now! A quick sword thrust, Axis, I beg you! Don't hand me over to those savages!"

Axis looked back at Ho'Demi. "Dead by nightfall, Ho'Demi. Throw his body on the refuse heaps outside the city for all to see."

"What is left of it," Ho'Demi said smoothly.

"Leave me two of your four soldiers, Ho'Demi," Axis said, watching Gautier crumple with fear. "I doubt you will need an entire unit to keep Gautier under control."

Ho'Demi saluted. "I thank you for this gift, Great Lord," he said, then signalled to the two Ravensbundmen who held Gautier to follow him, and strode out of the Chamber.

"Well, Jayme," Axis said, turning to the Brother-Leader of the Seneschal. "You seem to have presided over the virtual downfall of the Seneschal, have you not? The 'Forbidden'," and Axis almost snarled the word, "are coming home. Moving back to the hills and plains that the Seneschal has so long denied them."

He stopped speaking and stared at Jayme, almost unable to believe the change that had come over the man. As long as Axis could remember, Jayme had been strong and full of vitality. He had always been a man to take pride in his accomplishments and in his appearance.

Yet this man who now cowered before Axis looked like a broken-down ploughman, crippled by years of back-breaking labour and deadening poverty. He cringed under Axis' level stare, his clothes torn and stained, his hair dishevelled, pieces of food and spittle clinging to his white beard.

"Moryson? Gilbert?" Axis asked.

"Gone," Jayme muttered.

"Take him to a secure room," Axis instructed the two remaining Ravensbundmen. He could not send this cowering old man to the dungeons. "And lock him inside. Make sure the window is bolted so that he cannot throw himself from its ledge. I will talk to him later."

Axis turned and saw Rivkah, still supported by Magariz, staring at Borneheld's body.

Rivkah. Axis started to walk towards her. What could he say? He paused by Borneheld's body and glanced down. Borneheld's grey eyes, dull and blood-spattered now, stared sightlessly at the gold and silver moons that chased each other among the bright stars of the enamelled blue dome high above. Axis leaned down and closed them, catching the glint of gold among Borneheld's blood-encrusted hair. His gold circlet. The circlet of the Kings of Achar. Axis hesitated, then lifted the heavy circlet of gold from Borneheld's dead head and pulled the amethyst ring of office from his finger. Standing upright, he wiped them clean of blood and stared at them as they rested in his hands. His, Axis supposed. Both represented the entire authority of the throne of Achar.

Axis did not intend to take the throne of Achar. He did not want it, and he intended to make it redundant in the new Tencendor. Then what to do with these now-useless badges of office? Still considering, Axis walked slowly towards Rivkah.

Her eyes were riveted to his blood-stained face. So much blood smeared across her son, so much splattered about this Chamber. It made her think of the bloody births which had brought her sons into the world. How else could it have ended? How else?

"Rivkah," Axis said gently. He held the golden circlet and the ring uncomfortably in his hands, not knowing what to do with them.

Rivkah reached out a trembling hand to Axis. His torso had several deep wounds in it. Not serious, but they were still bleeding, and Rivkah could see the glint of a rib bone through one.

"You're hurt," she whispered and her fingers traced feather-light across his chest.

"These wounds will heal well enough once I visit the surgeon's tent and let him stitch me back together again," Axis replied.

Rivkah nodded and dropped her eyes. "I think it was hardest on me, Axis, watching you and Borneheld fight last night. I have never loved Borneheld, and I think I almost hated him for what he did to Priam . . . but . . . but . . ." Her eyes filled with tears and she could not finish.

Axis leaned forward and embraced her a little awkwardly.

"It is hard," she whispered against his chest, "to watch your two sons battle each other to the death."

On impulse Axis handed her the circlet of gold and the amethyst ring. "Here. Take the circlet and the ring. I will not use them. And you are the last of your line, Rivkah. Wear them, melt them down, break them up and sell them, I care not."

Rivkah sniffed and took the circlet and the ring. Her father had worn these, and her brother, as had so many Kings of Achar before them.

Axis looked at Magariz, dark and solemn behind Rivkah. "As soon as you can find some spare soldiers, Magariz, or perhaps use some of the servants still standing gaggling about here, take Borneheld's corpse and throw it on the refuse heaps outside the city walls. He belongs to the crows now."

Rivkah flinched, and her fingers tightened about the ring and the circlet.

It was not until late that night that Axis, his wounds itching and sore from the attentions of the surgeons, managed to find a quiet moment to himself. The palace had been subdued easily – there was no resistance. Belial and his men combed the palace from its gold-plated minarets to its shit-stained dungeons. They found mostly servants eager to please and courtiers eager to flatter. The servants Belial sent about their duties, the courtiers he sent back to their townhouses – time enough for flatteries later. Towards the end of their search they found a dozen Brothers of the Seneschal, as well as Earl Isend and an over-rouged woman cowering together in a room. Axis, who had experienced enough death this past day to last him many, many months, had ordered that they be shipped south to Coroleas.

Once the palace was secure, Axis spent the day in and about Carlon. Talking, soothing, taking charge of the city. The Carlonese had simply shrugged their shoulders and accepted that Axis had replaced Borneheld. They were far more enthralled by Princess Rivkah's return. Rivkah had spent part of the day in the streets, talking to the mayor and several of the Masters of the Guilds, as also to some of the ordinary citizens who hung shyly about, hoping to be noticed. Faraday accompanied her, and the widowed Queen and the resurrected Princess did much to calm people's fears about what the previous night had wrought. Several of the Icarii accompanied them, and the citizens' worries about the flying creatures were allayed by Rivkah and Faraday's assurances. The mayor was so enthralled by SpikeFeather he invited him home for dinner that night.

Belial cast open the gates of the city, as Axis had requested, and slowly the people of Carlon began to mingle with members of Axis' force. News, food, gifts and laughter were exchanged and mothers, wives and sweethearts learned word of who had and hadn't survived. By late afternoon there was a slow procession of women and children walking on the freshly turned graves of the fields beyond Bedwyr Fort, carrying flowers and last gifts, to say a final and quiet farewell.

Finally alone in one of the palace's guestrooms, Axis closed his eyes and let the warmth of the fire soothe his wounds. He was tired. So tired. Within a few days he would proclaim Tencendor, then move north to confront Gorgrael. Perhaps, he thought vaguely, his mind starting to drift off, it would be best to start sending troops north soon. Tomorrow morning. Who knew when Gorgrael would choose to attack. He must know of the troubles in southern Achar – *Tencendor!* This would be the perfect time to strike.

Faraday slipped into the room, wearing a deep blue cloak. Her hair was loose and her eyes shone. She smiled with love at Axis, asleep in the arm chair by the fire. He had washed and changed out of his blood-stained breeches during the day, but he still bore the marks of his fight with Borneheld. His chest and upper arms were bruised and marked in several places with the bristling cat-gut stitching of the surgeons. The joints of his sword hand were swollen with the effort of gripping the sword for so long.

"Axis," she said softly. She had waited so long for this. So long. Faraday had no intention of waiting any longer.

Axis opened his eyes, blinking slightly as he focused on her. "Faraday?"

She fiddled with the tassels holding the cloak at her throat, then suddenly it was free and fallen to the floor. She was completely naked underneath.

Axis stared at her. Stars, didn't she know how tired he was? He had not slept in almost two days – and had spent the last night grappling to the death with her husband. His entire body ached, and the freshly stitched wounds hurt more than he had been prepared to admit to the concerned surgeon.

But Faraday was a beautiful woman, and Axis slowly sat up, staring at her.

She smiled and knelt down at his feet, pulling his boots off, running her hand teasingly up the inside of his thigh. Then she leaned forward on her knees and kissed his breast, again teasing, and Axis physically jerked as his body began to respond to her touch.

Oh Azhure! he thought, carefully shielding his mind. It has been so long since you let me touch you, and you knew that it would come to this.

But as Faraday's hands moved more firmly over his body and her mouth grew insistent, Axis' internal turmoil grew. One moment he wondered, consumed with jealousy, if Borneheld had taught Faraday these tricks – these were not the actions of the young virgin he had kissed beneath the stars of the Ancient Barrows – and the next he writhed with guilt that his body should betray Azhure in this way.

Faraday laughed when Axis finally seized her, but as he made love to her on the hearth rug before the fire Faraday did not know that his ardour was driven by his desperate need to bury as deep as he could the guilt he felt over his betrayal of his Lover. It took all of Axis' self-control not to call out Azhure's name in his desire. And when it was over, and Axis had finally relaxed by her side, Faraday thought he cried for love of her, not for the love he had betrayed.

No-one, not Belial, not Rivkah, not even the Sentinels, had yet told Faraday about Azhure or about Caelum. And when the betrayal did come, Faraday would always resent very keenly that none had warned her. That none had thought to tell her.

As Faraday held the secret for the success of the Prophecy, so she also held the seeds of Axis' destruction in her power.

59

Shattered Vows

Timozel spent the night looking for Faraday, his mouth tight as he strode the corridors of the palace in Carlon. Borneheld had been good. Good. Brave. A true knight. To die like that had only underscored his goodness in Timozel's eyes.

He forgot that Borneheld had not wanted to listen to vision; had refused to grant Timozel command of his armies.

Occasionally as he wandered the corridors Timozel would have to flatten himself against a stone wall to avoid one of the Forbidden wandering through the palace. Filth! his mind whispered. Filth! They were already infiltrating the palace and before much longer they would take control of Achar. By winter all that the Seneschal had achieved would undoubtedly be lost. Before the year was out the Forbidden would have enslaved the good people of Achar again.

All was ruined. All was lost with Borneheld's death. The light had gone from Timozel's world.

He needed to speak with Faraday. Needed to remind her of her duty to her dead husband's memory, to tell her that the only suitable life for her now was one of serene contemplation in a quiet Retreat far from the excitement of Carlon. Faraday could not be trusted to control her own weaknesses. Especially regarding Axis.

He found Yr eventually – the slut was wandering back from the barracks in the early morning light – and asked her where Faraday was.

Yr raised an eyebrow knowingly. "Why, with Axis, no doubt," she said. "Last night was a night when lost loves were reunited. EvenSong and FreeFall. Jack and Zeherah. And Axis and . . ."

"No!" Timozel interjected, so angry he was tempted to strike her, but Yr's blue eyes blazed with such power that Timozel took a step back.

"Think not to strike me!" she hissed, and Timozel took another step backwards. "Now that we are five, now that we are whole, our power has increased dramatically. We will provide the weapon that Axis will use to best Gorgrael! Think not to touch me now!"

Gorgrael! Timozel's face darkened with fear, and then he turned and bolted inside the palace.

Yr looked after him, a puzzled expression over her pretty face.

Still Timozel roamed the corridors of the palace. He had checked most of the main apartments, startling many a sleepy occupant with his sudden entrances and then equally sudden departures. Timozel was sickened to discover noblewomen of court disporting themselves with the flying filth that Axis had brought into the palace in three separate apartments.

Where was Faraday? How could she have succumbed to Axis' seductions not twenty-four hours after her husband had been torn apart at her feet?

He found them eventually, in one of the lesser apartments normally reserved for visiting diplomats. They were curled asleep together, naked before the glowing coals of a fire.

"Faraday," Timozel whispered, aghast.

Faraday's eyes flew open. "Tim!" she gasped and sat up, her face red, her eyes hurriedly searching for her cloak.

Axis had been heavily asleep, his body desperate for rest after his duel with Borneheld, and his mind was so fogged with sleep that he did not realise immediately what was going on.

"You whore!" Timozel shouted, stepping forward and raising his fist threateningly. "Your husband has been dead less than twenty-four hours and you allow his murderer to crawl onto your body. You have violated his memory with your disgusting lust!"

Axis leapt to his feet, fully awake now. "Timozel," he grunted, reaching for the sword that hung in its scabbard by the fire.

"Stop it!" Faraday cried, reaching for Axis.

Axis turned before he was halfway to the sword and stepped back to grasp Timozel by his upraised fist. "What Faraday does is none of your business," he hissed. "Get out!"

"You have as much control as a rutting tom-cat, don't you Axis?" Timozel sneered. "Have you enjoyed the Queen, then? Have you impregnated her with whatever filthy diseases you have picked up from the whores you've slept with in the past?"

"Timozel!" Faraday cried again, but Timozel and Axis were now staring each other in the eye, almost totally unaware of her presence.

"I have heard of the licentious behaviour of the Icarii," Timozel grunted, his face only inches from Axis' now. "Heard of their filthy rutting ways. Have seen them assaulting fair women in apartments of this palace. Have you impregnated Faraday with disease of human whore, Axis, or Icarii?"

Axis' face twisted with rage and he literally growled, reaching for Timozel's throat with his other hand.

"*Stop!*" Faraday screamed, certain that one would kill the other before she had time to draw the next breath. "*Stop!*"

Both men paused, neither wanting to be the first to drop his eyes from the other's stare.

"Timozel," Faraday said more quietly, although her voice was still strained. "Timozel, look at me!"

Grudgingly, Timozel looked away from Axis and towards Faraday. What he saw made him step back from Axis in shock.

"Faraday, no!" he whispered in horror.

Faraday, standing straight and tall, held a large earthenware pot in her hands, and she was staring into Timozel's eyes unflinchingly. The time had come to end this charade of Championship.

"No," Timozel whispered again and took a step towards her.

"Stay back," Faraday said, her voice firm. Axis stepped back himself, his eyes swinging between Timozel and Faraday. What was happening between them? The power almost blazed out of Faraday's green eyes, while Timozel was abnormally ashen.

"I accepted your oath of Championship two years ago," Faraday said calmly, "when I was young and friendless and going into a marriage that I knew I would loathe. I thought that you would be a friend, a support, a pillar of strength who I could lean on through difficult times. You have proved anything but, Timozel. You supported Borneheld against me, you derided me when I needed love, you lectured me on my behaviour when I needed sympathy."

"No." Timozel reached out his hand to her. "No, Faraday. I have only ever done what was best for you. I have only told you what you needed to hear. You have been wayward, sometimes, and a Champion's duty is to return his Lady's steps to the correct path."

"I pity you, Timozel, and I grieve for you," Faraday said slowly. "I grieve for the bright-eyed, tousle-headed boy who I met riding across the Plains of Tare. Where did you go? What happened to you? Why this brooding hulk before me now? You are no Champion of Brightness, Timozel, but a

Champion of Shadow. You will wander strange borderlands until you lose your way and your soul completely." Faraday's eyes had glazed over until it appeared she was dreaming — even her words had the singsong quality of seer-saying.

"I have done with you, Timozel. If ever you find your way into the Light again, then wander my way, for I shall be glad to see once again the friend I have lost. Timozel. As this pot shatters," she said very, very quietly, "so then will the ties that bind us shatter."

She let go the pot and Timozel made a desperate dive for it. He almost made it, almost caught it, felt his fingertips graze its smooth surface the instant before it shattered into a thousand pieces across the stone floor.

"*No!*" he screamed, and both Faraday and Axis recoiled a little at the sound of his despair.

"So shatter the vows that bind us, Timozel. You are my Champion no longer. Begone."

In his ice castle so far to the north Gorgrael leaned his face to the wind and screamed in pure joy. Timozel! He was his! *His!*

Darkness swirled about the room and threatened to overwhelm Timozel. As the pot shattered across the floor he had felt the last vestiges of the boy he'd once been shatter and disappear. No-one mourned the loss of that carefree boy more than Timozel himself. And no-one hated more than he the man he had become.

But he was unable to resist the slow darkening of his soul. Thoughts that were not his crowded his head until he felt he would shriek in despair. Memories that were not his were taking over his life. Once, once . . . oh, once, Timozel had woken to find himself standing at the very lip of a well, listening to the screams of the young girl he had just flung down to drown in the waters far below.

That experience had virtually driven Timozel mad.

What had he become?

What forces were trying to take over his life?

Now, as Timozel raised his tear-stained face to Faraday, he knew that he need wonder no longer. She had shattered the vows that bound him to her, and she had freed him to Gorgrael's service.

"Get out," Faraday said flatly, stepping back. "Get out of my life."

Timozel slowly raised himself to his feet, staring at Faraday as she clutched the blue cloak around her nakedness. Had he treated her badly? Timozel had only tried to do what he thought was right.

"I'm sorry," he said vaguely, and he was not sure if he addressed the apology to Faraday or to Axis, or to both of them.

"I'm sorry," he said again, and then turned on his heel and walked out of the chamber, closing the door quietly behind him.

He walked down to the courtyard, mounted the first saddled horse he could find, then rode through Carlon, tears streaking his face.

All who saw him stood back and let him pass.

Once he was past the gates of Carlon, Timozel turned his horse's head north, for already he could feel Gorgrael's grip tightening.

Neither Axis nor Faraday would see Timozel again for a very, very long time.

60

Tencendor on the Shores of Grail Lake

Eight days after killing Borneheld, Axis proclaimed Tencendor in a grand and emotionally charged cere- mony on the shores of Grail Lake. It was later than Axis had wanted, but he had underestimated the time that he – that everyone – would need to heal after the war between himself and Borneheld. Virtually the entire population of Carlon moved to the fields that abutted the eastern shores of the Lake for the ceremony and the celebrations. Mingling with the people of Carlon (and the thousands of other Acharites who had journeyed to the city to see for themselves) were the individual members of Axis' army: Ravensbund men and women, Acharites and Icarii. Most of the Carlonese, never strong followers of the Seneschal, had accepted the presence of the Icarii with little trouble; indeed, they had welcomed the birdmen and women into their markets. Other Acharites – especially those from the rural areas – hung back, unsure, some even sullen, but overall there was surprisingly little fuss made about the presence of the Icarii.

Embeth, feeling slightly lost and overwhelmed by the events surrounding her, and missing Judith (who had elected to remain behind in Tare), had succumbed to StarDrifter's eyes and insistence and now shared an apartment in the palace with him. Embeth knew their affair would fade and die in the days or weeks ahead, but she desperately needed something, someone, to cling to. Soon, perhaps, she would move back to Tare. There was nothing left for her here. Her two youngest children were now married and lived far to the west; and Timozel . . . Timozel had vanished. Embeth turned her back on the excited crowd and slowly began to walk back to Carlon.

On the night of the duel, Azhure spent the entire time pacing the eastern shore of Grail Lake, watching the dawn gather, waiting, waiting, waiting. When the golden standard was finally run up the flagpole above the palace, Azhure had broken down and wept, both with relief and with wretched-ness, because she knew she had finally lost Axis to Faraday.

Azhure was more than a little bit nervous about today's ceremony. She had not seen Axis since he had rowed off into the night to face Borneheld, although she had heard most of what had happened from Belial. Today she would see him – and Faraday. She had heard that the woman had spent the past eight days laughing with joy – and why shouldn't she? She had spent those eight days with Axis.

And the problem of her pregnancy increased Azhure's nervousness. Axis had sent word that he wanted Azhure richly dressed today – and in a gown he'd had made for her. Azhure was now moving into her fifth month of pregnancy, and even though Icarii babies were small, this one bulged more than Caelum had at the same stage. Well, Azhure smiled a little bitterly, a gown it would be. She would no longer hide her growing pregnancy behind the armour of tunic and mail.

The rich, dark red material of the gown set off Azhure's pale complexion and blue eyes perfectly, and Imibe threaded tiny seed pearls through Azhure's hair to match the pearls that had been stitched into the gown. It was a noblewoman's gown, and Azhure stared at her reflection for a long time once Imibe had finished dressing her hair.

She heard a step, and a rose- and gold-brocaded Ysgryff entered to escort Azhure to the ceremony. Over the past eight days no-one had spent more time with Azhure than Ysgryff. He had spent his evenings with her, making her laugh, despite her sad-heartedness, with his stories of life among the Nors capital of Ysbadd and his early years spent sailing with the pirate ships of Pirates' Nest. In those hours when he sensed that Azhure simply needed companionship, Ysgryff would sit quietly, watching the fire crackle, perhaps scratching the head of one of the Alaunt.

Ysgryff complimented Azhure on her appearance, then stared at her belly for a long moment. "If you need anything, Azhure, *anything*, then ask me," he said, taking her elbow. "Axis is a fool ten-times over that he does not take you for his wife."

"Faraday is so powerful, so magical," Azhure began, but Ysgryff took her by the shoulders and shook her slightly. "There is *no-one* who can compare to you, Azhure! Axis risks losing his soul if he lets you fade away!"

It was a very strange thing for Ysgryff to say, and Azhure stared at him until Ysgryff's handsome face relaxed into a smile, and he patted her cheek playfully.

"Come, lovely lady," he said lightly. "Great happenings await us at Spiredore."

It was a twenty-minute walk to Spiredore, and Azhure, Caelum in her arms, moved slowly through the throng, Baron Ysgryff at her side. Axis had reserved seats for them at the very front of the crowd. People smiled and ducked their heads as Ysgryff and Azhure moved past them. Both were richly dressed and obviously noble, and the child in the woman's arms radiated such an aura of greatness that many gasped in wonder.

A dais had been erected at the foot of the tower of Spiredore and to its right a group of chairs were set up. Belial, Cazna, Magariz and Rivkah were already there, and they rose to greet Azhure and Ysgryff as they approached.

"You look splendid," Rivkah whispered in Azhure's ear.

"I look pregnant," she grumbled back quietly.

Belial kissed her cheek softly in greeting and glanced at her stomach, saying nothing, yet Azhure saw the flash of pain in his eyes.

Ho'Demi and Sa'Kuya arrived, both wrapped in snow-white icebear furs, the very tips of the fur tinted sky blue. Their hair was freshly plaited and greased, and more chips of blue and green glass and bright brass chimes hung among their braids than ever before. They looked splendidly savage with their blue tattooed faces and blood-red suns blazing at all from the centre of their foreheads and they kissed their friends and comrades enthusiastically. All the Ravensbund people had been looking forward to this day for a very long time.

The Sentinels, five now and content, sat to the left of the dais. Jack sat very close to Zeherah, and, although no-one had ever seen them touch, few had any doubts that their relationship was closer than that shared by any of the other Sentinels.

"My friends," called a voice slightly, and then StarDrifter alighted on the grass, followed immediately by EvenSong, FreeFall and FarSight CutSpur. Azhure had heard the tale of how FreeFall had been brought back from the dead in the Chamber of the Moons. EvenSong, shy but obviously excited, had brought FreeFall to talk with Azhure one evening, and Azhure had delighted in the birdman's company. He had been quiet and amusing, and had carried with him an air of such haunting beauty that most who found themselves in his company simply wanted to sit and watch him. Azhure had been no exception.

FreeFall had been so altered by death and reincarnation that the air of mysticism which most Icarii wore was strengthened tenfold in him. He remembered nothing of his time in the Halls of the Dead, and had only the vaguest memory of flying as an eagle. Axis, apparently, had refused to tell anyone of the mysteries he had concluded in the UnderWorld that had seen both FreeFall and Zeherah restored to the living world.

RavenCrest, still in Talon Spike, had received the joyous news of his son's return from the dead several days ago. He had not been able to fly south for the ceremonies to reforge Tencendor, but Azhure hoped that RavenCrest would re-meet his son again as soon as possible.

Azhure turned from regarding FreeFall and EvenSong and looked straight into StarDrifter's level eyes. She stilled at what she saw there. He stepped forward and embraced her, but with a shock Azhure felt his hand suddenly press hard against her belly and felt the light touch of power throb through her for an instant. She drew back silently; this was not the time or the place to make a fuss. And Azhure did not want for a moment to admit to herself the slight thrill of pleasure that both his touch and his power had given her.

"Azhure!" StarDrifter whispered so that only she could hear. "You are a wondrous gift to the SunSoar family! You carry not one but two babes within you. A son, and a daughter. Both will be Enchanters. Ah, Azhure, you are an enchanted woman yourself!" In the entire history of the Icarii race, only twice before had an Icarii woman given birth to twins.

Azhure's eyes widened. Twins! "Thank you, StarDrifter," she murmured and sat down in the chair behind her. What he had done to her was an undoubted intrusion, but both his touch and his words had comforted and strengthened Azhure at a time when she desperately needed both comfort and strength.

StarDrifter sat down beside her, Ysgryff hurrying to take the seat on her other side, and Azhure smiled as she settled Caelum comfortably on her lap. The boy was dressed in a suit of dark red velvet that matched her dress and, with his mop of black curls and blue eyes, looked every bit as striking as his mother. *Another son and a daughter*, Azhure thought. *Can* she *do that for him?*

She? Caelum's thought intruded into her mind. *She? Who is this 'she' who you have thought about so much recently? Is it Faraday?*

Pay attention, Caelum. Your father will be here soon.

StarDrifter had caught the exchange and was so stunned he literally rocked on his chair. He stared at Azhure. *How did she do that? How?* The ability to speak with the mind voice was one shared only by the most powerful of Enchanters – many of the lesser Icarii Enchanters never mastered the ability.

"Axis," Azhure said softly, breaking StarDrifter's thoughts.

A boat had drawn up to the shore and Axis and Faraday were stepping out. Azhure took a deep breath when she saw Faraday. She looked as wondrous as she had appeared in the vision Azhure had seen at Yuletide when StarDrifter had summoned Faraday to awaken the Earth Tree with him. She was dressed in a cream silk gown, heavily brocaded, its square neckline emphasising her pale breasts and neck. *Oh Stars*, thought Azhure in despair, *she is* so *beautiful!*

Faraday's face, indeed, her whole carriage, exuded happiness and contentment. She walked by Axis, touching his arm now and then, the dress swaying out from her hips slightly as she walked. Every smile she gave Axis, every step she took by his side, shouted her love for the man.

Axis looked fit and relaxed. He wore the golden tunic, the blood-red sun blazing in the centre of his chest, over the red breeches – now cleaned of any trace of blood. A golden sword swung by his side, and his hair and beard had been trimmed and brushed so that they caught the afternoon sun and glinted almost as gold as the material of his tunic.

The murmur of the tens of thousands gathered behind them grew to a swell of sound as Axis and Faraday approached the dais, and Azhure felt tears spring into her eyes. Faraday was so much the Queen that Azhure suddenly felt small and insignificant.

StarDrifter took her hand. "You are SunSoar as much if not more than Rivkah," he said. "You will always find a home and a welcome among us should you need it."

At the edge of the dais Faraday relinquished Axis' arm as he mounted the platform, moving to sit with the Sentinels.

"Why does she not stand with him?" Azhure asked. She moved Caelum closer to her stomach, delaying the moment when Axis would see her pregnancy.

"Borneheld is only a week dead," Ysgryff answered. "His bones are still to be completely picked clean on the refuse heap."

Beside him Azhure shuddered. As Axis had requested, Borneheld's body had been thrown to rot on the refuse heap and, as dusk fell on the day of his death, Gautier had joined him. Gautier had paid dearly and long for the crucifixion of the three Ravensbundmen in Jervois Landing.

"So it is better that Faraday sit apart from him rather than at his side. Otherwise people might talk," Ysgryff concluded.

Faraday smiled at the Sentinels as she sat down among them. Then her eyes drifted about the front row of chairs. She caught Rivkah's eye and smiled and nodded. She had enjoyed getting to know Rivkah very much. Both, as former Duchesses of Ichtar, had much in common and many memories to share. Faraday glanced at StarDrifter. Ah, his knowing eyes were enough to make any woman blush. And who was that striking Nors woman sitting by his side? She held a beautiful child, a boy, in her lap, and she smiled and chatted with Baron Ysgryff and StarDrifter. Faraday frowned a little. Was this the courageous Azhure who she had heard some gossip about? None of the gossip had mentioned a son – or how beautiful the woman was. A flash of gold at the corner of her vision caught Faraday's attention and all thoughts of the raven-haired woman faded from her mind.

Axis strode to the front of the dais and the crowd hushed. He bowed in the traditional Icarii greeting, turning to include all present. As he turned to the right he looked down at the row of chairs holding his closest friends and allies and smiled. His eyes caught Azhure's and she held her breath, her hands tightening about Caelum.

Axis straightened and faced the crowd. He slowly lifted a hand, his fingers beckoning.

Azhure gasped, as she heard Rivkah do so some few chairs further down. Both women recognised the gesture instantly. StarDrifter had used it to Rivkah and Azhure in his efforts to seduce both of them, and Axis had used it to Azhure, both at Beltide in the groves and on the rooftop of Sigholt after he had returned from the UnderWorld.

But now Axis was intent on seducing an entire nation, and from the intakes of breath that Azhure could hear behind her, she guessed he was doing a reasonable job of it.

"My people," he said simply, and his voice carried over the mass of people that stretched almost the entire way around the eastern and southern shores of Grail Lake. Enchantments Axis might have used to make his voice, and perhaps even the sight of him, carry about the crowd, but StarDrifter realised that those were the only enchantments that Axis was using. As with his success in the Icarii Assembly, Axis intended to reforge Tencendor using the sheer force of his personality.

"My people. A thousand years ago a nation died in this land. All suffered because of it – the Acharites, the Avar and the Icarii. One people lost beauty and music from their lives, and they lost the shadowed paths where once they had walked in search of mysteries and love. Two other races lost their homelands and those sites that remain holy to them to this day. My people," and all present understood Axis meant all three races, "let me tell you about the land of Tencendor that was lost to all of us."

Then he began to sing. Azhure remembered how Star-Drifter had sung to the Icarii Assembly in the first week she had arrived to live with the Icarii. Then she had thought his voice wonderful, magical. She had heard Axis sing before, too, but only softly to the accompaniment of his harp about a camp fire at night. Nothing she had heard before, whether from StarDrifter or from Axis, was quite as remarkable as how and what Axis sang now. Caelum sat still in wonder on her lap, his eyes locked onto his father, his little mouth open in a round "O" of astonishment. The baby inside her, *babies*, twisted slightly, hearing their father's voice at its full power for the first time, and they reacted strongly to it.

Axis sang of Tencendor, and where he had got the knowledge for it Azhure did not know. He sang of its beauties and of its music. Of the cities that had been lost, and of the woods and parklands that had withered and died over the past thousand years. He sang of the games that had once been held between the three races, and of the sky races that the Icarii had held to amuse the Avar and the Acharites. He sang of the learning and knowledge that Tencendor had fostered, of the schools and academies, of the study of the Stars and of the mysteries as well as of more mundane problems that, once solved, had improved life for all. He sang of the adventures that all had participated in, of the life and the loves, the music and the harmony, the flowers and the leaves.

But then Axis' voice changed slightly. It became sorrowful, and Axis sang of how distrust had destroyed the harmony between the races. He sang of how the Acharites had come to envy the Icarii and fear the Avar. Of how the Icarii had not realised that they sometimes unwittingly assumed an elite role within ancient Tencendor society, and how, knowingly, they sometimes laughed at the Acharites for their inability to fly.

"The Icarii ruled over ancient Tencendor society," Axis said, reverting to his speaking voice that, nonetheless, sounded every bit as beautiful as his singing voice. "And eventually that caused problems. I want to reforge Tencendor, yes, that is true, but I want to create a new Tencendor where the Icarii are but one race among three, where all three will share the wealth and delights of this new land. My people, I am the StarMan and it is my role to lead this new land into the future. I combine blood of the royal houses of both Icarii and Acharite peoples," and Axis explained for the benefit of those few who had not yet heard his story how he had been conceived and by whom. "I am both Icarii and human, I combine the compassion of the human with the arts of the Icarii. I am both human and Icarii," he repeated, "and my issue combines both Icarii and human."

Faraday frowned in some puzzlement. Combines? Surely, *will combine*?

"It will be my House which will lead the new nation. Not the House of SunSoar and not the House of Achar, but . . ." he paused, "the House of the Stars."

All – Icarii, Acharite and Ravensbund – stared at him, open-mouthed.

"Friends," Axis continued, "many of you do not know me, but many do. Many have fought with me, whether in the Axe-Wielders or my new-forged command. Many of you know me. You know what sort of man I am.

"My people," and again he held out his hand in the gesture of seduction, "will you stand with me to forge Tencendor? Will you accept me to lead you back into what was and forward into what will be? Will you ride at my back to defeat the Destroyer? To drive Gorgrael from this land so that we might all create the new land of Tencendor together? Will you stand behind the House of the Stars and behind the

StarMan? Will you offer me your loyalty? Your hearts? Your voice?"

For an instant the entire field was silent, then, far back in the crowd, someone screamed, "StarMan!" and in the next heartbeat the entire field had taken up the chant. "StarMan! StarMan! StarMan! StarMan!"

Azhure sat in her chair, breathless with excitement, listening to the sky erupt about her as the crowd chanted to their StarMan. Ogden and Veremund wept with joy and clasped each other's hands.

"Brilliant stroke, dear boy," Ogden whispered, emotion almost completely choking his voice. "Brilliant stroke. You show how in your blood you combine the two leading houses of both Acharite and Icarii nations, and, in doing so, create a third House, a new House for the new land of Tencendor. A House that, while combining the blood of the old, promises a new future beyond the hatreds of the past."

Axis stood back and let the acclaim ring through him. His face was grave, but his mind and soul sang with joy. He could feel the tug of the Prophecy here today. He had not entertained a single doubt from the moment he'd stepped onto the dais. He glanced down at Azhure and Caelum again. She looked immensely alluring in that dress, bouncing their son on her lap. How many nights had he lain awake as Faraday slept beside him, thinking of Azhure? Yearning for her?

What he felt for Faraday was so different to his consuming love for Azhure. For Faraday he felt gratefulness and friendship. Perhaps that could be called love. But it was like a dull child's toy compared to the shining love and devouring need he had for Azhure.

Oh my love, his heart cried, why is it that I cannot marry you? How it is that I will enjoy so very few years with you?

But what years he would have Axis was determined to have to the full. If Faraday had not heard any court gossip about his relationship, then she would leave the shores of

Grail Lake today in no doubt as to the position of this woman in his life.

Axis had opened his mouth on several occasions to broach the subject, but Faraday had always turned to him with such love in her eyes that he had swallowed his words and kissed her instead. Well, he thought, it's too late now to leap down and whisper hurriedly in her ear. She will simply have to accept it, as Azhure has learned to accept it.

Again he glanced at Azhure, and wondered desperately if he would be able to go to her tonight.

The shouting was now dying down and Axis held out his arms. "After a thousand-year hiatus," he said clearly, "and with your assent, I proclaim the reforged land of Tencendor. Tencendor!"

"Tencendor!" the shout came back at him.

Again Axis let them shout for a few moments, then he smiled and held up his hands for silence. "There will be few changes, apart from the new friends you see among you. Almost none of the Acharites will lose lands to the Icarii and Avar, and those who do will receive generous compensation in return for their land. Both the Icarii and the Avar realise that they cannot move back to what they once held and are willing to cede to you most of their old lands."

Again a cheer went up. The treaty Axis had signed with Ysgryff and Greville was common knowledge about Carlon now, and the people were already aware that the arrival of the Icarii and, one day, the Avar, posed little threat to them.

"Those of you with titles and hereditary lands will keep both rank and lands, although," Axis' face assumed a sad expression, "with the war that has enveloped Tencendor over the past months, and with those lost fighting the Skraelings to the north, land and titles have fallen vacant. My friends, over the past two years there have been many among you whose help has been invaluable. Without it I would not be standing here now and Tencendor would still belong to the realms of myth, not reality. My people, I want to create five first families, families whose members have, so much more than any others, helped myself and my cause."

He stared down into the first row of seats. "Belial," he said softly, "you are first among the five. Step here to me."

Belial stepped onto the dais, fell to one knee and offered Axis both his hands.

"Belial." Axis' voice rang clear and strong. "I owe my life to you many times over. I grant to you and to your bloodline henceforth the title, rank and privileges of Prince of the West. I cede to you the overlordship of Carlon, and of all lands that stretch from the River Nordra to the Andeis Sea and from the River Azle to the Sea of Tyrre. From these lands you may enjoy a tithe of all the rights, customs and duties. I also grant to you to own freehold the castle of Kastaleon and Bedwyr Fort, although," he smiled and his voice lightened a little, "I do expect you to repair Bedwyr Fort to its former glory."

Belial's face paled with shock. With this title and with the rights to tithe all customs and duties that were collected in the western lands, Axis had just made Belial, and any future children he might have with Cazna, very rich and powerful indeed.

"Belial, will you accept these lands, castles, titles and honours and swear me homage and fealty as StarMan?"

"I accept with honour, StarMan," the title came easily to him, "and I do so swear homage and fealty to you."

"Then, Prince Belial, stand and greet the people of Tencendor."

Belial stood, and Axis raised their conjoined hands above their heads. The crowd roared, loving it. Belial was almost as popular as Axis was himself. Jorge, Earl of Avonsdale, and Baron Fulke of Romsdale, the two noblemen whose lands, with those of Roland, Duke of Aldeni, would come under their new Prince's overlordship, shrugged their shoulders.

This new system was no different to that they had lived under with the royal house of Achar. One overlord was substituted for another. And Belial promised to be a considerable improvement on Borneheld.

Belial walked back to his seat and Axis turned back to the front row again. "Magariz," he said softly. "You are second among the five."

Startled, for he had not expected this, Magariz stepped onto the dais. As Belial, he sank down on one knee before Axis and offered him his hands.

"Magariz. You gave me loyalty and support when to do so risked your death. Magariz, I grant to you and to your bloodline henceforth the title, rank and privileges of Prince of the North. I cede to you the lands of the former province of Ichtar, stretching from the River Azle to the River Andakilsa, and from the Fortress Ranges to the Andeis Sea. All these lands will be yours, save the garrison of Sigholt, which I will retain as my personal residence. Of course, Prince Magariz, most of these lands are currently occupied by the army of Gorgrael. I hope it will add an edge to your commitment to driving Gorgrael from Tencendor knowing that these lands will be yours once freed of Skraelings."

Magariz already came from one of the ancient noble houses of Achar, but Axis had just made him immeasurably richer and nobler.

"Magariz, will you accept these lands, titles and honours and swear me homage and fealty as StarMan?"

"I accept with honour, StarMan, and I do swear homage and fealty to you."

As with Belial, so Axis now presented the newly created Prince Magariz to the crowd. The cheering for Magariz was as enthusiastic as it had been for Belial. Magariz's family was well-known to most of the Acharites.

Axis held his hands out for silence as Magariz stepped down from the dais. "The third family I name is my own, the

SunSoar family. FreeFall? Will you step forward to receive my thanks for what the SunSoars have given me?"

FreeFall stepped forward, and the crowd gasped at his beauty and the aura of peace he carried about him. FreeFall held out his hands for Axis to enclose, but he did not kneel.

"FreeFall," Axis smiled at his cousin. "You gave more than most for my cause. You lost your life to murder, and perhaps in doing so saved mine.

"FreeFall, your House and your people showed compassion to my mother, the Princess Rivkah, when foul treachery among the Seneschal would have seen her dead. Your House took me in and trained me in my heritage and gave me many of the skills needed to reforge Tencendor and that I will need to defeat Gorgrael. With the Treaty of the Ancient Barrows most of your sacred sites have already been restored to you. The Icarii will once again fly freely over the skies of Tencendor. FreeFall SunSoar, when all thought you lost and dead, your father, RavenCrest SunSoar, made me his heir to the Talon Throne. FreeFall, that title is yours by birthright and today I relinquish it back to you."

FreeFall opened his mouth to object, but Axis pushed on before he had a chance to say anything. "FreeFall, the title and throne of Talon in the newly fashioned Tencendor will not be what it once was. The Talon will still govern the Icarii people, but *not* the combined races of Tencendor. And, as Talon, you will still swear homage and fealty to me as StarMan and to my House of the Stars. Will you accept this?"

Axis stared into FreeFall's beautiful violet eyes. Never before had the House of SunSoar sworn homage and fealty to another; never before had the Talon, or heir to the Talon throne, subordinated himself to another. This was a critical moment for Axis. He had to get the Icarii and the SunSoars to back his vision for the future of Tencendor.

FreeFall dropped to one knee, his wings spread out behind him in the traditional gesture of respect and deference. "As heir to the Talon throne and on behalf of the Icarii people I do so swear homage and fealty to you, Axis SunSoar Star-Man. You have led us back into Tencendor when for so long we thought we would never again see the southern lands. You have restored to us our sacred sites. You have given back our pride. For that we gladly accept your House of the Stars above us. The Talon will accept your overlordship."

On impulse, FreeFall stood and embraced Axis, and again the crowd cheered.

As FreeFall stepped from the dais Axis indicated that Ho'Demi should join him. Ho'Demi had no hesitation about kneeling before the StarMan.

"Ho'Demi, as with the Icarii people, this is my chance to publicly acknowledge and thank the people of Ravensbund who have so long adhered to the Prophecy and who rode to support me and Tencendor. Ho'Demi, I grant you and your family the rights and privileges of one of the first five families of Tencendor, and the rights and privileges of the extreme north of Tencendor from the River Andakilsa to the Iskruel Ocean. Ah, Ho'Demi, it is only what you had previously and have now lost, but I swear before this assembly that I will fight to clean every last iceberg in the north of what Skraelings cling to them and restore your lands to your people. Will you swear me homage and fealty on behalf of your family and your people, Ho'Demi?"

Ho'Demi's voice rang out clear and true as he pledged his loyalty and that of his people to the StarMan and to the new nation of Tencendor.

Now Axis held out his hand to Ysgryff and the Baron joined him on the dais. Ysgryff's pact with the pirates that had sealed Borneheld's defeat in the Battle of Bedwyr Fort had reached almost legendary status, and none was surprised to see Ysgryff thus honoured.

"Ysgryff," Axis smiled, taking the man's hands as he knelt before him. "You have done much for not only myself and

Tencendor, but for the Icarii people as well. You saved the day when I battled against Borneheld, and for that alone I would honour you. But your work, and that of your family over the past thousand years, in preserving and protecting the Temple of the Stars on the Island of Mist and Memory places the Icarii forever in your debt. Ysgryff, you have already been well rewarded for your concessions to the Icarii and the Avar, but I now raise your family to the first five, and grant to you the title, privileges and rank of Prince of Nor. Ysgryff, will you accept this honour and grant me homage and fealty?"

Ysgryff grinned. What splendid theatre all this was. "I accept with honour, StarMan, and I do swear homage and fealty to you."

As Ysgryff stepped down, Ogden and Veremund again nodded to themselves. In his creation of the first five families Axis had included Icarii, Ravensbund and Acharite – symbolic of the united force that stood behind Axis and of the newly united nation of Tencendor. Of the Avar there was no mention, but then the Avar had refused to fight for Tencendor.

"But what of the eastern territories?" Veremund whispered to his brother. "What of the lands to the east of the Nordra? Will Axis govern those personally?"

Axis turned back to the crowd.

"There is one more acknowledgment I must make," he said softly, although his voice carried magically to every ear, "and one more grant that I must effect. It is the eastern lands of Tencendor that will be most affected by the return of the Avar and the Icarii. Guardianship of these lands will be a sensitive issue – although most of the territorial claims of all three races have been settled, no doubt there will be smaller day-to-day issues that will cause disagreement among the three peoples as they learn to live together once more."

Faraday nodded. Sensitive indeed. Faraday looked forward to the day when she could begin to transfer the seedlings from the Enchanted Wood to the eastern lands of Tencendor – already she had some twelve thousand names memorised and friendships cemented. But who would she have to work with?

"A sensitive issue and a sensitive guardianship," Axis repeated, "but the choice of Guardian of the East is easy. I would give it to the one among us who has lived among all three races and understands the problems of all three peoples."

Rivkah? Faraday thought, looking over to Axis' mother.

"Azhure." Axis smiled, and held out his hand.

Azhure blanched and stared at Axis. His smile widened, and his fingers waggled a little impatiently.

The crowd cheered approvingly. Of all stories about Axis' rise to power, of his battles with the Skraelings and with Borneheld, one of the best known and loved stories was of the raven-haired woman who rode at his side, who wielded the magic bow of the Icarii and who commanded the pack of enchanted hounds that ran behind her.

"Azhure?" Faraday whispered to Ogden beside her. "Azhure? Is she not this commander I have heard something of?"

"Ah, indeed," muttered Ogden uncomfortably. "Azhure commands the Acharite archers in Axis' army – and currently holds command of the army while Axis, Belial and Magariz reside in Carlon."

"But control of the East?" Faraday asked. "Surely *I* would have been better for that? I am the one who has been bonded with the Mother, am I not?"

Ogden's face reddened. "As Axis said, Faraday, Azhure has spent a great deal of time among all three races and she is already an accepted and respected commander within his army. She *is* a good choice, Faraday."

Faraday sat back in her chair, frowning, as the woman, obviously shocked, handed her baby to StarDrifter and slowly stood up. As she smoothed her dress down Faraday noticed that she was pregnant.

Axis noticed Azhure's pregnancy at the same moment as Faraday, and his eyes flew to Azhure's, stunned. Why? *Why* hadn't she told him?

Azhure stepped gracefully onto the dais, her eyes locked into Axis', and took his hand.

"Why?" he whispered.

"I did not want to hold you back from what you had to do, Axis. I thought that if you knew I was pregnant again . . ." her eyes flickered towards Faraday, " . . . you would hesitate in doing that which the Prophecy demanded you do."

Axis' eyes ran over her belly once more, confused. Even if she'd managed to conceal her thickening body from him, how was it he'd not felt the tug of the baby's blood? Caelum's tug had been so distinct, so strong.

Axis realised he was staring. "Azhure. I owe so much to you. You have given me such great friendship and support over the past nineteen months that I think I can never adequately repay you. You have given me my emblem, the blood-red blazing sun and you have fought courageously among my other commanders. Azhure, you have also lived among both Icarii and Avar. You know their problems and you know the problems that many of the Acharites will have in accepting the Icarii and Avar among them again. The position of Guardian of the East is one of great importance, and I would that you accept it. Azhure, will you shoulder this onerous load for me?"

"Gladly, StarMan."

Ysgryff, as Belial, Magariz and a number of others, stared a little. Not at the title and responsibility that Axis had given Azhure – all believed that she would do well as Guardian of the East – but that Axis had not asked her to swear homage and fealty to him. It almost implied . . . well, it almost implied that Azhure was of equal status to him. And yet Axis had demanded that FreeFall, as heir to the Talon throne, pay him homage and fealty.

Faraday, as politically astute as anyone else present, also noticed the oversight and realised the implications. Why would Axis not want this woman to swear homage and fealty to him?

"Azhure, Guardian of the East, you have no home, no lands. I will cede you no lands, but I will grant you a home that you may enjoy for the rest of your life but which will revert to me once you die. Azhure, I grant you Spiredore to do with as you will."

· "Oh, Axis," Azhure breathed, and the look in her eyes was all the thanks that Axis needed.

Faraday simply stared at her. I must get to know this woman better, she thought, if I must work with her to restore the ancient forests to Tencendor.

Azhure moved to sit down again, more than a little awed by her new responsibilities. This tangible evidence of Axis' trust and belief in her abilities, before all these people, had moved her deeply.

StarDrifter stared at Axis. Axis had hardly gone far enough! On impulse, he gave a single powerful flap of his wings and landed on the dais beside his son.

StarDrifter held out his hands and began to speak, his voice nearly as magical and as beautiful as Axis'. "I am StarDrifter SunSoar," he announced, "father to Axis SunSoar StarMan. Today is a great day. We have witnessed the reforging of Tencendor, a united Tencendor that will be strong enough to defeat Gorgrael and strong enough to move into the future. But my friends, there are still many trials ahead of us. Great battles to be fought as we endeavour to break the Destroyer's grip on the north. Axis will lead Tencendor into those battles. My friends and comrades, I do not want to inject a note of sorrow or despair into these joyful proceedings, but realities must be faced. What if Axis were injured, or, greatest sadness of all, killed?" StarDrifter turned to Axis and held out his hand in melodramatic appeal. "Axis SunSoar StarMan, will you name your heir today, before all present, so that there may be no doubts in anyone's mind?"

Axis glared at his father. *Did you think I had forgotten, StarDrifter? I was opening my mouth to do just that when you leaped so precipitously onto the dais.*

Ogden, as Veremund and Jack, stared straight ahead, completely unable to look at Faraday now. Yr's eyes widened in distress. This is what she had feared for a very long time. *Had* she and the other Sentinels done the wrong thing in forcing Faraday into an action which had kept her separated from Axis for almost two years?

"Sit down, StarDrifter," Axis said quietly, and again held out his hand for Azhure.

She stood as if she would simply hand Caelum to him, but Axis seized her wrist and pulled both her and their son onto the dais with him.

Faraday took a great, ragged breath and held it. She realised instantly who had bequeathed the black-haired boy his Icarii features. "Oh, Mother, what has he done to me?"

Yr leaned forward and placed a soothing hand on Faraday's shoulder.

Axis smiled and took Caelum from Azhure's arms, holding the laughing baby high above his head.

"I name my son, Caelum Azhurson SunSoar StarSon, as my heir to the House of the Stars and to the Throne of the Stars and to all ranks and privileges those titles hold. Welcome to my heart and to my House, Caelum StarSon."

Faraday's and Azhure's eyes met; Azhure looked away almost instantly, unable to bear the pain she saw reflected back at her.

The crowd roared. All they could see was the golden figure of Axis SunSoar StarMan, the beautiful woman beside him, and the son who Axis lifted high into the air.

"Hear me!" Axis shouted above the roar. "No other child born to me will supplant Caelum as my heir. He is my firstborn, and as bastardy has left no stain on my soul or on my claim to found the Throne of the Stars, then it leaves no stain on his soul or on his claim as my heir!"

Faraday sat, weaving back and forth through her own personal nightmare. Not only had Axis disported himself with another woman to the extent that he had got a son on her — and another on the way! — he had honoured the woman with great titles, great responsibilities, *and* had named *her* son as his heir, disinheriting any child Faraday would bear him.

She suddenly realised the full extent of the betrayal. Not only Axis', but all those about her. *Everyone* must have known of this! *Everyone*! Yet no-one had told her. Why? Why? Why had they let her believe the lie that Axis still loved her, still wanted her?

Borneheld's final words to her on the parapets of the palace in Carlon came back to Faraday. Axis did not truly love her at all. If he did, then he could not have done this to her.

61

Betrayal Confronted

"We need to speak, Faraday," Axis said, and Faraday turned to stare at him, her green eyes blazing with pain and betrayal.

"Yes," she said bitterly, "we do need to talk. But I hardly think this is the place for it, do you?"

And so they were rowed back in silence to the palace, where they climbed staircases and walked corridors in silence until Axis closed the door to their chamber behind them.

"We should be present at the celebrations," Axis said.

"*We* should be at the celebrations, StarMan? I hardly think there is any place there for *me*, do you?"

Axis flinched inwardly, although he kept his face impassive. Why hadn't he told Faraday about Azhure earlier? How do you tell the woman who has waited and suffered for you through two long years that you had fallen so deeply in love with another that you couldn't give her up?

"Faraday," he said again, and stepped forward and took her shoulders gently in his hands.

"Let go of me!" Faraday hissed, twisting her body away from him.

"Faraday, let me explain."

"No," she said, and Axis could feel her rage. "*I* shall explain to you. Axis, I can understand that for virtually two years we have been torn apart one way or another. That we have gone our separate ways for much of those two years. I can understand that perhaps you dallied with other women. Mother knows, Axis, I can understand that – especially after I married Borneheld. But what I cannot understand, Axis, and what I find so hard to forgive, is how you treated me today."

"Faraday," Axis tried to soothe, reaching out for her but halting his hand at the last moment. "You will be my wife. I promised to marry you, and I will."

"*Being your wife means nothing!*" Faraday screamed, her face twisting into ugly lines, "*when that woman across the Lake is your wife in everything but name!*"

She took a deep breath and worked to bring her temper under control. "Wife. What does that mean, Axis, when that woman across the Lake is *Queen* in everything but name! Over the past year at least, and longer by the look of that baby, she has shared your life, shared your adventures, shared your bed. Now you have given her the power, the recognition," she laughed a little, "even Spiredore, *and* you have given her your son. Again she is pregnant with your child. Do not try to tell me that she does not continue to share your bed and your heart, Axis."

Axis looked down at the floor. There was nothing he could say.

Faraday stared at him, a muscle leaping in her throat.

"*She* was the one to stand on the dais with you, Axis, not me. *She* was the one who took the cheers of the nation with you. Not me. Marry me, Axis? What a joke! Even as your wife, *I* would be the mistress, not her. She has everything. I have nothing. You humiliated me today, Axis. Can't you see what you did?"

Axis raised his head and looked at her. "I did not think to betray you, Faraday. Azhure was a friend when I needed one badly. She understood that I loved you . . ."

"You talked about me to her?" Faraday whispered. What other cruelties did this man have to deal her?

". . . and she fought to resist me. Faraday, do not blame her in this. I am the one at fault."

Faraday's eyes brimmed with tears. That Axis sought to protect Azhure and not himself told Faraday how deeply he loved her. "Strangely, Axis, I do not. I know how easy it is for a woman to fall in love with you. If I seek to apportion blame, then I must blame you." She turned away.

Axis stepped up behind her and wrapped his arms about her, gently rocking her. This time she did not throw him off.

"Will you give her up?" she whispered.

There was a pause. "I cannot," Axis muttered eventually.

"Do you feel *anything* for me?"

"Faraday." Axis turned her around so he could look in her eyes. He gently brushed some of the tears from her cheek with his hand. Wasn't this where they had started two years ago? "If I said I loved you, I would not lie. But what I feel for you and what I feel for Azhure are so different. But I meant what I said, Faraday. I *do* want you for my wife." He bent to slowly kiss her cheek, her neck, the soft rise of her breasts.

Liar, she thought. Liar. You want Azhure, but, honourable man that you are, you feel bound by the vows that you made to me so long ago. And how much do you want me because I bring the trees behind you? Do you fear, Axis SunSoar StarMan, that if you do not placate me with marriage then I might not fulfil my part of the bargain? That the Prophecy itself might fail if I failed?

Oh, Mother, Faraday cried to herself. You are the only one who has not betrayed me. All she wanted now was peace in the Sacred Groves, all she wanted now was to sit in the warm sunshine on the wooden seat in the nursery, Ur beside her reciting names and histories.

But for now Axis' fingers were sliding open the fastenings at the back of her dress. Does he think to placate me with his body? she wondered vaguely, but she did not resist him. One last time, perhaps, one last time.

62

Into Spiredore

Azhure lay sleepless in her tent, staring through the darkness. The excitement of the previous day had kept her tossing and turning in her camp bed for most of the night. Axis had held Caelum above his head and proclaimed him his heir – and named him Azhurson! The clamour from the throats of the tens of thousands present had surrounded her like the roar of the Nordra as it escaped the Forbidden Valley. And he had named her Guardian of the East, and given her Spiredore.

As she stood down from the dais Azhure had glanced again at Faraday. She was rocking backwards and forwards, her face pasty white, her green eyes enormous. Azhure had almost cried out with pain herself.

Axis was back in Carlon with Faraday this night, but Azhure was no longer jealous of her. Somehow Azhure knew that it would not be long before Axis was back this side of the Lake, come to visit his Lover in Spiredore.

Spiredore! Such a magical gift! It had been stripped of all the trappings of the Seneschal – and now it waited for her.

Throwing the blankets back, Azhure swung her legs over the side of the bed. She had not had the chance to go inside Spiredore yesterday – the celebrations for Tencendor had started immediately after Axis had closed the official cere-mony and Azhure had been whirled into them by StarDrifter who, with Ysgryff, had competed for her attentions all evening and into the night. She had slept a few hours, but now was awake – ready to investigate what she had been given.

Mama?

Azhure slipped a shawl over her white nightgown and leaned over Caelum's cot. "I am going to investigate Spiredore, Caelum. Do you want to come too, or are you still so tired you will whimper and fidget and distract me?"

I will be good, Mama.

Azhure smiled with love and picked her son up, nestling him close to her breast.

The camp was quiet now; hours before, all the revellers had fallen exhausted into their beds, or simply to the ground. Barefoot, and with only the shawl over her nightgown and a lamp in her free hand, Azhure picked her way through the camp, then up the grassy slopes to where the towering walls of Spiredore stood. Several of the Alaunt made to follow her, but she motioned them back. There was no danger in Spiredore, and she wanted to be alone with Caelum on her first visit.

The door was unlatched, and Azhure slipped inside, closing it quietly behind her. For a moment she simply stood and stared. From the outside Spiredore was obviously very large, but it appeared ten, twenty times the size inside. She walked into the centre of the tower and looked up, holding her lamp high. Stairwells, balconies, overhangs, all swirled to dizzying heights above her. Rooms, chambers, open spaces, all opened off the balconies surrounding this atrium. None of the myriad floors and balconies were level or even, jutting out in irregular squares, triangles, circles. It was an amazing sight, and should have been an eyesore, but somehow it achieved a subtle harmony that gave the interior of Spiredore great beauty.

"Stars," Azhure said. "I could get lost up there and wander about for days."

"Actually, it's quite easy to find your way, once you know the trick," a voice said lightly behind her, and Azhure spun about, the lamp swinging so violently in her hand that shadows leaped and danced about the atrium. Her hand tightened defensively about Caelum, who gave a squeak of protest.

An Icarii birdman walked towards her, an open book in his hand, as if he had been reading when surprised by Azhure. He was one of the most captivating Icarii she'd ever seen. His face was vibrant with power, far more so than Star-Drifter's face, and she realised he must be an Enchanter. Great violet eyes laughed at her from underneath a tumbled crop of dark copper curls. Behind him stretched golden wings; and not just dyed that shade, Azhure thought, numbed by the beauty of this birdman, they actually appeared to be made of beaten gold.

"I'm sorry," he said, closing the book with a snap. Azhure caught brief sight of the title . . . something to do with the Lakes. "I startled you." A contrite expression crossed his face. "And I shouldn't be here either. Axis ceded you Spiredore yesterday, and I am the intruder."

"You were at the ceremony?" Azhure asked, her hand lessening its grip about Caelum.

"Yes," he said. "I was there, but some distance from you, I think."

"I have not seen you before," Azhure said. "And you have a face one could not easily forget."

"As you have a face, Lady Azhure, that no man, Icarii or Acharite, could easily forget. You are a woman for whom your own Prophecy should be written – it is a shame that you must share one with Axis. Perhaps I will write one for *you* one day."

Azhure laughed. The man had a charming, if cunning, way with words. *She* shared the Prophecy with Axis? "Why have I not seen you before?"

The birdman's smile faded a little and his eyes became sad. "Ah, Azhure. I have been away. A long, long way away. I have only come home recently. That is why you have not seen me."

He stepped forward. "May I hold your baby for a moment? He is such a beautiful baby."

Azhure hesitated momentarily, then let the birdman lift an unresisting Caelum out of her arms. The Icarii Enchanter cuddled the baby, whispering to him, and Caelum stretched curious hands to the man's face, poking and prodding till the birdman laughed and handed Caelum back to Azhure. "All babies are curious, but he more than most, I think. You have a magnificent son, Azhure, and he a magnificent mother."

Azhure blushed and smiled. Abruptly she remembered he had not told her his name, and she opened her mouth to ask, but in the instant before she spoke the birdman took Azhure's arm and led her towards the first of the stairwells that twisted up into the heights of the tower, sundry balconies and chambers opening off it.

"I was going to tell you how to work the magic of Spiredore, Azhure."

Azhure smiled. Magic? How wonderful it would be if this Enchanter told her how to use Spiredore.

"My dear child," he said, as they reached the foot of the stairs. "It is very simple. If you wander willy-nilly in Spiredore you will, as you thought, get completely lost. You must decide where you want to go before you start to climb the stairs, and then the stairs will simply take you to that place."

Azhure's frown deepened. "But how do I know where I want to go if I don't know what the tower contains?"

The birdman laughed and his hand slid up her arm a little. It was very warm, his palm and fingers like rough silk, and Azhure found herself leaning a little closer to him.

"Then you have a lot to learn, Azhure." His tone became softer, deeper. "A lot to learn." He rested his arm on her shoulder, his fingers gently stroking her neck. "Where would you like to go, Azhure. Where? What would you like to see?"

Azhure smiled dreamily. His hand was soothing, his gentle breath on her cheek comforting. "I would like to see the view from the rooftop," she whispered. "I would very much like to watch the sun rise over the Avarinheim from the top of Spiredore."

"See?" he laughed, and the sound broke the spell between them. "You do have at least *one* destination – and you can spend the rest of your life investigating Spiredore. It was built just for you, Azhure. Just for you. Eventually you will remember where to go."

She smiled. "Your flattery goes too far, sir. Built for me? Why, this tower has stood for thousands of years, and I am only twenty-eight."

"Just for you," he whispered, and then he leaned forward and kissed her on the lips. It was a deep, absorbing kiss, and Azhure was in no hurry to break it – it was the birdman who eventually drew back.

He laughed shortly. "I should not have done that, Azhure. It was Unclean. But I was always the one to break rules. You must forgive me. Now," his manner became brusque, "if you wish to watch the sun rise from the rooftop you will have to begin to climb now. Sunrise is not long away."

Following his instructions, Azhure thought of the rooftop and began to climb, but, only a few steps into the stairwell, she turned and looked back down at him. "How did the Seneschal ever find their way about Spiredore?"

The birdman laughed. "To them, sweetheart, it was simply an empty shell. They built their own chambers and stairs, floors and libraries, but they never saw the true tower that you see before you now. They did not have the magic to see it. Now, go. Sunrise awaits."

Azhure nodded, and turned back into the stairwell. When next she looked down, the birdman had gone.

WolfStar backed against the doorway out of Azhure's sight, listening to her footsteps for a long time. What a remarkable woman – and what a son she had birthed.

As Azhure's footsteps slowly faded above him, WolfStar abruptly vanished.

Azhure stood atop Spiredore and watched the sky lighten to the east over the Avarinheim forest, her son cuddled comfortably in her arms. Her hair was loose, and the wind whipped both her nightgown and her hair about her lithe form. Above her head the morning stars whirled. Beneath her bare feet the tower gently hummed to itself.

Azhure had come home.

63

From Out of the
Dawning Sun . . .

As Azhure had not been able to sleep, neither could Axis. For hours he lay by Faraday's side, close but not touching, knowing she was awake as well, yet unable to speak to her as she was unable to speak to him. Finally, silently, he rolled out of bed, pulled on his breeches and boots, and went to talk with StarDrifter.

They stood on the balcony of StarDrifter's room, drinking in the cold dawn air as they gazed across Grail Lake.

"What are you going to do?" StarDrifter asked.

"I am vowed to Faraday," he said. "I must marry her."

"And Azhure?"

"I will not let her go. I cannot."

Both Enchanters could see Azhure atop Spiredore with their enhanced vision. The wind whipped her hair back from her face, and the white nightgown billowed about her body. She was laughing with Caelum, and pointing into the dawning sun as it rose above the distant Avarinheim.

"What does she have," StarDrifter mused, "that both of us cannot resist her?"

"It is as though she contains the Star Dance within her," said Axis softly, and StarDrifter dragged his eyes away from

Azhure at the tone of his son's voice. "Through her I can touch the Star Dance more powerfully than I can through any Song. StarDrifter, it is as though I hold the very Stars in my hands every time I hold her, as if it is their music that embraces me. Every time I lie with her, StarDrifter, the music grows louder."

StarDrifter was astounded at what Axis had revealed. He could touch the Star Dance through Azhure, through her body? Who, *what*, was she? He stared at his son, his eyes wide, his mouth half open.

The Gryphon circled high overhead. It was a mission fraught with dangers and traps, she knew, but it was an important mission, and Gorgrael had not wanted to trust it to a SkraeBold. Gorgrael had sent her south to spy out Carlon. What was Axis up to? Gorgrael had asked the Gryphon. What state his forces? *Where* were they? Could Gorgrael attack through the trench systems of Jervois Landing and expect little resistance from Axis?

To these questions and others the Gryphon had relayed her answers as best she could. Most forces were still concentrated about Carlon, and the soil was still red east of the city from a mighty battle. Borneheld lay dead and rotted on the refuse heap. Axis strode golden and assured and spoke at length of Tencendor. The woman, Faraday, walked by his side. Icarii and Acharite mixed freely. And Spiredore – Spiredore had wakened in much the same way that Sigholt had awakened. Tencendor was waking about Axis, and if Gorgrael wanted to move, he'd best do it quickly.

The Gryphon had finished her surveillance of Carlon and its surrounds and was ready to fly home and out of danger, but her attention was caught by the woman and baby atop Spiredore. There was something strange about them . . . strange . . . but the Gryphon did not quite know what it was. Should she fly closer for a look? Should she attack? There was no-one else about, and the Gryphon was confident of success. A woman. Alone. No weapons. Tasty.

And the Gryphon had the distinct advantage of being able to attack from out of the dawning sun.

She communed with Gorgrael with her mind, asking permission to ravage.

Gorgrael could see no harm in it.

Azhure stood atop Spiredore and laughed at Caelum. He was reaching out to the sun, it seemed so magically close, his eyes wide with wonder and joy.

She turned to look at the dawning sun, and blinked. There was a dark spot spinning out of the red orb. Puzzled, Azhure stared . . . and then screamed, wrenching Caelum to the floor of the roof in a futile attempt to protect him with her body.

Both Axis and StarDrifter saw and heard Azhure scream.

"Gryphon!" Axis cried, appalled. "*Azhure!*" he screamed . . . and vanished.

StarDrifter stared at the spot where Axis had been – then back at Azhure. The Gryphon was clearly hurtling down towards her now – and Azhure was surely dead if he did not do something very, very soon.

Without a single thought to his own safety StarDrifter lifted off the balcony and streaked towards Spiredore.

Axis materialised into a screaming fury of blood, bone, feathers and thick grey mist. He stared about him frantically – what enchantment could he use to overcome an attacking Gryphon?

A scream whipped through his consciousness and his vision began to clear. The scream had been Caelum's, and the sound was one of primeval terror.

"Caelum!" he shouted, and fought his way through to the sound. "Caelum!"

As he struggled through the grey mist Axis felt power being wielded on the rooftop, dark power, the power of the Dance of Death. How could he combat that? Were Azhure and Caelum dead already? He could hear no more sounds, save a peculiar splintering, tearing sound – oh gods! Was the Gryphon already feeding on their bodies?

He stumbled into an area free of mist, and the first thing he saw was Azhure, Caelum clinging desperately to her, lying with her back against one of the far walls of the parapets. She had a nasty wound along one arm, as if the Gryphon had struck as she raised an arm to protect her face, but otherwise appeared to be uninjured.

About five paces in front of her, the Gryphon lay writhing and twisting. For one stunned moment Axis thought an invisible beast was attacking the Gryphon, but then he realised that the beast was in the grip of an enchantment, and that this enchantment was literally ripping the Gryphon apart.

The enchantment used was of the Dark Music.

Behind him Axis dimly heard StarDrifter alight and scream his name, but his attention was all on the Gryphon and on the dark enchantments that were being used to tear it apart.

Slowly . . . slowly . . . slowly he lifted his eyes to Azhure. She was staring at the creature, ignoring the screams of the child in her arms.

The Dark Music was being wielded by her. *She was using the power of the Dark Music, the Dance of Death, to kill the Gryphon!*

"Azhure? Azhure? What is that you do?" he whispered in a voice papery-thin with fear, and he could feel StarDrifter's hand on his shoulder.

When Azhure replied her voice was flat and full of emptiness, making Axis recall the vast empty distances that lay between the stars he had seen in the Star Gate.

"What is this I do? I use the same Dark Music that was used to make this creature to unmake her. I unravel the enchantments that made her with the same powers." She looked up and met Axis' eyes – and Axis could see the stars circling in the great emptinesses of their depths.

"WolfStar!" StarDrifter gasped behind him, and Axis cried out. "No! *No!*"

But both the Enchanters, watching as the Gryphon was finally shredded to pieces by the power that enveloped it, remembered every single piece of evidence that indicted Azhure.

As one they remembered . . . Azhure walking graceful and confident along the rock ledge outside Talon Spike that any normal human would have fallen from in terror . . . Azhure's mastery of the Wolven . . . the Alaunt hounds, once WolfStar's, who now answered only to her call . . . the call of her blood that both Axis and StarDrifter were unable to resist – SunSoar blood? . . . the ancient Icarii script that she had decorated the cuffs of Axis' golden tunic with – how had she known that? . . . her ability to hear (and use, StarDrifter whispered) the mind voice . . . the Star Music that Axis heard whenever he made love to her . . . the depth of Caelum's Icarii blood, as if Azhure had contributed as well as Axis . . . the scars that rippled down Azhure's back, as if wings had been torn out . . . she had first found MorningStar's body, but had she killed her as well? And finally, the most damning of all, her easy use of the Dark Music. No Icarii Enchanter, and certainly no simple peasant girl, could use that.

"WolfStar," Axis whispered, and then white-hot anger enveloped him so completely it overran and negated his horror. *Had he spent his nights loving WolfStar?*

As the Gryphon finally blew apart in a cloud of vaporised tissue and blood, Azhure blinked and the stars faded from her eyes. A tremor ran over her face, and she became aware of her surroundings.

"Axis?" she whispered. Why all this blood? Why was Axis staring at her like that?

The Gryphon! Memories of the Gryphon attack flooded in and Azhure cringed and hugged Caelum tight. *Where was the Gryphon?* There had been a pain, a pain in her head, and then everything had gone dark. Strange whispers had shouted words through her mind. Where was the Gryphon?

"Dead," hissed Axis, and behind him StarDrifter's face was as implacable and as cold as his son's. "Dead, as you will be before long, WolfStar!"

It was not so much his words, although those were horrifying enough, but the tone in which he said them that tore Azhure's soul apart. Why did he hate her? What had she done? As Axis tore Caelum from her arms Azhure automatically dissolved into the welcome blackness that had always served as a refuge during her childhood whenever Hagen had sprung at her with similar hatred on his face.

In her last moment of consciousness Azhure realised her worst nightmare had come true. Hagen was not dead at all. He had simply assumed the form of Axis.

"By all the stars in the universe," the Dark Man screamed, *"what have you done?"*

Gorgrael backed up against a chair, almost falling over it. An instant previously, just as Gorgrael had felt the Gryphon blink out of existence, the Dark Man had materialised in Gorgrael's chamber deep in the heart of his ice fortress. He was insanely angry. Out-of-control angry.

And Gorgrael abruptly realised that an out-of-control Dark Man was a very, very, *very*, bad thing.

"Only a woman and a baby," Gorgrael whispered, scrabbling to keep his balance as the chair started to slip under his weight. "Only a woman and a baby. I saw no harm in it."

"No harm?" the Dark Man shouted. "No harm?"

Gorgrael thought he could see fire (or was it ice?) glinting somewhere in the depths of the Dark Man's hood. His tongue lolled out of his mouth in fear.

"You could have killed her!" the Dark Man shrieked. "You could have *killed* her!" He advanced on Gorgrael, his black cloak billowing, yet revealing nothing of the man beneath.

"What concern of yours is the death of a single woman and child, Dark Man?" Gorgrael hissed in fury. "What concern of yours?"

"*She* is a concern of mine!" the Dark Man snarled.

"A single human woman and child, Dark Man?" Gorgrael said, advancing himself now, and the Dark Man retreated a step.

"You fool," the Dark Man said quietly. "You may have undone everything now. Of all the people you had to set your Gryphon on you had to pick her. Of all the people."

"She lives," Gorgrael said, and peered as close as he could at the Dark Man. "She lives, and she destroyed the Gryphon. Is that not unusual for a human woman? To use the Dark Music to destroy my Gryphon? My beautiful pet? Who is she, Dark Man? What is she to cause you to storm my fortress in unconsidered rage? *What* is she?"

The Dark Man stared at Gorgrael. "She is exposed, now, Gorgrael. That is what she is. And, because of that, she may very well be dead."

64
....

Azhure (1)

"By all the gods in creation," Belial screamed as Axis raised his sword for the killing thrust, "*what are you doing?*"

"She is a traitor!" Axis yelled back. "She is WolfStar!"

Belial stepped back, appalled both by the scene before him and by the power and anger that blazed from Axis' eyes.

They were in one of the lower chambers of the palace – used, occasionally, as an interrogation chamber, and it was to this foul purpose that it was being put again.

Azhure, moaning in pain, was bound upright to a stone pillar, her head lolling on her shoulder. She was only barely conscious. Blood stained her nightgown in several places, and Belial could see that one of her legs had been heavily bruised. Mother knows what other contusions that nightgown is hiding, he thought distractedly.

"Damn you, Axis! Prove to me that she is this traitor! *Prove it!*" Belial shouted.

Axis stared at him, breathing heavily with effort and with rage. He shifted cold eyes to StarDrifter. "Shall we unmask the bitch?" His voice was as cold as his eyes.

"Best to kill her now, Axis."

"*No!*" Belial screamed and grabbed Axis' arm. "Prove to me that she *is* this traitor or, so help me Axis, I will raise every soldier I can to move against you!"

Axis swore viciously and threw the sword across the room. It hit a far wall and clattered to the floor. Apart from Azhure, there were only the three of them in the chamber. Belial had kept everyone else out.

"You want to see what she really is, Belial? You *really* want to see?" Axis snarled. He held Belial's stare for a moment, then he dropped his eyes and stared at his Enchanter's ring, twisting it slightly. StarDrifter scowled – what was Axis doing to the ring?

When Axis looked up again, his eyes were subtly different. He walked over to Azhure and twisted his hand in her hair, wrenching her head up so he could stare into her eyes.

She moaned again, and fear flickered across her face.

"I am going to unlock the traitor's mind," Axis said, his voice now so cold that Belial recoiled.

Music started to waft about the chamber. Harsh music. Music that StarDrifter at first thought was Dark Music, but then realised was a combination of fire and air music that was discordant and twisted. It was a song that unlocked a mind's secrets, but StarDrifter had never, never heard it before. It was a new Song.

"I am going to find out what secrets her dark soul hides," Axis said, grating out his words through clenched teeth, "and I am going to prove to you, Belial, that this . . . this *creature* is the traitor who murdered MorningStar and who intended to betray me to Gorgrael!"

A moment later Azhure screamed, her body convulsing, and she continued to scream as Axis tore her mind apart.

"Oh, gods," Belial whispered, appalled. He turned away, unable to watch, wishing that he could stop his ears as well, wishing that he had the courage to attack Axis and stop him from killing Azhure.

"He is sifting through her mind," StarDrifter said calmly. "Sifting through her memories. Searching for the key that will unlock her true identity."

Several minutes passed, and the intensity of Azhure's screams, if anything, deepened. Her body strained against the ropes so desperately that they burned through material and skin, and Belial, on the one occasion he found the heart to look, saw blood seep through to stain the white linen wherever the ropes pressed against her body.

"Ah!" Axis suddenly exclaimed in satisfaction. "I have found it!"

"What?" StarDrifter asked, stepping a little closer.

"A block. A shuttered grate. A welded door. A block. Behind this, StarDrifter, lies the true Azhure. Shall I open it?"

"Can you?" StarDrifter asked. "Is it possible? Should we?" What if WolfStar lurked behind that block, waiting to leap out? "Perhaps it *is* best to kill her now, Axis. It is enough to know the block is there."

"No, no," Axis grunted. "Belial wants proof. Well, he shall have it. Wait. I almost have it."

His face tightened in concentration and effort and the strength of the music doubled. Azhure abruptly stopped screaming and simply stared into Axis' eyes, so close to her own.

"Ah," Axis whispered, his hand still tangled deep in her hair. "I almost have you . . . almost . . . almost . . . *there*! It is gone!"

Suddenly his eyes widened, startled, horrified, staring at something that StarDrifter and Belial could not see. "Oh gods," he whispered, and then, without a sound, both he and Azhure vanished.

He was enveloped by her power, by the pure power of the Stars, and by some spark of compassion left within her, she did not let it immediately crush him. But she was also still caught in his enchantment — both were — and she was compelled to show him her secrets. All of them. Even those she had repressed and hidden in this dark hole of her mind because to let them free would have driven her mad. She opened her eyes and began to see. Began to see with the eyes of a five-year-old child.

And Axis saw with her.

The eyes blinked and opened. Blinked yet again, and opened wider. They saw the interior of the Plough-Keeper's home in Smyrton. It was a well-kept home, well furnished. The Plough-Keeper, Hagen, did well for himself.

It was early evening, and lamps and the fire burned merrily. A meal was set out on the table, but the food lay untouched on thick white plates. The eyes belonged to a little girl, and she was crouched in the furthest corner from the fireplace. She did not like the fireplace.

That was where Hagen was intent on the murder of her mother. He had her prone on the hearth, her head danger-ously close to the fire. Kneeling astride her body, Hagen gripped the woman's throat with his hands.

"Whore!" he screamed. "*I* did not father that aberration cringing in the corner, did I? *Did I?* Who, woman? *Who?*" And he thrust her beautiful head a little further into the fire.

Her hair was raven blue-black, and thickly coiled about her head. The Axis part of the mind that watched through the eyes in the corner saw that her face, even distorted with terror and marked by violence as it was, was very beautiful, her eyes a deep and mysterious blue, her skin creamy smooth in places, but blackened and burned in others. And soon her hair would go up in flames.

"Who?" Hagen roared, again driving her head yet further towards the flames and the coals, and Axis cringed in horror. Was this Hagen driving Azhure's mother into the flames, or was it he, driving Azhure to her death?

"Azhure, hear me!" the woman screamed, knowing she was near death. "Hear me! This man is not your father!"

"*I* know that!" Hagen yelled. "*I* know that. Ever since I saw those feathers sticking out of the girl's back this afternoon, the feathers that you have been binding for weeks now, trying to hide them from me, ever since that moment I have known she was not my daughter. Who? Who?"

"Azhure!" And the woman screamed, for in a burst of crackling her hair had caught fire. "Azhure," as the flames engulfed her head, "Azhure! You are a child of the gods. Seek the answer on Temple Mount! Ah!" Her hands beat frantically at Hagen's fingers clenched about her throat, desperately seeking release from the torment that engulfed her.

"Azhure!" her voice crackled horrifyingly from the ball of flame that now engulfed her entire head. "Live! Live! Your father. Ah! Azhure . . . Ah! Your father . . . *Ah!*"

Whatever she had been trying to say was lost in the expanding ball of flame. His own hands singed, Hagen recoiled, and for a moment or two the woman's hands beat ineffectually at the flames licking at the edges of her linen collar. An instant later her entire bodice had gone up, and the instant after that her skirts erupted in a roar of flame.

For minutes . . . hours? . . . the Azhure/Axis mind watched as the blackened body twisted and writhed on the hearth. It still made odd grunting noises, but the Azhure/Axis mind wondered if it were her lungs searching for air, or the sound of joints popping in the heat.

The smell was awful.

Only after the charred corpse stilled did Hagen turn to the little girl.

"Now you," he said softly. "Now you."

He lifted the bone-handled knife from the table, and bent down to the girl.

He ripped the dress from her body and twisted one hand into her hair. In his other hand he hefted the knife, seeking a firm grip.

As the little girl felt the knife sear into her flesh, so too did Axis.

As the little girl twisted and screamed and begged for forgiveness, so too did Axis.

As Hagen dug and twisted the knife deeper and harder, so too did Axis feel each and every twist in his own flesh.

As Hagen grabbed the slowly developing nubs of wings and twisted and pulled and wrenched, so too did Axis suffer.

Blade scraped bone, and Axis screamed and twisted and begged for forgiveness.

So too had Azhure.

As the knife rattled to the floor and Hagen seized every remaining vestige of wing and flight muscle and feather that he could find and pull and wrench and tear, so Axis begged, pleaded, screamed, twisted, fought, cried, despaired.

So too had Azhure.

And, as Hagen picked up the knife again, and began to dig and twist again, searching for hidden feathers, so Axis gave into despair.

So too had Azhure despaired.

And, as Azhure had, Axis lived through each moment of the next six weeks, weeks when the wing nubs kept trying to reform, weeks when each morning Hagen would tear off the grubby, blood-and pus-encrusted bandages and curse and reach for the knife and dig and twist and wrench and dig and twist and cut and scrape and tear and curse and . . .

I understand! Axis screamed somewhere in a dark, dark place. A place to which the Azhure/Axis mind had retreated because it was the only way it could survive. *I understand*!

Do you? her voice softly asked. *Do you*?

. . . and bandage up again to leave the child thin and weak and infected and pain-ridden to lie in the bed as he buried the charred corpse that had been her mother but yet to return the following morning and curse and reach for the knife and twist and scrape and tear and cut, cut, cut, cut and then leave to conduct worship in the Worship Hall, leave to give due reverence to the great god Artor, the good god Artor, and to guide the souls of the good people of Smyrton on their voyage into hell and to return to lift the Azhure/Axis head and force cool water down her/his throat.

"Why let me live?"

Hagen smiled. "Because I want to see you suffer," he said. "I like it. Shall I check your bandages again?"

I understand, Axis whispered, and this time he heard nothing but the sobbing of a girl driven to madness by the pain and the hatred and the loss and driven, as her only means of survival, to bury all of her memories and all of her enchanted powers behind a locked grate, a shuttered gate, a closed, silent door and repress, repress, repress and concentrate on being "normal", because that was the only way she would survive. The only way.

He was in a dark, dark place and he did not know how to get out. Azhure's strange power, long hidden, long fettered, had brought him here, and he did not have the skills to escape.

"Azhure?" he whispered into the darkness. "Azhure?"

Nothing.

"Azhure?" he called softly again, starting to crawl directionless through the dark. "Azhure?"

Nothing.

He sat and thought and listened. If he were Azhure, would he answer?

No. The darkness was the only thing protecting her.

What could he say? What could he say?

"Forgive me," he whispered. "Forgive me."

Nothing.

"For your mother's death, forgive me."

Nothing.

"For your pain and your terror, forgive me."

Nothing.

"For the loss of your childhood and the rape of your innocence, forgive me."

Nothing.

"For all the cruelty of the world that has ravaged you, forgive me."

Nothing.

"For my lack of trust and my lack of faith, forgive me."

Silence, and Axis knew that she was there.

"Help me, Azhure, for I am lost and I am frightened and I am lonely without you. Help me."

"Forgive me," a whisper reached him, and Axis burst into tears, appalled by *her* need for forgiveness. "Forgive me, Mama, that I cannot remember your name."

And then she was in his arms, the little girl and the grown woman all in one, and the girl and the woman and the Icarii Enchanter were weeping and seeking forgiveness and release and love and comfort and somewhere to hide, hide, hide from the pain and the injustice of the world.

Belial and StarDrifter stood, frozen. Waiting. Time passed immeasurably around them. Waiting.

And then, snap! they were freed from whatever bound them and the air shimmered and Axis stepped forth into the room and he bore Azhure in his arms and she seemed almost lifeless, for the skin and the flesh had been stripped from her back until the blood ran in colourful rivulets down Axis' breeches and boots to the floor.

"Help me," he whispered.

65

Azhure (2)

Faraday ran along the corridors of the palace, her skirts bunched in her hands, her breath heaving. She had fallen asleep sometime after Axis had left her and had then slept through until well past dawn. Only after she had washed, dressed and breakfasted did her new maid tell her something of the commotion in the palace.

What had he done?

The maid had heard only vague rumours, and eventually Faraday had rushed from the chamber, found one of the palace guard, and asked him where Axis was. Where he had taken Azhure.

In the interrogation chamber she found only blood and emptiness – but she could feel the horror and fear still resonating about the room.

What had he done?

From the interrogation chamber Faraday followed the trail of blood and lingering horror until now she ran along one of the main corridors.

Where? Ah, one of the principal apartment complexes, kept for visiting diplomats. He had taken her in there.

Faraday burst into the antechamber of the apartment complex and stopped dead.

In the antechamber were crammed StarDrifter, Belial, FreeFall, EvenSong, Magariz, Rivkah, Ho'Demi. All silent.

All pale. All shocked. Among them paced nervous Alaunt, as silent as the people, but just as obviously upset. One scratched at the closed door to the main chamber.

Frantic footsteps sounded in the corridor behind her, and a man collided with Faraday as he scrambled into the antechamber.

Ysgryff. Dark, angry, and only a breath away from violence. "Where is he?" he growled. "Where is he? What has he done to her?"

Before anyone could answer a baby whimpered, and Faraday glanced to one side. Rivkah sat patting Azhure's baby son ineffectually as he wailed and twisted feebly in her arms.

Faraday stepped over to Rivkah. "Give me the baby," she said softly, and held out her hands. Rivkah shrugged and handed the baby over.

Hello, Caelum. My name is Faraday.

The baby twisted around to look at her face. Her. *Will you help Mama? Her name is Azhure.*

Faraday smiled softly and stroked the boy's cheek. *Azhure. What a lovely name. Is she with your father?*

The boy's mind clouded. *He was afraid of her, Faraday. Why was he afraid? Will you help Mama?* He was quiet now, soothed by this woman who held him. He could feel the warmth and the love of her power and it comforted him.

If I can, Caelum. Shush now while I talk with the others.

She looked up at StarDrifter. "Tell me."

StarDrifter took an anguished breath. "Axis and I – and I am as much to blame for what happened here as Axis – thought that Azhure was WolfStar."

"*What?*" Ysgryff hissed.

"She started to use Dark Music, Ysgryff," StarDrifter pleaded. "What else were we to think? We had no choice. She *had* to be WolfStar."

"Ysgryff, wait," Faraday said urgently, stepping forward to lay a calming hand on Ysgryff's arm. "StarDrifter. None of us here know what you are talking about. Who is this WolfStar? And why would you think that Azhure was this person?"

Slowly, falteringly, StarDrifter explained about the renegade Enchanter-Talon, about his crimes against the Icarii race, about his return through the Star Gate. He explained how Axis, he and MorningStar believed that WolfStar was disguised as one of Axis' confidants, one of those closest to him. The traitor of the third verse of the Prophecy.

"MorningStar always believed it to be Azhure," StarDrifter said. "But Axis and I refused to believe her. Yet there were so many inconsistencies. So much hidden and strange. And Caelum," he waved at the baby in Faraday's arms, "has so much Icarii blood. So much. This morning . . . when Azhure used the Dark Music of the Stars to destroy the Gryphon . . . what were we to think, Faraday?" StarDrifter pleaded. "What were we to think?"

Encumbered with the baby, Faraday was able to restrain Ysgryff no longer. He leaned forward and literally hauled StarDrifter to his feet by the feathers on the back of his neck. "If he has destroyed her, StarDrifter, then by all the gods that live in the Temple of the Stars, I will destroy *you*!"

As Belial half rose to his feet, Ysgryff threw the shocked StarDrifter back onto the bench. "Personally, StarDrifter," he said through clenched jaws, "I hope that one day WolfStar will appear and hurl both you and Axis into the Star Gate in one of his crazed experiments, because that is all you two deserve for what you have done to that woman."

"Ysgryff, please," Faraday said gently. "Restrain yourself. Belial, what happened below?"

Belial told her what he could. "But that's all I know, Faraday. Not much. Azhure took Axis somewhere, showed him something, but I don't know what. When they reappeared the skin was hanging off Azhure's back in strips and Axis appeared half mad himself. He brought her up here and has allowed no-one in the chamber since. I think he will kill himself if Azhure dies – and even if she doesn't, I think he will kill himself for what he has done to her."

"Ysgryff, wait here," Faraday said, turning to the Prince of Nor. "I think you will have more to do with solving this mystery than anyone else."

She turned and walked towards the door.

"Faraday," Rivkah began, concerned. The last person who had tried to go inside had been confronted with an Axis so furious and so wild that they had literally slammed the door behind them in their haste to get out.

"No," Faraday smiled, her hand on the doorknob. "Axis will not throw out either myself or Caelum. Be calm. Wait."

Then she twisted the doorknob and walked inside, closing the door gently behind her.

The chamber was dim, the windows shuttered. Faraday stood still, adjusting her eyes to the light. Finally a slight movement caught her eye.

Axis rose from where he had been kneeling by a bed along the far wall of the room, a bloodied rag in his hand. He did not say anything, just stared at Faraday with sunken and haunted eyes as she moved towards him.

Faraday reached the other side of the bed, hesitated slightly, then sat down, looking at the woman lying curled up on her side.

"Hello, Azhure," she smiled, her face gentle. "My name is Faraday. I would we could have met in slightly happier circumstances."

Azhure was conscious, her blue eyes wide and dark with pain. She stared at Faraday a moment, then gazed at her son.

"Caelum is well, but he is concerned for you, Azhure."

Azhure reached out a trembling hand and touched Caelum. Faraday noted with concern how weak the woman was, how pale her skin, how it hung in loose, papery folds over her flesh. Azhure let her hand fall listlessly back to the bed. She was so weak and in so much pain that even her son could not interest her.

"You *have* made a mess of this, haven't you Axis?" Faraday said, her voice low, turning her head to gaze levelly at Axis.

Axis sank to his knees on the other side of the bed. He had been sponging Azhure's back with warm water, trying to stop the blood flow, but the water in the bowl was now deep red itself, and the flesh still hung in strips from Azhure's back. Bone showed in several places.

"I cannot help her," Axis whispered. "I cannot heal. It is one of the things for which there is no Song. Faraday," his voice broke, "do I have to wait for her to begin to die before I can help her?"

"Axis," Faraday said, making her voice as firm as she could. "Take your son and go and sit in the corner of the room. I would spend some time alone with Azhure."

Axis stood, dropped the bloodied rag back into the water, and reached over the bed for Caelum. The baby stiffened a little in Faraday's arms.

Go to your father, Caelum. He needs comfort.

As she passed the baby over Faraday stared Axis hard in the eye. "Caelum needs to know what happened, Axis. If you don't tell him then he will never trust you again. Now, go sit in the chair and talk to your son. Don't disturb Azhure or myself."

Axis nodded, cuddled Caelum to his chest, and walked slowly over to the distant chair, slumping down and murmuring to the baby.

Faraday reached down and took one of Azhure's hands in both of hers, rubbing it with her thumbs, gently, soothingly. "Now," she smiled. "I also need to know what happened. Tell me. Believe me, it will help if you talk about it."

Her touch comforted Azhure, and slowly, very slowly, her words heavy and awkward, she began to tell Faraday what had happened that morning.

"Wait," Faraday stopped her after only a few minutes. "Did you know what you were doing to that Gryphon?" Her thumbs continued to stroke the back of Azhure's hand.

Azhure shook her head. "No. It attacked. I was terrified. I was sure that Caelum and I would die. I had . . . I had no weapons. It lunged for us, and I raised my arm to protect myself," she lifted her free arm slightly to show Faraday the open tear that ran down the fleshy part of her lower arm, "and the creature tore into me with its beak. The pain, the terror, something . . . something broke inside of me. Something . . . opened. Faraday." Her eyes widened, pleading for understanding. "I don't *know* what I did! I am not WolfStar! Why should Axis think that I was? *Why?*"

"Shush, sweetheart," Faraday comforted, stroking the damp hair back from Azhure's brow. Faraday quietly told Azhure what StarDrifter had told them outside, and Azhure stared disbelieving at the woman before her.

"Oh," she said, inadequately. Had they doubted her *that* long?

"Azhure. What happened in the chamber below? I need to know, and you need to talk about it."

Azhure was silent for a long time, but Faraday was patient, and waited, holding Azhure's hand in one of hers, lifting the other to stroke the woman's hair, soothing, calming, quieting. Eventually, Azhure began to speak.

She spoke of Axis' anger, of his sudden revulsion, of his violence. It had reminded her, she said, of the man she had called her father, Hagen. She spoke of the nightmare that began on the top of Spiredore and continued in the interrogation chamber. Of the pain and the fear and the terrible aloneness she had felt when Axis had started to tear her mind apart in his efforts to find where WolfStar lurked.

And then the same thing that had happened when the Gryphon attacked. Something inside of her had . . . snapped . . . released.

"And it hasn't completely closed even now, Faraday. I can still feel something in the darkness there, calling to me."

"We will talk about that later," Faraday said gently. "Just tell me what happened next."

Azhure told Faraday of the vision she and Axis had shared. Of her mother's horrible death at Hagen's hands as he sought to discover the identity of Azhure's father.

"I can remember so much now, Faraday," Azhure whispered. "I remember that my wings had started to sprout some five or six weeks earlier. Mama had smiled and laughed when she saw them one day as she bathed me, and said they were a gift from my father, but she tried to hide them from Hagen. As they grew larger she would bind them to my back with a great linen bandage so my back would appear flat. But one day Hagen came home unexpectedly, and found me sitting on Mama's lap, the bandages undone and my back exposed."

Azhure's eyes were dark with guilt. "Oh, Faraday! It was my fault! I had complained that the bandages itched, and Mama had taken them down to scratch my back."

Faraday eyes filled with tears. "Go on."

Haltingly, Azhure told of how Hagen had come at her with his knife, day after day, determined to cut any remnants of the wings from her back. "Weeks it went on," Azhure whispered so low that Faraday had to bend down to hear her. "Weeks. Every morning Hagen would inspect my back. And if he saw anything . . . *anything* . . . that looked wing-like, then he simply cut it out."

Faraday was appalled. "Didn't the neighbours suspect? Didn't they ask what was going on?"

Azhure shook her head. "Hagen told them that Mama had run away with a pedlar – he buried her body secretly one night – and that I was sick with a simple fever. Sometimes one of the village women would come in with food, but even if they saw the bloody bandages on my back, they never asked what was going on. They believed whatever Hagen told them." She paused, then spoke again. "Even I came to believe the story that Mama had run off in the night with the pedlar. It was less painful, safer, believing that than the truth I had witnessed."

Faraday was almost overcome by her anger. Damn them! They *must* have realised what had happened! *How had Azhure survived her life in Smyrton without going mad?*

"I survived by becoming what Hagen wanted," Azhure said. "I lived the lie that he wanted. I became as normal as I could. It was the only way to survive – whenever Hagen thought that I acted in any way . . . 'strange' . . . then he would beat me until I screamed for forgiveness. I learned not to . . . not to use . . ."

"Not to use what, Azhure?" Faraday asked. This was an important moment. Azhure had to admit to who, to what, she was.

"Not to use my powers," Azhure finally whispered, and her head swivelled to look at Faraday again. "Faraday, Mama said that I was a child of the gods. That I had to seek the answer on Temple Mount to find out who I was."

"And so you shall," Faraday said. "But something tells me that you may find some of the answers well before you step onto Temple Mount. No, wait, Azhure. Later. Now I must do something about your back. Did it break open again during your vision this morning?"

Azhure nodded. "As I relived those weeks at Hagen's hands as he tore the wings from my back time and time again – oh Faraday! They were so determined to reform! So resolved! – so the scars on my back opened again."

"Well now." Faraday smiled. "Your Enchanter Lover has singularly failed to help your pain, but I think that the Mother will be able to help a little."

Faraday stood and moved around to the other side of the bed, noticing as she did so that both Axis and Caelum had fallen asleep in the chair on the far side of the room.

"Let me tell you about the Mother," Faraday said softly, gently lifting the rough bandages that Axis had laid in a few places and inspecting Azhure's back. As she did so she talked about the Mother, her voice as soothing as her hands.

Azhure closed her eyes and listened. Faraday spoke of wondrous things. Of Groves and Woods and fairy creatures. Of old women and strange gardens. Of the Mother herself and of her love for all nature and for the earth. Raum had told Azhure very little about the Sacred Grove, and what Axis had told her had only frightened her, but now Faraday's words made Azhure realise what a remarkable place Faraday had discovered.

Faraday's words slowed and her eyes glowed with power. Slowly, slowly, she began to dig her hands into Azhure's back.

Azhure stiffened, almost crying out with the excruciating pain that Faraday's probing fingers caused her, but Faraday continued to talk and Azhure clung to her words, using them as an anchor for her sanity. The room swam as she came close to fainting, but Faraday's voice strengthened, and Azhure managed to hold on to consciousness.

Gradually the pain receded and Azhure's back grew warm. Her body relaxed and she felt strength flow through her. Faraday's hands felt good. For a long time she lay there, feeling Faraday's hands, listening to her voice.

"Your wings are gone," Faraday said suddenly, breaking her tale of the Enchanted Woods and the Mother. "Hagen did a thorough task. I cannot bring them back for you."

The wings had caused her so much pain that Azhure truly did not care that they were gone for good.

Faraday was silent now as her hands traced long, lazy strokes down Azhure's back from shoulders to buttocks. There was no pain at all. Azhure closed her eyes and let her whole body relax against Faraday's touch.

"Come," Faraday eventually said, rolling Azhure over onto her back. "Let's get you out of what remains of this nightgown and wash you down. You are smeared all over with blood."

As she sat up and pulled the nightgown over her shoulders Azhure realised that her back was completely healed. She could not even feel the tug and pull of the ridged scars that had been with her for over twenty years.

Faraday found some clean, warm water set by the fire and washed Azhure down. She smiled her warm, lovely smile and Azhure suddenly laughed.

"Thank you," she said and grasped Faraday's hands momentarily. "Thank you."

"I have sometimes thought that I have lived a troublesome life these past two years," Faraday said quietly. "But I find that my own pain has been nothing compared to what you have suffered most of your life. Azhure, we both find ourselves at a crossroads here this day. It is the first time we have met, and we have so much to say each to the other, yet we must both continue on our way. I think that, after so much pain, you will walk a road into joy and happiness, while I . . ." Faraday dropped her eyes. "I think that I will find yet more pain before I find happiness again."

"Faraday," Azhure pleaded. "I am so sorry for what I have done. I would have given anything that I was not here, not standing between you and Axis."

"Hush," Faraday said. "We are all caught in this damned and cruel Prophecy. None of us can escape. I do not blame you for what has happened, although," Faraday's eyes and voice grew bitter, "I fault Axis for the way he has behaved. He has treated us both harshly. He is quick to action, a quality usually commendable in a fighting man, but not when combined with his temper and that streak of cruelty he sometimes displays."

She stroked Azhure's cheek. "I would that we became friends. I have seen the pain you have suffered, and I know that you will understand what I will have to go through."

"I would be proud to call you my friend," Azhure whispered.

"Come now," Faraday smiled. "No tears between friends. No recriminations. That we both love Axis is our misfortune, as is the fact that the man cannot choose between us." She sighed. "Azhure. I will leave. No, hush, let me finish. I would have left anyway. I have my own role to play in the Prophecy and it will take me far from here. I will leave you your Lover, and envy you your Lover, Azhure. I had him a week, and that week I will have to treasure for a lifetime."

She looked down at Azhure's swollen belly. "You make such beautiful children, you and Axis."

Azhure wrapped her hands about her belly. Had her babies been harmed?

"No," Faraday said softly. "They are well, although they would have experienced what you and Axis saw this morning, and I do not know how that will affect them." She paused, as if debating whether or not to go on, then shook her head slightly and closed her mouth.

Azhure relaxed. "A son and a daughter, StarDrifter told me," she smiled. "Axis must awaken them for me. Sing to them what they must know."

"But you can teach them as well as he, Azhure," Faraday said, her voice a little more serious. "You *are* an Icarii Enchanter yourself, after all."

Azhure's mouth dropped open.

Faraday patted her on the cheek. "Sit and think about that for a moment, and, in a few days' time, when Axis awakens them and you have some quiet, you can teach those babies as much as their father. Now, if I rummage about in the closet I am sure that I can find something for you to wear."

An Icarii Enchanter, Azhure thought numbly. No. No, no, no, no – I do *not* want to be an Icarii Enchanter. I want to be Azhure. Azhure. That's all. *I do not want to be an Icarii Enchanter!*

"Small choice," said Faraday, coming back with a linen nightgown and a crimson wrap. "You are what your father made you."

"My father?"

"One of the gods, your mother said?" Faraday quirked an eyebrow. "What a night that must have been when the gods got you on your mother."

"I have so much to learn," Azhure said quietly.

"And many, many years in which to learn it."

The full implication of what Faraday said took a moment to sink in. "Oh!" Azhure cried, and her hands went to her mouth. She stared at Faraday, her blue eyes wide.

"Many years," Faraday smiled, "in which to enjoy your Lover and watch your children grow. Azhure." She sat down on the bed beside Azhure. "I would that you do something for me."

"Anything!" Azhure said fiercely.

"Azhure. Love Axis for me. Raise his children for me. All of them." Her tone and expression was a little strange when Faraday said the last, but Azhure did not notice it. "Remember me to the children. Tell them of Faraday, who loved their father and who is your friend. Tell them of the Mother. Azhure, when I leave I will go to fulfil my place in the Prophecy."

"Faraday —"

"I walk a strange road ahead," Faraday continued. "But I do not want to lose the friendship that I have made here today. Azhure, you and I will meet again over the next months."

Azhure frowned. "How — ?" she started to ask, but Faraday hushed her.

"We will find a way, you and I. And perhaps, if I find the opportunity, I shall take you to the Sacred Grove. Icarii Enchanters are rarely welcome in the Sacred Grove, but for you I think the Mother and the Horned Ones, as Raum, would be delighted to make an exception. There are wonders there beyond imagining, Azhure, and I would like to show them to you. But, wherever, however, we will visit from time to time, perhaps you can bring your children occasionally."

Azhure looked at the beautiful woman sitting beside her, and felt totally insignificant. "Faraday," she said. "Thank you."

Faraday touched Azhure's cheek gently, briefly. "I am glad to have found friendship with you, Azhure. Now," her tone became brisk. "Lie down and sleep a while. You will need to rest a good deal over the next few weeks and months, I think. Perhaps until your children are born. Sleep."

Azhure lay down and closed her eyes.

Faraday sat with her for a long time, looking at the woman, occasionally stroking her hair as she slept.

You have a long and amazing journey before you, she thought, as has Axis, as have I. Pray, that after all the pain behind us and before us, at least some of us survive it.

Finally Faraday stood up, smoothing her gown over her knees. She walked to where Axis and Caelum slept, both sprawled out in the chair.

"Axis," she said softly, kneeling down by the side of the chair.

He awoke with a start. "Azhure?" His eyes darted to the bed.

"She sleeps. She is well. Axis." His eyes shifted back to Faraday, "I think I will leave you to your Lover."

"Faraday," he muttered and reached out his hand for her face.

"Axis," she smiled brightly, but Axis could see the tears deep in her eyes, could see the pain. "Axis, we fell in love, you and I, when I was but Faraday, daughter of Earl Isend of Skarabost, and you were but Axis, BattleAxe of the Seneschal. Now we are completely different people. So different. We cannot be what once we were. And perhaps we both needed Borneheld alive to be able to love each other." She paused, and Axis could see the bitterness deep within her. "How he would have smiled to know that his death meant, eventually, the destruction of our love."

"Faraday," he said again, but Faraday hushed him.

"No, Axis. It is too late for you to say anything to me. Nothing you say now would heal the hurt you have caused me. Axis, I still love you, but I will leave you so that Azhure can be your wife – and make sure that you *do* marry her, Axis. She is a jewel that you can ill-afford to lose."

She smiled, her eyes hard, finally letting her bitterness show. "I will still fulfil my part of the Prophecy, Axis. Never fear. Now, listen to me. Axis, I formally break the vows that we made together in Gorkentown, I retract my promise to marry you. I release you to Azhure. I do this for Azhure," she said harshly, "*not* for you. What we once had between us, Axis, is gone. No more. You are free." But am I? she thought. Am I?

She stared at him a moment longer, trying desperately to imprint his face in her memory, then she leaned forward and kissed him gently on the mouth.

"Goodbye, Axis."

She stood and hurried towards the door. Axis made to go after her but his movement woke Caelum and the baby began to cry. By the time Axis had soothed his son, Faraday had gone.

Faraday paused in the open doorway only long enough to let the largest of the Alaunt through, then she closed it with a sharp click.

The ante chamber was now distinctly crowded with concerned faces, all staring at her.

She smiled, although she thought her own face would crack with the effort. "They are well. Give them an hour, perhaps two, then go in. They will need to talk to you, and you to them." She glanced at Ysgryff, then smiled more naturally at Rivkah, noticing how Magariz had sat beside her and clasped her hand. "Rivkah? Can I talk with you?"

Rivkah nodded and the two women walked into the corridor for some privacy.

"Rivkah. I am leaving. I cannot come between those two. Ah, Rivkah, this Prophecy is a cruel thing," she said, her voice breaking.

Rivkah held her close, rocking her a little and soothing her. Finally Faraday stood back and sniffed, wiping away her tears. "I must go and speak to the Sentinels, Rivkah, but then I must leave on a journey. I do not know if I will ever see you again."

Rivkah's own eyes filled with tears. Faraday was right. This Prophecy *was* a cruel thing. As she regarded Azhure as a daughter, so also she regarded Faraday, especially because Faraday had been a Duchess of Ichtar too. Poor Faraday. She deserved to find happiness as much as Azhure did.

"Oh, I'm sure I will," Faraday smiled. "Sometime. Somewhere. But, Rivkah, did I see you hold Prince Magariz's hand in there? Should I assume . . . ?"

Rivkah actually blushed and Faraday laughed. "Rivkah," she said. "I would give you a gift before I leave."

Abruptly she leaned forward and kissed Rivkah hard on the mouth. Rivkah shuddered as a bolt of pure energy raced through her. She stared open-mouthed at Faraday as the woman leaned back; she felt . . . well, revitalised. Warm. Alive.

"A gift from the Mother," Faraday whispered. "Use it well."

Then she turned and was gone, leaving behind her a farewell gift that would, in years to come, cause Axis even more sorrow and heartache than Gorgrael would.

It was Faraday's parting gift for the man who had betrayed her.

66

Enchantress

Three hours later Axis convened a meeting of his senior commanders, the Sentinels, and his closest friends in the chamber. There were some things that needed to be said, and Axis was tired of having secrets. If WolfStar sat disguised among them, plotting and planning, then so be it. He, his parents and MorningStar had kept the secret of WolfStar close, suspecting all those about them. In the end their secrecy had almost killed Azhure.

Axis still found it hard to believe that Azhure had smiled and forgiven him so easily when she'd finally woken. He felt as if he would spend the rest of his life atoning for the pain he had caused her.

Now Azhure sat in the chair by the fire as the group waiting outside slowly filed in. She was wan and obviously weak, but she smiled at her friends and family, her heart easy. Rivkah, looking radiant, and Magariz; Belial, Cazna quiet and pale by his side; the Sentinels, all looking somewhat subdued; Ho'Demi and Sa'Kuya; the House of SunSoar – FreeFall, EvenSong, and StarDrifter, who, like his son before him, fell to his knees beside Azhure, crying for her forgiveness; Ysgryff, who, still grim with concern for her, touched Azhure lightly on the top of her head and glared at StarDrifter before he sat next to Rivkah and Magariz; FarSight CutSpur and several of his Crest-Leaders, together with SpikeFeather; Arne, even more dour than usual, and several of Azhure's unit commanders from the archers; and the remaining fourteen of the Alaunt who lolled between chairs and legs and made the chamber, once spacious, appear crowded and inadequate.

"Look," Axis said quietly, when all had seated themselves, whether on chairs or benches or on the floor. "Look. I want you to witness what I witnessed this morning. I want you to see where Azhure has come from."

The Song of Recall filtered through the room. As the circle of ghastly crosses had appeared before Arcen, now the interior of Plough-Keeper Hagen's home in Smyrton appeared before the assembled group.

All witnessed the dreadful events of Azhure's childhood. They witnessed the death of her mother – and Ysgryff cried out in horror when he saw the face of the woman who had been Azhure's mother. They witnessed Azhure's mutilation at the hands of her stepfather. They felt with Azhure the torment, both physical and emotional, that Hagen inflicted on her as she grew up. They realised why Azhure had buried her heritage so deep that not even she, eventually, realised what and who she was – if she had ever let the truth through then she would have died a death as appalling as her mother's had been.

StarDrifter eventually had to avert his head. As he did so he caught Axis' gaze. *The child will turn her head and cry – revealing ancient arts.*

Axis nodded imperceptibly. *Yes, StarDrifter. And where else is she in this Prophecy? Where else?*

"It saddens me," Azhure whispered, when the ghostly images had finally flickered and died, "that, of all I remember, I do not yet remember my mother's name. The loss of her name has tormented me all through these years since her death."

"Your mother's name was Niah, Azhure."

Everyone in the room turned to look at Ysgryff; even several of the hounds raised their heads.

Azhure leaned forward, stunned. *Niah!*

Ysgryff walked over to her, bending down by her side and taking her hand.

"Azhure, I was not totally sure until I saw your mother's face, but I had my suspicions."

"Ysgryff." Azhure's voice was distraught, her eyes wide and distressed. "*Tell me!*"

"Niah was my eldest sister, some eight years older than me. Like many women of the House of Nor, she elected to become a priestess in the Temple of the Stars rather than marry. She joined when she was fourteen, and became one of the senior priestesses when only twenty-one. Azhure, you do not remember your mother's name because she would never have told it to you. All the priestesses relinquish their names when they take their holy vows. She would not even have thought of herself as Niah. Even after she left the complex on Temple Mount."

"Niah," Azhure whispered. "Thank you, Ysgryff . . . uncle."

"I prefer Ysgryff, Azhure." He raised her hand to his lips and kissed it softly. "But I welcome you into the House of Nor. Later, when we have more leisure, I will tell you of your mother."

"Ysgryff." Axis leaned forward. "Do you know anything of the mystery of Azhure's conception? Of her father?"

Ysgryff shook his head. "Very little. Our family was contacted one year and told simply that Niah had left the Temple. It happens sometimes that a priestess will leave the Order of the Stars, but rarely, and we were all stunned that Niah had vanished. She had seemed so happy in the Temple. I went to Temple Mount to talk to the Sisterhood, but they could not, perhaps would not, tell me much. They said that Niah had simply left one day."

"And travelled to Smyrton to marry Hagen?" Azhure said. "Why? *Why?*" And why did he leave me alive when he hated me so deeply, she thought. Why?

Axis looked across at the Sentinels. "What do you know? Come, tell me." His voice was hard. "I will have no more secrets between us."

But Jack, who knew so much, knew that the Prophecy had always meant Axis for Azhure, not Faraday, was silent.

Veremund spread his hands helplessly. "Axis, believe me when I say that we know nothing of Niah, of why she would have travelled to Smyrton to marry Hagen of all people."

"You are not beyond forcing people into marriages that they do not want," Axis snapped.

Veremund hung his head. "Axis." He raised his head again. "I can tell you nothing; Azhure has always been a mystery to us."

StarDrifter stood up. "We cannot know why Niah fled to Smyrton when we still know so little about her, about her reasons for leaving the Temple and the Order of the Stars. Azhure, Niah told you to go to Temple Mount. Surely there you will find answers. Perhaps the priestesses will be more willing to talk to her daughter than to her brother." He took a deep breath and looked at Axis. "But I do not believe what she said about you being a child of the gods," he said, returning his eyes to Azhure. "Perhaps that is what she thought. Perhaps that is what she was told. Perhaps it was better that she believed that.

"Azhure, I think I know who your father is. It would explain so much about you, and it would explain – but not excuse – why Axis and I were so ready to jump to the conclusion that *you* were WolfStar this morning." Again StarDrifter took a deep breath. "Azhure, I think that *WolfStar* is your father."

Jack, sitting shadowed in a corner, raised his eyebrows in surprise. He had not thought StarDrifter so perceptive.

"You think *what*?" Azhure asked, but at her side Axis slowly nodded as he looked at his father.

"Azhure-heart," he said softly, "it would explain so much. The Wolven. The Alaunt." He smiled and looked back at Azhure. "Your SunSoar blood."

Axis took her hand. "Azhure, you know that both Star-Drifter and myself cannot resist you. Remember Beltide night in the groves. Remember how our blood sang each to the other – yours, mine, and StarDrifter's."

Axis' eyes caught his father's, then he went on. "If Wolf-Star is your father it would explain how you came to use the Dark Music. He must have learned to use it beyond the Star Gate and somehow he has bequeathed the ability to you through his blood."

Azhure leaned back in her chair and thought for a long time. It made sense, what they said. And it also made sense of her strange encounter in Spiredore.

"I met my father last night," she said softly.

"What!" Axis cried, and his query was echoed about the room by several other people.

"I did not know who he was then, but he could only have been WolfStar." She told them of her strange meeting, of his kiss, of his mention that it was Unclean. "As are relations between parent and child and as between brother and sister in the SunSoar family."

Her eyes softened. "He was a beautiful birdman. The power shone out of him. If he came to my mother, to Niah, like that then I can well understand why she lay with him and why she thought he was one of the gods."

StarDrifter looked at her, troubled by Azhure's obvious admiration for WolfStar. "He also murdered MorningStar, Azhure. And trained Gorgrael."

Azhure's eyes met his. "And yet he was kind to me and Caelum, StarDrifter. I do not seek to excuse his murders, but I think that he is a man of many disguises."

"Enough, uncle," FreeFall said, stepping forward from his corner. "We have many days in which to puzzle this mystery between us, but now we have a most important duty. Azhure," he brushed past StarDrifter and briefly stepped over the Alaunt at her feet to kiss Azhure on the cheek. "Welcome, Azhure, into the House of SunSoar. I am FreeFall SunSoar, your cousin. Sing well and fly high, Azhure, and may the years of the rest of your life bring only joy and happiness to counter the darkness that has filled your early years."

Azhure's eyes filled with tears.

EvenSong was right behind FreeFall. She kissed Azhure on her other cheek. "Welcome, Azhure, into the House of Sun-Soar. I am EvenSong SunSoar, and I am also your cousin. May the wind always blow at your back and your arrows fly straight and true."

StarDrifter bent down after his daughter, and Azhure blushed a little at the look in his eyes.

"Welcome, Azhure, into the House of SunSoar. I am StarDrifter SunSoar, and," he grinned, "I will be whatever you need me to be, but I am *not* your parent and I am *not* your brother." *And I am not Unclean*, Azhure could hear him echo in her mind. "May you pass on both your beauty and your allurements to the daughter you grow inside you."

Welcome, Azhure, into the House of SunSoar. My name is Caelum Azhurson SunSoar StarSon, and I am your son. Know that I love you and that if I am a child of the sun, then it was you who made me that way.

I thank you, Caelum, with all my heart, for your love.

Rivkah now stepped forward and kissed Azhure gently on her forehead. "Welcome, Azhure, into the sometimes fractious House of the SunSoars. May your compassion and courage in the face of adversity remind them all of their own shortcomings."

"Thank you," Azhure said as Rivkah sat back down with Magariz. She turned to look at Axis, expecting him also to welcome her into the House of SunSoar, but he merely smiled gently at her and glared at Ysgryff who hastily let Azhure's other hand go and hurried back to his seat.

"Azhure, my friends," Axis said at length. "There is a very special reason for my wanting so many people here, crowded into this room. I need witnesses for what I now do."

He dropped down on one knee and clasped Azhure's hand firmly between his own, interlacing their fingers.

"I, Axis, StarMan of Tencendor, son of StarDrifter, Enchanter of the House of SunSoar and Rivkah, Princess of the Royal House of Achar, do plight thee, Azhure, daughter of Niah of Nor and WolfStar SunSoar, my hand in marriage. Before these people here assembled and with my free will and consent I do take thee as my wife and promise to give thee an honoured place by my side and in my roost. In front of these witnesses I do promise to honour you, to remain loyal to you, and to pledge to you my respect, my possessions, and my body for as long as we both shall live. I promise never to lead you anywhere but into calm air, bright sunshine and rising thermals. My wings are your wings, my heart and soul are yours. You have my pledge of marriage, Azhure-heart, and to this may all the gods and Stars in Creation bear holy witness. May we dance through the years to the music of the Star Dance to find eternal peace among the Stars themselves."

The marriage vows Axis had spoken were an exotic mixture of Acharite and Icarii marriage vows, and they reflected the curious heritage that both brought into this marriage.

For a long moment Azhure was unable to speak. She gripped Axis' hands, staring into his eyes, unaware of any others in the room. Eventually she smiled.

"I, Azhure, daughter of Niah of the House of Nor and WolfStar SunSoar," she began softly, and her voice strengthened as she repeated the vows.

"My wings are your wings, Axis," she finished, "my heart and soul are yours. You have my pledge of marriage, and to this may all the gods and Stars in Creation bear holy witness. May we dance through the years to the music of the Star Dance to find eternal peace among the Stars themselves."

Axis leaned forward and kissed her. For the past few minutes, as he had begun to speak his vows of marriage, he felt, as Orr had said he would, the insistent urge to pass the Enchantress' ring on. This was the moment and this was the woman.

Axis let Azhure's hand go and pulled the Enchantress' ring from the small secret pocket in his breeches. He held the ring up so that all in the room could see it. The enchanted sapphire and the golden stars within it sparkled in the fire-light. The Icarii and the Sentinels all gasped, totally shocked – yet even they did not entirely realise what it meant that Axis now slid the ring onto the heart finger of Azhure's left hand. It fitted perfectly, made only for this woman and for this finger.

"Welcome into the House of the Stars to stand by my side, Enchantress. May we walk together forever."

The Circle was complete.

Glossary

ACHAR: the realm that stretches over most of the continent, bounded by the Andeis, Tyrre and Widowmaker Seas, the Avarinheim Forest and the Icescarp Alps.

ACHARITES: the people of Achar.

ADAMON: one of the nine Icarii Star Gods, Adamon is God of the Firmament and shares seniority with his wife, Xanon.

AFTERLIFE: all three races, the Acharites, the Icarii and the Avar, believe in the existence of an AfterLife, although exactly what they believe depends on their particular culture.

ALAYNE: a roving blacksmith in Skarabost.

ALAUNT: the legendary pack of hounds that once belonged to WolfStar SunSoar.

ALDENI: a small province in western Achar, devoted to small crop cultivation. It is administered by Duke Roland.

ANDAKILSA, River: the extreme northern river of Ichtar, dividing Ichtar from Ravensbund. It remains free of ice all year round and flows into the Andeis Sea.

ANDEIS SEA: often unpredictable sea that washes the west coast of Achar.

ANNWIN: eldest daughter of Earl Isend of Skarabost, sister to Faraday. Married to Lord Osmary.

ARCEN: the major town of Arcness.

ARCNESS: large eastern province in Achar, specialising in pigs. It is administered by Earl Burdel.

ARHAT: a Ravensbund warrior.

ARNE: a cohort commander in the Axe-Wielders.

ARTOR THE PLOUGHMAN: the one true god, as taught by the Brotherhood of the Seneschal. According to the Book of Field and Furrow, the religious text of the Seneschal, Artor gave mankind the gift of the Plough, the instrument which enabled mankind to abandon his hunting and gathering lifestyle and to settle in the one spot to cultivate the earth and thus to build the foundations of civilisation.

AVAR, The: one of the ancient races of Tencendor who live in the forest of the Avarinheim. The Avar are sometimes referred to as the People of the Horn.

AVARINHEIM, The: the home of the Avar people. The Acharites refer to it as the Shadowsward. See "Shadowsward".

AVONSDALE: province in western Achar. It produces legumes, fruit and flowers. It is administered by Earl Jorge.

AXE-WIELDERS, The: the elite crusading and military wing of the Seneschal. Its members have not taken holy orders but have nevertheless dedicated their battle skills to the Seneschal to use as it wishes.

Now most of the Axe-Wielders have abandoned the Seneschal to follow Axis in his alliance with the Icarii.

AXIS: son of the Princess Rivkah and the Icarii Enchanter StarDrifter SunSoar. Once BattleAxe of the Axe-Wielders, Axis has now assumed the mantle of the StarMan of the Prophecy of the Destroyer.

AZHURE: daughter of Brother Hagen of Smyrton. Her mother came from Nor.

AZLE, River: a major river that divides the provinces of Ichtar and Aldeni. It flows into the Andeis Sea.

BANES: the religious leaders of the Avar people. They wield magic, although it is usually of the minor variety.

BARROWS, The Ancient: the burial places of the ancient Enchanter-Talons of the Icarii people. Located in southern Arcness.

BARSARBE: a Bane of the Avar people.

BATTLEAXE, The: the leader of the Axe-Wielders, appointed by the Brother-Leader for his loyalty to the Seneschal, his devotion to Artor the Ploughman and the Way of the Plough, and his skills as a military commander. Axis was the last man to hold this post.

BEDWYR FORT: a fort that sits on the lower reaches of the River Nordra and guards the entrance to Grail Lake from Nordmuth.

BELAGUEZ: Axis' war horse.

BELIAL: lieutenant and second-in-command in Axis' army. Long-time friend and supporter of Axis SunSoar.

BELTIDE: see "Festivals".

BOGLE MARSH: a large and inhospitable marsh in eastern Arcness. Strange creatures are said to live in the Marsh.

BOOK OF FIELD AND FURROW: the religious text of the Seneschal, which teaches that Artor himself wrote it and presented it to mankind.

BORNEHELD: Duke of Ichtar, the most powerful noble in Achar. Son of the Princess Rivkah and her husband, Duke Searlas.

BOROLEAS: an elderly Brother within the Seneschal.

BRACKEN RANGES, The: a low and narrow mountain range that divides Arcness and Skarabost.

BRACKEN, River: river that rises in the Bracken Ranges which, dividing provinces of Skarabost and Arcness, flows into the Widowmaker Sea.

BRADOKE: a senior lieutenant within Borneheld's forces.

BRIGHTFEATHER: wife to RavenCrest SunSoar, Talon of the Icarii.

BRODE: an Avar man, Clan Leader of the SilentWalk Clan.

BROTHER-LEADER, The: the supreme leader of the Brotherhood of the Seneschal. Usually elected by the senior Brothers, the Office of Brother-Leader is for life. He is a powerful man, controlling not only the Brotherhood and all its riches, but the Axe-Wielders as well. The current Brother-Leader is Jayme.

BURDEL, EARL: lord of Arcness and friend to Borneheld, Duke of Ichtar.

CAELUM: a baby's name. It means "the heavens", or "stars in heaven".

CARLON: capital city of Achar and residence of the kings of Achar. Situated on Grail Lake.

CAULDRON LAKE, The: the lake at the centre of the Silent Woman Woods.

CAZNA: daughter of Baron Ysgryff of Nor.

CHAMBER OF THE MOONS: chief audience and sometime banquet chamber of the royal palace in Carlon.

CHAMPION, A: occasionally an Acharite warrior will pledge himself as a noble lady's Champion. The relationship is purely platonic and is one of protection and support. The pledge of a Champion can be broken only by his death or by the express wish of his lady.

CHARONITES: a race who live in the UnderWorld. They are related to the Icarii.

CLANS, The: the Avar tend to segregate into Clan groups, roughly equitable with family groups.

CLOUDBURST SUNSOAR: younger brother and murderer of WolfStar SunSoar.

COHORT: see "Military Terms".

COROLEAS: the great empire to the south of Achar. Relations between the two countries are usually cordial.

CREST: Icarii military unit composed of twelve Wings.

CRIMSONCREST: an Icarii male.

CREST-LEADER: commander of an Icarii Crest.

CULPEPPER FENWICKE: mayor of the city of Arcen in Arcness.

DARK MAN, The: Gorgrael's mentor. Also known as Dear Man. Gorgrael does not know his real identity.

DEAR MAN: See "Dark Man".

DESTROYER, The: another term for Gorgrael.

DEVERA: daughter to Duke Roland of Aldeni.

DISTANCES:
  League: roughly seven kilometres, or four and a half miles.
  Pace: roughly one metre or one yard.
  Handspan: roughly twenty centimetres or eight inches.

DOBO: a Ravensbund warrior.

DRIFTSTAR SUNSOAR: mother of MorningStar, grandmother of StarDrifter. Enchanter and SunSoar in her own right, wife to the Sun-Soar Talon, she died three hundred years before the events of this book.

EARTH TREE: a tree sacred to both the Icarii and the Avar.

EDOWES: a soldier from Arne's unit in Axis' force.

EGERLEY: a young man from Smyrton.

EMBETH, LADY OF TARE: widow, good friend and once lover of Axis.

ENCHANTED WOOD, The: the faerie wood beyond the Sacred Grove.

ENCHANTRESS, The: the first of the Icarii Enchanters, the first Icarii to discover the way to use the power of the Star Dance. The Enchantress was the founder of both Icarii and Charonite peoples.

ENCHANTRESS' RING, The: the Enchantress made use of an ancient ring to help establish the line of Icarii Enchanters. It was not hers, but she was granted the use of it for her lifetime. The ring has little or no power in itself, but it is a powerful symbol.

ENCHANTERS: magicians of the Icarii people. Many are very powerful. All Enchanters have the word "Star" somewhere in their names.

ENCHANTER-TALONS: Talons of the Icarii people who were also Enchanters.

EVENSONG: sister to Axis.

FARADAY: daughter of Earl Isend of Skarabost and his wife, Lady Merlion. Wife to Duke Borneheld of Ichtar.

FARSIGHT CUTSPUR: senior Crest-Leader of the Icarii Strike Force.

FEATHERFLIGHT BRIGHTWING: a Wing-Leader in the Icarii Strike Force.

FERNBRAKE LAKE, The: the large lake in the centre of the Bracken Ranges.

FERRYMAN, The: Charonite who plies the ferry of the UnderWorld.

FESTIVALS of the Avar and the Icarii:
Yuletide: the winter solstice, in the last week of Snow-month.
Beltide: the spring Festival, the first day of Flower-month.
Fire-Night: the summer solstice, in the last week of Rose-month.

FINGUS: a previous BattleAxe. Now dead.

FIRE-NIGHT, The: see "Festivals". Although now a fairly tame Avar festival, in Icarii and Avar legend, Fire-Night was that night tens of thousands of years ago when the ancient Star Gods (older and more powerful than the current Star Gods) crashed into the land in a fire-storm that lasted many days and nights. Legend says that these ancient gods still sleep in the depths of the Sacred, or Magic, Lakes of Tencendor. The Sacred Lakes were created from this fire-storm and their power comes from the ancient Star Gods.

FLEAT: an Avar woman.

FLEURIAN: Baroness of Tarantaise, wife to Greville. She is his second wife, and much younger than him.

FLULIA: one of the nine Icarii Star Gods, Flulia is Goddess of Water.

FLURIA, The River: a minor river that flows through Aldeni into the River Nordra.

FORBIDDEN, The: the two races, the Icarii and the Avar, that the Seneschal teaches are evil creatures who use magic and sorcery to enslave humans. During the Wars of the Axe, a thousand years before the events of the Prophecy of the Destroyer, the Acharites pushed the Forbidden back beyond the Fortress Ranges into the Shadowsward (or Avarinheim) and the Icescarp Alps.

FORBIDDEN TERRITORIES, The: the lands of the Forbidden, the Avarinheim and the Icescarp Alps.

FORBIDDEN VALLEY, The: the only known entrance into the Shadowsward (or Avarinheim) from Achar. It is where the River Nordra escapes the Shadowsward and flows into Achar.

FOREST, concept of: the Seneschal teaches that all forests are bad because they harbour dark demons who plot the overthrow of mankind, thus most Acharites have a fear of forests and their dark interiors. Almost all the ancient forest that once covered Achar has been destroyed. The only trees grown in Achar are fruit trees and plantation trees for timber.

FORTRESS RANGES: the mountains that run down Achar's eastern boundary from the Icescarp Alps to the Widowmaker Sea.

FRANCIS: an elderly Brother from the Retreat in Gorkentown.

FREEFALL SUNSOAR: son and heir of RavenCrest, Icarii Talon, FreeFall was murdered by Borneheld atop the keep at Gorkenfort.

FULBRIGHT: an Acharite engineer in Axis' force.

FULKE, BARON: lord of Romsdale.

FUNADO: a Ravensbund warrior.

"FURROW WIDE, FURROW DEEP": all-embracing Acharite phrase which can be used as a benediction, as a protection against evil, or as a term of greeting.

GANELON, LORD: Lord of Tare, once husband to Embeth, Lady of Tare. Now dead.

GARDEN, The: the Garden of the Mother.

GARLAND, GOODMAN: Goodman of Smyrton.

GATEKEEPER, The: Keeper of the Gate of Death in the UnderWorld. Her task is to keep tally of the souls who pass through the Gate.

GAUTIER: lieutenant to Borneheld, Duke of Ichtar.

GHOSTMEN: another term for Skraelings.

GHOSTTREE CLAN: one of the Avar Clans, headed by Grindle.

GILBERT: Brother of the Seneschal and assistant and adviser to the Brother-Leader.

GORGRAEL: the Destroyer, an evil lord of the north who, according to the Prophecy of the Destroyer, threatens Achar. He is a half-brother to Axis, sharing the same father, StarDrifter SunSoar.

GORKENFORT: major fort situated in Gorken Pass in northern Ichtar.

GORKEN PASS: the narrow pass that provides the only way from Ravensbund into Ichtar. It is bounded by the Icescarp Alps and the River Andakilsa.

GORKENTOWN: the town about the walls of Gorkenfort.

GRAIL LAKE, The: a massive lake at the lower reaches of the River Nordra. On its shores are Carlon and the Tower of the Seneschal.

GREVILLE, BARON: lord of Tarantaise.

GRINDLE: an Avar man, head of the GhostTree Clan.

GRYPHON: a legendary flying creature of Tencendor, intelligent, vicious and courageous. They were particularly deadly to the Icarii and it took the Icarii many hundreds of years to exterminate them. The Gryphon are inexplicably flying the skies above Ichtar again.

GUNDEALGA FORD: a wide, shallow ford on the Nordra, just south of the Urqhart Hills.

HAGEN: Plough-Keeper of Smyrton.

HANDSPAN: see "Distances".

HANORI: a Ravensbund elder.

HELM: a young Avar male.

HESKETH: the captain of the palace guard in Carlon. Lover to Yr.

HO'DEMI: the Chief of the Ravensbund people.

HOGNI: a young Avar female.

HORDLEY, GOODMAN: Goodman of Smyrton.

HORNED ONES: the almost divine and most sacred members of the Avar race. They live in the Sacred Grove.

HOVEREYE BLACKWING: an Icarii Crest-Leader.

HSINGARD: the large town situated in central Ichtar, seat of the Dukes of Ichtar.

ICARII, The: one of the ancient races of Tencendor. They are sometimes referred to as the People of the Wing.

ICESCARP ALPS, The: the great mountain range that stretches across most of northern Achar.

ICESCARP BARREN: a desolate tract of land situated in northern Ichtar between the Icescarp Alps and the Urqhart Hills.

ICEWORMS: potent creations of Gorgrael, instrumental in the downfall of Gorkentown. Fashioned from ice and snow and shaped like worms, from whence they got their names, these massive creatures carry Skraelings in their bellies. Rising twenty or thirty paces above men or walls, they can then vomit their cargo behind both lines and walls.

ICHTAR, DUKE of: the lord of Ichtar, currently Borneheld.

ICHTAR, The Province of: the largest and richest of the provinces of Achar. Ichtar derives its wealth from its extensive grazing herds and from its mineral and precious gem mines.

ICHTAR, River: minor river flowing through Ichtar into the River Azle.

IGREN FENWICKE: wife to the mayor of Arcen, Culpepper Fenwicke.

ILFRACOMBE: the manor house of the Earl of Skarabost, the home where Faraday grew up.

IMIBE: a Ravensbund woman, nurse to Caelum.

INARI: a Ravensbund warrior.

ISEND, EARL: lord of Skarabost, a darkly handsome but somewhat dandified lord. Father to Faraday.

ISLAND OF MIST AND MEMORY: one of the sacred sites of the Icarii people, long lost to them after the Wars of the Axe. See also "Temple of the Stars" and "Temple Mount".

IZANAGI: a Ravensbund warrior.

JACK: senior among the Sentinels.

JAYME: Brother-Leader of the Seneschal.

JERVOIS LANDING: the small town on Tailem Bend of the River Nordra. The gateway into Ichtar.

JORGE, EARL: Earl of Avonsdale, and one of the most experienced military campaigners in Achar.

JUDITH: Queen of Achar, wife to Priam.

KAREL: previous King of Achar, father to Priam and Rivkah. Now dead.

KASTALEON: one of the great Keeps of Achar, situated on the River Nordra in central Achar. It is of relatively recent construction.

KEEPS, The: the three surviving great magical Keeps of Achar, all built by the Icarii thousands of years ago. See separate entries under "Spiredore", "Sigholt", and "Silent Woman Keep".

KENRICKE: the commander of the surviving cohort of Axe-Wielders, left by Axis to guard the Tower of the Seneschal.

LEAGUE: see "Distances".

MAGARIZ, LORD: once commander of Gorkenfort, now one of Axis' senior commanders. He comes of a noble and ancient Acharite family.

MAGIC: the Seneschal teaches that all magic, enchantments or sorcery are evil and the province only of the Forbidden races who will use magic to enslave the Acharites if they can. Consequently all Artor-fearing Acharites fear and hate the use of magic.

MALFARI: the tuber the Avar depend on to produce their bread.

MASCEN, BARON: Lord of Rhaetia.

MERLION, LADY: wife to Earl Isend of Skarabost and mother to Faraday. Now dead.

MILITARY TERMS – Acharite (for regular army and Axe-Wielders):
Squad: a group of thirty-six men, generally archers.
Unit: a group of one hundred men, infantry, archers, pikemen or cavalry.
Cohort: five units, so five hundred men.

MIRBOLT: a Bane of the Avar people.

MONTHS: (northern hemisphere seasons apply)
Wolf-month: January
Raven-month: February

Hungry-month: March
Thaw-month: April
Flower-month: May
Rose-month: June
Harvest-month: July
Weed-month: August
DeadLeaf-month: September
Bone-month: October
Frost-month: November
Snow-month: December

MOONWALKER: the name Rivkah adopted when she joined the Icarii. She abandoned the adopted name of MoonWalker and resumed her birth-name at the request of a Charonite Ferryman.

MORNINGSTAR SUNSOAR: StarDrifter's mother and a powerful Enchanter in her own right. MorningStar is the widow of Rush-Cloud, the previous SunSoar Talon.

MORYSON: Brother of the Seneschal and friend and chief assistant and adviser to the Brother-Leader.

MOTHER, THE: either the Avar name for Fernbrake Lake, or an all-embracing term for nature which is sometimes personified as an immortal woman.

NARCIS: one of the nine Icarii Star Gods, Narcis is God of the Sun.

NEVELON: lieutenant to Duke Roland of Aldeni.

NIAH: a Nors woman.

NOR: the southernmost of the provinces of Achar. The Nors people are far darker and more exotic than the rest of the Acharites. Nor is controlled by Baron Ysgryff.

NORDMUTH: the port at the mouth of the River Nordra.

NORDRA, The River: the great river that is the main life line of Achar. Rising in the Icescarp Alps, the River Nordra flows through the Avarinheim before flowing through northern and central Achar. It is used for irrigation, transport and fishing.

OGDEN: one of the Sentinels. Brother to Veremund.

ORDER OF THE STARS: order of priestesses who keep watch in the Temple of the Stars. Each gives up her own name on taking orders.

ORR: The Charonite Ferryman.

OSMARY, LORD: husband to Annwin, Faraday's elder sister.

PACE: see "Distances".

PEASE: an Avar woman killed in the Yuletide attack on the Earth Tree Grove.

PIRATES' NEST: a large island off the coast of Nor and close to Ysbadd and the haunt of pirates. Some say the pirates are protected by Baron Ysgryff himself.

PLOUGH, The: each Acharite village has a Plough, which not only serves to plough the fields, but is also the centre of their worship of the Way of the Plough. The Plough was the implement given by Artor the Ploughman to enable mankind to civilise themselves. Use of the Plough distinguishes the Acharites from the Forbidden; neither the Icarii nor the Avar practise cultivation.

PLOUGH-KEEPERS: the Seneschal assigns a brother to each village in Achar, and these men are often known as Plough-Keepers. They are literally guardians of the Plough in each village, but they are also directors of the Way of the Plough and guardians of the villagers' souls.

PORS: one of the nine Icarii Star Gods, Pors is God of Air.

PRIAM: King of Achar and uncle to Borneheld, brother to Rivkah.

PRIVY CHAMBER: the large chamber in the royal palace in Carlon where the King's Privy Council meet.

PRIVY COUNCIL: the council of advisers to the King of Achar, normally the lords of the major provinces of Achar.

PROPHECY OF THE DESTROYER: an ancient Prophecy that tells of the rise of Gorgrael in the north and the StarMan who can stop him. No-one knows who wrote it.

RAINBOW SCEPTRE: a weapon mentioned in the Prophecy of the Destroyer.

RAUM: a Bane of the Avar people.

RAVENCREST SUNSOAR: current Talon of the Icarii people.

RAVENSBUND: the extreme northern province of Achar, although it is not administered by the Acharite monarchy.

RAVENSBUNDMEN: the inhabitants of Ravensbund, generally loathed by the Acharites as barbarous and cruel.

REINALD: retired chief cook of Sigholt, undercook when Rivkah lived there.

RENKIN, GOODPEOPLE: farming couple of northern Arcness.

RETREATS: many Brothers of the Seneschal prefer the contemplative life to the active life, and the Seneschal has various Retreats about Achar where these Brothers live in peace in order to contemplate the mysteries of Artor the Ploughman.

RHAETIA: small area of Achar situated in the western Bracken Ranges. It is controlled by Baron Mascen.

RIVKAH: Princess of Achar, sister to King Priam and mother to Borneheld, Axis, and EvenSong.

ROLAND, Duke: also known as "The Walker" because he is too fat to ride. Duke of Aldeni and one of the major military commanders of Achar.

ROMSDALE: a province to the south-west of Carlon that mainly produces wine. It is administered by Baron Fulke.

RUSHCLOUD SUNSOAR: father to RavenCrest and StarDrifter. The previous Talon of the Icarii.

SACRED, GROVE, The: the most sacred spot of the Avar people, the Sacred Grove is rarely visited by ordinary mortals. Normally the Banes are the only members of the Avar race who know the paths in order to find the Grove.

SACRED LAKES, The: the ancient land of Tencendor had a number of magical lakes whose powers are now forgotten. Sometimes known as the Magic Lakes. See "Fire-Night" for the legend of their formation.

SA'KUYA: a Ravensbund woman, wife to the Chief, Ho'Demi.

SEAGRASS PLAINS: the vast grain plains that form most of Skarabost.

SEARLAS: previous Duke of Ichtar and father of Borneheld. Once married to the Princess Rivkah. Now dead.

SENESCHAL, The: the religious organisation of Achar. The Religious Brotherhood of the Seneschal, known individually as Brothers, directs the religious lives of all the Acharites. The Seneschal is extremely powerful and plays a major role, not only in everyday life, but also in the political life of the nation. It teaches obedience to the one god, Artor the Ploughman, and the Way of the Plough.

SENESCHAL, TOWER of: headquarters of the Brotherhood of the Seneschal. The Tower of the Seneschal is a massive pure white seven-sided tower that sits on the opposite side of the Grail Lake to Carlon.

SENTINELS: magical creatures of the Prophecy of the Destroyer.

SHADOWSWARD, The: an Acharite name for the Avarinheim.

SHARPEYE BLUEFEATHER: Crest-Leader in the Icarii Strike Force.

SHRA: a young Avar child. Daughter of Pease and Grindle.

SICARIUS: leader of the pack of Alaunt hounds. The name means "assassin".

SIGHOLT: one of the great Keeps of Achar, situated in HoldHard Pass in the Urqhart Hills in Ichtar. One of the main residences of the Dukes of Ichtar.

SILENT WOMAN KEEP: The Silent Woman Keep lies in the centre of the Silent Woman Woods. It is one of the magical Keeps of Tencendor.

SILENT WOMAN WOODS: the dark and impenetrable woods in southern Arcness that house the Silent Woman Keep.

SILTON: one of the nine Icarii Star Gods, Silton is God of Fire.

SONG OF CREATION: a Song which can, according to Icarii and Avar legend, actually create life itself. In his address to the Icarii Assembly asking for their help to rescue Axis from Gorkenfort, StarDrifter claimed that Axis sang this to himself in the womb.

SONG OF RECREATION: one of the most powerful Icarii spells which can recreate life in the dying. It cannot, however, make the dead rise again. Only the most powerful Enchanters can sing this Song.

SKALI: a young Avar female, daughter of Fleat and Grindle. She died during the Skraeling attack on the Sacred Earth Tree Grove at Yuletide.

SKARABOST: large eastern province of Achar which grows much of the realm's grain supplies. It is administered by Earl Isend.

SKRAEBOLDS: leaders of the Skraelings.

SKRAEFEAR: senior of the SkraeBolds.

SKRAELINGS: (also called wraiths or Ghostmen) insubstantial creatures of the frozen northern wastes who feed off fear and blood.

SMYRTON: a large village in northern Skarabost, virtually at the entrance to the Forbidden Valley.

SORCERY: see "Magic".

SPIKEFEATHER TRUESONG: an Icarii Wing-Leader.

SPIREDORE: one of the magical Keeps of Tencendor.

SPREADWING RAVENCRY: Crest-Leader in the Icarii Strike Force.

STAR DANCE, The: the source from which the Icarii Enchanters derive their power.

STARDRIFTER SUNSOAR: an Icarii Enchanter, father to Gorgrael, Axis and EvenSong.

STAR GATE: one of the sacred sites of the Icarii people.

STAR GODS, The: the nine gods of the Icarii, but only seven of their names have been revealed to the Icarii. See separate entries under "Adamon", "Xanon", "Narcis", "Flulia", "Pors", "Zest" and "Silton".

STARMAN, The: the man who, according to the Prophecy of the Destroyer, is the only one who can defeat Gorgrael – Axis SunSoar.

STRAUM ISLAND: large island off the Ichtar coast inhabited by sealers.

STRIKE FORCE: the military wing of the Icarii.

SUNDOWN CROOKCLAW: one of the Icarii Strike Force killed in the Skraeling attack on the Sacred Earth Tree Grove at Yuletide past. EvenSong SunSoar filled his place in SpikeFeather TrueSong's Wing.

SUNSOAR, HOUSE of: the ruling House of the Icarii for many thousands of years.

TAILEM BEND: great bend in the River Nordra where it turns from its westerly direction and flows south to Nordmuth and the Sea of Tyrre.

TALON, The: the hereditary ruler of the Icarii people (and once over all of the peoples of Tencendor). For the past six thousand years a member of the House of SunSoar has filled the office of Talon.

TALON SPIKE: the highest mountain in the Icescarp Alps, the home of the Icarii people.

TANABATA: a Ravensbund elder.

TARANTAISE: a rather poor southern province of Achar. Relies on trade for its income. It is administered by Baron Greville.

TARE: small trading town in northern Tarantaise. Home to Embeth, Lady of Tare.

TARE, PLAINS of: the plains that lie between Tare and Grail Lake.

TEKAWAI: the preferred tea of the Ravensbund people. It is always brewed and served with great ceremony and is drunk from small porcelain cups bearing the emblem of the blood-red blazing sun.

TEMPLE MOUNT: plateau that once housed the Temple complex on the great mountain which dominated the Island of Mist and Memory.

TEMPLE OF THE STARS: one of the lost Icarii sacred sites. It was located on Temple Mount on the Island of Mist and Memory.

TENCENDOR: the ancient name for the continent of Achar before the Wars of the Axe.

THREE BROTHERS LAKES, The: three minor lakes in south Aldeni.

TIME OF THE PROPHECY OF THE DESTROYER, The: the time that begins with the birth of the Destroyer and the StarMan and that will end when one destroys the other.

TIMOZEL: son of Embeth and Ganelon of Tare, and a member of the Axe-Wielders. Champion to Faraday.

TREE FRIEND: in Avar legend Tree Friend is the person to lead the Avar back to their traditional homes south of the Fortress Ranges. Tree Friend is also the one who will bring the Avarinheim behind StarMan.

TREE SONG: whatever Song the trees choose to sing you. Many times they will sing the future, other times they will sing love and protection. The trees can also sing death.

TYRRE, SEA of: the ocean off the south-west coast of Achar.

UNIT: see "Military Terms".

UR: an old woman who lives in the Enchanted Wood.

URQHART HILLS: a minor crescent-shaped range of mountains in central Ichtar.

VENATOR: a war horse. The name means "hunter".

VEREMUND: one of the Sentinels, brother to Ogden.

WARLORD: title given to Borneheld, Duke of Ichtar, by King Priam to acknowledge Borneheld's *de facto* command of the armies of Achar.

WARS OF THE AXE: the wars during which the Acharites, under the direction of the Seneschal and the Axe-Wielders, drove the Icarii and the Avar from the land of Tencendor and penned them behind the Fortress Ranges. Lasting several decades, the wars were extraordinarily violent and bloody. They took place some thousand years before the time of the Prophecy of the Destroyer.

WAY OF THE HORN: a general term sometimes used to describe the lifestyle of the Avar people.

WAY OF THE PLOUGH, The: the religious obedience and way of life as taught by the Seneschal according to the tenets of the Book of Field and Furrow. The Way of the Plough is centred about the Plough and cultivation of the land. Its major tenets teach that as the land is cleared and ploughed in straight furrows, so the mind and the heart are similarly cleared of misbeliefs and evil thoughts and can consequently cultivate true thoughts. Natural and untamed landscape is evil; thus forests and mountains are considered evil because they represent nature out of control and they cannot be cultivated. According to the Way of the Plough, mountains and forests must either be destroyed or subdued, and if that is not possible, they must be shunned as the habitats of evil creatures. Only tamed landscape, cultivated landscape, is good, because it has been subjected to mankind. The Way of the Plough is all about order, and about earth and nature subjected to the order of mankind.

WAY OF THE WING: a general term sometimes used to describe the lifestyle of the Icarii.

WESTERN MOUNTAINS: the central Acharite mountain range that stretches west from the River Nordra to the Andeis Sea.

WIDEWALL BAY: a large bay that lies between Achar and Coroleas. Its calm waters provide excellent fishing.

WIDOWMAKER SEA: vast ocean to the east of Achar. From the unknown islands and lands across the Widowmaker Sea come the sea raiders who harass Coroleas and occasionally Achar.

WILDDOG PLAINS, The: plains that stretch from northern Ichtar to the River Nordra and bounded by the Fortress Ranges and the Urqhart Hills. Named after the packs of roving dogs that inhabit the area.

WING: the smallest unit in the Icarii Strike Force consisting of twelve Icarii (male and female).

WING-LEADER: the commander of an Icarii Wing.

WOLFSTAR SUNSOAR: ninth and most powerful of the Enchanter-Talons buried in the Ancient Barrows. He was assassinated early in his reign.

WOLVEN, The: a bow that once belonged to WolfStar SunSoar.

WORSHIP HALL: large hall built in each village where the villagers go each seventh day to listen to the Service of the Plough. Also used for weddings, funerals and the consecration of newborn infants to the Way of the Plough, it is usually the most well built-building in each village.

WRAITHS: see "Skraelings".

XANON: one of the nine Icarii Star Gods, Xanon is Goddess of the Firmament and shares seniority with her husband, Adamon.

YR: one of the Sentinels.

YSBADD: capital city of Nor.

YSGRYFF: Baron: lord of Nor, and a somewhat wild and unpredictable man like all those of his province.

YULETIDE: see "Festivals".

ZEHERAH: the fifth and lost Sentinel.

ZEST: one of the nine Icarii Star Gods, Zest is Goddess of Earth.